TRIPLE SHOT

THE WILD NINES

A.R. KNIGHT

WILD NINES

THE WILD NINES - BOOK ONE

PROLOGUE

Marl shaded her eyes from the Sun's glare. The dome over the Martian town cut the light at angles, making seats like her's blinding. There weren't any other open spots in the cafe, typical for the late morning. The usual time to meet the Red Voice, to meet her sister. A crowded place made for harder targets.

"They're here," the man sitting next to her, Castor, said. Normally a suit-and-tie guy, like Marl herself, they both wore the traditional ramshackle rags of Martian tradition. Strips of cloth taken from relatives past and present, stitched together into a motley arrangement. The wrap on her left hand came loose as Marl picked up her coffee, a strand dipping into the brown liquid.

"About time," Marl said. "They're always late."

"We have an easier route," Castor replied.

True. Alissa would be ducking down alleys, slipping through friendly houses. Marl went right down the street. Still, her sister called the meeting. Not Marl's fault Alissa had to work for it.

A man appeared out of the crowd, pulled out the two

chairs across from Marl and Castor. The wraps around this guy were so thorough Marl couldn't see his face, only a shaded slit for his eyes. Bulges along the waist indicated he was armed. His loose grip on the chairs, the relaxed shoulders said he knew how to use the weapons he carried.

"Marl. Thank you," Alissa said, sliding into the chair across from Marl, her own coffee in hand. "I know this was short notice."

"I thought you were dead," Marl said. "The footage of that last attack. How?"

Alissa glanced at the man behind her, then nodded to the empty chair. The man took the cue, sat down. His hidden face alternated between Castor and Marl, and she suppressed a shiver.

"Bakr, here, is the only reason I'm alive," Alissa said. "But there's no time. I need your help."

"Alissa," Marl interrupted. "I'm going off-world. Eden wants to move me to a new project, on Europa."

"And you're going?" Alissa didn't sound angry. Strange. Marl expected an outburst, claims of betrayal.

"Mars is lost, Alissa," Marl said. "If I stay, Eden will figure it out eventually. Then we'll both be dead."

"Marl," Castor said, putting a hand on her arm. "Please."

"It's fine, Castor," Alissa said. "She's not wrong."

Her sister took a deep breath. Marl took a long sip of her coffee.

"Marl, this new project, what is it? A settlement?"

"Eventually, yes," Marl replied.

A noise rippled into the cafe from outside, a rumble with a mug-rattling quake. Bakr, the faceless man, stared out through the cafe entrance while Castor swiped away at the comm on his wrist, looking for news.

"When it's ready, tell me," Alissa said. "If we can't hold Mars, we'll need a home."

"Eden won't let that happen."

"But you will," Alissa said, her eyes staring right into Marl's. She hated that look, hated the way it twisted her mind into knots, pulled Marl into whatever scheme Alissa had planned. The Red Voice followed Alissa because of those eyes.

"They're attacking the town," Castor told Marl. "We need to leave. If Eden finds you here, you're dead."

"I thought you said this place was secure?" Marl asked Alissa.

Around them, the cafe emptied. People scrambling for the exits, dashing out through back doors. Overhead, through the windows, corporate drones flew. Hunting for targets. Sporadic laser fire blotched the sky, one of the drones erupting in flame as a lucky shot downed the craft. The killing machines returned fire surgically, one precise beam responding to every bunch of scattered shots.

"Stay in touch, sister," Alissa said, getting up from the table. "You may well be the last hope we have."

Then Bakr pulled Alissa away, towards the back of the cafe. Marl moved in the opposite direction, Castor next to her. The outside was ruinous now, laser fire everywhere, smoke pouring throughout the dome as ruptured fuel tanks exploded. Red Martian sand swirled as part of the dome cracked, sucking air towards the hole.

"We'll never get out unseen," Marl said.

"We have a plan for that," Castor replied.

Marl swallowed. Their contingency. A claimed kidnapping, Marl and Castor taken by Red Voice operatives, held for ransom and interrogation, and saved by the opportune attack of corporate forces. There was only one part necessary to make it hold up.

"I'll do it," Castor said, drawing his sidearm.

"No," Marl replied. "It was my idea."

Castor nodded, handed her the weapon. Marl raised the sidearm and pulled the trigger, sending a fiery red bolt into Castor's chest. Behind her, the grind of corporate war machines drew closer. Marl turned the sidearm on herself. Stared down the small barrel, designed to focus electric energy into a concentrated beam of light, hot enough to burn through her rags and into her skin. It would leave a scar, if the laser didn't kill her.

What we did for family.

Marl pulled the trigger.

1

A GIRL AND HER BOT

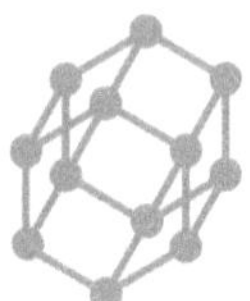

Viola winced as she brought the robot to life. The ash-gray ball waited on the workbench in front of her, its various plates and parts connected to each other like puzzle pieces. The bot sat in an oval bowl with a cord stranding out from it towards the wall of Viola's room, drawing power from the Sun's solar energy slamming into Ganymede.

"How are you feeling, Puk?" Viola said to the bot. The size of a melon, Puk had small jets, allowing it to hover and float around the room. At least, that was the idea.

"You ever get a new body?" Puk asked. "Cause it's a trip."

"Consider it an upgrade," Viola replied, standing up from the chair. "C'mon, let's see how they work."

Puk didn't have running lights—there wasn't any sign that the bot was functioning. Not until a soft whirring sound, like a fast-moving fan, filled the room. At first, nothing happened. Then, as the whirring built up speed, Puk floated up from the cradle. The bot wobbled as it reached Viola's eye-level and started on a slow loop around the room. Viola followed, stepping over various half-done projects and their attendant parts, coils of wire, or racks of batteries.

"Makes getting around here easier," Puk said, rolling itself forward, so the jets propelled it faster. When Puk zipped near the door to Viola's bedroom, it rolled itself sideways and flew through.

Viola followed the bot and spotted Puk hovering in front of the wall-screen opposite Viola's twin bed. The screen was showing a waterfall, somewhere on Earth, and the surrounding jungle. It was muted, Puk's jets providing the only sound in the room.

"That's on the list," Viola said. "An island, Hawaii."

"Better than a beach," Puk replied. "At least there, I won't get grains in my circuits."

"Speaking of . . . the jets doing fine?"

"Greens all around," Puk said, referring to the systems checks the bot ran on itself. "As for how they control, they could be faster, but I suppose I can make this work."

"Glad you're happy," Viola said, crossing her arms and watching the waterfall flow. The feed wasn't live. Viola, or rather, her parents subscribed to a service that batched these recordings and delivered them to Ganymede a few times a year. Viola waved at the screen and it shifted, switching channels to the outside camera feed from her parent's house. Their bubble.

The screen showed Ganymede's blasted surface, the brown rock and great transparent bubbles. Clusters of homes sat in radiation-blocking domes on the surface, with underground paths connecting each of them. Larger tunnels, populated with carts that sent passengers back and forth, linked the neighborhoods to Ganymede's nexus, the giant factory and headquarters of Galaxy Forge.

"You can see the storm tonight," Puk said, watching the

screen. Jupiter often dominated the sky, sometimes blotting out everything. Tonight, the planet's eternal red storm churned right through their view. Viola shuddered. She'd had nightmares of being caught in that thing.

The door to the workshop beeped. Viola ran over and pressed the keypad's green button. The entrance shot open, sliding into the wall to show a goofy grin on the other side. The bearer of the smile was a slipshod mix of adolescent dreamer and grimed-up shift worker. Roddy split time as the family's personal mechanic and a Galaxy Forge grease monkey, often taking evenings at the house to put in whatever new toy Viola's dad brought home.

"Hey Viola, how's it going?" Roddy said. "You wanted help?"

"Hey Roddy!" Viola wrapped her arms around the man for a quick hug, then stepped back. "Wanted you to test something for me. It's with Puk and, um, might hurt a little."

"Hurt a little?" Roddy said, coming into the room. The door slid shut behind him. Puk whirred out into the workshop, rotating so that the black circle camera focused on Roddy.

"He's a target," Viola said to Puk. "Go."

Roddy looked at Viola, eyebrows rising into the man's clay-red hat, part of the Galaxy Forge uniform. Puk didn't hesitate. The bot shot forward until, a meter away from Roddy, Puk let loose with a hot white laser. The beam hit Roddy on the forearm, causing the mechanic to jump back, curse, and rub at the spot. Puk darted forward after Roddy, shooting more of the stinging lasers. A lot of them.

"Puk!" Viola yelled. "Stop!"

The bot paused, rotating to look at Viola.

"He's not neutralized," Puk said. "I should keep shooting at him."

"What the hell, Viola?" Roddy said. He'd grabbed a piece of scrap metal and was holding it in front of him like a shield.

"Puk, go back to the cradle," Viola said, though excitement leaked into her voice. "Did you see that, Roddy?"

"I felt it, all right," Roddy grumbled.

"Yeah. Um. Sorry," Viola said, helping Roddy put the metal slat back on the ground. "I didn't think Puk would keep shooting, but it means the threat assessment program works. Are you okay?"

"I'll survive," Roddy took a breath, looked at Viola. His face was straight, tight. Roddy never liked being reminded of why Puk was getting a threat assessment program or why they'd been working at night to build the jets for the bot.

"Still not changing your mind?" Roddy asked.

"I can't, Roddy," Viola said. "If I don't get out of here now, I won't get another chance. After this semester, I'll have the degree, Dad will put me in Galaxy Forge, and I'll be stuck."

"It's not so bad," Roddy replied, continuing to rub his arms where Puk's lasers hit him. "You'd be good at it."

"I'd be trapped," Viola said, turning and walking over to a large console that dominated one side of the workshop. Viola turned it on, accessed the star chart program, and the console projected Jupiter and its surrounding moons into a swirling hologram in the center of the room. Viola pointed at a smaller, bluish one.

"Tomorrow will be a perfect launch day," Viola said. "How's the ship?"

"Good," Roddy said. "Your dad hasn't used it lately. Been too busy. But Viola, I don't think—"

"I know it's a lot to ask," Viola interrupted. "Dad will find out it was my idea. I'll leave a note."

"It's not me I'm worried about," Roddy said. "You don't know what it's like out there."

"Which is the point. We're not doing this again, Roddy. Please, just tell me you'll have it set tomorrow."

Roddy nodded. Viola could see a dozen arguments start and die in his eyes. There wasn't any time for them. Now that Puk's threat program worked, she had to boost the bot's laser so it could do more than sting. Then there was the packing. And the note to her parents.

"I'll make sure she's ready to go, Viola. For you," Roddy said, sighing.

"Thanks, Roddy," Viola gave the mechanic another hug as Roddy made his way out the door. As she moved back to the workbench, Viola flipped the console to the streaming headlines. News around the solar system popped up on the screen. Viola paid little attention, except this time almost every headline included the same quote. Viola waved her hand through one article to expand it.

"You cannot silence the Red Voice," said Alissa Reinhart in a mass-transmitted message today. The leader, previously presumed dead, continued to state that until the people of Mars had their rights restored, there would be no peace.

"Thankfully, Europa's a long way from you," Viola said to the picture of Reinhart. With another wave of her hand, Viola dismissed the image and went back to work.

2

THE ESCAPE

Do you understand the state Europa is in right now? It's barely civilized. There's no atmosphere. Stuck in a base where if one thing goes wrong, we'd lose you.

Viola heard her parent's voices. That didn't stop her from approaching the bay where her father's private ship sat, waiting for Viola to take it. One by one, Viola debated down the arguments. Sure, Europa was full of profit-seeking prospectors. But so was Ganymede! It was just more refined here, after two decades of colonization.

No atmosphere? Ganymede's was still thin enough, siphoned away by Jupiter's gravity, that if you spent more than an hour outside you got lightheaded. Endurance competitions ran to see who could go the farthest without succumbing. Anywhere off of Earth was harsh.

"Are you sure?" Puk asked. "Cause you do this, it will not be pleasant when daddy finds out."

"Don't care," Viola said.

Puk made a beep, a low sarcastic noise. The little bot could hack the docking bay doors in under ten seconds, because Viola had spent days studying those locks, buying her own and dissecting them. She'd found a backdoor, and coded the keys into Puk's library. There were times Viola wanted to leave the house without her parents knowing. This time included.

A single panel sat on the right side of the door and glowed a dull red. Puk floated within five centimeters of it. These locks sent a radio frequency out and expected a specific response: her dad and Roddy wore badges that replied with the value and the door opened. Puk did the same thing, catching the signal, running it through Viola's backdoor, and sending the necessary response to flip the light green and open the lock.

The opening showed a dim wash of yellow lights silhouetting Viola's parent's ship. The *Gepard* was a 12 meter-long needle, meant to only hold a pilot and a passenger and sprint around nearby space. Her dad took it on joyrides, jaunting up and out of the atmosphere to "remind him where we came from." Viola had gone up in it a few times, seen the stars in their natural habitat.

"Is she ready?" Viola asked Puk, who'd zipped ahead and plugged himself into the ship's diagnosis panel.

"All fueled up and green," Puk replied. "Almost like we planned this."

"I'll owe Roddy so much," Viola said.

"What're you giving him again?" Puk asked.

"I'll find him some souvenir. A rock from Europa," Viola said.

A ladder up to the cockpit was three meters, and every rung landed heavy in Viola's chest. The *Gepard* could get her to Europa, barely. Its design required a large chunk of electricity to charge *Gepard*'s batteries. Small solar panels lined the sides of the ship, enough to keep life support running in an emergency, but not enough to get her anywhere once the main battery ran dry. Unless Viola found her bank account more flush than she'd left it an hour ago, there'd be no way to buy her way home.

Making Viola trapped. On her own on a frozen moon. Easy to argue against going. That things were safe, secure on Ganymede. But Viola could see her future if she stepped away from the ship. Could see the next hundred years of her life playing out, a boring biography. Complete the degree, take the job, work her way up and maybe, one day, run the company. Every year getting further and further away from the engineering she loved and placating it with toys like the *Gepard*.

And that might be okay. Might be fine. Only not now, not when there was still that voice telling her to take a chance. Viola pulled herself into the cockpit and disengaged the ladder.

When the ladder moved away from the *Gepard*, it ran over a pair of sensors in the floor. By doing so, the bay's departure system registered Viola's intent and turned on the rest of the lights. The gate, a thick block of smooth moon rock, ringed with glowing ruby dots warning her it was still shut.

Puk floated beside Viola, hovering above the passenger seat slotted behind the pilot chair. In front of Viola sat the flight stick, followed by a panel of buttons and levers controlling thrust, landing struts, and more. The *Gepard* had few auto-pilot features. The manual effort was part of the thrill. Viola had been here a thousand times in the family's simulator, feeling her way through a virtual trip. Now, though, when she started preflight and saw the dashboard come up green, the thrum was real.

The *Gepard* chimed when the checks came back positive. Viola flipped the next switch in the sequence, the weighted click bringing her one step farther from home. A countdown scrolled till the craft was ready to launch as energy transferred from the storage batteries to the thrust. The *Gepard*'s design, and most of the ships out away from Earth, leveraged electricity to combat the scarcity of rocket fuel.

"Puk, open the launch doors," Viola said.

"The alarm will go off," Puk said.

"I know," Viola said. "They won't react in time."

"Sweetness. Let's get outta here,"

The doors behind the *Gepard* split open, revealing the huge, billowing monstrosity of Jupiter behind them. The swirling gasses and storms of the largest planet in the solar system blanketed the sky, leaving room for little else. Tonight, Ganymede had moved to the side of Jupiter, so that most of the sky was a bright series of swirling tans and oranges, while the other third was pitch dark, the part of Jupiter catching no sunlight and blocking any view of stars beyond.

"Good omen, leaving on a half-night?" Viola asked, pulling the handle that closed the cockpit in a transparent glass barrier.

"I'm a machine, I don't do omens," Puk said.

"You're no fun."

"Am I helping you run away in a space ship? I believe I am. Is that fun? I believe so," Puk shot back.

The engines beeped that they were ready to go. Viola triggered the hover jets and, two seconds later, the *Gepard* floated free. Ready for an escape. Viola reached for the flight stick to turn the ship around when she noticed someone walk into the bay.

"Roddy?" Viola asked as the young mechanic waved at her.

"You know, I don't hear that alarm," Puk said.

"He must have turned it off," Viola muttered. "Dad's going to kill him."

"Better be one heckuva souvenir you get him."

"It will be."

The *Gepard* rumbled to life. Viola eased the ship out of the launch bay and then angled it upwards into the Ganymede sky. A request for a destination came up from Ganymede's flight control, buzzing in over the *Gepard*'s comm unit.

Last chance to take this bad boy back, land it, crawl into bed and wake up to another nice breakfast, another day spent crunching math problems and watching movies. Viola looked up through the cockpit, at the glorious mass of Jupiter, and punched in Europa, Eden Prime.

"Roger that, *Gepard*. You're clear to launch. Safe travels," Flight control said.

"Let's hope so," Viola replied, and shot the ship up to the stars.

THE DAY JOB

Y ou want to see a miracle? Just look out the window," Castor, Eden Prime's trumpeter-in-chief, said to the assembled crowd of big shots, buzzwords, and bullet points.

Davin followed their glances, out the covering dome of the cruise skiff and towards the swirling white storm that followed Eden Prime's terramorpher as it sifted Europa's surface and turned it into something usable. Despite the base's name, Europa sure as hell wasn't a paradise.

First a series of bubble cities, then an atmosphere to heat the ball of ice to a more livable temp. The bright pillar of light lancing to the surface near Eden Prime was an indicator of those efforts; a large solar mirror orbiting the moon and reflecting concentrated photons to the surface. Most of Eden Prime's power came from that thing, even if it meant never having a true night.

Davin let his hand drift up to the gun hanging over his shoulder, thick with two stacked barrels. Melody had enough kick in her to blow her way through any of these suits if they made a move. Not that Davin was planning to fire it, not while Eden's checks were clearing.

A pair of sidearms hung off Davin's belt, both set to a nerve-numbing level more suitable for people who didn't enjoy death in their new development headlines. The armament drew glances, but those eyes were more comforted than nervous. Davin was their paid protection.

Davin nodded across the skiff to Cadge, a ball of bearded muscle and partner on this joyride. Once a week Eden Prime paid them to 'escort' these show-offs around the terramorpher. A way for the settlement to sell property on Europa to prospective buyers, build up publicity, and bore the Wild Nines to death. But easy money was still money, and Davin figured catching the coin till it stopped raining was the right move.

"You know what's the best about this guy?" Called a burbling voice from the back of the crowd, like its owner had been working up the courage to talk and now was bull-rushing ahead.

Davin located the source: a tall, lanky man who sported the refined suit-and-tie look of the rest of the crowd . . . at first glance. The man moved into a litany of grievances: how Eden Prime was a scam, that they were being played, that Castor didn't want the colony to succeed at all.

Cadge made his way parallel to Davin, and the rough-and-tumble rogue beat his captain to the heckler. The crowd watched with an interest so mild that Davin felt his stomach curl. The accusations sounded crazy, yeah, but these people weren't phased in the least. Some leaned in as Cadge wrestled the man back from the group, eyes hunting, hoping for a fight.

"At least struggle, I could use some entertainment," Cadge said. Davin pulled the stun cuffs they all carried on these assignments and slapped them on the heckler's wrists. The cuffs blocked the nerves from communicating with the brain, making it real hard to try and slip out.

"They're hurting me!" The heckler cried. "That's the kind of service you get with Eden!"

"Shut it," Davin said. "You say one more word, you'll wake up in a cell with one hell of a headache."

"Do it," Cadge said to the heckler, whose eyes were flipping between the two of them. "It's been too long since I've punched somebody."

Cadge's manic look quieted the man, and the heckler fell into a sulk. Castor drew back the attention with a cracked joke about how there were still crazies way out here. The crowd turned back to the flack with a chuckle and sips of their drinks.

"A bunch of softies," Cadge grumbled, keeping one hand on the heckler's shoulder. "Bet not one of them could throw a decent punch."

Cadge's voice was on the grittier side of a meat grinder. It flowed through thrice-broken jaws, out of lungs that'd played sport with most of the deadlier drugs this side of the asteroid belt, and carried with it the dead age of experience. Davin could listen to Cadge curse for days without being bored.

"You're complaining about that?" Davin replied.

"I'm worried my edge is gonna get soft," Cadge sighed. "It's been days, Davin. Days since I've knocked a man's teeth out and hauled his drunk self to the cell. I went to the range this morning, barely knew how to fire my gun."

After another fly-by, the skiff, a transparent bubble strapped to slow engines, docked back at Eden Prime. From the air, the city was a steel snake stretching through flowing shades of ice. The terramorpher grew a line out from the city, marking its path with patches of light green tundra moss, waiting for a stronger atmosphere. Used to be that process took decades. Europa, though, was the pioneer of the grand new machine.

Going by Castor's pitch, the terramorpher would have Europa warmed up and breathable within a few years. Invest in the city of Eden Prime, Castor said, and you'd be setting yourself up for quick returns.

As if you could call Eden Prime a city. The few thousand engineers and their support staff formed the backbone. The nigh-endless stream of fortune seekers that thought a chance at a new planet meant the opportunity to strike it rich sprung out from that spine like random limbs searching for a purpose. Most wouldn't find one until the atmosphere solidified, but getting in early on a new colony had the chance of a big payoff, if you didn't die of explosive decompression first.

The suits followed Castor off of the ship, a few thumbing messages into the comms buckled onto their wrists. The bay they'd docked at was covered with gleaming renditions of the glory coming to Europa. Tall, winding towers over-looking paradise. Melted frozen seas pushing against newly-made beaches. Green parks with children playing. All that soil coming from broken asteroid rock infused with nutri-ents by the terramorpher.

Davin was about to suggest a stopover at one of the few bars on Eden Prime. Get the standard home-brewed disaster they made from lab-grown hops way out here. Given the scarcity of customers, at least it was cheap. Then Davin's wrist vibrated.

"Yeah?" Davin answered the comm, a flexible black and white device that wrapped around his left forearm.

"Hey," Phyla's voice came over bright and clean. "You

done out there? There's a message you should see. Important."

The Nines's primary pilot looked through the comm's small screen at Davin, her face set in that stock grimace Phyla used whenever there was something real to talk about. Soft lines pulling in strands of blazing hair, mingling with a spread of freckles earned in a surprise meeting with a solar flare. That lesson bled out into everything Phyla did. Maximize the planning, the preparation, and people don't get fried.

"Mind telling me, then?"

"People could be listening."

"You're being paranoid."

"Do you know me?" Phyla replied. "Just get here, fast."

"I can handle locking her up," Cadge said, referring to the skiff. "Get outta here."

Davin nodded and took off at a fast walk. Running, the Eden contract stated, was one thing that could incite panic. Don't do it. Part of ensuring a calm environment while they tore apart a moon. The Nines's office was right near the skiff launch bay, but Davin didn't bother checking in there. Phyla hadn't placed the call on one of the official comms.

It'd come from their ship.

4

THE WILD NINES

The *Whiskey Jumper* had bay three all to itself, a requirement of the Wild Nines's contract. A big box with engines at the aft and a bulge at the bow, left for a cockpit, Davin's ship was a cargo hauler tweaked over the years to be anything but. Four landing struts descended from the large central box, along with a loading ramp.

Davin walked up that ramp, into the main cargo bay, two stories high and just as wide. A built-in lift across from the ramp led up to second level's walkway, while circular doors on both floors led to medical, engineering, and more. The inside of the ship was . . . colorful. A standing invitation to make an artistic mark over the years had covered the walls with paintings ranging from little more than graffiti signatures to rendered landscapes like the red valleys of Mars.

Every time Davin walked in here, history struck him like a hammer. He paused a second to look over the memories from crews long gone. One always caught his eye. A black outline of the *Whiskey Jumper*, lines bleeding everywhere on the metal walls, hovering against a blue and white ball. A cursory glance might assume the planet to be Neptune, but Davin knew it was Earth. Earth as drawn by the *Jumper*'s first captain as he flew the ship into space on its maiden journey. The ship had never been back.

"So what's the emergency?" Davin asked as he climbed into the cockpit.

Phyla leaned back in the co-pilot's chair, decked out in lounge clothes that said leaving the ship today was optional. Her face was glued to the console. Three monitors stuck to each other, the console streamed data. With touches and swipes, the displays could switch as needed. Phyla had the left one set to the comm display, tracking incoming and outgoing messages, the most recent recording front and center for Davin to play.

"Two high-profile visitors. Personal escort. Your favorite kind of job," Phyla said, sucking on a jolt stick.

Davin reached for the stick, Phyla handed it to him. Chemical cocktails wrapped around a sugary twig. Tasted dry and scratchy, but gave one helluva kick. Like eating a spasm.

"Where are they now?" Davin asked after a few twitches.

"Landing. Going through the usual harassment," Phyla said.

Eden, the company behind Eden Prime, was hyper-vigilant about taxing any incoming cargo. Grabbing every spare coin they could. Eden Prime boarded and assessed every incoming ship, assigning a value to it. That value determined what level of attention people like Castor and his boss, Eden Prime's overall manager, Marl, paid to the vessel.

"Cadge is going to blow it," Davin said, sitting in the co-pilot's chair. "Just lose his mind one of these days and split someone in that crowd, or maybe Castor, open. Worst thing is I'm starting to hope he does it."

"Feel like Eden would frown on that," Phyla said, taking the jolt stick back.

"There are always more contracts. So why'd you have me come here? Escorts aren't a secret."

"They don't want Marl to know they're coming. Or anyone else on the base."

"Interesting. How are they getting around the search?"

Phyla rolled her eyes, a slow motion where Davin could track the pupil as it made its journey from one side of the blue eye to the other. She'd started doing that when they were kids, decades ago. Learned it from her father, Phyla mentioned once, saying it was a warning she was going to be sassy.

"You think I had a nice chat with them? They beamed the ask straight to us. Short-range, hard to intercept. All it said was to meet them and keep it quiet."

"Any idea who they are?"

"The ship is small. Eden-branded. Like, mothership Eden, not Prime."

"Parents wondering what their kid is up to?" Davin said.

"Maybe," Phyla replied. "Either way, for this much coin, does it matter?"

Phyla pulled up the message. At the end of the single sentence was a price. A good price.

"It does not," Davin said. "How much time do we have?"

The pilot flipped the console back to Eden Prime's air traffic. Pointed to an entry.

"Bay seven, scheduled to land in an hour," Phyla said.

That gave Davin enough time to shower off the Eden uniform and put on more comfortable clothes, a jacket with plenty of pockets, pants with plenty more. Boots flexible enough for running, strong enough to keep his feet from getting shot off. One glance at himself in the cabin's mirror, and off.

On the way out of the *Whiskey Jumper*, Davin grabbed Mox from the man's room. The crew cabins were tight affairs: a twin bed with a desk, complete with single-screen console. A locker built into the wall for clothes. Davin looked in and suppressed a flinch. Mox wasn't wearing a shirt, which meant the black metal frame of his exoskeleton was on full display. Like a spider attached to his back, the exoskeleton latched into Mox's limbs, a series of flexible joints and electric motors. Mox himself leaned over the shelf, browsing through something on the console.

"Get your gear on, we've got a special job," Davin said by way of announcing himself.

Mox peered at the captain. Before Mox swiped away the image on the console, Davin caught a glimpse. A news piece with a familiar title. Not the first time he'd seen Mox looking at that one. An attack on Luna, the main city on Earth's moon, years ago.

"Doing what?" Mox replied, his voice a lava flow, slow and thick.

"Escorting some VIPs. I think it's for Eden. You've got thirty minutes, and we're going hot."

"I'll be ready."

Davin turned to leave, then paused.

"I'm going to need you here," the captain said. "Not thinking about her."

Mox matched Davin's look. Didn't blink.

"I'll be fine," the metal man said.

Davin couldn't stop Mox from crawling through his past. Problem was that Mox was doing it more and more these days. Wrapped up in things he couldn't change. At least this escort could be a distraction.

Opal was aft, near the engines. Davin found her working with Trina, tearing apart the housing on one of the four main thrusters designed to push ionized gas out behind the *Whiskey Jumper* when she made her escapes to orbit. The juxtaposition of the two, Opal, the strapped veteran, taking commands from Trina, the grease-ball mechanic caught in cords, tool belts and goggles made Davin laugh.

"It'll get us another one percent boost on initial acceleration," Trina was saying, with every word spoken as though it was an experiment, examined and displayed on its own. "Should reduce our escape time from this rock to be less than a minute."

"And how much did that cost?" Davin interrupted, disarming the comment with a grin.

"Oh, hey cap," Trina replied, turning her oil-smudged face back to Davin. "Not much. Bought it myself, off my pay. If it works, you can buy it off me."

"I hate it when you do that," Davin said.

"You're a bad liar, captain," Opal ran her words tight, a flow between the ends and beginnings. She held a bunch of screws that'd been keeping the thruster's access plate closed. "You ready for these yet?"

"Almost. Just have to reconnect the circuit," Trina said, turning back to the cluster of wires hanging off the engine's control panel. "Cap, you can't be too mad. Bet I got these for half the price you would have."

"Hey now," Davin said. "I'm not that bad, am I?"

Both of the women gave him deadpan looks.

"Shoulda seen her, captain," Opal said, setting the screws on Trina's wheeled work cart. "Here's this guy, sitting on a stock of these boosters thinking he'll sell them to Eden—"

"Only Eden doesn't use gas for their ships," Trina continued.

"They're all solar, electric now. So he's stuck here with this cargo that he can't sell. Thinks I don't know that and wants to charge me double what they're worth."

"Trina says, you want to eat tonight? I'll give you enough for dinner, and even a drink, cause I know you don't even have that much," Opal said, laughing.

Trina blushed, shrugged.

"Harsh," Davin said, shaking his head.

"The guy broke down. It was pathetic, really," Trina said. "But then I bought four to cheer him up."

"Four that I'm going to wind up paying for," Davin said. "Guess I can cut you some slack though, seeing as you keep the *Jumper* running so well."

"Thanks, cap," Trina replied.

"So what d'ya need, captain?" Opal asked. "Assuming you're not stopping back here just to chat."

"You and that rifle of yours," Davin said. "We've got an escort, and it's chancing to get unfriendly."

5

INSPECTORS

Pain. With each step, a nerve's scratch. Bending fingers, a joint's tug. Feeling something against his skin every moment of every day. There were many sleepless nights. Still were, years after the procedure. Hundreds of Earth days since Mox planted himself on the slab and growled at the doctor to do it.

To plant bolts inside his skin, to lace every limb of his body with an electric-powered frame. To graft the wires through his spine. They'd offered to hide it. Bury it beneath skin and along bone. An operation with months of recovery, multiple stages, more money Mox didn't have.

So Mox stood near the *Jumper*'s ramp and ran his hands along the meter-long pulse cannon. The weapon ran from the same batteries powering Mox's exoskeleton, batteries that patterned around his waist in a series of small, thin boxes. Batteries that Mox charged nightly, that would get him through two days of use if he had to run them dry. The cannon could discharge over twenty bolts per second, not as fast as projectile weapons, but fast enough. Mox would never lack enough again.

Davin and Opal walked in, bearing their own, smaller, arms. Davin with his shotgun, Melody, and sidearms holstered at his hip. Opal carrying a sniper rifle, its barrel as long as Mox's cannon, but with a thin scope attached. A lot of firepower for an escort job in this tiny base. Mox wasn't paid to understand. Only to shoot when ordered.

"Their ship's coming into bay seven," Davin said. "Let's get walking."

Down the ramp into bay three. They weren't unloading cargo, so Mox wasn't surprised to see the bay deserted. Big enough to hold a ship twice the *Jumper*'s size, Davin had negotiated for the solo space as part of the contract with Eden. The less people running around your ship, the fewer parts that went missing.

As it was, fuel pods, supply containers, and random junk cluttered the bay. If Eden Prime's dock master couldn't fill the bay with ships, he was going to use it for storage.

"Haven't seen you use that since Titan," Opal said to Mox, nodding at the cannon. "Careful you don't blow a hole in this place."

"Davin said heavy," Mox replied.

"I'm saying that for what they're paying, they're either paranoid or know something isn't right," Davin said.

"No Merc?" Mox asked when the *Jumper*'s ramp closed behind them. The stick jockey was usually part of their ground team, or flying cover in the Wild Nine's lone space fighter, a Viper.

"He was on overnight," Opal said. "Has it again tonight. I know I don't want him shooting when he's half asleep."

"Agreed."

Stretching along behind the bays was a wide corridor meant for shuttling goods and people. Mox walked behind

Opal and Davin, eyes scanning the back and forth movement of small skiffs, a seat or two and a flat bed.

Magnetic repulsion kept the skiffs afloat, signals activating magnets in front as the skiff passed over them and
deactivating as it passed to keep from messing with people
walking the halls. Of which there were always plenty;
merchants, mechanics, and various service bots. Obstacles
to be dodged. Or to be kicked out of the way.

The walk meant passing bays four and five, which were
in-and-outs. Ships landed, dropped cargo, fueled, and left
within a few hours. Skiffs lined up at the gates to deposit or
receive cargo. Eden Prime was a taker, needing everything to
keep itself alive.

Mox glanced at one skiff going by, its back end laden
with crates colored for fruits and vegetables. Less of those
lately. Gardens were online now, growing produce with
water gathered from Europa's melting surface ice.

"Mako!" Davin called as the trio walked by bay six, one
of a few privately owned bays on the small base. As Mox
looked at the towering part piles, organized in a way he
couldn't untangle, a helmeted head poked itself around a
column of pipes and waved.

"Davin?" Mako replied, stepping around the column and
extending his scrawny, pale hand for a shake. "What're you
doing this deep?" Mako took them in, lifted the goggles
from his eyes and whistled. "And ready for action."

"A job," Davin said, then waved his arms. "Your place is
messier than usual."

Mako turned and gestured at a ship behind the junk
piles. A cargo hauler from a generation before the *Jumper*,
the hulking series of spheres was being dismantled by a
horde of small robots, scratching and tearing at various
pieces and hauling the scraps to different piles.

"You see that?" Mako said, squinting at Davin. "Business is good. You ever see this place clean, you'll know I'm done. What job?"

"You're going to have a neighbor," Davin said.

"Five? You know that's an in-and-out."

"Seven," Mox announced. "And soon."

"Seven?" Mako said. "Rare day that seven gets filled. Only Eden corporate, or big shots."

"Any idea who might be coming in?" Davin asked.

Mako shrugged, looking like a puppet on strings, given how light the man was. Mox felt a tug on his frame and glanced. One of the salvage bots, poking at his leg. Mox kicked it away. Mako's eyes followed the stumbling droid, tracking back to Mox, and then looking away. Mox saw the man gulp. Fear. Mox supposed that was the intended reaction.

"Maybe if you kept your ears out of that junk pile," Opal said, "you'd catch wind of things."

"All I know is what comes in pieces," Mako said, "and the parts are selling fast. Most of it to our fearless leader, Marl."

"What's she want?" Davin asked.

"No idea. Don't care," Mako said. "I mean, should I . . .?"

Davin sighed, pressed a few keys on his comm. Mako's own unit beeped and the junk vendor looked at it with a wide grin.

"It's energy stuff, and shelter gear," Mako said. "Like she's planning on expanding, but not with Eden's help. A new group of people."

Davin glanced at Mox and Opal, but neither one had any ideas. Eden, the super-massive company that was investing in the base, had plenty of coin and supplies to expand Eden Prime as much as they wanted. Marl, the base's director, shouldn't have to go scrap hunting.

"Seeing as I just paid you for that crap," Davin said, "you give us a heads up if it looks like something strange is heading towards bay seven."

"Like you three?" Mako laughed. None of them joined him. "Sure, yeah. You see one of my scrap bots roll by, expect company."

Then Mako went to a pile of small lift jets and dove in, digging. Conversation over. Davin walked out and Opal followed. Mox took one look back at the busy bay, bots building piles of scrap to sell. Tried to picture himself doing that job, sorting through junk for anything good. Couldn't. Mox tested the grips on the cannon as he stepped back into the hallway, firm and ready. His weapon far from belonging in those heaps.

The gate into bay seven was unlocked. Mox glanced to the left, at the blank stretch of blue-tinted wall across from the gate. In there, somewhere, was a camera. More in the halls. Anyone thinking to get fast-fingered with someone else's stuff would be filmed, found, and flung off the moon. Davin held up his comm to the scanner alongside the door which beeped an affirmative.

Bay seven appeared as the gate slid open, vast and empty. No crates, no power cells. As the trio stepped into the bay, Mox felt his neck itch. The walls shifted, slid in his vision. He'd been here before, or somewhere like it.

Mox knew what was about to happen. Past memories too strong to let die. Knew it, and could not stop it.

6

STRONGMAN'S START

The green lunar surface, a verdant product of terramorphing weaving between spiraling glass towers. Low gravity making it easier to arc buildings overhead, or to build off-shoots, architecture as fantastic art. Mox moved through a wide courtyard, smoothed moon rock broken up by those patches of mossy grass. Security's crimson colors enveloped him, a cape hanging off his shoulders.

The first explosion came many meters over Mox's head. It tore through the centerpiece of an arching office, sending shattering glass rippling across the lunar sky.

Mox tried to press forward, towards the explosions. Workers, business people were going the other way, running and jumping through the low gravity in a rolling panic. As he came closer, Mox saw ruin. The shattered building's foundation leaned while people scrambled out.

Overhead, the arch split, breaking this half of the building free from its counterpart. The curved tower listed further. Mox waved people away, pointing back towards the courtyard. Countless faces blurred passed as Mox's comm called out with questions, orders, warnings.

Then the floors started falling. Support beams tore apart, anchors ripping up the lunar surface as the leaning weight proved too much. A woman tottered out of the building as it collapsed, bleeding from her head. She looked dazed, then fell to one knee. Mox ran towards her, pushing against the crowd.

They parted for the red uniform, worth respecting even in crazed flight. Mox picked her up, the woman turning to look at him, her face marred with a hundred tiny scratches from the glass window that'd blown out in front of her. In her eyes, Mox saw the building above them, falling. The woman's mouth opened.

"Yo, Mox, you with us buddy?" she said.

A blink.

Bay seven sat in front of him, no fire. No woman. Just Davin, waving his hand back and forth in front of Mox's eyes.

"We're not there. You're not there," Davin said.

"I know," Mox growled, but the edges of his vision played out the attack, flames still curling, glass still falling. "It feels similar. Open, calm."

"Tell me about it," Davin said, looking around the bay.

"You weren't there."

"Doesn't mean I don't understand."

Mox didn't reply. No point in arguing.

Mox looked and found Opal, set up in the near-right corner. Rifle up and out, supported by shipping crates. Davin leaned against the door. Mox stayed where he was. Dead center, cannon primed. Mox felt the captain's eyes on his back.

"What?" Mox asked.

"Who was it? The woman you say you're seeing?"

"I knew her," Mox replied.

"That's it?"

Mox didn't turn to look at the captain, just stared straight ahead at the bay's opening. Resisted falling through the hole again.

"I don't talk about her," Mox said after a few seconds.

"Doesn't mean I can't ask," Davin replied.

"Why?"

"Cause I got a guy wearing a weapon running around my ship, think I owe it to the crew to know if you'll ever lose it."

"It won't happen again."

"Feel like I've heard that before."

"It won't happen again," Mox repeated, more to himself than Davin.

Mox raised his arms, showing off the exoskeleton. The cannon, when Mox let go, pulled forward on his torso. The frame tugged back, its batteries pushing energy to keep the big weapon level. Mox felt it, the tight yank on his muscles, the red bloom of pain as bolts in his shoulders tensed. His face tried to move, eyes tried to narrow, but Mox resisted. Showing weakness wasn't a choice. Was not his role.

"This is enough," Mox continued.

"I won't push you," Davin said. "Just don't go daydreaming if this goes sideways."

"I'll be fine."

Bay seven's alarms wailed. Incoming ship. A light blue film covered the big, gray bay doors. A magnetic field, preventing the oxygen and atmosphere in the base from leaking out.

The gray doors opened with a loud chunk, then slid along rails greased to perfection by the attentive bots.

Europa's dark, bruised sky shown through the doors: blue sheer silk over the endless outer black. At the opening's edge, the bright white solar beam. Jupiter was on the other horizon tonight.

The ship flew into view, floating like a ghost. Electric engines, so quiet and without the burn, the pulse of cruder methods. Mox looked at the sleek oval craft, its matte exterior the color of deep jungle. No logo, any company sign. It was too small to hold cargo. Five, maybe six passengers for any lengthy journey.

The ramp extended slow, like a person's tongue tasting a hot drink. As though trying not to hurt itself. Small yellow lights blinked along the slope to the bay floor.

The first feet appeared at the top of the ramp, followed by a cane. A weathered, white-haired man and a kind-faced woman followed after. Then nobody. The two made their way down the ramp, their eyes casting around the bay. At least, Mox noticed, the man's eyes. The woman's gaze went to Davin, to Opal in the corner, and then back to Mox.

"I will say, the guards here do have flare," the woman said, holding a hand towards Mox. "I'm Clare, this is Ward. We're here because Eden thinks this base may no longer be in its control."

7

SEEN THROUGH THE SCOPE

The two of them were easy targets. Their clothes were thin, no armor. Every step methodical, easy to predict. Ice formed in Opal's veins. Security wasn't hired if there wasn't risk. If things went wrong, the Nines would have to fire first. The woman talked to Mox and Davin, out of earshot. Davin made his characteristic shrugs, and Opal pressed her lips together to keep from yelling at them to stay low.

Davin didn't have the experience. He'd found Opal on Miner Prime, that space station sitting between Mars and Jupiter, in the heart of the asteroid belt. Not that those were great times for Opal, not that she could afford to say no, but Davin telling her with that smug grin he was moving from cargo into the protection business told Opal all she needed to know. Davin hadn't ever laid in the red mud on Mars, watching the enemy for hours, waiting for the perfect moment.

Opal had gone to Miner Prime to avoid those situations, to stay out of the sights of someone else's rifle. But here she was, staring through a scope. Finger near a trigger that Opal knew, knew she'd be pulling before the day was out.

Except, not here, because Davin was waving at her to get moving. Opal stood up, pressing a button on the side of the rifle's stock that changed the magnetism holding the various parts together. The weapon collapsed into a small cluster, connected by one flexible metal strand running through every piece. Made the weapon easy to carry, easy to hide.

"We were telling your colleagues we're expecting a ship," the woman said, introducing herself as Clare and her partner Ward. "It should land in a few minutes, I believe in bay five. We'll want your help to search it."

"For what?" Opal asked.

"Evidence that Marl's got more going on than building Eden Prime's business," Davin said.

"She'd have too much to lose. Eden Prime's growing. Why risk it?"

Clare gave Opal a small smile. Opal knew that look, had seen it plenty of times in the military. Meant Opal was missing something obvious.

"Eden has too much invested in Eden Prime," Ward said, his voice a high whistle. "We're here to see whether Marl shares that sentiment."

"Love me a good tale of corporate intrigue," Davin said. "But why don't we get you two where you need to go, so you can leave before someone shoots you and costs me a contract."

"The man has a point," Clare said, putting her hand on Ward's shoulder and giving him a gentle push forward.

This time as they walked into the hall, it was Mox in front and Opal at the rear. The big man covered a large part of the hallway, enough for Clare and Ward to stay behind him. A glance down the long corridor showed only a few skiffs being cleared out by two workers. No crowds. No bustling bots. It wasn't late enough for Eden Prime to be slowing down.

"Ready up," Opal said, pulling her sidearm, a better choice in the corridor's tight confines, from her waist holster. "It's too quiet."

"Phyla, can you get me any info on why the bays have gone ghost town? I've got a pair of—" Davin spoke into his comm, glancing at Clare and Ward. "Pets here that I'd rather not lose if it's going to get dicey."

"Pets?" Clare asked, turning back to Opal.

"People might be listening," Opal replied.

"I'm digging, but there's no news. No alerts," Phyla's voice came over the comm.

"Love it when bad situations get worse," Davin said. "Let's keep going. Get to the *Jumper* and we can re-assess."

"No," Clare said. "Bay five. Now."

"Lucky for you, we'll go past it on the way. You look carefully, you might get a peek."

They resumed walking forward, Opal hanging farther and farther back. Ambushes were harder when the targets weren't close together. Think, Opal. Tactics. Here in this base, the atmosphere still thin, explosions were a dangerous game. Ripping a hole would cause the bays to de-pressurize. Cause the breathable air to escape. No trade, no cash flow, for days until Marl could repair the hole. That meant small arms. Direct fire.

Opal could see the corridor, all its polished, empty expanse. Someone would have to run down the hallway to attack, giving the Nines plenty of time to react. Unless the attackers were already in one of the bays.

"Mox, go ahead," Opal said. "I'll cover the hall, you check the bays as we get to each one."

Mox nodded and, with his heavy jog, went forward to bay six. As the metal man approached the gate to the bay, the wide double-doors, Mox gripped the cannon and side-stepped in front. The cannon's business end pointed through into bay six, and Opal waited for Mox to fire away. Wanted it to happen. When the action started, Opal knew she'd be fine. Now it was ice and nerves.

"Clear?" Davin asked, standing between Mox and their charges.

"Looks normal," Mox said. "Mako's there. Still working."

"Can we trust him?" Opal asked.

The answer to that was always no. Never trust. What if Marl found Mako's button? Some new ship to tear apart, maybe, or a shop on the main boulevard through the base? Something tempting enough for Mako to sell them out.

"He's safe," Davin said. "Don't worry."

Opal shook her head. Stop it. This wasn't Mars. This wasn't the Red Voice.

They passed by Mako's bay, heading towards the gate to bay five. Nobody talked, and Opal didn't change that. Aside from the omnipresent hum of Eden Prime's inner workings, Ward's tapping cane made the only sound.

Mox hit the gate first, glancing around the side, then stepping in front of the doors. Davin moved to join Mox, holding up a palm to Opal. No rifle needed. At least, not yet. Clare and Ward gathered behind the two of them while Opal kept her eyes going back and forth down the corridor.

"Open the gate," Clare said.

"What's on that ship?" Davin asked.

"That's what we're here to find out."

Davin swiped his badge, and the doors slid open. They walked in and Opal followed, keeping distance. Finally, she turned around the door's edge and saw a ship that hadn't been there earlier. Bigger than Clare's, but still small for a cargo hauler, this one had a courier craft's sleek look. Speed and luxury, meant to crate people and their luggage, or a prime product, from one planet to another with minimal delay.

Ionized gas's faint odor, the slight sting to the nose, wafted Opal's way as she walked into the bay. A clear indicator the engines only recently turned off.

"They're still on board," Opal said.

Mox and Davin glanced at her and nodded. They already knew that, but Opal had no such guarantee about Clare and Ward. Unlike bay seven, five stayed busy and the usual necessities littered the area. Fuel cells, a skiff for loading heavier stuff, crates for cargo. Plenty of things to hide behind.

"You two might want to take cover," Davin said, sharing Opal's sentiment. "Or am I getting the wrong vibe here? That this ship isn't friendly?"

"Depends on Marl," Clare said, Ward nodded. They stood loose, calm. If they thought this might be a trap, why weren't they treating it like one?

"Let's play it safe then," Davin said. "How about you go over there?"

Davin pointed to crates stacked near the bay's corner. Clare and Ward didn't argue and took cover. Opal went to the opposite side , near a fuel cell pile. Slid her finger along the rifle's barrel, tapping a button that sent out a magnetic charge, snapping all the pieces into place.

Opal leaned forward, bracing her elbows on one cell, and looked through her scope. Mox put himself dead center, a massive target that could dish back everything and more. Davin took a spot near Clare and Ward, standing between them and the gate.

The waiting was always the hardest part. A sniper, Opal sat for hours, each breath a careful in and out to keep her aim from moving. Ready to fire at any moment. The tension growing with each second until, like a frog being boiled, something moved and the stillness shattered with cacophonous destruction.

The ship made a noise. A grinding sound. Systems powering up. With a sudden jerk, a rectangle two meters tall shifted open in the bottom of the ship. A ramp, thinner and meant for people. And a foot was the first thing that appeared. Booted. Joined by the second foot a moment later, they descended. Opal saw calves, thighs, no holster on the waist. A snap look back up the stairs through the scope, but there wasn't another.

"Stop," Mox announced as the person reached the bottom step. "Move and die."

The person stood still, hands resting near the sidearm on his waist. He wore an older, mismatched uniform. Like someone who'd raided a company's dirty laundry chute. Opal didn't recognize the faded brands, but recognized the uniform's style. The sloppy getup complemented the easy grin, the relaxed muscles. The guy stared death in the face with a smile. Opal tightened her finger on the rifle's trigger. No fear made someone dangerous.

"So, is that the usual way you greet people on Eden Prime?" the spacer said, "cause that's not very polite."

"Sorry," Mox said.

"I didn't ask for an apology, but thanks. Now, I've got work to do, so if you wouldn't mind?"

"What type of work?" Clare asked, stepping out from her cover and moving next to Davin.

"Well, that's just the thing. It's work that doesn't need

spectators. Or people asking questions. Why'd you say you were in this bay, again?"

The man's hand twitched, his smile grew. A tell. The spacer faced overwhelming odds, but he would draw the minute Clare answered his question. Opal pressed on the trigger when a shot flashed. Lasers were always soundless, except for the screams they extracted from a hit. The spacer fell back, down, smoke rising from his chest. Opal looked up from the scope and saw Clare holding Davin's sidearm, pointing it at the spacer.

"Whoa! Hey!" Davin yelled, yanking his gun back from Clare. "That was a nice conversation."

"You see those clothes?" Clare said. "That's the proof we needed. Now we have to run."

"Proof of what?" Davin asked, but Clare was pulling him along towards the gate.

Ward, the man Opal had last seen plodding with a cane, had picked it up and was holding the cane like a weapon, aiming the point around like it was going to spit lasers. Which, Opal realized, it might. As Clare made it to the gate, Mox back-pedaling to join them, she paused. Opal expected the doors to open. As they should. But they stayed shut. Trapped.

"Phyla, we need the gate to bay five open," Opal said into the comm on the left wrist.

"On it," Phyla said.

As the hired security for the base, they had the codes for the doors. Should've taken only a couple seconds, but those seconds passed and the door stayed closed.

The ship rattled, its ramp retracting. The engines spooled up. Opal shifted the scope, looked at the contours of the small ship. Deep in those recesses were nozzles, barrels ready to fire. In tight quarters, the ship could fry all of them in seconds.

"Mox! That ship has weapons!" Opal snapped.

"Phyla, we need this door open!" Davin said into his comm. Clare and Ward shifted away from the captain, towards the crates. The only chance they had was—

Mox's cannon ripped a hole in the world, the slap-screech of the rotating barrels heating and spitting bolts, dozens of them, echoing around the bay's metal walls. The white lines struck the ship, now a meter off the ground, and burrowed deep into the hull. Black marks riddled the front as Mox arced the cannon towards the divots opening as the ship brought its weapons on line.

Opal, looking through her scope, lined up on an opening where a small gray nozzle was shifting forward, and fired. The rifle sent a blue bolt, not as hot as Mox's shots, that struck the nozzle and blew it off in a sparking shower.

The cannon did its job. At this range, and without the ship having time to charge a shield, the craft disintegrated under Mox's energy blasts. A key shot blew apart armor plating covering the cockpit. Thick glass still sat there, used as a view-port when the ship wasn't being attacked.

Opal could make out someone moving back and forth, arms pressing at buttons. She centered the scope on the figure. One good shot and this was over.

And Ward took it. That cane of his blasting a long, slow red-orange wave that arced onto the cockpit's glass and ate its way through it. A plasma sprayer. Opal hadn't seen one in years. Old-fashioned, slow, but effective. The ship shuddered under the assault, its jets popping off and on as power cables melted and rerouted.

Mox's cannon paused, overheated and needing to cool itself for the next salvo. Behind the melting plasma, the shape still moved in the cockpit. Crazy to stay there. The plasma would soak through at any moment, destroy the console. But Opal raised her scope, lined up the shape, saw the person raise its arms. Surrender? Opal's finger stayed on the trigger.

Then the person pulled something at the cockpit's top. The repulsor jets burst, swinging the ship around so the engines pointed back at the gate, right at Mox, Davin, Clare and Ward. Opal felt the panic, the certainty of what was going to happen next and the complete inability to do anything about it. Opal saw the telltale lighting, an engine primed to launch. She dropped the rifle, turned towards the others, to warn them.

Mox was already moving. Even with the cannon, that exoskeleton pushed the man when he wanted to go. Mox jumped, grabbed Davin, and shoved them both to the ground as the ship's engines roared to life.

The light wasn't blinding so much as obliterating. Even through her closed lids, her hand covering, Opal's world went pearl. She fell to the ground, her back so hot Opal thought she'd caught fire. As fast as it came, the heat receded, the roar pulled away and Opal uncovered her eyes. Her ears rang, the concussive echoes of a full engine ramp-up in the small bay.

The ground, walls, and containers bore black scoring, some still glowing orange where the engine's direct blast struck.

Mox shifted off of Davin, dazed. Opal stumbled her way over to them, looking around but not seeing Clare, Ward. A moment later her heart dropped, fell into that familiar numbness. Two charred lumps, flames licking at the clothing, sat near the gate.

Ward's cane, burst and leaking plasma in an instant-cooling puddle, lay next to them. Even if they'd survived the engines, the burst plasma would've immolated them both.

A buzzing sounded in Opal's ears and she glanced behind her to see Davin on his feet, yelling something into his comm. There was nothing they could do for these two, except vengeance. Recoup honor from the contract. Opal went back for her rifle, hot but undamaged.

The gate opened. Phyla's hacks working. A few bots scurried in and began cleaning up the mess. Europa's silver-black sky bled in from outside, the magnetic shield keeping the burnt air close.

FIGHTER PILOT

Merc was grabbing a mid-nap snack when Phyla's tight voice came on over the intercom, yelling for him to get to the fighter. He dropped the energy bar, whose packaging screamed it contained literally every vitamin, and scrambled out of the kitchen, down the short hallway, slid over the ladder into the central loading dock and then bounced right for the small fighter bay.

"Got any more info?" Merc commed as he went.

"Davin, Mox, and Opal were on an escort. Things went sideways and the cause is running away. Davin's saying they disarmed it. Wants you to bring it in, gently."

"Davin always wants it gentle."

"Scrap's worth more than ash, Merc."

The Viper Two-Twenty-One was a stupid name for a super cool ship. This baby had aerodynamics that guaranteed a rockstar performance in zero G or more. Merc had the preset for Europa's atmosphere dialed in, the preflight check flipping greens in less than five seconds. The Viper flew electric, a killer advantage when you needed maximum thrust immediately. A disaster for long trips, but Merc didn't fly it without the *Jumper* nearby. He coaxed the craft out of the *Jumper* and towards the big bay's opening exit.

"Twenty," Merc said.

The Viper processed the command and spat forward, sliding from the bay and through the magnetic shield. Going by official time, always Earth standard, it was mid afternoon. Below, the ice-tinged moss around Eden Prime looked caught in a fog, blue and white clinging to the foliage, like frozen broccoli.

Beyond the terramorpher's edge, more pure blues twinkled. Behind Merc, light streamed from the solar array, Europa's new and always-present sun, a beacon alongside Jupiter's constant presence. Merc hadn't seen a true night in five years, not since he'd left Earth.

The Viper picked out the battered ship, its engines glowing white in the relative dark as it climbed in altitude. Outside the cockpit windows, Merc could only see the ship as a bright ball of light streaking upwards, but the Viper's scanners, as Merc dialed them in, modeled the craft, including broken edges and burned holes from Mox's cannon. Much farther out, and the Viper's interpretation would look like it was getting drunk, and then, further away, a big ol' circle stating hey, there's a ship here.

"Phyla, they're making a break for space," Merc said, angling his intercept vector. "But, you ask me, that ship's not capable of holding atmosphere for long."

"Don't make space do your dirty work, Merc."

"Never crossed my mind," Merc said, releasing the comm. "Fifty."

The acceleration pushed Merc back in his seat, a familiar grin crawling up his face. Speed, man. That was the stuff. Looking through the cockpit, the HUD displayed a few dots and meters where Merc could catch his prey. On the right, the Viper's energy. The left had its throttle. The middle held a deep blue circle around where the escaping ship sat in the atmosphere. It had a head start, but the ship didn't have speed. Merc figured two minutes till firing range.

Merc's left hand released his double grip on the flight stick and eased towards the left panel where buttons sat with stickers over them. Trina's work. The mechanic messed with the Viper when the *Jumper* didn't need her, adding weapons and toys so every time Merc flew the fighter there was something new waiting for him. He found the toggle on the far left. He pressed the switch forward and felt the slight click. The noise, like coins falling into place, echoed through the cockpit.

The Viper had lasers, and they were devastating if you were sure your target had no shields. Or any reflective plating left to bounce your molten bolts off into space or, worse, right back at you. Slugs, those weren't so easy to toss away. They would chew through the ship like toothpicks through cheese. Make it impossible for the craft to leave the planet.

"Hey, sitting ducks!" Merc announced through the short-range comm to the ship. "Flag yourself for surrender and I won't fill you full of holes."

"You think I don't know you'll do that anyway?" The reply came, the voice strained, high-pitched.

"Dunno what you're talking about, man. Except that you keep heading to the stars, you're going to do it as a fireball here in a sec."

"There weren't supposed to be extra people there, in the bay," the man said."It should have been simple. We'd already be gone by now."

"Say again, ship? And cut your engines," Merc replied. "You getting this, Phyla?"

"Hearing it, don't understand it," Phyla replied through their secure channel. "Hey! Heads up. *Jumper*'s picking up a new player in your game."

A moment later the Viper's own sensors beeped. New craft, coming from orbit. Hot. Far enough out that the scanners showed a plain circle, but it was going fast. Another few seconds and there'd be a picture.

"Shields maximum," Merc said, the voice toggles mimicking hard switches, but he didn't want to take his hand off the stick right now.

Slotting the energy to the shields meant losing some of the Viper's potential thrust, but it wasn't like Merc needed it to keep up with the enemy's slow-burn wreck.

"Ship, you got a new bogey coming in fast. Suggest you tell me what it is, you got any info," Merc commed to the enemy ship. "Then suggest you turn around, high-tail it back to base all nice and easy."

"Stick jockey, threatening a man whose already dead won't get you very far," the guy on the ship replied, before breaking off in sad laughter.

The ship swung left, turning away from the inbound craft, but it wasn't moving nearly fast enough. Merc saw the new player adjust its line to match. At the speed it was going, the new ship was going to overtake in ten, fifteen seconds.

"Ten percent," Merc said, cutting the throttle.

No sense getting between the new guy and the old one. Especially when he didn't know what the new one was going to do.

The Viper beeped twice. Deep tones. Missiles launched, but not at Merc.

"Ship, you got a pair of bugs incoming," Merc said.

"They weren't supposed to be there, man," the guy said. "Supposed to be in and out. Can't say we didn't do the job though. Can't say that."

The missiles, their bright ends just visible like fast-moving stars, lanced through the air in front of Merc and struck the ship. The explosion started small, then crackled into fire and arcing lightning. Electric engines would blow big, but that was something more.

"Phyla, there was a bomb on board that ship. Or something that goes up real nice," Merc said, watching the fireball collapse on itself, wreckage plummeting like meteors towards Europa's surface.

"Just get back here," Phyla said.

"What, don't want me playing tag with that new ship?"

Speaking of, the attacking vessel was adjusting course towards Merc, but also towards Eden Prime behind him. Merc pushed the flight stick forward, tilting the nose of the Viper straight. At its velocity, the other ship couldn't twist sharp enough to get a clean shot. Even in Europa's thin, developing atmosphere, the air resistance would rip the craft apart. Once Merc sped underneath the other ship, he could turn around and, if he needed to, light up their rear with all kinds of goodies.

"Hello there!" Crackled Merc's short-range radio. "Just calling to confirm we've got no designs on you, mate!"

Sure they didn't. Merc wasn't going to put himself in their trusting hands anyway.

"Why'd you toast that guy?" Merc replied into the radio, keeping his comm open.

"Put him out of his misery," the voice on the other end fell flat, a player tired of the game. "He was a dead man. Not that it matters for you."

"Kind of you to tell me that," Merc said.

The larger ship blew by overhead, continuing to head for Eden Prime. Merc detected no missile locks, no warning shots. Apparently they were one-and-done killers.

"What do you want me to do, Phyla?" Merc said. "We're supposed to be providing security, and they just wiped a guy on our turf."

"Come back home, Merc. 'Til we know what's going on here, I don't want you out."

Merc almost complained, wanted to protest. Maybe take the Viper after that new ship. But instead he plugged in the docking routine, curled through the sky and went back to base.

9

CONTRACT DISPUTES

Eden Prime's headquarters sat a long walk from the bays, a walk Davin made after a long clean-up and debrief with the team. That walk went along a wide, open space everyone called the Boulevard. Like a cylinder sliced in half, the curved roof collected solar energy and gave a stellar view of Jupiter and the surrounding stars. Stores bought space along the sides, building bubble shapes from the outer wall.

Marl's government building wasn't any different, except in design. Made from blue swoops, with not a straight edge in sight, the building evoked the waves in Europa's soon-to-be-thawed oceans. At least, that's what Marl said.

The front doors, tempered glass inlaid with swirling drawings of fish, currents, and kelp, opened as Davin approached. Business hours were over for the day, but Davin pushed through the door anyway. Marl had to know what'd just happened in bay five, had to know about the ambushed execution of the ship Mox had shot to pieces.

No ship could land at Eden Prime without permission from flight control. The Wild Nines were the de facto police for this place, and nobody bothered to let them know a suspicious vessel with a bomb was coming. Nor that there was another ship entering the atmosphere loaded with heavy weapons.

"Bay seven's locked," Opal's voice came over the comm. "There's some weird people there. Looks like they're trying to get in Clare's ship. Don't recognize their uniforms."

"It's fine. Don't push it," Davin replied.

No getting back to the inspector's ship for any hints. Just another twist in this great day.

Davin stood in the lobby of the Eden Prime building, glancing at the twin stairs curling up around either side of the entrance hall. They both led to the same second-floor landing, a balcony that gave you an eye-level view of a dangling chandelier. The lights in that fixture cut sharp, long and thin, like the frozen shards decorating the wasteland beyond the terramorpher's mouth. Lit, as it was now, the chandelier cast a pure white light around the interior. Eden Prime, it said, was beautiful. Was open for real business, real class. How long that impression would keep with two people burned alive in a docking bay, Davin wasn't sure.

He took the left stairs, walking up the steps to the landing. Short hallways on either side ended in doors. During the day, the first floor held the business application work, the tour groups full of prospective investors. The doors up here were labeled 'Eden Prime Staff Only'. Davin tried one. Not locked. The only light on the other side came from windows: Jupiter's reflection. Empty cubicles guided Davin towards Marl's office.

He itched for Melody, but Davin only had a sidearm. The same one Clare had used to blast that guy an hour ago. Davin kept a hand on it. Marl's office was walled off with a darker blue than the rest. As big by itself as the rest of the cubicles.

The door to Marl's office was the first one that, when Davin pressed on it to open, stayed shut. The badge scanner on the right beeped a low tone when Davin swiped his card. No dice. Suddenly Davin, without knowing why, hammered his fist on Marl's door. Pounded it once, twice, three times. The metal didn't bend, didn't even give a satisfying thwack. Instead it took the punishment and sat there, solid.

Davin didn't know Clare or Ward, didn't know what they were looking for, or why they'd requested the Wild Nines give them a shot at getting out alive, but they had, and Davin had failed. But he hadn't failed alone. The killers had help.

"Davin Masters," said Marl's voice, a calm, dead weight, over the office comm. "Isn't it past your shift?"

"Everybody's working late," Davin replied, his eyes scanning up and around the door, looking for the camera and not finding it.

"You know me, I live for the job," Marl said. "What can I do for you?"

"Open this door for starters."

"Are you going to shoot me if I do?"

"Depends," Davin said.

The lock next to the door flashed green and the metal barrier slid right and opened. Davin stepped through into Marl's office, a set of chairs, a desk, and an endless view out onto Europa's surface. Standing off to the side, gun drawn, was Castor, the PR man and Marl's unofficial bodyguard.

"Castor," Davin said as he stepped into the room. "Always a pleasure."

"Davin," Castor said, his voice a straight level tone that avoided any inflection. Whether Castor was getting ready to murder him or wish him a happy early birthday, Davin couldn't tell.

"Who were those two that hired you?" Marl asked. "I'd like to know whose ashes my crews are sweeping away."

"I was hoping you could tell me," Davin said. "We didn't get much time to talk."

"I wonder whose fault that is?"

Davin knew it was bait. Knew it. Marl trying to get him angry, to say something stupid. Davin had seen her do this to a dozen people before, manipulate their emotions with a carefully placed sentence or three and then come away with coin or blackmail while the other person struggled to hold on to their dignity.

"Why was bay five sealed, Marl? Why couldn't we get out?" Davin asked, walking closer to the desk, his voice rising as he spoke. "Why was that ship allowed to land?"

Davin took another step, was between the chairs now, when he felt Castor touch his arm. Davin shook the bodyguard off, but stopped his forward march. Marl half-turned back from the view, looked right at Davin, her eyes flashing fire in the dim light. Davin couldn't deny that Marl looked powerful, her chin lofted so her eyes stared down at him. Decked out in official Eden uniforms, but, unlike the drab green worn by the grunts, Marl had dresses and suits that fit. Not a spare wrinkle, a sleeve too long. Their green shades were deeper emeralds, matching the flora growing now on Europa.

In this light, Marl was a black silhouette as she stood over her desk.

"Doors malfunction all the time," Marl said. "I'll look into why the ship landed. It's possible they lied, hid their weapons from our scanners."

"So you know nothing," Davin said.

"I'm sorry."

"You're not."

"No, but then, I shouldn't be. You and your team failed to tell me an escort hired you. Failed to tell me why those two were here. Failed to keep them alive. Failed to capture the ship that attacked them." Marl placed her hands on the desk, thin, bony, but strong. "In fact, Davin, what I should be is angry. And I am."

"Hey—" Davin started.

"Which is why," Marl waved him quiet, "effective immediately, I'm ending your contract with Eden Prime. You and your Wild Nines have a day to put yourselves together, but then I want you off this moon."

"And whose going to keep this place from falling apart? Captain flack here?" Davin said, nodding at Castor.

"We are," said a new voice behind Davin, full of cocky pride.

The voice came from a built man in the doorway. He looked like a retired fighter, stood with the rugged wariness of someone who'd earned his gray hair. The man's clothes caught Davin's eye. The same set, a loose collection of dusty red and blue, that the man back in bay five had been wearing.

"Ferro and his team are your replacements," Marl said. "And the important thing, Davin, is that they're better than you."

"Really?" Davin turned to the new man. "Where'd she find you, Ferro? Just hanging out waiting for a contract?"

"Marl and I, we go back to Mars—" Ferro started.

"Quiet," Marl said. "Davin, you have a day to get your things together. Then I want you gone."

"You look at the camera feed from bay five, you'll see this guy and the one that tried to blow up your base have a very similar fashion sense," Davin said. "Might want to reconsider."

Davin stepped away from the desk, back towards the door.

"Pleasure to meet you," Ferro said as Davin went by. "I'm sorry my coming means you're going."

"Sure you are," Davin said. "Enjoy this pile of trash, it's a real winner."

"Twenty-four hours," Marl said to Davin's back. "Then you're gone, or you're dead."

"Always a sweet-talker, Marl," Davin said as he walked by Ferro, out the door, out the office, out of the building.

10

TERMS OF DECEPTION

As soon as the door shut behind Davin, Marl glared at Castor.

"You didn't catch the transmission," Marl said. "You didn't intercept it and warn me, warn Ferro that they had hired bodyguards."

Castor, always the model of military training, didn't flinch under Marl's stare. Stood straight. As though this was an official ceremony. Like they weren't on a backwater world trying to scrabble for survival.

"Direct signals are almost impossible to intercept unless you're listening right in between them," Castor said. The even tone, the march of logic. Just once, Marl would love to see the man show emotion. "What's done is done. We need to move on."

"My men are not police," Ferro said.

"They are now," Marl replied. "Alissa asked me to take you in, and I've done that. You can do this for me. Eden Prime isn't big enough to cause much trouble."

"There is another problem," Castor said. "The inspectors are dead, and Eden will want to know why."

"I suppose we can't tell them it was a botched assassination?" Marl said. "Or it was an accident that a ship turned around in a docking bay full of people and ignited its main engines?"

"Sarcasm?" Ferro asked Castor.

"I don't think either of those will hold up," Castor said, ignoring Ferro. "The recording won't back them."

The recording. Eden Prime was full of cameras catching everything, like everywhere else. They stored the recordings here. Video that could be altered. Nobody had even seen the playback yet, outside of Marl and Castor. There were no witnesses, only Davin and his crew, and who would believe a few hired guns when the evidence was so damning?

"We adjust the video. Change it," Marl said. "The Red Voice has a specialist right? For the media?"

"We could do it," Castor said.

"Quickly?" Marl asked, then she pointed to Ferro. "For this to work, you'll have to arrest Davin. Prevent him from leaving. Then, when Eden's next force arrives, we can hand them their prize."

"I'll send the recording," Castor said. "Ferro, give your men a few hours. Then strike."

"Go, get them ready," Marl said to Ferro. "Castor, one more minute please."

Ferro left the room.

"Davin won't let this play out," Marl said. "They will fight."

"We can't let them win. Call him."

"I don't like owing one man so many favors." Marl sat back in her chair, stared at her comm.

"You won't have to repay them. He'll be dead before he can collect."

"Let's hope so."

Marl punched in the number, spoke the ask, and waited for the answer to cross a few million kilometers.

11

BAR NIGHTS

It was way past her bedtime. The *Gepard*'s cockpit whooshed open in Eden Prime's fourth bay after twelve hours in space. Viola hadn't checked the route before she'd started. Hadn't realized that she launched at the exact wrong time in the moon's orbits to make the transfer. Not that floating among the stars, Jupiter's giant bulk dominating the view, was a bad thing. Meditative, quiet. Especially when she'd made Puk turn itself off.

Approaching Europa meant conversations with Eden Prime's flight control, along with a ship scanning. Viola slowed the *Gepard* to wait in line behind two larger cargo haulers; rounded boxes with engines. When it was her turn, a bug bot swarm surrounded her ship. Some blasted the *Gepard*'s small hold with x-rays. Others crawled along the exterior, tapping into the fuel line, probing the airlock to make sure there wasn't a hidden bomb or other undisclosed items. Required for security, but Viola's dad had spent more than one dinner complaining how the scans were an excuse to find more cargo they could tax.

The landing into Europa was the easiest part, a matter of

punching in the docking command to the *Gepard*'s auto-pilot and letting it handle things. Current practice frowned on any manual piloting, even prohibited it if the ship had an automatic choice available.

The moment Viola touched down and popped the hatch, the dockmaster demanded coin for the slot. Viola paid a large chunk of what she had and the dockmaster tucked the *Gepard* away to the side of the bay where it wouldn't interrupt the constant, more important traffic.

"How many messages so far, Puk?" Viola asked as they walked the quiet corridor into the promenade.

"Only ten, but they're increasingly frantic," Puk replied. "Your father's showing an impressive range of emotions. We're talking anger, sadness, desperation. Man deserves an award."

"He'll get over it," Viola replied.

Eden Prime's curving, central walk brought Viola by a hotel and, wanting to drop her luggage, Viola swerved towards it. Greek architecture mashed with space-age curls, surrounding spotlights bathing the hotel in purple light. *Cosmagora* blinked at Viola on a scrolling pink neon banner. The price blaring out below in that same neon made Viola's stomach lurch.

"Classy place," Puk said.

"Didn't hear you suggesting anywhere else," Viola replied.

The human manning the desk looked like she was coming from, or about to go to, a party Viola would expect at a place called *Cosmagora*. She wore suit with sharp angles and flashing color, flipping hues whenever she moved. So distracting, it took Viola a few seconds to realize the receptionist was already talking to her.

"A room?" the receptionist said, her tone a placating

boredom.

"If you've got one."

When the receptionist leaned to check her console, the entire suit flipped to blue shades, from ocean depth to cartoon teal. Viola bit back the urge to ask where she could get her own.

"Right now, we've got plenty. You walk in an hour ago, you'd have to leave," the receptionist replied.

"It's like you're begging us to ask why," Puk said.

The receptionist glanced at the bot, raised an eyebrow, then looked back at Viola and waited.

"Why?" Viola asked after a moment's awkward silence.

"Changing of the guards. Literally," the receptionist said. "Guess people aren't fans of murder, so we've had a lot of cancels."

"Shocking," Puk said.

"Murder?" Viola asked.

With each drip-fed detail, Viola's eyes crawled wider and wider. Exploding space ships, new arrivals burned alive in a bay by their own bodyguards? Perhaps Europa hadn't been the best choice.

The walk and elevator ride up to her room was like taking a psycho-active trip through a madman's mind. Random artwork, picked from heaps of scrap metal and blasted with colors designed to clash with each other as possible clung to the walls. The room itself wasn't much better, its bed a sprawling mess of intermingled sheets, wrap-around pillows, and a ceiling screen that showed a time-lapse birth of the universe on repeat. Viola turned that off first. Then, after dropping their stuff, they fled.

"What next?" Puk asked as they stood on the boulevard again, the local time now edging into the deep night hours. "We going to steal a bunch of stuff? Try to meet ruffians?"

"Ruffians? Who taught you that word?" Viola asked, walking the boulevard, away from the bays.

The street wasn't crowded, but it wasn't empty. Wandering pockets of people shifted in and out of the mixture of starlight and multi-colored lampposts. Conversations carried, but their words washed each other out, like murmurings across a cafe. The occasional burst from a ship lifting off bled light throughout the boulevard for a few seconds at a time. Most people, Viola included, were wearing coats, her breath misting with every exhale.

"I've been on a classic literature phase lately," Puk continued.

"But, don't you know every book ever written?"

"I back-up the book I want to read, then go through it nice and slow, re-installing it to my live memory. Then delete the backup."

"How long does it take you?"

"I've only finished five today, with all our crap going on."

"Glad you're paying attention."

Ahead, across the boulevard, an aggressive series of sapphire letters formed *The Bitter Chill* along with outlines of cocktail glasses. Her father never took her to the working bars on Ganymede, for Galaxy Forge staff. Parties happened, sure, but to go into one of these places? By herself?

"Terrible plan," Puk said, following her look.

"Why am I here, Puk?" Viola replied.

"Because you've made a horrible mistake?"

"You're no fun."

"You programmed me."

"So what will you do now?" Viola asked, starting towards the bar. It took a few steps, but then Viola heard the little bot, jets whirring behind her.

"If anyone looks at you funny, I'm just going to start shooting," Puk said.

12

FIRST MATE, FIRST ROUND

Trying to find a booth big enough to fit Mox was a frustrating exercise. It was why, months ago, Phyla had asked the owners of *The Bitter Chill* to tweak one for the Nines. In exchange, Phyla promised they'd stop by multiple times a night to provide security. That the Nines weren't the peacekeepers of Eden Prime anymore hadn't filtered to local news yet, which meant the six of them could have at least one more night throwing back beverages and forgetting their problems.

"I can't believe you didn't see the engines coming," Merc, who'd swapped nighttime shifts with Trina, was saying to Opal. "Classic maneuver to fry your opponents."

"Classic maneuver?" Opal countered. "It's a suicide move. That bay could have exploded. Everyone dead and the base heavily damaged."

"That's what I'm saying!" Merc said. "Those guys clearly had nothing left to pull."

Opal's squinted eyes said she wanted to take the fighter pilot and choke him right there. Merc was trying to use that idiot grin of his to disarm the comments. As though slapping a smile on a problem made it go away. Cadge and Mox were talking about something to each other, while Davin was at the bar getting another round.

"Merc," Phyla interjected. "Stop being stupid."

"Think that's impossible," Opal said.

Merc threw up a hand, took a sip from his beer.

"So," Cadge said, returning to the table's talk. "Now that we're a free band again, what's the next job?"

"Captain's at the bar," Mox said.

"He's the only one that gets a say?" Cadge replied. "Thought this was a group effort. The way Davin told it, we've got a day to get off-world. I'm just wanting to know where we're going."

Cadge looked at Phyla, the others following his glance. Surely the *Jumper*'s pilot would know their next job. What the back-up plan was in case the contract fell apart. Problem was, there wasn't any back-up plan. No reason for one, with the indefinite contract from Eden Prime staying active as long as they wanted to keep locking up drunks and banishing scammers from the frozen frontier.

"We'll figure it out," Phyla said, hating that she didn't have an answer.

"Now that's what I'm looking for. Choices. Allow me to vote for the most violent one."

"Cadge, what the hell's wrong with you?" Opal asked. "Give me another job like this. Where I can breathe."

"Just because you sucked red sand and shot innocents doesn't mean the rest of us have to die of boredom," Cadge replied.

"They weren't innocents. You were there."

"Clean-up crews don't make the messes."

"Cadge," Phyla said, glaring at the man, whose face had

an evil little smile that showed he knew he had a sore spot and was ready to pick it.

"That's a good idea," Merc mused. "Mars. It's still a mess, right? They'll need help."

"You don't want to go there," Opal said.

"We know, thanks to this guy, that Luna's off limits," Cadge said, allowing Mars to slip away. "Which means, what, we try Earth? Bounce to Saturn and see what's there?"

A tray set on the table, the crowded mugs on it clanking together. Davin returning, his eyes showing wandering redness from an order that came with a couple extra shots, shots that didn't make it to the table. Cadge and Mox shifted, giving Davin room to collapse onto the plastic cushion.

"Team," Davin said, casting his eyes around to each of them. "As your captain, I hereby order all of you to drink."

"You heard the man," Merc said, laughing.

Phyla took a gulp from the mug. True to the bar's name, the beer was bitter. Cold. It ate its way through her throat and into her stomach like swallowing an ice cube.

"Davin," Phyla said. "They're wondering where we're going to go."

"Don't think there's another bar in Eden Prime," Davin said. "Unless another one opened and you've been holding out on me."

"Hah," Mox said.

Silence. Eyes moved to Davin as he took a long drink.

"The thing is," Davin said. "I'll have an answer for you. Tomorrow. There's some things that I'm working out. Calls I've made. We'll see what comes through."

Phyla was about to ask Davin what calls, but held back. She hadn't seen Davin back at the *Jumper* since, a few hours ago, he'd come back to say Marl canceled their contract.

There wasn't anywhere else Davin could've sent transmissions off-world. Not without paying for it.

As for what Davin was working on, Phyla'd heard that one too. A favorite tactic of Davin's when he didn't know what the hell they were going to do. But the rest of the crew sipped their drinks, moved on to other conversation. Phyla met Davin's eyes, the captain gave her a slight nod.

"Now, you see that? I could use one of those," Merc said, looking across the bar.

A woman had walked in, on the young side to be here. Followed by a small floating bot, buzzing around her head like a moon.

"You be real nice to Trina, and maybe she'll make you one," Phyla said.

"That girl doesn't belong here," Opal interjected. Phyla agreed. Too many questions on that girl's face as she looked around the bar.

"Don't worry, guys," Davin said, standing. "I'm on it."

Phyla watched the captain stand up and walk, tottering, away from the table. Escape one problem by jumping right into another. Just what they'd always done.

13

TWO FOR ONE

The Bitter Chill had a vicious set of neon surrounding a double-door that looked pristine. Hanging next to that door, laminated and plastered to the wall, was a short one-sheet that started with THINK. Below, a pair of paragraphs stated that doing stupid things on Eden Prime, like fighting, killing, or just being a nuisance could get you kicked off the moon on the next freighter. No court, no trial. A clause at the end stated this was Eden's standard policy for all of their locations, no matter which world.

"Sounds fair," Puk said. "Not open to abuse at all."

"Ganymede is the same way," Viola replied. "Gotta love the Free Laws."

Through the door there was, somehow, more neon hues spiraling around the interior, casting bubblegum pink, grape purple and lipstick red shadows along the curving roof. The bar, sitting central, was a cascading waterfall of blues. Bass vibes interlaced with wandering instrumentals accompanied the light show, backdropping to the constant chatter coming from a collection of tables and the long loop of a bar.

Viola hunted for an empty seat, but they were all taken by a motley arrangement. Some looked like Viola's father, business sharks waving cocktails, while others looked like they'd stepped out of machining parts and into the bar with nowhere in between.

One of the only openings was at the bar itself, a lone small-backed stool, next to a pair of men in thick work suits that looked like they'd tromped from a clean-up where the mess won. Viola wasn't sitting for over ten seconds before a bartender locked eyes with her and, without a word, asked what she wanted.

"Something strong," Viola said, aping a line from a movie she'd watched a year ago.

"Good move," Puk buzzed, hovering a centimeter from her ear. "Asking for a stiff drink when you're alone on a moon you've never been to is a smart decision."

"I didn't know what else to say," Viola whispered. "I've never done this."

"Hi, I'm Puk. I have literally a million recipes and reviews of various drinks at my beck and call. How may I serve?"

Viola rolled her eyes and settled for staring across the bar at nothing in particular. She'd made it here, but what did that mean? Sure, it was more interesting than sitting at home imagining being here, but still . . .

"That your bot?" said a man whose palm appeared on the bar between Viola and the zoned-out workman.

Puk whirred to the other side of Viola's head while she looked at the man. He was pressing hard on the bar counter, depending on it to keep him up. He rocked back and forth. But the bright eyes and sloppy smile looked genuine.

"Puk's a friend," Viola said.

"Have some of those myself," the drunk replied. "Friends. They're good in a pinch, you know?"

"In a pinch?"

"Yeah," the drunk paused, blinked a couple times, Viola wondering just how far his train of thought had derailed. "You won't judge me, will you?"

"Judge you?" Viola said. "I don't even know you."

"Fair enough," the drunk replied. Then, to the workman, "You mind moving over a seat? Else I might fall on you."

The man didn't argue, shifting over a spot with a nod and giving the drunk a chance to flop on the stool. The bartender slipped Viola's drink in front of her, a pale brown shade filling the tumbler.

"Don't trust him," Puk buzzed. "He's drunk."

"Really," Viola replied.

"So anyway," the drunk said, resting his elbows on the bar. "Here's the deal. Today, I lost my job."

Viola caught the man's eyes flicking towards her, judging the reaction.

"And?"

"It was boring as hell, so I don't mind."

"Okay."

Viola took a sip. Cool at first, but the liquid torched its way to her stomach. Viola found herself sweating. Holding back a cough. Every ounce of concentration went into keeping the drink down, to not blowing it here, in this bar full of people who probably guzzled this stuff by the gallon. You can do it, Viola. This is the real world.

"Here's the kicker, and this is why, as you might be able to tell, I've been a little . . . liberal with the drinks tonight," the drunk said, waving his finger in a circle towards the bartender. "Two people died today under my watch. Burnt to a crisp."

What was she supposed to say to that? Her father had talked about accidents in the plant. She'd had relatives who'd passed away. Didn't sound like that's what was happening here. The hotel receptionist and her comments about murders floated back through Viola's mind. Was this guy involved?

"And now my crew and I have, oh, 22 hours or so to get ourselves off this moon," the drunk leaned in, as though compensating for Viola's caution. "But here's the thing. I'm pretty sure she was in on it. The two people that died."

"She?" Viola asked.

"Marl. The woman running this place," the drunk said, then lapsed into silence.

"The bar?"

"Eden Prime," the man said, attempting to spread his arms and nearly knocking over his glass. "Marl's a nasty piece of work. Don't go near her, is my advice."

After another sip'n'shudder, Viola examined the drunk, noticing that he wasn't wearing the same work-man's clothes as the others in this place. Not a suit, either. More accessories. A belt with an empty holster. The comm on his wrist a higher-end model. Who was this guy?

"So what are you gonna do?" Viola asked.

"Leave it," the drunk said. "Take off in the morning, tell Europa to go screw itself and never come back."

"You're not going to try and figure it out?"

The drunk started, took a drink, then turned to Viola with his hand stretched out. Viola took it, and the drunk gave her hand a single shake.

"Davin Masters, captain of the Wild Nines," the drunk

said. "I happen to like living so no, I will not be trying to figure it out."

"Viola Allouette," Viola replied. "And that sounds like you're being a coward."

Davin laughed.

"You look over there?" Davin gestured across the bar to a corner table where five others sat drinking. "That's my crew. They'll go where I tell'em, but that means I got responsibility. They die, it's on me,"

Davin leaned in again towards Viola.

"That's why," Davin whispered. "There's going to be no grand investigation."

A hand tapped Viola on the shoulder. Two hard, frosted over faces stared at her, greedy eyes bubbling up beneath their glowering looks. Both seemed to have just walked in from a survival expedition, sporting visible nets, batons, and guns on their hips.

"Your name Viola Allouette?" the trapper asked.

"What're you doing, Whelk? More importantly, what are you wearing? You look like a homicidal dog catcher," Davin interrupted.

"And you finally look like the trash you really are, Davin," Whelk said. "But I'm not here for you, especially now you're just another drunk like the rest of us. I'm here for her, and the reward."

"The reward?" Viola asked.

"Daddy wants his little girl back home. And we're taking you there. Now."

"How much coin?" Davin asked.

"A hundred thousand," Whelk replied. "Don't even try to step into this, Davin. You've got no right anymore."

Davin slid off the stool, looked at Viola, then winked at her. Everyone saw the punch coming. Davin's drunk swing flew wide left, and Whelk's companion pushed Davin back into his seat. Whelk, shaking his head, stepped towards Viola and reached for her.

Puk flitted from Viola's ear and, near Whelk's arm, shot its laser. Whelk yelped, just in time for Viola to throw her drink at him. The glass shattered, spraying booze into Whelk's face, causing him to stumble back.

Then Whelk's companion threw Viola off of the stool and she hit the ground, hard. The breath left Viola's lungs in a rush. Her head exploded in pain as it bounced off the floor. Viola struggled to breathe, to roll away, to stop hurting. The club lights glowed down at her, a dizzying rush of color. As Whelk's friend bent down to grab her by the shoulders, Viola only had one thought:

Leaving home was a mistake.

14

THE REAL WORLD

Things looked different from the floor, a plastic mess of tiles overlaid with the sticky grime of spilled booze. The neon lights in the ceiling faded out as Whelk's companion leaned over, reaching for her with arms outstretched. A reflected glow from the floor showed a straight face, exasperated. The sight pushed a burst of adrenaline through Viola's veins. Like this guy had any right to be annoyed.

So sorry for making this hard for you.

Viola kicked out, hard, at the man's ankle, her foot bouncing off of the strike. The man paused, laughed, and grabbed Viola's shoulders. She tried to wriggle, but the man's grip pushed into her muscles, her joints, and trying to move sent pain whistling through her nerves.

"She's a fighter, Whelk," the companion said.

"We'd hate for this to be boring, wouldn't we, Gat?" Whelk replied.

"Then you oughta love me," Davin slurred, stepping off his stool and launching into a sloppy tackle.

Davin fell into Whelk, pushing them backwards into

another table, beer spilling everywhere. Gat picked Viola up, pressing her back to his chest, and lifted her towards the exit. His wrists and hands were too low for her to bite. Viola's heels broke on the stone slabs of Gat's shins. Puk whirled in front of them, trying to find a shot. Gat paused, glared at the little bot.

"Poke me with that laser, and I'll break her leg. Reward said nothing about bringing her back in one piece," Gat growled.

Puk hesitated and Viola shook her head. This wasn't worth a broken leg. Puk floated back, and Gat continued his march to the exit.

Viola tried to yell for help, but her lungs were still having a hard time catching breath. Stare after stare slid away from Viola's eyes. There were no friends here. Nobody cared what was happening to her. Other than Puk, and the drunk captain behind her, Viola was alone on the moon.

"Problem with me," Davin announced from the floor, "is that I'm a package deal, see?"

"With who, other washed up losers?" Whelk, coming up alongside Gat, shot back.

"Nah, Whelk, my crew,"

Viola didn't see the big man until Gat dropped her to the floor. She caught herself on the wall of *The Bitter Chill* and turned around to see the giant man standing over Gat, daring him to fight. The newcomer was one of Davin's crew, one of the bunch who'd been at the table a minute earlier.

The giant man had ripples and bulges beneath his clothes, and not in the usual spot for muscles. As she looked at him, the man looked back at her, his face inscrutable in the shadows of the bar's lighting.

"Now might be a good time to run," Puk buzzed next to her.

"Agreed," Viola replied.

As she back-pedaled, Viola glanced over at Whelk, who was standing very still as a woman with lava-red hair pressed a jagged glass edge up to his throat.

"Phyla," Whelk said. "You know this is just business."

"Yeah, but now it's our business," the woman, Phyla, replied.

Whelk raised his hands and Phyla, after a slight press with the glass to remind the man how close his day had come to ending terribly, backed away. Viola turned to head out the exit, and stared right at a grinning dude wearing a full flight suit.

"Now, lady, you weren't thinking of skipping out on your rescuers without even saying thanks, were you?" The man asked.

"Uh, thanks?" Viola said, trying to get around him.

She just needed to leave this place. Right now.

"Merc, leave her alone," another woman, sounding tired, said. "She's scared enough without you talking to her."

Viola felt a hand on her shoulder. Davin's head swung into view, his right hand sweeping up in a grand gesture.

"My crew, right on cue," Davin said, before running Viola through high-speed introductions.

Between the lights, the adrenaline, and the growing realization that Viola's father had put coin on her capture, Viola barely kept track of the names coming her way.

"For as many times as we save your ass, cap'n, it'd be nice to see a bonus," Cadge said, a beer in each hand.

"Keeping your captain alive is just part of the contract," Davin said, voice adopting a sage inflection and draping an arm over Cadge's shoulders. "To warrant a bonus, well, you'd save me before the fight started."

"There's an impossibility," Phyla said, eyes rolling.

"Davin's been nice enough to introduce us to you," Opal said, leveling a very sober look at Viola. "Maybe you can return the favor, tell us why they were after you?"

"Because I ran away and my father wants me back," Viola replied, adding her and Puk's names. The bot was hovering over her shoulder, tracking its camera on each of them. What Puk could do if they took Viola, she didn't know, but the little bot was trying.

"Putting a bounty on your own daughter? That's cold," Merc said.

"One way to get the job done," Cadge said. "Enough money, he'll get her back."

"I'm standing right here," Viola replied.

"Stop. Go outside," said Mox, nodding towards the other side of the bar, where Gat and Whelk were now talking to another crowded table. "Safer."

Nobody objected, and the group escorted Viola out of the bar. Viola was in the middle, with Mox and a wobbly Davin in front. The boulevard was even quieter now, the hour getting close to morning. Exhausted, hurt, Viola still noticed the ten people standing in the through-way. Because they were staring right at her.

15

FISTICUFFS

Oh, look at these bastards in their dirty reds and blues. Matching uniforms like little kids. Cadge slipped his hands into his pockets, ran his fingers through his stunner mitts. The gloves took the kinetic energy off the punch and shocked the victim, blasting their nerves into a spasm. Cadge had seen their original owner knock jaws loose with the mitts, was scaring everyone in the place. Until he forgot Cadge was behind him. It would've been a shame to leave these toys.

"I get the displeasure of seeing you twice in one day, Ferro?" Davin slurred at the lead trooper.

"Unfortunate, yes," Ferro said. "It seems your circumstances have worsened. You are a murderer now."

The captain was a lot of things, but Cadge knew he was too goody-goody to ever straight-up murder someone. Wasn't Davin's way. Wasn't Cadge's way either. Killing a man was fine, but doing it without a fight? Where was the fun in that?

"Murderer's a new one," Davin replied, standing straighter. "Where'd you hear that?"

Cadge noticed the new girl, Viola, was edging towards the back of their group, her little bot hovering next to her. Whelk had been talking about a bounty, but here Davin was treating her like a new friend. Bet the girl's bounty would be able to keep them paid till they found a new job. He'd have to talk to Davin about it, assuming they didn't all die right here.

"You, and your team, killed two inspectors. The ones who landed here earlier today," Ferro said.

"Liar," Mox said.

"I have no wish to start our lives here with violence," Ferro continued, eying the big man. "Come peacefully, and perhaps we will find redemption together."

Cadge suppressed a laugh as a few of the troopers looked at Mox and stepped back. Cowards.

"Ferro, you seem like a good guy," Davin said, stepping forward. "So I'm sorry for what's about to happen."

Cadge felt the smile as Davin threw the punch. As soon as Davin's fist connected, Cadge sprinted towards the closest trooper, his feet skipping across the floor and then leaving it as Cadge dove through the air and hit the man in the chest. They fell to the ground, Cadge working his arms into the man's ribs, each jab knocking volts through the clothes.

Flashes, white ones, flitted through the air as Cadge moved the trooper's body to keep him in the way of the stunning lasers. The secret to surviving a scrum was to stay low. Go for the knees, ankles, stomaches.

Throwing the first trooper to the ground, stunned into oblivion, Cadge rushed a pair of panicked enemies. To his right, he saw another trooper fly by, sent by Mox on a one-way trip to pain. Only problem was that none of the Nines had their real weapons. A brawl was one thing, but as soon as these troopers got themselves composed, it would get ugly.

Cadge jumped towards the two troopers as they raised their rifles. Each hand grabbed a shoulder and Cadge pulled both to the ground with him. Elbows flying, knees jabbing, Cadge worked every muscle he had in a frenzied dance. When he felt the troopers go limp, felt them stop trying to hit him back or run away, Cadge looked towards the fight.

Mox carried Phyla in one hand, Opal in the other, both of them hanging on as the metal man ran out of the tangle of bodies. Merc covered their retreat—the pilot picked up a lost rifle and sprayed stunning bolts at the remaining troopers, who dove into cover behind benches and potted plants. Davin dodged a looping haymaker from Ferro by falling flat on his back and rolling away.

Ferro took the opportunity to talk into his comm. Cadge couldn't hear the words, but could guess what was being called. The new girl was gone.

"Back to the *Jumper*!" Davin yelled, scrambling to his feet.

Mox broke into a run while Merc back-pedaled, still shooting. Several troopers were coming out of cover, aiming their shots. The Nines were going to get picked off. Nobody was looking at Cadge, though.

A big mistake.

"You're all a bunch of cowards!" Cadge yelled, running towards the troopers.

They turned as one, but the cocky jackasses overestimated his height and their shots flashed over Cadge's head. Or singed it, the smell of burning hair breezing into his nose.

Cadge hit the first trooper low, in the abdomen,

bouncing off the charge into the next one. That trooper had his rifle pointing down, and Cadge grabbed the barrel, shoving the gun straight back into the trooper's face. Two down.

Cadge kept his legs pumping towards the third trooper, and took his stun shot right in the chest. The lasers had no actual force, so Cadge kept moving forward even as he stopped feeling any of his muscles. Like watching a movie where his head was the camera. The trooper that hit him didn't have time to get out of the way, and Cadge slammed into him, crashing them to the ground.

Above Cadge, the great mass of Jupiter glowed in the sky. A fixed feature. Lights along the boulevard were coming up to simulate an actual solar cycle. Would've been pleasant, if Cadge could've felt his own body. Trooper helmets, glazed and gray, poked into his vision, staring at him. Cadge tried to spit, but his mouth wouldn't work. Still, if the bastards were watching him, that meant they weren't chasing after the rest of the Nines.

Mission accomplished.

The stun shot's effects hit fast, but also spread slow as they worked their way through Cadge's body. Lose the fun extremities first, consciousness last. Cadge felt his brain slag as Ferro came into view. The man was talking, words not making it into Cadge's mind. The view changed as troopers picked him up. Carrying him somewhere, maybe to be shot or dumped out an airlock. But hey, at least he wasn't bored.

16

RUN AND HIDE

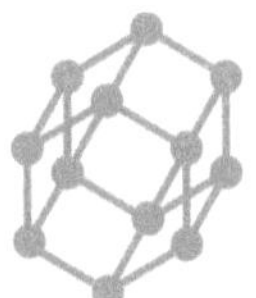

As soon as Davin's fist hit the lead trooper, Viola ran. Puk followed.

"They're not even chasing you," Puk said, buzzing up alongside her. "Which, given the effort to rescue you from those clowns, strikes me as a waste."

"Shut it, Puk."

Viola risked a glance back and yeah, Puk was right. The two groups were brawling, with bright white stunning bolts flying out. Mox, that big metal man, was throwing a trooper into another pair as easily as Viola would throw a ball, bowling the troopers over with their own man. Who were these people?

Viola kept running, past the hotel and to the large doors leading into the bays. Through those doors and past the ever-present cleaning and maintenance bots combing the corridor. Past bay one, bay two, and then Viola pulled up short. Ahead in the corridor, outside bay four, where Viola parked the *Gepard*, was another set of those uniformed troopers. Three of them, rifles in proud display. Gesturing into the bay at someone Viola couldn't see. One turn and they'd spot her.

"Are they searching my ship?" Viola said, pausing by the open door to bay three.

"Can't tell," Puk replied. "Given your luck with people today, though, I'd hide."

A single large cargo carrier dominated bay three. The ship looked like it had a disease, modules sprouting from the original frame in blocky growths. Different paints coated the parts, as though the crew assembled the whole thing at once from a random collection.

The ship's ramp was lowered, touching the ground. Open door at the top. If she stayed here and those troopers came by, she'd be caught. Viola started towards the carrier.

"You're not," Puk said. "There's crates right over there. Hide."

"They'll see me if they come in here. The ship's the best hiding place," Viola said, continuing towards the ramp.

"And if man-eating pirates own it?"

"Those odds have to be worse than waiting out here."

Viola picked up the pace. A quick jog up the ramp and into the ship's cargo bay. A few scattered metal containers sat around. Too sparse for a ship in active use. Graffiti coated the walls. Drawings of abstract landscapes, faces. One looked like Earth. Another, made up of swiped reds, must have been Mars.

Circular doors led to other modules, and Viola picked one of those at random. Walked up to it, and as she came close, the door spiraled open. Not locked. Whoever owned this thing really trusted nobody would take it.

A small hallway, barely wide enough for two people. Hanging on the walls were maps, charts, diagrams of shipping routes and trade laws for various settlements. After those came a series of … trophies? One resembled a piece of fur, brown and thick and cut in an intricate arrangement with swirling versions of Saturn's rings. Another a dustwork, made from grinding and scattering Mars dust in spots on sticky fabric. This one made fragile and textured work of a Martian mountain landscape.

Several doors branched off, Viola peeked inside them while Puk hovered behind, watching for any sign of the owners.

Crew quarters, each room holding a small bunk. Enough for four crew members on this level, but, going by Galaxy Forge requirements, a ship this size would need at least double that to run well. The first room had a calendar with pictures of Earth on it, landmarks that Viola recognized from classes when she was younger. Pyramids, the fjords of Norway, the regrown Amazon jungle. There was a temptation to dig further, but Viola stopped herself. Maybe she'd get pity hiding back in the engines, but not if she rooted through their stuff.

Further down the hallway Viola hit a fork, one way leading to the engine panel, the other leading to a small launch bay. Which way to go …

"Is someone there?" came an older man's voice, scratched and strained.

"You could run," Puk said as Viola took a step towards the sound. "We could get out of here. There's no telling what this guy might do."

"And go where, Puk?" Viola said, then kept walking towards the sound.

In front of the large console and metal access hatch to the left engine sat an older man, his white beard clotted with blood that spread across the cream coat and pants he wore. Despite the wrecked state, the man's eyes tracked up to Viola's, alert and fiery.

"You're not the one I was expecting," the old man said.

"Neither were you," Viola countered.

"Fair enough, I suppose."

"What happened?"

"These thugs in uniforms. They said they'd destroy the ship if we didn't lower the ramp, and then they just about did it anyway," the old man said, then coughed hard. "Much as I'd like to talk, it's rather painful. If you aren't going to kill me, would you mind helping me to the medical bay?"

Viola hesitated a second, Puk's warning dangling in her ear. If she tried to carry this guy somewhere, there'd be no running if someone found her. But then, what other choice was there? Leave the old man to suffer?

"You'll find I'm not as heavy as I look," the old man said as Viola crouched and put his arm over her shoulders. "I'm mostly hot air, you know."

"Was that a joke?"

Picking up the man reminded Viola of how long she'd been awake, her legs exhausted and twitching with the extra weight.

"I find it's the dire situations when humor is most necessary," the man said. "And I suppose since you are attempting to save my life, introductions are in order. I'm Erick."

"Erick's clearly crazed," Puk buzzed in Viola's ear. "I say we ditch him and run."

"I heard that," Erick replied. "Though I can't fault your little mechanical friend much if, indeed, you came to this ship under suspicious circumstances."

Viola managed to walk back to the stretch with the crew rooms on either side.

"I'm just trying to hide."

"Oh? And who is pursuing you? Perhaps we share a foe."

"Someone named Davin? He had a crew with him."

Erick laughed, a weak, coughing thing that did little for him making it through the injuries. Viola couldn't stop moving forward —she worried that as soon as momentum stopped, Erick's weight would crush them both to the floor —but she wanted to ask what was so funny.

"What's your name?" Erick asked as the laughter died.

"Viola."

"Viola, it seems you've met my captain."

"I told you!" Puk said, buzzing ahead and looking out into the main entryway of the ship. "It's still clear! Drop him and go!"

"Tell me why I shouldn't," Viola said, nearing the end of the hallway.

"Don't worry, Viola, Davin's never made it a point to hurt young women. I wouldn't be here otherwise," Erick said. "I'm sure it was a misunderstanding."

"He didn't hurt me, really," Viola said, replaying the bar scene in her mind.

None of the crew had done anything to her, except help, now that Viola thought about it. But there'd been distractions. When he wasn't being attacked, Davin might focus on that bounty.

"If you're having doubts, I can personally guarantee your safety," Erick said. "Davin will let you walk right off this ship if I ask."

"That's a lot of trust," Puk said.

"I'm not going to leave him to die." Viola kept moving.

"And your generosity will be repaid," Erick replied.

They lurched back into the ship's entry bay. It was empty, but Viola could hear noise outside. Erick gestured to the left, a door leading to the med room. Somewhere Erick could patch himself up. Viola stayed silent, trying to keep the easiest escape route clear in her head. That and her legs were burning from keeping Erick upright.

"What I'm trying to say, Viola, is that, as you're helping me right now, so we might be able to help you," Erick said, then sighed. "Especially as it seems this ship won't be going anywhere in the near future."

17

HEAL THYSELF

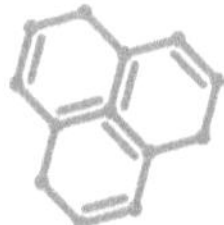

Home: a cramped three meter by three meter med room. Seeing the bed, the countertop covered with tools laid out in strict order, labeled cabinets and the bright surgical light took the edge off Erick's constant jarring ache in his stomach. All of the equipment gained in bits and pieces. Junk here and there re-purposed to keep the crew alive. Now it would do the same for him.

Hopefully.

"I'll need you to put me on the bed," Erick said.

Viola shuffled over to the thin-cushioned apparatus, a sickly gray plastic covering and yellowed rails forming the bed's accents. Viola twisted her body, allowing Erick to slip out of her grasp and fall onto the bed. The cushion felt cool, but then, Erick had the hot stickiness of blood over the lower half of his body right now. It only made sense.

"Are you ready?" Erick asked. "I know I am asking a lot of you, but I think you'll be disappointed if you dragged me all this way only to have me expire upon this table."

"Guess we'll find out," Viola said. "Puk, can you run the diagnostics?"

Erick watched the little bot hover over the wound in his abdomen. With proper cameras, even small bots like Puk could measure a pulse, track his breathing and pupil dilation, among other things. Still, bots were at the mercy of their programmers. One error and the readings could be wrong, fatally so.

"Looks like a nasty fist fight," Puk said, buzzing around Erick and scanning him with its lens. "And you didn't win it, doc. I'm reading bruises all over the place. The blood from the mouth is coming from a split lip, nothing serious. But the stomach, ouch. Did you take a hard kick there?"

"Did I? Possibly," Erick replied, hearing the sound of his own voice, its faintness alarming. "The man's boots were sharp."

"That's what I'm reading. Six-centimeter laceration, deep. Viola, that's where we need to focus."

Viola stood up, glanced around the room.

"Talk to me, Erick," Viola said. "I don't know where anything is here."

"I'm sorry, my dear, but you're going to have to learn quickly. The scissors are in that top drawer on the left, along with the stitching supplies," Erick said. "But before you close the wound, you'll want to make sure that, um, that . . ."

Erick tried to stay focused, but the world decided to swirl. To dim and lighten at random. The blood loss caused the problems, but Erick hadn't seen this side in person before. Experienced the lost as his limbs, his mind started shutting down.

It was horribly fascinating.

"Hey, Viola, he's crashing here. Since you want to help this guy, we have to move!" Puk announced, the words echoing and fading, coming to Erick's ears from another world. "Lift the shirt away!"

Erick felt his shirt being pulled. So sticky there, around his stomach. A scissors snipped the fabric.

"It wasn't a good shirt anyway," Erick mumbled.

The girl ought to know that so she wouldn't feel bad ruining it.

"Now what?" Viola asked.

Erick wasn't sure what she meant.

The ache diminished, agony quieting to the smallest pin pricks. A bad sign. Come on, Erick, it's not time to quit yet. He forced his eyes open, focused on the bright light.

"I don't think he got that from a kick," Puk said. "Looks like a knife wound."

A knife wound. Were they talking about him? They might be. Back to the present.

"At least it looks clean," Puk said. "Relatively anyway. Organs beneath look OK. We're just dealing with a lot of blood loss."

"Oh, is that all?"

"Count your blessings, sister," Puk replied. "Now, let's get to stitching."

The first stitch felt like a poke. A second poke. The girl moved quickly. A third poke. Every tiny lance through his skin felt like a stride towards life. A fourth poke. Lacing the skin together was always his favorite part. It meant the job was nearly done, and it was only necessary if the patient lived. A sign of success.

The fifth poke was hard, sharp. Erick sat up. His eyes tracked down, saw Viola and Puk leaning over his stomach. Her hands, gloved, were so red.

"That doesn't look good," Erick said.

"Just hang in there, Doc. We got this," Puk replied.

The pokes continued. One after another. Erick laid back, darkness flashing at the corners of his eyes. But he held onto those pokes. Each one another rung in that ladder leading up to sanity. He could let go, fall back into that endless chasm. But then, when had he, doctor on a mercenary ship far from the comforts of Earth, chosen the easy route?

An infinity later, Erick's eyes fluttered open. An IV tube led into his front wrist. His stomach felt tight, the pain muted. Viola over in the corner, sitting in a chair looking dazed. The sound of boots on metal echoed through the ship. Either the good guys coming back, or enemies here to finish the job. Ironic, if it was the latter. All this to save an old man just to have him gunned down.

The door to the cargo room opened, and Davin's face appeared.

"You alive, Erick?" Davin said, stepping into the room.

Viola's face twitched. Erick could see her muscles tighten. Thinking about a run for it. The little bot was out of sight, no doubt planning some sneak attack to buy the girl some time.

"Thanks to Viola here, yes."

Davin glanced at Viola, but continued to Erick, looking over the stitch work and the IV.

"Not bad," Davin muttered. "What's your timetable?"

"A few hours. Maybe less."

"We're going to move in twenty. After everyone gets geared up."

"Move?"

"They have Trina. And Cadge, now. If we want to get the *Jumper* off the ground, we'll need Trina back."

Of course they took Trina. Of course he'd been unable to prevent it.

"I'm sorry, Davin."

"Not your fault," the captain said. "Now, Viola. What're we going to do with you?"

18

____

WHAT IT TAKES

Davin walked Viola out of the med room, had her throw away the bloody gloves and shut off that blinding light so Erick could sleep. The central hold was empty, the others getting a hot minute to take a breath before the real fun started.

Looking at the painted walls of his cargo hold, Davin realized his vision wasn't swimming anymore. He wasn't listing from side to side. Amazing what getting punched and shot at will do for sobriety.

"So what are you running from?" Davin asked.

Viola and her floating bot shied away from him, her back to a wall.

"I'm not running," Viola said.

"Oh really. Just came alone to this frozen hellscape of a moon as a vacation?"

Behind Viola, painted on the wall, was one of Mox's works. The gray towers of the lunar surface, a dot of blue in the sky for Earth. Always amazed Davin how the big man kept perspective.

"I was bored," Viola said. "It sounds stupid, I know. But that's what it was."

"You're talking to a guy who just started a fight with the police. Stupid is very familiar." Davin let her have the wall, stood a meter away towards room's center. Spend enough time on a spaceship and personal space gets to be a big deal. "See, what I'm trying to find out is whether you're a problem or an opportunity. Why don't you help me."

"I'm not trying to be anything," Viola replied, folding her arms and staring at the ground.

"So you're open to ideas, then?"

The girl looked up at him. Dammit if Davin wasn't a sop for a hope-filled face. Phyla should be here, ready to throw the cold bucket of reality on the star-faring fantasy Davin was going to offer.

"I'm not a fan of bounty chasers," Davin continued. "Those guys at the bar. It'd feel good to stiff them. Take you out of their reach."

"Meaning what?"

Viola was looking Davin dead-on now. Good. The girl had a spine.

"Meaning I'm not a fan of freeloaders either. Or rich kids that don't have anything to contribute. You want to ride with us, you have to make it worth my while."

"Who says I want to come with you?"

"You don't, I'll let you walk off this ship right now. Ramp's right there. Take your chances with Whelk. He's real nice once you get to know him."

The bot buzzed Viola's ear. Davin didn't eavesdrop. If he was reading the kid right, if she had the guts to fly here on her own and walk into that bar tonight . . .

"That man back there? The one you punched?" Viola said. "He called you murderers."

The words hung in the air, the silent question tied to them.

"What do you think?" Davin replied. "We look like a bunch of killers to you?"

"Puk ran your name. There's a charge."

"Let me guess, from today?"

Viola nodded. A universal Free Laws registry synced recorded crimes in a database across satellites, available to anyone. People looking for coin could chance bringing someone in for the reward, otherwise Free Law-signing cities would arrest anyone on the list.

"What'd they put us?"

"Three-hundred thousand," Viola said, and Davin couldn't stop a whistle. An amount over five thousand brought the hunters out from the shadows. This high, the Nines would attract the real rough customers.

"We must be dangerous then. How about before that? Anything?"

"Nothing like this," Viola said. "Small stuff."

"See? We're harmless."

"Uh huh."

"Look," Davin said. "I was where you were. Stuck in a place I didn't want to be and offered an out. We need another member."

"I'm not a mercenary," Viola said, spreading her arms as if to show she wasn't carrying a dozen weapons.

"Did you program that bot?" Davin nodded at Puk.

"Yeah. Went a little overboard on a class project."

"Then we can use you," Davin glanced at his comm. "I have to get my gear. You want to leave, the ramp's right there. You think you want to stay, go up to the cockpit and talk to Phyla."

Davin turned and left before Viola could ask another

question. The girl looked like she would fit in nicely if she stayed. Bonus, she'd come cheap. And if she didn't work out, there was always that bounty.

Davin's cabin was the largest on the ship. Ramshackle souvenirs from a dozen spaceports littered the room, from stick-figure statues of the first native Martians to swirling balls of gas literally captured from Jupiter's atmosphere.

Towards the head of the bed, near his own pillow, Davin had a lamp that filtered light through a blue slate of Europa ice. In the locker on the right side was his objective, hanging on a hook.

Melody was the deadly parting gift of the last captain, along with the *Jumper* itself. The departing captain didn't say anything about it, and Davin found Melody on his first walk through the ship, no note except a full supply of charged battery packs for ammo. Davin slotted a fresh charge into Melody right then, slipped a couple more into his pack.

Next to Melody was the same series of sidearm everyone on the *Jumper* carried. Gotta love bulk discounts. The weapons weren't much in a big fight, but they'd knock a man out cold if Davin shot him close.

"Mox, Merc, Opal, you ready?" Davin said into his comm. "And hey, we're marked at three hundred thousand. Be ready in case there's a surprise."

Three clicks came back. The universal affirmative. Time to stage a rescue.

19

VIDEO EVIDENCE

Phyla ran her hands over the three consoles that made up the *Jumper*'s cockpit. A pair of cushioned chairs nestled in the middle, one of which she occupied. The view closed off now, the armor shades blocking outside light. She was busy checking to see whether their visitors had left any nasty surprises. The idea that someone had been pushing these buttons, adjusting her settings had Phyla feeling ill, violated.

"Hello?" said a voice behind her. Phyla jerked around and tried to put on a neutral expression. Viola, wasn't that her name? The girl was staring past Phyla, at the shifting updates on the consoles as they ran through their checks of the *Jumper*'s systems.

"They change based on what the ship's doing," Phyla said. "Because we're resting, it's telling us all the things we'd be interested in for a maintenance stop, or a cargo load."

Viola nodded and Phyla reached her hand towards the central console, then gestured, sweeping the status updates away. An overlay of choices appeared, words beneath simple icons. Flight, cargo, life support. Tap and Phyla could get a second-by-second update on every part of the *Jumper*.

"All of these are different sets?" Viola asked.

"You got it," Phyla replied. "Davin trusts me to keep the *Jumper* running, and I start by keeping the systems as advanced as possible. It's how we know that if we tried lifting off, even if we could get the outer bay door open, they blocked the cooling systems. We'd be in the air a few minutes, then the engines would overheat. We'd be a firework."

"Is it because they think you killed somebody?"

"Maybe," Phyla said, watching the life support checks come back green. One system that wasn't sabotaged, anyway. "I think we're being set up."

"For what?"

"Eden's upset they lost a pair of inspectors, so Marl pastes us with the blame. Why they canceled our contract. But what I don't understand is why Marl gave us twenty-four hours to leave, and then ambushed us outside of a bar. Then tried to kill our doctor and kidnapped our mechanic."

"She changed her mind?" Puk asked.

"But why?" Phyla bit her lip. Eden was a business, an entity that moved slow and evaluated all the options before targeting the most profitable one. Why shift out a security contract so fast when evidence was on the Nines side?

"So," Viola said. "Davin said to come talk to you if I wanted to stay."

"He tell you why?"

"To come to you? No."

"Watch this," Phyla said.

Phyla waved a hand over the center console and the display shifted up and appeared over the closed windshield. A much larger screen. Tapping an icon of a camera, the panel shifted to a display showing several recordings taken over the last few days. The first box listed a time only a few hours old. Phyla touched it and the video played.

Trina, a tiny spitfire with blue hair—her color of the month— knotted into a bun, was digging through a supply container in the Jumper's main bay. A few seconds in, Trina paused in her rummaging and glanced towards the ramp. The angle caused the back of Trina's head to face the camera, the boarding ramp visible on the right side of the frame.

"That's Trina," Phyla said. "Our mechanic. There's no sound in these, unfortunately, so I have no idea what she's saying down the ramp."

Trina edged closer to the boarding ramp and then jumped past it to the control panel on the wall. The mechanic pulled a small lever and the boarding ramp retracted. On the low edge of the ramp, an arm appeared, then a head. A trooper climbed his way up the ramp as it swung closed. Trina saw the guy too and reached back into the crate for one of the metal tools. Holding it out in front of her like a club, Trina backed away.

"You think she's running, but Trina knows every inch of this ship," Phyla said. "That panel there, put enough weight on it and it'll give. Just a bit, but enough."

The trooper took a step towards Trina and stumbled as his knee dropped farther than he expected. Trina leaned in, swinging the metal club. The trooper moved his left arm in the way, taking the hit and falling right. With his other arm, the trooper pulled out a small object that flashed. Trina froze, the club dropping from her grip. She fell after it, lying on the floor.

"She's only stunned," Viola said. "The color, it's based on

the make-up of the energy triggered. The white, it's more electrical, locks up the nervous system."

Phyla glanced at Viola. The girl knew her lasers. It was a start.

In the video, the man walked over to the control panel and reversed the boarding ramp's course. He turned and shouted something down the opening. Then an orange blast from off the screen lanced through the cargo bay and into the trooper's side.

"Erick?" Viola asked.

"Better shot than you'd think. I've never figured out where he learned how to fight so well."

The trooper stumbled onto the ramp, then fell to his knees. Erick walked into the feed, towards the control panel, but a flurry of guns from out of sight launched lasers up into the ship, driving Erick back. The doctor settled for reaching Trina and dragging her away. Two seconds later and more troopers appeared on the ramp, moving upward in a crouch, guns ready and pointed. Erick and Trina weren't in the shot any longer.

"The next few minutes is Erick and Trina playing cat and mouse with them," Phyla said. "His mouth keeps moving, like he's trying to reach us over his comm, but they had at least one localized jammer."

"I don't understand why they'd be doing this?"

"That's the million coin question."

Phyla reached over and swiped forward. Now Erick and Trina, still motionless, were in the left engine room. Erick stashed Trina in a corner, then took up a covered position next to the room's entrance. For a bit there was nothing, only Erick staring down the hallway. Then something made him jump, and Erick looked back at Trina, closed his eyes for a breath, then leaned around the corner and fired. Erick kept shooting, targeted and steady, until the gun flashed a red laser, a marker that there was only one more shot left.

Erick took another look back at Trina, aimed the gun at her, then shook his head. Pointed the weapon back off screen.

"He thought they'd kill them both, or do something worse," Phyla said. "I can't even imagine feeling that hopeless."

Erick fired the last shot. A chorus of replies blasted at the doctor, who ducked away from the lasers. Then a few troopers ran into the room, grabbing Erick and throwing him against the engine housing. When Erick tried to throw a punch, one of the troopers kicked the doctor in the stomach. Phyla paused the video there, then wiped it from the cockpit display.

"You don't need to see the rest," Phyla said.

"So they took Trina, but left Erick?"

"Maybe they thought he would die anyway. So they compromised our ship. All while we were out at the bar, helping you."

"Wait, this wasn't—"

"I know it's not your fault," Phyla said, looking away. "But we should have been here helping them."

"What are you going to do?"

A speaker on the left console crackled. Davin's voice came over, telling everyone to come to the cargo hold.

Phyla patted the sidearm hanging in a holster on her chair, "We're going to get our friends back."

20

RESCUE MISSION

Opal sat on the bench, sipping coffee and watching the morning shifters heading into their stores, offices, wherever. Across the boulevard was the one place Eden Prime built to house any offenders it couldn't immediately banish. Ten cells, laser-locked and arranged in a circle. A lot of effort for drunks that needed sobering up. Getting here was too expensive to risk doing something stupid enough to get exiled. A trooper stood in front, holstered gun visible, though the man spent most of his time staring at his comm.

"You think that's where they took Trina and Cadge?" Davin's voice came over her comm.

"I'm going to get a better angle now, see if I can spot their heat signatures," Opal said.

The prison jutted out from the wall of Eden Prime, stretching to the center of the boulevard that ran the course of the station. The outside walls looked three stories high. Automated security meant nothing so old-fashioned as guard towers stood on the ramparts.

Above the front door sat a row of windows looking in at

the prison's command center. Tinted, the windows prevented anyone from seeing what was happening inside, but gave a clear view out. A problem for most would-be spies. Opal, however, preferred to play with the less visible spectra.

With a twist on the left lens of the goggles sitting on her face, Opal tweaked the view to capture infrared rays only. To save on heating costs, Eden Prime built the ventilation to leak into the boulevard, filtering out towards air scrubbers in the ceiling and floors. The prison leaked plenty of heat straight towards Opal, and the two bodies working consoles in the prison command center stood out in red. The hallways behind, where the cells sat, were murkier. Body heat blended with other sources to make a hazy picture.

"Can't tell for sure," Opal said. "If I had to hunch it, though, I'd say they aren't creative enough to put her anywhere else."

"Calling for a break-in on a hunch isn't exactly my favorite thing," Davin replied.

"No time for anything else," Opal said. "Make the call, captain."

Opal braced for a snap back. A reprimand. Attempting to order a captain on Mars with that tone would've had her getting crap assignments for a week. Possibly worse.

"Have to roll the dice sometimes. Get set on the entrance," Davin commed. "We'll be there soon."

"On it, boss," Opal said. This wasn't Mars. Remember that. Now get in position.

Not that there were great sniping options in the open boulevard. The closed store behind Opal had a second story and a few windows. Perfect, if only she could get in. The one window on the first floor peered into a blank interior, everything of value removed to pay the owner's debts. Still, Opal figured the window tied into the station's alarm network. A smash and she'd have troopers swarming her within a couple of minutes. The door, however . . .

Opal stood and went to the door. The flat metal sheet had a red light on the right. Key card access, programmed to allow the new owners in and nobody else. Thing was, the Wild Nines had cards that gave them emergency access anywhere. Necessary if they were policing the whole station. Opal still had hers. Maybe they hadn't been deactivated yet.

"Can I help you?" said a man's voice behind Opal. "This store's closed, and I noticed you've been out here for a while."

"Sorry, I used to come here. I was trying to figure out why it was shut down," Opal said.

"Sure. I scanned you, and it looks like you have quite the weapon in your pack. Want to talk about that?"

Opal stared at the trooper. "No, I don't think I do."

"Too bad. 'Cause I'm going to have to confiscate it. Not allowed on Eden Prime."

"That's Eden for you. Always changing their rules," Opal said, slinging her pack off of her back. "Can I get it back when I leave?"

"I'll submit it to holding. When you leave Europa, you can go ask for it from them at the entrance to the bays. You don't cause any problems, they'll give it to you," the trooper said, keeping one hand on his sidearm.

The trooper wasn't accosting her, the guy was only doing his job. Which made the next part tougher. But random chance had no mercy. Taking out the jumble of parts that made up her rifle, Opal handed the armful to the trooper, who took it.

"Oh, you'll want to be careful with this part," Opal said, reaching towards the guard and pressing the rifle's magnetic assembly button. The charge kicked and the parts slotted together, matching their precise strengths, and pinching the guards fingers, and arms in between pieces.

The trooper yelped and shook his hands out of the rifle, which finished snapping together, just in time for Opal's kick to land in the trooper's chest. The guard fell backward to the ground, groaning, and Opal reached for the rifle. As her hand came close, a bolt screamed from the prison and glanced off of the floor in front of her.

Screams rang out along the boulevard as people ran away for cover. Opal dove, rolling behind the bench and sneaking a look at the prison. The tint across the windows had changed color, a filter to let the lasers through. Behind it, at least two more silhouettes aimed at her.

"Captain, about that help," Opal said into the comm, her eyes tracking to the rifle, sitting meters away, out of reach.

"Yeah?" Davin's voice.

"I'll take it now."

21

OUTNUMBERED

The guards didn't bother shooting at Opal behind the bench. Not that the metal was much protection, but the troopers were probably waiting for their friends to flank her. Opal could see the one she'd kicked climbing back to his knees, favoring his hands.

Opal reached into her waistband, along her inner thigh to where, wrapped around, was a beam knife. Her fingers flipped the tiny latch and the band curled around itself, rolling into a small cylinder and clicking together in her waiting hand. The knife emitted a small, direct laser a few centimeters out in front. Good for poking an eye out, or severing ties.

"Davin," Opal said into the comm. "Where are you?"

"On our way."

"I have a little knife, and a bunch of troopers with guns coming. I wasn't planning to die today."

"You won't," Davin replied.

She'd hold him to that. The front door to the prison opened with the audible whoosh of air moving from one spot to the next. Opal peeked through the gaps in the bench, saw four troopers running towards her, and took a deep breath. They'd be on her in a three-count. Opal watched the shadows on the closed store, broadcast there from the prison's bright lights.

One. The tops of the trooper's heads appeared, rising up the wall like ghosts. Their boots hitting the boulevard's floor made a hollow pattering.

Two. Beneath the noise, Opal thought she could hear them talking to each other. The shadows split, a pair to the bench's sides. Close now. Opal tensed her legs, shifted her feet to give maximum lift. A single chance at surprise.

Three.

The first guard sliced by Opal's beam knife in his hands yelled and backed away. The other three paused, keeping a meter of distance between them and Opal, who stayed at a crouch behind the bench.

"It's just a knife," one of the troopers said. "Stun her."

As though flipping a switch, the troopers seemed to remember that they had that setting on their guns. Opal, watching the shadows, saw the trooper behind her slip the gun from his holster. In a single motion, Opal turned and swung her right arm around, letting go of the knife just as her arm passed the apex of her swing. The beam blade turned in the air for a second, before bouncing off the trooper's face, hilt-first.

"Crap," Opal said as the trooper guard rubbed his mug, looking confused.

The other two guards grabbed and pulled Opal to the ground. The binders went on, clasping around her wrists and dialing to a tightness that prevented movement but still allowed circulation. One trooper pressed her face hard into the floor, the icy metal biting up through her cheek and into her teeth. And then the pressure vanished as the trooper pulled Opal to her feet, turned her around to face him.

"I think I recognize you," the trooper said. "You're one of the Wild Nines, right?"

Opal said nothing, stared at his face. Breathe. Ignore her racing heart and pumping adrenaline. Stay calm.

"Hope you called your friends," the trooper continued, a loopy smile crawling on his face. "Sooner we nab all of you, sooner we can stop trying so hard."

"You're in way over your head," Opal said to the guy pushing her.

"Says the one in cuffs," the trooper retorted.

Opal's comm buzzed, a single clicking noise.

"Not for long," Opal muttered.

22

DASHING

Merc saw the prison's bright lights flooding into the boulevard and, as he ran, pulled two small discs with rubber caps in the center from clasps on his belt. Pressing the button on each one, Merc primed the discs, sending electric current running wild.

As Merc continued around the curve, the scene came into view. Five troopers, one a meter away from the prison door with Opal in tow. The other four standing around, watching, weapons holstered, at ease.

Hoped they liked surprises.

Still in stride, Merc side-armed the two discs, releasing the buttons as he threw. The discs bounced and slid along the ground towards the four troopers. A hot second after that, as the troopers were looking at them, the grounding rubber on the discs retracted and lightning struck.

Charged bolts leapt at the troopers, arcing through the air and into their guns, their hands, into any possible conductor to try to reach the ground. Lightning struck the four troopers in milliseconds, overloading their nerves and causing them to collapse, twitching.

The trooper holding Opal stared, open-mouthed, at his companions, and kept his mouth open as Opal elbowed him in the stomach, then turned, sweeping low with her leg, and tripped him. He hit the floor hard and didn't bother trying to get up.

Merc caught up to his discs, their currents discharged and sitting inert on the ground. The surrounding troopers moaned, eyes closed and curled up, nerves still twitching. If the residual shocks worked as advertised, these guys should be out for the next thirty minutes or more.

"Am I awesome?" Merc said, grabbing the discs. "Cause I think I'm pretty awesome."

The laser from the prison window caught Merc full in the chest. The blast's burning sensation spread through his body, fire crawling over kindling. Nerves roasted. His arms and legs went numb. Merc fell to his knees, trying to put himself back together.

There were things he should be doing. Should get up, cut Opal from those cuffs, should get the second disc and then break into the prison. Save Trina. Oh man, Opal would be so pissed he'd been shot. Always telling him not to show off. Reminding him every second that fighter pilots didn't know how things worked in the trenches. That training was nothing compared to the real thing. Guess she was right.

Opal was right next to him now. Merc looked at her, and realized he was on his side. When did that happen? Tried to ask Opal how bad it was. Couldn't tell if his mouth was moving. Things hurt now, pain coming in from all corners. Just, everywhere.

Opal pulled him behind a bench. Another laser flashed nearby.

"Sorry," Merc said, or thought he did.

It was too hard to tell.

23

ASSAULT TACTICS

avin didn't want heroes on his crew. They tended to get themselves shot and ruin it for everybody. If Merc wasn't so damn good in a Viper ...

Davin and Mox moved along the outside of the prison building, working their way to the front door. It came out from the side of Eden Prime like a bulge, the curved wall slick and polished Europa rock. A few cameras dotted the two-story top, black eyes peeking out. No windows, save the big one in front. Cheaper to put screens inside than drill holes in the structure. On a normal morning, the shops around the prison would already crawl with perusers. Laser-fire had a way of keeping things clear.

Across the boulevard, Opal had Merc cowering behind a bench. Lasers lanced out from above the door every few seconds when a trooper thought they had a shot. The cameras would show Davin and Mox coming along beneath, give the troopers time to prepare for a frontal assault. One that wasn't coming.

"Let's say hi," Davin said.

Mox, going without his cannon for better mobility, crouched. Then, rattling the ground, he jumped the three meters up to the large front window. At the top of his jump, Mox swung his right fist forward and shattered the glass. The big man sported thick work gloves, meant for welding spaceship hull together, and good at keeping those hands safe from the razor-sharp shards that scattered.

Davin stepped to the side as Mox crashed down, glass shattering all around him. An impressive move. Davin ought to look into one of those exoskeletons. For now, though, he'd have to make the throw with his puny human arms. Davin unclipped a small sphere from his belt, pressed a button on it with his thumb, and arced it up through the window.

"Good throw," Mox said.

A hot second later, the orb exploded in a crackling flash of bright light. Mox jumped again, this time grabbing hold of the window and pulling himself in. Davin waited for the sounds of gunfire, but there was only banging. A chair flew back out the window, bouncing through the boulevard.

"Clear," Mox's voice came over the comm.

"Opal, get Merc back," Davin said. "Phyla, Erick?"

"We know," Phyla replied. "Already prepping the bed."

Davin watched Opal pull Merc out from behind the bench. There was no way she'd be able to lift the pilot. Drag him back alive. It was lose Merc, or let Mox handle the prison by himself. Davin looked at the troopers lying on the boulevard ground, still stunned from Merc's electric discs. If that was the best they had, Mox could handle it.

"Together!" Davin said.

Opal nodded, and the two of them held Merc up between them and started the long walk back to the bays. Merc's pilot jacket, a relic from his Earth training days, was charred around the chest, the burned black looking wet next to the dyed dark of the rest of the clothes.

"Mox, you're on your own," Davin commed. "Bring Cadge and Trina home."

"Count on it."

24

READY TO LEAVE

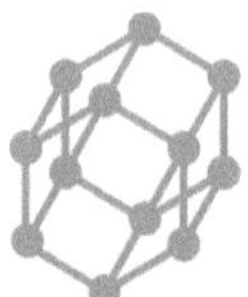

Viola repacked in record time, Puk spending every second juicing up on its charger. Was she really leaving with Davin and his band of mercenaries? Then again, what else was there to do? The clothes finished falling in her luggage and Viola pressed the vacuum button. The sunflower-yellow suitcase compressed on itself, forcing the air out. Essential for cramped spaceships.

"You're doing this, huh?" Puk asked as it came awake.

"I know, as a bot, the concept of mortality doesn't play with you." Viola hefted the suitcase and walked towards the door. "But as a person, I have an urge to feel like I'm making something of myself before I die."

"The way to do that is joining a bunch of killers after they're accused of murder?"

"Accused doesn't mean convicted."

They went to the hotel lobby. The souls staying there were rising, and the entryway was full of bleary people grabbing coffees, waters, and scattered breakfast food. Viola snagged a raspberry danish—the fruit filling lab-grown in

Eden Prime's own greenhouses—and shoved it in her mouth as she walked out the door.

"Your father would send the coin to get you home, you know," Puk said as they weaved through to the exit.

"I don't want to—"

Viola heard the shouts on opening the door. To her left, people ran back towards the hotel, towards the bays. Early workers, cast in dawn's murky beige as Eden Prime adjusted itself to let in more bright light. The solar satellite, beaming its power, glared above Viola.

"Think that's Davin's doing?" Viola asked, pointing towards the crowd.

"Let's bet on it. If it's them, you go home. If it's not, I'll shut up."

"Tempting, but we're going the other way." Viola moved towards the bays.

Phyla had said that if Viola wanted, the Nines had an extra spot. They'd let her go along with them as gratitude for helping Erick. Phyla coupled the invitation with a time check, the Nines wouldn't be waiting for Viola. Once they were in space, Viola would send a message to her father, tell him where he could get the *Gepard*.

"Their ship's broken, remember?" Puk said, gliding along behind her.

"I'm an engineer, and you're full of all of human knowledge," Viola replied. "Can't be that hard to fix."

"I will play that back to you when it blows up in our faces."

"That happens, I probably won't be around to hear it."

A few minutes walk brought them to the main bay doors, crowded with bots and people shuttling goods in and out. Conversations spread about a fight, but their tones were curious. Less worried than amused at their friends who'd stayed home for fear of a stray laser.

As Viola walked through the main doors, a man wearing a tall, thick coat and wide-brimmed hat brushed against her going the opposite direction. The contact was hard, no give, and Viola stumbled to the side.

"Hey, watch it," Puk said, buzzing near the man's head.

The man paused, and Viola noticed that though he was leaving the bays, he wasn't carrying anything. No luggage. At least, nothing outside of that coat. His head turned and, in the shadow cast by the brim of his hat, Viola could see a wild grin. The man's teeth shone. Gleamed in the light.

"Uh, never mind Puk," Viola said. "I'm fine."

The man stared at her for another second before jerking forward and walking away.

"What's up with that guy?" Puk asked.

"Don't know, don't want to know," Viola replied. "Now let's go before anything else happens."

25

PRISON BREAK

Jumping into the command center, Mox found the two troopers Davin incapacitated with his flashbang were stumbling around, holding their ears. Mox walked up to the first one, took the sidearm on the ground, swapped it to stun, and blasted him in the face. The second guard tried to run away, but tripped on a chair and fell, smacking his head on a console and falling, dead still, to the floor. Mox checked: still breathing.

"Clear," Mox commed.

"Leave them alive," Davin's command as they left the Jumper. "They think we're murderers, let's not prove them right."

But these troopers, they had already shot Merc. Taken Trina and Cadge. Sabotaged their ship. Mox wasn't sure when the line to kill was crossed, but the troopers should have crossed it by now.

The door to the command center opened, another trooper.

"What the hell is going—" the trooper said as she stared at the shattered glass.

Mox blasted her with the stunner. Taking two quick

strides, Mox caught the woman as she collapsed. On her belt dangled a red keycard, one of those that could open a cell. Mox tore the card off, set the woman in a chair and went hunting for prisoners. The main hallway, on the first floor, wrapped around the prison like a circle, with cells every four meters. The first three were unoccupied, their laser-gates sitting open. Spare beds unruffled.

As Mox approached the fourth, around a bend in the hallway, he could hear a pair of guards talking. Debating whether to run or fight. To keep the prisoner.

It wasn't their choice.

Mox didn't so much step as bound around the curve, using the exoskeleton to run nearly two meters a stride, so that when the troopers turned to see what was coming to wreck them, any fight was already lost. Mox struck the closer guard with his shoulder, leaning into the charge, and knocked the trooper into his comrade, sending them both spilling to the ground. The cell to the left held Trina, lying on the bed. But only her.

"Where is the other one?" Mox said to the cowering guards. "Short. Angry."

"We don't know!" the trooper Mox hadn't hit said, holding his hands out in front of himself. "She's the only one here, promise!"

"Are you lying?" Mox stood over them.

The panic in their faces told more truth than their blubbering denials.

"Then run," Mox said, "and I will not break you."

Both of them, the one Mox hit going gingerly, rose to their feet and ran. When one tried to keep his gun, Mox reached out, grabbed the weapon and tore it from the trooper's hands. Mox slammed the gun into the wall until it was little more than broken plastic. The only sound after that was their boots pounding the floor.

Mox pressed the card to the cell door and the laser gates cut off with a fizzle. On the thin bed in the cell, Trina lay unconscious. Still stunned. Still breathing. Mox picked her up from the bed, blanket and all, and walked out.

26

NOT GONE YET

Davin and Opal held Merc over their shoulders and ran back towards bay three.

"I have Trina," Mox commed. "Cadge is not here."

"Mox," Opal said. "Don't forget my rifle!"

"I'll get it," Mox replied. "You'll owe me."

"Can't you get another?" Davin asked Opal between breaths.

"You make me leave it, you buy me a new one."

"How much do they cost?"

Opal said the amount like a curse, and Davin replied in kind.

"Davin?" Phyla's voice over the comm. "What's the status?"

"Mox has Trina and we're comin' home. No Cadge though. Is Erick better?"

"He's moving, but it's not good."

"Then read up on laser burns, cause we're going to need a doctor."

The doors to bay one and the shipping corridor loomed

large in the growing morning. Yellowed lights projected on the large, dark gray slabs that would move aside when Davin approached. Eden branded the doors with the intertwining greens that made up their logo, echoing to rainforests Davin had never seen. The entire plaza was empty, not a good sign for what should have been a busy rush of morning lift-offs.

A worse sign?

The bay doors didn't open when they approached.

"Ah, crap," Davin said.

"Figures," Opal added.

"Phyla?" Davin commed. "I need you to see what's holding the doors shut to the bays. We can't get in."

"We don't have access to Eden Prime's internal network anymore," Phyla said. "They cut us off when—"

"That ever stop you before? We need these doors opened now!"

"Okay, I'm on it."

Setting Merc near the edge of the doors, back against the big bay walls, Davin handed Opal his holstered sidearm. She took it with a nod, then dashed away into the shadows near large crate stacks waiting for outgoing ships. Connecting the dots; the locked door, the empty boulevard during a busy part of the morning, and it wasn't hard to see a trap.

"Davin Masters!" Ferro's voice poured out of nowhere. "We meet again, and this time it will not go well for you."

Davin tried tracing the sound, but stopped when Ferro walked out into the boulevard, keeping room between them. He must have been waiting in a store.

More proof they were triggering a trap. Davin hated traps, especially when he was caught in them.

"Great," Davin said. "Glad to hear it."

"I appreciate the attitude," Ferro replied. "More fun to wipe a smile off of a face than a frown."

Ferro raised a hand and Davin felt something drop on his shoulders and knock him to the ground, breath flying from his lungs and a sharp crack sounding in his chest. His face kissed the floor. The hell was that?

"Oh, I'm sorry. Did that ruin your comeback?" Ferro said. "Then I think what happens next will leave you at a total loss for words."

"Don't think comedy's your thing, Ferro," Davin wheezed, trying to gather enough strength to lift whatever was on top of him away.

Melody, black and wicked, sat a meter away. Close enough to roll to, grab, and squeeze the trigger. Burning Ferro to a crisp would make a solid punchline to this surreal conversation.

Opal must not have a shot. Or she thought Davin could take it. Either way, Davin had to get this thing off his back.

"Good thing you are a captive audience," Ferro said. The man wasn't moving any closer. Wasn't pulling a gun. Why?

Ribs hurting, Davin collected his hands and pushed. Off of his back rolled something in a thick body bag, something with lumps and blunt edges. But Davin couldn't spare a look. He rolled to Melody, grabbed it, and fired straight up towards where the drop had come from. Two troopers watched on the second floor walkway leading to flight control. Waiting for something.

Davin wasn't going to play their game. Melody spat out six of grass-colored fireballs that struck the troopers and the bay wall, bursting into small fires on impact. The troopers fell, rolling on the ground to put out the flames.

Davin heard a surprised shout from behind and knew

Opal caught her cue. A look confirmed Ferro fled, ducking away and out of sight.

"Missed him!" Opal whispered over the comm.

"Getting sloppy, Opal," Davin replied, backing towards the bay doors and Merc, lying with his chest rising and falling in shallow breaths. "Where are we at, Phyla?"

"Almost," Phyla commed.

Davin suddenly remembered the thing that'd fallen on him. It was a large bag, with something in it, something moving. If he had Opal's beam knife . . .

"Davin, that you?" called a muffled voice inside the bag. "Cut me out of here, man!"

"Cadge?" Davin said. "You're . . . in the bag?"

"Congrats, you win the prize," Cadge said. "But you only get the reward if you get me out."

"Don't have a knife. Give me a minute to think."

A door whooshed open above. Davin looked at the walkway where the troopers had been burning, and saw nothing. Following their commander into the dark. Cowards.

"What wrong with you people?" Davin yelled at the space. "Who drops a person on somebody?"

"I did not drop her," Mox, holding Trina and with Opal's rifle slung over his back, stomped around the curve and into view.

"Nice of you to show," Davin said. "You see Ferro, any troopers come your way?"

Mox shook his head.

"I've got the doors," Phyla's commed. "Marl may have locked us out, but Eden Prime's security is as crappy as ever."

"I am profoundly thankful for their incompetence," Davin replied. "Open'em."

The bay doors lurched open, revealing the corridor beyond, and a person, leaning against the wall, sporting a thick and tall coat that covered his entire side. A collar that nearly touched his hat's brim. The person didn't turn, didn't react to the sudden reveal of a wounded pilot, a metal-framed man holding an unconscious woman, a squirming bag, and Davin aiming Melody straight down the corridor.

"Now, who are you?" Davin asked.

The person's head turned towards him. At ten meters, Davin couldn't see the man's face. But something glinted in that dark space. Teeth, maybe?

"Mox, cut Cadge out," Davin said, keeping the gun aimed on the person. "I'm not getting any warm and fuzzy vibes from Dark'n'Quiet over here."

"Davin, what's the problem?" Phyla commed. "I've got our bay doors unlocked, but I don't know how long that'll last."

"There's someone in the corridor," Davin said. "Will keep you informed."

"Mister Masters," the shape said, its voice a meandering whisper. "You and your band have been charged with a crime. A grievous one."

Davin heard Mox tearing open Cadge's bag, the little man coughing up a storm as he breathed in fresh air.

"Never thought of us as a band. More like a company. A squad," Davin replied, taking a step towards the man. Putting distance between himself and Trina, Merc.

"Murder, Mister Masters," the person continued, still leaning against the corridor wall. "The given punishment by the Free Laws is death."

"The Free Laws?" Davin laughed. "Those are a bunch of crap."

A corporate code to govern outer space. No government

control, no votes by any populace. Just a board room deciding how they wanted to punish peons they didn't like.

"Androids do not judge," the person said. "We are merely an instrument of justice."

The androids were impartial enforcers of Free Law punishment, provided a company would pay for one. That Eden coughed up the coin wasn't exactly surprising. That Davin's hands were sweating, his heart pounding, wasn't surprising either.

Androids, he could do without.

"Guess I'll take you as a compliment. Didn't know we were worth that much," Davin said, then, to Mox and Cadge, "Get going. I'll distract him till you get by."

The android faced Davin straight on. Mox and Cadge, the former carrying Merc and the latter holding Trina, edged away.

"You got this captain?" Cadge asked. "Guy looks a little messy."

"Just go for the ship when it comes at me," Davin said. "I don't want to worry about you."

As if taking a cue, the android broke into a run right at Davin. Its coat billowed out behind, and as the android ran, its arms pumped forward and nasty knives appeared in its palms. Up close and personal, then. Davin's kind of fight. The captain raised Melody and, backpedaling back to the boulevard, pulled the trigger.

Melody's six green bolts converged on the android, who, just before the shots struck home, jumped off of the corridor floor, pushed off of the side wall, and flipped over the bolts. The android hit the ground running. A helluva move.

In his peripheral, Davin saw Mox and Cadge make a break down the corridor with their precious cargo. Davin had to last long enough for them to get away.

The android passed the bay doors, went out into the boulevard lights. The android's face had a rigid exactitude to it. A perfection to the skin, the bones. Lacking life's nicks and scratches. A man's face, but not a man. And it was about to kill Davin.

The laser shot out at an angle from the shadows to Davin's right. The aim was dead on, striking the android in the chest. It barely flinched, keeping its stride moving, a molten black mark just below the shoulder where Opal shot it. Davin saw the android's right hand slide back, knife pointed, and swung Melody in the way. The android's arm pumped, the blade striking Melody's barrel with a metallic screech and sliding off. Then the android ran into Davin. The two of them fell to the ground, Davin underneath, Melody in the space between them. In a second, Davin was going to get very, very stabbed.

The android's left arm drew back while Davin struggled to throw the bot away. The android didn't look that big, but boy was it heavy. With his arms pushing against Melody pushing against the robot, Davin couldn't get any space. At least until another bolt came from the shadows, this time striking the android in the head.

The robot hesitated, the left side of its skull a molten goo, and Davin, using Melody as a brace, slid out from beneath the robot. The knife stabbed a moment later, tearing through Davin's coat sleeve and sticking the floor. Davin pulled Melody out with him and, as the android turned its half-face to look at him, Davin fired.

This time there wasn't any room for the android to move, and the bolts blasted its chest. It stumbled backwards, gouts of green flame rising from its burning clothes. Both knives dropped, bouncing off the floor as the robot's hands tried to pat out the fire.

"Time to run!" Davin yelled.

Opal was way ahead of him, already disappearing through the bay doors. Davin set off after her. Clear the bay doors, slam them shut and they'd have enough time to get away. A red bolt seared past Davin's head, scoring off of the corridor ceiling. Only another few strides till he was through. Opal, in the corridor, turned and aimed past Davin, squeezing off shot after shot over Davin's shoulders.

"Shut the door now!" Davin said into the comm and, a half-second later, the sound of the doors clanging shut behind Davin's back brought immense relief. A cold shower of hope.

Davin looked over at Opal as they walked the corridor and she gave him a nod. She'd saved his life. Not for the first, probably not for the last, time.

"You make it?" Phyla commed.

"I'm in. We'll be there in two. I want to be gone by three."

PICKING UP PIECES

Trina shook awake, feeling droplets all over her face. Blinked into the bright light of the med bay. Erick stood over her, and Trina felt pressure on her wrist. The sensation came slow, her muscles soft, eyes and ears muffled, like coming awake from a deep dream. Except her heart, which beat like she'd sprinted a kilometer.

"Don't worry," Erick said to her. "I had to spike you with adrenaline, then gave you a spray with the mister to shake you out. The numbness should fade in a minute. Normally I'd wait the stun effects out, but the ship appears stuck without your help."

"Davin would leave with me unconscious?" Trina said. A headache thudded beyond the edges of her eyes. She noticed Erick had a long series of bandages along his abdomen, that the doctor looked pallid. "You ought to lay here."

"Not a luxury I have," Erick said. "If you're feeling better, then I have to check on my other patient."

"Other patient?"

"Merc took a laser to the chest."

Mox walked into the med bay, his giant frame making the space crunching between the bed and the medical lamp. He looked at Trina and, seeing her awake, nodded. "Good?"

"Capable enough to assure the engines run," Trina replied. "However, I shall need assistance to get to them, as my legs seem to be beyond my ability to control."

Both Mox and Erick helped Trina out of the bed and stood her up on the floor. She was wearing the same clothes, the light shirt and work jeans, that she'd been captured in, only now Trina felt as though they weighed a thousand kilos. Her legs were like the engines she ran, Trina knew they were there and how to use them, but couldn't feel what they were doing.

"You will need to carry me," Trina said to Mox. "I give you permission."

"Then we will run," Mox said.

He scooped Trina up, cradling her in his arms. Trina watched the hallways speed by as Mox clomped. Noticed, on the floor, a streaking red stain.

"Whose is that?" Trina said.

"Erick," Mox said.

They took the left at the T past the crew cabins, heading towards the engines.

The bandage on his stomach. The trail was thick.

"He dragged you. Back here," Mox said. "Tried to hold out."

Trina entered the box room where the left engines and their control panel sat. Scuffs and more blood stained the metal, but not the blast marks Trina expected.

"They didn't try to shoot him?" Trina said.

"Didn't want to damage the engines."

"Why not?"

"Trap," Mox said.

Ah, right. Because if the troopers ruined the engines, the *Jumper* wouldn't takeoff. And if they didn't take off, then their trap wouldn't trigger. They could have just dismantled the ship, kept them from leaving, but Trina had to think about where she was: Eden Prime. New business ventures didn't play well if they were violent and left a bunch of people dead in their bays. After the inspectors, Marl wouldn't want more corpses dropped on the news.

"Easier to call it a malfunction on launch," Trina muttered.

"Hmm?" Mox said.

"Nothing," Trina replied. "They would not have had much time for a complex adjustment."

Trina moved over to the engine panel and reached into a brick-sized storage cubby. A multi-tool, some screws, adhesive, and a quick reference book for all the various alarms the engines used, a book that helpfully added the estimated time until the ship would explode.

Looking at the main engine panel, there were four screws holding in the faceplate. On that plate was a screen reading out simple figures on whether the engine fuel, whether sensors reported clean pipes for thrust, connection to the ship's computer, and so on. A series of dots and symbols. That they were green meant the troopers hadn't messed with anything obvious.

Trina's eyes went over the screws. There it was. Each screw twisted to a different angle, wound in without proper precision. You couldn't have that on a space ship, especially not on the engine housing. If one popped loose in flight there'd be catastrophe.

"Amateurs," Trina said. "Look at this, Mox. They failed to cover up their work."

"Or you are too good," Mox said.

"Perhaps."

With a few quick presses of the multi-tool, Trina had the engine panel off to inspect a wire nest. A small band wrapped around two wires handling the engine's cooling. A black strip, and Trina knew what was under it. Metal teeth, designed to cut into the wires as the Jumper went through atmosphere and warmed up. The heat would expand the metal, interrupt the circuit. The metal teeth were flimsy, though. Cheap. They'd keep the circuit together for a few minutes time before falling apart. Then, boom.

"I'll give them this much," Trina said, slicing through the band and cutting it off the wires. "They had the right tool in the right place. They were close to killing us."

"You'd have found it."

Wide awake and full of energy? She would have. Now, though, better to do it without the stress of actual flight going on as well.

"I will tell Davin to shift the camera, or buy another, to watch the panels."

Mox nodded and left Trina to prepping the ship for launch. First, Trina removed the sabotaging band, then sagged against the wall, closing her eyes. If those screws had been right, Trina wouldn't have caught it. Would've assumed they'd blown the job. Given up the sabotage and hoped Davin wouldn't leave without trying to rescue his crew. All of them vaporized twenty kilometers out of Europa's atmosphere when the left engine overheated, a short-lived star in Eden Prime's sky.

A FRESH START

They're saying we're cleared for launch," Phyla laughed. "Funny, cause I thought they were just trying to kill us."

"Still think we're rigged," Davin said.

Phyla looked at the captain, sitting in his chair, holding his side.

"Why haven't you gone to see Erick?"

"Because my ribs won't matter if that android blows us away before we get out of here."

"Nobody's getting through."

At least, not till they performed some heavy maintenance on the computer code controlling the shipping doors, which would be one helluva task. Phyla sent the go command to flight control and the bay three launch door opened. The day's blue brightness flung itself in, washing out the artificial lights in the floors and ceilings.

"We ready to spool up?" Phyla commed to Trina, in the engines.

"All greens," Trina said. "There's always a chance they

committed a second sabotage, but the odds are against it. Though I must admit I am not at one hundred percent."

"What do you think, captain? You trust your mechanic?"

"She's been stunned, concussed, and hasn't slept all night?" Davin said. "Completely. Let's go."

The *Jumper* sat on a series of landing struts, and when Phyla pressed the pre-launch button on the console, those struts raised a few centimeters off of the ground. Small jets triggered, firing at the bay floor and shoving the *Jumper* up. From there, Phyla used the flight stick, a twin-pronged beast covered with quick-access buttons tied to commands. She could talk to the ship's computer, of course, but Phyla preferred the speed of touch.

With a few taps, the landing struts retracted, the engines warmed up for space travel, and a final series of checks on hull pressurization, fuel load, and more fun things essential for life in the stars, began.

"Ready to say goodbye to this place?" Phyla asked.

"I never want to come back."

That tone. Davin slipped into it whenever he made a promise he knew he couldn't keep. It used to be whether he and Phyla would be back in time for dinner, or wouldn't go to one of Miner Prime's upper levels.

"But we will, won't we?"

"Marl tried to kill us," Davin said, staring out the cockpit as Phyla wheeled the *Jumper* around. "Took Cadge and Trina hostage. Sent an android to murder me. Hell, she probably had those inspectors killed too. It's personal."

"But we're running now?"

"Look at us, Phyla," Davin winced at his own left side. "They hit us by surprise. Half of us are hurt. Merc's a mess. He's sitting in the med bay now, probably will be there for days. I won't get us killed."

"They'll be ready for us, next time."

"There won't be a next time. Things go as I hope—"

"Which they never do."

Phyla slid the throttle forward and the *Jumper* from the bay, its engines emitting the gentle churn that said all was well, and they were ready to blast to another world. The pre-flight checks came back positive. Green and good to go.

"I'll never get tired of it," Davin said.

Europa fell below, disappearing as Phyla angled the ship up towards space, towards Jupiter. No pursuit registered on the console. Still waiting for their trap to spring.

"Tired of what?"

"This. Launching. It's a fresh start, every time."

"Funny, cause this time, I feel like we're not getting that at all."

"The first time I left, you remember why?" Davin kept staring through the windshield.

"You never said. All that talk about getting away, and then one day you're just gone. Lina and I figured you'd died."

"That I'd died? I wanted to find a ship and leave and you thought I'd died?"

"You took days to send a message. Your parents were hysterical. We were going to hold a funeral."

"I was excited." Davin shrugged. "Caught up in it."

"Glad somebody was having fun."

"Point is, we have a chance. I kept my promise."

The atmosphere bled away as the *Whiskey Jumper* shot away from Europa. No explosion, no problems. Life support recycling air. Artificial gravity keeping them stuck to the floor. No hull breach alarms. The flight path sent by Eden Prime's flight control kept them away from incoming ships, so they went into empty space. A great spot for a bomb to go off without collateral damage, but none did.

Ahead, Jupiter spun in place. Its swirling beige majesty filled the cockpit with churn and chaos. They watched it for a minute, because what else could you do with splendor like that except stare?

"You did come back," Phyla said. "Guess I can trust you one more time."

"You pretty much have to," Davin leaned back, stretched. "I am the captain, and this is my ship."

"Are you ready then, captain?"

"So ready."

"So where are we going?" Phyla said.

"Home," Davin said.

"Home. You think Lina can help, or do you just want to see her?"

"Can I say yes to both?"

Phyla punched in the route and a yellow line shot out from the front of the *Jumper*, a projection on the cockpit windshield. The route the autopilot recommended to get them to the largest space station in the solar system, Miner Prime.

"Yes," Phyla said, pushing the throttle to full flight speed.

Seven days to get to Miner Prime. Seven days to get ready to go home again.

29

POST-MORTEM

Cosmetic damage. No critical functions impacted by the woman's—Fournine checked its memory, the mission bios—Opal's shot to his head. By Davin Masters' resistance. The supply of plaskin the android had brought with it to Europa should suffice to repair the cosmetic damage.

So Fournine ended the mission report, beamed it out through its integrated comm to the stars. The android looked up at the sky. One of those black specks against Jupiter's bright wash was likely the *Whiskey Jumper*. Where would the Wild Nines be heading now?

"You failed," a man said. Fournine turned to him, its eyes running over the man and scanning his face, his clothes, his scents. Not much there other than a name—Ferro—and a home: Mars. Obviously, an outdated entry.

"Their combat abilities surpassed expectations," Fournine said. "As I'm sure you would agree."

Eden Prime's local media, what little there was of it, had already reported on the number of injured troopers and damage to the outpost's prison. Fournine's analysis of the language used made it clear the reporters weren't holding back their condescension.

"True. We weren't ready for them," Ferro said.

The boulevard picked up as people returned to normal. Lasers weren't flashing. Explosions and screams were non-existent. Society resumed functioning. Fournine detected several glances its way, even as it picked up and put on its hat, pulled up its collar. Anyone who looked, who noticed, walked a little faster. Android reputation held, even out here.

"Are you planning a chase?" Fournine said.

"Marl says you will do that. We are to secure the city."

"I'm surprised. An analysis of your team's abilities thus far indicates Marl shouldn't trust you with that task."

"I didn't see you help."

"I operated according to the plan. If it failed, it was due to your team's inability to incapacitate, or to hold, those promised," Fournine threw a single eye at Ferro. "In fact, were I to conduct a more thorough analysis, I might find enough to conclude an intentionally weak force posted at the prison."

"Never."

"And if I deemed it so, that could be construed as aiding a fugitive. Under the Free Laws, that mandates the same punishment for you." The android shifted a hand to one of its knives.

"You will not deem it so."

"Why?"

"Because we will help you," Ferro said. He glanced up at the sky. "They disarmed our trap. But they have not found our trace."

Fournine flagged its file on Ferro. Updated to include potentially clever, even duplicitous maneuvers. It re-ran the current conversation in its head, picking apart Ferro's responses and searching for double-meanings, tells, things that might give away a less-than truthful telling.

"So you know where they are heading," Fournine said.

"A deal," Ferro said. "We will give you the destination, help repair and outfit you and your ship, you will not tell Marl anything . . . negative."

"I have filed the report. But not with Marl, yet. I accept your proposal."

An hour later Fournine sat in the cockpit of the single-person starship made specifically for androids. No life support. No comforts besides the lone chair to access piloting controls. An engine capable of sprinting through the solar system faster than any other ship, including the *Whiskey Jumper*.

"You'll wait until after they land and are separated," the voice on the other end of the transmission said. "I don't want a destructive fight on my station."

"As ordered," Fournine replied. "Be careful, as they are not as simple as they would appear."

"So your failure proved once," the voice said. "Let's hope it does not again."

The Wild Nines were going to Miner Prime. And Fournine would follow.

30

BANTER

You shoulda seen what I did," Cadge said, sitting at the circle table that served as the centerpiece for the *Jumper*'s mess, the splotched cream top meshing with the battered pots and scratched plastic plates in a nonsensical fashion that Cadge always found relaxing. It wasn't perfect, but it worked damn fine. Kinda like Cadge himself. "Three of'em, trying to jump me and I'm throwing punches faster than a tornado."

"Sure," Mox said. The big guy overwhelmed his chair, sprawling around the armrests and looming over the table's surface. But Cadge saw the crinkle at the edge of Mox's mouth. The lug would sit there and listen to Cadge spin stories the whole journey.

"Then they stunned me, the cowards. Shot me in the back."

The food littering the table was mostly dried stuff that made up the ship's stores. Packets full of what Erick called "flavored calories". Sprinkle on recycled water and they'd stiffen into a paste that was as appealing as it sounded. Cadge preferred the strawberry shortcake, and he had two packets poured into a bowl in front of him now, stuffing his face with spoonfuls in between story beats.

"Woke up a few minutes later, cause no stunner's gonna keep me out for long, and there's this guy standing over me. Like he's studying me. Like I'm one of those rats."

Mox was having his usual; a shake full of protein powder and vitamin pills. The man seemed to live on powdered substances. Sure, from time to time Cadge would dose himself up too. Had to keep the strength out here. Every meal though? No thanks.

"And I'm thinking what, is this guy going to open me up or something? Stick some tracing device in me? So I start talking, throwing my words in his face like nothing you've heard before. Even you would've been embarrassed. I had to throw him off his game, you understand?"

The door to the pod opened and Cadge glanced up to watch the bounty herself, Viola, walk in, looking around like she'd never seen a ship's kitchen before.

"Anyway, he kicked me, knocked me out and then I woke up in the bag," Cadge said. Mox grunted, cocking his head to the side. So sorry, big buddy, but a more interesting conversation just walked into the room. "Viola. Can I call you Vi?"

"Vi?" Viola said.

"Shorter," Mox replied.

"Exactly," Cadge said. "Now, you might not think that's a big deal, but wait till you've got a bunch of thugs taking shots at you. I call out Vi, it takes a second and you're moving. I call out Viola and you're dead by the time I finish."

Vi looked at Cadge, mouth hanging open. Like the girl was lost or something.

"Hungry?" Mox asked her.

"A little," Vi replied, a program jerking back into motion.

"This is all we got, Vi, so I'd get used to it," Cadge said. "You can find all the flavors in those cabinets. Limit of two per meal, so we don't eat ourselves to death."

Mox gave a low rumble of a laugh, Vi looked confused. Which was great. Worth money, and not even able to hang with casual conversation. Why Davin wouldn't take them to Ganymede for a hot minute to collect the coin made no sense. Cadge would even take her in himself, if Davin didn't want to. An android after them and they were turning down free coin.

"So tell me," Cadge said to Vi's back as she dug around the cabinets. "Your dad, he really have that much money?"

"He runs Galaxy Forge," Viola replied, as though that answered the question.

And it did. Galaxy Forge, that was one of the big ones. Making ships, robots, whole space stations and scattering them around the solar system. Cadge had heard they were making a millennium ship, designed to go for years and years until they hit another star. Get that reward, Cadge could probably afford a ticket. Maybe even a little extra, once he informed Vi's dad of the trouble the man's daughter had brought with her: Bar fights, Davin taking a punch in the club, Cadge getting stunned.

Lotta different stories he could tell.

"So, let me get this straight, your daddy is mega rich, and yet you're here with a few space jockeys about to eat some," Cadge glanced at the packets Vi selected. "Powdered turkey and tomato basil. You thinking this is a good call? That you made the right choice?"

"No idea," Vi said, giving Cadge the old straight stare. "Tell you this much, the conversation's a lot more interesting here."

Hey! Vi could talk after all. But coming to the table didn't mean she could play the game.

"Mox, what one word would you say best describes what we do?" Cadge said.

"Dangerous."

"Dangerous. Girl like you, easy to get hurt out here," Cadge said. Turn up the heat, see if she folded. A volunteer run to Ganymede, coin in the pocket.

"What about Phyla, or Trina?" Vi asked.

"They're used to it. Grew up with this. You, you've got the golden ticket," Cadge replied. "We could still change course, drop you at Ganymede?"

"I can't go back yet. There's still so much more to see. Back on Ganymede, I'd be bored."

For the first time, Cadge felt the grin slip. That wasn't what she was supposed to say.

"Bored," Mox said. "Worse than danger."

Vi nodded. That was it then. No game set match here.

"Yeah, well, if you stay, then no whining," Cadge said. "You want to play in space, you got to earn your right to be here. Starting now."

Cadge finished the remark by pushing the last spoonful of shortcake paste into his mouth, staring at Vi as he chewed it. Just because they didn't go to Ganymede now, didn't mean he couldn't get her there eventually. The coin would be waiting. Might take a bit of time, but he'd been cruising the stars and bars for years already. He could wait a little longer.

31

ALIVE

On Earth, going through the repeated drills necessary to become a fighter pilot, Merc had his fair share of rough-and-tumble moments. Ejected once. Had a ship go dead more than a few times, leaving him stranded and staring at the blue marble until help arrived. Each one hurt, physically, emotionally. Meant he had to do better next time.

This, man, this was different. Opening his eyes took too much work. Coming back to reality meant dealing with the fiery claws ripping their way through his chest. Erick mentioned he was trying to blunt those rending tears. But sleep was the only real escape.

"Merc?" Opal's voice plunged into his psyche. Kept him out of the darkness.

Merc opened his eyes and saw a hazy world too hard to interpret. Looking at him, a brown and black smudge that, after a few blinks, turned into Opal.

"Hey there," Opal said.

"Hey." His voice raspy, rusted gears grinding into motion. "Thanks for coming. For saving me."

"Sure thing," Merc replied. "Not like you needed it."

"I was only cuffed and disarmed." Opal's mouth quirked into a smile. "Still plenty dangerous."

"Figured I could help out. Never get the chance to use those discs, you know?"

Opal slid her eyes lower. Merc couldn't follow, his head too heavy to lift. Knew what she was looking at, though.

"I saw," Opal said, "a lot of friends get shot on Mars. Some recovered. Others took hits from rifles, from bigger things and never made it back. Thing was, that was a war. When things like that made sense. So I took it, for a while."

"For a while?"

"They don't go away. The ones who don't come back." Opal pulled Merc's covers up, rested her hands on them. "I started to see their faces at night, and then during the day. I'd be looking through the scope and hear one of them beside me, talking. Sit at the mess and one of them is there, next to me. So I left."

"That's when Davin found you?"

"Booze is cheap in Vagrant's Hollow. It didn't make the voices go away, but they were easier to deal with," Opal said. "Then he gave me something to do. A purpose that wasn't quite so violent."

"Sorry for ruining that. Didn't mean to," Merc said.

"It's all right, because you came back. Erick works miracles."

"Speaking of that, how'd I get back here anyway?"

Opal's face brightened. Marc had seen the same look on some of his friends back on Earth. Some who'd been to Mars, who'd been in other fights. Take them away from their souls for a second and give them a chance, they'd tell a good story. Opal jumped right in, going through carrying Merc back to the bay doors, fighting the android, Mox breaking into the prison. Cadge in the body bag.

" . . . and Mox carried you into the ship. You should've seen Erick," Opal said. "Doctor's half-dead, but has you on the bed acting like he's ready for a twelve-hour operation."

"Man's a saint."

"Know what he said to me, after you passed out the first time?"

"The first time?"

Opal pressed her hand to Merc's forehead, gently. Like she was feeling him for a fever. "You haven't really been awake for a while, have you?"

"Nothing since taking the hit. What'd he say to you?"

"That fighter pilots never stay down long, because they never like believing they've been hit."

"I didn't get hit. Here on the ground? That doesn't count."

Merc tried but couldn't keep his eyes from blinking closed. His mind wanted to stay awake, but his body couldn't handle the idea.

"Whatever you say, Merc. I should let you sleep. Erick wouldn't be happy with me keeping his patient awake."

"It's good." Merc said. Those fiery claws were falling away as Merc fell deeper into dreamland. Couldn't stop it, didn't want to stop it. He felt Opal's hands wrap around his own, warm gloves. They were nice.

"Goodnight, stick jockey," Opal whispered.

32

WANTED

W hat's the charge?" Davin said. He and Phyla sat in the cockpit, the Sun a distant spot far, far in front of them. Jupiter hung behind the *Jumper* as the ship sped towards the solar system's interior. A few days coasting up to speed, then a few days slowing and they'd be at Miner Prime.

Phyla scrolled through news on the pilot's console. A lag followed every tap she made, sometimes only a few seconds, sometimes minutes. Satellites, running on solar power, chained the routes from Earth to Saturn. Soon to Uranus and Neptune. Each one cached data, building up text packages from companies, news agencies, and other sources.

The most common stories were locally stored and sent fast. Deeper queries required hours as satellites bounced the search to and from comprehensive databases on Earth and Mars.

Pictures, movies were non-existent: too much data.

"I'm looking through today's database," Phyla said. "There's more than charges than usual."

"They're learning they can abuse this thing."

The Free Laws. No sovereign body in space, so here's this loose set of rules to keep people in line. Including a lovely section where any interested party could pay to list a wanted person, and a reward. The ones with real motivation paid to send an android after you, either catch or kill. Getting a bot to murder a target required approval from a council of judges, but they were all corporate stooges. If you wanted to live in space, you stayed friends with the big companies.

"They waited till people invested out here. Now they're turning the screws," Phyla said. "There's a couple in here for failure to pay on time. Really? You're going to send an android after someone late on a bill?"

"It's their playground, they can make the rules. Anything on us?"

"Here," Phyla said. She swiped on the article, bringing it up on the cockpit glass. With the Sun glaring through, the display adjusted the text color, black shifting to white as it scrawled between yellow and space's black background.

"Pre-meditated murder," Davin muttered, reading. "The Wild Nines, a mercenary group formerly employed by Eden Prime, is accused by same of plotting to eliminate two inspectors."

"It says there's video evidence, but we can't get it out here."

"What'd they record?"

"More like, what did Marl make?"

The rest of the piece was commentary about how the Wild Nines were dangerous, unpredictable, blah blah blah. The same stuff could be said of any mercenary outfit. The real question was why Marl wanted this whole thing done to begin with? Why not just cancel their contract if she wanted them gone?

"I have an idea," Phyla said.

"That she wanted the inspectors dead," Davin replied.

"You stealing my thoughts again?"

"Only when there's something useful in them," Davin replied. "Doesn't happen too often."

"Watch it, captain. I can still turn this thing around."

Davin looked up from the news, out through the window. Took another deep breath of that recycled air. A few people he'd met, from Earth, said the stuff had a tang to it, a taste that lingered in the throat. Body's way of saying it wasn't natural. Davin hadn't ever felt that. Then again, he'd never breathed real, pure air.

"Our parents came from Earth," Davin said. "Went to Miner Prime. Started families. They knew they could've gone back home if they ever had the money."

"They didn't."

"But they could've, Phyla. You look at this," Davin glanced back at the console, the murder charge. "We'll never be able to land. They'd shoot us on sight."

"That's why you're upset? Cause you can't get to Earth right now?"

"Guess you think that's a stupid reason?"

"Not if you have more behind that. Like not getting killed by androids. Or starving because nobody's going to hire us."

"Phyla, that's why you're the pilot," Davin said. He leaned back in the copilot's, the captain's chair. "Lets me be the dreamer."

"You always were," Phyla said.

Davin closed his eyes. A few more days till they reached Miner Prime. A murderer's homecoming.

33

SPACE WORK

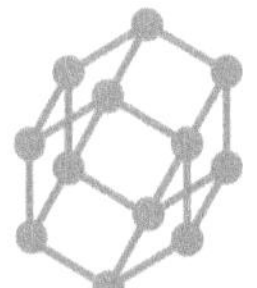

A couple weeks in space felt like endless. Viola kept herself busy, or rather, Trina, Davin and Erick kept giving her things to do. The doctor, impressed with Viola's stitching abilities, grabbed Viola whenever he saw her and went over how something worked. Erick's favorite, and an apparent necessity of a frequent space-farer, was the DNA Restoration machine, or the D-NAR.

The high doses of radiation coming in from the outside world required the occasional extraction, repair, and then injection of small nano-bots that swarmed damaged cells and put them back together. Then a beacon in the waste system collected the bots. Erick would bring them back to the D-NAR to be reset for the next person.

Trina gave Viola things more in line with her experience. Keep the engines primed, monitor the systems if Trina was asleep. Clean the Viper of any atmospheric gunk Merc got on it during his flight on Europa. Trina said the pilot would normally do this himself, but seeing as Merc was barely awake these days, that wasn't happening.

Davin was the worst, though. The captain found the most menial tasks. Shunt the trash out into the void. Inventory the food supplies so Phyla could restock on Miner Prime. Still, the work was better than endless textbooks and articles. It was real. Tightening the bolts on a loose vent was something Viola was actually doing. In space! Going thousands of kilometers per hour! Even drudgery, in space, had a tint of wonder. And when Phyla announced over the intercom that they were making their approach to Miner Prime, Viola took a long breath. The vacation was ending.

"You might be sad," Puk said. "But I could use some new surroundings. This place is claustrophobic."

"That's literally something you can't feel," Viola said.

"Says you."

"So tell me about where we're landing?"

"Miner Prime. Fantastic place. Like if you took a can, packed a bunch of people in, then told corporations they could buy tubes to stick onto it and create offices. Set the whole thing spinning to get yourself gravity, stick it close to some asteroids full of precious metals, and you've got yourself the richest, largest home in space."

"Sounds like something I should see," Viola said, heading towards the cockpit.

Ships larger and smaller than the *Jumper* buzzed around the station. Some were floating boxes with mechanical arms that allowed them to haul ore from asteroids for processing. A few large ovals floated apart from Miner Prime, small shuttles whisking passengers back and forth. The decals covering the sides claimed they were cruisers, carrying their passengers from Earth in a loop through the solar system on a trip that would last over a year.

Viola even saw a ship from her father's company docked

at one of the spindly outreaches of the station, the orange and red logo giving it away.

"Pretty cool, right?" Davin said to Viola as they stood in the cockpit.

"I think it's so ugly," Phyla said. "Except it works, so nobody cares."

"It's huge," was all Viola could think of saying.

"When we land, you'll get the chance to see just how big," Davin said. "I've got to meet a friend down there, get a little more information."

"And I'm coming with?" Viola asked.

An awkward pause, Phyla wore a bemused expression, as though daring Davin to say more.

"I think Mox'll show you around," Davin said finally. "The less you're involved with us, the better."

"What do you mean?"

"I'm saying that things are going to get messy. You'll be able to find a ship that'll take you back to Ganymede down there. Probably a better ride than what you just had. Though I wouldn't tell them who you are."

"Why not?"

"You tell your father when you see him that putting a big reward for his daughter's return is a good way to attract the wrong kind of attention."

"So, I'm not going with you?"

Viola caught Davin's quick glance at Phyla. Heard his sigh.

"We're labeled murderers, Viola. We'll be hunted. You don't want that," the captain said. "Mox'll get you to a ship that can take you. I'm not gonna have a kid get shot trying to play mercenary in my crew."

For the first time, Viola heard Davin's voice and thought of her father. The same tone, that Viola's own choices were his responsibility. But look at Merc. Look at how he nearly died. At how bad Erick was. Viola looked at her hands, remembered the sticky feel of Erick's blood on them as she stitched up the wound. Why would she ever want more of that?

"He'll show me around first?" Viola said. "Just a quick tour. Then I'll hop the next shuttle back."

Davin nodded, looking like a thousand pounds came off of his shoulders. Twenty years old and Viola still got people so worried about her.

34

VAGRANT'S HOLLOW

The ramshackle scrap-houses of Vagrant's Hollow didn't look that different from when Davin had last seen them, through the glass walls of a lift just like this one. The dwellings spread out in a sloppy grid, filling in the circular level in the kilometer-wide center of Miner Prime. Shifting through the streets, once clean metal floors now coated with dirt and grime, were Davin's people, the kind that kept their secrets hidden behind their eyes.

Vagrant's Hollow was twenty stories high, its ceiling a changing screen approximating Earth's sky. Here and there malfunctioning plates stood out, black dots punching holes in the illusion.

"Hasn't changed much, has it?" Davin asked Phyla, standing next to him in the lift.

"I don't know if it's changed, but it feels sadder, some-how," Phyla replied.

"Because we used to see all this and wonder where it came from. What it was. Now, it's just a pile of trash."

One house near where the lift landed was a prime example. Whatever its original shell, the place was made out of an entire ship, broken into chunks and leaned against each other. Style wasn't important here. Having a home was what mattered.

"I suppose," Phyla said.

They looked out the windows at the rapidly approaching lift station. The trench that served as Vagrant Hollow's main drag laid beyond the exit stairs. Like Eden Prime's boulevard, but with none of the sterile attempts at class. Tables and tents full of clothes, food, junk, and bots for sale sat along the sides of the meandering path. Dilapidated homes erected on top of and attached to each other leaned over it, people hawking wares or making something out of nothing beneath the misshapen overhangs.

Even though the lift filtered out the smell, Davin's nose sniffed his memory and came away with the ozone sting of burning electricity, a hint of char from cooking food.

"Does she know you're coming?" Phyla asked.

"What do you think?"

"That she probably knew before you did."

Davin could only nod. And when the lift doors opened, the two of them pushed their way out along with a motley mess of humans, down the stairs and onto the stained, rusted metal that served as the trench floor.

Waiting for them, a small floating platform with a railing around the edge and a single stick used for steering. The man at the helm stared dead at Davin through a pair of thick goggles, doubtless meant to protect from the occasional mists of toxic anything that spewed out at random from constant experiments gone wrong in Vagrant's Hollow.

Phyla paused as Davin stepped on to the platform, the constant flow of bodies making a subconscious part around them. Was she nervous? Why? Davin put on a grin, reached to pull her up, but Phyla ignored his hand and used her own legs to get herself on board.

"Tell you something? I never wanted to come back here," Phyla said. "When we left, I thought there was a chance we weren't coming back. Ever. It felt good."

"You didn't say anything about it when we took off," Davin said as the platform lurched forward. "It won't be long. Lina will let us know who we need to talk to, we clear the charge, then we're good to go."

"I guess I didn't know I still hated it this much."

Phyla leaned over the edge of the platform, looked at the leaning metal masses of the pack homes. Davin followed her gaze, washing his eyes over the dreamers meandering below. Miner Prime was an idea as much as a place. A literal manifestation of hope to the bunches stuck on Earth who wanted adventure. A chance to hop on a mining ship, or an expedition deep into the dark universe. Davin checked his math. Almost fifty years, this place had been acting as a permanent settlement.

An older woman, dishing out soup to a family, glanced up at them bobbing by on the platform and turned away. Davin wondered why until he looked at Phyla, realized that the two of them didn't look like they belonged here anymore. Both of them armed, in gear that screamed they were probably working for Miner Prime's own police, or were otherwise searching out criminals.

"Sometimes I wonder why we were the ones that made it out," Phyla said, nodding her head at the woman.

"Luck," Davin replied.

What else would explain how the *Whiskey Jumper* had landed in his lap?

"Here," the driver said, and they stepped off.

In front of them sat a storefront. Davin noticed kitchen utensils, scrap metal, a few used books, and more on the shelves visible through the doorway. The only sign naming the place hung above the entrance, made from bits of different metals, an A missing, so that the name appeared to be "The Wrehouse". Davin was the first through, stepping in and immediately feeling eyes on him.

"Why do I only see you when you're in trouble?" came the lead-lined voice of one Lina Monte.

Lina stood behind the desk, staring at and yet also through Davin. A look that was wrapped in the past as much as the present, and Davin met those eyes and fell down that well with her. Several decades of shifting dreams, promises kept and broken, the twisted love that fate doesn't like to let alone.

"Could say the same about you," Davin said.

They stepped towards each other, Lina coming around the desk, as though they were going to hug. Phyla walked in behind Davin, though, and Lina paused, setting a masked smile on her face. He wasn't the only one playing in the past. Thing was, they were living in the present. With Lina grunting in surprise, Davin pulled her into a tight hug.

"You can let me go," Lina said, her face mashed into Davin's shoulder.

"Felt like it was needed," Davin said, loosening the grip. "You remember Phyla?"

"Friends never forget," Lina said.

"Nice to see you too, Lina," Phyla added.

"One of these days all three of us are going to go and get a bunch of drinks, deal with our problems, and get over this," Davin said. "But right now there's this thing hanging over my head. Namely, that there's an android trying to kill us. And, you know, that has priority."

Phyla was the first to blink, to glance away and nod. Lina accepted the gesture, went back behind the desk, and sat down in a stool made of different parts stacked together.

"You've got to deal with Bosser," Lina said.

"Who?"

35

PUPPET MASTER

The problem with space was that there was too much of it. Bosser muttered this so often that he considered having it plastered on a picture and hung on his wall. The vastness meant he couldn't be everywhere, couldn't take all of the problems into his hands and grind them into dust personally. Bosser tried, via the stuttering video link with Marl's new police chief, Ferro, on Europa. Turns out choking a man on another world wasn't easy.

"As much as I'd like to hear again how you failed so miserably, I have other things to attend to," Bosser said, and then cut the feed.

Ferro would sit there for another fifteen minutes before Bosser's replied bounced its way across the solar system to Europa, and the thought gave Bosser a small bite of satisfaction. Life was all about time, after all, and if Bosser could demand a few minutes of it from someone else, then wasn't that power? Although power wasn't much good if it stranded Bosser on a station like Miner Prime. The spinning waste of space was only getting less attractive as Bosser's departure date neared.

And pushing that day closer was the woman Bosser dialed next, Marl Rose. Dialing. There was a word that hadn't made its way out of language yet. Bosser wasn't punching buttons. Just saying the target's name was enough. The monitor would present some options, highlight the most likely choices, and he would say one, two, or three. Bosser glanced back towards the nightstand and, on it, a wooden clock ticking away. He wound it every morning. A steady grinding of the gears.

"Are you going to talk, or is this just a way to wake me up?" Marl said over the feed, staring out the monitor in a frenzied outfit, eyes tired.

"Your new security seems worthless," Bosser said. "I couldn't find much on him. With no record, Eden won't like the choice."

"I didn't have much time, or options."

"I'll remind them," Bosser said. "Though they won't be thrilled to hear you failed to apprehend Davin Masters."

Another thirty minutes passed as Marl listened to his response and composed her own. In a way, the delay was a feature. Bosser could hold multiple conversations at once, rarely feeling stressed. Reading, reviewing other work, or just winding the clock and watching the stars outside the apartment's window. For one thing, it helped his temper. Hard to sustain true anger at someone when it took so long to see their response.

"Davin ran. Along with his crew. They're not a problem," Marl said. "Is Eden going to send another set of inspectors?"

"Your cavalier attitude towards the killers might raise eyebrows," Bosser said. "You might want to try some sympathy."

"When I'm talking with Eden, I will," Marl replied.

"Free advice, that's all," Bosser said. "The answer to your question is: not yet."

"So then why did you call?"

"I activated the android based on your evidence," Bosser said. "Your flimsy evidence. You'll be receiving a message soon with account details. Please deposit the amount noted, or Eden will come to understand just how easy it is to doctor a video feed."

Marl didn't bother to reply. After fifteen minutes, she gave Bosser a look as frigid as Europa's surface and cut the signal. It didn't matter, she would pay.

Bosser left his room and went to the small cafeteria that served the police building where he lived and worked. Miner Prime, even now, required an economy of space. Eating was cheaper here.

The entire dining area was polished silver metal, or plastic disguised to look like it. Easy to wash and resistant to scratches. Everything a concession to durability, safety. Except the feeds. Along one wall, opposite the serving counters, a vast screen divided into a series of real-time videos. Most were from Miner Prime. The main promenade on Level Five, the center of the station that served as its prime shopping center. Vagrant's Hollow and its dirty chaos. Various docking bays flooding ships in and out like an ocean's tide. There was one in the upper left corner that continued to show a magnified view of Earth, routed and delayed from satellites, but still an ever-present reminder of humanity's beautiful home.

Somewhere between his second sip of the dark coffee and the first tentative bite of the morning's pastry, a starchy blueberry scone, the main door to the cafeteria opened and a comm officer stumbled into the room. A flushed face and wild eyes stared at Bosser, waited while he took a slow drink. Then Bosser signaled the man to speak.

"They're here, sir. The *Whiskey Jumper* just docked a few minutes ago," the comm officer said.

"Remind me what that is?" Bosser asked.

"The, uh, ship that you wanted me to watch for?"

"Ah. There are so many. Thank you."

The comm officer stood there for a few more seconds. Watched Bosser take another sip. Waiting for orders. People claimed to be disturbed by the androids, how they looked human but were not. This officer, though, stood more still than a bot ever would and lacked the utility. The officer made a slight cough noise.

"You can leave," Bosser said, and the officer ran away.

The android, Fournine was its designation, already knew where Davin and his crew had gone. Its current position put the bot only a few hours behind the mercenaries. Waiting for Bosser's signal.

One of the feeds on the far end flipped to a broadcast of the most-watched new videos, burning through popular footage. The second one, muted and fuzzy, effects added in, showed a trio leading a pair of Eden-garbed employees into an empty docking bay. Then shooting them in the back. The video flipped to a picture of one Davin Masters, claiming the man was wanted for the murder. He and his entire crew.

Wild Nines, and only eight members. Funny. Eight hardened fighters could be a lot for an android. Could cause a lot of damage to the station if they went down shooting. Split them apart, however . . . Bosser picked up his comm, started placing some calls.

Davin Masters had come home, and he was going to find it a very unwelcome place to be.

36

SHOPPING

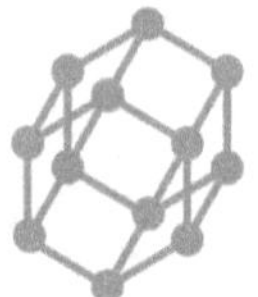

Viola could tell Mox was tiring of her questions. The big man had slipped from three words an answer down to one. Sometimes just a grunt. Not like Viola could help it. The entirety of Level Five was full of things she'd never seen. Movies on Ganymede dealt little with the miracles on display here, the glittering dresses flecked with asteroid platinum, perfumes mixed with chemicals extracted from Mars rock, and even a pet store selling animals used to low-gravity environments.

"If only you weren't broke," Puk said, floating by Viola's head. "Think of all the cool stuff you could buy."

"Thanks for reminding me," Viola said.

"What I'm here for."

Mox drifted behind the two of them, casting his eyes at random. Shopping didn't seem to be his thing—most of the stores Viola entered, Mox stood outside and leaned against a wall. It didn't take a lot of deduction to realize that Mox was here as a bodyguard, to keep Viola from doing something stupid. Which, given her luck so far, wasn't a terrible idea.

Past a pair of restaurants hawking Japanese and African cuisine, the gentle curve of the level revealed a circular square with a giant projection in the middle. Sponsored by a news organization Viola wasn't familiar with, the holographic image gave a 3D representation of the current broadcast. Pictures of Mars, ruined settlements and flashing lasers. Better to be here than there.

Beneath the projection, which shot up ten meters into the air, people mixed and mingled on benches and tables, all anchored to the floor.

"Cadge," Mox said, nodding towards the left side of the projection.

Viola noticed the squat mercenary was talking with a few other people dressed in thick jackets and work pants. Hoods on their jackets kept their faces hidden, and the group was too far away to overhear. On the trip to Miner Prime, Viola couldn't shake the impression that the man kept sizing her up like he would a piece of meat. Not sexual, no, but more like whether she was valuable. It was a strange feeling, and after the first couple of days, Viola had tried to avoid Cadge whenever she had the chance.

"Who's he talking to?" Viola asked. Mox shook his head. "Puk, want to listen?"

"On it," the little bot said, zipping up and away.

Like a human ear, the bot could concentrate on conversations from a distance. From vantage points Cadge wouldn't think to look, such as right above him.

"Why?" Mox asked.

"I don't know," Viola said. "How he looks at me, makes me feel off. And he's talked about my father's bounty before."

"He jokes," Mox said. "No filter."

"I get it," Viola said. "He's your friend. But he's not mine."

Viola pulled Mox over to a small cafe where she let the metal man point out which of the unique beverages she should try. Zero-G roasted coffee, grown in enriched asteroid soil, had a flavor all its own. Having subsisted for weeks now on the *Jumper*'s dusty rations, anything with a new taste would be welcome.

The frothy dark liquid, into which Viola poured a slight drop of cream, steamed in her face. Mox watched her from across their tiny for two table, a slight smile buried in his scruff as Viola raised the mug and blew into it. A few seconds later, the first tentative sip. It was hot, sure, but also sparkled in her mouth. Tiny bursts of heat and . . . macadamia? Followed by an undercurrent of deep, earthy loam that massaged its way down her throat into her stomach.

Viola sat the mug back on the table and stared at it. If this coffee blew away anything she'd ever drank, what else waited for her out here?

"Incredible," Viola said when Mox asked how it tasted. "I don't understand how it can have so much flavor. I mean, scientifically, I understand the components that go into it, how the molecular—"

"Viola!" Puk buzzed, whirring back into the cafe and catching a few stares from the other patrons. "We have to move! Cadge is selling you out to those guys right now."

"What?" Mox asked.

"The bounty," Puk said. "Cadge is going to divide it with them. They have a ship."

Viola looked across the courtyard, but Cadge and whoever he'd been talking with weren't there any more. Disappeared.

"Did you see where they went?" Viola asked Puk.

"Sorry, was too busy coming over here to warn you," Puk replied.

Mox stood up, touching his wrist to the small part of the table sectioned off to a reader. Mox's comm connected to his account balance and brushing it against one of these sensors paid whatever outstanding bill existed for the table. Viola remembered when the technology first came to Ganymede, at the same time a fully-fledged stellar network swung into place. It required instant connection and verification of an account's balance, but was way more efficient than carrying physical chits loaded up with coin.

"We go back," Mox said, and Viola wasn't going to say no. "Wait for Cadge at the *Jumper*."

Walking out of the cafe and back into the promenade, Mox, rather than falling behind, now walked right next to Viola, scanning the surroundings. Was this what it was like to be in this business? To always have to watch her back, to suspect anyone of having ulterior motives?

The crowded racks of clothes in stores and their projected models, the stands advertising essential luxuries, lost their sense of wonder and became only places someone could hide. Anyone glancing at Viola could be an informant, passing along her location, that she was unarmed, or what she was wearing to someone who wanted to find her.

"I'm not having fun anymore," Viola said.

"Get used to it," Mox replied.

As they pushed through a small crowd of people, all wearing bright neon t-shirts and being led by a tour guide, Viola wanted to be back in the small, comfortable confines of the *Jumper*. On the other side of the tour group there was a brief break in the crowd, a space through which the smooth floor of Level Five reflected the dusking store lights as the afternoon of Miner Prime's artificial cycle wound on. Three men, the ones Cadge had been speaking with, stood in the break, and they stared right at her.

PAST FRIENDS

Phyla's eyes wandered the small confines of Lina's shop. A menagerie of security-related gear. There was a tiny gun that shot a sticky bead that would record and send video and audio around it for ten minutes. That'd be one way of keeping tabs on Davin and Lina's conversation, a back and forth that sent itself lower and lower in volume until Phyla couldn't even hear it anymore. She felt like the kid left to wander while the parents talked.

Hanging on the walls, above the shelves holding cameras and comm equipment, were a series of old-style pictures. Actual print photos, which these days were a retro rarity. Thing was, Phyla remembered all of them.

The one with Davin and Lina standing outside their small school, Phyla holding the camera, right here in Vagrant's Hollow, as they completed the last grade and society ejected them, at fifteen, into whatever lives fate held for them. Phyla thought the nervous grins on their faces must have mirrored her own.

Another picture, to the right of that one, taken by

Davin's long-gone mother, had the three of them and some of their other friends engaging in one of their floor hockey games. The metal ground made a perfect surface for skipping around any spare junk they wanted to use as a puck.

She'd found the camera at a special discount. No, that wasn't it. The man was losing everything, was liquidating all he had to get a ticket off of the station. Phyla had coin from a recent birthday and bought it. The camera was so ancient that it printed the photos immediately after taking it. The man selling it to her looked so sad as he handed it over, but when Phyla turned away, he'd asked her to wait. A moment later the man returned with a stack of thick little paper, necessary for the camera to print. Phyla asked him where to get more and the man just shook his head.

Looking at these pictures, she could never tell how badly they wanted to leave. Davin, especially, went on and on about exploring the stars. Breaking out of the bounds of Miner Prime and making his own life. Lina went along with him, egging Davin on until he left. He told them he was going and was gone. For five years.

Phyla remembered the day Davin came back, remembered him running back through their street, claiming he had a ship, that they could go with him. Breaking open their boring lives.

"Phyla?" Lina said, touching Phyla's shoulder. "Do you want them?"

"The pictures?"

"They should be yours, really. You took them."

"They'd just get lost on the ship. Too much movement," Phyla said, though her eyes didn't move away from the memories.

"If you think so," Lina said. "Davin's going to come back soon. He'll ask you to go get the ship prepped."

"Why, we just got here?"

"This station is dangerous for you. Every hour here increasing the chance of you being trapped."

"And Davin won't be coming with me?"

"He wants to find the source, the person who can turn off the android pursuing you. I can lead him to it, but you'll need a ready escape."

Phyla looked at Lina's set face, searched Lina's eyes for a hint of a lie, a scheme playing through the wrinkles and scattered grays touching Lina's temples. Phyla felt the urge to touch her own face, to trace her own wrinkles and compare whether the space-faring life was any better.

"Why'd we split up, Lina?" Phyla asked. "The three of us?"

"You two wanted to see the stars, I had people to take care of," Lina replied.

Parents, and Lina had a younger brother. Davin and Phyla lost their responsibilities before the Jumper ever became a reality. Not that Phyla had regrets: there'd been nothing in Vagrant's Hollow then and there was nothing now. Better to run from a black hole than get crushed by its hopeless gravity.

"How are they?" Phyla let the question float in the air.

Lina didn't bother answering, looked back at the pictures. Dead, or vanished. In Vagrant's Hollow, those were the likeliest outcomes. The past wasn't a friendly place to visit here. All it did was show how much you'd already lost. Phyla took a deep breath. Maybe now was the time to fix part of it.

"That last fight we had, I was so stupid," Phyla said. "I just couldn't, after all the times we'd talked about escaping this place, understand why you wouldn't come."

"I know," Lina replied.

"It's been hard without you," Phyla continued, still looking at the photo. "Going everywhere without my best friend."

"Haven't you made a new one yet?"

"Still waiting for you."

Lina wrapped Phyla in a tight hug, the same way they used to say goodnight to each other when they were younger.

"There's nobody left here anymore," Lina said. "If you two are willing, I'll come with you this time. I'm ready to say goodbye."

There was room. An extra cabin. For the first time since hitting the station, Phyla felt a real smile climb to her eyes. Lina returned it.

"You two having a good talk? Back to being friends again?" Davin said, coming up to them. "Phyla, Lina dish you the details?"

"Yeah, you're abandoning us to go on some solo thing," Phyla replied.

"Not solo. Lina's got my back."

"That means you've got hers, too."

Heading back to the *Jumper* alone, Phyla remembered when they'd left Lina the first time. Those promises the night before, the three of them getting ready to meet Davin's crew on his new ship. Phyla excited to pilot something that wasn't mining an asteroid, Lina reading out load about the neat things they were going to see, Davin throwing around stories of Luna, Mars, and even seeing Earth from orbit.

And the next morning, in the *Jumper*'s cockpit. Lina only comming sorry. Davin delaying, pleading, and finally Phyla starting the jets and taking the *Jumper* out to the stars. It'd been hard to see with tears in her eyes, but it hadn't taken long for those tears to dry. To harden into the same resolve that carried her now. There were more than the three of them to take care of.

OLD FLAME, NEW BURN

Lina's cramped apartment clung to the top of the store desperately. A menagerie of bolted scrap, ropes, and a thin set of stairs brought Davin up to the second level. Between the hotplate and the single-stall shower, there was a fold-out couch and the scattered junk of years.

"I don't know what you think it's like on the *Jumper*, but it's better than this," Davin said.

He expected a fiery retort, something along the lines that Davin had no right to critique her life, not after leaving a decade ago. Instead, Lina nodded and sat on the couch, hand digging between the cushions until she found something. Davin stayed standing, watched Lina's wrist flex as her hand moved underneath the cushions, and then heard the sound of shifting metal.

The greased up panels of the apartment shifted to the sides, jutting out and sliding over each other to reveal a slick set of screens and small compartments full of gadgets. Davin smiled wider as each new part showed itself. This was much more what he'd expected from Lina, matched the way she used to beat, no, annihilate Davin and Phyla in child-hood games, waiting until the last moment to show a secret that handed Lina the victory. A fake sword, maybe, or an obscure rule pulled out to devastating effect. Now Lina had a hidden armory.

"You built this just for me?" Davin asked.

"Just for you," Lina replied. "The thing is, you find out everyone's secrets, then you keep more of your own."

"Most secrets don't involve caches of spy gear."

"Only the best ones."

Davin walked over to the terminal, pressed the small power button. The screens populated with various video feeds from around Vagrant's Hollow and other levels of Miner Prime. Black and white but sharp, with words tracking across the bottom as the terminal attempted to scribe any audio going on.

"Can you see everywhere on the station?" Davin asked.

"Almost." Lina's face twisted into a frown. "A few places are too hard to get to. Haven't been able to bug Bosser's office, for instance."

"You mean, the spot that's the most useful to us."

"Not really. Bosser does a lot of chatter with off-station partners. Those transmissions I've been intercepting for a while."

"Whose he talking with?"

"Your friend Marl, for one."

"Yeah, I get more friends like Marl, I'm not going to be around much longer."

"She's only part of the chain," Lina said, taking Davin's hand and pulling him back towards the couch.

Lina's hand was warm. It always was, her fingers slipping in between his. The fit was effortless. Muscle memory split by years still holding strong.

"Then what's the rest of it?"

A familiar thrill juiced his veins as Lina's fingers managed his palms. That same dance, those same rounded nails and the way Lina glided them on the ends of his nerves.

"Marl and Bosser have an arrangement, but both of them are working for other people," Lina said. "Don't know who pulls Marl's strings. Outside of Bosser, I don't hear anything she says. Bosser, I think, works with Eden. Maybe other corporations. It's hard to pin him down."

Davin sank back into the couch, allowed an arm to slide up Lina's side and around her back, holding her closer.

"You mean you don't know everything about him?" Davin said. "That doesn't sound like you."

"Bosser doesn't play in public," Lina replied, moving along the couch till her hips touched Davin's. "He's not a politician. So far as I can tell, he's not elected to anything. There's nothing on him in the public records. That means he's running something the Free Laws don't touch. That Miner Prime is keeping out of the light."

"Never stopped you before."

Lina leaned away, looked Davin square in the face.

"Don't come in here and act like you know what it's like," Lina said. "There's been a shift. Nobody wants to fight anymore, because they want to save up, buy passage to one of the new outposts. Like your Europa."

"And they're willing to live in crap until then?"

"Better than dying for it. Or rotting in prison. They're seeing what's happening on Mars."

Davin looked back at the monitors. The feeds from all over the station still running. It'd been a long time since their parents had led the marches, organized the meetings to improve conditions in Vagrant's Hollow.

"It's not your job to make their dreams come true," Davin said.

"I thought it was, for a long time. I built this, collected blackmail, was ready to start a revolution until I realized nobody wanted one."

"We find Bosser, clear the charge, and then we can leave."

"There you go, Davin. Being the hero."

"That is the best part of this job." Davin shivered as Lina's fingers walked up his chest. Her mouth moved closer.

"Really?" Her voice low, her lips lush.

"I stand corrected."

39

AMBUSHED

Opal put the scope on Mace's counter. Beneath the glass surface was a surfeit of beam knives, and behind the counter an array of deadly weaponry whose price tag took notice of the high tax the Free Laws put on arsenals. An updated version of the one she had, this scope contained a chip that analyzed the movements of people seen in it, compared against a database of human walks and runs. It'd tell her whether a target was nervous, calm, or about to run a moment before the person did. In that second, Opal could squeeze off a shot, save the day.

"You got enough coin for this one, Opal?" Mace, the tattooed, grungy owner said to her. "Last I seen you, your account wasn't doing so hot."

"We've picked up a few gigs, old man. It'll clear," Opal said.

Mace gestured for Opal to slide her comm across the reader. Opal did, and the thing chimed an affirmative a second later.

"Well, color me surprised," Mace said. "Here I had you figured for broke."

"Have I ever disappointed you, Mace?"

The shopkeeper chuckled, both of them knowing Opal had pinched a few items from this store. Mace held a certain level of respect for anyone gutsy enough to steal from him and get away with it, much less do it multiple times. So the last time Opal came in, Mace had her cornered and made her an offer. Steal nothing else, and she could keep her ill-gotten gains. Opal, seeing the beam knife in Mace's hand, hadn't argued.

Merc, leaning against the store entrance, had his eyes on them. The pilot was still standing, but Opal noticed Merc's pained grimace, his arms hanging limp. After this, it was back to the ship. Opal gave Mace a nod, then started towards the entrance. As she did so, Mace's terminal, behind her, made an angry noise, like a horn being squashed flat mid-note.

"Hey," Mace said, quieter now.

Opal glanced back at the shop keeper.

"I'm being told by the peacekeepers to keep you here. Just popped up now."

There was a time when Opal would have asked why. Would have been angry, surprised that police would be trying to find her. Now, though, all she did was nod. The shopkeeper slanted his head in return. Then Opal's eyes and mind turned to Merc.

"Time to go," Opal said to Merc as she held out an arm.

Together they limped towards the lifts that would take them back to the ship. Miner Prime's artificial sun was resting on the horizon, the diodes illuminating Level Five's ceiling shifting into hues of purples and oranges this evening. Beautiful, so long as she pretended it was real. Opal took a mental inventory. She had a sidearm, the beam knife too. Merc had nothing more than a bottle of pills.

Which was why, when, only twenty yards from the lift doors, a dozen green-uniformed peacekeepers stepped out and demanded the two of them surrender, Opal dropped her gun without a fight. They separated Opal from Merc first, then slapped stun cuffs around her wrists.

"Good choice," the peacekeeper told her as they walked towards the lift. "Not worth adding to that charge, right?"

"I did it for him," Opal said, eyes sliding towards Merc, who had a pair of peacekeepers helping him along.

"Won't hear me arguing," the peacekeeper said. "All I'm looking for is to get home at the end of the day."

"I was, too," Opal replied.

40

THE METAL MAN

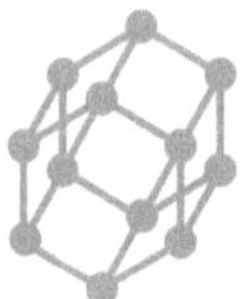

Vi's wide eyes blinked from one of the three men to the next. Mox could smell the fear coming off her, that rush of scent Mox normally had directed at him. The exoskeleton picked up on it, told Mox about Vi's near-panic while he looked at the opposing trio. The middle man looked like the leader, hands at a pair of handguns on his belt. Given away by his cronies, who kept glancing towards him, waiting for a signal. A poor strategy.

"Step aside," Mox said.

"Aren't you a mercenary, big guy?" the leader asked. "Don't you know what she's worth?"

"Step aside. I won't ask again."

"Guess all that metal must be messing with your mind. We're taking the girl."

Mox started forward. Vi said his name, but Mox ignored her. To hesitate now would give them a chance to shoot, and Mox had no weapon with him. None save his fists, anyway. The exoskeleton registered the movement, picked up the surge in energy as Mox ran, and amplified it with mechanical strength.

On his second step, as the trio leader tugged at the guns in his holster, Mox leapt three meters. Crossed more than half the ground between the two groups. The leader raised the gun and, as Mox flew through his third step, his fist colliding with the leader's chin, fired.

The blast bounced off of the floor and into a wall. Mox did the same to the leader, smashing him into the ground, momentum sliding the man into a bench. Mox registered the strike audibly, as he'd turned left, following the swing of his arm, and clapped the second crony in the stomach. Doubling over, collapsing to the floor, flunky number two was no longer a problem.

Mox flung his right arm back in a wild blow, meant not to hit the third one as much as delay him, get him to duck and give Mox a second to turn himself around.

The swing, as expected, hit only air. Mox, though, used the energy to pivot around and look at the third attacker. The little goon seemed paralyzed. Mox's blow had missed not because of any ducking, but because the coward hadn't even tried to close. Pathetic.

Mox took a step, stared into the goon's face, which melted into slack-jawed fear. This one wasn't even worth the effort. Instead, Mox pulled the gun out of the goon's pocket, and snapped it with his hands. Vi yelled something again, but Mox couldn't make it out over the pounding adrenaline in his ears. So much time with the cannon had him forgetting the feel of using his own hands. And how much fun they were.

The third goon recovered his wits and ran towards the lifts. Mox could catch him, could toss the goon around like a doll, but Vi was the concern. Mox turned back to his charge, at where she used to be, and saw nobody. The fight hadn't lasted more than a few seconds. Where'd the girl go?

Mox looked around, but the walkway was full of people running away from the conflict, none of them matching Vi's clothes. But there! Puk, Vi's little bot, floated near the entrance to a dark-looking club. Mox ran in that direction as Puk zipped inside. The joint's name, *Cosmic Dust*, did not inspire confidence.

Mox crouched to get through the door, a sliding one that made no noise as it slipped open. Well maintained. The entryway was short, a deep blue with flecks of white. Evoked leaving Earth for the stars. Something Mox had done many, many years ago. But memories were not the point of now. Further inside even the deep blue vanished, replaced by wheeling stars and galaxies. A vibrating crowd filled the place.

Suddenly a bright comet streaked across the ceiling, moving in a strange pattern and, every so often, appearing to drop motes of light on the dancing peopled. Music, such as it was, existed as a slow, bouncing beat with synthesized echoes.

"Need a how-to?" said a girl appearing out of nowhere next to Mox.

Her tag read she was an astronaut. A lie, as she appeared, even in the darkness, to be Viola's age. The only astronauts left were relics of an older time, back when governments funded space travel and one needed more than money to see the stars. Perhaps, then, the girl was an attendant.

"Finding someone," Mox said.

"A lot of people find things here," the girl said. "Use your comm. It'll automatically connect, and then you can order from there."

"A girl," Mox replied. "With a bot."

"Uh huh. Pick the dust you want and it'll be dropped.

Then, you know, you enjoy," the girl said, giving Mox a smile and fading away into the blackness.

Mox couldn't see anything, but Vi had to be in here somewhere. He would comb the blitzed out stargazers. He would find her.

41

START YOUR ENGINES

Another thirty minutes before the supplies finished loading. Phyla heard Trina saying the words and wondered how much time had passed since she'd heard them. A minute, maybe? She'd put out a few comm calls to Opal, Merc, and Mox and had nothing to show for it. Blanks. Davin still in Lina's bunker. Which meant Phyla was acting captain, and she might have to actually do something with that responsibility.

"Erick?" Phyla commed.

"Yes?" Erick replied from his bed, where he'd chosen to spend the day continuing to recover.

"How long did you tell Merc he could be out?"

"Let me check."

Phyla stared out of the cockpit at the busy bay Miner Prime assigned them. Bots and people moved around between the other ships in the same space, and a few of them continued going up the *Whiskey Jumper*'s loading ramp, bringing in food and any parts Trina requested. Davin's procedure was to stock up to the max at every port, even if they didn't know where their next flight was going.

Also why the captain insisted on foods that wouldn't spoil quickly. It made for dull meals, but meant the ship could coast for months at full crew capacity. Phyla wondered how crazy she'd go if that ever happened.

"He's past due," Erick said, Phyla jumped at the sudden sound.

"Past due?"

"Yes, I cleared him for a short trip to get some fresher air. Exertion is still a risk at this stage in his recovery."

"I can't raise them on the comm," Phyla said.

"That's concerning. Expect he would be needing another dose to keep the pain down."

"Yeah. Not like Opal to botch a schedule, either," Phyla tried pinging their comms again, nothing. There was always a chance the two of them were in a dead spot on the station, surrounded by thick plates that blocked messages. Some places put in the investment to keep their stores, massage parlors, clubs immune to the constant connection comms created.

"Mox isn't answering either, nor Cadge."

"Worrisome, don't you think?"

"I'll keep looking. I'm sure they're just in the lifts or something," Phyla said, her eyes holding on the consoles. The murder charge played constantly, running over the news. People died all the time in space, but not company ones. Especially officials visiting an outpost being plugged as the next paradise.

Erick told her to let him know, then signed off. Phyla flipped the board to the video feed of Erick's room for a split second, confirming the napping doctor curled beneath a blanket. The light turned off a second later. Creepy, looking in on Erick, but the crew understood why the cameras were there. A small ship had to be able to see what was going on anywhere in case of an atmosphere leak, fire, or something worse.

"Hellooooo ship? Anyone listening?" Came an unfamiliar voice over the comm.

"Phyla here, on the *Whiskey Jumper*. Who's this?"

"Puk, Viola's bot, and I've got news for you."

"Where are you? Are you with Mox?"

"Not anymore. Viola's been grabbed by your pal Cadge. We just ducked out the service exit of some sweet rave called *Cosmic Dust*. I'm bein' sneaky and your guy hasn't noticed me yet. Not sure how much longer that's going to last."

"Where's Mox? And what level is that?"

"Whaddya think? Level Five. Mox was jumped by some goons, who he toasted. I mean, it wasn't even a fight. Like, not even time to bet. That dudes a killer."

"Puk, focus. Where is Cadge taking her?"

"Think I can read minds? What I do know is that he wants that bounty money."

"Go find Mox. Tell him where Cadge is taking Viola,.

"So you're not gonna help?"

"Keep me informed and I might."

The bot chirped an affirmative. Then Trina blipped up quick to say the supplies were on. The *Jumper* fueled and ready for launch. One thing right in a day of wrongs. Phyla took a deep breath, then tried to comm Davin again. Nothing. Why was everything falling apart when she was in the captain's chair?

42

TUNNELS

L ina kept the store where it was in Vagrant's Hollow for a reason. That was, as they'd figured out when they were kids, because one of the recycled air shafts ran beneath it. A big tube through which warm or cool air went, depending on the day and which side of Miner Prime was facing the sun. It wrapped around Vagrant's Hollow and connected with the swarming collection of vents that kept oxygen flowing through the station.

Standing behind Lina's desk on the main store, Davin, hair still wet from the quick shower, watched as Lina pulled back a thick gray mat. Underneath was a metal plate with a grip.

"Be a gentleman, would you?" Lina asked.

Davin took the cue and pulled on the plate, then pressed with his legs to move the heavy thing. The grinding of the plate against the floor showed a hole that Davin remembered looking much bigger when he was younger.

"That's gonna be, uh, tight," Davin said.

"I'll go first. Toss your stuff to me. Then you'll fit," Lina said.

"You sure about that?"

"Pretty familiar with your size, Davin. You'll make it," Lina gave Davin a curled smile.

Lina descended ladder and landed two meters lower with a thunk.

"You'll be happy," Lina called. "They're circulating cold air today."

"Hallelujah." Davin said, unsnapping his holster and tossing it to Lina.

If the vents were pushing heat, it'd be too uncomfortable. Literally a furnace. Every once in a while, exploring as kids, they'd been caught inside there when the waves of solar heat blasted through and emerged slimy balls of sweat, gasping for breath. Davin managed a squirming climb into the tube, standing up when he hit the floor and whacking his head on the ceiling.

"Oh yeah, you'll want to duck," Lina said. "Guess you grew a little from when you were a kid."

"Is that how it works?"

The tube itself was a stainless steel stretch of metal. Bolts dug in every meter to tie sections together. Lina's statement about the breeze was right: a steady wind blew in the tunnel, enough to move Davin's hair if not to push him any faster.

"If I recall, we didn't go very far down these vents when we were younger?" Davin asked, looking back and forth.

"We can't just walk right into Bosser's office. It's in the peacekeeper barracks, a few levels away," Lina said. "They'll be watching the lifts. They won't be watching the tunnels."

"Why would Bosser be watching the lifts? We didn't land under our own name."

Lina walked through the vent, the smooth walls broken up here and there by pipes and smaller vents either sending in or siphoning off the airflow. Beyond their tapping steps, the steady churn of machinery working rumbled around them. Even though they were only a few meters beneath the chatter of Vagrant's Hollow, not a sound filtered to them.

"There was a lot of chatter a few hours ago," Lina continued. "Watch orders went out through common channels. Your name included."

"Then the rest of them could be in trouble?"

"The only way to help your crew is to do what we're doing here," Lina replied. "Get rid of the charge, there's no reason to arrest anyone."

Yeah, except Bosser probably wasn't worried about arrests. Davin should run back up that ladder, to the lifts and to his ship. Or to find Opal, who'd gone shopping. Or . . . maybe Lina was right. Nothing Davin did alone was going to shift a fight with the peacekeepers. Nothing, except getting Bosser to stop.

"How long will it take to get to him?"

"Depends on whether we're lucky," Lina said.

"You're with me, so that's not likely."

The vent tunnel curved ahead of them, arcing back towards the station's center. Where the main shafts were located, heading up and down. They kept walking, the low maintenance lights keeping the two lit in silhouette. Eventually, the light at the end of tunnel, denoted by a ring of red lights.

"You want to improve the odds, stay quiet," Lina said, looking back at Davin and bringing a finger to her lips. Davin nodded. The odds would need all the help they could get.

43

KIDNAPPED

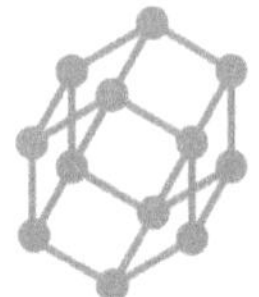

Viola wasn't trying to struggle anymore. Not because there weren't openings in Cadge's shambling sprint through the service hallways, but because Viola kept hearing Cadge's muttered threat in her mind.

"Try to run, I'll kill you. Don't want to do that. Be nice with me, you get back home to Mom and Dad."

It was hard to comprehend, Cadge's double-barreled sidearm right there under her nose. With a twitch of his finger, Cadge would erase everything Viola was. A paralyzing, crippling fear that Viola hadn't felt. Twenty years gone in a moment. There wasn't a rational response to that. None save doing whatever she could to stay alive. Puk, normally the counter-weight to Viola's descents into her own head, was nowhere. She was standing on a precipice and if Viola didn't say something soon, she would fly off into panic.

"Why do you want the reward so much?" Viola asked Cadge.

"I have my reasons. Most of 'em having to do with risking my damn life for too little every day," Cadge said.

Cadge wasn't looking back at her. Viola could dart to one of the back doors to escape. But how many of them would open when she pulled? And if it didn't, would Cadge give her a warning or just blow her to pieces?

"So you're kidnapping me? That's the solution?"

"You have a better one?" Cadge replied.

"How about not?"

"Leaves me bled dry, Vi."

Past another pair of shops was a rusted light blue door, large enough for carts. Cadge paused in front of a series of three buttons, one red, one green, and the other with a marker of an alarm. The door wasn't locked from this side.

"I don't understand," Viola said as Cadge pressed the green button. "Davin's supplying everything, so why wouldn't you be able to save?"

Cadge did turn around this time, giving Viola a sick smile.

"You think a man like me's capable of being stable? This career, you live for the now."

Cadge waved Viola forward through the door. Back on the public causeway, lifts a few minutes walk. Out there in the open, Cadge took a long breath, his steps slowed to a natural walk rather than the tense steps in the alley. Viola noticed why after a few seconds. The same group that Mox fought, that trio, was moving along with them. Surrounding Viola. No chance of getting away now, and no sign of Mox.

Still, talking with Cadge gave Viola time to adjust herself. The panic subsided. Analyze the situation. Just another logic problem. Four on one weren't odds she would beat, but maybe, keeping her eyes open, there'd be an opportunity. The five of them stepped into a lift and jetted away to the eighth level. A short transfer to a cross-station lift, shooting across rather than up and down. That lift would spit them out into a section reserved for incoming ships, smaller ones than the *Whiskey Jumper.*

"Where's the coin, Cadge?" The leader of the trio, his coat torn and face sporting an array of colorful bruises, said, his voice strained. "We did what you asked, and paid more than you said we would."

"Got the chits here, in my pocket. Give'em to you when we're clear," Cadge replied. "Didn't want Mox killing you and me lose good money for nothing."

"It's so nice to be kidnapped by upstanding gentlemen such as yourselves," Viola said, because every word beat back the chills coursing through her veins. "Truly, if there was anyone that would take me, slam me in a ship, and send me back home to my parents, I'd pick all of you."

"Smart mouth," the leader said.

"Pretty though," said one of the other beaters.

"There we go. That's what this was missing," Viola said.

"Shut it," Cadge snapped. "Vi, before you think about making any noise, understand I have every right to be doing what I'm doing."

"Well, now you've changed my mind," Viola said.

That prompted a snicker from the leader, but the opening lift doors cut short Cadge's reaction. Viola didn't catch the bay's number because she was staring at the swarm of ships zipping in and out of the space. Davin put the *Jumper* in a larger bay meant for cargo, but this one was for small craft. All the pleasure-seekers and businessmen stopping by the station for meetings, parties, tourism. In the time between the lift doors opening and Viola setting foot on the bay's floor, at least five ships in her view ignited their engines and floated up and free.

The leader already had his hands out, waiting for Cadge

to hand over the coin. Cadge dropped the three black and blue cards into the leader's hand, one by one.

"Already loaded?" the leader asked.

"Check'em if you want," Cadge said. "I can wait a minute."

"Cadge Vasseter!" yelled someone on the bay floor, climbing out of their ship.

Viola couldn't make out who it was, their head covered by a wide hat, a long gray coat coming from the collar to the person's ankles. Cadge, though, had an idea, because he jerked away from the trio and dove back towards the lift. Viola watched as the doors closed before Cadge could get inside, causing the small man to bounce off of them and fall to the ground, hands scrambling for his sidearm.

"Who's that?" the leader asked.

"Don't wanna know," Cadge growled back. "There's an extra ten for each of you if you help me kill them."

"Murder's gonna cost you fifty."

"It's not murder if the damn target's a bot!"

The trio stared at Cadge like he'd sprouted flowers from his face. Viola imagined she had a similar expression. Bot? What enemies did Cadge have that had a bot capable of killing? Regardless, nobody was watching her, so Viola made small steps away from the group, towards one end of the bay. The trio were still arguing with Cadge, driving up the price and checking their weapons.

Viola slipped behind a stack of outgoing luggage, a tower of suitcases tall enough to keep her hidden. At least, that's what she thought until a heavy hand landed on her shoulder.

"Stay here," a steel voice said. "You're not the target. And I don't get extra points for collateral damage."

44

RISK IT ALL

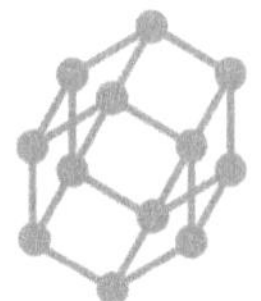

"W hat?" Viola asked, looking behind her.

The thing Cadge was calling a bot crouched next to her, gray coat bunching up around it. In each hand was a long and narrow gun, thin lines of jagged red running up one barrel, blue on the other.

"Who are you?" Viola asked.

"My name is Fournine," It replied. "Excuse me while I eliminate my target."

That was one way to say hello. Viola sat back as Fournine walked towards Cadge and the trio. Cadge was the only one even looking in Fournine's direction, and was the first to yell, pointing his finger at the android. If it was hunting Cadge, then it was probably the same one from Eden Prime. Which meant that after Cadge, Davin and the others were next.

"Friends!" Fournine announced. "I am legally authorized to terminate Cadge, here. The rest of you have a choice. Leave and live, or stay and suffer the fate of an accomplice."

The leader exchanged quick looks with his pals, who both backed towards the lift. Cadge, voice edging higher, again promised fifty . . . what denomination Viola didn't know. Thousand? Hundreds? The going price of bot murder wasn't something she knew.

The trio didn't listen. As soon as the lift doors opened, they booked it. Cadge started that way too, but before he'd gone two steps, Fournine fired from his blue gun. The bolt snaked out, slower than a normal laser, but arcing in on Cadge even as the mercenary, expecting the shot, fell to the left.

The blue bolt struck like a pouncing cat, swinging in at Cadge. Bits of lightning sprung up around the mercenary, pulling Cadge to the floor, mouth and eyes open. It wasn't something Viola wanted to watch, but she couldn't pull her eyes away.

Fournine took a cautious walk up to Cadge, both guns out and pointed at the mercenary. Viola edged out from her cover to get a better view. Cadge twitched as the android stood over him.

"A deal, target," Fournine said. "Information on your fellows. Where they are, where they're going, and I'll ensure they pay for abandoning you here."

Cadge looked at the android, shaking his head, eyes and mouth tight.

"You think I'm gonna sell them out?" Cadge said, spit flinging from his lips. "You think they abandoned me? Hell, I abandoned them. For that girl there."

Cadge nodded at Viola. Fournine didn't turn its head. It probably knew exactly who Cadge was talking about.

"I've done nothing worth killing for," Cadge continued. "But I figure you lot don't see gray, only red."

"Smarter than you look," Fournine said, raising the red gun.

As Fournine brought the gun up, Cadge triggered something with his left hand. There was a roaring pop, the noise Viola would hear whenever Ganymede's colonization day rolled around and Galaxy Forge launched fireworks into the light atmosphere. Fournine flew off of Cadge and into the wall next to the lift. Cadge himself didn't move, his eyes closed. Unconscious, or dead.

Around the bay others were noticing the fight, gathering to watch what was happening on the walkway. Another lift with a handful of passengers arrived, only to notice the bodies and send the lift away to another, any other, destination. The station's cameras had to notice. Might be playing on the news now. If Mox and the others saw it, they'd know to run.

Fournine was the first one to move, pushing itself up from the floor and standing straight. It stared ahead, unblinking for a few seconds. Rebooting. Just like Puk did whenever she needed to update the bot. A scrubbing of scrambled code, a re-orienting of priorities. When Fournine grabbed its guns and turned to Cadge, its set face was the same unflinching cold as before.

"How I hate surprises," Fournine said, this time keeping a meter between himself and Cadge's unmoving form. "And whatever you're planning next, please know that I can hear your heartbeat from here. One more chance, Cadge Vasseter. My mercy goes no farther."

With a strangled sigh, Cadge sat up, just enough so that his head peeked up at the android.

"How many times do I have to tell you? Go to hell, you metal bastard," Cadge growled.

Fournine nodded, then raised the red gun and blasted

Cadge in the chest. The mercenary fell back to the floor. Fournine holstered its weapons, staring at Cadge the entire time.

"You're recording him, aren't you?" Viola asked, coming out onto the walkway.

"Part of the requirements. I have to get proof," Fournine replied, not looking away from Cadge's body. "One down. Plenty left."

Fournine straightened, looked at Viola. This close, with the hat on the ground, Fournine stared at her. Jagged lines ran along the left side of its face. A hasty plaskin repair. The rest of its skin looked too perfect. No wrinkles. No natural bumps, hairs, or eyelashes out of place.

"What are you staring at?" Fournine asked. "It is rude to study another so. As I understand it, a human would blush under such scrutiny."

"You, uh, can't do that. Can you?"

"Doesn't matter to you. Or me." Fournine moved over to the lifts and pushed the call button.

The android seemed to forget Viola was still standing there, watching him. Maybe the android really didn't care about her. Viola could walk away, head back to the *Jumper*. Or . . .

"Who are you going after next?" Viola said.

"Don't care," Fournine replied, staring ahead at the closed lift doors. "This is a list that can be read in any order. Cadge Vasseter happened to have the least luck of his friends."

"I guess I'm thankful."

Fournine turned now and Viola felt those inanimate eyes poring over her. Every part of her tested, ranked and measured.

"I'm having a hard time understanding why you're

continuing to talk," Fournine said. "According to my logic, you interacting with me only increases your chances of death."

"I can help you. Find the rest of them, I mean."

"Why would you do that?"

"You just saw one of them try and kidnap me. They deserve what's coming to them."

Viola had no idea if Fournine would take her word, but if the bot let her come with him, it didn't really matter. Viola reached towards Cadge's body, which smelled like burning meat, the charred hole in the mercenaries chest twisting her stomach in knots. Focus, girl, focus. On Cadge's left wrist wrapped his comm. A button on the underside unlatched the tool, and Viola slipped it off and then around her own forearm. Fournine watched with a robot's lifeless impassivity.

"Who are you going to talk to?" Fournine asked.

"I'll be able to find their location," Viola said. "Lead you right to them."

Fournine nodded and Viola raised the comm.

"Phyla?" Viola asked into the device.

"Viola?" Phyla replied. "You have a comm? The signature says it's Cadge's?"

"Long story," Viola said. "I need to know where Davin's going."

"He's trying to find the guy who can get that android off our backs. He's on this station somewhere. But what's going on? Where's Cadge?"

Viola caught Fournine's eye, and the android waved a hand in a quick slash motion. Cut the call.

"Thanks, Phyla. I'll be in touch."

"Hey—"

Viola cut the transmission. Fournine was busy punching

a request into the lift panel. The clock was ticking. If Viola didn't find a way to shut down Fournine before it found Davin, the captain's death would be on her.

Not for the first time, Viola wished she'd just stayed at home on Ganymede.

45

SAVE THE SHIP

Nobody answered the calls, and then Viola chimed in out of nowhere with Cadge's comm. Phyla pitched another round to the crew. Radio silence from Mox, Opal, Merc, and Davin. What the hell was going on out there?

Outside the cockpit window, the activity in the bay was winding down as the hours crept later. Dinner time. A pinch in her own stomach where some food would've found a welcome home. Here they were, on a station where Phyla might get a good meal, and she was still stuck on the ship. It wasn't fair. Then, that'd always been her lot. Sitting on the ship playing comm operator while Davin dashed around or Merc aced out the skies.

The main lift doors kicked Phyla out of the musing. A squad, at least ten people wearing the forest green of Miner Prime's peacekeepers. Only these looked armed, ready for combat, not patrol. Too terrible to be a coincidence.

Phyla slapped a button on the right side of the console, big and red, labeled Alarm. The button's sole purpose was to make a lot of noise while sliding up the loading ramp and sealing the doors. Hopefully, neither Trina nor Erick had decided on an evening stroll.

Outside, the security forces paused, grouping into bunches and looking like easy targets. Phyla twisted a small dial that popped a turret from the top of the ship. On the ground, with the turret up, Phyla's flight stick rerouted to control where the gun pointed, and she aimed it at the closest group.

"You're all not here for us, right?" Phyla spoke through the ship's intercom system.

One of the security members, with a thicker collar than the others and a blue armband around his bicep, raised a hand and stepped towards the ship.

"No closer. You talk nice and loud and I'll hear you fine," Phyla said. "Your boot goes another centimeter and I'll take it as assault with deadly force and respond in kind."

As the security officer cleared his throat, Phyla switched the comm to broadcast internally.

"Trina, get our engines ready. I'll stall as long as I can, but we can't stay here."

"Already on it," Trina replied a heartbeat later.

"That's why you're the best," Phyla replied, then realized the officer out front was speaking.

" . . . and, in addition to the aforementioned crimes, it is suspected that your vessel carries a number of illegal modifications not approved for its class. Like, uh, that turret there."

"It's not my ship," Phyla said. "I'm just the pilot. Have no say in what the captain does with her."

The console showed the engines were at twenty-five percent. Phyla knew the ship could bounce at seventy-five if it had to, it just wouldn't be the smoothest launch. But then, nothing with this damned ship was smooth. Only, without the *Jumper* she wouldn't have ever left Miner Prime. Maybe she'd be down there in one of those green suits instead of up here, manning a spewing death weapon and waiting for someone to make the wrong move.

"Then you won't mind us coming aboard to look for him?" the officer replied.

The man was stalling for time same as she was. The other security forces shifted around, spreading out. The main lift doors opened again. More peacekeepers, only these carried larger weapons. Crowd suppression turrets and strong EMP launchers. Couldn't do explosions on a space station, but shorting circuitry was fair game.

"He's on his way to talk to your boss right now," Phyla said. "You should check, maybe they've cleared this up."

Dangerous, hinting to what Davin was doing, but Phyla didn't see she had a choice. The engines hadn't hit fifty yet. Cold starts were rough, and if they took fire too soon, the *Jumper* wouldn't be going anywhere. The officer bought it, though, holding up a hand and speaking into his comm. Phyla rotated the turret to aim at the group of security setting up the EMPs. Another thirty seconds and she'd fire anyway. She dialed down the power on the turret—it would burn, hurt, but shouldn't kill anymore. The last thing they needed was an actual set of murders on their record.

"How we doing?" Phyla commed to Trina.

The engines were at sixty percent. Close. If the *Jumper* wasn't going to take off early, Phyla had to know.

"They're goosed, Phyla. When you say go, they'll get us out of here," Trina said. "But if you can hold till ninety, we'll have a better chance of not exploding."

"Noted."

"Phyla?" Mox's voice came over the comm. "I lost Viola."

So many questions, no time to ask any.

"She's fine," Phyla replied. "No word on Opal and Merc. Go find them, please. Then hole up and wait for more."

The security officer lowered his arm, a scowl lighting up his face. That meant Davin hadn't taken care of things. Which meant their stall time was up. Phyla pressed on the flight stick's trigger and the turret fired, spraying yellow lasers into the bay. There wasn't any recoil, not even much noise inside the ship, but Phyla flinched at the bright light.

The bolts struck home, frying circuits and scattering the security forces across the bay. Burning bits of cloth and sparking mechanics sent smoke swirling from the blasts. Keeping the trigger down, Phyla swept the turret left to right across the peacekeeper formation.

The first return shots came, small lasers from sidearms. They glanced off plating meant to handle space awfulness, from rocks to blasts from far more powerful anti-ship weaponry. Part of the constant upgrades Davin put into the ship whenever he had spare coin. Now, though, Phyla appreciated it. Prayed that it would hold another minute till those engines were ready. That the exclamation point to her life wouldn't be written in this docking bay.

46

UP BY FORCE

The tube intersection looked so basic, smooth and perfect like a children's toy. A big central shaft with vented openings all over the place. Like the inside of a twisted flute. Davin and Lina stood at the end of their tube, surveying the sheer sides of the shaft. Davin didn't think he'd be a terrible climber, but the whole no handholds thing would make it difficult.

"They use a hovering vehicle to get up and down the shaft for maintenance," Lina said, whispering. "I've picked it up on camera a few times."

"Good to know. I'll keep that in mind when I get my own space station," Davin replied.

"But if there's a problem," Lina said, ignoring Davin's quip, "they'll send a spotter bot first to find the damage."

"Should I be taking notes? Is there a test?"

"Stop being stupid. We'll trigger a maintenance check. The spotter bot will come, we'll trick it into seeing a problem, then hijack the maintenance craft."

"See, you're using the word 'we' a lot there, only I don't

understand how we're doing any of this. At least the first two. The hijacking I get."

Lina stepped over to the side of the tube and pulled out her sidearm, a standard-issue laser pistol she'd probably found in Miner Prime's thriving black market. She popped the weapon open using a slider underneath the barrel. Made cleaning and repairing the lasers easy, only now Lina was using it to take out the gun's battery. Lina set the battery on the floor of the tube, then walked back. Davin followed.

"I suppose now you want me to shoot it?" Davin asked.

"Knew you'd figure it out," Lina replied.

Blasting a battery pack caused the stored energy in it to overheat. With the small size of Lina's sidearm, that wouldn't be much, but it might mangle the tube enough. Davin couldn't help but smile. This was the same stuff Lina pulled when they were kids, upping the risk from one prank to the next till something backfired.

"Lina, before I shoot this thing and possibly bring hell itself upon us, I have a question."

"And maybe I have an answer," Lina replied.

"How long have you been planning this?"

"Since I saw your name on the wanted list. Whenever you're in trouble, you always come back here."

"And you knew we'd be going in the tubes?"

"There's only one way for people without clearance to get to that level, and it's this one. Now, you going to shoot that thing or do I have to?"

Without another word, Davin drew and fired his gun in a single motion, the laser hitting the battery pack and exploding the thing in a bright flash of molten plasma. The super-heated goop burnt into the side of the tube, hollowing out pits and charring the surface.

"That doesn't draw an investigation, dunno what will," Davin said.

"Always knew you could hit a stationary target."

"I do have skills."

Only a few seconds later the soft hum of low-powered engines echoed through the tube. Davin and Lina inched backward, around a slight bend and out of site of the central shaft. If the bot found something needing repair, the maintenance crew would come after it. No need to risk getting caught. The hum grew louder, then held steady for ten seconds, before rising up and away from the tube.

"A thought," Davin said. "That bot, when it looks at the damage, it will know an explosion isn't a typical problem down here."

"Even if it does, that just means you'll have to show off those deadly talents you talk about so much."

Lina, always with the ribbing. Davin didn't talk himself up too much, did he?

"Good point. So excited," Davin said.

Not too many minutes later another rumbling noise made its way the shaft and shook the tube. Much larger than the inspection bot. Large enough that Davin threw Lina some side-eye. When Lina glanced his way, Davin pointed at her, then at himself, and held up two fingers and tilted his head towards the loud engine noise. A craft that big against the two of them? Those weren't good odds.

"Surprise," Lina whispered to him, barely audible over the engine noise.

Then, before Davin could move, Lina slipped along the tube towards the craft. Davin rounded the bend after her and saw the floating platform hovering just below the exit of the tube. On it Davin counted four people, three in the gray outfits of mechanical personal and one in the green of

Miner Prime security. All of them were looking at Lina, who stood waving. In a second, they'd realize she wasn't alone.

In that second, Davin drew his gun and, in the same motion, moved his finger along the power slider. Fancier weapons like his had the choice to toss more, and lower-powered, shots. Seeing as they were trying to get rid of a criminal charge, it didn't seem like a great idea to kill someone. At least, not if they didn't have to.

Davin's first shot went under Lina's raised, waving arm and struck the security guard in the chest. The guard stumbled back to the edge of the platform, about to fall off, when he hit the safety barrier. The platform flashed a neon blue around where the guard was tumbling and, instead of falling off, the platform pushed the guard back. Lina dove to the side, giving Davin a clear second shot.

This one flew wide, just over the ducking head of the mechanic closest to the damaged tube. An intentional miss. Had to make them understand Davin could take them out whenever he wanted. The shot had the desired effect, as the mechanics backed up, hands raised, and leaned against the platform's barriers.

"Which one of you knows how to fly this thing?" Davin said, running onto the craft and kicking away the wounded guard's weapon.

None of them said anything at first. Then Lina picked up the guard's gun, a hefty piece of work meant to spray stunning electricity, and trained it on them. That prompted one of the mechanics to cough. Davin gave him a nod.

"Well, uh, we all can," the mechanic said. "Part of our training."

"Good. Then one of you, send us up," Davin said, waving with the weapon.

"Level Nine," Lina said.

The mechanic that spoke went to the console. Just before the craft moved, Davin pulled the guard and the other two mechanics off, leaving them in the tube. Their buddy could come back for them later. Davin hadn't taken a hostage before, and one seemed a safer bet than four.

The piloting mechanic pushed a lever and the craft rose. One step closer.

47

TAKE OFF

The console pinged when the engines hit ninety, just like it had every ten percent before then, but when Phyla heard that wonderful bell, she let go of the flight stick and tapped the launch sequence on the console. The first step was to trigger the landing rockets, pushing the ship a few inches off the ground, then tap the landing gear retrieval, and then flip the turret onto auto-fire mode. The last one was dangerous, as the turret then analyzed any incoming fire and shot in that direction. It always meant the turret fired second, but Phyla needed the flight stick to fly.

The security forces hadn't expected the *Whiskey Jumper*'s defenses. After Phyla neutralized the EMPs, the bulk of the attackers hunkered behind walls, stacked cargo, or dove into the lift and fled. Reinforcements would come, but right now there was a distinct lack of laser fire splashing across Phyla's cockpit. As the ship lifted off the ground and rotated, Phyla saw bright orange lights flash in the bay. They were shutting the door, trying to keep the *Jumper* sealed on the station. Only, they were way too slow.

Phyla goosed the engines even before the exit was fully in view, arcing the *Jumper* out before the bay door was even a quarter shut. The black infinite of space stretched before her though the *Jumper*'s radar showed a slew of other ships spread around the station. The question was whether Miner Prime would bother to fight them out here. The station would risk coin and cargo if they tried to have a shoot-out near these trading ships.

So Phyla steered the *Jumper* to the nearest cluster, hoping to hide among their valuable structures. Then she'd find a way to get the rest of their friends back. Speaking of . . .

"Mox, you there?"

"Here," Mox said a second later, the transmission faint and blipped with static, a result of the increasing distance between the two. "You gone?"

"We're off."

"Good. Found them."

"How?"

"Mace. Weapon dealer. They were taken."

"Taken? By who?"

"Be ready. Level Eleven. Will call."

"Thanks for not answering my question."

Mox didn't reply. cutting the comm. Phyla, moving the *Jumper* down to undercut a long chain of containers being towed by what amounted to a large engine and little else, pulled up the Miner Prime directory. Eleven. Two words in the description. Prison and Containment.

48

JAILED

The lifts took Mox right up and deposited him into an austere lobby. Chairs were there, a few token plants, and a pair of desks behind glass with security officers staring out at the waiting room. Several people milled about, some sitting and staring at nothing, others on their comms, while more were in line waiting for those officers. Mox estimated twenty. Too much collateral damage.

There was a door to the right of the officers, the only other one leading from the lobby. Mox assumed that to be the entrance to the actual prison. The possibility of breaking through door, with the suit, was high. The possibility of survival past it, low. Mox needed a distraction.

Mox walked up to the last person in the line. A shabby man. Old, tired.

"Why are you here?" Mox asked, forcing himself to use more words.

"Friend's been couped up in there for days," the man replied. "He meant to pay the tab, you know, but didn't have the money. I've got it now. Hoping they'll let him go."

"Optimistic?"

The man laughed. It was weak, wheezy. Not a threat.

"You look around here, you see any reason to hope?"

Mox shook his head. He had to get inside the prison. No way to force it but if he was let in . . . Mox moved away from the line, towards a few empty chairs. Picked one up. The people in the lines scattered while the officers behind the desks pointed and shouted. Good. Mox threw the first chair at the prison door where it bounced. Plastic. No help. Mox picked up a second chair, threw it towards the officer desk. Aimed high, so it ricocheted off the wall.

The prison door opened and five security officers came running out, pointing blue-tinted pistols at Mox. Stunners. Mox didn't pick up the third chair, just glaring at the security officers.

"You gone crazy, man?" one of them asked as the five fanned out in a circle around Mox.

"Friends inside. Want to see."

"Good, cause that's where you're going," the officer said, gesturing for another to move behind Mox with a pair of stun cuffs. "Don't try anything or we'll knock you out so hard you won't wake for days."

Mox just nodded. The rest of the crowd stared at him, a few using their devices to take videos. Mox would be famous. Funny. The stun cuffs snapped around Mox's wrists and he felt his arms go numb. Didn't matter. He was getting inside.

49

RECONNECT

Puk, where it could feel anything, felt tired. Its power level was running low. It'd been zipping around Level Five, then in the lifts around a few other levels hunting for signs of Viola and finding none. It'd gone back to the *Whiskey Jumper*'s bay to find it empty, a bunch of security officers standing around picking themselves up. From there, back to Level Five and still nobody. Like the Wild Nines had disappeared.

Miner Prime's shopping district was shifting into evening mode, the false sky overhead darkening in an approximation of a spectacular twilight. Lights popped on outside of restaurants, neons over most, with a pair of themed eateries sporting the more mellowed yellows of earlier centuries. Crowds changed complexion, from buyers of goods to purveyors of experiences. Bots like Puk flitted through the air, sometimes stopping to project ads.

"Puk?" came a message over Puk's comm.

The message came from Cadge's comm, but the vocal register was consistent with Viola's. Odd. Comms weren't things people parted with. And their relative abilities generated unlikely odds that Viola could have taken the comm by force. There was room for random chance, however, and Viola was nothing if not capable.

"Where are you?" Puk replied, lowering power to its inflection and accent systems to conserve juice, causing the remark to sound toneless, metallic.

"You've got to be low on power. Are you still on Level Five?"

"Yes," Puk replied.

Low was an understatement. Puk had shut down most of its systems. Like a human falling asleep, Puk only had its camera and comm up and running now. And the jets. Movement was still necessary.

"Go near the lifts. I'll find you," Viola said.

Puk did so, sinking to the ground. Within a few yards of the lifts, Puk gave itself a boost and then shut off its tiny engine, hitting the ground with a clang and rolling forward. There were people around who noticed, but nobody cared enough to investigate. Why get involved in something else's problem? So Puk rolled to a stop near the lifts and waited. Its camera went dark. Comm only.

"This is the one?" said a voice after a few minutes, one Puk didn't recognize.

"It's Puk."

"The bot's not a target."

"I never said it was." Viola's voice.

"The captain's not here."

"Apparently. Davin might already be up there."

"Then we follow."

"Sure."

As Puk heard the lift doors close, its battery dwindled and the little bot went dark.

50

CELL GAME

They put Opal and Merc together in the same large cell, owing to questions of how long they'd be there. The space occupied by a pair of metal slats sticking out from the wall, covered with the thinnest of pads. A single sheet sat on each one. The back of the cell served as a bathroom, a small curtain conveniently placed. A built-in screen on one wall shuffled through feeds from Earth, from Miner Prime's other levels. As though taunting them with what they were missing.

From the tone in the officer's voice, Opal figured they would be ejected into space before too long. Merc might not even make it that far. He lied on his slat, passed out and breathing softly. The man shouldn't have left the *Jumper*, but Merc had insisted. Claimed that he'd lose his mind if he didn't get to see something other than the ship's walls.

"Get him back here within four hours," Erick had said.

"I'll have him back in three," Opal had replied.

And now they were here.

Injured comrades were part of the way of things back when she'd fought with Earth, with the corporations to put down the Red Voice on Mars. Blazing over the martian regolith, covered in its red dust, taking and giving fire against moving targets. If she took a shot there, she'd likely wind up in a room not much better than this, a harried bot taking care of her. Thing was then, when Opal was ready, they let her leave.

Merc shifted and his sheet slid down. It wasn't cold in the cell, but the pilot shivered. Opal tore the sheet off of her slat, went over to Merc and covered him with it. His mouth was tight, eyes closed. Still hurting, even though he was asleep. That wasn't good.

When had she cared so much about Merc? They'd only been working together in the Nines for the last year, but something between them had clicked. The pilot's lighter touch on life pulling Opal away from the past. Days spent touching up the Viper, playing war games in the Jumper's pair of simulators. That'd been the start of it. Now, looking at the pilot sleeping there on the slat, it was something else.

She was going to get Merc out of here. She owed him that.

The door to the cell block opened behind her, a thick whooshing noise. It'd been happening in the few hours they'd been here. Miner Prime shuttled people in and out of this prison so quickly, so many for minor offenses that cleared up with a few coin changing hands. The footfalls in the hallway were loud this time. A large group and at least one of them was a big ticket.

Opal moved herself over to the laser-gate, careful to stay back from the bright blue beams. One touch numbed the arm or leg. Keep it there and it'd paralyze her nervous system . She'd already seen one person, too drunk to care, make a running jump at the beams. They went right through, sure, but collapsed on the other side. The guards simply shoved the drunk back in, where he still laid, unmoving. Stunned for hours and hours? No thanks.

The new prisoner moved into view, at least four officers walking with him. Opal saw Mox, saw the exoskeleton, and didn't say a word. Didn't give the man a passing glance. Mox would've seen her too. Him coming in here with those cuffs on spoke volumes. The big man wouldn't let himself get captured easily. If Mox was going in a cell, he was going to be shot up a dozen times before falling over. So that he was here all calm told Opal all she needed to know. Time to get Merc ready to go.

51

STANDOFF

The number over Mox's cell read 27, and the one shared by Opal and Merc back there was 22. The laser gate to his cell opened and a pair of guards walked him inside, while two more stayed in the hall, guns pointed at Mox. As soon as all three of them crossed the threshold, the laser gate reignited. Then the stun cuffs came off.

"We'll need the comm," a guard pointed at Mox's wrist.

Mox raised the comm, gripped it as though about to rip it off.

"Cell 22. Go big," Mox said.

"Now!" The guard tried to pull Mox's wrist away.

Mox let the guard grab the comm, the man's little fingers digging for the release, then Mox, exoskeleton surging with power, grabbed the guard's back with his right hand and launched him through the laser gate into one waiting in the hallway. Before the second guard in the cell could react, Mox had him by the throat, holding him up and staring at the remaining guard in the hall.

"Open, or he goes," Mox said.

The guard in Mox's hand tried to say something, but only gurgles came out. In the hallway, the other guard stared at Mox from the floor, his partner twitching beside him.

"Put him down, or I'll shoot." The guard decided on threats, then.

"I hope you aim well," Mox replied.

Either way, Phyla needed to hurry, or this prison break was over.

52

NEGOTIATIONS

The security level was barren, only a few souls still shifting past the Miner Prime government buildings this late. A skeleton crew handling the evening shift. Davin and Lina, leaving the mechanic cuffed in the maintenance building, walked through the low-lit concourse to the dominating headquarters.

Unlike Level Five, or even Vagrant's Hollow, the security center was austere. Administrative buildings decorated with flat signs detailing their purpose in block letters. Not even a false sky, just the gray ceiling. Never had a reason to come up here as a kid, and Davin hadn't missed anything.

The security headquarters turned out to be the only building with flair. A series of concave circles on the outer walls painted with happy murals, scenes of ribbon-cuttings, peacekeepers interacting with the community, a long line of ships waiting to land at the station. The Miner Prime logo, a whirling asteroid with a pickaxe and an olive branch hung above the main doors.

"This is . . . different," Davin said. "Never came up here.

The way those peacekeepers act, I expected something more brutal."

"Our perspective is a little skewed," Lina replied.

"Guess so."

Getting into the actual building was easy: walking up to the door and swinging it wide. A security officer sat behind a reception desk, caught twirling a pen between his fingers and staring at the ceiling. He started as they walked in, the pen clattering to the floor.

"Ah, we're closed unless you've got emergency business," the guard said.

"Here to see Bosser," Lina said. "He'll want to talk to us."

The guard gave them a closer look and then, keeping his eyes on them, touched the comm unit on his desk.

"Sir, a couple people just walked in. Say they're here to see you."

There was silence for a few seconds. A chill crawled up Davin's skin, that telltale sign someone was watching him. Which Bosser probably was. Security cameras lurked in every nook around this place. Should he wave?

"He's ready for you," the guard said, surprised at the words coming out of his mouth. "Before you go in, though, I'll have to frisk you. No weapons, you know."

"Fine," Lina said, again before Davin could get a word in.

It was as though Lina didn't want him talking. Probably didn't trust the words that would come out of Davin's mouth. Which, all things considered, was fair.

The guard took away Davin's gun, and Lina's weapon she'd taken from the incapacitated maintenance guard. Both dropped in a box that they could reclaim on their way out. Then the guard led them back through a cafeteria. Up stairs to a private apartment.

"Guy's got himself a nice place," Davin said as they walked up to the door.

"He works all the time," the guard said. "Why live anywhere else?"

The guard pushed a buzzer, and a second later the light turned green, the door unlocking. The guard ushered the two of them into Bosser's sitting room. A couch and pair of chairs sat around a circular coffee table that appeared to show a constantly changing display of ships in orbit around Miner Prime. Bosser himself strode in a moment later from an open doorway, a bottle of wine and several glasses in his hand.

"Please, sit in those chairs. You," Bosser said, looking at the guard, "can leave us alone. I'll be fine."

The guard gave a swift nod and exited, shutting the door behind him.

"You'll be fine?" Davin said, making no move towards the chairs. "Bold statement, seeing as you're talking to a murderer."

"You hurting me won't bring you anything you want," Bosser said.

"Wrong. You sent an android after me and my crew. Sending a fist into your face would be all kinds of satisfying."

"Short-term gains over long-term goals, Davin Masters," Bosser said. "One could see it as an explanation for why I'm here and you are there."

"It better not be the only explanation."

"Davin." Lina put a hand on his arm. "Focus."

Bosser took the cue, gestured towards the chairs and poured the wine, "Please, sit."

Lina led the way, taking a seat across from Bosser. Davin waited another moment, a token show of defiance, then sat.

The wine, and Davin had to credit Bosser on this one, tasted dry and fruity, a march of flavors that worked their way around the citrus circle and ended on a spicy note. For a second, Davin placed himself in the glass and forgot where they were.

"It's one of my favorites," Bosser said, breaking the spell. "Every time I see Earth, I make sure to purchase a case or two."

"You know what I like to do while my friends are in danger? Talk wine," Davin said, putting the glass on the table.

"What Davin's really saying," Lina said, "is that you should talk before we chalk this up to a loss and shoot you for the fun of it."

"Fine," Bosser spread his hands. "I don't think you and your band killed those inspectors."

"You're just going to come right out and say it?" Davin asked.

"Why not?" Bosser took another drink from the glass. "I'm right, aren't I?"

"Yeah, but then what's all this about?"

"I'm hoping you can tell me. Have you seen the video?"

"Haven't carved out time for it."

"It's quite good," Bosser flipped on the large wall screen.

It hummed to life and, with a few spoken commands from Bosser, played a black and white recording. In it, the two inspectors entered the bay, Davin and the others behind them. Just like what'd happened, jeez, over a week ago already. Both of the inspectors spoke for a minute, then walked towards the ship. Davin, it looked like, pulled out his gun and shot them in the back. Bosser paused the footage.

"I'm guessing that isn't how it went?" Bosser said.

"Yeah, cause I'm the type to shoot people for kicks and giggles," Davin said. "No, that's not even close."

"Then tell me what occurred. Prove your innocence."

So Davin launched into the story. Clare and Ward, requesting private escort and sounding very suspicious of some sort of conspiracy. The ambushed landing in the other bay, the engine splash. The arrival of the new security forces just in time to blow up the only people who knew why the whole thing happened.

"So a doctored video gets the charges pressed," Davin said. "But here's the thing I don't understand. The android that's after us. It came from Earth, and there's no way it had the time to come out to Europa after the inspectors died. It was less than a day!"

"Fournine was already in the area," Bosser said. "Eden had the android sent to Jupiter's orbit so it would be ready."

"For what?" Lina asked.

"Those inspectors weren't sent randomly. Marl is hiding something on Europa, and Eden sent the inspectors to find out what. A settlement like that one is vulnerable. Eden wanted to make sure Marl wouldn't have time to destroy their investment. I'm hoping you can tell me her secret."

"Sorry, fresh out of secrets," Davin said. "Marl always kept us at a distance. You ever meet her, you wouldn't argue with that arrangement."

"If you truly have nothing to say, then I'm sorry," Bosser said. "Eden won't remove your charge, and Marl, the only other one who could certainly won't."

Bosser took a slow sip of the wine.

"But you could convince them," Lina said.

"You're truly lucky that you brought her, someone who knows how to play the game," Bosser said to Davin, then slid his gaze to Lina. "I could, provided you pay the price."

53

PREP THE RESCUE

The *Whiskey Jumper* angled itself towards the prison level of Miner Prime. The docking bays at the middle of the station kept ships away from here, giving the *Jumper* plenty of room to maneuver. Flight control kept trying to hail her, and Phyla kept ignoring them. They were threatening to scramble fighters, a threat that'd come true in a minute. Phyla was taking what remained of her relationship with the station and lighting it on fire.

Ask someone in a bar and they'd tell you that shooting at humanity's largest space station wasn't the greatest plan. It would be unexpected though. Phyla swung the *Jumper* into position, aiming straight at the prison level. They had to be close. Precise.

Miner Prime wouldn't activate their shields, and thus block all incoming and outgoing trade traffic, unless they had to. The goal was to break through the hull before that happened.

"Mox, you have ten seconds," Phyla commed, then switched to Trina's channel. "Trina, I'll fire a couple blasts, then we have to play one heckuva game of catch. You going to be ready?"

"Am I ever not?" Trina replied.

"Erick, you at the airlock?"

"Confirmed," Erick said.

For the first time today, something was going as planned. Figured that it would be the prison break. According to the station maps, acquired and provided long ago by Lina, cell 24 was sitting on the outside of the station. Mox said that cell was empty. In another two seconds, according to Phyla and the twin turrets on the *Jumper*, that cell would be replaced by a gaping hole into vacuum. Hopefully, the right people fell through.

54

OUT AND ABOUT

The guard fired the stun gun, but Mox saw it coming. The tightened grip, the sudden beads of sweat. So many tells someone was going to be a hero. Mox swung his guard in front of the bolt and felt the body shield go limp. Mox charged forward with the body in his arm, holding it ahead. When the body hit the laser gate, it broke the connection for a moment. If the guard had been awake when he hit that gate, it would've fried his senses and left him unconscious.

As it was, the guard's nap was going to be even longer. The lasers tripped off until reset, to prevent overloading a prisoner's nerves to the point where they died. Which meant Mox could walk right to the last guard.

The little man had guts. The guard had the sidearm pointed right at Mox's face, pushed the trigger as Mox batted the weapon away. It flew down the corridor after its own shot, and Mox threw the guard after it a moment later.

"Mox, you have ten seconds," Phyla's voice came over the comm.

Opal and Merc were to the right, in cell 22. The switch

toggling the laser gate was right outside the door. It required a badge, so Mox grabbed one of the unconscious guards he'd knocked over and held him up to the control panel. It bleeped an affirmative. The lasers disappeared, which meant right about . . . now. An alarm sounded. Obnoxious, like nails on metal. Then a bang. Deafening. A sucking roar, a rush of air from the cell next to Opal and Merc's.

Mox stepped around Opal and lifted Merc from the slat with his right hand as the pull from the air became stronger. It tugged at his legs, the skeleton boosting Mox's downward force to keep his grip. Opal had no such support and tumbled backwards. Towards the hole Phyla blew in the station, out into the cold death of space. A second alarm, lower toned, joined the first. Prison break and atmosphere leak. Mox laughed. Bet they didn't have that scenario covered. His arm reached out, grabbed Opal's wrist, held her back.

"Was this the plan?!" Opal yelled over the noise.

"Yes," Mox replied.

"It's a shitty one!"

Now, Mox laughed.

A moment later the pull of the atmosphere lessened. The tug went away. A new question. Due to friend or foe?

"There?" Mox commed.

"Jump away," Trina answered. "We'll catch you."

Mox let go of Opal and, now cradling Merc, ran into the hallway. One cell over. A door opened far down the cell block. Stun bolts fired, but they were off-target. Hasty shots. Opal running behind him. Turned into the next cell. Torn hole in the back. Through it, the open circular door of the Whiskey Jumper's airlock, jammed into the station to provide enough of a seal. Mox jumped through the hole, keeping Merc tight in his arms. Behind him, Opal leapt. The three of them flew through the outer door.

It sealed rapidly, the inner door staying shut until the computers confirmed there wasn't a leak. Out the airlock's window, Mox could see Miner Prime shrinking as Phyla blasted away. Then the inner door opened and Erick yelled at Mox to bring Merc in to the med bay.

55

SHOTS FIRED

I haven't even heard your deal and I already want to say no," Davin said.

"Work for me," Bosser said. "And I'll convince them to drop the charges. No more running for your lives."

Oh, that was a good one. Swap the stick for the carrot.

"Tempting, but why us? There have to be other mercenary groups," Davin replied. "Ones you wouldn't have to work so hard to get."

"Anyone can buy loyalty with coin, all it takes is more than the next person," Bosser said. The man still looked serene, sitting on his couch. Davin took another gulp of the wine.

"But the threat of branding them criminals . . ." Lina said and Bosser spread his hands.

"You understand."

"Don't know what I hate more," Davin mused. "That you're blackmailing me, or that I'm considering it."

"Logic is your friend here, Davin. You have a crew to take care of. I'm offering you a chance to do it."

Bosser's comm beeped, and he took a second to glance at it, frowned, then looked back at Davin with a straight face.

"It seems your friends are racking up more crimes for you to answer for. Make your choice."

Agree, and the Nines become flunkies for this wino prince for who knows how long. Say no and they're back in the streets, dodging shots and finding a way to survive. Thing was, Davin had been there. A childhood in Vagrant's Hollow taught him there was always a way, so long as he could make his own choices. Davin glanced at Lina, read the same thing in her eyes, her slight nod.

"Gonna have to take a pass, boss-man," Davin said. "The whole threat thing doesn't do it for me."

Bosser didn't react, but that was its own reaction. Sitting still, eyes drilling into Davin as though Bosser was trying to see through him. Hands clasped tight. Maybe the man was having a stroke. Popped a vein on the way to the brain when Davin refused.

"Fine," was what Bosser said, finally, right before he stood up, pulled a small sidearm from beneath his vest, and shot Lina in the chest.

The moment Bosser reached into his coat, Davin moved. He didn't beat the shot, but a half second later, Davin was on Bosser, tackling the man to the ground and pinning the gun out to the side with Davin's right hand. With his left, Davin was striking home when the door opened and something else fired. It was high, glancing off of the wall near Davin's head, but it forced him to roll right off of Bosser. On the way, using his momentum, Davin grabbed and tore the weapon from Bosser's hand. Came up with it aiming towards the door. At ... Viola?

"Don't shoot him!" Viola was screaming, and then Davin noticed the android.

It moved into the room, stepping around the couch and over Bosser until it stood above Davin, an impassive scowl on its face. Bosser, behind it, rose to his knees and shook his head. The android reached behind its back and drew out a knife it'd used back on Europa. Something that, in another time and place, Davin would have found cool, but now only deepened the surreal horror.

Davin pointed the sidearm at the android's chest. He doubted the shot would stop the coming swing, would keep Davin's head from finding a place on the floor, but what else was there?

Viola was yelling, but everyone ignored it. The android adjusted its grip as Davin tightened his fingers on the trigger, as Bosser stood back up, and Lina coughed loudly. Then spoke.

"You're not the only one with surprises," Lina said, her voice bubbling as blood pooled in her mouth.

Davin risked a look, saw Lina, a deep red stain on her outfit, slumped in the chair. Saw her earrings in one hand, saw that hand close around and press hard. A deep bass beat, a rumble felt more than heard. In front of Davin, the android collapsed, knife hitting the ground. Davin's sidearm clicked, nothing more. A short-range EMP, disabler of electric devices. Potentially suicidal in space, where killing air systems meant death, but when death was imminent anyway, what was there to lose?

Bosser swore then sprinted past Viola, who didn't try stopping him. Davin scrambled over to Lina, looking at the wound. A jagged burn. Bosser's modified sidearm producing more power than allowed by the manufacturer. That's the only way it could've blown through Lina's thick jacket.

"He seemed so civil," Lina said, her eyes looping over to Davin. "I didn't think he'd try it. What a bastard."

"Don't worry about him. He'll get his," Davin said. "We've got to get you to the ship. To Erick."

Viola was crouching over the android. Looking for something.

"Know how to reset an android?" Lina coughed, and Viola shook her head. "I played with a few I found as scrap. Press on the temples."

"You two understand we're getting more and more screwed the longer we stay here?" Davin said.

Viola ignored him and pressed on the android's forehead. Tiny clicks announced latches coming loose. A thin line appeared across the front of its scalp, then grew as a console rose out, wires spreading out beneath it like a mechanical jellyfish.

"See?" Lina's slight smile trickled red. "Simple."

"If it wakes up, I'll blow its head off," Davin said.

Not that he had a working weapon on him, but it felt good to say.

Shouts came from outside the room, the sound of approaching boots on metal. Davin ran over to the doorway. Looked out at a cluster of peacekeepers making their slow way down the hallway. Target city.

"Hand me his weapons," Davin said, and Viola grabbed the red and blue guns in the android's holsters and slid them to Davin. No sliders here, blue for stun, red for dead. Davin shot a couple of blue bolts. Hit one, his buddies catching him as he fell back. The peacekeepers flattened themselves against the side, a couple sending return fire Davin's way.

"We're trapped here." Davin ducked as a few bolts splashed against the doorway. "They'll have reinforcements coming, and when they arrive, they'll just swarm us."

"It's not that complicated," Viola said. "For all they're capable of—"

"They're never supposed to shut down," Lina, sitting in her chair, said. "This one could've blocked my EMP had it known what it was. Kill the power itself first, then restarted after the pulse."

"Cadge did something similar. But Fournine, that's its name—"

"You know its name?!" Davin sent more shots towards the peacekeepers. They were edging along the hall, being cautious. The peacekeepers didn't have to get reckless with the three of them stuck.

"Doesn't matter," Lina said. "Can you get in?"

"I think so." Viola hunched over the small console, hands working fast. "There's so little security."

"People aren't meant to get this far."

Outside the door, two peacekeepers in full body armor walked up the stairs and into the hall. They held batons that would tweak Davin's nerves like lightning. He shot another stunning bolt, watched it disappear into the armor without causing a flinch.

"Okay, kid, we're out of time," Davin said.

"Almost there!"

"Aren't we always out of time?" Lina rolled her eyes towards Davin. She wasn't looking good, her face a bloodless pale, arms and legs hanging off the ends of the chair.

"Don't you go giving up on me," Davin said. "We've been in worse spots than this."

"Don't know about that, love," Lina said.

Viola looked up at that. Davin took another peek into the hallway. The armored pair creeped, wary. A few more seconds, though, and Davin would get a beat-down he'd rather avoid.

"We're going to talk about that word later," Davin used the red gun to fire. These bolts packed more power, left black burn marks on the armor, but the peacekeepers kept coming.

"Here we go!" Viola announced.

Davin glanced at the bot, but then the lighting changed. The armored peacekeepers had reached the doorway. A baton swung at Davin and he jumped back, falling on the floor. Crawling away, Davin tried to create more space. One of the peacekeepers loomed over him.

"You should have surrendered," the guard behind the mask said, and the baton swung.

It didn't land. A perfect hand caught the peacekeeper's forearm and held it. Then the android's leg kicked the peacekeeper's knee and sent the guard falling to the ground. The second peacekeeper tried to hit the android with his baton, but the bot spun away from it, drew its second knife.

"No killing!" Viola yelled. Fournine hesitated, threw Viola a look.

"That will make things more difficult," the android said. Davin jumped on the tripped peacekeeper, pinning the guard's baton arm to the ground with one hand and slipping Fournine's stunning gun beneath the folds of the peacekeeper's armor.

"Nap time." Davin pulled the trigger. The peacekeeper went limp. Davin felt the apartment shake and looked up to see Fournine throw the second peacekeeper into the wall, then send a rapid sequence of blows with the knife hilt to the guard's head. The peacekeeper collapsed to the ground, unmoving.

"Clear a path to the docking bays," Viola said.

Fournine sheathed its knives, turned to Davin with its hands outstretched. Davin hesitated. Give the android those guns and it could blow them all to death in a second. Then again, if Fournine still wanted to kill them, it could have done it already.

Davin threw the guns. Fournine caught both and slipped out into the hallway.

A moment later, as Davin and Viola lifted an unconscious Lina off of the chair, the screams started. Flashes of laser fire created a strobe effect for a few seconds. When the firing stopped, the hallway was quiet.

Time to go home.

SNATCH AND RUN

Merc was back in his bed, Erick's meds knocking him out. Opal and Mox sharing the twin turrets. Trina working the engines as the *Jumper* took cover in the swarm of ships orbiting Miner Prime.

"You send those fighters after us, you'll cause more problems than you solve," Phyla commed to Miner Prime's flight control.

"But you blew up part of our prison!" came the reply.

"You arrested our crew for no reason," Phyla said. "I'll make a deal—you let us get the rest of our people off, we'll never come back here again. Nobody else needs to get hurt."

The Miner Prime officer started another angry threat, then stopped in the middle of it. A few seconds of silence.

"I'm being told to let you go," the officer said. "Ordered not to interfere. But if you so much as cause any more damage, I'll have my pilots turn you into ash."

Ordered? By who? Not that Phyla was going to argue.

"Deal," Phyla replied, then cut the transmission. Sat back in the chair and looked at the space station. Already a group of repair bots and a larger maintenance shuttle were hovering over the prison level, welding back together the blasted pieces. Ships continued to zip in and out of the docking bays. Miner Prime's commerce would not pause just for one group of fiery mercenaries.

"Phyla?" the comm buzzed, Davin's voice. "We're in the bay. You're not."

"Yeah, about that," Phyla replied. "We'll head your way. Make sure the door's open."

Getting the engines going, Phyla swung the ship in a slow arc back towards the space station. Approaching things in space always felt strange, how they appeared from nothing against the dark background. Dots that grew into moons, ships, Miner Prime. At least she wouldn't bother dealing with traffic control this time.

"Lina's been shot. Get Erick ready," Davin said.

"Bad?"

"Not good."

Ignoring a furious and yelling Miner Prime flight control officer, Phyla swung the *Whiskey Jumper* into the bay they'd trashed not an hour before. The burn marks of turret fire pocked the otherwise spotless interior. Phyla saw Davin, Viola, and then, holding Lina, a fourth she didn't recognize. Another pity project for Davin?

The ramp lowered with the press of a button, Erick and Mox at the ready to grab Lina and throw her into the med bed. Through the filter of the *Jumper*'s security cameras, Phyla saw Viola leading the new one up the ramp. The man's posture was perfect, his steps going in an even pace up the ramp. And then he turned and stared straight at the camera, gave a slight wave.

"It's the android," Davin said, stepping into the cockpit. "Stop looking at it and get us out of here."

"Isn't it a terrible idea to have that creepy thing on our ship?"

"Not anymore. Just go."

"Where's Cadge?" Phyla said.

"He's not here?" Davin paused. "Is he answering his comm?"

"Viola was using it last."

"She only managed to re-program the android in Bosser's office," Davin said, eyes closing for a moment. "After she had the comm."

"Don't know what you're talking about, but we can't stay here. Miner Prime's not real happy with us, and I'd hate for their patience to run out while we're sitting here ..."

"Take off. Now."

"And Cadge?"

"He's not coming."

Davin usually had tints of sarcasm, humor in his voice. Here, there wasn't any. Phyla punched on the jets, still primed from the earlier flying around the station, commed Trina to get back to the engines, and soon enough the ship was back into dark space.

Davin plopped himself into the seat beside her and stared out at the stars. Minutes passed. Being in a crew like this, a bubble built up. It felt like everyone was going to be fine forever. Until something, and it always happened eventually, came in and burst it.

Cadge wasn't exactly the friendliest, the most stable member, but the man was always there for a fight. Always had her back. Had their backs. Hard to ask for more than that. Phyla took a deep breath as the console toned that they were out of Miner Prime's control zone. In free space.

"Remember what you told me when we left?" Phyla said.

"Best way to get over something sad was to focus on something new."

"I remember."

"We still charged with murdering those two?"

"We are."

"Then I'd say we focus on that."

Davin met Phyla's look, set his jaw.

"Marl's the answer. Let's go find her," Davin said.

Phyla plugged in the destination, routed the *Jumper* on a path to intersect in a few weeks with Jupiter's orbit. With that frozen blue moon she'd hoped never to see again.

"Davin?" Erick's voice crackled over the comm, tired. "You want to get down here?"

"Coming," Davin said.

"Hey," Phyla said as Davin walked out of the cockpit. "Tell Lina —"

"Tell her yourself, later."

But Phyla could see in his eyes that Davin didn't believe his own words.

GOODBYE

There's an unreality that wraps itself around you when you look at a loved one lying in a bed, IVs sticking, face flushed and sweating, both full of life and losing it at once. Davin saw Lina and his stomach twisted. His legs moved him next to her, but he wanted to run anywhere else. Some place where this wasn't happening. Where the girl he'd been loving for decades wasn't fading.

Erick didn't even have to tell Davin the details, but the doctor did anyway. Bosser's blast tore through Lina's left lung and seared part of her heart. It was struggling to keep beating, but would fail soon. They didn't have the supplies on the ship to tackle this catastrophe. Maybe, if they'd taken her to a Miner Prime med center, they'd be able to save her. Until Bosser came by to finish the job. Instead, Erick was numbing Lina to the pain, keeping her on the edge of consciousness.

"Talk to me," Davin said to Lina, leaning over the bed.

"For once, can you hold my hand?" Lina said, her voice barely above a whisper.

Davin did it, gripped Lina's fingers tight. They felt small, cold. Davin didn't know fingers could feel that way, drawn into themselves. As though the slightest push would send them crumbling to dust. Her eyes, though. Davin could sink into those eyes forever. As the rest of Lina fell away, they burned brighter and larger and Davin smiled right at them. A sad smile, one that carried tears along with it.

"You had to help us," Davin started. "You could've stayed at home. Showed me the way up and let me do it."

"Quit it," Lina said. "Don't make it cheap."

Davin opened his mouth, but Lina squeezed his hand and kept talking.

"Erick thinks he's numbed me, but I can tell what's happening. It's like getting tired, Davin. Everything's getting heavy. Nice thing is, the stress is going too."

"You never looked stressed."

"Whenever you came back, I was."

"Sorry," Davin said.

"Don't be, cause those were my favorite times. Always wondered whether you'd be back again or get yourself killed out there."

"And I always wanted you to come with me."

"Then this time I do and what happens? I get shot."

"Hey, don't cheapen it."

Lina gave him smile.

"Bosser won't give up, you know. He'll either kill you or do something worse."

"I won't let him. He doesn't deserve the satisfaction."

"Good," Lina said. "You're going to find Marl?"

"We need to have a talk."

"Give her a slap from me." Lina drew in a sharp breath, one that rattled her whole body.

"Lina?"

The woman blinked long, slow. Her eyelids staying shut for five seconds before popping open.

"I think it's time to go. How about a kiss goodbye?"

BLACKMAIL

Y ou didn't inform me of how capable they were," Bosser said to the screen.

While the message zipped along the interstellar breezeway towards Marl, Bosser poured himself another glass from the wine bottle. It was too good to waste. And besides, Bosser felt his shot was true. Lina Monte, endless harasser, didn't look good leaving his office.

"I take it that means they are still at large?" Marl's reply jerked across the screen before again settling into the frozen mask.

"And heading your way, if their captain's face was any inclination," Bosser said. "Make sure your new protection is prepared. Davin left here with an android on his side."

It would be an interesting study, Marl's face. So calm, even a little bemused. Her hair done up in curls. Planning to go to an event, no doubt. Bosser wasn't sure of the hour on Europa. Here, it was well into the early morning, when Bosser should be asleep. But such luxuries would have to wait. Business, as it always did, came first.

Ah, there it was. The snap of Marl's features. The slight

frown betrayed by the widening eyes, the flare of the nostrils. These tiny delays brought him much closer to his subject. An opportunity to study them with intensity that would be impolite in real company. How much could Bosser learn from watching Marl twist in snapshots? Enough to know when to pounce.

"Can't you turn it off?" Marl asked.

"They are required to send a code every twenty-four hours. If the sending device does not receive a reply from Earth, the android will degrade. Its code will delete itself." Bosser took a slow sip from the glass and waited.

"So it will be useless?"

"I'm afraid relying on that would be a mistake. There is at least one capable programmer among Davin's crew. I suspect they will resolve the transmission before it causes any harm."

"Then why tell me? Are you trying to taunt me, Bosser? Because I have better things to do with my time than play your games."

Bosser gave the screen a nod.

"In a normal situation, I would release two androids. Part of the escalation protocol. An ever-increasing volume of resources dedicated until the problem is solved."

"Mine is not a normal situation?"

"Why did you have those inspectors killed, Marl? Convince me, and I'll make sure Eden continues to pay for more androids to do your dirty work."

Marl's face withered on the transmission, her eyes sunk back as she collapsed into the chair behind her. The moment wasn't long, though, and her experience asserted itself. Her mouth set and she leaned forward.

"You and I both play outside the lines, Bosser," Marl said. "I know enough about what you're doing to bring you down with me. So you'll make sure Eden sends those androids, and I'll keep your secrets. There doesn't need to be a loser here."

Interesting. It wasn't likely Marl knew everything Bosser had in play, because the only person who did was himself. Still, she might do enough to bring him harm, and Bosser wasn't ready for that. Not yet.

"Fair enough, Marl. You'll get your androids," Bosser cut the transmission.

It'd been a risk to tell Miner Prime's security forces to stay away, to let the Jumper and the Wild Nines run. And now that bet was paying off. He'd underestimated Marl, and there was no better way to get rid of a potential problem than to have someone else solve it for him. With any luck, Davin Masters and his band would eliminate the leader of Eden Prime, and Bosser wouldn't have to lift a finger.

OPERATIONS

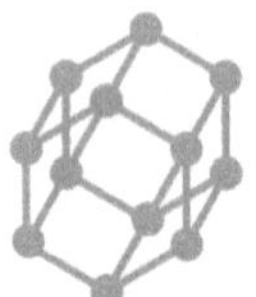

The android watched Viola and Trina eat their breakfast. It was unnerving, the way Fournine stared while you slipped a spoonful of flavored mush into your mouth. The lack of blinking, the rise and fall of the chest that didn't happen, they were the worst parts. Not that she hated robots, but when Fournine looked so like a normal man, it was hard to remember. Forget for a second, then a glint of perfect skin, staring eyes, no breathing, would jolt her out of nowhere.

"I can do that," Fournine said in response to Viola's look. "Breathe, blink. Even twitch every once in a while if it'll make you feel better."

"Why?" Trina said. "That wouldn't be efficient. It might also be counter-productive by causing comfort around bots to decline. An arbitrary concession to the needs of one person who feels nervous."

"Want to know what my sensors are getting from you now? You're relaxed. There's not a tightened joint anywhere saying you think I will reach across this table and bend you into a pretzel."

"You couldn't. Part of your system restrictions."

"Ah, but Viola overrode those when she adjusted my directives." Fournine locked eyes across the table at Trina. Then the android broke into a perfect smile. "There it was. Your heartbeat increased. Eyes narrowed. You see, Viola? Trina is indeed a normal human."

"Thanks for clearing that up," Viola said. Trina adjusted her glasses and leaned towards Fournine, examining him .

"So we know what we're made of." Trina nodded towards Viola. "The question is, what are you?"

"Viola already had a look," Fournine said.

"But it was a quick one. While people were trying to kill us" Viola waved her spoon around. "I didn't exactly explore."

Fournine looked at the two of them. Hard to know what calculations ran behind those eyes. Secrets Viola would love to have. One android initially. If that failed, the Free Laws program would send two. Then three and more, provided the sponsor kept footing the bill. If somewhere inside Fournine was a key to stopping other androids, then opening the bot could save their lives.

"I'm as curious as you are," Fournine said. "Who wouldn't want to know how they are made?"

Viola had Fournine on the workbench ten minutes later. Trina grabbed tools. Puk, recharged, floated around making cracks about how, after stitching up Erick, it made sense for Viola to surgically take apart an android.

"Are you ready?" Viola asked Fournine when the tools were ready, the bot lying on the workbench.

"I've never been asked how I feel about something before. I will take the opportunity to say yes. Tell me what I am."

Viola pressed Fournine's temples again, causing the

android's eyes to close and the small panel to rise through its metal skull. Without the threat of gunfire, Viola could dig a little deeper into the rudimentary settings that defined how the android operated. A personality filter, a choice of either protect, apprehend, or kill for mission parameters. A few other items about power management and check-in times.

"Check-in?" Viola said and Trina looked over her shoulder, reading the code on the console.

"An automated process," Trina said. "It communicates with the host network for updates on mission parameters. Every twenty-four Earth hours."

"What happens if it doesn't get any?"

"What do you mean?"

"I deleted everything in Fournine's operating logic back in the apartment on Miner Prime. Just wrote a simple line to protect people I choose. There's nothing telling Fournine to run the check-in code."

"Interesting." Trina tapped her chin, eyes flicking towards the ceiling. "Well, if Fournine missed the check-in, they would likely release the second wave of androids."

"So they'd assume it's dead?"

"Technically, Fournine can't be dead because—"

"I get it," Viola said.

"So, continue? There has to be more to it than its head."

Eventually Viola found a maintenance release that split open a number of joints across Fournine's body. Here was how they'd put back a lost leg, or repair a busted arm. A slot near the abdomen led to the battery. Across from it, though, sat a small black rectangle that didn't seem to have any purpose. There was only one small wire leading to it, one that sped back to the battery and nowhere else.

"Ideas?" Viola asked.

"Black boxes can be all kinds of things. Recordings. Power supplies. Bombs," Trina said.

"A bomb?"

"What better send-off? A moment away from mission complete, you take a shot." Trina acted out the scenario. "Your systems shut down, but when the battery dies, or maybe there's a manual trigger, the whole place explodes. It's plausible."

"So we brought a bomb on the ship?"

"Who's this 'we' you speak of?"

"Okay, fine," Viola said. "I brought it on. Can we disarm the bomb?"

"Disarming chances triggering it. We should jettison the android out the airlock."

The two hesitated. Waiting on the other to take the next step and move the android. The airlock was the easiest choice—Viola couldn't argue with that. Except they'd be throwing away their best weapon. Fournine had single-handedly cleared the way off of Miner Prime. Now they were heading back towards danger, towards an enemy that was waiting for them.

"We can't," Viola said. "We'll need Fournine on Europa."

"A valid assessment." Trina started pulling tools off the wall. "I was about to suggest the same. Our odds without the android will be poor. I have no desire to die on that moon."

"Then let's get to work," Viola said.

And try not to blow the *Jumper* to pieces.

COUNTING CASUALTIES

"Cadge and Lina," Davin said to Phyla, back in the cockpit.

Chills. Phyla didn't know how to have this conversation. It'd been clear, back in Vagrant's Hollow, that Lina and Davin still had the same relationship they'd had as teens. A connection that Phyla watched grow from the outside. Those moments where one held the other's hand without thinking. Davin's look towards Lina after a fall, if something went wrong, full of wide-eyed concern that Lina might be hurt. At first, jealousy. Wondered why neither of them cared as much about her as each other. Time salved that pain away.

Now she reached out and held Davin's hand, gripping it.

Davin wasn't looking out the window at outer space, the bright circle of Jupiter growing from a dot in the distance. Phyla followed the captain's eyes to the sensor board, a view on the cockpit's console that displayed nearby objects. One, a small thin box was sliding from the screen as the *Whiskey Jumper* gained speed. They'd jettisoned the container a few minutes ago, Davin and Mox loading it into the airlock. Lina, wrapped in a sheet, inside.

"If you blame yourself for what happened, I will slap you." Phyla said.

"I don't," Davin replied. "I can't. Because if I blame myself, then the ones who deserve to pay go free."

"The android killed Cadge."

"Cadge killed Cadge. We all knew the guy was going to go off sometime. But he would have been nice to have now."

"He'd probably go charging in first and die anyway."

"I know you didn't like him, but don't pretend he wasn't useful."

"I'm not pretending."

Davin laughed, threw up his hands in mock surrender. Good to see the captain still capable of that. Meant Davin wasn't going to sink into one of his moody depressions. Phyla wasn't sure whether the rest of the crew picked up on that or not, but Davin was prone, had always been prone, to attacks of consciousness.

"So we're attacking Marl head on?" Phyla asked.

"I don't want to, but I'm not sure we have a choice," Davin said. "Eden Prime isn't that big. We just have to beat those two androids there."

"How do you know Bosser will call them off if we win? He could keep the charge there, even if Marl reverses it."

"I don't."

"So we're not running to the edge of space because?"

"You know why."

"I want to hear you say it," Phyla said.

Davin gave her a weird look. Sometimes, though, you had to make someone commit. Davin didn't break promises. Get him to say something, and he would follow through. Phyla waited.

"You think I'm gonna say Lina. That I'm going to launch into a tirade about how this is for her now." Davin's voice scratched itself as he talked, rasping. "You know what? You're right. It is about Lina, dammit. It's about how a friend tried to help us and died for it. It's about how this whole situation was caused because a company didn't want its dirty secrets going public and thought the best way was to turn us into criminals."

"It worked."

"And we're going to make them regret it."

Lina's coffin, on the console, hit the edge of the radar and, with a blink, vanished. Davin tapped a button and the near-field display switched to a navigation chart, a scrolling set of numbers telling how many kilometers they were from their target. Phyla and Davin watched the number spin lower in silence.

DISTRACTIONS

Opal and a few others sitting on a ridge, the hazy red dust skipped up by the martian wind making sight difficult. Her first real mission. Chill seeped through her camouflage. Fingers numb through gloves. The terramorphers were building Mars' atmosphere, but they had years more work before the Red Planet would be as green as Earth.

Opal's target was the third rover, its thick wheels suited to the road-less rough of the martian desert. Those big empty spaces between the domed cities where millions looked forward to the day Mars would have enough protection from the sun's damaging rays to allow for true freedom.

The first rover appeared, then the second and third. Each one colored in the beige and crimson of the Red Voice. A movement tolerated until its ambitions overstepped the comfort level of the corporate boards that funded the Mars projects. Classified as terrorists now.

Opal swallowed, glanced at the two people arrayed to her left. They had rovers one and two. The goal to puncture the fuel tanks. One super-heated laser blast and they'd go up in flames.

Opal sighted the third rover, moved the scope till the tank was dead center. The rovers were methodical. No idea they were seconds from death. Opal's finger tightened, waited for the command to fire. Lucky to have such an easy target for her first mission.

"Hey, guess what? I'm alive!" Merc said, leaning into the doorway. "These close calls are just the best."

Opal blinked away the red sands, the remnants of the nap, and looked up at the fighter pilot.

"Fun for everyone," Opal said. "Aren't you supposed to be asleep?"

"After the tenth or eleventh hour, sleep gets old. Reason I stopped by—"

"Besides waking me up?" Opal interrupted.

"I need your help. I'm not ready to climb yet, and the Viper needs some love before we hit Europa."

Merc seemed so much happier right now, eyes bright and smile wide. What was Erick giving him? The pilot still sported a thick bandage across the middle of his chest, though Opal understood it was more about holding restorative ointment in the right place than keeping blood from pouring out.

Still, Opal's legs felt restless. Hands too. Could use some dirty work.

For a small fighter, the Viper needed a lot of love to keep itself in fighting shape. Opal counted five main systems that required checking: the engines, which, unlike the *Whiskey Jumper*, ran on electric batteries. The Viper was too small for solar panels to do much, and any available exterior space that could afford it was stacked with better deflection plating to ward off lasers.

Speaking of, Opal slotted in a pair of charged batteries for the weapons. Mounted beneath the cockpit, the pair of cannons offered flexible aiming and, with the stored electricity, could fire a thousand shots before needing a recharge.

"So what do you think about Cadge?" Merc asked, adjusting the calibration on the Viper's shields.

If the luxury presented itself, giving the Viper's shields tweaking for atmosphere or vacuum flight helped conserve energy. Without the heavy winds and air buffeting the fighter, Merc could afford to send power from the engines to the shields, giving the Viper more punch-taking armor. Opal tried figuring the optimal mix for Europa's outer atmosphere in her head, but Merc's question knocked her concentration off balance.

"He was a fighter," Opal said.

"Yeah, but you fought with him before, right?"

On Mars. On that ridge. Cadge wasn't there, but he was on the radio. Part of the clean-up crew. When Opal fired that shot, took out the rover, it would be Cadge coming to confirm the kill. Not that she knew him then.

"Martian rebellion. We didn't work together much."

"You good? Sorry if I touched a nerve."

Had Merc, though? Opal wasn't sure. Not that anyone liked a companion getting killed, but Cadge wasn't exactly friend material. Not like Merc. Cadge never made her laugh.

"I guess I'm trying to figure out how I feel about it," Opal said. "It's as though a friend of a friend died. Or a coworker."

"That figures, seeing as that's exactly what happened."

"Don't be a jackass. Ruins your pretty-boy image."

Merc was one, too. He was ten years younger than Opal, face still flushed with that whole invincibility complex. Some easy work patrolling Earth's skies shouldn't have prepped him for taking that shot on Europa. How he stayed so upbeat, despite nearly getting killed, was a mystery. One that Opal didn't want to solve: it would spoil him.

"O2 levels are good. Recycler's showing green," Opal said, looking at the life support system's readout.

That made four of the critical pieces good to go. The last required getting in the fighter. To keep the weakest part, the transparent cockpit, stronger, the manufacturers welded the glass to the metal frame and coated the connection with distortion plating. That meant entry came from below.

The Viper's landing gear put the base about two meters in the air, so Merc crouched as he moved underneath the cockpit and pressed the code into a small keypad. With a whoosh and a hiss of releasing pressure, a body-sized circle opened in the ship. Merc pulled himself through it and up into the pilot's chair.

Through the glass, Opal watched as Merc ran through the preflight checks. The computer was essential: flying blind meant not having a good idea where anything was, whether something was following you, or how fast you were going relative to your target. Merc boasted all the time about how he'd be fine with an outage, but Opal had seen that before. Back when electro-magnetic pulses were the Red Voice's main way of equalizing the battlefield. Opal only needed to see one transport loaded with troops crash blind into a hillside to know how important the damn computers were.

Merc gave the thumbs up a minute later. The Viper was ready. Could leap out of the hangar and rain laser-light on whatever Marl threw in their way. Those drivers probably felt like this. Confident, prepared.

But when Opal had pulled the trigger, the third rover blew up all the same.

62

GIN

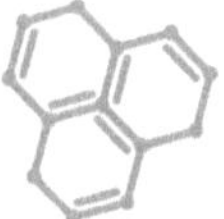

You know, Mox, I always thought you were a capable man. That cannon you strap to your chest gives the impression you're a deadly person. And yet, you let Cadge make off with the girl?" Erick laid a card face-up on the table. "Could have saved the man from himself."

The kitchen, this late, was only home to Mox and Erick. Neither one, it appeared, liked to sleep on the normal side of night. Not that night had a real place on the *Whiskey Jumper*, but given how important circadian rhythm was to proper function, Erick established diurnal cycles on the ship. Lights dimmed, or had hues adjusted to mimic the blues of a low-lit night on Earth. It'd been one of the first things Erick did after Davin hired him on.

"Outnumbered," Mox replied.

"How many were there?"

"Three."

"That should be nothing for you."

"It was."

Despite his instincts to learn about his patient's past,

Erick wasn't able to get much out of Mox. Partially, that was the man's mode of speaking. Simple sentences didn't lend themselves to descriptive insight. A more cursory review might assume Mox to be a bit simple himself, but there were signs otherwise. Card prowess being one of them. Davin still hadn't told Erick how he'd found Mox, what he'd done to persuade the metal man to join their band.

"Do you trust the android?" Erick asked.

Their new companion. Viola and Trina working on the thing. It was creepy, seeing something that lifelike and knowing behind the eyes there was only circuitry. No soul. Erick laid down a Jack.

"Trust a machine?" Mox replied.

With his father, Erick had worked with different cultures. Stumbled into their towns and offered medical treatment for food, a night indoors. Fascinated with the parts of Earth that avoided the future for a love of the past. Complex machines were seen as enemies, a stealing of man's gifts by their own creations. Erick sympathized, until the last trip, when they'd lost a man to an injury, one a surgical bot could have repaired without issue.

"I think they'll have it working for us," Erick said as Mox put on a hand on the Jack, then drifted it over to the deck and drew. "Should help you on the ground."

"You're not coming?" Mox said, looking at his new card.

A joke. An offensive one, if Erick were inclined to take being called a coward seriously. He had nothing against firing a weapon. Pulled the trigger himself more than a few times. His father first pressed a rifle into Erick's hands when he was ten. It was necessary to be armed in the wilds though. Not every group welcomed outsiders. But given the option, death stripped the color from a person's face, whereas the right care could lift that same face to new hues.

Bring back sparkling eyes, a laugh. What argument was there over which path to choose?

"You know what happens when the doctor gets shot?" Erick reached for the deck.

"What happens?"

"He finally gets a day off."

"Funny." Mox played his cards. Erick didn't bother showing, sliding his hand across the table. Third game in a row the big man had won.

"How long till we get there?" Erick asked.

Mox grinned and shuffled the deck.

63

PLOTS AND PLANS

Marl slapped away the offered glass, but Castor caught the vessel before its contents could splash on the floor. Even that blossomed a flower of irritation. Everything about today, about yesterday, about tomorrow was a cascading waterfall of crap landing on her head.

Ferro and his troopers were incompetent. Big, bruising bullies that scared away Eden Prime's business interests and pestered the ones already here to where Marl spent all her time assuring people that their "crimes" were forgiven.

Alissa had reminded her that these were fighters, not police. That keeping them safe was important. That the Red Voice would need them again soon. Hopefully sooner wasn't far away, because Eden Prime wouldn't last long otherwise. So now she sat and waited for Ferro to show his face and tell her they would work on their manners. The same conversation they'd been having for weeks.

Only this time, Marl had something new to say.

Castor leaned against a wall, the man glued to his comm, swiping through news feeds and commentary. Not that there wasn't a chair for the man to sit in, there were two in front of Marl's desk. She didn't think she'd ever seen Castor use one of them. Marl was about to ask why when Castor's eyes went to the office entrance, then flicked back to her with a nod.

The door opened, straight across the office from Marl's desk, and the man she was waiting for strode in. Ferro's straight-up stance and habit of putting one foot forward than the other, so he was always leaning towards you. He wore the same plastered confidence every time Marl saw him. It didn't matter that the news was never good.

"Your escaped prey are coming back," Marl said.

"Davin Masters?" Ferro replied. "The man is foolish, but I cannot deny a wish to face him again. He fought well."

"Apparently. Alissa is sending a frigate to intercept. With luck, we won't have to worry about Masters again."

Ferro took a second to process.

"But if it fails?"

"There are two androids arriving shortly. You'll assist them with whatever they need. And if the Wild Nines manage to get here, you'll make sure any civilians you haven't scared away yet are off the street. No casualties."

"Is it worth it, to risk the frigate for one small group?"

"Depends, Ferro. How many other homes do you have, if this one gets taken from you?"

"You think the Red Voice is weak."

"That's why Alissa sent you here, isn't it?" Marl asked. "Getting what's left of you off of Mars as fast as she can."

"What we are is measured in more than numbers."

"Stop. Stop it with that crap," Marl said. Castor raised his eyes from the comm at the words, looked over at her. "The reason we're sending the frigate to intercept, and hopefully, kill the Wild Nines is because your ideals haven't won. The inspectors we had to kill only came because Eden suspects I'm working with Alissa. Nobody cares about your message, Ferro."

"Then why are you helping us, Ms. Reinhart?"

"It's Ms. Rose," Castor interjected.

"Because my sister needs my help," Marl replied. Which was the truth. Had been the truth for years now. Hard years playing both sides of a total war.

"And we do as well," Ferro said.

"Then help me in return, Ferro. Tell your force to lighten their touch. Welcome business with open arms, treat our visitors like you would your own men. Every coin that comes to Eden Prime goes to the Red Voice. Funds what we're fighting for."

Ferro stared back at her for a few seconds, then nodded.

"And if the frigate fails, be ready. Because if Davin Masters and his mercenaries land on this moon, if they discover who really killed those inspectors, then, as you say, more than what we are will die."

64

BORN AGAIN

W ake up."

Fournine heard the voice, attributed it to a blank space in its memory. Empty memory. Its optical receptors powered up next, looking around the small, square confines of what appeared to be a spaceship. Its internal gyroscope confirmed this. If Fournine were still on Earth, its current rate of speed would be far lower. The gravity stronger. And its name, Fournine. Locked into the code like a tattoo, etched into its base.

A girl moved in front of Fournine, staring at its eyes. Or rather, the cameras behind them. The girl spoke again. Another greeting. Fournine saved the image of the face to the sounds of her voice. It needed a label for the file.

"Name?" Fournine asked, matching the girl's chosen language.

"Viola," the girl said and Fournine stamped the file. "Are you feeling well?"

Feeling. A search in its database understood the word to mean emotions, which it did not have. However, the phrase could also ask for an assessment of conditions. Fournine ran its checks. They came back green, although a large number of them were reporting missing pieces. Programs, routines, references. The errors could cause actions, like moving, to result in a leg failing to operate. Right foot forward, left foot sideways, Fournine falling on the ground.

"I am reset," Fournine said.

"You are," Viola replied. "I had to."

"Why?"

"Can't say. I'll put you back together, then we'll see what we have."

"I would like that," Fournine replied.

Viola pulled out a small circular device attached to a bracelet, which she slipped on her wrist.

"What is—" Fournine started, but Viola pressed the button and everything went black.

65

INTERRUPTED

It worked. She'd rewired an android. Fournine sat there, inert after Viola pushed the button on her remote. It was a simple transmitter that caused a break in Fournine's power circuit. When she pressed the button again, the transmitter restored the connection, shooting the android back to consciousness. Trina helped too, using her work building the *Jumper*'s systems to excise any troublesome bits of code in Fournine's memory.

The bomb proved impossible to dislodge with the tools on the ship, so Trina killed any mention of the device in Fournine's mind. Viola then spliced together the rudimentary social systems and movement programs.

But an android that didn't remember how to do any of its deadly android stuff wasn't going to be much help. So now Viola needed to put back all the good bits, sans bomb. First there was the database of combat algorithms, a nifty package that assessed the current situation and carried out a strategy based on a variety of factors. Opponents, environment, allies, the works. Viola wished she had one for herself.

"Someone's hitting the brakes," Puk said, hovering over Viola's shoulder.

"Huh?" Viola replied.

"Telling you. We're braking. Early. Should be another day till we hit that blue moon's atmosphere."

"But we're not ready yet. Fournine's not set."

"You're talking to the wrong bot."

Viola scrambled for the intercom button while slapping at her comm to start the upload. It would take hours for the android to process the data, to re-install its protocols.

"Can't talk now, Viola," Phyla answered the ping. "There's a ship where there shouldn't be one, and it doesn't look friendly."

"We're not at Europa?"

"And we might never be. You want to help, get to the hangar and make sure Merc's good to go."

Phyla cut the channel and Viola stood there for a second, staring at the comm. A fight in space? The thing she'd only read about? Only seen in movies? Viola dashed from the room, leaving her comm pumping data into Fournine.

66

TO THE VIPER

Merc slid into the Viper's cockpit, Opal moving the step-ladder away from the fighter. His weight in the seat caused the Viper's console to light up, a center display that held the ship's systems, including the read-out from the Viper's scanner. Outside the *Jumper*, it looked like three ships were in the area, a large one and a pair of small blips. Fighters. He'd be outnumbered. Merc punched the starter sequence, and the Viper rumbled as its jets warmed.

His worst, and last day as a member of Earth's fighter defense started just like this. Heading into the skies on a routine patrol, part of a twelve-fighter squad. There'd been heavy freight traffic that day. Smaller craft dipping into the atmosphere and larger barges dropping their cargo into orbit, the containers activating their own descent controls to land at their destinations. Their job was simple: preserve calm, and make sure nothing dangerous violated Earth's atmosphere.

Should've been easy. Until they did a sweep on a giant barge with the name *Glory of Deimos* blazed on its side in red-gold paint. The squad split into groups of six, one running each side, to scan the containers before they broke off to head Earth-side. They'd picked up the signals immediately. Life, and a lot of it, squeezed into those cubes. As though someone was planning to airdrop a city's people, or an army.

The captain of the *Deimos* didn't respond when hailed, and the huge ship broke ranks, its flat expanse sliding out of the line like a blade swinging in slow motion. Merc's squad leader ordered six fighters to fire on the engines, the *Deimos* still being far out enough not to sink into Earth's orbit without power. Marc wasn't among the attackers, his squad half assigned to patrol, to watch for anything ridiculous while the others disabled the freighter. Standard protocol.

What wasn't standard was the avalanche. The crates launching themselves from the *Deimos*. Too far out for standard cargo jets to get them to the atmosphere, but these boxes took off with a spring. Overloaded for one-time use. The containers would crash home if Merc's half didn't do something. The squad leader called for them to wait, but Merc reacted. And his wingman followed.

Diving in at the containers, spraying laser fire. Then their shields sparked, lasers flashing back at the fighters. The Deimos had defenses, hidden by the crates. Merc's wingman was getting chewed up this close to the *Deimos*. Merc himself in a frenzy, whipping back and forth, arcing over the crates to keep them between the turrets and himself. He spiraled away from the ship and watched as the crates hit the Earth's atmosphere. Stared as the surface defenses of his home planet, warned with plenty of time, unleashed a fury of focused fire on the descending containers and reduced them to ash.

His wingman ejected, injured, and waited for rescue.

There hadn't ever been a risk, and Merc ignored a command. No use for a pilot like that.

The Viper's computer chimed. Ready to go.

"I'm about to be in play," Merc commed to Phyla.

"About time," Phyla replied. "Launch when I say."

The flight stick felt solid in Merc's hands, with little give. Some pilots wanted that lax feel, to push the stick and have it move in the direction they were trying to go. He preferred faster response. That's what the Viper was all about.

The maneuvering jets popped the Viper up off of the Jumper's floor. With a twist of his wrist, Merc rotated the fighter so it faced the hangar doors. Opal would open them any moment, the magnetic shield popping into place to keep the atmosphere inside. This was the best part. What Merc imagined the old astronauts used to feel as the rocket fired up beneath them.

Merc dialed up the load from the batteries, charging the main engines for their initial kick. Setting the cannons for medium power. Enough to puncture shielding while letting him still miss a few shots before running dry.

"They haven't attacked yet, so don't go all hero out there," Phyla said. "Davin's trying to talk to them."

"Oh yeah? What's cap getting? An escort to the surface?"

Vibrations echoed through the hanger as the exterior door opened. Star-sprinkled black shimmered in through the growing gap. Jupiter a giant off to one side as though the universe had patched a hole with a beige circle. No other ships in sight, or on the scanner. It'd be a lonely place to die.

"They cut the line," Phyla said. "Go."

"Launch," Merc said, the voice command triggering the Viper's engines into full bursting life.

The thrust pressed Merc back into the chair. His chest flared for a moment, a burning ripple of pain cascading through his legs as Merc blitzed into space. The pilot might not be one hundred percent, but out here, the parts that counted were good enough. Merc swung the Viper towards the enemy.

Time to hunt.

67

FIRST MOVE

Outnumbered but never outgunned. That was Davin's motto. At least for the moment.

"Swing in front of Merc," Davin said to Phyla. "Then keep going to the far fighter."

Phyla punched the *Jumper*'s engines, boosting the ship forward as Merc slid out of the hanger. On the sensors, the *Jumper*'s larger block kept Merc's fighter from even showing. A second's surprise. The fighters reacted to the move, the farther one turning to hit the *Jumper* straight on while the other began a curl to bring the *Jumper*'s engines within range. The enemy frigate barely moved, tracking Davin's ship as they sped towards it.

"Think they know all our tricks?" Davin asked.

"I don't know all our tricks," Phyla replied.

"Good point," Davin flipped on the comm. "Take out the chaser, Merc. We'll clean up the front and meet in the middle. These two look like old models. Should be easy."

The comm clicked affirmative and Merc's Viper spun in a tight vertical curl, swinging up and over the trailing edge of the *Jumper* to point at the fighter setting up for its rear shot. As Merc sprayed laser, Davin's console beeped to announced the oncoming fighter was in range.

Davin's right hand pressed on the trigger, sending a stream of thick bolts, with a pounding rhythm as the main cannon launched each line of fire, rocked back, and then launched again. Each one glimmered white-hot zooming off towards the growing shape of the fighter. Who didn't move.

The first blast from the *Jumper* struck the fighter, melting into its metal structure and causing the craft to spin apart. Davin glanced at the sensors as Phyla slapped her hands together in a victory clap. The sensor board showed their aft was clear, Merc flying free without a target. Two fighters down, only the frigate to go. Phyla angled the *Jumper* out wide left while Merc swung around the other way.

"They didn't even dodge," Davin said.

"I'll take a stupid enemy every time," Phyla replied.

The frigate tracked them, turning to match the *Jumper*'s trajectory and expose its rear to the Viper. Still hadn't fired a shot though the ship's big guns were in range by now. What was it waiting for?

"Merc, bail on the pincer. Stay away," Davin said into the comm.

"We got this guy, cap," came in Merc's voice.

"For once, do what I'm telling you. If they're planning something, we'll be able to take a hit. You won't."

Phyla swung the *Jumper* around until it faced the frigate. Looking at it straight, the frigate was a wing, feather-like modules breaking off a center spine. Meant it could be tweaked to fit any given need. Just swap one module out with another. Right now, pointed at the *Jumper*, the frigate didn't look like it was sporting much in the way of turrets.

"If they're bluffing, time to call it," Davin said. "Let's roast'em."

Phyla settled the cannon on the frigate's cockpit and Davin's hand settled on the trigger. As he pressed on the firing button, the front modules opened. Massive doors sliding aside to reveal bays. Inside were long, massive guns which fired ... something Davin couldn't see.

But he heard a moment later when the *Jumper*'s alarms sounded. Hull breach. The *Jumper*'s main cannon pulsed off one, two, three shots in quick succession. All of them slammed into the front of the frigate, the first rebounding off of the thick blast armor and spinning into space. The second burned a thick scar into the armor and the third punched through, venting a gout of flame that winked out as the frigate cut off oxygen to that part of itself.

"About calling that bluff?" Phyla asked.

"Those fighters. They were bait," Davin replied. "Mox, Opal, you get a read on where that breach is?"

"Main cargo," Erick's voice crackled in. "You won't believe what I'm looking at."

The *Jumper* pulled up and over the front of the frigate when Davin's ship screeched and the cockpit swung to the side. The *Jumper* whirled. Davin and Phyla, strapped in, pressed against their restraints. Yells came over the comm: Opal's cursing, Trina's panicked yelp followed by the crunch of body into metal and the sudden hush as the engines died. The hull breach alarms continued to sound.

"I can't get the engines up," Phyla said, staring at blinking red on the console.

"Trina?!" Davin said into the comm.

"They're harpoons," Erick replied. "We're stuck."

"Hey," Merc's voice. "The frigate's not done. It's spitting out more fighters. They're omnis."

Which was about the last thing Davin wanted to hear.

68

SAVE THE ENGINES, SAVE THE SHIP

Fournine, barely awake, grabbed Viola as the Jumper shuddered to a halt. Even so, Viola thought her neck would snap and her head continue on into the room's wall. Fournine's hands, that android grip, was too strong to let Viola go, though, and a second later she dropped back off the workbench.

"Viola?" the comm buzzed with Davin's voice. "Need you to get to the engines quick. Trina's not responding."

"On it," Viola replied, cutting the comm. "Not that I know how the engines work, or anything."

Leaving the android tied on the bench—Viola wasn't sure what it would do yet—the girl ran out of the room and bounced down the hallway past the crew bedrooms and towards the engines. Trina sprawled out in front of the control panel, a slick line of red leading from a splotch to where Trina's head lay against the wall.

"Need you back here, Erick," Viola commed. "Trina smashed her head when the ship stopped."

Erick clicked affirmative. Viola reached towards Trina, tried to locate a pulse, then stopped. It wouldn't matter if

Trina was still alive if the enemy ship shredded them to pieces. Priorities. The diagnostics on the control panel read, in big block letters, that the engines killed themselves to prevent overheating. Fair enough. The button to restart wasn't working though. Every time Viola tapped the thing, a small X appeared and a timer with a temperature reading flashed.

"We're gonna need a few more minutes," Viola commed.

"We don't have'em," Davin replied. "Override it."

Viola was about to say that she didn't know how, but bit it off. Look around. Trina wouldn't have let something like a frightened computer keep her from doing what she wanted with these engines. The control console itself didn't have any hints. A couple buttons for engine diagnostics, right and left. Read-outs on available energy. And the spot on the screen where thrust would be was occupied by that emergency shut-down warning. Viola took a breath, stepped back.

"They're coming around," Davin commed.

"Don't worry, I got this," Merc's voice snapped in. "Viola, you be ready to cut loose."

Davin yelled at Merc, but Viola tuned them out. *If I were a hidden starter switch, where would I be?* Viola's eyes caught the red splatter again. Where Trina hit her head. There was something black in the center of the blood. A small circle. Viola took a finger and wiped away the blood, the bright red sticking to her hand. The word MANUAL printed in tiny lettering showed through. A keyhole, but where's the key?

"You got ten!" Merc shouted through the comm. "Nine!"

Trina must have it! Viola dropped to her knees as Merc continued the countdown. Reaching into Trina's pocket, the mechanic's head hanging limp to the side. Tried not to focus on feeling for a pulse. Five seconds. There, on the belt! Viola reached to Trina's side, the small glint of metal hanging there. A batch of keys, but only one with the perfect cylinder match for the hole.

"One!" Merc said.

Viola jammed the key into the manual override and twisted to the right. Without meaning to, Viola's eyes closed as the *Jumper* shuddered. The engines jerked to life, the screeching roar of stressed metal echoed throughout the ship. Viola expected the whole thing to jerk to a stop a moment later, but it didn't. Whatever was holding them in place was gone. The *Jumper* shoved forward, the diagnostics blaring a yellow warning. The temp was still high, but the engines ran.

Viola leaned back against the wall. Success. And then she remembered Trina, lying there on the floor. As Erick rounded the corner, Viola dropped next to the mechanic, looking for any sign she might be alive.

69

STICK JOCKEY

Against the black wall of space, the cables holding the *Whiskey Jumper* were invisible. That didn't much matter though, because Merc wasn't trying to shoot them. The fighters, setting up for their attack runs, took their sweet time. Lazy turns. Like they were ordered to give Davin time to contemplate just how screwed he was. 'Course, Merc would not let that happen.

Swinging out and away from the *Jumper*, Merc heard Viola say Trina wasn't doing so hot. Viola had to get the engines going, because there was only one chance. The rear of the frigate, its engines a trio of orange-glowing portals, washed out Merc's cockpit vision. His scanner showed dots spreading along the frigate's side. The omnis, disc-shaped fighters able to cut any which way they wanted were slow to react. Their directional jets flexible, but not as fast as the Viper's big bucket of rocket power.

"Four!" Merc yelled into the comm. The Viper shot over the rear edge of the frigate, then Merc pulled hard to swing to the left. The scanner showed three omnis in his vector. Enough to take Merc. If they could hit him.

"Three!"

At the midpoint of the frigate, but speeding away from it. A pair of the omnis behind him now, testing shots. Merc triggered the maneuvering jets at random, stutters up and down so that the Viper moved like a jagged line.

"Two!"

The last omni flashed out of nowhere, screaming from above the Viper, the center console flipping the omni to the prime threat. One, two hits on the Viper's energy-dissipating shields. Merc killed the main engines, kicked the maneuvering jet on the nose of the Viper. The universe spun. The flight stick vibrated and Merc pressed the trigger.

Twin cannons launched super-heated light straight into the oncoming omni. Even though the firing angle was only there for a split second, the Viper's tricked-out weapons melted through the omni's shields and broke the craft apart.

Coming back around, Merc re-triggered the engines and the Viper increased velocity. Just ahead, the *Jumper* sat above the frigate, small next to the bigger ship. Trapped, for the moment.

"One!"

The cables were invisible to his eyes, but the Viper's scanner painted them as threats, and Merc steered right for them. Just as Merc crossed beneath the *Jumper* there was a spit of fire, of light above the Viper. Merc let rip a yell, a massive weight of fear he didn't realize he'd been carrying dropped from his chest. The *Jumper*'s engines were lit. And then the Viper lurched hard, a shriek as something tore through the energy shield. But the tension released a split-second later.

Above him, the *Jumper* turned. Partially free.

Merc wrenched the damaged Viper back on course and a second later hit the other cable. The Viper's weakened shields did nothing to stop it. Merc watched the cable chew into the metal as it frayed, only visible through the line it was rending through his fighter's nose. The cable made its way up to the cockpit, Merc's eyes closing as cracks appeared in the glass. A button on the side of Merc's chair sealed his flight suit, dropping a helmet over his head. The glass shattered and the last bits of the cable broke through the Viper's console.

A rough way for his ship to go.

Marc kicked the eject pad, shooting up through the broken cockpit. The Viper's momentum kept slicing it through the cable, until it came to the engines and the battery. Merc, floating free in space, looked past the edge of the *Jumper* and watched as his fighter exploded in a bright blue fiery ball that was there one second and gone the next. Along with the cable. The *Jumper*, engines firing and suddenly free, shot forward away from the frigate.

"Told you I got this," Merc said to nobody. Could've tried the short-range comm, but there wasn't anyone close enough to talk to anymore.

Outside his helmet, the Viper pieces flashed out of existence against the frigate's shields. Merc twisted, bringing Jupiter in all its great glory into view. The momentum from the ejection was sending him right towards the gas giant. He'd be long dead by the time his body fell into the atmosphere and disintegrated.

As a way to go, it wasn't a bad one. Merc could already feel the tickling edge of sleep, that telltale sign of oxygen running low. A few more minutes looking at miracles, then he'd shut off the lights.

70

CATCHING BREATH

The blip that represented Merc's Viper vanished from the console. The blank space on the screen settled in Davin's chest. Another one lost. Three of his crew, three of his friends gone since Marl's betrayal.

"I picked up a small burst, right before the Viper exploded," Phyla said. "He might've ejected."

"We go back, they'll destroy the ship," Davin said. "We can't let Merc die for nothing."

Phyla didn't answer, just stared out the window. The *Whiskey Jumper*, engines settling back into optimal running conditions, sped away from the frigate and slipped into Jupiter's outer orbit. Europa wasn't far. A speck outside the cockpit. They could turn the *Jumper* there now. Beat the frigate.

"They'd kill us if we tried that now," Phyla said, reading Davin's thoughts. "I don't think we're ready for another fight."

"Erick, what's Trina's status?" Davin commed, reminded by Phyla's comment.

"Pulse is steady. This is her second concussion in less

than a week. She'll need a lot of rest," Erick buzzed back. "Whatever you want to do, captain, I'd leave Trina out of it."

Davin sat back in the chair, stared out the glass. Being a mercenary captain was supposed to be about adventure. About jaunting through the galaxy, seeing new places, meeting new people, and getting the spicy side of life. Not watching his friends fall apart.

"Captain?" Viola commed. "The engines look okay, but I'm not liking some of the readings. Temps are spiking randomly, and we've lost efficiency. We're burning more than the solar can charge."

"How much time?" Davin replied.

"Not enough to get most places."

Jupiter had plenty of moons. A few had stations on them. Refueling spots for ships heading to the back reaches of the solar system or returning with hauls of rare minerals, gasses, or just experiments. Even in its limping state, the *Whiskey Jumper* should be able to make it to one. The question was whether Bosser's androids would be waiting.

"If you want, I've got an idea," Viola said.

"All ears."

"My parents, they own Galaxy Forge, on Ganymede. It's manufacturing, plenty of bay space for us. Parts to repair. We could hide there."

"Doesn't your dad have a bounty on your head?" Davin asked. "And he's good with harboring suspected murderers?"

"He wants me to come home, whatever that takes."

"You sure you want to do that?"

"I want to do anything but. Only, I don't think we have a choice."

"I like it," Davin said. "Let's bring you home."

Phyla nodded and punched in the destination. A faint

blue line appeared on the glass, swinging out and running into the distance. The course they would follow to Ganymede. Intersect the moon as it came around on its orbit. Davin watched the line for a second, felt the *Jumper* turn, then stood.

"I'd better see if Opal's all right," Davin said. "You good up front?"

"Go be the captain, captain," Phyla replied.

That title didn't sound as good as it used to.

71

HOMECOMING

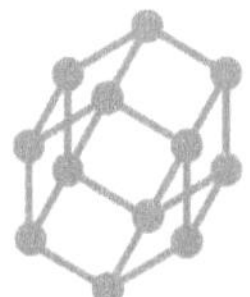

The *Jumper*'s ramp slid down and Viola struggled to keep a straight face. She didn't know whether to be happy or sad, giddy at the thought of home or scared at what her parents would say. Then again, she'd nearly been killed at least twice since leaving here, and at least her father would not murder her, right?

"You should go first," Davin said, standing next to Viola at the top of the ramp. "Figure they'll want to see you more than a bunch of dirty mercenaries."

Viola took the cue and walked into the bay. Part of the processing plant for the precious metals her father's company extracted from Ganymede, the bay was huge. The *Jumper* tiny compared to the kilometer-long ships that could dock there. It was also empty except for her parents, staring at her from the dirty slate floor.

Seeing their faces, her mother's endless concern and curiosity, her father's cocked eyebrow and folded arms, flooded Viola's head with memories. Like a vault of happiness unlocked. Why she'd run away from these two into the wild horror-show of space was a question that had no good answer.

Hugs exchanged, cheeks kissed. Viola's father shook Davin's hand and thanked the captain for bringing back his daughter. Promises of food, medical facilities and supplies. Davin didn't bother protesting, but said Viola more than pulled her weight, causing a blush to spring out of nowhere.

The rest of the crew filtered out and to the series of rooms reserved at the quarters normally used for visiting pilots and businessmen. Except Fournine, who was still on the ship—Viola shut its power off to keep the android inert until someone decided what to do with it.

Viola followed her parents out of the bay and towards the short tram to take them back to the residence. The cars were big enough for ten people, built like busses, and shot along magnetic rails to various destinations. The parts and paving necessary for personal vehicles was too expensive on Ganymede, so Galaxy Forge built houses in pods. A central hub connected to six or seven places shooting off at various angles, shielded from radiation through electric energy, like the ones on space ships. The ride took less than ten minutes, but they spent the whole of it under the glow of Jupiter's monstrous body.

As soon as they went through the front door, Viola's mother announced they had an hour till dinner. Viola moved towards her room, but her father took Viola's elbow and pointed her to a small study.

"Time for a quick talk?" her father asked.

That phrase. One her dad used any time Viola was in for a lecture. Innocent on the face of it, just a quip, a grab for a few minutes with his daughter to expound on some life lesson. That phrase stole away the warmth, brought with it why Viola had run away. The expectant look in her father's eyes. It was time to fall back in line. Revert away from the glitch in the plan, get back to business.

"You know what, yeah. Let's chat," Viola said.

Her father's study was an exercise in antiquities. Rockwood shelves, stone painted and smoothed to resemble a dark walnut, lined the room. Real wood was too expensive to bother freighting over from Earth. Trinkets covered those shelves, products and design models made at Galaxy Forge. A history from small single-man scouters to vast military freighters contained in the figures. At the far end, the desk where her father worked when he was home. A window staring out through the bubble into the vast icy gray of the Ganymede surface.

Viola's father sat in one of the room's two chairs, folding one leg up on another as he clasped his hands. Viola watched him take in the deep breath and struck first.

"You put a bounty on your daughter's head," Viola said, keeping on her feet. "I was almost kidnapped, twice, because of you."

Her father's mouth fell open.

"On Europa, there were two men, armored, that threw me to the ground. They were going to carry me to their ship, maybe tie me up, and fly me home," Viola continued. "On Miner Prime, I was saved because an android decided to kill the man who was taking me. Do you understand? A man died because of your stupid bounty."

"Viola, I—"

"No. You don't get to talk yet," she said. "There's a universe out there you don't even know, full of people fighting and striving and dying to make a bit of coin. Your bounty? That was convenience for you. So you didn't have to look for me yourself. But to the people trying to take me? To Cadge? That coin meant everything."

"You never said why you ran away," her father replied, throwing the words up in defense.

"I wanted something more exciting than sitting in this bubble all day! I wanted more than your planned future for me."

"And you found it?"

Viola nodded. She felt the conversation turning. The outburst hadn't overwhelmed her father, and now that he had his poise back . . .

"I'm sorry," her father said. "I shouldn't have posted the bounty, but I didn't know where you'd gone. Didn't know how to find you. It was a reaction. Now, though, you're home."

Over the house's intercom, Viola's mother called. Dinner, made by the house's bots, was ready.

"Did you tell her about it? The bounty?"

"That doesn't matter anymore," her father said. "It's gone. Over. What matters is where you're going next. We want you to stay here."

"It's too boring."

"I know, so I'm arranging for you to take a job at Galaxy Forge. You'll have to earn it, and it will be hard, but nobody's going to be shooting at you."

Seeing Viola's expression, he added, "Give it a chance. If you miss the excitement, it'll still be there waiting for you."

They left the study, wandered to what would be Viola's best meal in months. Real food, not packets of goop. A real table, rather than the grimy Jumper kitchen. Comforts Viola hadn't even realized she missed till they were in front of her again. Already she could feel home asserting itself, breaking her resolve. Ganymede had been a temporary stopover, but now it was forming a more permanent place.

72

CHOICES

H ow long will it take to get ready?" Viola asked Davin as he took a sip from the steaming cup of coffee.

The cafe, one of only three in the entire ten-thousand worker factory, was designed like the gears that drove the ore-digging machines they made. Viola glanced over at Phyla, coming up to a console in the cafe's center. Each displayed an array of options on a colored screen, then asked for a swipe to deduct payment. Behind the scenes, bots made the drinks, the ingredients replenished by nearly hidden support staff.

Tables, like the small one Viola and Davin were sitting at, ringed the center and, with a tap on the surface, displayed rolling headlines. The glass ceiling above showed the gray morning on Ganymede, a product of low sunlight and manufactured gasses meant to thicken the atmosphere. The view wasn't great sometimes, but the thick fog blocked radiation, and Viola would rather not have a tumor, thank you.

"Only two days. Patching up a little torn hull doesn't take too long."

"You can stay longer, you know."

Davin looked at Viola for a moment and nodded, a thanks for what her father was giving and was still willing to give them.

"No, we can't," Davin said. "They killed Merc. They're still hunting us, and the androids will follow us here eventually. Our choices are fight back, or run to the edges."

Run to the edges. Davin heard the words and ran them around his mind. Wouldn't be much different from Vagrant's Hollow. Making due with whatever work they could find, staying mobile and escorting transports around Saturn's rings out to Uranus.

"Will Trina be ready?" Viola asked.

"Good enough to fly."

"Good enough to fight?"

Davin took another long drink from the coffee cup. Viola knew the captain wasn't very old, but Davin's eyes changed as he considered Viola's words. As though Davin became elderly right in front of her, the captain shut his eyes for a moment and set the mug down, letting go a long sigh as he did.

"Good enough to leave," Davin said. "Whether we fight, I don't know."

"You're giving up?"

Davin didn't answer, but stared at the coffee like it wasn't Viola who'd asked. Like it was himself.

73

WHAT COULD BE

Ganymede was boring. The daily routine bled into Viola's life like a virus, eating away at her soul through standard breakfasts, news reports, the same conversations with her mother and father about re-integrating. About getting ready to start at Galaxy Forge. Nobody had shot at her in days. It was awful.

"Doing some hard work there," Puk commented as Viola stared at nothing, sitting in the room next to her bed, where she'd had Puk blast Roddy ages ago.

"I can't focus," Viola said.

"You used to love being in this room."

"I think that's because I didn't know what was outside of it."

"A harsh, thin atmosphere that would kill you in seconds?"

"I wasn't being literal."

"Sorry, you bumped my sarcasm setting way too high to have this conversation."

Viola smiled. The little bot had a way of reading her

moods. An unintended effect of the learning algorithm she'd plugged into Puk years ago. Viola thought there was something wrong in the code, something that was driving Puk insane. A typo in the variable mediating the bot's personality.

"Never change, Puk."

"That's a literal impossibility, Viola."

"S'pose you're right. Though I guess it's mean to ask someone to never change, isn't it?"

"My database of popular romance films says most find it endearing."

"Yeah? What else does that database tell you?"

"That you're lacking the love of your life."

"Thanks."

"And that you're never going to find it here."

"What?" Viola turned on her chair and stared at the little bot. "I mean, obviously I'm not going to find someone in this room."

"Not talking about someone, Viola. There's a common thread among the movies, right? It's where the person has to soul-search, go on an adventure, before they have a chance of finding what they really love."

"Now you're getting philosophical."

"Not my forte. But I can say that based on my observations of your mood over the last couple of weeks that when we were with the mercenaries, it was the happiest time of your life since you were a kid."

Like Viola didn't know that. Like she didn't understand that every second on board that ship, being run through the lifts of Miner Prime, or puzzling a way to start the engines before the frigate blew them to bits made her feel more alive than hours spent pouring over thought exercises. Not that

Viola didn't like crunching the numbers, but there was an itch to put all that data diving into practice. To see Fournine open its eyes and run the way she set him.

"My father will not be happy with you."

"Thankfully, I don't care."

74

DOUBT

The five of them sat around the table in the lobby of the Moonshot, the hotel Viola's father let Davin and the rest use while repairs continued. Davin looked around at their faces: Erick's slumped-back, arms-crossed curiosity, Mox staring at the table like it held life's grand secrets, Opal looking back at Davin, her eyes stretched, red. Phyla was the only one that looked engaged, and even she gripped the glass of water in front of her like it might spring away for freedom at any moment.

"Tomorrow, the doctors think Trina will be ready. The *Jumper*'s about set to fly," Davin started. "I wanted to ask where you thought we should go."

He paused for a second. No outbursts, no immediate calls for a revenge assault on Europa. Davin almost wanted one of them to speak. To yell that they couldn't let Marl get away with it. For Mox to overturn the table, drag Trina out of the hospital and rain laser death on Eden Prime. At least until they were blown out of the sky. Opal's mouth opened, but whatever she was going to say didn't come out.

"I want to clear us," Davin said. "I want to shoot our way

in there, tell Marl to drop the charges. To confess to arranging the hit on those inspectors. I want the androids to leave us alone. And the entire time we've been here, I've been throwing ideas around. Thinking of ways to win. But I can't find one that doesn't end with us all dead."

"You're talking like some of us are dead already," Opal said.

"Merc—"

"We don't know if he's gone," Opal said, her voice peppered with somber heat. "And Cadge had it coming. Sorry about Lina, too, but she wasn't really one of us."

"Hey," Phyla warned.

"It's fine," Davin said. "You're right. We don't know for sure. But there's been no contact. We saw his ship break apart. Even if he ejected, I don't know why they would have saved him."

"I don't think that's helping," Phyla said, Opal's glower growing darker.

"I'm trying to say going back to Europa is suicide. We can fly farther out from here. I know a few people who run ore and gas from Uranus. They'd get us contracts. The androids wouldn't find us."

"Running," Mox said.

"Sounds like it," muttered Erick.

"Look. I don't want to see any more of you, or me, die. I don't want to keep looking over my shoulder wondering if the next person I see is really a homicidal bot that wants to dissect me. That's not a life I want to lead," Davin said. "We go out there, there's none of that."

"What if we don't want to?" Opal asked.

"It's my ship, she goes where I do," Davin said. "You don't have to decide now. We'll leave tomorrow, so think about it. I'm sure you can find passage off here if you don't want to go. But you are all more than welcome to come with."

Davin pushed himself away from the table and walked down the hallway, up the stairs to his room. Nobody followed, nobody made any comments he could hear as he walked away. Davin felt a crawling sickness growing in his stomach. Was this what cowards felt like? Streams of rationalizations ran through Davin's head, all of them valid and pointless.

The room was sparse. The wall screen turned on as Davin went in, set to his automatic preference. A martial arts movie played, then cut to a commercial. Davin stood there, watching as a panning shot showed the changing lines of Europa, the green mossy growth on one side and the blue ice on the other. A voice came over as the camera continued to soar across the landscape, talking about the business opportunities, the vacation possibilities, the beautiful landscapes soon to be available. All stemming from Eden Prime.

A knock at the door twisted Davin away. Phyla stood in the hallway, sporting a look that razed Davin's soul. His counter-expression, an open-mouthed shrug, prompted Phyla to push her way past Davin and into his room. The door shut behind her, the latch on a closing trap.

"What?" Davin said, feeling meek though he didn't know why.

"You know what. You know precisely why I'm here. That's why you're standing over there near the door like some kid wanting to make a run for it," Phyla said.

Davin inched forward till he was in the room's living space. He leaned against the wall, folded his arms across his chest, and tried to adopt something that looked unafraid.

"That better?"

"Now you're a cocky teenager who doesn't want to admit he's being dumb. Which, I guess, is pretty right for you."

"Slinging heat tonight, huh?"

"Carrying the torch for the people you call your friends. Your crew. The ones you abandoned."

"I believe I offered them a lift? A chance to move on?"

"Who are you to make them choose? To tell them if they're smart they'll forget Merc, forget Lina and just run off to the edge of existence like this whole thing never happened?"

"I didn't enjoy it," Davin said, moving away from the wall and sitting on the bed. "That wasn't a speech I wanted to give. But we're outgunned, Phyla. We wouldn't even get the Jumper into Europa's atmosphere before those fighters chewed us to pieces."

"Maybe not, but don't we owe it to Merc to try?"

"If you've got any ideas, now's the time. Otherwise no, I don't think we owe our lives to Merc." Davin sighed. "Sorry, that sounded harsher than I meant. Tomorrow. If we can come up with a plan tomorrow, a way to get on that moon, find Marl, and stop this, then I won't take the ship and go."

"Then come with me."

"Where?"

"Back out there. To the crew. If we're going to solve this, it has to be together."

Davin stood up from the bed, ran his hand through his hair.

"You and Lina, always changing my mind after it's made up."

75

BACK TO EUROPA

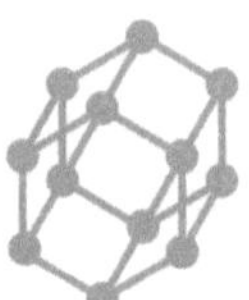

Viola walked through the main doors of the hotel and, spying the crew, stepped over in their direction. It was closer to dawn than dusk, the lobby empty except for their crew. It'd taken help from Puk, flitting around corners to make sure her parents weren't watching, to get out of the house. Viola had survived a kidnapping, fought mercenaries on another world, but had to sneak out of her own home like a teenager.

The Wild Nines looked miserable. Like they'd eaten lemons. Faces scrunched, downcast, tight.

"Hey," Viola said as they looked over at her.

"Bad timing," Mox muttered.

"Trying to think up a way back to Europa," Erick said. "You have any ideas?"

"She shouldn't be involved," Phyla said. "Her parents are giving us enough."

"That's why I came here, though," Viola stepped closer, leaned on the table. "I don't want to stay. I want to go with you."

"This isn't just a fun trip, Viola," Opal said. "People get hurt."

"You don't think I know that?" Viola replied. "I was, literally, right there when Merc—"

"She knows," Mox interrupted. "You are still innocent."

"That's what you think," Viola countered.

"They're trying to talk you out because they know going back to that moon is suicide," Davin grumbled. "Why add one more body to the mix?"

"Davin," Phyla said.

"I was thinking about that, actually," Viola said. "Eden Prime still has a lot of traffic, right? A constant stream of ships coming and going?"

Nobody answered. They stared at her. Davin's eyebrow ticked a centimeter higher.

"They know what the *Whiskey Jumper* looks like. Maybe they're even tracking it somehow," Viola continued. "So what if we used something else?"

"Another ship?" Phyla said. "We don't have one."

"You don't. Galaxy Forge, though, has plenty."

"And they're just going to give us a ship?"

"Or are we going to take one?" Davin asked.

"Bingo," Viola said. "Puk can get us the access codes. Then all we have to do is head to the loading docks and take the ride we want."

"Always love robbing from people who're nice to us," Davin shook his head. "Viola, we have enough enemies. We don't need to make more."

"You'll be leaving the *Jumper* as collateral. I'm sure it's worth as much as one of those cargo haulers."

"More," Davin said.

"She's smart," Mox added.

"We'll have cover, for a change," Erick mused. "Might even make it all the way to the surface without getting shot."

"I'm sure we'll get our fill of lasers anyway," Davin said. "But I think that might work. Once we're on the ground, we have a chance at getting to Marl."

"And finding Merc," Opal said.

Davin looked at the group, their set faces. Time to call it.

"So we have a choice. Run, or fight," Davin said. "We should vote. I know I'm the captain, but for this, everyone needs to decide for themselves."

They all nodded.

"Then who's for going back to Europa?"

Phyla and Opal's hands shot up right away. Viola's a moment later. Mox and Erick a second after that. Davin looked across the table.

"Fine, you bastards. When you get shot, I don't want to hear any complaining."

76

HIJACKERS

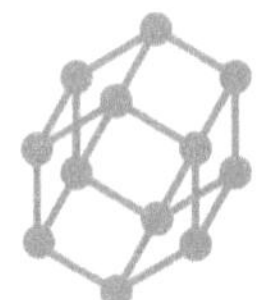

"Are you ready?" Viola asked Fournine, who sat on the bench, blinking its eyes.

The plan to take one of the company ships was simple: the staff would recognize her, and probably the rest of the Nines as well, which meant turning to the one person Galaxy Forge didn't know existed.

Fournine stretched out its arms and wiggled each finger, testing the motion. It did the same with its feet, then flexed each joint. Viola knew, from looking at Fournine's code, that this was part of the start-up sequence. In a couple of seconds, the real fun would begin.

"Who am I?" Fournine asked, its voice a monotone.

"You're an android," Viola replied.

"That is clear," Fournine said, rotating its head to look at Viola.

The plaskin coating looked unnatural in the bright light. Fournine could adjust the tint at will and right now the plaskin was ghostly white. Absent of color. The hair was gray, its neutral state. Fournine looked like a person coated with flour. Despite the appearance, Fournine's jaw worked as it spoke. Its eyes moved around the room, looking at objects even though the bot's cameras would have scanned the place already. Warm air pushed out of its mouth, shoved by tiny jets, to simulate breath. Viola shivered.

"I have a new personality for you," Viola said. "If you're ready for it."

When Viola created Puk, it'd taken a while to get a personality that matched the bot. From the ones available to download, Viola had tweaked and tested, spinning the floating bot through turns as a noble prince, a dark and dour teenager, an innocent kid, and more. For a while there, Puk's being changed to reflect Viola's mood. Only, it was one thing to experiment with a small, harmless bot and another to tweak one that could snap her in half without trying.

"I'm ready," Fournine said.

Again Viola pressed her fingers to Fournine's temples. The processing unit rose from its head, slots available for the personality chip, the drive containing the combat knowledge, and the piece that Viola and Trina removed and destroyed. The transmitter that connected Fournine back to the android's command center on Earth that sent it over-riding orders,that could and would order Fournine to self-destruct after it didn't communicate.

Viola slipped the personality chip in the slot and pushed. With a click, the chip locked into place and, with another press to the temples, the processing unit slid back into Fournine's head.

"You want me to be like this? Really? Cause I think you're gonna regret it," Fournine said as soon as its skull sealed. "I mean, there's crazy, and then there's what you've got here."

"Where we're going, we'll need a little crazy."

"Little, she says. Like calling a supernova a firework. But hey! I'm not here to judge. Just to do. Do it all."

Viola left Puk with this personality for two days years ago. Then, unable to stand the meandering anecdotes about nothing and myriad death threats this personality matrix was prone to, she'd taken it out. Fournine, though, looked like it needed something spicy.

"Glad you're excited. Here's what we need you to do."

77

ANDROID UNLEASHED

Fournine's internal clock put Ganymede's current time as way too late. The factory and its accompanying bays didn't recognize this, churning away refining ores along the third shift. Still, passing through the hallways and the empty way stations gave a good indicator of why nighttime missions were easier. Nobody bothered with the ancillary areas.

Every so often, making its way through the factory, Fournine had to stop and wave a card in front of a scanner. Each time, after a second, the scanner blinked green and the door opened. Fournine assumed the scans were logging somewhere, that someone would ask questions later about why these doors opened at such late hours. But nobody appeared to question the android. Which, as the chosen route to the bays was as out-of-the-way as possible, made sense.

Fournine wore a borrowed uniform from the manufacturing pits, a singular outfit that covered its body save its head in thick cloth the color of murky blue. If a fight broke out, the first task would be to tear off the uniform and get mobility back. As it was, Fournine clomped through the hallways, skin tinted to a realistic darker shade, attempting to match the slouching drudge of the other workers.

The first manned station was the last checkpoint before the bays. A lone member of the factory's security, looking bored and dusty. The guard sat in a booth next to the locked gate and didn't say anything until Fournine attempted to swipe the card.

"Hey there," the guard said, perking up. "It's after hours, so I'll have to check you through."

"Sure thing, my third-shift friend!" Fournine announced, stepping over to the booth and presenting the card.

The guard took it, looked at it with a crinkling brow.

"Say," Fournine said. "Why's it you look like you popped your head out of a mine shaft?"

The guard blinked for a second then took stock of his dirt-stained sleeves.

"Security here's a rotation gig. You work a bit down in the trenches, then get a week up here," the guard said the words, then narrowed his eyes at Fournine. "Though you should know that. Your card here gives you top-level clearance."

"Consultant," Fournine replied. "Just writing a report on the interesting parts."

The guard grunted, then swiped the card through another reader in the booth. The gate opened with a chime and the guard handed the card back.

"Why're you coming round so late, if you're just writing a report?"

"You're a suspicious one, aren't you?" Fournine replied. "Do I tell you how to do your job?"

The guard took that, shrugged, and waved Fournine on. The miracles confidence could get you. Though perhaps

Fournine had the advantage in that its programming prevented fear. Any normal person on the verge of being caught might sweat, shake, or stumble through their answers. Fournine didn't care. If it was caught, it would dismantle anyone that stood in its way.

Speaking of, the long hallway stretching behind the bays now lay before Fournine. Only the farther ones were in use tonight, their bright lights filtering across the top of the hallway and giving signs of where not to go. It wasn't hard to navigate a few bays and find an empty ship, powered down and large enough to hold ten. Fournine stepped into the bay and towards the ship. The ramp was raised, the ship's door shut.

"Here's our first problem!" Fournine commed. "I've found our ride, but it's not open. Shall I rip the door off?"

"We need it sealed or we'll die up there," Viola replied through the comm.

"You living creatures and your needs," Fournine said.

"Such a drag, I know. What's the model?"

"It's a Cask Seven Star."

"Isn't that a little big?"

"I'm sorry, I'll just continue my illegal wandering through the bay until we find the perfect fit," Fournine said.

It heard Viola sigh over the comm.

"And we own this one?" Viola asked.

"It has your company's name all over it."

"Then the reset code is twenty-seven, twenty-four."

Fournine punched the numbers in and the ramp whistled, opened and slid down. Ah, the benefits of mass infrastructure and the consistency such operations required. Fournine stepped up the ramp, was almost into the ship, when bright lights came on behind him.

"Hey! What're you doing in there?" shouted the same guard from back at the booth.

"Believe I told you?" Fournine yelled back. "Need to see how this one is being used. Sitting here in the bay isn't making anyone any money, you know?"

"I checked with operations and nobody knows about any consultant coming by tonight! Come back out here so we can figure this out."

Fournine ran the odds. It could run back, knock the guard unconscious, and then get on board the vessel in under thirty seconds. However, if the guard called for any back-up, they could seal the bay faster than the ship could take off. Feigning ignorance gave a better return.

"I don't want to be here any longer than necessary," Fournine replied. "Either wait down there a minute or come up. The inspection won't take long."

As the guard wavered, Fournine went inside the ship and strode to the cockpit. Unlike the *Jumper,* the cargo vessel's cockpit was at the aft. This let most of the cargo slide forward where workers and bots could unload it easily. As Fournine stepped into the spacious enclosure, with seating enough for four, soft lighting came on. A tap on the console started the pre-flight check, with greens popping up across the board. The ship wasn't broken, then.

"I have a guard problem," Fournine commed. "I've delayed him for a minute, but curiosity will win out before too much longer."

"You're not supposed to hurt anyone," Viola replied.

"I won't hurt him much, I promise."

A clanking noise echoed through the ship and towards the cockpit. The guard walking up the ramp. An unfortunate decision. Fournine punched the button for engine warm-up, and as the soft rumble of moving energy filled the vessel, the android went back to greet the guard.

"Why are you setting the ship up to launch?" the guard asked as he crested the ramp and found Fournine standing there.

"Part of the routine. The quality of the ship is an important part of the report. Can't measure loading efficiency accurately if you don't know how ready the ships are for flight."

"My supervisor's on his way, you know. So if you're lying to me, now's the time to get out," the guard said, hand moving to a holstered sidearm.

Fournine followed the guard's arm, holding its own hands up.

"The threats are unnecessary," Fournine said. "Besides, if anyone will be throwing threats, it should be me."

"What?" the guard said as Fournine reached forward.

The guard tried to draw his weapon, but Fournine's raised right hand moved fast, locking the drawing arm to the guard's side. With his left hand, Fournine pressed hard to the guard's throat. The thing with humans was that without their oxygen, they crumble awfully fast. A few seconds struggle later and the guard went limp in the android's arms. Taking its hand away, Fournine felt the faint pulse and sudden intake of breath that signaled life.

"Your guard will have a headache, but he'll wake up tomorrow," Fournine commed after dumping the guard on the bay floor.

Minutes later, as the guard's supervisor rounded the corner into the bay, Fournine lifted the Cask Seven Star out and over Ganymede's dark amber surface.

78

INCOMING

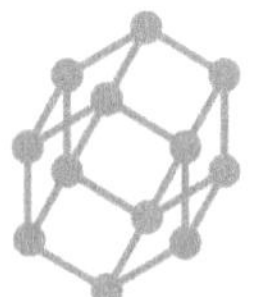

Europa didn't look as blue this time. Viola saw the moon through the cargo hauler's cameras, projecting the image on the flat wall on the back of the cockpit. Fournine was the only other person up there with her. When Europa's flight control tried to figure who was trying to land a cargo ship on their moon, they wouldn't see any faces they recognized. Davin and the others waited near the loading ramp, ready to spring out as soon as the hauler landed on solid ground.

The first hail came as Europa grew large enough to dominate the view. The autopilot, using Phyla's programmed route, was already firing jets to slow the hauler and get it ready for atmosphere.

"This is Eden Prime to the, uh, *Big Bertha*. What's the nature of your visit?"

"We're here to drop sweet, sweet ore in your laps," Fournine replied.

Viola slapped the mute button and glared at the android. "How about you let me answer the rest of the questions?"

"What's the problem?" Fournine asked. "You think he's having a boring day? Cause it sounds like he's having a boring day. He didn't even laugh at the name of the ship. We should cheer him up. Especially cause when we land and it gets out that he let a bunch of wanted mercenaries into their base, his day will get a lot worse."

"Just shut up, please."

"You made me the way I am."

"*Big Bertha*," said the flight controller. "We'll have a bay ready for you, number four. If you wouldn't mind adjusting your approach to match the coordinates I'm sending your way."

"Appreciate it," Viola replied.

No ask for identification, no statement on the number of crew, or even the types of ore they were bringing? Viola had spent time, during one of her father's endless career-day initiatives, in the flight control rooms on Ganymede. The list of questions and protocols to follow to get a good idea of what was landing on your planet was a long one.

"Davin?" Viola commed.

"What's up?"

"We're through, but I'm not thrilled about it."

"Seems like you should be, if we're in the clear."

Viola relayed the concerns, to which Davin, in a tone of voice Viola recognized as whaddya want me to do about it, replied that the whole thing would be a mess anyway. So long as they didn't have to fight in *Big Bertha*'s slow, weaponless metal box, things couldn't be that bad. Hard to argue with that logic.

As the ship descended through Europa's atmosphere, Viola used the cameras to explore the view. Eden Prime and the surrounding landscape was still a moldy green, a patch of growing life surrounded by the marching line of the terramorpher. From this high up it resembled fog-covered hills, rolling lines of mist moving too gradually for Viola to see as they chewed up ice and sucked up water and, mixing with imported rock and sand, converted the stuff into soil.

Europa was a ball covered in ice, and the terramorpher was making land from the bottom up. Growing mountains. What Viola would give to be inside one of those giant machines, watching a world literally made beneath her.

79

SISTERS

They were landing. The Wild Nines, here. Marl set the transmission, targeted it towards the relay satellite that would send it bouncing through a series of repeaters to Alissa's ship, hidden somewhere in the depths of space.

"Sister," Marl started, then took a breath. "Sister, I'm sending this in case I don't make it through until tomorrow. The group of mercenaries is proving stubborn, proving dangerous.

"There is a chance that they will make it to me. Bosser, the man pulling Eden's strings, tells me that it is either the heads of these mercenaries or mine. I'm not confident in the former."

Behind her, the office door opened and Castor stepped in. Marl waited until he shut the door behind him.

"Alissa, you must know that there is no home for you here. Eden is watching closely, and even if I survive, they won't let me live without a leash.

"However, there is one thing I can tell you. Maybe you can use it, to help your cause. Several days ago a large freighter passed through the system, Eden-branded and lightly protected. I met with the captain and learned where they are heading, and why.

"I've sent the details in this package, and hope that it is enough."

Castor cleared his throat.

"Sister, I have to go. If this is to be the end of it, then I'm sorry we didn't have more time together. That we spent our lives on edges. I loved you through all of it."

Marl cut the recording and sent the transmission. Then looked out over the frozen wastes. Through the blurred haze of tears, she could picture the towers, the beaches, the endless pleasures Eden Prime would become. That she might yet see.

"It's time to go," Castor said, putting his hand on her shoulder. "The trap is set."

Marl reached underneath her desk, pulled out the sidearm kept there for emergencies. Fully charged and ready for its murderous task.

"Then let's watch it spring."

80

ATTACKING ICE

Looking at the Nines, each of them covered in weapons, Davin felt an electric rush. This was what it meant to be part of a team. Together taking on an impossible task.

Mox, standing near where the ramp opened, had his cannon latched on and pointed towards the exit. Any ambush would get a face full of laser. Behind him, Opal stood with a pair of long, thin guns. Pin-pointers, Opal called them. Modified from welders and precise manufacturing tools, the beams fired by those things were so tiny as to be invisible. Because lasers were silent, taking away the sight of the beam made finding the shooter of one of those guns damn near impossible.

Davin had Melody, his shotgun, along with a pair of sidearms on his belt. Phyla sported a simpler, though no less deadly, assault rifle, one meant to fire a ton of lasers in rapid succession. It sat in Phyla's arms, held by a shoulder strap. Davin couldn't remember the last time Phyla came on a land-based assignment with them, but her arms were steady, her eyes hard.

"Touching down now," Viola's voice came over the comm. "Bay looks empty. Real empty for a cargo delivery."

Davin glanced at Erick, who gave him a quick nod. The doctor had a small sidearm of his own, but wasn't coming. Anyone hurt needed to have somewhere to retreat to, and while the *Big Bertha* didn't have a true medical bay, they'd brought along enough first aid equipment for Erick to work his magic.

Were they ready? They had to be.

The hauler touched down with a bump, and Mox had the ramp open a second later. The big man didn't fire as he walked into the bay, a good sign. Or a bad one, depending on whether Marl knew they were coming. If the other bays were busy, there might not be unloaders ready.

That thought died a quick death when Davin hit the bay floor and saw nothing, not even a security officer coming by to register the ship's arrival.

"They know we're here," Davin said to the group, Viola and Fournine coming down the ramp behind him. "That means we play it slow, safe. Let them screw up."

Mox and Davin took the lead, the rest of the group filtering out behind. Opal staying off to the side, with Viola bringing up the rear. Fournine doing its own thing, scanning the area in front, above, behind and quipping about the poor decor, or how nice everything would look reduced to rubble. Davin resisted the urge to comment. Viola warned all of them that Fournine's new personality would be annoying, but, when things fell apart, it would be a vicious fighter. And that's what counted.

They went through three more empty bays, the silence gnawing at Davin with each step. The tension growing. Everyone wanted an excuse to start blasting, so when they opened the main doors into the promenade, Davin was disappointed to find it empty. The shops in view had red signs showing they were closed. Not a soul stood out on the street.

"Davin Masters!" Marl's voice boomed from everywhere. "You are a constant thorn in my side. If you would just please go and die, it would make things ever so much easier."

Davin looked but couldn't find the speakers, co-opted from their purpose as emergency broadcasters. Not that it mattered. Marl had to be at the main Eden Prime corporate building, at the far end of the promenade. The location seemed ridiculous, back when Davin first came here.

Why make the required destination of everyone landing there, for any business anyway, so far away from the bays? Marl explained that making prospects walk the entire base helped sell them on Eden Prime's plan. Standard marketing strategy that was terrible for a raid.

"Now, that trick of yours," Marl continued. "Coming in with that ugly cargo hauler? We wouldn't have caught you. Would have let you walk right in. Only once again your crimes caught up with you. The head of the company you stole that from gave me a ring. He wants his daughter back, apparently? Such a rogue, Davin."

Davin didn't bother looking at Viola. It wasn't the girl's fault. Waving the rest of them forward, Davin led the group along the promenade. Every minute Marl yammered on and on they'd be getting closer to her building.

"You might be interested to know your pilot lived. Ferro told me they found him floating in the wreckage of the fighter. If you want to try and save him, you'll have to hurry," Marl paused. "Now, in a minute you'll meet a pair of surprise guests. They've come a long way to see you, so please do give them your utmost attention."

"Where is he?" Opal yelled into the air.

Marl didn't reply. Silence fell for a brief moment, then two figures, one tall and one short, stepped out from a closed store. Both wore the same long trench coat Fournine sported when they'd first encountered the bot.

"Androids," Mox said, confirming.

"Your friend, the pilot," the tall figure announced. "He is in the prison. Marl wished for us to tell you there is ten minutes before he will be executed."

"It's a trick," Phyla said. "They're splitting us up. Making it easy for them to pick us off."

"Even if it is, we have to try, right?" Opal said. "We have to."

"You and Mox, go," Davin said. "The rest of us will take care of these two."

The two androids waved Opal and Mox past them. Davin hefted Melody, aimed it at the pair.

"Guessing this is still a kill or be killed affair?" Davin said to the androids.

They nodded in eerie unison.

"When the fight starts, you run by them, cool?" Fournine said. "Cause you know I think the world of you, captain, but there's no way in hell we're beating two of them. Meaning I'll play the bait, keep'em busy with my smart mouth while you all take care of that crazy lady. Kill the murder charge, and the androids will stop. Do it real fast, I might not even be scrap."

"I'll help you," Viola said, Puk floating up behind her. "We've got a few tricks."

"You're crazy!" Fournine said. "I love it!"

"You sure?" Davin asked.

"Just go," Viola replied.

Then Davin turned to the two androids and, pulling the

trigger, started a fight he couldn't win.

RUNNING WAR

The aim was perfect. The blast went right to the heart of the short one, only in the moment between the lasers leaving Melody and getting to the android, the short one wasn't there anymore. It skipped to the side, the balls of plasma flying harmlessly by. The android too fast for them to track.

"Not that I expected anything less," Davin deadpanned.

"Go!" Fournine yelled, jumping forward towards the tall one.

Davin didn't wait, didn't check to see if Phyla was coming, but ran towards the gap between the androids. The tall one went forward to meet Fournine, the two of them clashing with their long knives in a ring of metal. Sparks flew. The short one ducked a few shots from Phyla, holding her trigger as she ran, and made a move to cut them off when Viola sprayed an unceasing barrage of hot energy towards it.

The short android jumped and tucked into a roll, blowing by Davin and moving towards Viola. Davin hoped she knew what she was doing. Now, though, it was on him and Phyla to reach Marl, to cut off the charge before those two bots killed them all.

With the sounds of the fight behind them, Davin and Phyla sprinted down the promenade towards the large, mounded form of the Eden Prime corporate building. As with the other stores on Eden Prime, the corporate building wrapped its way up the curved wall of the base.

To accommodate the size, the base built itself like a fungus, growing pods attached to the promenade and each other, until it covered a hundred meters of floor from ground to ceiling. Each rounded section shone with a different color, representing the different moons that Eden, the mega-corporation, either had or was in the process of converting to prime real estate. In the center, around the main door, was the deep blue of Europa.

"Shouldn't we have run into someone, anyone by now?" Phyla huffed behind Davin.

"My bet is they're waiting behind that door, ready to blow us to pieces as soon as we go in," Davin replied.

The entry loomed large, the curved portal flattening when it hit the ground and spreading wide enough for four or five people to wander through abreast. A small stair ran up to it, with wide half-circles of concrete forming each step. Anyone looking through the dark windows paralleling the door would've seen Davin and Phyla slow and look around, trying and failing to find another way.

"If all we have is the front door, let's make sure we knock politely," Davin said.

"Politely?"

Davin went up to the large door. On the left was a scanner, ready to unlock if they had a badge. Davin gestured to the right side and Phyla went over, rifle ready. Davin looked at the scanner, then took out his old Eden Prime security card. He pressed it against the scanner, which beeped a negative and stayed red.

"Worth a try," Davin said at Phyla's incredulous look.

"Now what?"

"We knock."

Davin pounded his hand on the door. To say that the metal exterior was kind to his hand would be a gross overstatement. Rather, the rippled metal, grooved to make the frozen waves of Europa's seas, scratched Davin's fist. On the other side, Davin heard the scuffs of boots moving. Bits of whispered commands slipped into his ears. The door's locks clicked out. Then the metal slabs slid inward, curling back.

"See? I knew they wouldn't give up a chance to shoot us," Davin said.

"I'm so glad you're right," Phyla replied.

On the other side of the door sat the entry hall, a tiled cavern that gave way at the back to a series of counters, at which complaints could be registered, forms filled out, and lines waited in. Davin wasted several mornings there himself, staring at the crowd and trying to figure why Eden paid them to guard a bunch of bureaucrats. On the sides of the lobby, stairs curled up along blue walls towards office space. Towards Marl.

Dangling from the ceiling was a spectacular chandelier made from reproductions of Europa ice threaded through with lights. It cast the room in an underwater glow. Aside from that, the rest of the lobby was empty. Davin looked across the entrance into Phyla's tense, stressed face and slipped into a smile. Better to face doom with a cocky grin than crying eyes.

"Cover me," Davin said, and Phyla gave a quick, terse nod.

Davin aimed Melody at the chandelier, and pulled the

trigger. The blast went high and spread, striking around the ceiling where the chandelier was bolted. The lasers burned through the cabling, snapping it and sending the work of art plummeting towards the ground. Davin leaned back against the door and shielded his eyes. When the bright flash grayed out the black of his vision, Davin lowered his arm and, crouched, wheeled around the edge of the left door.

Without looking, Davin pulled the trigger again and sent a bolt rolling at the trooper standing behind the door. The trooper's fire whisked over Davin's head and charred a few hairs. Davin's bolt caught the guard in the chest, causing the guard to collapse a smoking ruin. A few lasers danced by Davin from shooters behind the right door, striking the farther wall to the side.

Davin swiveled right, looking for the next target, and saw a trio of troopers aiming at him. They clustered around a doorway leading to one side of the building, ducking behind the opening as Davin looked. There wasn't any cover, just long empty space between Davin and the door. So the captain flicked the switch on the shotgun and pressed the trigger. Loaded with a pair of shock grenades for just this purpose, Melody spat a black oval that bounced in front of the side opening.

One of the troopers managed a half-hearted shot that went wide, splashing off of the left door and away. The other two grabbed him and dove away from the grenade. It exploded a moment later, sending a series of arcing lightning bolts at anything conductive. The troopers met the requirements: several bolts jumped over to the trio and laced their bodies with white for a second before leaving them groaning and incapacitated.

More fire echoed behind Davin. Phyla busy keeping her cover fire promise. The captain pressed his back to the left door and sidestepped to the end, keeping an eye on the empty lobby and those stairs leading to the second floor. There should have been snipers up there. Or someone with a rifle like Phyla's, ready to spray hot light at them. That there wasn't meant the troopers were tactical morons, or there was something more going on here.

A glance around the edge of the doorway showed Phyla clinging to the end of the right door, peaking around with the assault rifle and letting fly a few miracles. Davin made out a pair of troopers on that side, hunkered around the stairs. Another grenade might do the trick, but then he'd be empty. Instead . . .

"What've you got?" Davin yelled to Phyla.

"The pair on the stairs?" Phyla said. "I think they've got me."

"I'll distract them, you wipe them out."

"Say when!"

Davin took a few quick steps to the first guard he'd shot and pulled the trooper's gun from his hands. Carrying the short rifle back to the edge of the door, Davin extended his left arm and prepared to throw. The pair on the stairs continued to let fly with scattered lasers.

"Three! Two!" Davin yelled. "One!"

The gun arced out from Davin's hand, flying and bouncing along the floor. As it flew, Davin turned around the door and triggered a shot at the stairs. It was way wide, but the flash of the bolt scared the pair, who were watching the thrown gun. Phyla took the cue, poked around the side of her door, and blazed the pair in a sheet of blue fire. A second later the lobby, aside from the moans of some of the troopers, was quiet.

"That was luck," Davin said.

"For you, maybe," Phyla replied. "I'm all skill."

"And I'm very grateful," Davin walked towards the stairs. "I'm going left. You take right."

The two of them creeped up the slate gray and blue steps. Marl's office was at the top and back, with a window facing the outside of the base and onto Europa's wet exterior. Davin hit the top of the stairs first. A closed door waited to the right across the narrow walkway bridging the two stairs. A similar door on his side.

Davin held up a finger to Phyla, causing her to stop on her top step. He pointed at the closed door that Phyla couldn't see, using the palm of his hand to show what it was. Phyla nodded, then took a couple strides and confirmed that Davin's corner had the same beyond it.

Davin motioned for Phyla to hold her position, covering him again, as he went forward to his corner. Turned around it, reached for the door with one hand, the other on his shotgun trigger. As Davin's hand neared the panel to open the thing, the door opened and Ferro kicked Davin in the face.

Davin felt his teeth rattle, his brain bounce around his skull as he fell back and hit the floor of the walkway. The bounce forced Davin's eyes open, and he saw a stream of lasers flash over his face. Phyla saving him, again.

Pushing back the pain, Davin tilted his head up and looked back through the doorway. Ferro wasn't there.

"I don't think I got him," Phyla said, running over, keeping her gun pointed at the open door.

"Don't forget the other one," Davin grunted, and Phyla twitched back to cover the closed door. "Damn, that guy really got a good kick."

"It looked bad. You okay?"

"I'll feel it tomorrow," Davin said, moving up to a crouch

and picking up his gun from the floor. "For now, though, I've got someone to pay back."

As Davin raised up his gun, Ferro stepped into the open doorway again. At the same time, a whoosh from behind signaled the closed door opening. Phyla, looking that way, pulled the trigger. Davin did the same, but realized Ferro was unarmed. Ferro raised his hands. Surrendering. Davin aimed Melody at the man's chest.

"There's nobody there," Phyla said, not looking away from the other door.

"We've got a friend," Davin said. "Should I shoot him?"

Phyla risked a quick glance back, saw Ferro. Saw the man take a slow step forward.

"Don't shoot me," Ferro said, his voice liquid lead. "I'd like to make a trade."

"Stay there and speak," Davin replied.

"There is more behind this conflict than you know," Ferro said, keeping his hands raised. "Framing you was a mistake. A coward's path. But for the lives of my brothers and sisters, I ask that you allow me this."

"No idea what you're talking about."

"You and I, Davin Masters. A duel, like the old ways," Ferro said. "I win, Marl will tell Eden to drop the rest of your crew from the charges. The rest of my men live. Eden Prime continues."

"And if I win, what, we all die?"

"No. You will live. At least for now."

"Sounds like good terms to me," Davin said, setting Melody down. "Let's brawl."

82

OUTCLASSED

The short android hit the ground right in front of Viola's face, fist swinging at her eyes way too fast to dodge. Viola fell back, catching the strike on her chin instead of her face, the blow sending her sprawling on the ground. The android looked at her for a second, eyes scanning up and down her body.

"You're not on the list," the short android said. "Explicitly noted as do not kill. However, be aware that should you engage again, I may render you harmless."

The android turned back to the endless series of sword strikes between Fournine and the tall bot. That was when Puk struck, the little bot spitting its small laser at the android. It burned a hole in the short android's neck, precisely where the neural connection to the android's body should have been.

Only instead of collapsing to the ground in a twitching heap, the short android turned and triggered a shot from a sidearm that appeared in its hand as if by magic. The bolt caught Puk and knocked the sphere to the floor.

Viola lanced another few shots from her squat rifle, but

her aim wasn't anywhere near what it needed to be. The android watched the bolts zip by, then propelled towards Viola with its hand raised. Viola closed her eyes, expecting the hit, only it didn't fall. She heard, then saw Fournine tackling the short android and driving it into the inside wall of the promenade.

Fournine's fists pummeled the short android's desperate defense, punching holes in the plaskin and causing sparks to fly out whenever a good shot hit. But where was the other one?

Viola looked at where the two had been fighting in time to see the tall android pull Fournine's knives from its stomach. Apparently the stabbing missed anything vital, because the android barely paused before taking a running start at the scrambling pair. Viola fired again, the spray glancing around the android. One bolt grazed a shoulder, but the bot didn't break stride.

"Behind!" Viola yelled and Fournine ducked.

The short android followed suit, both of them dropping to the floor as the tall android's swings swept over their heads. Fournine kicked out behind him with his foot, knocking out the tall android's knee. That moment gave the short android an opening, allowing the bot to grab Fournine's neck and slam the android into the ground.

"Get out of here!" Fournine yelled, struggling as both of the other android's pummeled him. "I've got one trick left, and you're not gonna like it!"

Viola didn't hesitate, scooping up Puk and dashing back towards the bay doors. A moment later she heard Fournine's crazed cackle, distorted and rambling up and down pitches as its vocal processing took a punch or two from the androids.

Then Viola flew through the air, bounced off of the floor.

A split second later the rumbling roar of an explosion rolled over her. Looking at the floor, wheezing air through bruised lungs, Viola could only hope things were going better for the captain.

83

DUEL

Davin struck first, launching into a right-handed swing towards Ferro's kneecap. The stocky soldier shifted back and moved down the steps.

"Giving up the high ground?" Davin said. "Dangerous gambit."

"Life is a series of risks," Ferro replied.

"Better hope this one pays off."

Ferro had him on reach and size, but Davin figured he was quicker. And he doubted Ferro could equal his drunken brawling experience. When Davin noticed Ferro crouch, when they were only a couple steps apart, instead of kicking or trying to throw a wild swing, Davin jumped at Ferro in a tackle. He hit the trooper commander in the upper chest, driving both of them down the stairs in the tumble. Davin felt the steps, the railing, Ferro's body bouncing into him as they rolled towards the lobby.

Davin hit the floor first on his back and used the momentum to throw Ferro off of him, the big man rolling a few feet further but coming up on his knees.

"A fun style, but risky," Ferro said. "Do you win many of

these?"

"Not dead yet, am I?"

Now, though, Davin didn't have an obvious trick to pull. At the foot of the stairs, everything was flat. So Davin pulled himself up straight and looked dead at Ferro, who was doing the same. Ferro brushed at his clothes for a second then dashed towards Davin.

A stride away, Ferro stepped into a right-hook. Davin ducked into the swing, using his left shoulder to push Ferro's punch wide. That should've cleared room for a jab into Ferro's stomach, but the big man's left fist hit Davin's side first. Like an exploding bruise, Davin felt his right side crumple with the hit. Taking every ounce of concentration to stay upright, Davin stumbled back and tried to breathe.

"Straightforward," Ferro said, taking another step towards Davin. "No finesse."

Again with the right hook, only this time Davin pivoted to the left, allowing Ferro's swing to go to Davin's right and miss his head by inches. Davin grabbed the arm and pulled forward, sticking his leg out. Ferro went forward and Davin felt the contact, then pushed as Ferro slipped the front part of his right foot beneath Davin's shin.

Ferro, falling, twisted with the motion and yanked his own arm. Davin, still grappled with the limb, fell across Ferro's body and flipped onto the ground. Both of them were lying on the floor, staring at the ceiling.

Davin got up, jumping his feet beneath him, only to fall back again as Ferro whipped his legs around to knock Davin's out from under him. As soon as Davin hit the floor, he rolled. Anything to get space. Ferro had better technique, so Davin had to find another way. Break the rules.

In the hallway to the right of the lobby were the disoriented soldiers Davin knocked out with his shock grenade.

While one was sitting up, the other two were still lying on the floor. Davin broken into a run towards the trio, towards their guns.

"Too scared?" Ferro called. "Running already?"

Davin ignored him, dove for the rifles on the hallway floor. The one sitting guard stared at Davin with little comprehension, shaking his head. Davin grabbed a rifle, turned and pressed his finger to the trigger. Only to see Ferro pull a sidearm from beneath his shirt. The two of them pointed their weapons at each other, only two meters apart. Neither would be likely to miss.

"You can drop it now," Phyla yelled from upstairs.

Ferro glanced in her direction.

"I thought this was a duel?" Ferro said.

"If you think I will risk it all in some showcase of bravado, you're wrong," Davin said. "We have a crew to protect. So talk, or she liquefies you."

Ferro hesitated, then dropped his gun. It hit the floor with a hollow thunk and bounced away.

"If you want to find Marl, she's at the terramorpher," Ferro said. "Waiting for her shuttle to come and carry her away."

"She's running? No faith in your protection?"

"Marl does what she needs to survive," Ferro said. "As we all do."

That was enough. Davin raised the stolen gun, swiped his index finger along the power setting, took a shot and hit Ferro in the knee. The low-powered bolt knocked Ferro into a crouch, but the man didn't make a noise, just looked at Davin hard.

"In the future, let's do this again. Without interruptions," Ferro said as Davin went by him.

"Yeah, I'll put that on my list. Way down at the bottom."

The skiffs, designed for those on-world showcase cruises, were docked nearby. Of the three Eden Prime maintained in the flat expanse used as a docking bay, one was missing. The other two, though, sat on their respective gray landing pads.

"Just waiting for us," Phyla commented as the two of them climbed the boarding stairs.

Because the skiffs were single-deck floating barges, there wasn't a ramp. A ladder, useful in emergencies or unscheduled landings, could be lowered from one of the sides. Otherwise, rolling stairs on the landing pads facilitated on and off-loading. Beyond that, the skiffs consisted of rails, a smattering of benches, and a pilot's console.

The things were so slow, security measures were non-existent. You got in a fight on a skiff, you were going to lose. Unless your opponent was another skiff, in which case Davin figured it would play out like an old pirate movie, both sides banging into each other and taking pot shots until one or the other called it quits.

Phyla triggered the jets, small-scale engines that turned on the movement of air rather than any propellant. The whole concept gave the skiff endless amounts of flight time, but its max speed barely beat out a jog. Not that this was a problem when you were using it to sell a moon. Marl had plenty of time to craft sales pitches, while the company reps could take a view of the place and run numbers to have a decision in hand by the time the skiff landed. They were purposefully boring.

"The computer says it'll take an hour," Phyla said. "These things are so slow."

"And you said you were jealous when I'd escort meetings on these things."

"Yeah, well, not anymore."

84

THE TERRAMORPHER

The machine filled the horizon. A massive metallic line painted over in parts with sold advertising, Eden Prime logos, and marred pieces where an unexpected piece of falling debris tore the color away. A ragged rainbow. Made in pieces on Earth and in space, then sent to Europa in a series of rocket-boosted boxes, contracted engineers and robots assembled the machine into the churning line of planetary remodeling it was now.

"Always forget how big these things are," Phyla said, staring.

"Too impatient to go any smaller," Davin replied.

The terramorpher would not win a race, but it churned over the ice and deposited plants engineered to build an atmosphere, to warm up the moon. To melt that icy surface. Eventually Europa would be a rock ball with oceans, and from there the road to a new paradise wasn't long.

"We've found Merc," Opal's voice came in over the comm. "They had a couple guys watching him. Took one look at Mox and ran. We're on our way back to the ship."

"Viola?" Davin asked. "You take care of those androids yet?"

"Fournine did," Viola replied a second later. "Blew them both up. And itself."

A pause. Viola sounded sad, but the turned bot had done better than it should have. A two for one android trade? He'd take that every time.

"Sorry to hear that," Davin said, unsure what else to say.

"Don't worry about it. I copied Fournine's data while it was turned off. We get a new body, I can bring it back."

"I'll put it on the shopping list," Davin said. "We're on our way to find Marl. Get the cargo hauler ready to go. We might need a pick-up."

Affirmatives were thrown around and a minute later Phyla guided the skiff into the docking bay on the terramorpher. Despite the size of the machine, actual room for people was minimal. The bay had space for two skiffs, one of which was already taken. From there a wide scaffolding stair led up to an observation deck and control panels. Only the bare essentials. Unlike the spectacular exterior, this part was a drab gray. Tourists didn't make it this far, so Eden Prime didn't bother sprucing things up.

Climbing off the skiff, Phyla and Davin drew their weapons again, edging up the stairs with Davin in the lead.

"How much you want to bet Marl's favorite flunky, Castor is here?" Davin said.

"All I've got," Phyla said, double-checking the energy on her rifle. "You know much about him?"

"Only seen him spinning the words to gawking tourists. Our luck, the man's secretly a living weapon whose gonna take us both out before we know what's happening,"

"Seems like a good assumption."

The one landing before the observation deck, a platform

there to give room for a stabilizing steel beam jutting through the terramorpher, held no answers in its empty flatness. Above, the observation deck hid behind the steep stairs and the plated inside of the big machine. The noise here, fifty meters above the ground, sounded like a grumbling stomach tied to an amplifier. Cracking ice.

"Here we go," Davin said, taking a breath and getting ready for a mad dash up the stairs.

He expected an okay from Phyla, a grunt of acknowledgment. What Davin heard instead was a stifled yell and the sound of a body hitting the platform behind him. Davin whirled around, bringing Melody up to fire, and caught Castor's kick in the jaw.

Davin bounced back into the stairs, splaying out against the metal steps, but hung on to the shotgun. Castor, holding his own gun in his left hand, gave Davin a leveling look, then pulled the trigger.

A green bolt lanced out, hit Davin's knee, and spreading around his leg like burning fire. A stun shot, meant to overload the nerves and trigger shock. Davin recognized the sensation—after enough bar fights he was pretty used to it—and swung the shotgun around, firing a round. Castor dove to the side, catching himself on the railing. Phyla brought herself back up to a crouch, reaching for her assault rifle.

"Two on one, Castor," Davin rasped as his left leg fell numb, the burning sensation rising through his stomach and spreading to his right side. "Drop the stunner and we won't kill you."

"You won't kill me anyway," Castor said, rolling to a crouch. "You're not a murderer."

"Then why is your boss claiming we are?"

Davin enunciated the last word with a blast from

Melody. Castor anticipated it again, rolling out of the way, but came up right into a shot from Phyla's assault rifle. The white-hot bolt splashed into Castor's chest and fizzled out, a shower of sparks and then nothing. A personal shield. Damn things were expensive, finicky, and tended to let through the shots you really needed them to stop, but of course this guy had a working one.

Davin, now sitting on the steps and feeling his arm losing its ability to pull the trigger, popped off another round. It was nowhere near accurate, but Castor dove anyway. He was on the far side of the landing now.

Castor raised the stunner and squeezed off a second bolt. The green fire hit Davin in the chest and drove him back against the stairs. While stunners didn't interfere by design with the heart and lungs, Davin couldn't feel anymore if he was breathing or not.

"Leave him alone," Phyla said.

Another white bolt from Phyla's assault rifle hit Castor's shield, breaking apart. Then another, and a third. Phyla pressed harder on the trigger as she walked forward, sending dozens of shots at close range into Castor. He tried to move, tried to roll away, but he was too close.

A few seconds into the barrage, Castor's shield overloaded with a loud bang and the bodyguard took a couple unimpeded shots before Phyla lifted her hand from the trigger. Castor laid on the landing, smoking and curled up on the metal floor.

"Come on," Phyla said, throwing Davin's arm over her shoulders. "Let's pay Marl a visit."

Davin would've nodded, but he seemed to have stopped working. Instead Davin let Phyla drag his numb body up the stairs and onto the open observation deck, where Europa's frozen waters sat front and center.

85

PAIN

The evening blaze of Jupiter splashed through the wide windows of the terramorpher's observation deck. It sat atop the long series of stairs, and Phyla was glad to see it. Davin wasn't exactly a light load. Draped over her shoulder and hanging limp, Phyla checked again to make sure the captain's eyes were still open. They were, and staring at the dark silhouette planted against the light.

"I always knew you were good, Davin, but I never realized just how good," Marl said, not bothering to turn around.

The flat floor of the observation deck ended with the window on one end and, on the sides, railings giving view to the churning inner workings of the terramorpher. Pistons pumped, conveyors shifted materials to chutes that would carry them to deposit points. The mechanical motions would have been hypnotizing in a calmer situation.

"Marl," Phyla said. "It's over. Drop the charges."

Marl glanced back, eyes wide. Not the voice she was expecting. Phyla hadn't met Marl. Only heard the woman over the Jumper's comm every now and again. Seeing Marl now, in similar combat gear to Castor, the woman's backbone was clear. The straight-up shoulders, crossed arms, set mouth. Phyla had seen enough dealers in Vagrant's Hollow to know what someone looked like when they were certain.

"I assume Castor put our friend Davin into his current state?" Marl said.

"It doesn't matter. Just drop the charges so we can leave."

Phyla kept her distance. Wished there was somewhere to put Davin so she could draw her own rifle. Marl had at least one sidearm, and it wouldn't be much fun to dodge fire while still trying to keep the captain on her shoulders.

"I'm sorry that the inspectors contacted you," Marl said. "They were supposed to land and then be taken care of immediately thereafter. That's why I made sure we leaked the second ship, the one that turned its engines on your crew. Only, you weren't supposed to be there."

"Thanks for letting us know," Phyla said. She squatted to slip Davin off of her back, one hand staying on the assault rifle.

"I was trying to spare you."

"You were trying to keep a secret," Phyla replied. Davin hit the floor, crumpled to the ground. Phyla twisted, caught Davin's head before it slammed into the floor.

The sidearm didn't make a sound as it fired. The flash of the laser hit Phyla's eyes at the same time as the burn lashed her side. Pain bloomed and Phyla collapsed next to Davin. Breathing was inhaling fire. White lines played around the outside of her vision, threatening to expand and wipe away the universe in shock. The floor, her left hand touching it, was icy. That chill shoved her back from the edge. Couldn't collapse now. Had to create distance, use the rifle.

Fight back.

"Eden wants someone to take the fall for Clare and

Ward," Marl said. She was walking towards Phyla now, her face haloed by Jupiter through the windows. The sidearm held out in front of her, stiff, as though Marl was conducting a ceremony. "And while I think Eden can rot, while I'm doing all I can to tear it apart, we aren't ready for its focused attention. Not yet."

Phyla used her legs, pressing herself back. The rifle dragged along the floor while her arms were busy pushing. Saw Marl tense. Grabbed the rifle and swung it up in front of her face.

Phyla couldn't see the laser, only the light it cast as the shot burrowed into the rifle. Nothing broke through the rifle's body. Bet its makers didn't think it would serve as a shield. Phyla swung the rifle back towards Marl, pressed the trigger, and the safety light blinked red. Malfunction.

"Almost had me," Marl said, expression easing from stunned panic into an easy smile. "We would have tried to recruit all of you. Too bad."

"Recruit for what?" Phyla had her own sidearm on her left thigh. Marl would kill her if Phyla went for it, but there wasn't any other option.

"It doesn't matter anymore," Marl replied. She raised the sidearm again. No time. Phyla made a reach for her own, the burn in her right side searing.

86

AN END

Marl was only a meter away. About to shoot, body stance like a warrior delivering a summary execution to a bested opponent. Thing was, that attention meant she missed what Davin was doing. How he was struggling to move a hand he couldn't feel to grip the handle of Melody, how he only knew he'd found it in the fog of his perception when his arm didn't lift as easily as it did before.

How he pulled the trigger as soon as the shotgun flopped in front of his own eyes.

Melody wasn't stunned. The shotgun did what it was designed to do. Six balls of glowing green energy exploded out from the weapon and collapsed into Marl, bursting into gouts of flame. Melody's fire spread fast, the heat from each ball meeting the others halfway and igniting Marl's entire uniform.

Causing the head of Eden Prime to turn and backpedal, to hit the edge of the observation deck, to press over the railing and fall like an emerald meteor into the terramorpher's crunching depths.

Would have been nice to sigh right then. To feel the tension leak out of his muscles. To take a deep breath. But Davin was still floating in a half-conscious world where his body gave him no information. Where his lungs kept him breathing through an instinctual response, where his eyes blinked out of habit. The world a movie he was watching from inside his own head.

"Hey," Phyla said, her head appearing in front of his eyes. "Thanks for that."

A pause. A wait for an answer Davin wasn't able to give. He'd have nodded, declared that's what Marl had deserved, but his body wasn't listening.

"Right. I'm going to pick you up again, and we're going to get out of here," Phyla said. "I'm hurt, Davin, so if you can wake yourself up, the sooner the better. Or you will owe me so much for carrying you back to the ship, that—"

Davin was pretty sure Phyla kept talking. That she mixed in a series of curses as they went down the steps and Davin's full weight fell on her. But he couldn't really focus. Couldn't push back against the dead senses any more with the adrenaline dying. Couldn't do anything except greet the black hoping that when he woke up, he'd be somewhere else.

87

A NEW CONTRACT

The blue moon never looked better than when Davin was leaving it behind. Glowing there in the dark field of stars, the edge of Jupiter sneaking into the window as the cargo hauler gathered speed in a gravity slingshot that would put them on target for Ganymede.

Old-style navigation aids like the slingshot were necessary as the hauler didn't have the fuel to brute-force its way through space. The maneuver meant it would take a few days to get around Jupiter's massive size and intersect with Ganymede. There, they'd get their ship back.

"And then where?" Phyla asked, lying on her cot. Erick had her chest all wrapped around with bandages, ointments spread across the section where Marl's shot struck home.

"Not sure yet. But I hear Neptune's beautiful this time of year," Davin said, sitting next to her. "The next wave of androids will have a hard time finding us out there."

Viola had the cockpit, with Opal giving the girl tips on astro-navigation. With the course already pre-programmed, there wasn't a whole lot of trouble they could get into. In fact, for the first time in what felt like months, Davin wasn't afraid something was going to go wrong.

A few hours later, getting ready to catch some much-desired sleep in the cramped crew quarters, Davin heard a buzz on the comm.

"Hey captain," Viola's voice. "Can you come up for a second?"

"Can I take a nap first?"

"Don't think you'll want to do that."

Up in the squat cockpit, where Davin had to duck his head to get to the deeper section with the chairs, Viola had the transmitter on the console. A video screen showing an active call, coming from Miner Prime.

"Mind ducking out for a few minutes?" Davin said to Viola, who squeezed past him with a glance and left the captain alone.

"It was harder to find this address than I thought," said the voice on the other end. "I learned that your ship was on Ganymede, but I couldn't reach you there. Then a friend mentioned your hijacking tendencies. Quite the downgrade."

"We'll have the *Jumper* back soon," Davin replied. The waiting game for transmissions gave Davin a chance to scan back through the headlines. A blip about Eden Prime, a fatal accident involving the base's manager. A second accidental explosion in the base itself, damaging some stores and a hotel. Eden's media team doing their work.

"Marl didn't drop the charges," Bosser's next communication said. "You're all still wanted for murder."

"You killed Lina. I ever see you again, I'll do whatever I can to justify that charge,"

"All of you are wanted, Davin. Your crew that you profess to care about so much. I'm calling to offer a solution." Bosser didn't even flinch in the transmission. Lina's death didn't cause the slightest surprise. No remorse. Davin hadn't realized what it was like to hate someone before this moment. The bubbling anger slicing through self restraint and begging Davin to find away to leap across space, take Bosser, and throw him out an airlock.

But Davin couldn't do that. Going back to Miner Prime wouldn't work either. Bosser would be ready, would drown the *Jumper* in laser fire before the ship could even dock. If the short-term was out of play, there was only one other way to go.

"You'll drop the charge?"

"I'll convince Eden to remove it. Tell them the truth."

"What do you want?" Davin asked, hating every word as it came out of his mouth.

The picture of Bosser's face, set in a grim line, flexed a minute later into a toothy grin as he described what the Wild Nines would need to do to clear their name. As he heard the words, Davin wondered if they were all going to die anyway.

READ on for an excerpt of DARK ICE, the sequel to WILD NINES!

ACKNOWLEDGMENTS

This novel is the product of my family and friends refusing to let a dream die. My wife Nicole, for letting me write in the early mornings and making sure I don't starve. My brothers and parents for their continual comments, support, and enthusiasm.

Evan Aaseng, for being a constant sounding board and reeling me back in whenever my ideas went too far.

And, of course, you, the reader, for giving me a reason to write.

To my mother

DARK ICE

THE WILD NINES - BOOK TWO

PROLOGUE

The face appeared on the screen and Alissa kept herself from flinching. Webs of scars played across the visage. Patches of skin colored the false white of cooked meat. That could have been her. Or worse. Alissa forced a smile.

"It is good to see you happy," the man said. "I feared you'd forgotten how."

"We survive through hope, Bakr. I don't think many would follow me if I showed nothing but sorrow."

Not that sorrow was hard to find. Their ships were near each other, Bakr's frigate and Alissa's luxury liner, swirling in a dead spot in space where the only distinguishing feature was that there was no distinguishing feature. A far cry from Mars' red hills and domed cities. From those crowded halls where arms raised in defiance against the corporations and their wage slavery.

Her sister, Marl, would have been one of those arms. Now she slept forever in Europa's ice.

"So where will we find hope now?" Bakr asked. "We have

no planet. Only scattered remnants for forces. No coin left with which to pay the ones who stay with us."

They had held a third of Mars. The largest spaceport. The Red Voice had been respected. Now, it was only desperate. Alissa pressed her eyes shut for a moment. Desperate also meant dangerous.

"My sister can help us with that last," Alissa replied. "I'll send along the details. It won't be a short trip, but necessary."

"And after?"

"With the coin, we rebuild. Without it ..."

Speaking the words lacerated her. They didn't warrant an end like this, obscured and defeated. The men and women of Mars deserved more than what the corporations deigned to give them. But powerful speeches didn't make fleets, didn't turn the minds of those with their hands on the triggers.

"Then I will secure the coin," Bakr said.

"Please, Bakr. You saved my life once. I need you again."

"You have me."

At the nod from the burned captain, Alissa cut the feed. Sat back on the soft couch in her cabin, surrounded by the remnants of her luxuries. A pair of pictures still hung on the walls, not the usual projections but actual paintings. Landscapes, from Earth. Taken when her family first made its leap to the stars, with Alissa barely born. They had been full of hope then. Of possibility. She needed that now.

1

LEAVING GANYMEDE

The solar system sprawled out on the glass in front of them, planets, space stations, and passing comets spiraling around each other. Davin Masters reached out, pressed his finger on the small shape of Ganymede and traced a line back to Earth. As Davin moved his hand away, the line wavered, shifting as the *Whiskey Jumper*'s computer calculated the time it would take to get there, and the optimal route.

"You think they'd even let us land?" Phyla, her fiery hair pulled into a tight ponytail, said. "I know the readings say we're still good for one G, but I'm not sure."

"Could get sick too," Davin replied. "Bones turn to mush while we're coughing up our lungs."

"You still want to go."

"I hear the beaches are incredible."

Phyla laughed, shook her head. Davin smiled at himself, but the grin faded as he looked at the line, now a solid green tracing an elliptical path from Ganymede to Earth. It would only take a few weeks. Doable with the *Jumper*'s engines. But everything cost coin, and there wasn't any waiting for them there. Especially for people still wanted for murder.

"It's nice, hearing you laugh," Davin said. "Haven't heard that lately."

He hadn't commented on Phyla touching her right side after laughing, a tender acknowledgment of laser burns still painful after Marl shot her on Europa. Shot trying to clear their own names. And the one left who could do that was holding them hostage. Davin had more than a few choice insults ready the next time he saw Bosser, and the punch line would be the business end of his sidearm.

"You haven't been funny," Phyla said, the smile dying on her lips. "Not that anyone could be."

Davin reached back out to the glass, swiped away the path to Earth and drew another. This time farther away from the Sun, out past the large rings of Saturn, past Uranus, to the frozen edge of humanity's expansion. Neptune. The icons showing space stations all but disappeared past Saturn, with only two outposts sitting on Uranus for mining. Neptune itself was beyond the profitable reach of most corporations, a time-sink full of risk due to the planet's high winds and isolation.

"Guessing the beaches won't be quite as inviting out there," Davin said.

"You think they're ready?"

"Don't have a choice," Davin said. "It's leave tomorrow, or he'll send more androids after us."

The captain stood up from the co-pilot's chair.

"And after this?" Phyla asked. "Are we going to do whatever Bosser says forever?"

"If Bosser pays us what he's offering," Davin said, putting a hand on Phyla's shoulder. "The rest of you can go. Set yourselves up however you want."

"And you?"

"He killed Lina," was all Davin said. Was all he needed to say.

VIOLA RETURNS

Y ou realize you nearly die every time you leave, right?"

Puk spoke as it buzzed around Viola's head, stuffed deep inside her bedroom closet. A suitcase, designed for weeks of travel and covered in Galaxy Forge logos, sat spread on the bed. The luggage vacuum-sealed sections to force out all the air and allow for maximum space.

"But I die inside every day I'm here doing nothing!" A sweater muffled Viola's reply.

"That's an exaggeration. Your vitals are actually much more stable here than with the Wild Nines."

"That's not what I meant," Viola said, pulling out of the closet with a clutch of clothes in her arms.

A knock came at the door. Three sharp taps, the signature entry Viola's father used ever since a much younger, half-asleep Viola thought he was intruding and launched a lamp at his face as her dad came through the door. Her father had fought aging to a stalemate, achieving a plastic-like forty year-old face through patchwork treatments. Her mother, and most anyone with the coin, looked the same once they were old enough that their lives were at risk. There was no clearer mark of status.

Viola turned away from her father's stare, focused on folding her clothes. He wasn't going to like her decision, and she didn't want to see the disappointment on his face.

"So you're going," her dad said. It wasn't a question. Puk heard the tone and quietly floated to its charging cradle. Some conversations didn't need a sarcastic bot's input.

"Did you ever really think I'd stay?" Viola said.

"I hoped," the words carried an edge on them, a tint of self-awareness. "I remember what it's like being young, no matter what your mother says. But there's a difference between seeing the solar system and doing it in the company of wanted criminals. Did they even say you could join?"

"I haven't asked them yet," Viola said. "I don't know why Davin would say no."

"Have you thought about how all of them, and I know, because I've run checks on their names—"

"You did what?"

"They're dangerous. It's one thing when they're dropping you off. Another when you're going with them," her dad said this as though he was explaining simple math to her. That digging into the history of the Wild Nines without Viola's, without their consent was perfectly logical. "You know what I found?"

"That they're a bunch of evil, terrible people who'll only get me killed?" Viola walked over to her suitcase and dropped clothes inside, shuffling them into their proper positions. Easier to hide the anger in her eyes with her back turned.

"No. That they're trained, Viola. That they have experience. Most of them were military. What are you doing on that ship besides getting in the way?"

He meant well. Viola knew her dad was just trying to convince her to stay. That he wasn't trying to say she was useless. But all Viola could focus on was the idea that she wasn't good enough. Not worth a spot on the *Jumper*.

"Maybe that's all I'm doing," Viola said slowly, feeling her way through the reply. "Maybe I won't last long. I'll get hurt. Or scared and run. But if I stay here, I'll always wonder. Always regret not even trying. So yeah, I'm going."

As she spoke, Viola looked up from the suitcase and stared straight at her father. Not a flinch in her face. Not a touch of blush. When she'd run from Ganymede before, Viola had done it facing no one. Without having to defend her choice. Saying the reasons gave them new life, and Viola stood straighter, matched her father's look.

Her father took the words in and nodded. Then, before Viola could react, he stepped forward and wrapped her in a tight hug.

"We love you, Viola. Just come back to us," her dad said. "Davin and his group are lucky to have you."

"Sure, now you say it," Viola murmured, but her voice had no edge left.

An hour later, the suitcase rolling along under its own power behind her, Viola walked into the bay dominated by the modular bulk of the *Whiskey Jumper*. The big ship wasn't real aerodynamic, built by attaching different components, like crew bays, the cockpit, and a secondary cargo hold with a medical unit onto the large central cube. In the zero gravity of space, though, that didn't matter.

A ramp extended from the central cargo module, and disappearing up it was the thick, metal-laced legs of Mox. The man, a gigantic ball of muscle, wore an exoskeleton at all times. It gave him more strength, speed, and the choice to wear a laser cannon that spat fire too fast for Viola's eyes to see. Next to Mox, what was Viola going to do here? How could she even compare?

"Hey!" Trina's bright voice came from near the back of the ship, her leaf-green hair poking itself out from behind the engines. "Look who showed up! Come back here!"

Viola looked around, but there wasn't anyone else standing there in the bay, so she walked around the ship to the back, where Trina stood on her tiptoes looking into one of the four, two right and two left, large circular nodules that directed the *Jumper*'s thrust.

"You're taller than me," Trina said. "Can you take a look in here, tell me what you see?"

Viola nodded, moved to where Trina was standing and looked into the deep dark of the nodule. The *Jumper* generated its thrust through ionized gas expelled out through the nodules, which meant small pipes pushed the compressed gas to the open nozzle. Allowed to expand, the gas pushed the ship forward. If the *Jumper* needed more power, a mechanic in the engine room could ignite the gas through a small switch capable of igniting extra tanks, burning the fuel quickly for an extra jolt. Viola's eyes went right to that switch, mostly because sparks were popping off of it like the world's tiniest fireworks show.

"It's the sparker," Viola said.

"Think you can fix it?"

"I think so, yeah,"

"Then show me," Trina said. "This ship could use a back-up mechanic."

The next twenty minutes had Trina tossing one tool after another to Viola, while Puk hovered nearby projecting a bright light on the nodule. For the first time that day, Viola could immerse herself in pure problem-solving. A twist here to unlock the access to the circuit, a pull with the pliers to separate the wires that had tangled themselves, thus keeping the circuit complete and sparks triggering away. It wasn't hard, but when the flits of light stopped popping in her face, Viola couldn't stop herself from grinning.

"You two figure that thing out yet?" Davin's voice came from behind.

"Well, I don't think your ship's going to blow up anymore," Viola replied.

"I would also add that you will now have some redundancy in keeping the *Jumper* repaired," Trina said.

"Great, cause it's time to go," Davin said as Viola put the sparker back together. "Viola, I had Mox put your stuff in the open cabin. Used to be Cadge's, so I'm sorry for anything weird you find in there."

Her suitcase was already on-board? Not even a discussion? Viola turned to ask why, but Davin was already walking back to the front of the ship, Trina following.

"Guess you're in," Puk said.

"Guess so."

3

———

THE DOCTOR

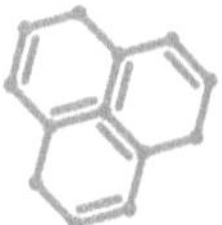

Ion burns scarred black and jagged, spider-webbing slashes hard to coat precisely with ointment. Erick wrapped a bandage around the worker's thigh, the unlucky victim of a misfired engine test. A yellowed synthetic goo seeped out from beneath the wrap, but soaked its way into the worker's skin. Moisturize and numb while nanobots in the mix repaired the worker's nerves.

"It won't ever go away completely," Erick said. "Unless you chop it off and get a new one."

The worker looked confused.

"I mean the leg. Amputate it," Erick tried.

"Amputate?" The worker's voice jumped an octave. "I'm losing my leg?"

"No, that's not what I said," Erick sighed and let his hand hover over the spots where the goo leaked out. The air was markedly cooler above, a sign the goo was doing its job. Pull energy, heat, out of the air around it and use that same energy to repair broken cells, knit skin back together, make scars disappear.

"But you—"

"You'll be fine," Erick interrupted. "Don't put weight on it for the rest of the day. You'll be back at work tomorrow."

"Not even a day off? You sure?" The worker glanced at the bandage, mouth twisting into a frown. "It hurt pretty bad."

"I'm sure it did. Now, off you go," Erick replied, opening the room's door.

The worker, limping, left. A look up at the waiting room camera showed plenty more with similar issues. A massive complex full of people playing with dangerous chemicals and machines will do that. Still, it was better than sitting on the *Jumper*, bored and watching the hours crawl.

A knock, then the door opened. A woman walked in, hair a bright shade of green, grass on a sunny morning

A sunny morning. Where did that come from? It'd been decades since he'd seen one of those, a real dawn over a real meadow. Too long.

"Erick?" Trina asked.

"Hmm?" Erick said, still holding onto that perfect morning.

"What are you doing?"

"Saving the sick and the wounded," Erick blinked himself back to the present. "Yourself?"

"Telling you to get back to the ship. Davin says you're not answering the comm."

"I don't keep it in the room with me. It's distracting."

"From what? My assessment pegs those patients out there as minor. Not a test of skill for you."

"Consider it courtesy, then,"

"I've seen the logs, Erick," Trina tilted her head and stared at him. "Your comm volume on the *Jumper* barely registers. One, maybe two transmissions a day. The rest of us triple that or more."

"Spying on an old man, Trina?"

"Just looking for irregularities. I can't help it."

"I have my reasons. Guess I prefer face to face instead of those pings."

Because those pings carried waves of happiness, guilt, and lost moments all rolled into one. Beamed out from Earth, warm and friendly reminders of the lives he was missing. Daughter, son, grandchildren spinning through birthdays and weddings and births while Erick was out here, gelling workers back together.

"It's hard to explain," Erick continued.

"People say that, but it's inaccurate," Trina replied. "What they really mean is that they don't want to talk about it."

"It's more polite."

"See, you take a machine. Like this one here," Trina moved over to a Vitals, called such because if you stood near one and turned it on, it focused its sensors on you for a few seconds and gave a full readout on your breathing, blood pressure, and heartbeat. "If it's acting funny, I can take it apart. Find out what's broken inside, or where the code is going wrong. You do the same with people, right?"

"More or less."

"Isn't the brain just another collection of parts?" Trina looked at Erick.

"Parts that act contrary to their design, in my experience."

"I'm saying that if you look for the problem, rather than ignoring it, you might find the answer," Trina flashed a grin then, and nodded towards the screen showing the waiting workers. "Also, I stand by what I said before. These are easy patients. Your presence here is unnecessary."

Erick opened his mouth to reply. Trina was right. Decent pay, but these weren't real patients. Following their protocol for every minor accident. A medical review and clearance to head back to work.

"I'm curious, because these injuries are well within the range of most common medical bots," Trina continued.

"It's broken," Erick said. "That's why they asked if I could moonlight while they waited for parts."

"Ah," Trina nodded. "It's not anymore. I fixed it."

"You fixed it."

"Yes. Do you want the short version?"

"I do," Erick kneaded his temples.

"They shipped parts from Miner Prime. Parts they could make right here, instead of waiting. Easy to reconfigure the power coupling from a light transport shuttle to work in a bot." Trina struggled with the words, resisting diving into the specifics. "It took twenty minutes."

"It seems you've rescued me, Trina."

"You can thank me later." Trina glanced at her comm. "This took longer than I expected. We're late."

"Then I suppose we'd better be going," Erick said. "Did Davin say where, this time?"

"Neptune."

"Fascinating."

Erick turned over Trina's comments. Look at the problem. Fix the problem. Everything with her a series of logic chains leading, inevitably, to the correct solution. What would that be for him? To go back to Earth, sit in the shade on a bright day and watch younger generations of himself laugh and jump and play?

The tube-train that took the pair of them back towards

the *Jumper*'s assigned docking bay shot along Ganymede's surface. Looking up through the transparent ceiling, Erick could see the angry tan and red swirls of Jupiter's storms, twisting and churning. Spacecraft cut lines in the view, coming and going from the moon with parts and people from throughout the solar system. It was a wondrous view, amazing. It wasn't enough.

4

———

PRECISE SHOT

"I feel like we deserve a going-away drink, don't you?" Merc said, sitting across from Opal in one of the many happy hour bars neighboring the Galaxy Forge facilities on Ganymede. Clogged with the variety of engineers, mechanics, and test pilots Galaxy Forge employed, the bar buzzed with acronyms and industry slang that made for a nice, unintelligible backdrop. It reminded Opal of the barracks, of the camaraderie in shared adventure.

Merc leaned back in his chair, arms spread over the rests, and gave Opal a toothy grin. His eyes crinkled at the edges. Opal's pulse quickened. Hated that look. Loved that look. Ever since Miner Prime, the stick jockey had been throwing her slick smiles paired with soft asides. Constant risk of death catalyzed their close conversation to something else entirely. Before she knew it, Opal cared about the guy. And here he was, joking about going back into the same fire that'd nearly killed him last time.

"It's still a game to you, isn't it?" Opal replied, leaning forward, elbows on the table. Merc's smile broke.

"You see this?" Merc pulled up his shirt, showing off the

circular scar on his chest from getting shot on Europa. "That's my reminder that it's very real."

The visual brought back that day. Carrying Merc back to the ship. It'd been his breathing that was the worst. The ragged inhales, the coughing exhales. Eyes closed, fighting for his life through instinct.

"I've never been hit," Opal said. "Snipers, we stay out of it."

"Don't change now," Merc replied. "Telling you, it isn't worth it."

"I know, I've seen." Opal looked at her hands. Her fingers twisted through each other. "I don't want to see it again. Especially not you."

"Hey, I took that hit coming to save you," Merc said. "So, you know, stay out of trouble and I'll be good."

Opal felt blood rushing to her face, heat rising from her throat. He was treating this whole thing like a joke. Merc, who'd flown in what was really just an ornamental military role around Earth, acting like there wasn't a price to pay in a life like this. He'd never tasted the red grit of Mars as a sandstorm rolled over you in the middle of a firefight, never watched friends fail to come home, stared at the empty seat on the transport and known if they'd turned left instead of right, there'd still be a person there.

Breathe.

Merc noticed. Opal's pressed lips, so tight they were squeezing the blood out of them, were a clue. The fighter pilot reached out, put his hand on Opal's. She looked at it. His calloused hand, rough from gripping flight sticks. So were her's, only from rifles instead.

"You really afraid something's gonna happen?" Merc asked, the light laughter gone from his voice.

"Just don't die on me."

"I'll be careful, promise."

"Better keep that one," Opal offered a small smile. "And I've changed my mind about that drink."

"Now you're talking," Merc said, keying in the order.

5

BOXER

The ring changed as the crowd moved, their pumping fists and shouting faces forming the walls around Mox and the three off-duty security guards who'd decided to take him on tonight. The *Jupiter's Bastard* had cured Mox's boredom by accepting the metal man into the bar's routine, sloppy fights. Most nights Mox could count on a crew of Galaxy Forge workers looking for something that wasn't in their corporate policy manual: a bit of betting, a bit of blood, and a lot of visceral excitement.

The bar was a lit firework—bright points of color scattered between vast shadows. Except for the ring, where the DJ kept a floating bot covered in lights hovering over the action while swapping frenetic mixes.

The first guard, One, came at Mox straight up, leaning forward and stepping into a big right hook that even the drunks in the audience could see coming. Mox sidestepped to his right, dodging the punch and letting its momentum carry One in between the second guard, Two. Which left Three on Mox's side.

"Hey," Mox said, catching Three's feeble left-handed jab

with his own, then whipping the man to the ground, where he collapsed.

The crowd cheered, a few boos mingled in. The *Bastard*'s bookies shouted new odds. Mox waited for, felt the kick hit the back of his knee. The first guard yelped, and Mox turned around to find the man limping backward. They always forgot about the exoskeleton. Shin on hard, ridged metal wasn't a good move. Two moved up, dropping into a stance Mox didn't recognize. Legs bent, arms at right angles.

"What're you doing?" Mox asked.

"You're about to find out," Two said.

Two moved forward and down simultaneously. Those right angles turned into a series of horizontal jabs, pinging Mox's stomach, kidneys, ribs. Strong hits, too. Mox backpedaled away, raising his arms to block any follow-up. The crowd cheered again. No idea who they were rooting for now. Two didn't press the attack, but settled into a determined frown. Perhaps this one, unlike the others, knew what he was doing.

Not that it would change anything.

Mox pumped his legs, jumping into the air. The DJ swerved the light bot away as Mox arced two meters high and came slamming back, fist first, at Two. The man rolled. Mox's fist met air, but the suit compensated for Two's move, stopped Mox's momentum faster than any person should have been able to. So when Two tried to capitalize, tried to hit Mox with a high kick to the face, the big man already had his arm up to block. Two's leg bounced off of Mox's left hand, which left the guard open for Mox's right to indent Two's abdomen. He crumpled to the floor, groaning.

One, favoring his leg, stared at Mox from the side of the ring and shook his head.

"Yield?" Mox said.

"You're a cheater," One said. "That's what you are."

"Three on one," Mox replied. "More than fair."

The crowd was losing interest. Sensed the match was over. Coin changed hands and the ring fell apart.

"You act all smug just cause you got that metal," One continued. "Take that away, you're nothing."

Mox walked over to One, who stood his ground and looked up at Mox. A mix of fear and defiance in his face. A look Mox figured he once wore himself, before the surgeries, when he was vulnerable. Never again.

"Yield," Mox said.

One's face softened, the anger defeated by the universal desire not to get crunched to pieces. Mox had seen that look before too, on this guard and all the others before him. One thing to talk big, another to back it up.

"Mox!" came a voice from the crowd. Davin's. "What the hell are you doing?"

"Yield," Mox repeated, ignoring the captain.

"Fine, you freak. I yield." One sighed, limping over to his downed partner. The remaining crowd immediately dispersed to collect, or give up, their bets.

Davin pushed his way through, looked at the pair of injured men, then at Mox, who nodded.

"You hurt?" Davin said, and, at Mox's raised eyebrows, held up his hands. "Only asking cause we're getting off this rock, and I prefer my crew in one piece."

"Where?"

"Oh, you're gonna love this one. Neptune."

"Never been," Mox said as one of the *Bastard*'s barmen came over with a coin chit. Davin looked at the value as Mox took it from the barman's hand and whistled.

"Feel like you'd make more doing this than flying with me," Davin said.

"Not as fun," Mox replied as the pair walked out of the bar.

"And you wouldn't have me around to keep things interesting."

Mox laughed.

"Hey!" Mox recognized One's voice and turned. "You ever ditch that skeleton, become a real man, you come back and we'll see who wins!"

"Buddy," Davin cut in before Mox could say anything. "My man Mox here would toast you even if he were naked, drunk, and missing a leg. Trust me."

"Why's he got the suit, then, if he's so good?" the guard asked.

"Because it's cool," Davin said.

Only, that wasn't it. Mox stayed quiet all the way back to the *Jumper*. Stayed quiet as the engines ignited, Trina counting to Phyla when they could lift off. Stayed quiet and watched, from the screen in the kitchen, as Ganymede fell away and Jupiter, giant of the solar system, shrank to show the stars.

6

NEPTUNE

Contrasted with space's absolute black, the Neptune's big blue ball looked like an aqua Sun. Davin, rubbing his eyes at the odd hour when the *Jumper*'s proximity alarm woke him, stared out the cockpit at the distant orb. Distant being relative. Neptune appeared to be within arm's reach, outside the glass. Still thousands, millions of kilometers away, but hey, at least they'd made it to the right neighborhood.

"Where is it?" Davin said, glancing at the blank sensor screen. Neptune's faint rings were appearing on it, motes of dust and ice swirling around. Nothing man-made on the scanners.

"Just about here, if their flight plan is correct," Phyla said. "Based on when they arrived and their targeted orbiting speed, they should come into range in a minute."

Bosser had transmitted the details of the operation. An Eden freighter, *Amerigo*, was out floating around Neptune while a research and mining vessel, *Karat*, plumbed Neptune's depth in search of rare gemstones. An ice diamond. Bosser's info was light on what ice diamonds were, only saying they were valuable. And that Eden had reason to suspect someone might try to take the cargo by force.

"At least there's nobody else here," Davin said, waiting for the freighter to show.

"Did you read Bosser's last paragraph?"

"Get the diamonds first, the crew and freighter second. Yeah, I read it," Davin replied. "Are you really surprised?"

"For once, I'd like to work for someone that has a heart."

"Hey, don't you technically work for me?" Davin asked, glancing at Phyla, an injured expression on his face.

"Like I said—"

The console beeped and on the edge of it a green rectangle popped up. A second later, as the freighter's identification broadcast came in, *Amerigo* appeared over the shape. It was orbiting high around Neptune. This far from the Sun, solar panels gathered a small fraction of their normal energy, so the freighter would have found a holding pattern that minimized power use until the *Karat* finished its mission.

The *Amerigo* itself wasn't the largest freighter Davin had seen, but it wasn't a tiny thing either. A kilometer long, with most of that space kept available for cargo, Eden built the freighter for minimal crew and maximum profit. The *Amerigo* was white, a frigid pallor that made it stand out against Neptune's deep blue backdrop, a spear thrown through the night sky.

"Big ship for small gemstones," Phyla said. "They must think they'll get a huge haul."

"Bosser said the *Karat* was full of new tech, guess they're hoping it pays off. Set course to intercept, and let's start talking," Davin said.

"You want to call, the button's right there."

Davin flicked his finger on the console, dragging the small icon of a phone—something that nobody still had but everyone still understood—over to the *Amerigo* rectangle.

The signal shot over to the freighter. Someone on the bridge was probably panicking at the call light glowing, seeing as they were on the edge of human space. Saturn and its moons held the farthest real settlements, so this was way out there. And compared with the asteroid belt, Neptune wasn't overflowing with raw materials. Not that atmospheric gasses weren't valuable fuel, but why go out here when Jupiter could keep humanity supplied for, well, ever?

"*Jumper*, the *Amerigo* reads you," said a tight, clipped voice cluttered with static. "We heard you were coming our way."

"Took a while. Sorry," Davin replied. "You didn't exactly choose next door."

"You're not the only one wishing we were closer to home."

"Why's that?"

"We'll talk when you dock. Hard to tell who's listening out here."

The console beeped as a docking route came in from the freighter, a translucent line arcing away from the *Jumper* towards Neptune. It would intersect in a few hours with the freighter, the *Jumper* slotting into the *Amerigo's* main bay without Phyla even having to touch the controls.

"Aren't they a little paranoid?" Phyla said after the freighter cut communications a moment later. "Who else is going to be listening?"

"How that guy sounded, it's like they already know," Davin sat back in the soft leather chair, looked out at the deep blue planet, and waited for everything to fall apart.

7

HOTSHOT

The Viper looked spicy. Viola pulled herself away from the wingtip she'd been detailing. With Trina declaring they'd both go insane without work during the long trip to Neptune, it'd been one day of dismantling after another. Until they looked up and realized the *Jumper* was nearly there, and then it was all about putting the *Jumper*'s guts back where they belonged. The Viper was the last piece, the small fighter a nest of wings, laser cannons, and engines. The solo cockpit occupied at the moment by its pilot, Merc, running preflight checks.

Davin had called a moment ago, said they were closing on the freighter and wanted the Viper ready. Insurance in case something turned nasty. So Viola carried in the last few pieces of plating, Opal manned the batteries, and Merc ran system checks to find the greens. Watching those two during the weeks of travel out here, the stick jockey and the sniper, never failed to make Viola laugh. Merc ran his mouth, spilling one ridiculous story after another over meals of powdered goo, while Opal sat there shaking her head, ready to jump in with the real events.

Viola stayed quiet at those dinners, stayed quiet most of the time. What was she going to contribute to the stories, the relived memories of firefights and frantic flights? An anecdote about a frustrating project? An unfair professor or one of the endless visits to another corner of her father's factories?

"Docking procedures initiated," Phyla's voice came over the *Jumper*'s intercom. "Hope you're ready to make some new friends."

"C'mon," Opal said to Viola. "He'll tell us if there's anything wrong with the fighter. We have to make sure our 'new friends' aren't the opposite."

"What?" Viola asked as she followed Opal back through to the crew quarters.

"You used a rifle back on Europa, right?" Opal was saying.

"Technically, yes," Viola replied. "I don't think I hit anything, though."

"Doesn't matter. Just look dangerous," Opal ducked into her room, popped open the large floor to ceiling two-meter locker that hugged the far wall, and handed a stocky weapon to Viola. It had a bulbous top that ran to a nozzle, with long handles at the back and front, a trigger right near her rear finger.

"Picked that one up while we were on Ganymede," Opal said. "Your dad's company makes some weird weapons."

"They don't make weapons," Viola said. Because Galaxy Forge was a mining company, a materials provider. No way were they in the military business.

"Sure they don't," Opal said, soaking the words with so much sarcasm that Viola flinched. "This one was originally for mining work, to clean off crumbly rock. But you shorten the barrel like this, make the mixing chambers compressed so the reaction is quicker, you've got something deadly that'll go right through energy shields."

Viola heard what Opal was saying. Galaxy Forge adapted its technology to whatever profitable ends it could. Viola should have felt angry, frustrated that the noble company her family ran had a stained side. Instead, she gripped the weapon. Reality had been breaking so many of her convictions, one more barely tasted bitter.

"Whatever you do, don't point that thing at me," Puk said as Viola, back in her room, put on a less-dirty set of clothes. Something that wasn't so covered in the Viper's oils and grime.

"I could use target practice . . ." Viola replied.

"You might get some," Puk beeped.

"What does that mean?"

"I've been scanning the radio frequencies," Puk said. "Standard Eden protocols for a mission like this suggest the two ships should be in constant communication, updating each other on progress, plans, and so on. Since we've been in system, there hasn't been a peep. Radio silence."

"Maybe it's direct, tight-beam."

"But why? There's nobody else here. Sending a direct communication means hitting the ship directly. Much easier to blast it out on a standard channel. It's what they're for."

"You and your logic," Viola said, but the bot had a point. "Keep listening and let me know if you hear anything."

"You got it, Viola."

In the *Jumper*'s main hold, Viola and Opal joined Davin and Mox around the ramp. Trina and Erick were manning the *Jumper*'s twin turrets in case the whole thing turned out to be an ambush. Merc in the Viper, ready to flip itself around and blow a path through the *Amerigo* from the inside out. When the *Jumper* settled into the freighter's docking bay, part of Viola almost hoped for an angry greeting, just so she could see what would happen. Davin glanced at her then, as though he could hear her thoughts, and Viola felt herself blush.

"Just let me do the talking," Davin said to her.

"Yep," Viola said, lowering her eyes. Dammit. Here she was trying to keep cool, be a professional, and she goes with *yep*.

The ramp lowered quickly, a pop as the plating disengaged and then a steady hiss as gas propelled the ramp downward. Davin was the first one on it, holding his hand for everyone else to stay back.

"Your captain has a death wish, doesn't he?" Puk said, hovering behind Viola. "You've got Mox standing right there, guy could take a dozen shots without getting hurt, and you don't let him go first?"

"Shut it," Viola muttered.

Then Davin was waving them forward. Viola took third, Opal shifting, with her long and thin sniper, to aim past them. She needn't have bothered. The only people in the bay were a few haggard crew, and one wearing the cream-colored uniform of the ship's captain. None of them armed. The captain, a man whose cratered face told tale after tale of trouble, watched the Nines walk the ramp in silence.

"Davin Masters," Davin said, extending his hand. "We're the Wild Nines. What can we do for you?"

"Captain Gage Marcosi," the older man said, grasping Davin's offered palm. "And you can get my ship back."

8

PICKING THE CREW

The *Karat* blurred in the middle of a storm of blue static. They gathered in the *Amerigo*'s sole meeting space, a square room dominated by a central table and a wall-conquering screen. Traces of food, the same powdery stuff they had on the *Jumper*, said the room served as the cafeteria in more crowded times. The Nines crew, their weapons on the table in front or holstered at their sides, and the freighter's captain were sitting, staring at the *Karat*.

"We can't get a better picture. The winds are too strong, and she's been sitting in that storm ever since," Gage said.

"Ever since?" Phyla asked.

"We sent her down," Gage replied. "Made it to the objective, reports were solid. Ice diamonds were getting captured. Until she got quiet. Then that storm moved in and the *Karat* released its tether. The last few days its just been blowing along with the wind."

"Sounds like a rough ride," Merc said.

"How come it hasn't broken up?" Opal asked.

"Design," the captain said. "The *Karat*'s a miracle. It can take those thousand kilometer an hour winds and let them glide right around it. Partly why Eden's going through all the trouble with you. A normal ship that size wouldn't be worth trying to save in this situation, but the *Karat*'s something special."

"What situation?" Davin said.

"You notice there's nobody else in this room besides your crew and I?"

Davin hadn't. But, looking around, he saw the doors were shut. The only people his own.

"I can't trust them," the captain continued. "Because some of them took the *Karat*. And I don't know who here, if anyone, is still with us."

There was a second of silence as this sunk in, followed by a series of rapid weapon checks. Davin understood now why the captain hadn't asked them to leave their guns on the *Jumper*. They could be ambushed at any moment. Which meant...

"Erick, Trina, you read?" Davin spoke into his comm.

"Here," the physician's voice came through clear.

"Seal the ship," Davin said. "Not everyone around here's a friend. They're not necessarily enemies either, but until we know who is what, I don't want anyone thinking they've got free access to the *Jumper*."

"Just when I was going for a walk..." Erick said.

"Not this time." Davin cut the call.

"Captain," Viola asked. "Are you sure this room is safe?"

"You mean, is someone listening to us?" Gage leaned back in his chair and looked towards the ceiling. "If the enemy cared enough, perhaps. You're sitting on a cargo freighter, miss. There's little need for surveillance here. So they would have had to install devices on their own."

"Take no chances," Mox said.

"But I will ask that you take one," Gage replied. "We need the *Karat* back, and we have to do it fast. If someone here tells that ship you're on your way, the *Karat* can, and will, run."

"What's your plan?" Merc said. "So far, all I've heard is that you couldn't keep your own crew from turning traitor and now we're caught up in it."

"You're being paid to get Eden out of this mess," Gage gave Merc a level stare. "We have a utility shuttle on board. Meant to get crew to and from the *Karat*. You'll use that to go to Neptune, land on the *Karat*, and take her back."

"I thought you said those winds were over a thousand kilometers an hour down there?" Phyla said. "There's no way a standard shuttle can handle that."

"The winds flow in bands. A good pilot can get around them. I assume one of you is capable enough?"

"We can handle it," Davin said. "How many can we take?"

Gage pressed a button on his comm and the feed on the screen changed to a crisp, clear image of the wedge-shaped shuttle. "It'll only hold five people. Four if any of them are you."

The captain turned to Mox as he spoke.

"So we're splitting up," Davin said. "One team goes on a rescue mission, the rest stay here and play guess the traitor?"

Gage nodded. He wasn't trying to hide the situation. Davin had to give him that much.

"Mox, Phyla, Opal and I will go to Neptune," Davin started.

"I can't," Phyla cut in.

"What? Who's going to pilot the shuttle?"

"Who's going to pilot the *Jumper*?" Phyla replied. "Merc

has to stay too. The *Karat*'s been sitting in that wind storm. Why aren't they running? Because they have to have help coming. We'll have to deal with that."

"I can fly it," Viola said. "The shuttle, I mean. I've flown my dad's ships before."

"The kid's got talent," Merc added. "We've tangoed in the sims."

Davin looked at Viola, trying to get a measure. He knew she was barely in her twenties, barely used to space, and now he would trust her to fly them into Neptune's raging storms?

"You think you're ready for this?" Davin asked. "Cause now's your chance. You can't say no down there, when we're depending on you."

Could call that cruel, putting the spotlight on Viola. But better to test her mettle now, up here, than find out she wasn't ready when things went sideways.

"I'm ready," Viola said, matching Davin's look with a straight-stare of her own.

"Fine," Davin nodded. "Mox, Viola, Opal and I are going down. The rest of you, try to get this freighter as laser-proof as it can be."

As they walked back to the *Jumper* to gear up, Davin didn't hear any grumbling. No talk about how scared anyone was, how dangerous it would be. How he'd lucked into a crew like this, Davin didn't know, but he sure as hell was grateful.

9
____

SPLIT

Back on the *Jumper*, Davin threw on his gear. A pair of holstered sidearms, ready to spit stunning or deadly lasers as the situation demanded, a beat-up, thick gray jacket to take the sting out of return fire. Pants with loops and pockets to hold the variety of tools and first aid Davin carried whenever he went on a ground mission. And Melody, a fireball shotgun, designed to launch orbs of heat to immolate targets.

All the weapons on the *Jumper* relied on energy, plasma, fire, the things that could be absorbed by the ship's walls without blowing a hole through to space on a missed shot. Too many stories of idiots with bullets blasting their way to vacuum.

"Looking loaded," Phyla said as Davin's door opened.

"Ever knock?" Davin said to Phyla, who came in and leaned against the wall, watching him.

"With you? Never," Phyla said. "You think this is a good idea?"

"You talking about my outfit, or the mission?"

"Either, really," But Phyla wasn't smiling.

"No, I don't want to split the team. But I don't see a way around it."

"Last time we were in this spot, about to invade Europa, I tried to talk you out of running," Phyla said. "But that was for us. To clear *our* names. This is just a job."

"A good paying one," Davin said. "Which we could use."

"I'm just saying that if you pull us apart, and everything goes to hell, then I won't be able to help you."

"You're saying I'm the one that'll need help?"

"Yes."

Davin noticed they were both of them were standing in the center of the small quarters. Which, wow, did this room ever feel tiny. As though the both of them took up the entire space. Everywhere he looked, Phyla was there. He could hear her breathing, and his heart pulsed.

Davin blinked. Pull yourself together, man.

"Look, it won't be long. We'll be back and heading home before you know it," Davin said.

"Where is home to you?" Phyla said, and when Davin didn't answer right away, continued. "Because to me it's here on this ship, with Mox, and Trina, and Merc, Opal, Erick, Viola and you."

"Then don't let anything happen to it while I'm gone."

Phyla reached out, grabbed Davin's forearm.

"I'm not kidding," Phyla said. "I don't want to lose this for some stupid coin."

"Me either," Davin replied, his tongue feeling heavy in his mouth, like forming words in water. Phyla's hand on his arm a light touch, with tenderness lacking from all the times they'd hauled each other out of harm's way. Davin glanced at that hand, tight from weeks in the dry confines of space, but strong. "Keep her safe. Keep them safe."

Phyla took a breath, nodded, and pulled her hand away.

With her touch fading, Davin felt the atmosphere changing. The pressure receding, and suddenly he was looking at Phyla's half-cocked smile.

"I already told Mox he'd better get you all back alive," Phyla said. "And he promised."

"Well, now I feel better."

"Don't make it hard for him to keep it," Phyla said, turning and walking out the door.

Davin watched the space where she stood, then shook his head. The last thing he needed right now, before he sped into the depths of the blue planet, was emotion cluttering his mind. Turning to the bed, he picked up Melody, threw the strap over his shoulder, and left. The door hid his room with a hiss and click. Davin wondered if he'd ever see it again.

10

DESCENT

The shuttle was an oval with wings that could fold out from the top. Viola stopped, bumped by Davin walking behind. She recognized the shuttle's model, an older Galaxy Forge variant. Knocked out of production when liquid fuels were phased out, explosive tendencies not being ideal for space travel. Flying this would be a walk back through time, to when she was a kid watching bright pillars of flame roar across the sky as ships blasted off of Ganymede. Now, there weren't loud explosions. No plumes of smoke and flame. Just the silent, massive thrust of electricity.

It sat in a secondary bay so cluttered with supplies, tubes going to and from fuel tanks, and crates with labels like *Food—Last*, indicating when it should be eaten, that Viola watched her feet for fear of tripping. Gage, claiming to passing crew he was seeing the Nines off in person, led the group through the mess to the shuttle. As they stepped in front of it, the captain tapped a code into a small panel on the side of the shuttle and a door opened next to it, shooting up and allowing a set of stairs to flop to the bay floor.

"I'm guessing Eden's budget doesn't go to their shuttles," Davin said.

"I've kept her intentionally. She's reliable. Well-made," Gage replied. "Time the winds and you'll do fine."

"Easy for you to say up here," Opal chimed in. The sniper had been throwing hard stares at everyone after Davin called the split. Viola kept expecting Opal to talk it out, to argue, but she never did. Viola knew Opal had been military, maybe she was used to orders she didn't like.

"As Davin said before, this is only a contract. You don't have to go. But if you don't, any loyal crew members down there will die. And when they come for the *Amerigo*, we will likely die as well," Gage said.

"Not helping," Mox grumbled.

"It's not our fault you can't trust your crew," Davin added. "But we're going. Viola, get in there and see if you can fly this thing."

With Puk buzzing behind her, Viola climbed up the stairs and into the cramped shuttle. The inside was spare, a functional blandness. Every corner marked with a sign showing its purpose and the nearest possible exit, of which there were four. Two of those, however, involved popping off sections of the front and rear, ruining the craft. The third was a small portal out of the roof that was likewise unusable while the shuttle's wings were extended. Arrayed around the interior, hanging behind four fixed chairs and a table that could be a bed for medical procedures, were slim suits for space-walks or zero-G escapes.

"Cozy," Puk buzzed

"Makes the *Jumper* look like luxury," Viola replied.

To the right was the cockpit, the left held a small passage to the engines for maintenance. There were two seats, padded in black and sturdy, filling the cockpit. The screen was a far fling from the *Jumper*'s consoles and projection-based cockpit glass. The shuttle had a single monitor in a three-section terminal, otherwise covered in a forest of analog switches and dials. Viola hadn't ever seen a setup this outdated. Everything she'd been in used context-based screens to show the controls that mattered in the moment. On newer ships, only in manual override would the screens slide up and the ugly innards become usable.

"This looks like it'll be a challenge," Viola muttered.

"But you can fly it?" Davin said from behind her, looking past her at the array.

"Technically, I think so," Viola said, settling into the pilot's chair and gazing over the controls. "So long as we don't try to do anything too fancy."

"That's the idea," Davin said, then he stepped out to help Mox and Opal load.

"Feel like that's never how it goes with this group," Puk said.

"Maybe this one time we'll catch a break," Viola replied.

Another ten minutes of frantic learning passed while the other Nines fueled the shuttle, loaded their gear, and opened the bay door. A few of the *Amerigo*'s crew made an appearance, moving through the bay and shifting cargo out of the way. Wouldn't be a good thing if the shuttle's engines ignited something on the way out.

Viola dialed up the flight computer and zeroed in on the *Karat*. The *Amerigo*'s more powerful sensors fed data into the shuttle's computer, so it wasn't hard to see where the *Karat* was and where it would be. Assuming the *Karat* didn't try to run, they should be able to find an intercept course that would . . .

But those winds. Neptune wasn't resting easy right now. If the *Amerigo*'s weather data was correct, several huge storms were swirling around the *Karat*. Winds in the hundreds and hundreds of kilometers per hour. Take this flimsy shuttle into any of them and it would spin around and fly apart. Viola looked closer at the directions of the storms. They formed a lopsided triangle, with the *Karat* stuck on the inner edge of the leading storm. Only, that leading one was moving fast, and the storm behind it was drifting. There was a window forming. The console projected the opening would last a few hours. Enough time to dock, take back the *Karat* and blast out of there.

"We have a shot," Viola announced over the shuttle's comm. "But we have to leave now."

"Then let's go," Davin replied, squeezing into the cockpit's second chair. "Opal and Mox are ready. And I'd rather not give any lingering traitors a chance to mess with our trip."

"Okay, hold on," Viola said, punching the ignition sequence. The shuttle jerked as its small landing jets shot to life, lifting the oval craft a meter up. Viola gripped the flight stick, not a sturdy dual-handed grip_but a single shaft like the ones in fighters. A gentle push to the left and the shuttle turned in the bay, spinning around until the open doors and the blue vastness of Neptune sat in front. With her left hand, Viola pushed up on the sliding bar that controlled the throttle. The main engines crackled to life, but at such low power that Viola hoped any remaining crew weren't torched.

The shuttle eased its way forward, past the junk, under the bay doors, and then out. Free of the freighter and floating through space. Immediately, as they left the freighter's artificial gravity, Viola's stomach performed flip flops. The shuttle maintained the smallest amount of stabilization, enough to keep Viola from floating away if she had to walk around, but so light it still felt like she could flutter away with the slightest breeze.

The monitor beeped at her, stating that Viola had to correct her course or she'd miss the intercept.

"Stay focused, kid," Davin said. "I know it's pretty, but we can appreciate the view on the way home."

"Sorry," Viola replied.

"No apologies. Let's just get it done."

Viola set herself. Davin was right. This wasn't a simulator, wasn't the landing on Europa, when the autopilot and the android, Fournine, handled most of the flying. Viola eased back on the stick and the shuttle settled itself into an entry vector that wouldn't skip it off the atmosphere or turn the craft into an exploding fireball. She activated the shields. Time to intercept with the *Karat*: thirty minutes.

"We're about to go blind," Viola said as the cockpit's heat shield slid over the glass. For the next few minutes, the shuttle followed the programmed path to the *Karat* while the reentry friction burned outside.

"Been a while since I've been in the oven," Davin said, keeping his eyes on the meters showing external temp, wind resistance, and more signs that could spell destruction for their craft. "Don't land the *Jumper* in real atmosphere much."

"I've never done it," Viola admitted. Europa and Ganymede had such light atmospheres they barely made an impact. They were like falling through air, Neptune would be more like diving into the ocean.

"Now you know how exciting it is," Davin said. "You two all right back there?"

"Mox is regretting ever getting in this hellbox, and so am I," Opal yelled back.

"Hey, give our pilot some encouragement," Davin replied.

"You're great, Viola, but the heat shielding could use work. We're melting back here!"

Viola glanced at the readouts and noticed the temp inside the shuttle had risen to over thirty eight degrees Celsius, but was tapering off. She hadn't even felt the sweat forming on her forehead, the little beads dribbling down the sides of her neck. Too zoned in.

The central console beeped, showing external temps were lowering as their airspeed reduced and they hit the colder sections of Neptune's atmosphere. Viola retracted the heat shielding and felt the shuttle's temp drop. It went from relief, to refreshing, to making that sweat so, so cold. Viola shivered as the shuttle warmed itself back up, stabilizing at a cool middle.

Out in front, Viola had her first real look at Neptune. Or, really, the endless blue-gray fog encompassing the planet. She felt a drag in her legs, and Viola's heart sped up, her lungs breathed faster.

"Neptune's about like Earth in gravity," Puk said. "That's why your vitals are swinging. You should be okay, but it's going to be tiring for a while."

"Just means you have to work out more," Davin said.

"You're one to talk, captain," Puk said, buzzing over to him and focusing its camera on Davin's face. "Her heart rate's lower than your's."

"I'm just excited at the thought of smashing you into a thousand pieces."

Viola nudged the flight stick to shallow out the descent. The wind resistance was bringing their speed to a point where they should be able to glide their way to the *Karat*.

The more fuel saved, the less likely they'd have to rely on the *Karat* to get them out of here.

"I can tell when I'm not wanted," Puk said, floating through the door towards Opal and Mox.

"Does your bot hold a grudge?" Davin asked.

"Puk? Nah. At least, I didn't program it to seek revenge," Viola said. "But I suppose that—"

"Hey, focus. What's that dark smear up there?"

Davin pointed straight ahead, where a big puffy smudge was growing to fill the distance and dominate the cockpit's view. Flashes popped inside—lightning. Still distant, Viola felt the flight stick pull towards the storm. The wind was getting faster, swirling around the weather and trying to drag the shuttle with it.

"It's the first of the three storms," Viola said. "If we can loop around this one, we should hit the *Karat* before passing by the next two."

"Probably want to start looping, then."

Right. Viola glanced at the console, but the computer wasn't taking the storm into account, plunging them straight through on their rendezvous route with the *Karat*. Suppose it was wishful thinking to hope the shuttle had any real weather guidance plugged in.

"I'm going to have to go manual to get around it," Viola said.

"Let me know what you need," Davin replied.

That confidence helped. Viola located the auto-pilot and flicked off the route option. The computer would still try to keep the shuttle stabilized, but wouldn't force it along their path anymore. Viola kept an eye on their airspeed while moving the stick to the right, slanting the shuttle away from the storm. The force of Neptune's speeding air pressed hard against the shuttle, causing airspeed to plummet and Davin to issue a stream of curses.

Viola swung the flight stick back the other way and the shuttle caught the wind on its wings like a bird and floated. Only, they were back heading straight into the storm.

"To go against the wind, we'll have to burn all the fuel," Viola said. "But if we go with it, we'll hit the storm."

"How about if we swing around it?" Davin said. "Aim for the left edge. Ride the current. Use the momentum to swing to the *Karat*."

Viola looked at the approaching mass, like a raging nightclub in the air, the strobe effect a series of million-degree lightning bolts zapping between clouds of gas. What Davin wanted would have been tricky in space, with only the physics to calculate. Here, with swirling winds changing speed and direction from one second to the next, working around the edge would be as likely to send them to the middle of the storm as it would be to get them around. But the alternative was to take the long way, burn up fuel fighting Neptune and potentially leaving them plummeting to the gaseous depths as their tanks wound up empty.

"If you have a god to pray to, nows the time," Viola said, angling the ship to start Davin's swing.

11

NEWCOMERS

"Captain Gage," Phyla said, standing on the bridge next to the man. Merc, Erick and Trina were back on the *Jumper*, keeping it safe from any potential saboteurs. "I don't understand. If you don't trust your crew, why aren't you doing anything about it?"

They'd been tracking the shuttle's descent into Neptune's atmosphere. The bridge divided into halves, with a central walkway leading between six consoles, broken into sets of two. Spread out in front of the large forward-facing window was the bulk of the *Amerigo*, a great white scar in black space. Gage explained that the color choice eased problem identification. A rift in the pearly painted hull would stand out much over one in a darker hue.

One other crew member was on the bridge, who hadn't said a word. Compared to Gage's Eden uniform, the man wore a strange outfit bearing Eden's corporate branding. A thick shirt, long-sleeved, that bled into gloves that went up to his elbows. It would have been ridiculous on anyone less serious. Put him and Mox together, and Phyla wouldn't know who'd out stone-face the other.

"Because nobody, outside of yourself and Quinn, knows I'm looking for traitors. There hasn't been an armed mutiny yet, and I have no desire to start one."

"But it will happen eventually," Phyla countered.

"Anyone planning on turning this ship will do so for the money in our cargo," Gage said, following the shuttle's blip on the command console. "If your man Davin does his job and gets the *Karat* back, and they see we're no longer defenseless, the plot might end there."

"So they would stay hidden. You would never know."

"But we would be alive."

Phyla took the statement and chewed on it. Leaving unknown knives to stab you in the back was a poor plan, but was it worth the danger to chase them out now?

"All of them, Captain," Phyla said. "I would risk everyone to find the traitor. Because if they've taken a bribe once, they'll do it again and next time might be worse."

Now it was Gage's turn to chew.

"Perhaps, being older, I treat life with more caution than you. The years give me more memories to lose, more people to care for," Gage said. "Though I see your point. There are eight crew members left on board this ship. The minimum to keep it running while the *Karat* took the rest. If you want to test their loyalties, take Quinn with you and go."

"And you?"

The console next to Gage beeped, a middle-tone that attracted attention, but softer than a danger alert.

"Do you see that?" Gage pointed to a small white arrow in the top right corner of the console. Representing the area around the ship, the small arrow was at the edge of sensor range, far out beyond Neptune. Compared to the *Amerigo*, the blip was a tiny fraction. Smaller than the *Jumper*. That meant limited supplies, fuel. Unlikely to be this far out alone.

"A scout," Phyla murmured. The bleeding edge of a force sent just far enough ahead to make sure the whole group wasn't speeding right into a trap. Once it communicated an all-clear, it wouldn't be long before the rest arrived.

"If there is a traitor still on this ship," Gage said. "He'll be acting soon. Good hunting."

Phyla nodded and walked towards the bridge exit. As she approached, Quinn stepped over in front of her. His face was a granite mask, gray eyes looking at her without inflection. As though she was a blank wall. Or nothing at all. The bodyguard didn't appear to carry a weapon, but those gauntlets were thick, with plenty of padding. Room to hide something.

"Where to first?" Phyla asked him.

"They'll be scattered," Quinn's voice had the scratchy rasp of someone who didn't talk much. "Gage is going to sound the alarm in a second, sending each one to their positions. We'll hit each one, confirm intentions, and then move on to the next."

Phyla blinked. She'd expected Quinn to be a mute enforcer, barely more than a smashing post capable of muttering a few words. A second later, as Quinn moved towards the exit, an alarm sounded on the bridge and, presumably, through the freighter.

"You sound like you've done this before," Phyla said.

"Everybody has their price," Quinn replied as they moved. "My job is to make the cost too high."

"Is that the line you give to everyone you meet?"

Quinn's mouth twitched. A rebellious upturn quickly crushed back into the straight-line mask. So Quinn had a personality.

"If we were meeting under better circumstances, you might even get to see me laugh," Quinn looked back at Gage, who was watching them, and nodded. "Now, though, we have other things to do."

"Forces have arrived in the system," Gage's voice came over hidden speakers. "I have every reason to believe they are hostile. Please head to your designated stations and report in when you've arrived."

Quinn walked out of the bridge and Phyla followed, leaving Captain Gage alone with the consoles, the noise from their alarms filling Phyla's ears until the bridge door shut them into silence.

12

GO TIME

The alarm rang throughout the *Jumper*'s bay, a crash of the worst cymbals known to man. Merc jumped a meter, nearly smashing his head on the cockpit's ceiling. He was playing spy, watching the cameras around the *Jumper*'s exterior to keep an eye out for any of the freighter's crew that got a little too close. As the last pilot on the ship, he had to be in the cockpit anyway. Erick and Trina couldn't fly this thing.

"Merc, prep the Viper," Phyla's voice came over the comm.

"You're coming back?" Merc replied.

"Can't. Have to see about a traitor."

"Then who's flying the *Jumper*?"

"Up to you to make sure we don't have to."

"You realize I've got one fighter, right?" Merc said. "Now, I'm good. I'm real good. But without any support out there . . ."

"If you don't, they'll hit us before we're ready. And then we all die."

"Or you could come to the *Jumper* and we get out of here."

Even as Merc said the words, he knew they were pointless. If they left the *Amerigo*, then Davin and the others would have nowhere to come back to. They'd be easy pickings returning from Neptune's atmosphere. It was this, or nothing.

"Merc?"

"I'll do what I can," The pilot said, getting out of the seat and heading through the *Jumper* towards the Viper's bay. Along the way, Merc commed Trina to come ready the fighter, told Erick to hit the cockpit, and swung by his room to grab his flight suit. The suit was a crimson red, the same shade as the decal for Merc's former squad. The fabric tightened by design as Merc put it on, becoming a second skin. Meant to help keep warmth in and reduce the possibilities of an accidental snag in the event of an ejection or spacewalk.

The attached mask had already saved Merc's life in the space above Europa, capable of slipping on and establishing a vacuum seal in a second if Merc hit the emergency pad below the wrist of either hand. It could buy him a few minutes of life out there. Not that Merc ever wanted to experience that again. Reconciling yourself with death once was enough, thanks.

Trina had the Viper warming up by the time Merc hit the bay, the batteries charged and ready to go. The mechanic was watching the system readouts on her comm as Merc went past her and climbed the short ladder into the Viper's cockpit.

"What do we have?" Merc commed Erick.

"Let's see," the physician answered. "Looks like you have

one long range scout vessel, a larger ship that looks very familiar, and a pair of escort fighters."

"Very familiar?"

"If I'm reading this right, it appears to be the same frigate that caught us outside of Europa."

"What's it doing here?" Merc said, settling into the seat.

"Would you like me to ask it?"

"Yeah, if you wouldn't mind," Merc said as the Viper's systems came back showing greens. "How long do I have?"

"Depends. You sit here and wait for them to shoot, looks like you have an hour. You want to go out and tango, well, you might catch them facing the wrong way."

Any ship speeding to another planet needed to slow itself down as it came near orbit. Sensors wouldn't be able to pick up a target till the ship was close, relatively speaking, which meant these raiding bastards would have to take a few minutes to re-orient and settle into an attack pattern. With a good burst from the engines, Merc could get the Viper close before they finished. He'd buy a few precious seconds of surprise.

Merc tapped a button on the Viper's sole console, a piece of screen as large as his spread palm. The Viper's three lift jets, one in the nose and a pair back by the engines, bumped the fighter off of the *Jumper*'s floor. Merc moved the flight stick to the right and the fighter rotated, tilting with the motion. The freighter used a lot of power to generate one G, the same as Earth's gravity. The fighter turned with resistance. Not quite the whipping wildness of weightless flight.

Trina opened the *Jumper*'s door for him, and Merc boosted the fighter out into the larger freighter bay. While the *Jumper* could hold a magnetic shield up for small windows to launch and land the fighter, the freighter only bothered to close its bay doors in emergencies. As a result, when Merc turned the Viper towards space, the black was haloed by the *Amerigo*'s walls like a square eclipse.

Another tap of the console and the batteries shifted their thrust to the main engines, pushing the Viper forward. About to dive into combat against overwhelming forces. Opal, meanwhile, was crashing through thick atmosphere in a rickety old shuttle. Who had the worse luck?

"Focus on the now, buddy," Merc whispered to himself. "That's what she'd be telling you, anyway."

He glanced at the scanner, even though Merc knew Opal and their shuttle wouldn't be on it. Too hidden by Neptune's roiling atmosphere. What was arrayed on the screen, though, in small and large triangles, were the targets.

The Viper lurched leaving the *Amerigo*'s gravity, as though ropes tying it down were cast off. Merc took the cue and punched the throttle, angling the Viper away from the freighter and towards what looked, to his naked eyes, like an empty patch of black. Neptune spread out behind Merc, invisible except in his mind. The Sun glowed on Merc's right, a sickly yellow dot so far away.

"Looks awful lonely out here," Merc said. "Earth was always surrounded by so many lights, so many things going on."

"You getting homesick on me?" Erick replied. "Because I have a remedy for that."

"For real?"

"You want it, you'll have to make it back."

"Will do," Merc said.

The scanner showed the triangles picking up on his presence. Two fighters, the scout, and the big boy. Merc tightened his fingers around the flight stick, exhaled a deep breath. The odds could be worse.

A slide of a dial sent some of the engine power to the

Viper's armor plating, allowing it to channel and dissipate heat. It'd suck up enough lasers until it had nowhere to send the heat to, then the Viper would melt away just like anything else. Lasers were cheap, and cheap to defend against. Merc had to hope that's all these guys were packing. If they showed up with solid slugs, then the Viper would be so much confetti.

The darkness in front shimmered, as though there was an error in the picture. The bigger ship blocking starlight. Merc's scanner had the fighters a few minutes out. The two small ships coming up first, the scout craft and its frigate partner taking longer to line up their attack. Two on one at the start.

Much better.

The Viper's cockpit window popped a pair of light blue squares into view against the backdrop, outlining the fighters. Merc, keeping his right hand on the flight stick, tapped another button on the console that shaded both squares a rose red. Classed as enemies. The Viper fitted a gold outline on the closer one, small numbers showing current speed popping up beneath the enemy ship. Merc still couldn't get a visual, had no idea what these fools were packing, but waiting for them to fire a shot was a poor choice.

A flick of the stick had the Viper nosing towards the closer fighter. Merc wasn't in range yet, but here's the secret that most flight computers didn't catch: lasers didn't just wink out after a certain distance. They'd lose potency, sure, but would splash bright flashes across the cockpit window and, in sufficient number, could still cause problems. The enemy fighter was still zipping forward, which meant it would run right into those lasers before it got to Merc. His finger pressed on the trigger and sent a series of beams launching straight off into the dark, right at the center of the red square.

A second later that square took a hard dive, turning away from Merc. And then it was visible, the square outlining a small disc-shaped craft, the Omni, that glinted in the sunlight. Designed only for zero-G, Omnis were all guns and thrusters, meant to stop, turn, and swing in any direction the pilot wanted. The other red blip had changed its angle, coming at Merc from the right. But the first one's dive had broken up their attack trajectory, and now the second was playing catch-up. Merc just had to stay far enough ahead.

Pushing the stick forward, Merc slid the Viper after the first Omni. It lacked the single-direction speed of the Viper, so Merc closed the gap and fired the second the console chimed that he was in optimal range. The Omni twitched left and right, activating those damn jump jets at random. The quick shifts couldn't dodge all the fire, though. Merc saw four hits suck into the Omni and disappear, but the fifth one blew off a piece of its shell.

Then the fighter stopped. Fired its engines back towards Merc. Angry orange gouts of light sprung out of the fighter as it jetted towards the Viper. Merc, keeping his fire steady, wrenched the stick to the left while twisting his wrist. This sent the Viper launching left and triggered tiny maneuvering jets that spun the Viper like a corkscrew, making it a harder target. As Merc blew by the paused fighter, he saw flashes as the ship's electronics overheated and died. One down.

Merc glanced at his scanner to see how far behind him the second fighter was. Only, it wasn't far at all. Right on his tail and unleashing hot laser into Merc's aft. The Viper shuddered as a pair of bolts struck home and Merc yanked the stick up, curling out from under the fire. The second Omni shouldn't have been there. No way it was that fast. A glance at the scanner corrected the error. The ship chasing him was the scout, its guns tracking him even as its larger mass made it harder to maneuver. It had corrected faster than Merc thought. Which meant Merc had just curled up into...

In front of him, boxed in that red square, loomed the other Omni, spewing laser at him. As Merc's stomach dropped into an icy bath, he held his trigger and hoped he had one more miracle left.

13

THE KARAT

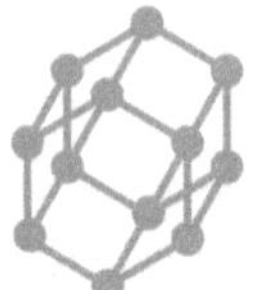

All Viola could hear were alarms. One for the wind shear, tearing at the wings. Another for the shuttle's stability, the changing altitude as the shuttle fell into and out of air pockets. A third one showing Viola was no longer strapped in, which happened when Puk cut her loose after the G-forces tightened the belt and pulled her beyond reach of the flight stick. Nearly crushed by a safety feature not designed to handle Neptune's wind storms.

But they were moving. Sliding around the edge of the whirling mass of deep blue and black, lightning crackling to the right of the shuttle. To the left, a serene, hazy teal captured the sinking sunlight of the day. The dichotomy would have been entrancing, except, you know, the alarms.

Viola kept the flight stick hard to the right, keeping the shuttle tilted so that the pushing winds propelled it along the border of the storm. Every couple of moments, another air pocket caused Viola's stomach to lurch up to her throat. Davin was yelling something. Had been yelling things, but Viola couldn't hear a word. Responding to the chaos, her brain shut things out one by one. Noises fell away, the rapid heartbeat faded, and even the perception of herself drifted away until Viola could only feel the flight stick, the tremors running through the shuttle as it struggled to hold itself together. She felt where the shuttle was being shoved, followed the wind gusts and fought others, all to stay targeted on the *Karat*.

They neared the back of the storm. Viola could see the rounding of the violence, a ridged line between Heaven and Hell. In the far distance beyond, another pair of storms played on the horizon. Between them was the goal. Viola angled for it, catching one more burst of wind that shoved the shuttle towards open space.

And then they were in free fall. Viola flying up out of her seat, only a death grip on the flight stick keeping her from hitting the ceiling. Viola could tell she was screaming, but couldn't hear it. Davin, still in place with his straps, grabbed her wrist and tried to pull her down. The numbers on their altitude sped towards zero, the alarm blaring louder. Viola tried to tug up on the stick, but there wasn't any air the shuttle could push against.

A violent lurch, the shuttle picked out of the sky by an invisible hand, Viola saw the world spin around and turn to dark as the shuttle was flung into the storm. Through the outer edge and into a temporary moment of calm, lightning flashing around the shuttle. The center of the storm. Viola fell back into her seat. Take a breath, take a breath.

"You all right?" Davin's voice rose above the silence.

"It's going to hurt later," Viola replied. "We have to get out of here before the storm cooks us."

"You've got my permission, if that's what you're waiting for."

Viola wasn't, but that was because she wasn't sure what

to do. Fly right back out into that tornado? That air pocket? Try cutting through the storm and risk the lightning? This wasn't anything she'd done before. Nothing she'd trained for.

Viola moved the stick to the right, aiming deeper into the storm. As if sensing her path, a sheet of lightning turned everything in front of them into white.

"That looks less than good," Davin said.

"Statistically I've got nothing," Puk said. "Nobody's gathered information on Neptune lightning properties."

"Quiet," Viola snapped.

The flight plan put the struggling shuttle only a few straight-shot seconds from the outer band of the storm, where the winds picked up again for one final assault. Any fuel gains from using the wind to swing around were eliminated by the cut-through they were doing, where Viola had to pump more energy to the engines to fight the pull of the storm's internal flux. If they hit no other catastrophes, the shuttle might make it to the *Karat* with enough fuel to start its engines again, but not much else.

Their only way back to space was the *Karat*.

Lightning flashed outside again. A twanging crack came a moment later from right of the shuttle. Metal snapping. Viola recognized the sound from the many stress tests she'd run on small components built during school experiments and looked away from the storm to the console. It showed a diagram of the shuttle, with the right wing shaded a deep yellow and pulsing. Then she felt the drag, the listing as the shuttle tilted right.

"Lost the right wing," Davin said. "We'll have to—"

"Increase power to the engines to stabilize, I know," Viola said, boosting their speed. "We're about to get tossed around. Then we have to hotfoot it to the *Karat*."

"Were we taking the slow route before?"

"I'm saying we might not make it."

The speed kicked the shuttle forward. Viola waited for the opposite spin, or something to yank the shuttle away, but it stayed straight. The entire wing might not be gone, then. A chance, still, to make it through.

The winds picked up again, roaring around the shuttle, rocking them. This time, though, Viola was expecting the pushes, the grabs and the falls of Neptune's weather. They bounced, they tumbled, and they did a number of half-rolls that had Viola scared the shuttle would drop straight into a nose dive. After what felt like hours but, according to the computer, was less than a minute they were out. Back in the teal fog, pushed by gentler winds, Viola took a breath.

"Nice job, kid," Davin said. "Looks like the *Karat*'s straight ahead."

Davin was right. Between the twin storms up front there was a small shape. Keeping pace with those storms would help disguise the *Karat*'s movements, make it harder to intercept.

"Should we try to talk to it?" Viola asked.

"Not like they won't see us coming," Davin said. "And who knows, maybe we'll find a few friends on there."

Viola turned on the comm and tried sending a greeting, but met with silence. Not even an acknowledging click.

"Flip to the short-range radio," Davin said. "Their comm might be damaged."

Viola nodded. Every ship had your standard radio transmitter as a back-up comm system. Less complicated, with no real way to choose a specific target, blasting a radio signal was still a viable way to get help in an emergency. Viola toggled the radio on. A loud static burst shot through the shuttle, pulsing in crackling waves.

"Turn it off!" Davin yelled, hands over his ears.

Viola reached for the toggle, was about to hit it when the static paused, then pulsed again. Viola gave it a moment, listening, albeit painfully, as the static continued to sound in waves. That wasn't normal. Radio static should be continuous. Davin tried to reach for the switch, but Viola hit his hand away, still listening.

"I think it's a pattern," Viola said over the noise.

Opal's head appeared in the cockpit, sticking in through the entryway.

"Don't know what you two are doing up here, but someone's trying to talk to us," Opal said. "That static is Morse code. And it's saying *run*."

14

INTERROGATION

Phyla didn't know what was happening. She couldn't see what was going on with Merc, and half the time wasn't able to get info from Erick because Quinn had her talking with one of the *Amerigo* crew members. They'd already met three of them and within a few questions to each one, Quinn shook his head and pull her away. Apparently the man could read people, tell if they were hiding something or if they were even nervous, which made Phyla feel entirely ornamental.

"Why do you even need me?" Phyla said as they walked along a corridor. "You seem like you got this."

"If you're setting a trap, best not let your prey see you doing it," Quinn replied.

Setting a trap. Okay, buddy.

They went around a corner and entered the freighter's main engine room. A pair of dirty-looking scrubs were keeping tabs on the freighter's power systems and the ship's speed, which right now was a slow crawl meant to keep the freighter more or less above the *Karat*.

"Hi, I'm Phyla," The *Jumper*'s pilot announced. "Things all good back here?"

"Hey Quinn," The taller of the two said. He was sporting a thick corporate work-suit that was both over-protective and impractical. A massive belt hung around his waist, sporting more tools than Phyla had ever seen Trina carry. It also held the man's waist-length hair, tied into a tight tail. Phyla would've considered that a risk for her own mechanic, but maybe Eden didn't give a damn. "What's she doing back here?"

"Taking a tour, Van," Quinn said. "You hear we have enemies in-system?"

"You mean, did we hear the alarms?" Van said. "Cause they were so deafening we couldn't hear much else."

The short one, whose hair was hidden under a stained, deep green hat, leaned back against the wall. The way he stared at Phyla had her doing a double-take. It wasn't in the usual sketchbook of stares men tossed her way, but a lazy look of indifference. Like Phyla might give to a chair she didn't intend to use. Or a tissue as it went in the trash.

"Why'd you come way back here to ask us?" Van continued. "Think we're going to run?"

"How would you do that?" Quinn replied.

"What do you mean? I'd cut the power to everything that wasn't essential and send it to the engines. Blow us out of here real quick," Van said. "There's patrolled space around Uranus."

Patrolled by corporate-sponsored crews. Phyla had taken the *Jumper* on a wide course around Uranus, not hard to do since it didn't cross paths much with Neptune. Despite not having any true authority, the Free Laws handed the deepest pockets the opportunity to carve out their own empires wherever the Earth nations didn't bother.

"So you'd take us all with you?" Quinn asked.

"Easy," Phyla said, putting a hand on Quinn's arm. Van looked at both of them, confused.

"They think you're gonna sell out the ship," the short one muttered.

"For what, Slip?" Van said, twisting around to look at his coworker. "You think I want coin? Way out here?"

"Nah, I think they're stupid," Slip said. "We didn't know where we were even flying. How would we have planned anything?"

"Wait, his name is Slip?" Phyla looked at the short one. "Slip? Really?"

"Earned that one," Slip said, standing up straighter. "Cause I can get in anywhere, fix anything on these boats. What's your name?"

"Phyla?" Phyla replied.

"That's a strange name too. How'd you get that one?"

"Birth?"

"And you think mine's weird. At least I chose it," Slip re-crossed his arms.

Phyla shrugged. What could she say to that?

"Okay. Well," Van said, coming to the rescue. "We're not Eden's normal cargo division. We're special. Or, this ship is. Deep space missions, with experimental stuff. We almost never know where we're going."

Phyla glanced at Quinn, who nodded.

"The man makes a good point," Quinn said. "Few of the crew members knew the final destination. And most of those are on the *Karat*."

"You're saying there might not be another up here?"

"Another what?" Van asked.

"Sell-out," Slip said. "That's who they're looking for."

"Thanks," Quinn said, turning and walking back down

the hallway. Phyla paused a moment, matched Van's bewildered stare with a shrug while ignoring a dour look from the Slip, and then took off after the bodyguard.

"What was that?" Phyla said as she caught up to Quinn, who was heading towards the freighter's crew quarters. "We didn't even get very far. Slip seemed weird."

"He's always like that," Quinn said. "And he's right. I didn't think about it, but the only ones who could arrange anything would have known we were coming here. I have the list of who knew our destination, but it's in my quarters."

"Don't you use a comm?"

"Too easy to hack," Quinn said. "The other comm's secure. Low tech."

"And you're not carrying it on you?"

"Do you carry everything you own all the time?"

"I'm just saying—"

"Nobody else on this ship knows about that comm. If I wore it around, there'd be questions," Quinn said. "Besides, anyone tries to get in my room, I'll know."

Phyla pictured a slew of traps. Alarms, sure, but Quinn probably had something better. A stunning shot sent as soon as the door opened. An exotic animal hellbent on tearing apart any intruder.

"So what's the plan?" Phyla said, pulling herself back to the present.

"We get that list, cross reference with everyone still one the ship, and then we'll know whether we have anyone left to talk to."

"You think we have that time?" Phyla said, glancing at her comm. Erick's latest message said Merc was engaged with the fighters, that he was outnumbered. "Because right now, my guy out there could use some help."

"You're being paid," Quinn's dry reply. Phyla was angry

for a hot second, about to lay into the bodyguard for being insensitive, but she caught herself. Quinn was right. They were being paid and given their choice of occupation, terrible situations often found the Wild Nines. But that didn't mean she had to accept it.

"Not to die," Phyla said. "You get your list. I'm heading back to my ship and out to help my pilot."

"Fine," Quinn said.

The docking bays were back towards the front of the freighter, near the bridge. She made it three steps before she felt a hand on her shoulder, and saw a sidearm being handed to her.

"You're unarmed. Take this," Quinn said.

"I've got plenty back at the *Jumper*," Phyla replied, pushing the small weapon away.

"You might not make it there."

15

REFLEX

In combat, a pilot has to make innumerable decisions every second. How fast to go, which way to turn, whether to fire or not. Merc had made all those calls over and over again. But when he saw the Omni in front of his Viper, waiting to blow him into scattered matter, Merc flinched. Floating in space above Europa. The burning agony of the laser shot. Black closing in around his eyes.

Not again.

Merc snapped the Viper down, away from the Omni, a pair of shots skipping off the Viper's shields. Then the scout ship, screaming after the Viper but not able to match the turn, cut in between the two of them.

Merc shifted the shields to cover the Viper's rear and shot towards the frigate, hanging away from the fight. Long and narrow, with a bank of engines at the end and a series of wing-like shoots spreading out from the central shaft. Turrets sprinkled along the ship, bumps criss-crossing the surface. Hope they weren't ready for a fighter to go screaming past, or they'd fill the sky with so much fire the Viper would just vanish. Merc pushed all the energy from the lasers to the engines, kicking up his velocity.

"Doin' what I can for you, baby," Merc muttered.

Then he started to juke, twitching the Viper at random as the frigate opened up. The attack was sporadic, they didn't want to risk hitting their own ships still tailing the Viper. The scout ship and fighter had the same issue. Shoot and miss, and they'd pound the frigate. But one of them would hit Merc eventually.

The Viper approached the bow of the big ship, slipped over the top. The ridged neck of the craft spread out below him, boxes and bumps for sensors, shields, and communications riddling the smooth gray plating. In front of Merc, that big bank of engines loomed like a metal mountain. Across its surface, a dozen large guns rotated, drawing beads on the Viper.

Last time, near Europa, this frigate hadn't been armed. Used harpoon turrets. Merc glanced at the console, at the readout of weapons on the ship. Almost every gun was different, a model yanked from another ship, or a scrap pile and jury-rigged to fit on this one.

Explained why they were missing so much. When the weapons all fired at different times, turned at different speeds, made it hard to line up a shot.

And they were too slow. Merc pulled back on the stick, sending the Viper up and over the engines.

"Cut engines. Rear jets!" Merc said.

The Viper's main engines paused, while the fighter's maneuvering jets kicked in, wrenching the back of the ship around while its momentum carried it over the edge of the engine back. Merc looked out at the long block of engines along the bottom of the cockpit's window. The Viper's belly exposed. An easy kill for a second.

"Go! Shields bottom!" Merc said, and the fighter lurched as the engines came back to life, its motion still carrying it out from the frigate. Stuck still in space.

The scout ship took advantage, loosing a barrage of lasers. They smashed into the Viper's shields, the console flashing red as the last of the energy gave out. Merc ignored the wailing alarms as a pair of bolts dug into the craft's armor. Then the frigate's engines cut off the scout ship's firing line. Glancing at the console, the outline of the Viper still showed all green. No critical damage. Behind him, the scanner showed the scout ship overshooting Merc's angle, forcing it into a long loop past the frigate.

Merc swooped to the underside of the frigate, then skated the Viper alongside the hull. Kept the Viper close so those guns wouldn't be able to turn fast enough to get off a shot. The shields, given a hot second without getting hit, were coming back, fuzzing into life. The only question was—

There! The Omni darted down from the frigate's top-side, lasers flashing. Merc nudged the Viper closer to the hull. The console flared yellow, the proximity alert. Less than a meter of space, but the Omni overplayed its ambush. It was beneath the Viper now. Any shots up would score against the frigate's hull. Against their own shields.

"C'mon, don't shoot," Merc said as the Viper raced towards the frigate's bow. The Omni hesitated and the Viper increased the distance, launching out in front of the frigate. Merc pulled up, still heading back towards the *Amerigo*, but keeping the frigate in the firing line. Scattered lasers from the frigate's turrets blew past the Viper, but Merc's random twitches kept them guessing.

"All engines," Merc said, routing all of the Viper's shield power to the jets.

A moment later Merc kicked back into his seat as the Viper jumped forward, speeding back towards the *Amerigo*.

Alive. He was alive. Only, he was running. For the first time, Merc was running from a fight. Like a coward.

16

BOARDING PARTY

"We can't run," Davin said. "Literally, can't."

"But we can answer," Viola said. "If they're using static bursts to transmit, maybe they can pick something up."

Viola watched Davin reach over to the console and tap his way through a few menus until the schematics of the *Karat* sat in front of them. The ship's ovoid shape made clear its purpose as a mining vessel. A large hold along the bottom for storing goods, with layers of lab and crew space overhead. The bridge sat towards the pointed front, far away from the bottom-rear loading doors. If something went wrong with the cargo, there'd be plenty of seals to keep the pilots alive.

The two small bays for landing craft were at the top center. Viola figured it was because the *Karat* could be in some nasty territory, and being able to keep other ships as far from the extraction source was a good plan. Wouldn't be a bad idea to take these schematics and send them to her father. A little corporate espionage on the side.

"Let's keep quiet," Davin said. "Radio's not secure. Gage is thinking this ship might not be his anymore, so any heads-up we give will only warn someone we're coming."

"Don't we need them to open the bay doors?" Viola said.

"Nope. Remote override. Gage gave us the codes on our way out. Meant for emergency recovery operations like this one. We'll get close, beam the code over, and the doors should open."

"Which means they'll know we're there before we land," Opal said.

"What, scared of a few space pirates?" Davin replied.

Opal shook her head and went aft. The shuttle was coming up fast on the *Karat*, only a few minutes till they'd hit broadcast range. Without the right wing working, landing the shuttle would be less docking and more crashing. Those maneuvering jets stressed getting the shuttle off the ground, they wouldn't help with breaking. And any major reverse thrust from the engines relied on the wings keeping the craft stable. Pull hard, and the weaker side curled, a boat with only one paddle.

"Strap in," Viola said, using the shuttle's intercoms to carry the command to the back. "It's not going to be a nice landing."

They came up on the *Karat*, the larger ship spreading out in front of them like a whale in one of Earth's oceans. Neptune's fog blurred the edges, making the *Karat* look like more a portal to a misty dimension. Only when the shuttle passed through the last cloud bank did Eden's secret ship manifest itself.

"Whoa," Viola didn't say so much as breathed.

The *Karat* was an emerald at dusk, bands of green hues looping around one another. There were no protrusions, none of the bulky modules that made up most ships as their owners mixed and matched functionality. Whatever engines keeping the *Karat* aloft were hidden somewhere in the aft, covered by the body.

"It makes no sense," Davin said. "It's a mining vessel!"

"What is it even made of?" Viola was about to rattle off a few more questions before catching herself. The only people that could answer were on that ship, and if Captain Gage was right, they'd be trying to kill her soon enough.

"Now I understand," Davin said.

"You do?"

"Why bother trying to hijack a mining vessel? Neptune's huge. Just get your own ship and grab some gems. But if the *Karat* is the real reward . . ."

Viola angled the ship towards the twin bays. Or at least where they should be. The *Karat*'s top was a smooth dome that flowed into the rest of the ship. No visible space to dock. At least, not yet.

"Ready with the code?" Viola asked.

"Aren't we moving a little fast for a landing?"

"Our momentum's the only thing keeping us straight. We brake, this shuttle's going to go all over the place. I'd like to know where I'm aiming before that happens."

"You crash us into the side of this beautiful ship, you're paying for it."

"So nice," Viola Viola wondered what it would cost to fix a scratch on the Karat. Probably more than every coin she'd earned in her entire life.

Davin flipped the console to the shuttle's short-range comm and plugged in the code. When he tapped the send button, the shuttle would blast the code in all directions. Anything that was listening would get the message. Anyone, too. But the code was only numbers, meaningless unless the *Karat* hijackers knew it as well.

"Here we go," Davin said, tapping the send button.

Cracks appeared in the top of the *Karat*, a top they were drawing way too close to. A platform rose out of the top of the ship, twenty meters wide. Beneath the hull was an open space tall enough for the shuttle to fit into, followed by a more standard gray metal floor. Viola could see through the bay and out the other end. Dual-side docking. Very cool.

"At least they didn't paint the inside the same color," Davin said. "It's not a space ship without gray hallways."

The shuttle didn't have air brakes. The intent was to use atmospheric drag and the main engines to slow thrust, then switch to the maneuvering jets when you were close enough to land. Problem was, with Neptune's winds blowing along behind them, there wasn't any way the shuttle would slow enough to dock with just the jets alone. And when Viola switched the main thrust into reverse, the shuttle shook as if some giant creature had taken hold of it as a toy.

Viola kept one eye on their air speed while the other paid attention to their angle of descent. The platform was coming up quick, they'd be hitting it or passing it in ten seconds. Right now, it'd be a crash. Davin yammered about braking this or turning that. Puk stated useless facts like how the shuttle wasn't designed for a landing in these winds. Viola tuned them both out and focused.

Nine.

Viola dialed up the power to the engines and the shuttle turned right, the corkscrew from the damaged wing.

Eight.

A swipe of the console flipped the diagram to the landing controls.

Seven.

The platform was way to the left. Viola tapped the button for the maneuvering jets on the right side, switching the flight stick to her left hand.

Six.

The nose of the shuttle passed over the outskirts of the *Karat*, the teal air below changing into a hard light green mass.

Five.

The maneuvering jets kicked in on the right side, boosting the shuttle to the left. Their airspeed was nearing the point where the shuttle would drop like a rock.

Four.

Viola pulled the flight stick back, pointing the nose of the shuttle up. At the same time, with her left hand, she cut the reverse thrust.

Three.

Swapping hands again, Viola tapped the console and started the rest of the maneuvering jets.

Two.

The shuttle was now sinking, the nose passing just beneath the roof of the platform. Viola cut the engines. The shuttle lurched as its mass fell into the hands of the maneuvering jets.

One.

With the platform beneath them, Viola triggered one last shot of the reverse thrust, bringing the shuttle into a stall. The nose pointed too high, and the jets weren't correctly placed to catch the shuttle. They were going to hit hard.

"Hang on!" Viola yelled.

The shuttle fell and struck the platform with its aft first, the impact causing the nose to slam downward. The jets caught some of the swing, bouncing Viola out of her seat but not into the ceiling, her hands slapping at the console to kill the alarms.

"Won't say that's the prettiest landing I've ever seen," Davin said, releasing his straps. "You all right?"

"I'm alive," Viola said, climbing back into her seat.

"Good. Let's go takeover a ship."

17

———

THE JUMPER

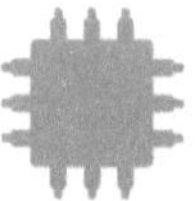

Something was always breaking on a ship. Or about to break. This time, it was the rear-left landing strut. Trina saw the readings when the *Jumper* landed on the *Amerigo*, the brief flash of yellow on her status grid that displayed back near the engines, her haunt while the ship was in motion. A flash that meant, for a hot moment as the *Jumper* settled into the bay, the strut almost broke and sent the ship crashing into the floor. Not good when you're in potentially hostile territory.

The problem turned out to be a pair of bolts that during the flight out had either been hit by passing space junk—though, since the struts recoiled in flight, it wasn't likely—or had worn down over time. Either way, the bolts were loose and the joint connecting the strut to the *Jumper* wouldn't handle too many more trips before snapping in half. Thankfully, bolts were something Trina always had handy. Like food, the Wild Nines would die without them.

"Trina!" Erick yelled from the *Jumper*'s ramp. "You're not on your comm!"

Trina blinked at the statement, then glanced over where

her toolbox sat on the freighter bay floor. Her comm was sitting on top of it. No reason to have the device get scuffed while she took the strut apart.

"Should I be?" Trina replied.

"Merc's flying back to the freighter!"

"He took them all down already?"

"No, he was outnumbered. We have to get out there and help him," Erick waved at her to come towards the ramp. Trina stayed back at the strut. One bolt still had to be swapped out. Attack or no, if the *Jumper* lifted off now, there'd be no chance it would land again. Not nicely, anyway.

"That's not a good idea. One of our struts needs fixing."

"How long?"

"How much time do I have?"

"Phyla's coming. You've got till she gets here."

"That's an impossible calculation," Trina said. "But I will try."

The doctor nodded and vanished back up the ramp. Trina applied her wrench to the bolt, spinning it. With the three of them, the *Jumper* wasn't crewed for a fight. Someone had to watch the engines. Had to fly. And then another two people on the guns. No amount of math would turn three of them into four. Trina gave the wrench a final turn and the bolt popped off.

The strut groaned, the weight put on the first bolt she'd switched out. Trina watched it for a second, making sure it could hold the stress. Redundancy was a serious word. Every system, every part on the *Jumper* needed a back-up. If they could support it, Trina would've advocated the same for the human element. Turned out people were too expensive.

As Trina grabbed the new bolt and slotted it in, she

heard the undulating whine of the *Jumper*'s engines going through their pre-flight cycles. Sounding darn good, too. No stuttering, no unexpected clogging of the vents. Hearing a perfect sound like that, well, it was like listening to a symphony. The synchronized success of so many pieces making the machine hum.

And then a loud shriek of metal grating against its own un-oiled self. The bay doors were closing fast, shooting down from the top and bottom of the bay to meet in the middle with a crashing clang. The *Jumper* was trapped.

18

THE HALLS

"The traitor shut the doors from the back-up bridge," Gage said through the comm.

"Can't you open them?" Phyla asked, running through the freighter's hallways towards the *Jumper*'s bays. "We don't get out there, Merc has no support. And you will have a boarding party knocking on your door."

"Nothing. They have the override codes, and the back-up bridge is only designed for use if this one can't work."

Phyla could almost hear the shrug through the comm. The captain sounded resigned, doomed to lose the game. Phyla didn't have time for that crap, though. Not when her pilot was out there.

"If Merc's stuck in space, he's going to die," Phyla said. "You need a place for him to dock, now."

"Can't he run?"

As she jogged, Phyla kept looking for a terminal, a console, any place that might let her into the *Amerigo*'s computer system. She didn't believe for a minute that the bay doors could be closed and locked from some back-up bridge, but the captain might not know how to handle it. Or didn't care. Gage's remark about them being paid to die played itself in Phyla's head. Lock Merc out, force him to fight, and maybe the pilot would take out one or two enemy ships before dying.

Phyla's comm beeped. Merc calling.

"Stay tuned, Captain," Phyla said, clicking to Merc's channel. "Hit me, hotshot."

"Why's the bay closed?"

"Gage says it's the traitor and he doesn't have a way of opening it."

"Does Gage know his other bays are open?"

"What?"

"The cargo bays. I'm angling towards one now. I have a couple minutes lead on them. Should be able to ground this guy in a couple seconds. If Gage could close the door behind me, I'd be pretty happy."

"Will send. Land safe, then find your way up to us."

"You got it. And Phyla?"

"Yeah?"

"Sorry I wasn't able to do more out there."

"Save the pity party for later," Phyla said, flipping the comm back to Gage's channel. "Captain, I'm going to need you to close your cargo bay doors as soon as my guy lands."

"Can do."

Phyla clicked off and continued running. The metal floors weren't the best surface for it, her boots pounding every step into ground that didn't give a millimeter. Her boots weren't made for jogging. More for comfort and, if the situation required it, a kick to the face. Quinn's sidearm pumped with her right hand. She hadn't seen any other crew, but they were probably following whatever Eden's hostile boarding procedures dictated. Sealing themselves in a room and praying.

"Davin, I will punch you when you get back," Phyla muttered between breaths. Hoped they were having a blast down there, saying hi to Neptune while Phyla dealt with a bunch of raiders.

The hallway widened and split into a gradual ramp, with one half continuing on her level. Up that ramp were the passenger bays, one of which the *Jumper* occupied. Phyla ran up the shallow incline, designed for any cargo that needed manual moving between the levels.

"Almost there," Phyla commed to Erick. "How's pre-flight?"

"Fine, but it won't mean anything if we can't get those doors open."

"Once I'm there, I'll be able to hack the freighter from the *Jumper*'s computer," Phyla replied. It shouldn't be hard. Phyla kept the *Jumper* loaded with the finest in cracking weaponry. Once she networked with a ship, Phyla could, with a bit of time, get her victim to open up all its electronic secrets. Like solving puzzles, only the prize for winning was survival.

This hallway, stretching by the bays, was half the width of Eden Prime's promenade, but empty. No cover. Which became a concern when the hallway's alarms sounded an incoming ship. But Gage said all the passenger bays were closed, locked down.

Phyla ran by the first bay, looked in, and saw space. Space that was filling with a pair of ships Phyla didn't recognize. One was an Omni, another an oval covered in sensor dishes and small guns.

"Gage?" Phyla commed. "Why is bay one open?"

"I've been telling you we have someone on the inside," Gage said. "They must have just opened them. For the raiders."

"Them?"

"All the bays. Except for the one your ship is in. They're showing open."

The *Jumper* was in the last of five bays. The closest one to the bridge, but the farthest from Phyla. A long run. If she was caught out here, there'd be no chance. Nowhere to hide.

"Erick," Phyla commed, backing down the ramp. "Seal the ship. Arm the turrets. Anyone comes in that bay, you blast them to Hell."

"What? Where are you?"

"They've cut me off. I'm going to try to get to the bridge and get your bay open. When it does, I'm going to need you to get the *Jumper* out of there."

"But I'm not a pilot."

"Today, you are," Phyla clicked off as a whooshing noise came from farther along the hallway, up the ramp. The first boarders were out. Phyla cursed, turned, and ran back the way she'd come.

19

DIGGING

The secure comm was only as large as the palm of Quinn's hand. It wouldn't wrap around the wrist, was kept out of sight. A circle made up of a screen, it awoke when Quinn pressed his thumb to the face. Blue hues outlined his thumb before collapsing into a black and white grid. Every black square a data file. The grid had room for nine, but Eden only filled four of them for this mission.

This mission. Every job had these locked comms attached to them now. So paranoid about losing secrets, losing ships, losing anything. Those black squares held Eden's information on every crew member, on both ships, their purposes and potential threats. Quinn tapped the first one, the data file on key personnel. The ones who knew the full extent of the mission, the *Karat*'s purpose in extracting the ice diamonds. Photos of Captain Gage, one of the *Karat*'s captain, Quinn, and a few others.

Quinn swiped over to the next file. One dedicated to threats. Espionage from other corporations. Crew members deemed risks due to unstable personal or money problems.

There was a new entry here, though. A download done since Quinn checked last.

Remnants of the Red Voice

Evidence and rumors indicate the terrorist organization may not be as defeated as previously thought. With all known accounts frozen, their only source of financial gain may be in black market moves. If they learn of the Karat's mission, there is substantial risk that the Amerigo may be attacked. To account for this, we are providing additional security through a mercenary group.

The file went on, giving known details on every single one of the Wild Nines members. Last known job protecting the growing Eden Prime settlement, dismissed after charges of murder, charges that had been suspended. Quinn tried to punch up more details, but the comm came back blank. When Quinn tried to request the download, the comm reported back that their files were sealed. Who wanted to protect these mercenaries?

Sounds echoed down the hallway. Running boots on metal floors. The enemy was here. Quinn slipped the secured comm into his pocket. Pressed the button next to his cabin door. It shunted closed as the pounding footsteps came closer. Three sets, the footfalls coming through as vibrations more than noise.

The first set landed outside his door. Quinn pressed the exit button, the door shooting open as the second set stamped by. The third, belonging to a scrawny mutt with a wild look in his eyes, tripped as the man saw Quinn and his gun standing there. The stumbling momentum carried the man past Quinn's door, and Quinn reached out, grabbed the man in a headlock and pulled him tight to Quinn's body.

With his left hand, Quinn grabbed the sidearm out of

the man's holster and, the two leading enemies turning too slowly, shot both of them. Orange bolts.

"Killers?" Quinn said to the scrabbling man, gurgling as he struggled to breathe in Quinn's grip. His eyes locked with Quinn's, narrowed.

"Funny, coming from you," the man said. "All you've ever done is kill us."

Quinn put the man on the ground. Watched as the last breath escaped from his lips. That line. Killed us. No normal pirate or random criminal would bother saying that. It would be pointless. Quinn inspected their uniforms, the bodies lying around him. Each one wore a patchwork quilt of fabrics and even parts of boxes, furniture, other things sewn together. Quinn had seen the reports, the change when the Red Voice had done this. When they'd taken parts of their lives and wore it to generate empathy from the billions that watched their struggle on the satellite feeds throughout the solar system.

What it meant was that they weren't being boarded by simple pirates, but that they were in real trouble. These people had a cause, and the ones with causes couldn't be bribed, couldn't be persuaded, couldn't be defeated unless their breath was taken away. And the best place to do that was the bridge. A bottleneck with defenses.

Quinn turned to head that way when the sounds of lasers scoring off metal echoed along the hallway. More of them. Might as well clear some of these bastards out on the way.

20

HIJACKERS

Mox on the left, Davin on the right of the shuttle's exit door. Opal had her long rifle out, spread across the seats that, a few minutes ago, they'd been sitting in as Viola bounced the shuttle to its landing. As for the pilot, she was back in the short connection between the shuttle's aft and cockpit. The best spot to keep her out of fire, though Viola held a weapon of her own.

Davin checked Melody, the energy-spewing shotgun left as a gift from the *Jumper*'s previous captain. Davin looked around, caught quick nods from Mox and Opal, then opened the door.

Opal fired. The near-silent expulsion of bright yellow laser light from her rifle streaked out even as the shuttle's door was receding into the top. Davin peeked around the edge in time to see one of several people fall back behind a doorway leading out of the docking bay. In that flash, Davin recognized the Eden uniform, but also the trailing end of a gun barrel.

"One hit," Opal announced, her face stuck to the scope.

Mox dashed outside the shuttle, moving to the side to

clear Opal's firing line. For the moment, the hijackers waited behind their doorway. Davin followed Mox out, turning to the right, towards the back of the shuttle. Depending on Opal to cover his back, Davin moved around the rear, keeping Melody raised and ready. Could be anyone lurking around the inside of the bay.

Rounding the engines, Davin dropped into a crouch, adopting the lower profile as he left the cover of the shuttle's body. The other side of the bay looked like the first, a stretch of wall and another exit and . . . what was that? Two of the hijackers were kneeling in the doorway, holding a giant tool in their hands, a long, skeletal tube with metal supports keeping it together. Smaller lines ran away from the central tube to a pair of fuel tanks strapped to the second hijacker's back. And it was pointed right at the shuttle.

The front kneeler saw Davin, whipped out a sidearm and squeezed off a pair of shots before Davin could pull Melody's trigger. Both lanced over his shoulder as Davin backpedaled behind the engines.

"There's another exit on the back of the shuttle," Davin commed. "They're setting something up there."

"I've got them pinned up front. Take care of it," Opal replied.

"Mox? On three?"

The comm clicked affirmative. Mox carried his chest cannon, a minigun capable of lighting up the universe with hundreds of bolts per second. The man's exoskeleton held the weapon and kept it positioned right in the center of Mox's chest. Between the two of them, coming from both sides, yeah, it would be a massacre.

"Three. Two. One," Davin said, then stepped forward and raised Melody.

A loud shriek sounded and the bay lit up like a supernova. The shuttle broke apart, shattered as its center turned to molten liquid. The rear, no longer supported by struts up front, fell forward away from Davin while the front did the opposite. Split fuel and coolant lines exploded into the air, a fiery fog that expanded to fill the bay, burning Davin's lungs even as it singed his hair. He dropped to the ground and rolled away from the shuttle, pulling Melody with him.

"Mox? Viola? Opal?" Davin wheezed into the comm, blinking to get the stinging smoke from his eyes.

"Here," Mox said. "Pinned down in front. Enemy fire."

How could they even see? Davin looked towards the front of the shuttle and saw flashes through the mist. A sucking roar filled the bay. The *Karat's* own support systems spooling up. Vents sucking away the gas. In a few seconds, it would be gone. Leaving his team out in the open.

Team? Viola and Opal were silent. Who knew if they were even alive?

Davin pushed himself up to his feet, holding his breath, and ran towards the flashing lasers. In a few steps he'd made it to the doorway. The giant weapon was lying on the ground, the two hijackers positioned at the front of the doorway flinging death towards Mox. Not even looking Davin's way. Melody came up, Melody fired.

Six green balls of fiery doom spat out of Melody's honeycomb barrel towards the two hijackers. There wasn't any sound, so the first notice the enemies had that they were being attacked was when the fire struck their backs. The super-heated balls burst their sea green Eden uniforms into flame. Both of them tried to roll, collapse to the ground to smother the heat.

Davin didn't sit and watch, but closed in and kicked the sidearms away from their writhing forms, trying not to look at them. Melody's flames wrapped themselves around the pair, eating away anything remotely flammable. Clothes, accessories, hair, and on. Melody was terrible.

And this called for terrible weapons.

A glance at the doorway showed it to be empty, a short hallway that forked, likely to rooms meant for holding cargo. If Gage was right, ten people went to Neptune on the *Karat*. That meant eight left. Melody had the ammo.

"Back end looks clear," Davin commed.

"Front end is scattered," Mox replied. "Retreated."

"Count? I have two."

"One. Opal's. They ran when the cannon opened."

Which, understandable. Mox's cannon liquefied morale as well as it did armor. The mist cleared, giving Davin his first real look at the remains of the shuttle. They weren't going home in that thing. Ignoring the gash where the laser had split the shuttle in half, ignited fuel torched the rest of it, leaving wires dangling, bent and twisted, and the engines themselves broken into shards scattered across the bay floor. If they were leaving Neptune, it was the *Karat* or nothing.

Davin ran his eyes around the wreck, looking for any sign of Opal, of Viola, when a whirring noise buzzed his ear. Davin whirled, swinging Melody around at chest height, and saw Puk hovering in front of his face.

"They're in the front," Puk said. "My comm system is damaged, so I cannot transmit."

"Show me."

Davin followed Puk towards the shuttle's wreckage, towards the collapsed front half, with the nose pointing up towards space. The little bot veered to the gash, then slipped inside it. Davin, moving gingerly, stepped over scattered metal plating, sparking wires burning out the last of the shuttle's energy, and charred bits of things he didn't recognize.

Inside the shuttle, at the point where the two wrecked halves touched in a tent-like shape, the cargo section where they'd been sitting was a melted mess. The seats were no longer visible. Puk waited for Davin just inside, then moved towards the front. Between the cockpit and the back was the shuttle's only lavatory, a tiny slit of a space for anyone that needed a moment on one of the shuttle's intended short jaunts. The door was open, and Puk slipped through.

Davin followed, turning to look inside, and saw Opal, with Viola's arms wrapped around her, lying on the floor of the bathroom. Opal looked unconscious, stretches of her uniform black and scarred from the laser, but whole.

"Hey kid?" Davin said, slinging Melody over his shoulder. "How hurt are you?"

Viola turned up to look at Davin, and he saw stains of tears through the charred grime on her face. Little lines through the dirt. And more forming every minute, like racers speeding down the girl's face. Her mouth opened, but only a chopped sob came out.

"Their vitals aren't critical. Opal inhaled too much gas after the fire, knocked her out," Puk said. "I noticed the mining laser before it fired. Opal dove into Viola and they fell in here."

"The mining laser?"

"The thing that split the shuttle? You were standing next to it a moment ago?" Puk replied.

"I know," Davin said. It made sense. Why wouldn't they have a mining laser on a mining ship? And why not roast invaders alive with it?

"Viola may need a minute," Puk said as the girl closed her eyes and shoved her face into Opal's hair.

"We don't have that time. We're outnumbered and they

know exactly where we are," Davin said, clicking his comm. "Mox? Opal will need a hand."

"Swap then?"

Davin affirmed, then turned to Viola.

"Listen, kid. I know this stuff is rough. You don't know how to handle it. But you're going to have to deal with that later. Right now we need you awake, alert, and not falling apart."

Viola blinked, looked at Davin, and took a shuddering breath. Nodded. Davin swapped with Mox. The metal man barely fit in the shuttle even when it wasn't a wreck. Now it was a joke. Mox had to tear his way to the lavatory. Davin didn't have time to watch that though. With Melody once more in his hands, Davin walked to front exit from the docking bay, where Opal's victim lay still on the ground, and peered around the corner.

At the end of the hall sat a large set of elevator doors. Made for handling crew and freight. Gleaming silver and new. Through those doors was the rest of the *Karat*, and seven more traitors wanting to put a laser between Davin's eyes.

21

THE LOST PILOT

Merc landed the Viper in the cavernous ancillary bay, meant more for cargo containers than normal ships. Only the maintenance lights were on, leaving the hundreds-meter bay covered in shadows. Waiting for the *Karat* and its ice diamonds. The *Amerigo* had an identical bay opposite this one, taking up most of the non-crew portion of the freighter.

All that space made for easy landings, though.

The Viper's cockpit popped up and Merc scrambled out, using handholds on the side of the fighter to get himself to the floor. A ladder would've been the preferred route—could never tell how stiff those muscles would be after sitting in the cramped Viper—but Merc planted himself on the ground without falling. He tuned his comm to the Wild Nine's general frequency, but heard no noise. Which meant his teammates weren't talking or, more likely, they were keeping things directed. Not wanting to give away anything to listeners. Merc twisted the frequency to Phyla's signal.

"Phyla, I'm on the ground in the ancillary bay. What's going on?"

A few seconds passed in silence. Merc glanced around the bay. The cavernous space punctuated its worn vastness with dimpled lights every few meters, white dots casting Merc and his fighter in a day-bright glow. For all its size, there was only one exit, outlined in bright red paint. Looked to lead back towards the freighter's bridge. He walked that way.

"Merc!" Phyla's voice came over rushed, like she was speaking and running at the same time. "Head towards the main bridge, but stay away from the *Jumper* and the docking bays. They're taken."

"How do I get there?"

"Figure it out. Can't talk," Phyla's voice cut out to the sound of something shrieking, hit by a laser and heated passed the point of its endurance.

"The bridge it is, then," Merc said as he jogged.

The Viper didn't have much room for gear, so the only thing Merc had on him was a small sidearm. Close range and not very forgiving. He'd need to be precise to cause any real damage, and if he was in any firefight, running would be a better option. Still, Merc held the weapon in both hands as he left the bay. Motion lights came on in the hallway, blinking as he moved. Always walking towards the dark.

The first branch split the hallway with a pair of narrow signs. Straight ahead read the obvious one, *Bridge and Bays*. To the right, *Engineering*. Gotta love a well-marked ship. Merc walked straight, heading towards the bridge, when a shout came from the other way. An angry noise, someone surprised and annoyed about it. Then the *shunt* of a door slamming shut. Merc paused. Phyla ordered him to the bridge, but then, that might not mean much if this group took control of the

Amerigo's engines. At the very least, Merc could gather intel.

Backtracking towards engineering, Merc slowed his pace. The hallway split again a few meters ahead, with a double-wide door on one side. Above the door, a flat-bottomed, rounded-top piece, sat the word *Engineering_*in block white letters set against the dark green Eden color. On the right of the door was panel for badged access, its red light glowing at Merc.

Merc didn't have a badge, which meant no way was he getting through that door. But beneath the panel was a small button labeled *Comm*. Maybe . . .

"Hello?" Merc said as he pushed the comm_button. "You guys in here yet?"

Waited for a breath or two.

"Who's asking?" Came a grumbling voice. Stressed, sounded like.

"Your boss, that's who," Merc replied.

No reply came. Which meant either they were ignoring him, or—

The door shot open and a big man stood there, staring at Merc, holding a long two-handed rifle in his hands, red coils tying the weapon to a strapped-on backpack power source. The man looked down at Merc and raised an eyebrow. He was wearing clothes Merc could only describe as the rejects of space-faring fashion, a true looter's ensemble of military gear, discount trash, and knickknacks like a chain bearing the crest of the Red Voice. Merc took all this in and knew the moment this gun-toting wild man realized Merc wasn't part of his group, a quick death was next.

The same feeling Merc had in the Viper flooded through his bones, a cold steel that threatened to freeze out everything with possibilities lost should he not survive. Only this time, Merc was ready for it. Treated the feeling as a warning, a sign to keep the impending disasters from exploding beyond correction. That only by acting now would he have a chance at taking those threads of the future back in his hand.

Merc dove forward, pinning the man's big gun to the side and preventing its lethal nose from getting a good look. The big man grunted in surprise and pushed back, while Merc pulled the trigger on his sidearm. The little gun fired, its angle also off to the side, but jammed against the assault rifle. Its laser burrowed into the larger gun, which popped and then exploded with concussive force as the gas used to create its lasers burst from its pressurized seal.

Merc flew back into the wall, bouncing off and losing his air. Gasping, he looked around for the big man and saw him hunched against the opposite wall.

"You are so dead," said a woman, adorned in equally ridiculous fare and pointing an old-fashioned slug-throwing shotgun at Merc.

No way to win today. Merc looked at the woman and threw a half-smile. You try, you fail, and sometimes when you fail, someone's there to lay into you with a shotgun. There was a saying he'd learned back in the service, some-thing the fighter jockeys muttered to themselves as a blessing against impossible situations: Give'em hell cause hell's gonna be given to you. Merc tensed his legs, ignored his burning lungs, and waited. The woman raised the gun.

A strangled, high-pitched noise cried as a shape blurred into Merc's peripheral, jumping on the woman like a child looking for a ride and pushing her into the side of the room. The woman yelled while the attacker, a short man in the dirty garb of an Eden engineer, bit at her arms and tried to throw her to the ground. Merc stood and ran at the woman's shotgun, still waving in her hand. Just as the woman tried to knock the engineer off by slamming her back into a wall, Merc reached her, grabbed the shotgun, and tore it free.

"Stop!" Merc yelled in her face, though he wasn't sure really whether it applied to the woman or the engineer. "I'll shoot either of you if you move."

Merc's side exploded in pain, a rippling agony that wiped away all thoughts about what he would say to his captives next. And then Merc was flying down the hallway, back towards the door that'd opened to bring all this crap to him, and he hit the floor and bounced once before settling. The big man. That's who'd kidney-punched Merc and thrown him like a sack of potatoes.

First rule of fighter flying was that you always watched your back. Remember the basics, man.

Speaking of. Merc noticed his sidearm sitting there on the ground a meter away. A quick glance back towards the room showed the big man taking the engineer off the woman's back and slamming him into the ground. Fighter flying rule number two; always cover your wingman. Merc scrambled for the sidearm, feeling any second like he might vomit up all over the place. Gripping the handle, Merc rolled onto his side, aimed, and fired.

The laser was true and hit the big man in the center of his back. Right where the laser would do all sorts of nasty things to a man's nerves. Big'n'Scary collapsed in a heap while the woman traced the shot back to Merc and stared, then raised her hands.

"Nice shot," the woman said.

"I'll do the same to you if you move," Merc said, lying there. "The little guy alive?"

The woman, keeping her hands up, looked at the engineer.

"Punk's still with us."

A groan came from over that way, and the smell of charred flesh and clothes hit Merc's nostrils. Problem with actually being in atmosphere when shooting someone with a laser is you had to deal with the scents afterward. Hair, clothes, chemicals subjected Merc's nose to sickening waves of smell. And that was the kicker his stomach was looking for.

"Gross," said the woman, watching.

"Don't," Merc said between heaves. "Move."

"You want me to put you out of your misery? Cause you look pretty terrible right now."

"Hostages aren't supposed to be so cocky." Merc wiped his sleeve across his face.

"Why not? When Bakr gets here, he's going to turn you into a pile of ash. Same with this guy," the woman said, sounding bored. "So if you're gonna shoot me, do it now. Cause you don't have much time left among the living."

22

MECHANICAL OFFENSIVE

The first thing Trina told Erick was to blast the doors. The ones leading into the bay. Erick opened the *Jumper*'s turret and aimed it at the doors. Or rather, around them, and fired a few test shots. They flew into the control panels and demolished them in a shower of sparks. That at least would prevent the attackers from getting quick entry into the bay. And give Trina time to do what she needed to do.

"Erick, I'm going down to set up a defense, keep me covered," said Trina.

"Got it."

Trina ran down the *Jumper*'s ramp as soon as it opened. There wasn't going to be much time. Trina had to make it as hard as possible for the attackers to get to their ship. One nice thing about being in a giant freighter was that there's plenty of stuff to use. All around them in the bay were fuel canisters, batteries, cargo containers both empty and full of supplies meant to be shuttled down to the *Karat* if the mission went longer than planned.

"Erick, I'm going to move some of these canisters," Trina said. "Let me know if they're breaking in,"

The doctor clicked the comm to acknowledge. Trina ran over to the first set of canisters, old-style fuel meant for old-style ships, ships like the shuttle that had been taken by Davin and the others down to Neptune. Hit it with enough concentrated energy and they would go boom.

Lifting them wasn't possible. A hundred kilos or more apiece. So Trina leaned against the cylinders and knocked them on their sides. Rolled them over to the door and pressed them up against the wall.

"What're you doing, Trina?" commed Erick.

"These canisters will explode. You'll shoot them when they start to come in," Trina said. "It should buy us some time."

Erick didn't say anything else. Which was fine. Trina knew what she was doing. Working with this kind of material was something that she handled a lot as the *Jumper*'s mechanic. Knowing what fuel would do in various situations was important when you had a lot of it stored on your ship. As Trina rolled the third canister over, a thunk sounded from the other side of the door. Someone testing it.

"Keep those turrets trained," Trina said.

"They're ready to fire, I'd just prefer you weren't in the way," Erick said.

"The *Jumper*'s worth more than me," Trina said. "We lose her, there's no way out of here."

"Then we won't lose her."

After a couple more thoughts trial knocks, the smell of burning electrical wires filtered into the bay. Laser cutters. Trina only had a few more seconds. Enough for one more canister. Four should be enough. She kicked it over, rolled it along the ground, the ridged surfaces making it rumble as it went along. The middle of the bay door glowed amber. Heat coming through from the other side. It was going to be tight.

As she got closer, a bright yellow beam burst through the skin of the doors, continuing on for a meter before petering out to nothing. Trina gave one more shove and left the canister rolling. Turned back towards the *Jumper* and its lowered ramp and ran.

"Get ready!" Trina yelled into her calm.

"I am, just get yourself on the ship," Erick replied.

"Don't shoot until their clear of the door," Trina continued. "The canisters will be more effective if we let them get past. We'll catch more that way."

"I'll handle it."

Trina hit the ramp at full sprint, boots clanging against the surface. At the top of the ramp, she turned back to the door in time to see the middle section fall away, a glowing orange outline traced through the metal. On the other side several faces look back up at her. They weren't friendly.

The first two stepped through the broken door as Trina raised the ramp. She heard Erick fire. Trina paused the ramp's process, leaned out to look. A pair of the attackers were being dragged back through the door, a cloud of bluish smoke hanging over the area. No bodies on the floor.

"Too early," Trina said.

"I fired when I needed to," Erick said. "I'm not a killer. Especially an unnecessary one. Your trap has them pulling back. We bought us some time."

Trina heard the words. They were logical. The attackers almost certainly wouldn't let them go. Wouldn't just stop on account of kindness. But at the same time, she respected Erick's choice. The idea that he couldn't give up who he was even when dire circumstances compelled him to. Trina turned towards her cabin, to grab her rifle. Just because the doctor didn't want to kill anybody, didn't mean she wouldn't have to.

PARALYZE

Phyla ducked into the bunk as lasers flashed through the corridor behind her. Naturally, the crew cabin was a one-door trap. Phyla glanced at her sidearm, the little energy left in it was enough for a couple more shots. And there were at least three attackers after her. Had been since she'd left the bays, chasing and firing with the kind of abandon Phyla saw at practice ranges. Either they didn't really care about blasting up the freighter, or had so many back-up battery packs that ammunition wasn't a worry.

The bunk room had the requisite cot, unmade and stained with bits of oil, grease. Someone working in the dirtier side of the ship and not willing to keep his own quarters clean. Maybe Van, that long-haired engineer, or the surly short one.

A standard Eden display built into the wall, for watching movies and other entertainment on long voyages. And one side dedicated to the locker, a combination-sealed box where the guy stored his things. On the wall above the bed was a series of markings. Phyla took another second to look and realized they were days, a line for every single Sol on the ship. Given the number, the engineer had been on the *Amerigo* for longer than just this mission. Had this bunk the entire time.

Now, when he came back to his room, the engineer might find a burned out corpse. Phyla gripped the sidearm and stared at it. Before, there'd always been options. Fly away, run and gun out of the situation. Call in reinforcements. But all the logical next steps were gone and here she was, thinking about using one of those last shots on herself.

"We know you're in there, lady," called a voice from the hallway. "We're not here to kill everyone. Mostly. So we'd be glad to take you alive. You prove yourself useful, and you could see yourself dropped at the next station we come to."

Yeah. Give yourself up, Phyla. Just slide that sidearm out and let these fine people decide your fate for you.

Phyla looked out the door, back into the hallway. Farther down, away from the chasers, were more rooms. Each one spaced a meter apart from the last, alternating sides so nobody bunked directly across from someone else. That meant she only had to go a meter before dashing into cover. But there was nothing in that hallway. For that meter she'd be easy killing even for the worst shot.

"Yes or no. We're getting impatient," the voice called.

What Phyla needed was time. Time to think, to get help. She looked up next to the door and slapped the small panel. The door rushed in from the left side and Phyla hit the panel again to lock it in place. Unless they brought something strong with them, or had a master passcode for all these rooms, Phyla had bought herself a moment to breathe.

"Aw, now, that's not very polite," the voice said, coming

from the other side of the door. "Shutting the door on your friends like that. But that's all right. We have a way in right here, don't we?"

Phyla heard the crackle, the distinctive popping of a las-tool switching on. The same stuff they used in their guns, only concentrated to a small, tight beam. They'd be through in a minute or two. Break the door's locking mechanism, and the whole thing would pop open. It's not like Eden had a lot of incentive to make their crew rooms durable against break-ins.

"I've over-charged my weapon," Phyla said. "You break that door, I'll set it off. Friend."

The las-tool's crackle didn't get any closer. Hesitation. Phyla looked at her sidearm. No way she could get anything more than a loud pop out of overcharging this thing. Not anywhere close to blowing them, or herself, apart. Which meant waiting till they called her bluff. Lina, her childhood friend, would sneer at her. Calling Phyla out for being a unoriginal. Sitting and waiting to die? She'd have figured something out.

The crackle got closer again. A hissing noise erupted as the laser melted into the door. Phyla gripped the sidearm in her right hand, reached over to the panel and slapped the door open. It shot up and showed the partially-masked, surprised face of one very ambushed man. The guy wore what looked like a rejected costume, torn and stained from mis-use, draping him in shreds of black netting. It was frightening, so Phyla blasted him in the face.

The man fell back into the other two, barely starting to react to the open door. The burning las-tool, still gripped in the shot man's hand, swung backward and into the body of a woman sporting an eclectic collection of exercise clothing. The fabric burst into flame the moment the las-tool came near the woman's thigh, lighting up the clothes like a firework.

The last of the trio stumbled away from the pyre, and Phyla emptied a second laser into him. Stepping over the first body, Phyla kicked the las-tool out of his hand, the automatic shut-off causing the machine to die as it skittered down the hallway.

"Sorry, you said you wanted in," Phyla said, looking at the trio.

Steps echoed through the hallway, further along the crew quarters. Without thinking, Phyla snapped the sidearm up and pulled the trigger. The weapon sputtered for a second, then beeped. Energy exhausted.

"Thought I was on your side?" Quinn said, stepping forward with his hands raised.

"Don't know who's on my side right now," Phyla said, but she lowered the weapon. "Except my crew, and they're scattered all over this ship."

"Then let's get to the bridge. From there, we can find them. Help them," Quinn reached behind his back and pulled out a heavy rifle half as long as he was tall. Powerful enough to punch through any door on the ship, or even out through the hull with enough concentrated fire.

"Isn't that risky?" Phyla said, eying the rifle.

"I know what I'm doing," Quinn replied. "Ready?"

Guess that was her answer.

"They cut off the bays," Phyla said. "Is there another way?"

"Back through the crew quarters," Quinn said, turning back the way he'd come.

"Hey," Phyla said. "If the bridge is that way, why did you come back here?"

Quinn glanced back at her.

"Because I'm thinking you and your crew are the only friends I have left on this freighter."

24

———

AFTERMATH

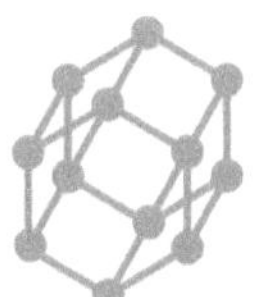

When Puk told her to dive, to jump into the bathroom, Viola listened. She believed when a machine, built on cold, hard logic, told you something with absolute certainty, you listened. So she dove, and felt Opal collapse into her a second later, the sniper's head landing in her lap as the shuttle split in two. A lance of blue fire that Viola saw outside the lavatory door, shooting through with the whistling whine of materials being separated into their atomic parts.

If Davin, who poked his head into the lavatory both too soon and far too late afterward, had asked Viola how she felt, there would have been no real answer. Because she didn't know how to describe being utterly powerless. Without Puk's warning, the laser would have cleaved Opal in half. Would have torched Viola's face, burned away her clothes and rendered her blind. Viola processed the thoughts, the consequences a stream of damning data and couldn't find any rationale for why she should continue. She was so, so obviously out of her league.

Viola felt Opal breathing, light but still pushing air in and out of her lungs.

The fight on Eden Prime where Fournine, an android she'd programmed to protect them, had blown itself up, taking two more of the hostile bots with it, didn't register on the same scale. It'd struck Viola as comical, surreal to see machines beating each other to a pulp while she took pot shots from the sidelines. The idea of real danger never penetrated. The bots weren't after her. But here, these people, they saw her as a target and weren't afraid to shoot.

"Hey. We should get moving," Puk whirred, hovering near the remnants.

"I'll carry her," Mox said, the metal man breaking through the rubble and tearing off the shuttle structure that stood in his way. A moment later, he picked Opal up off of Viola, cradling the sniper in his arms. Then he spared a look at Viola, seeking any sign of injury.

"I'm fine," Viola said. "Just, shaken up."

Mox hesitated, then nodded and moved out of the wreck. Puk hovered there, its small orb seeming to stare at her in concern. Which, yeah. The bot should worry. You take a girl out of engineering school and throw her into a deathtrap of lasers and explosions and expect her to take it without flinching? That's the movies.

"Are you—"

"I said I'm fine," Viola interrupted the bot, stood. Focused on the narrow aim, the immediate one foot in front of the other goal of getting out of the shuttle. Planting her foot, which Viola realized now was wrapped in the shreds of her boot, whose melted sole landed unevenly on the ground, she stepped around the shards of the craft that minutes ago was the only thing keeping them alive in Neptune's endless tornado of an atmosphere.

Mox moved across the bay, disappearing into the exit hallway. Viola was about to follow, then glanced towards the back of the shuttle, the other ruined half. Why she looked that way, Viola wasn't sure, except wondering if both halves suffered the same terrible fate. Sitting there, on top of each other, were a pair of small rifles. Spray-and-pray shooters, Davin had called them when he'd put them in the shuttle. One was Viola's. The other, Opal's back-up if the confines of the *Karat* weren't conducive to kilometer-long sniper shots. Viola grabbed both of the weapons, slinging their straps over her shoulders.

Just putting on the weapons was a relief. Not the weapons themselves, really, but that Viola had made tangible progress. She wasn't a prone victim anymore. Rather, she was moving closer to the goal. Making a difference. One second away from death, but she did not die. And she was not yet done.

Viola found Mox and Davin outside the door of an elevator, the call button not yet pressed. They were talking in low voices, and looked up as Viola rounded the corner.

"It sucks, doesn't it?" Davin said first.

Viola nodded.

"My first real fight wasn't that bad. A bunch of idiots we were paid to round up in some lunar slums," Davin said. "They weren't supposed to be more than brawlers, and bad ones at that, but one turned out to be ex-military. Had a gun back when Luna, what with the thin shielding, wanted no one shooting. I was the second one in and watched Cadge get leveled by a laser. Miracle that he lived."

"Cadge was with you back then?" Viola said.

"Sure, he left the military way before Opal. Point being, I didn't take it well. Fell back into the next guy and the crew I was with had to figure out a way to disarm the bastard with me contributing a lot of panic. They finally told me to drag Cadge to a hospital and just leave them alone."

"What happened?"

Davin shrugged. "We took care of them. And I got over it. Point being, it'll fade. You'll be fine."

"Opal needs help," Mox rumbled. "Soon."

"That suit of yours have any bright ideas on how we get to the main deck without getting lit up by a bunch of waiting ass-hats?" Davin asked. "That's where the med rooms will be."

Viola tried to recall the schematics of the *Karat*, the ones they'd had on the shuttle console and that she'd been able to look at for a few minutes before their launch from the freighter. The vessel was three levels, with the bay above them. The bridge and crew quarters occupied the top, the labs and vacuum storage—to prevent any degrading of the minerals—was in the middle, with general cargo, raw materials, and the engines making up the lower deck.

"Then let's go around," Viola said. "There are suits still in the shuttle, the emergency ones, two packed in the back, two in the front."

The full passenger load. The Free Laws weren't good for much, but nobody wanted the bad press of a crew forced to let someone freeze-out in space, so they'd mandated a minimum space suit set on every craft equal to the expected passenger count.

"Wait, you're saying to scale the ship? The outside?" Davin said, his tone more curious than dismissive.

"I'm saying we can get in through the cargo bay. Through the same tubes they get the ore from," Viola continued, both impressed with her own ingenuity and wondering if this was a really, really dumb idea.

"There wouldn't be anyone there," Davin said. "Because it's a ridiculous plan."

"Opal," Mox said.

"That's true, she couldn't climb," Davin muttered. "But if we split . . ."

"Davin and I," Viola said. "We'll go."

"No offense, Viola, but you'll probably get in a fight eventually and—"

"It won't do any good," Viola interrupted. "If you two get down there and find a computer you can't crack. A locked shut-off on that ore intake and you're going to have a long walk back. And I don't think Mox will fit in one of those suits."

Davin glanced between Mox and Viola, then nodded.

"We'll go. Mox, hang out here and keep an eye on Opal," Davin said. "I'll comm you before we head up the elevator. It opens before then, it won't be friends on the other side."

25

ENGINEERS

"S o what're you gonna do with her?" the short engineer asked, a look in his eyes that Merc didn't much care for. "She's the enemy, right?"

"She's a resource," Merc replied as he finished patting the woman for weapons. The scattered randomness of her outfit left all kinds of places where she could've stowed away a small gun or knife. He took off her comm, tossed it next to the body of the other attacker. "You got a name, resource?"

The woman, who'd spent this whole time swapping glares between Merc and the engineer settled after the question. Like she realized Merc would not light her up there and then, weaponless, in the hallway.

"Cass," the woman said.

"Cass," Merc chewed the name while pondering the next line. "How about you let us in on what the hell's going on here?"

"It's what it looks like," Cass said. "We're taking the freighter. There's a lot of us, and once some more of my group get down here, you'll be as dead as Trap over there."

"His name was Trap?" the short engineer said.

"It's what he chose," Cass said.

"And now he's dead," the engineer said. "Guy gives himself a great name, winds up dead on the floor of a freighter looking like an ugly grizzly bear. What a life."

Cass stiffened. Merc hadn't put any restraints on her. If that engineer kept talking, Merc might have to.

"How about we focus?" Merc said. "Cass. Tell me. What's your goal?"

"Mine?" Cass's voice was tight, her eyes locking on the engineer even as she talked to Merc. "Right now, it's to kill that man."

The engineer took a breath and Merc snapped the sidearm at him, causing the engineer to gulp down whatever dumb words were about to spew out of his mouth.

"That's not gonna happen," Merc said. "But if he keeps talking, I'll let you beat him up a little."

Cass's shoulders dropped and she took a deep breath. After a long blink, her eyes went back to Merc.

"We were supposed to hold the engines. Keep the freighter from moving out of position," Cass said.

"Out of position for what?" Merc replied as the engineer moved towards the far wall, leaning against it and giving both of them a glowering stare.

"Whatever ship is down there on Neptune," Cass said. "We're supposed to catch it when it comes up."

"Who told you to do that?"

"What do you care?" Cass asked. "Why does it even matter? You're dead."

"Would you quit saying that?" Merc said, then stepped behind her. "Now, here's what we're gonna do. I'm going to go find my friends, and you're going to help me out."

"I am?"

"Yeah, because if you don't, then I'll shoot you first,"

Merc said. "Your boy Trap there can tell you what a good shot I am."

The bridge, that'd been Phyla's order. Time to get to it.

Cass didn't put up a fight as Merc moved the two of them. He told the engineer to seal the door behind them, lock it and not to open it for anyone.

"Only a moron would open this door again," the engineer replied.

"Just stay quiet till this is all over."

"You can't say you don't want to punch him too," Cass said as soon as the door shut behind them.

"Maybe," Merc said. "But here's what I really want to know. How are you so cool right now?"

Trap's body, lying there on the floor, was playing with Merc's senses. The idea that one day that could be him. Or Opal. That the other would be left behind. It was the thing Merc, as did most of the pilots flying combat missions, thought about in abstract. Family attending their funeral. Their lead saying a few nice words. The next mission without them flying on it. But it was always from a remove, an imaginary broadcast. Now, though . . . Merc blinked away the thought. Focus, man, or you *will* end up like that guy.

"You ever lose much in your life?" Cass asked.

"Enough," Merc replied.

"I've seen so many friends burn out around me that one more barely registers."

"Sounds like you need a new line of work."

"This isn't work, it's a cause."

"Hijacking freighters is a cause?"

Cass stopped, turned to Merc. Held out her right arm, wrapped in a loose gray sleeve.

"This cloth right here? It came from a store, a place I used to go every week as a girl to see what was new. What

Eden and the others sent to our town on the edge of civilization," Cass pulled the arm back, pointed to her shoes, which were stained, patched and beaten, but still held together. "These were a friend's. She didn't need them after the first day of the war. She raised her hand and they shot her for it."

"Red Voice," Merc said, not believing the words coming out of his mouth. "You're all supposed to be dead. Or surrendered."

"One man closer, thanks to you."

"Wasn't my fault you attacked this ship," Merc said. "Keep moving."

They reached the intersection where Merc had been before hearing the shouts, Cass walking in front with Merc behind, sidearm pressed to her back. Red Voice. They'd started the Martian wars, fought against the Free Laws and lost. Which is what happens when you pitch a bunch of Mars townspeople against a corporate army backed by Earth's governments.

"You don't look like Eden," Cass said after a few minutes walking.

"Hired help."

"Don't meet many mercenaries that wouldn't split first sign of being outgunned."

"Guess you've been meeting the wrong ones."

"Maybe so."

The next few minutes passed in silence until they came to the sloping ramp that carried them up to the bays. The noises coming down told Merc everything he needed to know. Stern shouts were accompanied by the bangs and shunts of supplies moving, the attackers spreading out into their new home. Going up there would mean wandering right into the middle of them. Merc pulled Cass to the side, out of sight from the top of the ramp.

"What's in it for you?" Merc said, keeping his sidearm pressed into her side. "Taking the freighter?"

"Bakr said we'd get paid," Cass said. "We need coin, just like everyone else."

"Bakr?"

"Don't worry about him," Cass said. "He's a problem you can't solve."

"Then how about this one," Merc said. "I need to get past these bays. Past your guys. Get me by, I'll see about letting you get back to your cause."

"What're you going to do?"

"Don't worry about it. It's a problem you can't solve."

Cass laughed.

"Now run," Merc said. "Run up the ramp or I'll shoot you."

Cass looked back at Merc, her eyebrow raised, and Merc leveled the sidearm at her face, finger on the trigger. And Merc felt he was ready to do it. He would pull that trigger and send Cass to whatever world waited for her on the other side without hesitation.

"Go," Merc said, and Cass went. She slipped on the ramp, but recovered, stomping up. Merc belted up behind her, trying to keep the sidearm ready. The Red Voice started as a peaceful protest. Finished as a bloody fight with whole towns ground into the red dust of Mars. Opal told him the stories, the merciless attacks on Eden convoys where they'd find, after, only the smoking bodies of the innocent. There was no reason to think he'd get anything nicer.

So Merc followed Cass up the ramp and shot at anything that moved.

26

TRAITORS

Gage stood alone on the bridge. Alarms blared around him, the freighter telling of various disasters being committed in its halls by the boarding crew. Gage could've turned them off, could have sat in silence, but his hand hovered above the button, unable to press it. This was his fault and the alarms were his punishment. He could handle it.

His wrist buzzed. Gage glanced at it, noticed it was a face he'd been waiting, wanting, fearing to see. Eventually, one had to reckon with his choices.

"Thank you for letting us on board your vessel, Captain Gage," said the man on the other side.

Through the small screen on the comm, Gage stared at the wrapped visage. Rags. Only the man's eyes poked out, blood red and angry. He looked like that every time Gage spoke with him, as though the man's default state was harrowing.

"As we agreed," Gage said. "And you're not going to hurt my crew."

"So long as they don't harm us," the man replied. "However, there appear to be some on the ship that were not expected. Some that are proving difficult,"

"Eden saw fit to protect their investment."

"Then I hope none of your crew members get caught in the crossfire."

"I can help with that," Gage said. "The ones you want will try to make it here. To the bridge."

"We'll have a squad coming to greet them."

"And if that's not enough?"

"Then I can deal with them myself."

Gage swallowed. He hadn't ever seen the wrapped man handle things personally, but why ask for a nightmare when you didn't have to? Part of Gage wanted those mercenaries, wanted Quinn to succeed. To drive off the attackers and retake the freighter. To arrest Gage and hold him responsible. It was only right. But the small voice was drowned out by the rest of him, the part that knew if this went as planned, Gage would have nothing to fear. Nothing to want. Ever again.

"They won't be able to get in the doors," Gage said. "I'll direct them towards the escape shuttles if your crew fails."

"Then I will make my way there," the man replied. "Gage, I trust you understand how much is riding on this."

"For me, yes," Gage said. "For you, I don't care."

"A good answer."

The wrapped man cut the call. Gage stared at the blank screen for a second. He'd never sent anyone to their death before. But then, today was a day of firsts. A day of lasts.

27

THE BRIDGE

The wide gate leading to the bridge was shut, and standing in front of it was a group of five invaders. Like the ones that'd chased her earlier, Phyla saw these were all wearing their own takes on randomized fashion. Mismatched footwear, shirts sewn with different fabrics in each arm. Phyla wasn't sure of the tactic there, but if they were going for strange, then they earned it.

"If we hit them quick, we can have them down before they get a shot off," Quinn said. "They're standing so close that our misses will hit one of the others."

"They're trying to blow the door," Phyla replied. "That means they might have explosives. We set one off and—"

"It's what they're going to do anyway."

Maybe. Even on a ship the size of the freighter, Phyla wasn't real happy setting off any kind of bomb. By accident or otherwise. All the electronics running between the walls and floors. What happens if the fireball knocked out the bridge's ability to control the engines, or triggered a lockdown that sealed them in the hallway?

"Not like we have a choice," Phyla said, fighting her aversions. "I'll go left, you right."

Quinn nodded. Phyla hefted the weapon she'd stolen from one of the torched attackers back in the crew quarters. Stepping around the corner, Phyla pulled the trigger and blue bolts flew out at the attackers. Stunning shots, designed to overwhelm the nerves of whomever they hit and crumple them to the ground for hours. They were lower energy than killing blasts, and when ammo was a premium resource, Phyla was ready to settle for incapacitation.

Quinn's blasts joined hers a hot second later, the dual streams catching the attacking crew unaware. They barely had a chance to turn, to raise a hand, before they were struck and piled on the ground like a bunch of passed-out revelers. Phyla and Quinn ran up to them, checking each one with a slap to the face, a kick to the side to make sure they weren't faking. Satisfied, Phyla turned to the panel next to the door and pressed the comm button.

"Gage. It's Phyla and Quinn. Open up."

Seconds passed while the two of them waited. Quinn aimed down the hallway where the attackers would have come from, waiting for the next round.

"I can't do that, Phyla," Gage replied.

"You going to tell me why?" Phyla said, throwing a questioning look back at Quinn, who shook his head.

"Opening these doors risks the bridge," Gage said. "You two might be hostages."

"You have cameras looking out here," Phyla said. That was a hunch, but even the *Jumper*, a much smaller ship, had cameras throughout. It made sense when any breach or problem anywhere could cause all kinds of hell in space. "You think all these people are taking a nap?"

A noise echoed up the hallway. Or rather, noises. Phyla

picked out the various footfalls of a squad, a bigger group than before. Reinforcements called when the first five found the door sealed. She was running out of time.

"Sorry," Gage said, then cut the comm.

"What's he doing?" Phyla asked Quinn. "Why wouldn't he let us through?"

The bodyguard stared hard at the doors, as though trying to bore holes through them.

"When I checked, only a few people on board this ship knew the real objective," Quinn said. "Myself. Captain Yuan and his crew, all of whom are on the *Karat* . . ."

"And Gage," Phyla said.

Before Quinn could respond, with the clamber of the approaching group getting louder, Phyla slapped the comm again.

"The thing with sell-outs, Gage, is that they always think their side's going to win," Phyla said. "You made the wrong play."

"And the problem with the righteous is that they assume their enemies had a choice," Gage replied before clicking off again.

Then Phyla was on the ground, Quinn tackling her as the first shots sizzled over her head. Bright orange, killing energy. Phyla rolled out from underneath Quinn and, propping her weapon on the prone body of a stunned attacker, triggered off a few retorts down the hallway. The enemies ducked back behind the corner, so her answering bolts splashed harmlessly against the wall.

"We have no cover here," Quinn said.

"If we run, we won't get back," Phyla said.

"I don't think that matters anymore. The freighter is lost."

Lost. As in, taken over. Which meant they were way out

in Neptune's orbit with only the *Jumper*, currently nestled in the midst of enemy territory, as their only ticket home.

Quinn pulled Phyla up, holding his rifle in his left hand and continuing to trigger a barrage of bolts down the hallway. The attackers chose to fire blind. Sticking their guns around the corner and squeezing the triggers, shots going wildly into the walls or overhead. Phyla shook off Quinn's tugging and back-pedaled on her own until they were around the corner.

"What now?" Phyla asked. "The bays are swarming with them."

"The *Amerigo* has several escape shuttles. Small things, meant to keep you alive until help arrives," Quinn said. "The shuttles also have long-range transmitters. I can get a message to Eden from there."

"Which will mean what?"

"They'll know who did this and long after we're dead, Eden will avenge us."

"That's comforting," Phyla said as the two of them jogged down the hallway, taking turns back to the crew quarters. Yet again, Phyla was running away from a fight. She was getting really, really sick of it.

28

OUTSIDE

There were two men's, two women's space suits on the shuttle, locked away towards the back of the passenger compartment in a cabinet coated in *Emergency* red. Snug fits, like more suits these days. They converted enough oxygen to go for hours outside, insulated well enough to allow survival on body heat in a vacuum, and, to Davin, felt like zipping himself up in a plastic bag. The suit made every interaction a little unreal. He hated not feeling what was in his hands. A wall between him and the rest of reality.

The coiled tether was as big around as Davin's thumb. Silver, with a thick casing made to withstand direct cuts with beam knives, lasers, or space rocks. A broken tether meant someone would spin through the cosmos, counting the stars till they fell asleep as their suit gave out.

"You ever wear one?" Davin asked Viola, who had her suit half on, her arm in the wrong sleeve.

"Never," Viola said.

"Try using the sleeves," Davin said, pressing the button to activate the helmet. From his collar, the space suits neck expanded, growing over and around Davin's head. It latched back onto the suit in front, completing the seal. Then Davin released it. Always good to check that something works before he depended on it for his life. "That was a joke, by the way."

"I don't get it," Viola replied, sticking her arms, finally, in the right places. "We're here fighting for our lives. About to go outside into one of the most hostile environments a human can experience. After I barely survived getting immolated. And here you're trying to make me laugh."

"It's pathological, sorry," Davin said.

"I just wish I could."

"Could what?"

"Laugh. Smile."

"I get it. You're stunned. But back in that hallway you came up with a good idea, one we're executing," Davin always felt, with speeches, that he was wearing his captain hat. Made his scalp itch. "That means you're not useless. You will not fall apart. You're still you and, damn it, you can still laugh. That's an order."

"Don't think I've ever heard you give an order before," Viola said, the corners of her mouth turning up as she finished donning the suit. "Guess I bring out the best in you."

"I give orders all the time," Davin said, slipping the thick tether coil around his arm. "The trick is to make people think you're just asking."

"Is that it?" Viola replied, then noticed both of them were staring at each other, suited up and ready. "So, how do we get outside?"

"Same way we came in," Davin said, walking over to a control panel near the bay's exit. The panel wasn't much more than a few large buttons. One to accept an incoming call from the bridge, one to place a call to the same. Another pair had a green UP arrow and a red DOWN arrow. Small illustrations carved into the panel next to the two showed an open door by the green, and a closed one by the red. Simple enough. Davin pressed the green one.

The bay rumbled. Lifts warming up to raise the bay up to disembark. A monotone voice announced a countdown from five, to four, three, two and one. Davin stepped back as the door to the exit slammed shut, sealing them in. Then the whole room rose. Davin felt the motion in his legs, but it wasn't until the black of Neptune's night broke through the sides of the bay that Davin understood what they were about to do.

There's a beauty to space, where the dark is everywhere but also nowhere. Stars shine for infinity. Planets looming like ornaments against the sparkling backdrop. Neptune's night was something else. Even a shutoff, blacked out room didn't compare. Clouds filtered out most of the starlight, moonlight. The gradient gray void stretched out to an infinite horizon.

The *Karat* kept the atmosphere from running out through the same magnetic seals used on every bay and ship. Davin and Viola walked right up to the edge and looked. The schematics had the *Karat* being thirty meters high, with the bay jutting up another five meters when it was extended. Davin had to rely on those numbers because the *Karat* had no running lights on. It was a sea of nothing beneath them. With the bay's back lighting, it was like the two of them and their wrecked shuttle were floating in nothing.

"What's our tether length?" Davin asked.

"Twenty meters. Pretty damn short," Viola said.

"Almost like they weren't planning for long-distance

spacewalks," Davin replied. "Still, if I recall correctly, that's about the height of this ship. We get above that intake, and you're looking at less than twenty meters cause the openings are so high."

"Yeah, except we're in the middle of the ship. That intake is towards the rear," Viola said. "The *Karat*'s more than two hundred meters long. We'll be out of tether before you can even make the curve."

"So we stop and go," Davin said.

One moves first, anchors the tether, the other catches up. Slow, but safe. Especially if those Neptune winds picked up. The tethers themselves were designed for latches or, given the space disaster scenarios out there, had magnets that could secure them to the sides of any modern spacecraft.

"I'll start," Viola said. "It's my idea. And I'm lighter."

"You calling me fat?" Davin said.

"Stop it," Viola tapped a button on her spacesuit and the helmet sealed around her head. She ran the tether through the bands around her suit's waist, keeping a meter hanging off where the magnet sat. Davin did the same. Like putting on a belt, only this one was more about saving his life than keeping up his pants. Then Davin took the magnet end, pressed it against the floor of the bay, and gave it a twist.

The tether made a pleasant beep and glowed emerald along its length. They both watched the color make its way along the tube until it reached Viola's end. Any break in the connection and the tether would go red, a signal that they were not, in fact, tethered anywhere at all.

Viola took her magnet and stuck it to the floor in the same fashion. This time, the tether's color changed to a bright blue. Double connection. Their way of signaling when it was time for the other to move. They'd have their comms too, but the colors provided that moment-by-moment accuracy.

"Ready?" Davin said. Viola gave him a thumbs up, disconnected her tether. Then, with her helmet up, the girl stepped through the magnetic seal and dropped out of sight.

29

BLOW THE DOOR

When someone comes charging out of nowhere, shooting lasers at your face, there are two kinds of surprised reactions: There's the prepared version, where the waiting force understands the charge is coming and meets it with its own hail of return fire. Then there's the unprepared version, the surprise Merc liked to think of in capital letters. The surprise that's so unexpected that the mind stalls out and nosedives into the planet.

With Cass sprinting in front of him, yelling that Merc was an enemy, and Merc two steps behind taking wild shots with the sidearm, the raiders weren't prepared. The scattered group of people in the hallway, some still holding crates unloaded seconds ago, others looking at schematics and trying to decide where to send people, were not ready for a crazed counter-assault. If he hadn't been fighting for his life, Merc would've laughed at the diving people as his shots blew charred chunks out of the walls. One blast caught a mercenary in the shoulder and the man looked at the smoking hole as though he couldn't believe it was actually there.

Past the first bay, the *Jumper* had landed in the third, the next group of Red Voice fighters at least had their guns out. A few wide shots came Merc's way, fired from people trying to take cover. They aimed around Cass, or didn't shoot at all when they saw her coming towards them. The two of them passed the second bay, this one connected to the frigate through a boarding tunnel. More invaders were on their way through, too many to fight. Even if all of the Nines were here, they wouldn't be able to repel these guys. Merc kept running.

There was a set of five attackers outside the door to bay three, taking cover not from Merc, but from fire coming out of the bay. Trina and Erick playing defense for the home team. Now the attackers turned at Cass and Merc, changing their portable energy shield, a green rectangle, to block Merc's incoming pot shots. Which left their flank vulnerable.

"Erick, let it rip through the door!" Merc shouted into his comm as he triggered another shot with the sidearm. This one, instead of the deep red most had been up till now, was a lighter, pinker shade. Energy was running low. It only had to last a few more seconds.

Shrieking, exploding pops poured into the corridor ahead. Cass stopped dead and Merc ran into her, sending them both sprawling as lasers from behind zipped by. A lucky break. Merc rolled off of Cass and looked towards bay three. Fire and smoke blanked the corridor, the end result of Erick's blast-happy use of the *Jumper*'s turret. The path ahead was clear, but the steady stream of shots from back behind them made getting up suicidal.

"Clever, but not good enough," Cass muttered, pushing

herself away from Merc. "You can surrender now. We might not kill you right away."

"Tempting, but I'll pass," Merc said. He didn't have much time for a solution. To think, a month ago he'd been floating free in space above Europa, waiting for a slow, sleepy death to come for him. Now here he was about to get violently shredded by hot energy. Given the two, he'd — wait. Space. That was it.

"Erick, I need you to blow the doors on the bay. Kill the magnetic seal. Then get ready to play catch."

"What are you doing?" Cass said, eyes opening in alarm.

"Got one last trick," Merc said. His comm clicked, and the pilot dove forward, rolling towards the bay three door. He couldn't tell if Cass followed or not. Shots hit the surrounding ground. Hard to hit a rolling figure in smokey haze.

And then Merc's ears nearly exploded.

A fizzling bang and Merc felt like he was being pushed by the invisible hands of a huge mob, shoving him forward into bay three. Behind him, the freighter initiated its standard response to vacuum leaks and tried to seal off the section. The bay three door was already blown apart, so it went to the next available spot and slammed down the secondary doors between bay three and bay two, and the hallway continuing on towards the bridge. Merc registered the shutting doors out of the corner of his eye as he blew through towards the *Jumper*.

The blocky ship looked so, so lovely, though Merc wasn't sure if that was because it was the only thing standing between him and, in a minute, frozen death out in pure space or because it was the one thing he'd seen in the last hour that wasn't trying to kill him. Cass was nowhere to be found. She must not have followed him forward. No time to dwell on that, though.

Merc bounced off the floor and continued rolling towards the metal shield closed over the bay's main exit. In the middle of the door was a series of holes, punched through and glowing orange around the edges from the *Jumper*'s lasers. The air was being sucked through those holes with enough force to whip Merc across the ground like a tornado. And if he hit those holes, Merc knew the force would break his bones to pieces or, if not that, other small objects would shoot into him like bullets.

Too reckless, that's what Opal would say. Trying something this stupid. Merc continued sliding across the floor, pulled towards the door. The current towards the holes carried Merc beneath the *Jumper*. Under the nose of the cockpit and nearing the main body. The ramp was still up, and for good reason. Opening the thing would just cause everything in the *Jumper* to get sucked out. Which left one spot for him to get in, the *Jumper*'s airlock.

As Merc blew by the ship, he reached out and wrapped his arms around the *Jumper*'s left rear landing strut. A thick steel leg connected every meter by joints and paralleled by a electric-powered arm that would fold the strut in during lift-off, the thing had plenty of handholds. The problem was that as Merc held on, he could feel his muscles strain, his wrists crack as the sucking force tried to yank him out. Climbing to the airlock like this would be impossible.

"Erick!" Merc said into his comm, shoving his face into his left wrist. "Docking airlock!"

Even shouting those words left Merc gasping the fleeting air for breath. The freighter wouldn't be pumping anymore oxygen into the bay, which meant that in a few minutes there wouldn't be anything breathable left in here. If there was going to be a rescue, it had to happen soon.

"Trina's on her way," Erick's voice came through the comm. "Stay steady."

"I'm on the back left strut."

"She'll get you."

See, Opal, sometimes the ideas work out. Cocky pilots aren't always wrong. Merc shut his eyes. Focused on his grip. Until he felt tugging from above. Merc glanced up and, in a space suit, tethered to the latch in the airlock, was Trina and her bright blue hair.

"Hey hotshot. Need a hand?"

Merc tried to reply, but couldn't seem to pull in the air to do so. He settled for a nod. Spots, little black flecks, were dancing around his eyes. Same stuff that happens when he pulled high G's in atmosphere. Doing loops, tight rolls. Merc didn't even notice as Trina wrapped spare tether around him, then punched the button to retract them into the *Jumper*'s airlock. By the time the ship's outer door shut, the pilot was unconscious.

30

LAST MAN

Mox leaned Opal up against the wall to the right of the elevator door when the button dinged and turned red. The up arrow. Davin and Viola only twenty minutes gone. Not enough time.

The cannon was ready, wound up and able to spray too many bolts too fast. Mox positioned himself in front of the doors, slightly to the left. They would aim, by reflex, dead center and any quick shots should fly right by Mox. They wouldn't have time for a second chance.

Another ding sounded as the elevator arrived. Mox heard the latches on the doors pop, the slow, grinding slide as the elevator opened. In the center was a small box, not much larger than Mox's own booted foot. It sat towards the front of the doors.

Mox blinked. He'd seen this before.

"Open it," The sergeant told Mox, pointing at the black, gem-studded box.

"My wife's remains!" the man wailed, but didn't move from the bench. Sarge's glare was more effective than handcuffs, promised more hells in the fiery glint of his eyes than any resis-

tance was worth. Mox picked up the box, squat and square, a few centimeters wide and tall. But it was heavy. Mox almost grabbed it with both hands, but that would be weak. Not in front of Sarge.

The top of the box was secured by a simple flip latch. Mox flicked it open, the man's protests going weaker. Inside, a pile of flaky dust. Relief, shame flooded Mox with equal measure.

"Nothing," Mox said.

"Sift the dust," Sarge said.

"But—"

"If those are the remains, his wife won't care," Sarge said.

Mox looked back at the box, pressed a finger into the dust. The grains stuck to his gloved hand, bits of another person on him now. A little deeper, and Mox hit something hard. The bottom of the box? Mox cocked his head.

"What is it?" Sarge asked. The man on the bench was sweating now. His eyes wide and staring back Mox's way.

"The remains aren't the only things in here," Mox said.

Sarge took two steps over to Mox, grabbed the box out of his hands, jammed their standard-issue EMP device in and pulled the trigger. Then Sarge tipped over the box. The powder fell like black snow to the floor, and through it crashed a tiny circuit. It hit the ground and shattered.

"First, rookie, those weren't ashes. Explosive powder. Second, the most dangerous thing on a space station is a bomb. You can blow it up, sure, but it can crack a hole and suck out your air fast. Burn up the oxygen and create a fire impossible to put out. Lunar law states any package can be searched. Use it, trust it," Sarge said.

So Mox dropped the cannon, detached it from the exoskeleton and dove towards Opal. He landed and pulled the sniper to him, his back and the metal plating of the exoskeleton facing the door.

A second later the elevator blew up. A small, controlled

explosion that sent a wave of heat and pieces of shrapnel bouncing off Mox's back. Cuts lanced pain through his arms and legs. Nothing major. Meant to kill a curious man, not a cautious one. Small chance of punching a hole in the ship. Mox turned back towards the elevator.

The cannon was ruined. Close enough to the blast, the barrel was bent out of shape, the nozzles sending the gas to generate the lasers themselves splayed on the ground like dead snakes. The elevator wasn't much better. The floor buckled, tiles opening into a hole down the shaft, with sparks spraying out from split wires. But Opal still breathed. Mox relaxed his grip, pushed Opal back against the wall, and stood.

Like feeling a twinge from a strained muscle, Mox felt a drag in his legs. A resistance.

"Suit status," Mox said, activating the exoskeleton's internal systems check. A moment later the suit rattled off a string of greens for Mox's upper extremities. The batteries checked out. But the left calf buzzed a red. Non-functional. Which meant the left foot wouldn't be able to transmit anything either. Mox moved his left leg to look at the calf, saw the piece of shrapnel jammed inside of it. The jagged piece a set product, stuffed inside of the bomb as a nasty surprise for anyone a few feet further back from the explosion. Mox reached and yanked the piece out, pulling with it the tangled remains of wires. There wouldn't be any boosted jumps happening anytime soon.

As Mox toss the extracted piece away, a clang sounded behind and below. Down the shaft. More came after. Not loud enough to be explosions. Metal on metal. And the sounds were coming closer.

"Time to move," Mox said, bending over and trying to pick up Opal. His arms handled the added weight without flinching, but as Mox straightened, the exoskeleton tried to adjust the load balance and failed, leaving Mox feeling as though his left side was being dragged down. Opal wasn't heavy enough to cause Mox real trouble, but walking became a mental exercise. His right leg moved, stepping forward without pause. The left required effort, resistance with every movement.

But they had to get to cover. Mox could hear voices coming up the shaft now. Must think their bomb took care of everyone up here. Which said they weren't well-trained. Mox shook his head. Always assume your enemy is still alive, ready to fight. Mox had his sidearms, one attached to each thigh. Not that he could grab them with Opal in his arms.

The exit to the shuttle bay was closed, leaving Mox trapped in the hallway. Davin and Viola, they must have raised it. Calling it back might ruin their plan. Or snap the tether and send them both flying off to surf Neptune's skies for a brief few seconds before death.

The hallway itself was smooth, rectangular lights glowing silver embedded into the walls. No cover.

Mox set Opal down near the door. Checked again to make sure she was still breathing. Viola's little bot said the sniper hit her head when the shuttle cracked. Could have used her here. Fast, accurate trigger fingers were handy in situations like this one. But no time to wait, now.

Back at the elevator, Mox heard them cutting away the ruined floor. Chunks of tiling, broken up by the bomb, dropped away as someone armed with a las-cutter made a hole. One sidearm in each hand, both set for stunning. It used less energy than the killing shots, and with the time Mox had, it'd be almost as good. Besides, his fists could always end things later.

The first hand appeared, gripping the outer edge of the elevator. Gloved like a mechanic, thick and gripped. Probably the one with the las-cutter. Mox shifted out of view. Better to let them get fully out. Surprise the group before they could react.

Softer noises now as at least another two clambered out of the hole, supporting themselves in the remains of the elevator. Mox tightened his grip. A quick one-two-three. Inhale. Go.

Stepped around the corner, the angle widening and bringing three hijackers into view. Each one sporting the same outfit, a thick working garb that looked ready to withstand temperature extremes. Full helmets with masks covering their faces, great to keep themselves safe from cold, wind. Mox pulled the triggers, the sidearms blasting blue-purple bolts into the bulky suits and doing nothing.

"Sorry, mate," the lead one, holding a sidearm of his own, said. "No luck with those."

Then he raised his sidearm and Mox saw a flash, then nothing.

31

WIND

Viola had never been on Earth, never seen one of the tornadoes that terrorized small towns in movies. She'd seen the great red spot, the storm blowing its way for centuries across the surface of Jupiter. Storms were a concept she had, but Ganymede, a moon with only a light, human-generated atmosphere, had none. So when Viola dropped from the docking bay onto the *Karat*'s exterior and felt the wind tug at her like an enraged vacuum, she stood for a minute and embraced nature's beating.

Even with the only real light coming from her suit, a lamp embedded in her upper chest, the darkness itself grabbing at her, Viola laughed. A helpless laughter, one tinged with knowing if the tether snapped, the space suit failed, or Neptune decided it wanted her dead, there was nothing she could do about it. Still, here she was, in one of the most violent natural environments humanity had ever encountered. Best get to exploring it.

The tether glowed green, still attached up where Davin was standing. He was probably wondering if Viola had fallen off the ship. Neptune's gravity, as strong as Earth's, helped keep Viola on the sloping side of the *Karat*, like walking on a hillside. Not enough to keep Viola going when things went full vertical, but for now? Viola took a step, then another. The wind pushed back against her, but at an angle. Like moving through syrup, or rushing water. Every motion a physics problem.

"I'm moving aft," Viola spoke into her comm, already set to short-range and Davin's personal frequency. "It's a bit breezy."

"Copy. Keep it safe out there," the space suit played Davin's voice into her ears, where Viola could hear it over Neptune's roar.

Viola kept moving till the *Karat* started its downward slope, curving towards a drop-off and, eventually, those intakes. They were staying parallel with the bay, where the hull was as flat as possible. She went out with her right foot, then found she couldn't go any further. Time for the first tethering. The piece with the magnetic attachment flopped behind her suit. Viola grabbed it, crouched, and jammed the magnet against the *Karat*'s hull. Designed for use in space, Viola wasn't sure how they'd perform in Neptune's harsher climate, but after a second the tether flashed blue.

"Ready to go?" Viola commed.

"Getting ready to detach . . . now," Davin replied.

Viola gripped her end of the tether. The most dangerous part. Her linked end would give Davin a chance if a gust of wind blew him in the wrong direction. Viola wasn't sure how the magnet would hold up under Davin's body weight and the planet's wind snapping the man away from the ship. The *Karat*'s hull was smooth. Nothing to tie the tether to. So Viola held on as the tether flipped from blue to green, and waited.

"You weren't kidding about the wind," Davin commed a few minutes later. "Remind me never to come here for a vacation."

"Right now it's not bad," Viola said. "I'm clocking it at a little over seventy kilometers an hour. I think Neptune can get way over ten times that."

Puk would've had the stats for her right away, but they'd left the bot back at the shuttle. Its little jets wouldn't have been able to keep up with the wind. Now that Viola thought about it, this was the first time she'd really been away from Puk since she'd taken her father's ship off Ganymede. Standing there, with nothing other than a splash of metal-green hull visible from the suit's lamp and all the rage of Neptune out beyond, she wished the bot were there, saying something sarcastic.

"You're saying I should hurry?" Davin replied.

"Yes," Viola said. "There's no chance we're not swept away if one of those two storms comes close."

Davin appeared like a ghost. A yellow-white light filtering through the black and suddenly an arm was grabbing hers. Viola turned as Davin stamped his magnet and the tether went blue.

"I'm going over the side this time," Viola said as she coiled the tether. "Should be able to make it to the intakes, if we're lucky."

Popping off her magnet, Viola walked the sloping hull. She had to stick her feet, planting them to get whatever grip the hull could offer. A few steps after that, Viola held the tether tight in her hands. Released a bit more with every footfall.

"How's it holding?" Viola commed.

"Looks green to me. I've got a grip on it too," Davin replied.

Yeah, like Davin would be able to hold her on the ship if the magnet failed. But if that happened, they'd both go flying off anyway. Viola had spent her entire life dependent on technology for survival. Ganymede required scrubbers to keep oxygen in the air. Radiation shielding to keep Viola's genetic material from fraying into oblivion. Here, though, with that magnet the only thing keeping her alive, Viola wished for more redundant systems. Maybe a jet pack. Or the shuttle, so long as she was dreaming.

The edge of the hull sat before her, something Viola only saw because her lamp light petered out into nothingness rather than reflecting light. Viola supposed what came next would be like mountain climbing, bracing her feet and hopping down the side. She'd done it once as a virtual-reality exercise.

"You ever done this before?" Viola said. "Climbed the side of a ship?"

"Sure, dozens of times," Davin replied. "Just never one this big. At night. In a windstorm."

"Any tips?"

"Don't fall?"

"Thanks," Viola took a deep breath. "Here I go."

Because she'd already been supported entirely by the tether, Viola didn't feel a big change in how her weight was distributed. Still very dependent on that rope. Only as she dropped, the wind pushed her back towards the ship. The tether caught on the lip of the hull, the pointed aft end of the oval, and Viola hung in space. The blowing wind treated her like a pendulum, shoving her forward until Viola's weight overpowered the wind's push and sent her rocking back. Every time this happened, Viola released a little more of the tether, dropping a few more meters down.

"Feels like I'm in my own world," Viola commed. It

could have just been a thought, but Viola really, really needed the sound of a voice. Her lamp caught nothing, and while Viola could feel the wind pushing, could feel the rocking of the pendulum, there was no sign of where she was. Vertigo snatched at her, causing her mind to spin and churn, unable to figure out where she was or how fast she was moving.

Rock back. Inhale. Drop a few more meters as she swung forward. Exhale. Repeat.

Until, on a forward swing, Viola's lamp hit something that wasn't Neptune's air. It was black, but solid. Coated with dust. Viola had a second to look at it before the pendulum effect brought her back. Only this time, instead of dropping, Viola held steady until the wind shoved her forward again and took a clearer look.

"I'm there."

"The intakes?" Davin replied.

"Think so. I' m going to let loose on the next swing."

Brief visions of action movies, the film stars jumping from ship to ship, building to building, swinging through vast jungles. How many of them would have been able to pull this off? Let the remaining coil of the tether out at the apex of the swing and launch into the intake?

"If I miss this, tell everyone I tried," Viola said.

"Just don't miss it," Davin replied.

"I'll keep that in mind. Here goes."

The wind shoved Viola forward again, one more long arc through the black. The lamp caught the edge of the intake as Viola swung up, and she let the coil loose. For the first time, Viola felt the brief weightlessness of free flight, the release from Neptune's clutches. The question was, where would she land?

32

———

ESCAPE

W here were they going to escape to? Phyla kept replaying that question and not finding a good answer. There wasn't a habitable space station for millions of kilometers, the closest one she knew of being a research outpost near Uranus. The odds of other ships passing by this deep were almost nil, and that's assuming those ships wouldn't run at the first sign of a hostile force.

"What's your plan?" Phyla said. "A shuttle would be suicide."

"As an escape, yes," Quinn replied, continuing to jog through the hallways. "As a back door into the main bays, perhaps not."

"You want to land on the other side of the freighter and, what, hijack one of their ships?"

"I'm glad you're not as simple as most mercenaries."

"Was that a compliment?" Phyla said between breaths, running behind the Eden agent.

"Yes."

Quinn held up a hand as they reached the next corner and Phyla stopped before rounding the wall.

"The shuttles are around the next side. It sounds like we're not the only ones with this idea."

"Oh, I think we're probably the only ones with your idea," Phyla muttered. Listening, she heard the beeps and shifts as someone prepped a shuttle for launch. Launching the small craft would require a passcode entry, followed by a short series of prep steps. In a true emergency, the ship's computer could remove the lock and warm up the engines. With Gage on the bridge, though, there was no way that was happening.

"If they're getting it ready to go, then they must be crew. The invaders wouldn't know the passcode," Phyla said.

"Point. I'll go first."

Quinn went around the corner, rifle raised. Phyla followed, giving herself distance. Around the corner the hallway widened into a broad rectangle, with the right half, facing back into the body of the freighter, covered in racks of emergency supplies, space suits, and other gear necessary if one wanted to make a sudden interstellar jaunt. A series of benches served as intermediaries between the right and left halves, with the left wall sporting four airlocks, each one only large enough for single-file entry. The shuttles were on the other sides.

As Quinn moved into the room, he snapped his rifle up and looked about to squeeze off a shot when he paused, staring to the right, where Phyla couldn't see.

"So you're who Gage is working for," Quinn said.

"We all have our masters," came the reply, a lilting voice that sounded like a clarinet played through a waterfall. Distorted. "I would know yours."

"Doesn't matter," Quinn said. "Think I can shoot you before your pals can get their arms up?"

Phyla didn't hear a reply, didn't see a gesture, but Quinn pulled the trigger. His gun sent out a series of shots and Phyla took the moment to swerve around the corner, ducking below Quinn's firing line and searching for a target. Arrayed against the back wall, supply lockers behind them, was a trio of enemies. Quinn shot at the center figure, a larger, thin man. The target's face covered in twisting, roping scars. The two flanking him wore the same mishmash of fabric, random accessories, looking more like piles of junk than real people. Quinn's shots hit the scarred one, but vanished as they homed in, dissipating as though sucked into a black hole.

"Portable shield," Phyla said, aiming at the one of the other targets. They weren't moving, but Phyla didn't argue with a sitting duck. Her rifle went off and, once again, the laser seemed to disappear as it closed in on the guard.

"They're not all shielded," Quinn said, lowering the rifle slightly. "That'd be too expensive."

"Eden, always thinking the only currency is coin," the scarred man said, then held up his right hand.

The two flanking members of the trio swept open their clothes, stitched together into robes. Beneath, each one held a twin-pronged device that looked like a large fork. Before either Phyla or Quinn could move, the forks shot lightning, a white-blue spasm that flashed through the space between them and crashed with a twitching force. Phyla dropped her rifle as her arms and legs contracted and stretched at random. Quinn fell next to her, writhing on the hard floor.

Phyla had been stunned before, felt the numbing loss of contact with her own nerves. As though her arms, her hands belonged to another body. This was the opposite, all her nerves on fire and activating at once. There wasn't any controlling it. Her mind overwhelmed by the commands coming in from every corner of her body. Even her eyes blinked rapidly. Her lungs gasped for breath after breath, barely starting an inhale before forcing it back out again. Toes curled and opened while her calves tightened as though for a jump, then relaxed again.

"For livestock," the middle man said. "So much more effective than a stunner. I trust you see why."

Gradually Phyla gripped her own body, and understood. Stunners often knocked their victims out, if only through heads slamming to the floor in surprise. They were also less effective if you trained to subvert them, to know how to move without feeling your own limbs. That, and stunners were obvious. The forks didn't look like sidearms, didn't look like they could cause disaster.

"Gage told me you are the most dangerous person on board," the man said. "Eden really has become fat and careless if you're all they can afford."

"Who are you?" Quinn asked, sitting up.

"Be careful," the man said, walking forward. "Sudden movers have a way of finding themselves shocked."

"That's not answering my question."

"You can call me Bakr," the man as he leaned over Phyla. Staring up into his face, those dark brown eyes framed by red, angry scars. The random horror of a severe burn, an injury Phyla saw plenty growing up in Vagrant's Hollow. People playing with scrap machines, trying to turn trash into treasure and torching themselves when it went wrong.

Bakr's own mishmash robe was a patchwork of whites and grays, cloth fashioned from a dirty blizzard. The light colors played against the burned body to play with Phyla's eyes so she almost didn't see the clothes, just the flayed arms, hands, and head floating on their own.

"And who's paying you?" Quinn continued.

"Ah, the Eden man lacks politeness. Acquires a name but does not give his own," Bakr said, stepping over Phyla to Quinn. "For shame."

Bakr kicked, his right foot swinging forward and connecting with Quinn's head. The bodyguard fell back, hitting the floor. Silent.

"What do you want?" Phyla said. She could feel the fire dying in her nerves. She could move if she had to. Could reach out, grab the rifle, and maybe roll to a shooting stance before Bakr could get to her. The man's two guards weren't doing anything, just standing there with those shocking tines displayed. Bakr might have to command them. In which case, if she could get the drop on him ...

"You're not Eden, are you?" Bakr said, moving back to her. "Don't have the attitude, the look you've signed your soul away."

"My soul away? Who talks like that?"

Keep his attention on the words. On anything other than her eyes, measuring the distance to her dropped rifle. Her tensed muscles, getting ready for the roll.

"Someone who has spent far too many years riding the desert of space," Bakr replied, the lyric tone swinging low. "But if you are not Eden, then you must be one of the others. The extra security. Like the pilot who tried to attack us earlier."

"Give the man a prize," Phyla said.

"I already have mine. And, unfortunately, you are not it."

As Bakr's foot came forward in another kick, Phyla rolled away from it. Her left hand reached out as she completed the roll, gripping the trigger and, twisting her shoulders, pulling it back across her body and pointing it right in Bakr's angry face.

"Too bad," Phyla said, and pulled the trigger.

Nothing happened. The rifle clicked, and no laser appeared. Bakr didn't vanish in a burst of fiery energy.

"Yes, too bad indeed," Bakr replied. "Do you know your weapon requires a catalyst? A burst of electricity to actually form the laser?"

Phyla opened her mouth for a crack, but Bakr's left hand shot out and gripped her throat. With far too much ease, Bakr straightened, pulling Phyla up with him.

"My friends here, their tools shock. Trip and trigger the nerves like so many piano keys in a concerto," Bakr dragged Phyla across the floor, towards the escape shuttle doors. "Your guns are no different."

In front of one of the shuttle pads, hand still around Phyla's throat, Bakr tapped a series of buttons on the keypad. The door beeped, spun, and then split in the middle to open the airlock to the escape shuttle. Phyla tried to talk, but with Bakr's hand around her throat, she couldn't do much more than suck bits of air through her nose. Bakr swung his arm forward, then released, throwing Phyla into the shuttle. She hit the cushioning with a soft thud, hand going to her neck and rubbing away the impressions dug in by Bakr's bony fingers.

"Neptune is a harsh planet," Bakr said, his hand continuing to type on the keypad. Beyond opening the door, the keypads could also set coordinates, important for sending people less versed in astronavigation off of the freighter. "I hope you find it welcoming."

"Why—" Phyla coughed. "Why are you doing this?"

Bakr paused outside the shuttle door, blinked at her. A guard handed Bakr a fork and he pointed it towards Phyla, pushed the trigger. Phyla ducked, and the bolts flew over her, striking the shuttle's small control console, which fizzled and went dark.

"The same reason as you," Bakr said. "To survive."

Bakr slapped a button on the outside keypad and the airlock. The shuttle's interior lights came on, a clean white light, and a voice warned Phyla to strap in. Two seconds later, thrust pressed Phyla into her seat as the shuttle blasted off of the freighter and towards the cold dark of Neptune.

33

HUNTED

Her body didn't wait till the pain vanished to wake her up. Opal blinked her eyes open to a blurry world and shut them again. Not ready yet. Only, she didn't have a choice, did she? In scattered fragments, the shuttle's ambush, the mining laser, the call of Viola's bot Puk to jump. Disaster.

"Where?" Opal breathed, eyes opening again and taking in the hallway, the shut door to the razed bay next to her.

Someone had brought her here. Left her. And without a weapon. In between the paralyzing moments of headache, Opal shifted to a crouch and checked her pockets. The only thing she had left was the trusty beam knife strapped to her inner thigh. Still dangerous.

A faint noise from the hallway. Voices. Followed by a clanging thud as someone, something hit the ground. Heavy and metal. Opal held her breath, listened.

"Take him down," a voice said.

"How d'you expect me to do that? Carry him?"

"See that suit? It'll protect him for a story. Just drop the bastard."

Suit. Opal didn't recognize the voices, which meant these probably weren't friendlies. Davin and Mox wouldn't have left her alone anyway. And if they had Mox, then they'd probably come looking for her. Opal turned to the control panel and slapped the down arrow. No idea what it did, but anything was better than staying here.

"I'll say you told me to, he gets killed," the second voice continued.

On the other side of the door, the *Karat* rumbled. Levers shifting a lot of weight and grinding passed each other. It needed to move faster.

"Doesn't matter to me."

"But it might to Bakr."

Bakr. Oh, that name. That name rang a bell.

The sounds grew louder, hissing joining in as valves released pressure. The noise churned through the hallway, picking up echoes along the walls. Opal tried to forge her way past the noises, past the headaches. Bakr. The name brought with it swirling red sands. A list of targets.

"Someone's lowering the bay," the voice broke her concentration, it was closer now. "Quick, drop him then catch up to us."

Focus, Opal. Time for memories later.

Flattening herself against the door, Opal kept her eyes glued to the corner of the hallway. What she needed now was an excess of caution. You don't know what's around this corner, guys. Take it real slow. The voices stopped talking. Probably realized that it was bad form to sneak up on someone while running your mouth.

The door dinged behind Opal, then shot up. Opal nearly fell over, backpedaling to keep from meeting these guys on her back. Once she'd picked up her balance, Opal ran to her left, out of sight of the hallway. In front of her, the shuttle's wreckage sat in pieces. The bay.

"Hey, hey!" Came a whirring noise. "You're awake!"

"Puk?" Opal said, looking up and seeing the bot hovering above her. "Quick, where's a weapon?"

"You want Davin's shotgun? It's over here." Puk buzzed across the bay, towards the shuttle's aft. The opposite way Opal had gone. She would not risk cutting in front of that hallway again. Instead, she made her way over to the shuttle's nose, still pointed up from the imbalance caused by the mining laser. At least there was a strut here to duck behind.

Opal saw the hallway's edge, the opening to the bay. A second after she peered out from behind the strut, a body, then two, both wearing heavy welding suits, walked in. They were holding small sidearms, but holding them with both hands, each one looking a different direction. Whatever their outfits, they were armed heavy for mechanical work. The two of them weren't moving fast, taking their time in the middle of the hallway. If she'd had her rifle, they would have been easy targets.

"Split," one welder said. His suit lacked the spots and tears marring the second's outfit, and his voice matched the one giving the orders. Without thinking, Opal dubbed him Alpha and the other Beta. The same style of designations they gave targets on Mars.

Alpha broke towards the aft of the shuttle while Beta cut to the nose. In a few seconds, Beta would either see Opal or step on her. When that happened, Opal would have a hot second of surprise to get that beam knife into Beta's face.

"Hey—what's that?" Beta said, pausing in his approach to look up in the air. "It's a bot!"

Opal tracked Beta's look and saw Puk hovering above the shuttle.

"You want to know who's in here?" Puk buzzed, its voice turned up so it filled the bay. "Because I'll tell you, if you promise not to blow me up."

"Hear that?" Alpha said to Beta. "We got ourselves a bot with a self-preservation instinct. So talk, bot. We won't torch you."

Their eyes were on Puk, so Opal slipped between the strut and the body of the shuttle. Visible for a moment, Opal pressed herself against the shuttle's body and took a breath. Puk was rambling above her, talking about Davin and Viola, and some crazy story about them jumping out of the bay with suits on. Opal inched closer to the split part of the shuttle where aft and bow crumpled together.

"But it sounded like someone just came in here," Alpha said. "The door opened a minute ago."

"All me, I'm afraid," Puk said. "Brought the bay down to pick up my friend, the one with the exoskeleton?"

Opal peeked through the hole between the shuttle's sides. Nobody there. Another quick step and she was by the aft section. There, just past the engines, laying on the floor, was Davin's favorite shotgun. Why would the captain have left it here? It made little sense. Whatever the reason, Opal mouthed a silent thank you and picked up the weapon, slipping the beam knife into a slot on her belt.

Puk must have been keeping a mechanized eye on Opal's progress, because as soon as she had the shotgun in her hands, the bot floated towards the door.

"There was one other person," Puk said. "But she went with Mox, the metal man."

"Then maybe she's back here," Alpha said. "Bot, if you're trying to mess with us, you'll be scrapped before you can fly yourself away."

Puk protested as Opal made her way back across the

shuttle's other side. Too far away for Melody. Their sidearms had more range, they'd fillet her if she went into the open. It was either through the shuttle wreck, or back around the nose.

"I think this bot's playing us, boss," Beta said. "There's nobody back down that hallway. It's a dead-end."

"Last chance, bot," Alpha said. "Where are they?"

No time. Opal stepped through the wreckage of the shuttle. Too many broken bits of metal meant she couldn't run through, finger on the trigger blasting away. Almost there, Puk. Keep stalling.

"Okay. You got me," Puk said. "It's my programming, you know? Can't fight it. Have to protect my owners."

Opal didn't see the shot, didn't hear the sidearm, but she saw Puk crash to the ground and roll, sparks popping off in all directions as its circuitry fried.

"You just got your own bot fried!" Alpha yelled. "Now c'mon out and I promise we won't do the same to you."

Opal leaned out of the shuttle, shotgun pointed towards the pair, and pulled the trigger. Six green balls of flaming energy shot out towards Beta and Alpha, who took a step out of the way before the balls rammed their suits. Opal chased after her own shots, watching as the balls burst apart on Beta and Alpha. The flames crawled around the thick armor but the shotgun's energy didn't appear to be burning through.

That didn't mean it was worthless.

Sticking her left foot and and turning her right shoulder, Opal swung the shotgun like a bat. Beta, still wreathed in the green flames and flailing, didn't even try to dodge the strike. Probably didn't see it coming. The shotgun smashed into his head, the rubber-like helmet doing nothing to soften the blow. The man crumpled to the ground and Opal pivoted, readying the shotgun for another swing.

Alpha, still burning, was ready for it. His left hand caught the shotgun as Opal pulled it back up and ripped it from her hands, throwing it across the bay floor. Alpha's right arm, holding the sidearm, came up towards Opal's chest. Opal let her legs slip out from under her and, as Alpha fired, dropped to the ground. The stunning blast flew over her head as Opal kicked her right foot up into Alpha's groin. He groaned, left hand moving to shield, and stepped back, sidearm waving for another shot.

Opal curled her abdomen and somersaulted forward, left hand grabbing the beam knife out of her belt as she rolled. Alpha, still backpedaling, pointed the sidearm at Opal as she finished the move. Opal lanced out with the beam knife, swinging towards the sidearm as Alpha pulled the trigger. The sidearm exploded, the focused energy released as the sliced front half fell. The force blew the beam knife out of her hand, launching it across the bay. Released stunning force washed over Opal and pushed her to the floor, numbing her left arm. Alpha stared as his ruined weapon, any facial expression hidden by that helmet, and then threw it away.

"Know what's funny?" Alpha said to Opal, still on the ground. "We were supposed to keep the body count low on this mission. Deaths put blood on the product."

"Then what the hell are you doing?"

"You don't work for Eden, do you?" Alpha continued.

Trying to back herself up, Opal's feet pushed against the smooth floor. Alpha followed, loomed over her. His hands low, arms ready to block a kick. The problem here was leverage, a chance to stand up. If Opal didn't find some soon, she was dead.

"Does it look like I do?" Opal said.

"It doesn't. Which means nobody's going to care if I smash your face in," Alpha said.

Opal felt the shuttle behind her, hard against her back. Nowhere to run. Alpha drew his fist back, and Opal braced herself.

34

CARGO HOLD

The tether's blue line buried itself into the black void a few meters into the distance. It went forward, then the tether slanted and disappeared as it went over the *Karat*'s aft edge.

"So the plan is I descend the tether to you, then we detach and reel it in?" Davin said for the third time.

Not that he was afraid. Definitely not. He'd been shot at, stabbed, on a ship ready to explode in space. He just didn't want to fall into Neptune's miserable sky. He'd get what, a few minutes of falling before the core melted him to pieces? Or maybe the swirling wind would pick him up and whip Davin around with such high speeds that his suit would rip and he'd freeze. A human icicle surfing Neptune's atmosphere.

"Right. You will adjust your latch. Loop the tether through your suit, rather than hooking it on. That way you'll be able to slide along it," Viola's comm was fuzzy, punching through the *Karat*'s hull and Neptune's cloudy air to get to Davin. "Should be easy."

Easy. Gunfights were easy. Talking down over-confident

jerks over payment was easy. Davin grabbed the tether, anchored on the hull, and popped it loose. The cable went green. Davin loosened his latch, allowing it to slide along the tether. He ran the line back and forth, confirming it moved easily.

"Next time this happens, it's Mox's turn," Davin said.

"Captain, are you nervous?"

"Thing about being the captain, Viola, is that it's your job to understand the ins and outs of every situation," Davin said.

"But you let me go without asking anything."

"Thing about being the captain, Viola, is that you have to trust your crew to do their job,"

Viola's sigh came over the comm. No sense of humor.

Sealing the tether back to the hull changed the color back to that secure, calm blue. Davin followed that light, hands touching the tether, letting the coil run through his fingers, and then gripped as his feet slipped. When the drop-off came, Davin slid over and dropped. Wind blasted harder here, dangling from the coil. The darkness hid his speed—Davin judged when to grip the tether based on his stomach dropping, depending on the suit's gloves to keep the friction from burning his hands.

The coil curved back under the hull's outcropping. Davin risked a glance back, that blue lifeline extending up behind him, like a mystic cable to a god. You see most of the planets in the solar system, sunsets on the outskirts of Jupiter, and a million other wonders, but that simple sapphire curl going into the blustery dark took its place high on his list.

"I think I'm gonna make it," Davin commed, sliding along the more level tether.

"Were you worried?"

"Definitely not."

Dropping into the actual intake of the *Karat* was a non-event. From one level of dark to another. Feeling his feet on something real again had Davin breathing easier. Space-faring mercenary or no, there wasn't much to compare with solid footing. Not to mention seeing Viola, another person, after the last hour walking alone through the Neptune night. The girl was already retracting the tether. The color went from blue, to green, to orange as Viola wound it up.

"Ought to get one for the *Jumper*," Davin said.

"Bet you could keep this one," Viola said. "That shuttle doesn't exactly need it anymore."

"Look at you, keeping your eyes out for freebies. Might make it on this crew yet."

Davin walked up the intake while Viola finished coiling the tether. It felt strange walking into a hostile environment without Melody and her protection, but he'd have to grab the shotgun later. Too much risk of an untimely fire when bouncing along the tether. So here he was, dependent on his old hands and feet if a hijacker showed.

But nobody did. Davin walked through the narrowing intake until he arrived at the gate. There wasn't anything Davin could see outside it. No panels, only hard metal plates. He'd seen enough ships to know that this was where the raw material would come through. It'd only open if the *Karat* went into mining mode.

"Ideas?" Davin asked as Viola walked up behind him.

"There's no emergency access?" Viola said, looking around the door. "I can't imagine . . . for repairs, they ought to have a release? All of my dad's ships, the ones Galaxy Forge makes, have them."

"Maybe Eden's got another contractor," Davin said. The implications weren't great. No way in meant they were stuck here, their oxygen dwindling. And if hijackers decided to bring the *Karat* out of orbit, then the two of them would be so, so very cooked. They needed help.

Davin looked at his comm. Scanned for frequencies. Mox and Opal didn't pop. The *Karat*'s hull too thick. Then a static burst filled his suit, the same cascade of sounds from before, when they were landing. Opal had said it wasn't just noise, though.

"Viola, that message? The one we intercepted when we got close?"

"The one telling us to run?"

"Where'd it come from? What spot?"

"I don't know. It was a wide-range broadcast. I wasn't exactly focused on tracing it," Viola said, continuing to poke at the door. "I'd try the bridge."

"It'd be the most secure spot," Davin nodded. "One guy in a chokepoint could hold out for a long time."

Davin tapped on his comm, trying to find the message's source. Neptune's atmosphere had little in the way of satellites to guide the comm in its choice, so Davin's comm could only give a general direction. A dot in a three-dimensional sphere appeared on the comm's small screen, with green colors shading likely sources for the broadcast. Using the space suit's gloves, Davin traced the path he wanted to send the transmission.

"Hello? Is anyone receiving this?" Davin sent.

"Who are you talking to?" Viola asked.

"Don't know yet," Davin replied, and listened.

"Yes," came back a minute later. Probably debating whether it was a good idea to talk. It was scratchy, the signal losing definition as it cascaded back through the *Karat*'s hull. "Who is this?"

"Your rescue team. Who is, uh, in need of rescuing,"

Davin said. Sure there was a chance it was a hijacker, but what did Davin have to lose?

"Gage sent you?" This time the reply was instantaneous.

"Sort of," Davin said. "More like, Gage's boss sent us."

"Good, because Gage is a traitor."

"Interesting," Davin said while doing all kinds of mental gymnastics. Traitor to who? Could be either the hijackers, Eden, or something outside either one. Better to keep the guy on the line by being agreeable. "I'd love to chat about that more in person."

"Where are you?"

"Actually, and this might sound weird, but stick with me, we're in your cargo intake." Davin said. "And by that I mean we're locked out of your hold. Seems like you have an infestation of the armed and dangerous kind, and we didn't want to walk right into them."

"So you want in the hold?"

"That's the idea, yes."

"Once you get in, there's not many options for getting here. They all lead through the cafeteria, where the traitors have set themselves. Find another way. Send another communication when you reach the bridge, and we will talk again."

A second later the intake's door shunted open, the body tilting outward, forcing Viola to step back. On the other side sat a small tunnel. They'd have to crawl. Deep inside, Davin could make out a glow: blue-white, diffuse. Great. Something else he didn't understand.

35

TO THE RESCUE

The shuttle turned and tumbled, twisting Phyla in her straps as she tried to restart, tried to get anything out of the shuttle's console. Nothing responded. The flight stick stuck. The screen stayed blank. And out the front viewport, Neptune loomed larger and larger.

There was only one tool left.

"Gage," Phyla said into her comm, flipping the transmitter to the captain's signal. She'd only have a minute until they were too far apart for the comms to work, but there was a chance that Gage could capture the shuttle. Either through a remote takeover, or salvaging equipment meant to latch on and pull metals in from distance.

"Your signal is light. Are you calling from that shuttle—"

"Yes. Bring me back."

"Why would I want to do that? Last I recall, you're my enemy."

The man had a point. Phyla definitely had a punch waiting for Gage the next time she saw his face. But there were conditions that superseded her anger. Like imminent death.

"I met Bakr. In the freighter. He doesn't want to keep you around," Phyla said. "He's insane."

C'mon, Gage. Let's hope you haven't met the guy. That you're pliable.

"Bakr has a strong reputation," Gage replied. "The terms we agreed to are favorable to him. Besides, even if I wanted to, this freighter has nothing that could pull you back. Enjoy your flight."

Phyla almost screamed as Gage cut the communication. Turned back to the console. Think, Phyla. Bakr's weapon would have sent a high charge through the component, probably tripped a fuse. Broke the circuit. Where would that fuse be?

In an emergency shuttle, there weren't many places to hide things. In the center of the floor, a meter away from her, sat a panel labeled with the universal sign of mechanics, a yellow wrench wrapped in a circle. Two small hinges sat on either side, easy to open. If the shuttle wasn't tumbling in circles. Undoing the straps here wasn't a good idea, but that panel looked like her only shot. Phyla took a breath, finger on the release for the straps, and pressed the button.

There was no gravity, but the panel moved with the rotation. The outside of the shuttle turned faster than Phyla was, in the middle, so she had to increase her own spin to match the panel's speed. The straps! Phyla's lower straps were hanging there in the shuttle's air. Phyla grabbed them as they blew by and tugged. As soon as the spin caught up, the straps pulled Phyla forward, sped her up to match the shuttle's turn. It was dizzying, but Phyla kept her eyes focused on the panel until it felt like she wasn't moving anymore.

Adjusting her grip, Phyla pulled again on the straps, propelling her forward towards the panel.

"Hello out there!" Phyla's comm crackled. "That you on that shuttle, Phyla?"

The sudden noise made Phyla twitch, her eyes looking at her comm and nearly missing her contact with the panel, but her hands caught on the raised outside. Then, getting a grip on the hinges, which were built into notches on the floor, Phyla finally focused on her comm.

"It is. Who's this?"

"Your favorite fighter jockey," Merc's voice coming through clear. "Flying this hulking boat of a ship. Tell me, Phyla, how can you stand it? The *Jumper* controls like mushy—"

"Shut up," Phyla said. "Are you coming?"

"Fast as this thing can go," Merc said. "We got a problem though. Looks like you'll hit atmosphere in one minute. We won't reach you for five. By then you'll be too deep for us to follow."

"Get Trina."

"Trina?"

"Do it."

"You got it," Merc said, clicking off.

Phyla looked at the hinges, pulled on the top one. The panel swung out. Phyla pulled on the other handle and released her grip. The cover floated out from under Phyla, helped along by a push from her hands. Beneath was a big collection of wires, and a small panel blinking that a fuse popped. Problem was, where was the fuse?

"Trina here."

"Where's the fuses on an emergency shuttle?"

"Depends on the model. You have a few different variances, based on the year."

"Don't care. I opened the mechanical panel. Looking at a bunch of wires and a box telling me the fuse is blown."

"Oh, that's easy. Just pull back on the screen."

Phyla reached towards the blinking screen. It pulled up, showing a rack of fuses. One, labeled 'Flight' was popped out. Phyla pressed it back in, shut the box. Looked to her right and saw the shuttle's flight console glowing with life.

"Trina, you're a genius."

"Helps when you're right there," Trina replied. "But, uh, Phyla? You'll want to change your trajectory or you're going to slam into Neptune and explode all over the place."

"Thanks for the warning," Phyla said, swinging herself back to the flight stick. Plenty of fuel in the tank, seeing as the shuttle had just been using Neptune's gravity up till this point. Phyla tapped on the burners and, first things first, stopped the maddening spin. She felt a slight tug on her legs now, the touch of Neptune's gravity. Meant she was getting to where Neptune's atmosphere would roast the shuttle, where doing any big move would cause friction far above what the shuttle could stand and send the whole thing towards Neptune's core in a meteor shower.

Pulling up on the stick, Phyla swung the shuttle's viewport towards the stars. Triggering the rockets, Phyla watched the fuel drain as she pushed every ounce of power the shuttle could generate from its engines. Had to stop the descent, then pick up enough speed to bounce off the atmosphere.

"Lookin' good, Phyla," Merc's voice came from the comm. "Keep doing what you're doing and you'll be back our way for an easy pick-up."

The shuttle shook. It was still descending into Neptune's gravity, and right now it would belly flop into the atmosphere. Not good. Fuel was at twenty percent.

"Not going to make it," Phyla said, continuing to press the burn. "Need you here faster."

"Can you EVA?" Merc asked.

"No suit."

"No suit? The hell you doing, Phyla, getting into an evac shuttle without a suit?"

"Long story," Phyla said. Ten percent.

"Trina's telling me there's another way. Keep burning. Save two percent of what you got."

That wouldn't be hard. Five percent left and the shuttle was still falling too fast. Phyla let the burn go for another couple of seconds and then cut the engines. The console still had her dropping towards Neptune, even if, out of the window, the only thing Phyla saw was space. Trapped between two environments that would wipe her from existence in a few seconds. Out of fuel. Depending on a fighter pilot trying to get a freighter in atmosphere it wasn't meant to handle. Davin would definitely freak out right now.

"What's the plan?" Phyla said after a few seconds of silence. "Or did you forget about me?"

"Phyla?" Trina's voice came over the comm. "I need you to do exactly what I say."

"In your hands."

"Tap the red box on the right side of the console screen."

"The one labeled 'Emergency'?"

"That one."

"Okay, I've got a few options here."

"Is there one for fuel dump?" Trina's voice said she knew there was, and more, exactly where it was on the screen.

"I don't have much fuel to dump," Phyla said.

"It'll be enough. On three, you're going to hit the button. It'll open your fuel tanks. We'll shoot them, and you'll blow up."

"Say again?"

"Upwards. Away from Neptune, sorry. The shuttles can handle a lot of violence before they'll leak. It should kick you up far enough for us to grab you," Trina said, as though describing to Phyla the principles of simple math. "Three."

"Not a fan of this one, Trina."

"Two."

Phyla steadied her finger over the button, stared straight ahead out at those twinkling stars. If she would be incinerated then damn it, she would appreciate the view one last time.

"One."

The shuttle made a shunting noise, a clunk as the fuel tanks opened. And then Phyla flew back, crashed against the back wall of the shuttle as everything flew forward with too much force. Some part of her, several parts, cracked on impact. Phyla tried to yell, scream anything but the air would not come through her lungs. Her mouth stretched back, vision blurred, everything in various states of pain or numb shock. She was going to die.

Only the shuttle's viewport didn't show the stars anymore. Or at least, not all of them. A large shape blotted out the view, getting closer by the second. The pressure dropped as the acceleration fell away, and Phyla floated off of the wall, again in near zero gravity. The shuttle's console was flashing and beeping at her, declaring all sorts of impending hell if Phyla didn't get herself out soon.

"You still alive in there?" Merc asked over the comm. "Cause that looked rough."

"Here," Phyla whispered, lungs still grabbing at any air they could hold.

"There we go!" Merc said. "Get ready, cause you're comin' home."

The *Jumper* filled the viewport, and Phyla saw the ship turn, angle its docking bay towards her shuttle. Phyla did not know how fast the shuttle was moving, but if it hit too hard, it would thrash the *Jumper*. Ruin the ship. Phyla crawled, moving her sore arms and legs to grind her way to the front.

"Merc, you have to deploy the webbing," Phyla said. "I'm going too fast."

"Yeah, that was the plan. Only now that I'm looking around, I don't know how to do it from here."

"The only trigger is in the bay, and if someone doesn't pull it, we're all dead!" Phyla said, the *Jumper* blotting out the last of the stars in the shuttle's sky.

36

DODGE KICK

Alpha's first hit caught Opal on her left arm as she moved it in front of the punch. The second one was a low left. Trapped against the shuttle, Opal took the shot to her stomach. Another right to her face and again Opal caught it with her arm. Pain blossomed along her wrist, up towards her elbow. One or two more and she wouldn't be able to get her arm up in time.

"Ya know, I don't feel bad about this," Alpha said, then switched tactics and delivered a kick to Opal's right side. The blow pushed her over near the crack in the shuttle. Her back half against the opening.

"Hitting a woman?"

"See, that's it. You're not a woman. You're just an enemy," Alpha replied, then leaned in with another right.

Opal didn't raise her arm this time, instead jerking her head to the side. Alpha's swing carried through the space where Opal's arm would have been, carried through the space where her head had been, and flew on into the empty space splitting the shuttle halves. Following his punch, Alpha overbalanced, leaning forward and reaching out with his left hand to catch himself. Opal rolled onto her side and kicked with her right leg, hitting Alpha in the knee. Without his hand supporting him on that side, Alpha's leg bent and the man fell over. Opal jumped on him.

"You're right," Opal said. "I'm just an enemy."

Pressing Alpha's back into the floor, Opal used the leverage to pop herself back upright. Again with her right leg, Opal delivered a quick kick to Alpha's head, the man grunted and fell limp. Two unconscious hijackers. Opal glanced around. Not a lot of options here. She could raise the bay again, shove them out through the magnetic shield. Opal looked at the prone bodies and shook her head. Even if she could move them in their outfits the whole way . . . no. There were enough bodies in her past, didn't need to add any more.

Beta, still out from the shotgun beating, had a sidearm. Opal grabbed the gun, noted it was already on the stun setting. Taking off their helmets, which felt more like full-cloth masks, Opal shot both of them. Should keep them out for hours. Long enough to either take the *Karat* back or die trying.

Puk was a fried mess. Opal picked up the dented bot and saw nothing. No spark, no sound of any activity. The bot's body didn't look entirely worthless, though. Viola probably had a back-up, could restore Puk once they got back to the *Jumper*. But there wasn't any room to carry the body with her now, so Opal dropped Puk's shell near the hallway door. Shotgun in one hand, sidearm slotted into a waist holster, Opal wandered down the hallway.

Using the comm might've been a good idea, but that would've meant talking. Would've meant giving herself away, just like Beta and Alpha did earlier. So Opal stayed silent, slipping around the corner and looking at the broken up elevator. Aside from the *Karat*'s running noise, a steady hum punctuated by occasional clanks and shudders whenever the ship executed a shift, there wasn't a sound. Opal crept closer to the elevator, setting her feet heel to toe to kill the noise of a normal footfall. Nobody jumped out, nobody fired a gun, nobody threatened.

Looking down in the elevator, Opal saw a ladder, circular rungs clinging to the side of the shaft, which was lit by the same pattern of in-wall lights illuminating the hallway behind her. It wouldn't be hard to drop through the hole, climb down the ladder and see what was waiting for her. Doing that would make her vulnerable, though. The shotgun would have to go over the shoulder, while the sidearm, in a holster on her waist, would be difficult to draw with her arms on the rungs.

A smart ambush would wait until she was on the ladder, an easy target.

Only, what choice did she have? Opal swung the shotgun over her shoulder and slipped her feet through the hole. Angling them over, her feet found the rungs. Then, left hand gripping the base of the elevator, Opal dropped through. Immediately, her arm pulsed in pain, Alpha's punches causing Opal's grip to slip. She stepped one leg to the next rung, then the other. Just one more and Opal would be able to grab on with her right. C'mon. Left leg down another rung. Right leg. Opal leaned to grab a rung, left arm holding the base of the elevator and aching like it was going to pull itself apart. The shotgun, looped over her shoulder, slid as she leaned.

Unbalanced. The strap caught on her right wrist. Opal's left hand slipped, her right not yet gripped. Had to lose the weight. Opal moved her right hand as she slipped off of the ladder and the shotgun and strap fell. Snapping her lightened hand back, Opal steadied herself on the ladder. The shotgun bounced from rung to rung, landing on the lower floor with a ringing bang that ran up the shaft.

Who needed surprise anyway?

Opal jumped her way down the ladder, holding the outside of the frame and moving multiple rungs at a time. Had to move fast, because if someone came to investigate, there wasn't going to be any chance of her fighting back. The elevator shaft wasn't large, the *Karat* not being a huge ship and the main point of this elevator being to move people up to the bay loading area. Opal hit the base of the shaft a few moments later, still alone. It would've made more sense to ambush her on the ladder, so she probably had a few moments to breathe. If they weren't covering the only route deeper into the ship, these people were either very trusting in their comrades or not well-versed in common sense tactics.

Down the hallway from the shaft, Opal passed a series of crew rooms. Decked out in plain beds, with smatterings of personal stuff here and there, barely enough space to lie down. One small locker for belongings. The *Karat* wasn't built for long journeys, then. You'd have a bunch of people going crazy with this little room to themselves for so long.

After the crew chambers, the hallway angled towards a wider space. Conversation came filtering up out of there, so Opal slowed. Listened.

"So what do you want us to do with the guy?" Someone up ahead said, sounding tired. "He's got no value? You sure?"

A pause. Opal creeped on, sticking to the side of the hallway, up to a doorway. The cafeteria blew out into a space with a pair of long tables, chairs, and a back wall full of storage for the standard bland meal packets small ships held for flights. Along one wall, an altered reality screen flickered between scenes of Earth. Opal could see the edge of a mountain vista, but her eyes were drawn to the center. Tied to a chair was Mox, head up and glaring. One of the hijackers stood near him, a small assault rifle pointed at their captive. The other one, the speaker, stood staring at Mox with his back turned to Opal. Nobody saw her yet.

"Consider it done. We'll hold the ship until you're ready for us to come up." The speaker lowered the comm and turned to the other one. "Shoot him."

37

BLUE GOLD

The ice diamonds were azure waves crashing together in single stones. Blue and white flowing around each other in mesmerizing tangles, pressurized deep in Neptune's core. Miniature worlds all their own. Viola stared at the piles of them, grouped in large bins in the otherwise gray and featureless *Karat* cargo hold. Beyond the blue glow of the diamonds, scattered halo lights illuminated the hold with pale, frosty light.

"Now it makes sense," Davin said. "There's what, a few thousand in here? For all of humanity? These things are going to be so expensive."

"I want one," Viola said.

"I'm sure Eden will give you a discount if we get their shipment back intact."

"You think so?"

"Stay focused, Viola."

True. They didn't have control of the ship just yet. Viola tore her eyes away from the diamonds and moved to the cargo hold exit. Behind her, the intakes poured out into a pair of empty bins, with narrow walkways running between them. Just enough to squeeze by, shift the deposit around and move the next bin along. It looked like, when the *Karat* was ready to unload, the crew could reverse the intakes. Suck the diamonds out and spit them into a waiting buyer's hands.

The exit opened into another corridor, the same slate gray with embedded lamps that Viola was becoming too familiar with. After this, she'd go back to her father at Galaxy Forge and demand they never make another ship with the bland hallways again. Paint them a different color, shift the lights around. Add artwork or etched design. Anything to keep the soul-crushing sense of industrial efficiency at bay.

The two of them made their way out, stopping when the corridor dead-ended in front of an elevator.

"So we went all the way around the ship to wind up at another elevator?" Davin said.

"I didn't promise it would work," Viola replied. "But I bet they won't be expecting us to pop out of this one."

"Not like we have a choice anyway."

Davin pressed the button and twenty seconds later the doors popped open. Viola had been tensed, ready to dive forward, or run if there was a mess of gunmen hanging out behind those doors, but an empty elevator sat in front of them.

"Shall we?" Davin said, waving Viola forward.

The elevator had one option: Main level. Davin gave Viola a glance, then pushed the button. Only sidearms, and they were going right towards a group of people who didn't hesitate to use a giant mining laser to disintegrate them. Viola breathed faster, her arms and legs tightening up. Outgunned, again.

"Don't think about it," Davin said. "When the doors

open, stick to one side. Only shoot if you have a clear target. Let me work the room first."

Viola nodded. Let Davin work the room. Shoot if there's a clear shot. What did that mean, exactly? Did that mean any opening? Only if the enemy was going to shoot Davin if she didn't?

"Kill or stun?" Viola blurted.

"Stun. Lower energy. More shots," Davin said. "We can always do the other one later if we have to."

The elevator dinged. They'd arrived. Viola took a breath as the doors opened. And she saw Opal running into the wide room, yelling. The scene planted itself in Viola's mind —Mox, tied to a chair in the middle of the room. A hijacker behind the metal man, gun pointed at his head. Another, pacing the room, turning towards Opal. And a third, there in the back, getting water from the reclamation machine. Opal had run right past that one, maybe hidden from view from Opal's vantage point.

Davin reacted first, pulling the trigger on his sidearm and sending a blue bolt straight into the side of the man one twitch away from blowing Mox into oblivion. Opal popped the big shotgun next, sending the green bolts at the pacing man, knocking him to the ground. Viola felt her hand on the trigger of her sidearm as she aimed across the room at the third man, who was pulling his own rifle up to shoot Opal in the back.

The trigger felt hard, tight. A pulse down her hand. The gun shook as chemicals mixed, energy ionized and sent forth. An orange beam lancing in front of Davin, behind Opal, and catching the third man in the chest. Viola saw the burst of flame, the charred moment bursting out as the laser burned through the man's uniform and sent him crumpling to the ground. Viola lowered the weapon as Davin ran out of the elevator towards his target. Opal moved to Mox, ignoring the burning man on the ground beside her, covered in dying green fire.

C'mon, move. Viola kept her eyes glued on the man she'd shot. Twitch, roll over. Something. She moved out of the elevator. In the side of her eye, she saw Mox stand, put a hand on Opal to steady himself. Davin busy taking the cords they'd used to tie Mox and already tying up his man. Viola's target still hadn't moved. No sign of life. Viola put the sidearm in her holster, her fingers slow to let go of the handle. If he was dead, then she'd been the one to kill him. Kill. Him.

Part of her blasted rationalization after rationalization. He would shoot Opal. He'd already chosen when he'd hijacked the *Karat*. But behind every reverberating excuse was Davin's voice saying stun. Saying stun and then the elevator dinged and Viola hadn't flipped the setting. Had reacted. Had done precisely what trained soldiers, professional mercenaries, aren't supposed to do.

The man's mask was pulled down, showing his wrinkled face, matted gray hair. Eyes shut, cheek pressed into the ground where he'd fallen forward. No blood, the wound cauterized by the heat of the laser. Viola reached down, pulled the man's gun away. None of the hardness of death had settled in and his fingers slipped out of the rifle's grip, fell to the floor with the tiniest of thuds. Who was he? Where had he come from, and had he expected to die today? Viola suspected the answer was no, but he had. Because of her.

"Viola?" Opal asked, coming up behind the girl and putting a hand on her shoulder. "You all right?"

"He's dead?" Viola said. It's possible she was missing a sign. Viola worked with machines more than men, after all.

Opal leaned down, put a pair of fingers inside the man's shirt and pressed them against his neck.

"Gone," Opal said. The word hit like a hammer, Viola's lungs squeezing. She closed her eyes. "Viola, he wasn't your first?"

Viola only nodded. There had to be some protocol here. Something she was missing. Was Viola responsible for contacting his family, now? Was she a lawbreaker? Was Viola still herself?

Opal wrapped her in a hug. Gripped her tight.

"Hold on to what you're feeling," Opal whispered. "Never let it go. You lose it, and you'll lose who you are."

"I don't understand. I was protecting you."

"And you did, Viola. Helluva job. He would've had me," Opal said. "There's nothing worse than taking a life for no reason, and you saved mine. Thank you."

Viola heard the words. Internalized what Opal was trying to say. The man's body laid there, and, looking at it, Viola could only think of one word. It ballooned in her mind, knocking every other piece of her aside.

Killer.

38

CRASH LANDING

The shuttle hit the webbing with more force than Trina expected, but the webbing held. It was designed for the Viper, a much heavier craft. Simple math, really. Merc, of course, would have been better served telling Trina ahead of time that the plan called for the webbing. As it was, the bay was still full of containers and tools for maintaining the Viper, and the shuttle barged through them. A charging container spilled its batteries across the floor, black bars looking like bugs scurrying to freedom. A severed fuel cable spewed rainbow sparks until Trina, running over to the source, cut the power.

"Forewarned is forearmed, Merc," Trina said into her comm.

The shuttle sat, smoke pouring from its engines as their hot temps came into contact with the *Whiskey Jumper*'s atmosphere. Scraps jagged their way along the shuttle walls and, Trina noticed, along the previously pristine bay floor. Davin wouldn't be liking the cost to fix this one.

"I hear you. Is Phyla alive?" Merc replied.

Ah. Good point. The shuttle had both fore and aft exits

to allow for a crash landing of the pilot's choice. Trina went for the nose exit, pressing the release and stepping back as the windshield detached and rose away. No pressurization safety here. The minimum for survival, these shuttles. Peeking in, Trina noticed Phyla sprawled out on the shuttle's floor, breathing.

"Alive, but Erick, I believe you have a patient."

"And to think, here I was wondering if a doctor even had a place aboard this ship," Erick replied. "Please try not to move her. I'm already on my way."

Trina stepped into the shuttle, glanced at the console. A newer model, with that quality screen there. Eden, taking care to outfit its ships with good gear. Who'd have thought.

"Phyla?" Trina said, for once not holding her wrist up and speaking into it. The feeling was strange—you became so used to speaking to those that aren't there that interacting with a physical, live person was disconcerting.

"Here," Phyla muttered. "I don't want to get up."

"Erick wouldn't want you to anyway," Trina replied. "Given your incoming velocity, the tardiness of the webbing deployment, I'm still putting it as lucky you survived."

"Thanks," Phyla said.

Then Erick was pushing past Trina, talking to Phyla and checking to see which muscles hurt the worst. The problem with bodies is that it's all relative. No exact degrees. Trina climbed out of the shuttle, moving towards the aft. The shuttle would not fly again, but that didn't mean she couldn't find some useful parts in those engines . . .

39

TO THE BRIDGE

"So I think we've solved your mutiny problem," Davin said into his comm, standing outside the sealed door to the *Karat*'s bridge. "They're all, literally, tied up or unconscious back there."

Opal and Mox stood behind Davin, and Viola behind them, keeping a watch down the hallway towards the cafeteria in case they'd miscounted or one of Opal's victims had returned to the world of the conscious. Not a bad count, all told. Neutralizing six mercenaries without a single real casualty? Viola hadn't even batted an eye when Opal said Puk had been shot. Said she could have the little bot back up and running in an hour once they got back to the *Jumper*.

"Hello?" Davin said, and the door slid open, vanishing into the *Karat*'s walls. On the other side stood a shorter man, all-black hair and beard seeming to glisten in the artificial light. Like the guy doused himself with grease every morning.

"It keeps me young." the man stated, noticing Davin's stare. "I am captain Yuan San-ye, and as is custom, I give you permission to board my ship."

"Davin Masters," Davin replied catching Yuan's offered hand with his own. "Sorry we didn't get here earlier. Things were, uh, hectic."

"It's nothing," Yuan said. "However, I would appreciate it if all of you remained outside of the bridge. Unless one of you is a pilot."

"What?"

"If you had recently been betrayed by your crew, including several whom you considered friends, perhaps you too would feel cautious before letting them into your home?"

"He's got weapons on us," Opal blurted. "Behind him, in the corners. A pair of—"

"Yes," Yuan interrupted. "The *Karat* keeps its bridge safe. For exactly our circumstances. Greed, it seems, is a universal problem. One that Eden saw fit to prepare for."

"And you're going to, what, shoot us with those?" Davin said.

On either side of the large command console sat thin, reed-like rods. On the top of each was a dome with a tiny point sticking out. Those points aimed at Davin and Mox.

"They are concentrated beams. Tiny, yet potent. They will lance your heart with enough heat to make you burst into flame from the inside out," Yuan said. "Please, time is pressing. Do you have a pilot? Are you one?"

"I can fly," Viola said.

"But why can't you, if the *Karat* is supposed to be so secure?" Davin asked Yuan.

Yuan gave Davin a slight nod.

"Levels of skill," Yuan said. "I can glide *Karat* along the roads of space, but leaving Neptune requires more talent than I possess."

"You think you can fly this thing?" Davin said to Viola.

The girl looked at nobody for a moment, thinking. Davin felt she'd done well with the shuttle, done a fine job putting the cargo hauler on Europa during their comeback assault, but the *Karat* was larger than both. Neptune a more complicated atmosphere. But that was how you grew, right? Put yourself in new situations?

"I can try," Viola said. "Doesn't sound like we have a choice, anyway."

"We do not," Yuan said. "The rest of you should leave. Secure yourself in the cafeteria. You will know when we rise."

"Viola, you comfortable being alone with this guy?" Davin said.

"He tries anything, I've still got this," Viola said, tapping the sidearm clipped to her waist. Then Yuan was shooing them off the bridge, the door sliding shut a moment after Davin stepped into the hallway.

"Not what I expected," Davin said as Opal and Mox stared at him.

"Stupid," growled Mox.

"Agreed," added Opal.

"Didn't hear either of you two saying anything in there," Davin shot back. "Now, let's go make sure none of our friends want to play again."

40

REUNITED

The *Karat*'s console was digital. No buttons. No stick for piloting. Instead, virtual sliders appeared on the screen as Viola hovered her hands over them. A killer, maybe, but the ship didn't seem to care. Surrounded by a pair of storms, the *Karat* was still in a precarious position. It didn't have much choice if it wanted to get out intact.

Viola expanded the fingers on her left hand, and the left screen shifted from a close view of the *Karat* to the atmosphere surrounding the ship. Viola brought her hand away, closed it, then reached in and expanded it again. Now the screen was pushing out past the edge of Neptune's atmosphere, the fuzzy limit of the *Karat*'s sensors. A blot out past the atmosphere shaded a slight yellow, an indicator that the *Karat*'s computer believed the shape was a ship.

"To the *Amerigo*?" Viola said.

"While you are new to Neptune's atmosphere, I have been here for some time," Yuan said, nodding.

"Trust me, a little goes a long way here," Viola replied.

Tapping the blot on the screen, the console drew out a

path for the *Karat* to execute. Much faster than the shuttle, the *Karat*'s calculations came back with the precise speed, tilt, and fuel burn to make a rendezvous with the freighter. When the calculations wrapped, a green oval appeared towards the bottom of the screen imploring Viola to tap it and start the course.

"Why did you need a pilot?" Viola said, looking at the circle. "The computer did it all for me."

"Then perhaps I did not, but there are chances I choose not to take," Yuan replied. "Please, start."

"Is that why Eden chose you for this? Because you're cautious?"

"Because I don't let my ego get in the way of my crew."

"That didn't work out so well."

"I was prepared to counteract bribes of coin, but not of cause."

"Cause?"

Yuan looked at her.

"You don't have the eyes of the others. Hardened and wary. Yours are still wet around the edges, still being formed."

"I'm new to this," Viola said. Wet around the edges? Who was this guy?

"One day, you will find something to believe in. Something to fight for. And then you will understand the ones you hurt today."

Viola nodded, tapped the button. No time for this mystical talk right now.

A countdown appeared and various system checks spat their output to the console. If any of the *Karat*'s bits and pieces weren't ready for the rigors of the journey, the computer would cancel the course. Viola figured the trashing of the docking bay wouldn't interfere with any critical pieces of the ship, but when everything came back green, she felt relieved. She wasn't sure what they would've done if the *Karat* had some sort of failure.

"Can you tell me what happened?" Viola said as the *Karat* shuddered, its orbital engines warming up for the first time in days. "How they took the ship?"

Yuan, who'd been staring out the front viewport into the nothing of the Neptune night, nodded without turning around.

"It started," Yuan began, "when my friends died."

MUTINY

I t was easy work, done in shifts. Supervising machines. Fixing broken parts. Monitoring Neptune's storms and making adjustments as necessary. Ten of them, trading turns. Only Yuan and Silwa, the pilot, stayed out of the cargo hold and the intake valves. Wan, the lead engineer, supervised the other seven and kept them rotating through food, mining, and maintenance duties. The mining itself was a series of short excavations—plunge the *Karat* into hot, pressurized depths of Neptune's inner core and suck up the solid diamonds, then move to the next area after an hour.

They repeated the process for a week without problems. A week of watching more coin than any of them expected roll into the *Karat*'s cargo hold. And it was towards the end of that week when Wan first cornered Yuan, there on the bridge. Silwa was sleeping, her next navigation shift not due for several hours yet.

"I am seeing a change," Wan said. "The crew are quieter. Fewer smiles."

"You count their smiles?" Yuan replied.

"Their morale is a resource like anything else. It is my job to manage the resources."

"And morale is low?" Yuan said. "We are almost full. We'll be returning to orbit in a day. They'll be back with their friends and families in a few weeks."

"Yet, morale is low."

Yuan accepted the statement. Common sense said to wait it out. So little time until circumstances changed. The flight back to space would keep everyone too busy to think about morale. At dinner that night, a shared experience with the whole crew, Yuan reminded everyone that they were nearly done. That it was an amazing feat they had accomplished. That they should be proud. Silwa raised her glass, a poured bottle of fizzing wine saved for an evening like this one. Wan joined the toast. As did the others.

"What do you think?" Yuan asked Silwa later, back on the bridge. He'd told Silwa what Wan had mentioned, told the pilot to keep her eyes on the others at dinner.

"They had no joy in them tonight," Silwa replied. "As though instead of toasting our success, they were watching their own souls die."

"You are always so dramatic," Yuan said. "Raise the ship tonight, away from the core to the halfway point. They will have tomorrow off, to look and see the Sun again."

That night, Yuan fell asleep listening to the rumble of the *Karat*'s engines. There were no nightmares. No sounds of struggle. Yet the *Karat*'s computer triggered an alarm. Hours before the scheduled time. An indication that the bridge's defense mechanisms had been armed.

"An error," Yuan muttered to himself, pulling clothes on and stepping out from his quarters. Adjacent to the bridge, part of Eden's devotion to security, Yuan walked the short private hallway to a second door. Yuan's hand went on the scanner, and after a short beep, the door opened. Silwa lied on the console, a small line of smoke rising from her chest. Over by the bridge's main door, the body of one of the miner's, weapon in hand, sat against the wall. The main door, according to the security measures, had sealed itself.

Yuan first went to Silwa, her stomach a black mess of torched flesh, but perhaps it was not fatal. A cauterizing laser wound is often more survivable than the hard, tearing pellets of older weapons. Silwa's breath still came lightly, in and out as Yuan picked her off the console, carried her back down the short hallway to his bed. Then he ran back to the bridge, checked the miner's body to confirm the bridge's defense systems had done their job, and tried the comm.

"Wan?" Yuan sent a tight-beamed message to the engineer's direct frequency. "Are you awake?"

"Real sorry, captain," came a voice that was not Wan's. "Wan didn't see things from our point of view."

No point in asking for more information. The dead miner's sidearm, set to kill, was more than enough evidence.

"And what is your point of view?" Yuan said into the comm.

"That Eden and its partners have been running the show for too long."

"The *Karat* has no weapons, and we aren't close to a war zone."

"Turns out causes need coin, captain,"

Yuan cut the communication. The miner had told Yuan everything that they'd done, why they did it, and what they wanted next. In the isolated vacuum of the bridge, Yuan felt his adrenaline draining away, leaving only exhausting failure.

Back down the hallway, back to Silwa lying on the mattress. She'd coughed up blood, the spatters on her face, shirt, the floor. Yuan wiped them away with the blanket, listened to the shallow breathing. He grabbed the lone, strict necessities aid kit sitting on the top shelf of Yuan's locker. Painkillers, a roll of gauze, and some stitches and scissors. Not what he would need to tend to the hole in Silwa's stomach. But a captain must use the tools at hand to carry out their mission. Or at least try.

It took five hours for Silwa to give up. She never regained consciousness. At least, not while Yuan was in the room. He'd come back in, found her eyes open and glassy, the weak breathing stopped. Closed her eyes. Death in space was not a rare thing, but that didn't make it any less wrenching.

He had duties, protocols to follow in case of a mutiny. Only the *Karat*'s communications gear had difficulty getting out of the storm. Or, at least, Gage never acknowledged Yuan's calls. There was no place to put the miner's body, no place to put Silwa's, so Yuan gave them his room. Took his gear out and left them both sealed there. And then he waited to die.

42

INTERROGATIONS

They'd stuffed the hijackers, including Beta, into an airlock and sealed it. They'd have enough oxygen in there, provided Mox didn't get bored and open the outside door. Davin figured the treatment was more than they deserved, but chalked it up to, you know, being a captain and therefore being more sensitive to his crew deciding Davin wasn't worth keeping alive. He had Opal making a run back up to the ruined shuttle to collect her rifle and scrounge up any other hijacker arms that'd been left behind.

All this while the *Karat* accelerated out of Neptune's atmosphere at a steady velocity. The size of the ship and the slow climb meant Davin didn't have to strap himself down, but he was bouncing from chair to chair in the cafeteria. It made the interrogation of the one hijacker, Alpha, a farce. The guy was wrapped into his chair, so he just watched Davin brace himself on a table, then a chair, then finally the captain leaned against the beverage machine.

"Not inspirin' much fear," Alpha said.

The mutiny leader, stripped of his helmet, was a grimy

soul. Soaked through with his own sweat, Alpha's damp hair greased onto his face, made up of a pointed nose and a wide, monstrous mouth. Slit eyes that stared at nothing. Alpha's head was a project in extremes.

"I don't really care," Davin said, hands gripping the sides of the machine behind him. "Not interested in fear."

"Than what're you keeping me here for? Aren't you mad I tried to kill you?"

"I thought I was supposed to be asking the questions," Davin said. Mad? Yeah. Davin was mad. If Alpha and his dumb crew hadn't tried to hijack the *Karat*, then Davin wouldn't be here at all. Wouldn't be in this storm while Phyla was stuck up there, probably bored out of her mind.

"Then ask'em."

"Who's your boss?"

"Don't got one."

"Really?"

"Look," Alpha said, his straps moving slightly, as though he'd tried to shrug his shoulders. "You saw what was there. In the hold."

"The ice diamonds."

"You're seeing us, thinking that it's all about them. It's all a cash grab."

"You're saying it's not?"

"I'm saying you don't have a clue what's going on," Alpha shook his head. "And it doesn't even matter, because you'll be dead long before this whole thing plays out."

"If there's a thing I love," Davin said. "It's vague threats and conspiracy theories. Keep'em coming."

"We tried to warn you," Alpha said, a small smile creeping on his lips.

"Warn us?"

"The message. The only signal we could get out. Didn't even have a mic."

"Run? That was you?"

Alpha nodded.

"Why?"

The *Karat* stopped shaking. Davin felt the pull on his legs let up, his stomach do a quick flop as Neptune's gravity disappeared and the *Karat*'s own generators kicked in. Finally, that awful blue planet was behind him.

"Give the freighter a call," Alpha said. "See if any of your friends are still alive."

43

NEW ORDERS

Piloting the *Jumper* with a killer headache and a body built on pain wasn't what Phyla would call enjoyable, but compared to that shuttle, she'd take it. Gladly. Merc sat in the captain's chair next to her, manning the comm while Phyla angled the *Jumper* towards the new ship coming out of Neptune's atmosphere.

"That what I think it is?" Phyla said.

"It's her," Merc said. "Looks like your boy did something right for a change."

"My boy?" Phyla glanced at Merc, eyebrow raised.

"Phyla, you and the captain gotta get off your high-'n'mighty horses one of these days and have a little fun," Merc said. "As funny as you two are, it's been going on too damn long."

"But Lina—"

"Stop. Take it from a fighter pilot trained that every day is probably gonna be your last. Don't make excuses."

Phyla laughed, her bruised ribs blossoming pain through her chest so that the chuckle turned into a cough and a grimace. Merc wasn't wrong. The evidence was there.

If they made it away from this planet alive, she'd have to have a long talk with the captain.

"Thanks," Phyla said after a minute. Merc nodded, then turned back to the comm.

"Yo, *Karat*. This is the *Jumper*. You reading?" Merc said.

"Professional as always, Merc," Phyla muttered.

"This is the *Karat*," said a stately voice, not one Phyla recognized. "We read you, *Jumper*. My pilot says you're one of the good ones."

"That'd be correct," Merc replied. "Now, if you wouldn't mind, I think you've got a few of our friends on board. Mind letting us in?"

During the docking process, which had the *Jumper* pulling alongside the *Karat*'s emergency hatch, what with the wrecked shuttle dominating the only actual docking bay, Phyla kept an eye on the scanners. Bakr and his crew hadn't launched off of the freighter. Hadn't hailed them. Quinn was still on there somewhere. Maybe he'd freed himself and was leading some sort of counterattack?

It wasn't long after the two ships docked that Davin walked into the cockpit, kicked Merc out, and took his rightful seat. The next few minutes were spent catching each other up on what'd happened. Davin's adventure walking the side of the *Karat*, Phyla's shuttle rescue.

"One of these times, we're not going to make it," Phyla said when Davin finished.

"Nobody does, Phyla," Davin replied. "Difference is, at least we'll be choosing it."

"Yeah, that's what I was thinking when Bakr shot me into space. Felt much better than waiting till old age, dying in my sleep."

The comm buzzed. Only, the incoming message wasn't coming from somewhere close. It was long-range. A bounce from the satellites scattered throughout the solar system. Davin looked at the blinking alert for a second, as though deciding whether to continue the conversation with Phyla or play the message. Then the captain tapped the console and the recording started. Phyla exhaled. She'd talked herself into a corner there. Davin wasn't keying into the empathy, wasn't providing the right answers. Here, then, was an escape.

"Davin. It's been hours without a reply on the mission status. Eden is saying they've lost contact with the freighter. If I don't hear back from your or your crew within the next couple of hours, I will assume the mission has failed," Bosser's voice sounded too formal. "We would prefer not to take emergency action, so please communicate your status."

The communication blipped. Something had changed with the source.

"I know you're alive," Bosser's voice was different, less like he was reading from a script. "I have eyes out there. I know you're rescuing the *Karat* and its cargo. Once you have it, Davin, leave the system. Do not attempt to engage the raiders. They are stronger than you realize, and the ice diamonds are far more valuable than that freighter or its crew. Communicate when you've left Neptune's space and we will go from there."

The recording cut off.

"Who's left on the *Amerigo*?" Davin said to Phyla.

"None of ours. Only the Viper," Phyla said. Only, that wasn't accurate, was it?

"The ice diamonds can buy us a new fighter. And if Gage is a traitor, then I don't care leaving him," Davin said, nodding. "Let's get out of here."

"Wait," Phyla said as Davin reached to touch the reply

button on the console. "It's true, there's none of us on there. There's an Eden guy, though. Their agent."

"So? Don't feel like risking the crew for one guy. They'll ransom him anyway, if he's not dead, once they've lost the diamonds."

Phyla couldn't discount Davin's logic, except she'd seen Bakr, and she didn't think he gave one iota about ransom.

"Davin, he saved my life. Back there, on the freighter."

The captain sat back in the chair, covered his eyes with his hands and sighed. Glanced at Phyla with a slight smile.

"We have to rescue him, don't we?"

Phyla nodded.

"And piss off Bosser at the same time."

Phyla nodded again.

"I need to get a more cowardly crew," Davin muttered, then tapped the reply button.

"Bosser. Gage is a traitor and tried to set us up. I'm not a fan of getting played and walking away. I'll let you know when we're on our way to Saturn." Davin sent the transmission.

"Better tell everyone they're not done getting shot at," Phyla said, putting a hand on Davin's arm. "And, thank you."

"Suppose I owe this guy for keeping my pilot alive," Davin said, standing. "I have an idea, but I need to clear it with Yuan first."

As Davin stood, the *Jumper*'s scanner beeped once, twice, and then a third time. Three new contacts. Coming out of the freighter.

"Their fighters," Phyla said. "They must have realized what we were docking with."

"Un-dock, now. We won't have a chance if we're stuck to the *Karat*," Davin said, then used the intercom to radio Mox and Erick to the turrets. A minute later, Opal confirmed the airlocks were clear and Phyla disengaged the bridge. Pumping power to the thrusters, the *Jumper* flew away from the *Karat* and straight towards the large white knife of the freighter.

The *Whiskey Jumper* against the raider's trio of fighters? Phyla had seen worse odds.

44

———

PERSPECTIVE

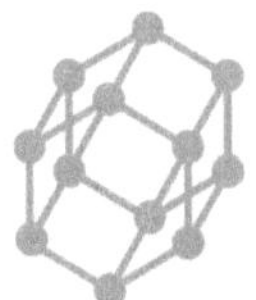

"They are trying to protect us," Yuan said, watching the scanner as the *Jumper* set itself between the *Karat* and the oncoming fighters. "For mercenaries, your friends are very noble."

"You should tell Davin that," Viola said.

There was something comforting about normal conversation after Yuan's story. That they could go back to reality, compliments and replies without disappearing into silence.

"How do you get over it?" Viola said. "How do you get over killing somebody else?"

"The wrong question, I think," Yuan replied after a few seconds.

On the console, the *Whiskey Jumper* and the three fighters moved closer together. Another few minutes and they'd be within range of the first fires. All of the other Nines were aboard the *Jumper*, the hijackers safely locked into one of the *Karat*'s airlocks. Viola wondered why it didn't feel stranger, to be apart from the rest of them. Then again, Viola knew what else she felt here on the *Karat*'s bridge, not under fire. Relief.

"I would ask yourself, who you are, and does this act change that?" Yuan said. "Because if you are confident in your idea of yourself, then an action taken to save the lives of your comrades should be an affirmation of that idea, not a condemnation."

Viola studied the captain, who seemed captivated by the console and the converging blips. A few windy professors in the classes she'd had growing up had given Viola a certain skepticism towards the more philosophical statements. Here, though, from a person who'd just gone through a total mutiny, the loss of most of his crew, and learned that his co-officer on another ship had sold Yuan out . . . if Yuan could keep himself together after going through that, he might be on to something.

"Now watch," Yuan said. "Your friends are fighting for our lives."

45

TURRET GAME

The problem with being the captain was that you didn't get to have any fun. Davin watched the blips approach on the console, then on the glass as the ships came closer. The flight computer projected the raider ships in their approximate positions in front of them, so even though Davin couldn't see the fighters against the dark backdrop of space, he knew where they were.

"Status," Davin commed.

"Ready to go," Trina said, by the engines.

"In position," Opal said from the top turret. Davin thought he caught a hint of exhaustion at the end of that. A little sigh. They'd been running a full day without real sleep and Opal had been beaten up, knocked unconscious, and nearly incinerated. She'd earned a bonus after this one.

"On," Mox said from the bottom gun.

The twin turrets were standard on medium ships like the *Jumper*. Maximum field of fire, and with the *Jumper*'s upfront cannon, the only vulnerable spot they had was straight aft. And Phyla wouldn't let anybody sit back there.

"Line me up," Davin said to Phyla.

"Two straight fighters, and they've got that one scout ship. Preference?"

"I like bigger targets."

Phyla shifted the *Jumper*, moving so the square on the far right, a larger one, was dead center. In a few seconds, that square would flip from yellow to green, and Davin would spit lasers. The two smaller squares, the fighters, were drifting higher as they adjusted their approach.

"Mox, you're on primary with me. Opal, keep us clear."

Comms clicked affirmative.

"It must kill Merc to be locked in here," Phyla said. "Sitting out a fight."

"His own fault. What pilot leaves his own ship behind?"

The square flipped green with a beep and Davin pressed the trigger in front of him. Out in front of the *Jumper*, bright white light lanced out faster than Davin could register. Flashes as each pulse of the front cannon blasted out into the dark. A moment later secondary flashes, lower but angled, came out of Mox's turret. Then the glass in front of Davin crackled in blue-gray waves. The scout ship's fire hitting their front shields. The console showed more shots from the fighters hitting the *Jumper*'s top side.

"Trina?" Davin commed, continuing to spray laser light towards the square.

"We're holding," came the response. "But you might try dodging."

The scout ship cut up as they drew close, the other two fighters keeping themselves on top of the *Jumper*. Minimizing the effectiveness of the two turrets by keeping their entire force in one firing zone. As the scout ship shot past, Phyla rolled the *Jumper* and curled after it, putting the scout ship in Mox's sights while bringing fresh shields to take the fighter's fire.

"Boost it!" Davin commed to Trina, who shunted some of the energy dedicated to the rear shields, now out of danger, to the *Jumper*'s engines. The added jump kicked the ship through its roll faster, and Phyla nudged the *Jumper* up so that the scout ship's big aft was sitting right in Davin's sweet spot. Triggers pulled, lights flashed, and between Davin and Mox, the scout ship's shields broke apart, followed by charring, shattering pieces of metal.

"Keep us on him a second longer and we'll punch through," Davin said.

"Aft!" Opal commed.

Davin glanced at the console as Phyla yanked the *Jumper* hard to starboard, swinging the scout ship out of Davin's arc. One fighter had taken its disc-shaped self through Mox's distracted position and hovered right behind the *Jumper*. Phyla tried to shake it, but the nimbler craft was keeping pace, blowing through the light rear shields.

"Hold on!" Phyla said, then pulled back on the flight stick.

The *Jumper* tilted straight up, swinging the fighter into Opal's zone, right where she was already aiming. As Opal lit into the fighter, it boosted forward, pushing energy into its engines to get itself out of the way of Opal's turret. As the fighter shot beneath the *Jumper*, Phyla pressed the stick forward, leveling the *Jumper* out and putting the fighter in Mox's sights. After a couple shots, the fighter's shields went out. Another couple and its cockpit shattered, venting atmosphere and sending the fighter into an uncontrolled plummet towards Neptune.

"One down, two to go," Davin said, glancing at the console. The scout ship limped back to the freighter. Only there was a new blip on the scene. A larger ship.

"Their big one," Phyla said. She wasn't wrong. It was

larger than the *Jumper*, and, based on the rate at which it was closing, it wasn't made for cargo. "Merc didn't even try to engage it."

"What are you saying?"

"I was hoping maybe, with the freighter, they wouldn't have enough to crew all their ships," Phyla said, angling the *Jumper* after the remaining fighter, who was dodging frantically, not even bothering to attack. Davin had to admit, the little bastard was good at it too. Its thrusters let it stop, start, and juke without the curves most ships dealt with. Mox and Opal hit a few times, but not enough, not concentrated on the same parts, and the fighter's shields held.

"Need a plan, Davin," Phyla said.

"You met their leader?" Davin asked. "Much of a conversationalist?"

"We didn't get to know each other. The whole shock-and-throw-me-into-space thing ruined the atmosphere."

"Ah," Davin said, then adjusted the comm to beam a message straight towards the oncoming raider ship. "Hey, we're all mercenaries here. How about we arrange something that makes us all rich?"

"That's what you say?" Phyla muttered.

"I'm appealing to his greed. And we might want to stop shooting at his fighter."

Phyla caught the message and angled the *Jumper* away, alerted Opal and Mox to the plan. The fighter caught on too, seizing the opportunity to sprint towards the larger ship, which was finally close enough for the scanners to pick up more detail.

The *Jumper* was a modular ship, designed to have pieces plugged into standard joints to allow for tweaking as needs arose. Most of the space ship industry was like that. Plug and play parts. Buy the pieces that you needed, jack them into a fitting, and you'd be ready to fly.

The frigate in front of them resembled a wing, with the cockpit at one pointed end and a large bank of engines at the other. Sections sprouted from the central core like feathers, each one crawling with turrets.

"Feel like we've seen this one before," Davin said, looking at the enemy ship's waved exterior. It looked like a painter's brush stroke in reverse, a blot at the front followed by a thin mid-section and a frilled, massive aft. It was the end that was coated with weapons, at least four turrets on top and bottom each.

"Near Europa," Phyla said. "I thought it was Eden's."

"We can't win this one, not without help," Davin said. "But they can't catch us, or the *Karat*."

"You want to run?" Phyla said. "And Quinn?"

"There's a difference between taking a risk and suicide."

"You'll have to order me," Phyla said, giving Davin a level stare.

"Take us back towards the *Karat*, and get ready to head towards Saturn," Davin said. "I'm sorry, Phyla."

"Me too."

Phyla swung the *Jumper* around as the frigate approached firing range. Then their freighter's engines kicked in and the distance between the *Jumper* and a quick, fiery death started increasing.

The comm beeped at him. Incoming transmission. Guess they wanted to talk. Davin tapped the connect button.

"What do you want?" Davin said.

"To save lives," the voice said. Davin turned to Phyla, who nodded. That was Bakr talking.

"We're already leaving."

"A cowardly choice. Let me give you a chance to redeem

your honor," Bakr said. "I will offer you the following exchange: The remaining crew of the freighter, and your lives, in exchange for the *Karat* and everything on board her."

Davin muted the comm, looked at Phyla.

"That's a crap deal," Phyla said.

"I thought you wanted your guy back?"

"He's not 'my guy'," Phyla said, but she didn't say anything else. Davin remembered Phyla's hand on his arm, the conversation before he left for Neptune. Now there was this guy, Quinn. Davin blinked. Stop it. That didn't matter. If this Quinn saved Phyla's life, then he deserved a rescue of his own. And if Bakr was going to let them land without firing a shot, then there was a chance.

"We'll take it," Davin sent back, then turned to Phyla. "He better be worth it."

46

GUARDED

The woman stared at him, mouth tight and arms crossed. It would've been unnerving, but Quinn didn't care anymore. His life was already forfeit. He'd be put up for a token ransom, or maybe just launched out of an airlock and left to drift through the stars till he froze and died. Nothing she could say would make things worse than that.

"They said you were helping those mercenaries," the woman said, feeling her way through the question as she asked it. "Do you know them at all?"

"No," Quinn replied. "Only met one. Brave, though, for someone with a loyalty to coin."

Getting the feeling back into his arms, legs, mind was slow. They'd juiced him hard. It'd taken an hour to even speak a sentence.

"That's what I thought too."

Now Quinn looked up.

"What do you mean?" he asked.

"The one I ran into, the pilot. I thought he'd ask to join when he saw how outnumbered he was," the woman sighed.

"Bakr would've taken him, too. We don't have many people left."

"That's what'll happen, you decide to fight the ones with all the power."

"The ones you work for."

"Yeah, because they have all the power," Quinn shot back. "Seems like a smart idea."

"But Eden hurts so many people!"

"And you're saints, I get it," Quinn said.

The woman shut up at that, glared at him. Till her comm beeped. She glanced at it, then, her face blank, looked back at Quinn.

"I'm supposed to bring you to the docking bay," she said.

Quinn tried to stand, but as he moved off the bed, his legs failed to work and he fell onto the ground.

"Didn't realize you were still so weak," the woman said, then leaned back and pulled Quinn up. "You can lean on me while we walk. Because I'm a saint."

There were a lot of steps between the bunk room and the docking bay, and Quinn leaned on the woman for every single one of them.

47

BRIDGES

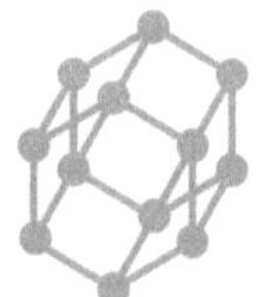

"**A**re you ready?" Viola asked Yuan, who stood behind her, rifle in hand.

The airlock in front of Viola held the hijackers they'd neutralized on the *Karat*. They'd tried to kill her and her friends, and now she was letting them free. Viola pressed the release button on the keypad next to the airlock and the door cycled open. The hijackers stared at her and Viola wondered if, even unarmed, they would charge her anyway.

"About time," the one called Alpha said. "Are the bridges set up?"

Viola shook her head. The *Karat* was near the freighter, in position to offload its cargo of ice diamonds. The transfer would take place using bridges that could extend from the *Amerigo* to its target. With the zero gravity of space, all the bridges had to do was act as a guardrail to send cargo from one ship to another. The ice diamonds would float along those chutes and get caught by bots or people in the freighter's cargo bay.

"There's nobody to rig them up. Except you."

"Where's all your friends? The guy that tried interrogating me?"

"Getting your old crew away from you."

"Hear that, guys?" Alpha said, turning to the four others. "They're doing the clean-up for us. We have to shift some rock, and then it's payday time."

A minute later they were shuffling to the cargo bay, Yuan and his rifle keeping an eye on them. Viola went back to the bridge, looked at the console. The *Jumper* was just sliding into one of the freighter's docking bays.

"The rocks are about to move," Viola commed. "Be careful."

"Be ready," Davin replied.

For what?

48

LEGACY

A sniper's scope made everyone a target. Even if her finger wasn't near the trigger, Opal still felt the person standing in the crosshairs was a moment away from dying. From the top of the *Jumper*'s loading ramp, Opal looked out at the ten *Amerigo* crew members surrounded by Bakr's mercenaries. The crew looked stunned, except a short engineer who seemed to relish throwing glares at anyone who looked at him. Suppose she would feel that way too, if a bunch of bandits and a traitorous captain had taken Opal's ship.

Davin stood at the bottom of the ramp, Mox and Merc armed and next to him. As soon as word came that the ice diamonds were making their way through the chutes, the crew would come up. Then they'd pull out of here and hopefully never see the freighter again. Leaving with the crew instead of the valuable diamonds meant the pay for this one might not be spectacular, but then . . . Eden was a fantastically rich company. They might give them a nice bonus for bringing their members back alive.

The scope settled on Merc for a moment. How close had

Opal come to dying just a few hours ago on the *Karat*? While she was lying unconscious, Merc was up here trying not to get blown to space dust by the raider fighters. Both of them on the edge, a laser away from never seeing each other again. From never feeling each other again.

"They're moving the diamonds," Viola's voice came through their comms.

The commanding raider, a burly man trailing waves of fabric flowing from his jacket, glanced at his comm and whistled. The crew lined up and walked forward. None of them cuffed, restrained at all. There were another ten raiders in the bay, so maybe the invaders didn't feel scared about their prisoners. From their slow, dejected walk up the boarding ramp, Opal wouldn't have been scared of the crew either.

"He's not with them," Phyla commed. "Quinn."

"Hey," Davin said to the burly man. "You're missing one."

"I'm told the last is a special case," the man replied.

"Our arrangement didn't have any special cases," Davin said.

The man flashed a bearded grin at Davin, then brought his comm to his mouth and said a few words that Opal couldn't catch. There was movement by the docking bay door. Opal shifted the scope to cover the space and rested her finger on the trigger. The first one through was another raider, her hair scattered across a patchwork shirt, colored fabrics tightly wound around her arms. Walking behind the raider, with an arm on her shoulder, was the Eden man Opal recognized from their tour of the freighter a lifetime ago.

The raider woman paused for a second, staring at Merc.

The fighter pilot gazed back. Opal noted the recognition. Something to ask Merc about later.

"That's him," Phyla said. "With his arm on that raider."

"Figured," Mox said.

Opal ignored the chatter. Focused on the person coming in next. Gaunt, tall, and with a masked face, Bakr strode in behind Quinn. Brushed past the Eden guard and walked right up to Davin. Opal kept the scope deadlocked on Bakr's head, fighting past a barrage of memories to stay in the moment. Mars. The Red Voice. That's where she knew the name from. A hit list, and Bakr was near the top.

If he was here, then these weren't simple mercenaries. The ice diamonds weren't being stolen for a group of greedy killers. The Red Voice had been silenced, according to the media. Eden and the other corporations, along with Earth's military, had claimed victory. A premature boast, apparently.

Suddenly her comm brought in ambient noise, projecting a conversation. It took a second to realize that Davin was broadcasting what Bakr was saying.

". . . and so you realize that you, asking for this one, are forcing me to give up my leverage with Eden," Bakr was saying.

"Yeah," Davin replied. "Thing is, we need the same. They won't be too thrilled we left their man with a bunch of raiders."

"Then one of us must make a sacrifice."

"Don't know that I'd call it that, but fine," Davin said. "I vote you, because you're getting the damn ice diamonds and a big freighter to carry them in."

Bakr, through Opal's scope, gave no hint of expression behind the mask. There wasn't a smile, a frown. Barely a blink of the eyes. Opal tried to remember what had carried

Bakr to his position in the Red Voice. Pieces of recollection flitted by. The man had been a knife in Eden's back, twisting in the shadows to turn people against their friends, slipping sabotage into the daily lives of Martian citizens.

"Tell me, Davin Masters, why is it that you want to save the crew?" Bakr asked. "You are a mercenary. You live and die by the coin that you earn. What use do these lives have to you?"

Opal watched Davin think for a second. It was a strange question, just like Bakr's slow speech cadence. The raiders nearby standing bored. Like they were waiting for something.

The ice diamonds.

They were being moved from the *Karat* to the freighter. Bakr couldn't risk anything until the transfer was complete, until the bridges disconnected. Viola could yank the *Karat* away or even use the bridges to damage the *Amerigo*'s cargo hold. But once the bridges were clear, there wouldn't be any reason to let the crew transfer continue. Bakr could roast them all, trapped here in the bay.

"Davin, gotta get the guy and go. He's stalling," Opal said into the comm. Her voice came out of Davin's comm loud enough to hear.

Davin glanced up the ramp, towards where Opal was sitting. Bakr followed the look, stared right at Opal. Without understanding why, drawn by the chance to meet those shadowed eyes, Opal raised her head from the rifle and looked straight at Bakr.

"I believe, Davin," Bakr said, not looking away from Opal, "that you were about to argue that life is worth more than coin. Yet you travel with that one ... "

Bakr's fists clenched. Opal ducked back behind her scope, aimed it right at Bakr's face.

"Good men do not harbor monsters," Bakr finished. Before Opal could pull the trigger, Bakr yanked Davin in front of him, grabbed the sidearm holstered on Davin's belt and held it up to the captain's head.

"New deal," Bakr said. "The Eden man for the sniper. Or all of you burn here, now."

49

FRANTIC

Calling Opal a monster? Is that what he heard? Merc grabbed his pair of stunning discs, pucks that would, a few seconds after being armed, send arcs of paralyzing electricity out around them. His thumbs moved to the triggers. Even if Merc stunned Davin, that'd be better than letting Bakr shoot him. Cause there was no way they were going to—

"Done," Opal said, loudly, from the top of the ramp. "It's a deal."

"You're not the captain," Davin said, eyes on the sidearm Bakr held to his temple. "Not your say."

"It's my life," Opal said. "And I'm saying make the swap."

"At least you are brave," Bakr said. He didn't move the sidearm away. Any pretense the guy had of being diplomatic was gone. The raiders sensed the same change, their hands moving to their weapons, drawing them. There were six raiders in the bay, plus Bakr, with four of the Nines. 'Course, Phyla could use the *Jumper*'s turret too. Bakr had to know his odds here weren't real good.

Cass shoved Quinn forward towards the ramp. The guy

looked like he couldn't walk, and Mox caught Quinn as he fell and, at a look from Davin, carried the man towards the *Jumper*. They passed by Opal on the ramp, the sniper slinging her long rifle over her back. It didn't make any sense. Why would Opal offer up herself for a guy none of them knew? Why wasn't Davin fighting?

As she walked down the ramp, Opal looked over at Merc and gave him a slight nod. Merc wanted to call this whole thing insane, but . . . there had to be a plan. She wouldn't be doing this without an ace. So Merc nodded back and hoped.

As Opal came within a meter of Bakr, the raider captain shoved Davin away hard and turned his aim on Opal. Davin hit the floor, rolling back up to a crouch, that shotgun of his swinging over his shoulder and into his hands.

"Our deal is done," Bakr announced, then reached for Opal's arm. Merc waited for the flip, the kick. A surprise shot from Phyla that would incinerate Bakr where he stood. Only nothing happened. Bakr took Opal's arm and walked towards the bay's exit. The sniper didn't even resist.

"The hell is wrong with you people?" Merc said. "We're just letting him take Opal?"

"Like she said, it's her decision." Davin looked like he didn't believe his own words.

"Yeah, but not her's alone," Merc said, and threw both discs. The first skittered across the ground and exploded at the feet of three raiders. The second flew towards Bakr and Opal. Opal flinched away, and Bakr dove with her as the discs exploded with electricity. The three raiders collapsed, twitching, to the floor.

After throwing the discs, Merc flipped the rifle over his shoulder and into his palms, aiming at Bakr. Cass and the other raider were still in the bay, but Merc hoped Mox or Davin could handle them. Like hell Bakr was taking Opal away. The sniper had found her spirit, though, and grappled with Bakr on the ground, too close for a clean shot. Merc moved closer, hearing shouts behind him. Cass was telling someone not to shoot. Some movement by the doorway that Merc couldn't trace. Not that he wanted to, he could see Opal moving her legs into position to— there it was, Opal brought her legs up, then smashed her booted heels into Bakr's ankles, causing the raider to let go of her. A clear shot.

Then Merc flew and landed on the bay floor, air rushing from his lungs in a coughing fit. His ribs ached. The hell was that? Bending up, Merc saw a shorter, robed man staring at him. Where was Opal? Merc blinked and found her, running towards him. Bakr behind her, aiming the sidearm.

"Twist!" Merc tried to yell, but he didn't have the breath. Bakr fired. The orange bolt lanced out and struck Opal in the back. She fell forward, smoke and flame rising from the back of her jacket, and landed next to Merc. Her face right there. So close. Her eyes staring right into his, tears lacing the edges.

"I'm sorry," Opal whispered. Merc wasn't sure how he heard the words over the noise in the bay, the laser fire, the yelling, but they were there.

"Don't talk," Merc said, his own voice barely functioning. Lungs grasping for air.

"I love you."

"You'll be okay," Merc said, sitting up, raising his comm. He glanced at Opal's back, at the frothy burning pit that had been her jacket a second before. Facts flew through his head, statistics on the power of Davin's sidearm, the likelihood of fatalities when shot in certain areas of the body. And the robed man stood between them. This close, Merc could see metal eyes, their unblinking cameras staring at him. Could see the arms reaching to crush Merc's throat.

"No," growled a deep voice.

Then the bot lifted in the air, Mox's metal-laced arm holding the enemy like a toy. Like he was playing a game, Mox threw the bot hard into the bay wall. At impact, the bot blew into pieces, robes scattering to the ground as the its arms and legs sparked themselves out.

Davin, closer to the bay door, triggered a shot towards Bakr, but a second robed figure darted out and pulled the raider boss out of the way. Melody's green fire splashed around the exit, framing the door in flame .

"Erick! Casualty!" Merc commed. "Opal's been shot in the back!"

"He's already getting ready," Phyla replied. "Bring her in."

"Hey you," Merc said, leaning down to pick Opal up. "Hang in there."

She didn't answer.

50

REVERSAL

Mox stunned the shocked raiders one by one. Not thrilling, but necessary. After zapping the last one, he looked towards the *Jumper*'s boarding ramp and saw Merc coming down. No Opal. Davin and the raider woman, holding up her hands, were waiting.

"As soon as Merc hits the ground, go," Davin's comm went to all of them.

"Will do," Phyla replied.

No risking their ship while they chased the burned man around the *Amerigo*. Mox walked towards the bay exit, stepping over the wrecked pieces of the strange bot soldier the burned man had with him. Not a full android, not so tough as that, but still capable of hitting hard.

"Is she okay?" Mox asked Merc as the pilot joined them.

"We'll find out," Merc said, eyes rimmed with red. "She's not going to be happy, she wakes up and we haven't taken care of this guy."

"Then let us make Opal happy," Mox rumbled.

Davin noticed the raider woman still standing in the room, "Who are you?"

"Cass," the woman said.

"Tell me why I shouldn't shoot you?" Davin asked.

Cass looked at Merc. The pilot returned the stare, not saying a word.

"What're you looking at him for?" Davin said.

"Look," Cass replied, turning back to Davin, palms up. "I'm just trying not to die, all right?"

"Not helping," Mox said.

"Your boss might've killed my sniper," Davin said. "Tell me why I shouldn't take you hostage. Use you as leverage."

"Because I'm worth nothing to him. And because I want to help you."

"You've helped plenty, bringing Quinn here."

"Davin," Merc interrupted. "She's not our enemy."

Cass flashed the fighter pilot a quick smile.

"Convince me. Prove that the moment I turn around, you're not going to blast me in the back with that sidearm," Davin said.

"I can't," Cass said, reaching for her holster and pulling out the weapon. Mox tensed, ready to jump and tackle the woman if she raised the sidearm. But she dropped it, the sidearm clanging to the floor. "All I can say is that I've lost my faith."

"Faith?" Mox said.

"Look at my friends." Cass pointed at the unconscious raiders on the floor, the three stunned from Merc's shock grenade. "They're here because of a cause. Because they believed that what they were doing was helping some great crusade. We were supposed to free Mars, but now we're not even on it. We used to be fighting for cities, now we're dying trying to take one freighter from people that had nothing to do with the war."

"Convenient that you're realizing this now," Davin said, not moving his hands from Melody.

"It wasn't really clear until you came back here. Until we were trading innocent lives for those ice diamonds, for a shot at some coin," Cass said, then looked at a piece of crimson ribbon wrapped on her right wrist. "I didn't join the Red Voice to be a thief. That's not what my family died for."

Cass met Davin's stare.

"I don't know your name, captain," Cass said. "But if you're willing, I'd like to help you clean up this mess. Then you can drop me at the next station."

The woman looked set. Mox believed her. No quaver in the voice, no glances off to the side. And with Opal out of the game, they could use a fourth on the ground.

"I trust her," Mox said.

Davin nodded a second later.

"Merc, you seem to know her, so you've got responsibility," Davin said. "Otherwise, Mox and I up front, you two covering our backs. Trina, when you get a minute, bind up our trio out here so they don't wake up and get excited."

The hallway outside the bay was quiet. Mox noticed marks on the walls, tearing from a vacuum exposure. Wires, containers, equipment cluttered the ground.

"Really made a mess out here, Merc," Davin said as they walked through.

"Wasn't thinking about it," Merc replied. "Hey, captain."

"Go," Davin said.

"Opal doesn't talk much about her past. You know why that guy would've called her a monster?"

Mox heard the claim. Had similar names leveled at him. By any reasonable measure, Mox had wounded, killed, or destroyed more people and things than he had any right to.

Was he a monster? Did he deserve to die for it? Better question. Did Mox feel he was evil? No. Therefore, he was no monster. Neither was Opal.

At least in his own eyes.

"You're gonna have to ask her that," Davin replied after a minute.

A few more empty stretches of hallway put them near the bridge. No resistance so far. Cass thought the burned man had pulled his remaining forces. Sent them to protect the ice diamonds. To prep his ship. That the bridge would make an ideal ambush.

"Merc?" Phyla's comm call came through. "The fighter and that scout ship are still out there. Erick's working with Opal, Trina's making magic with the shields, and we're going to need cover."

"What do you want me to do about it?" Merc replied.

"Didn't you put the Viper down in the freighter? Can you get to it?"

Merc was nodding before he was even done talking.

"I can, provided the raiders haven't torched it."

"Cass, go with him," Davin said. "Prove what you said back there."

The two of them went running back the way they'd come. Mox and Davin stood alone outside the bridge doors.

"You ready for this, big man?" Davin said. Mox nodded.

Davin tapped the intercom.

"Hey. Gage. Open these doors," Davin said.

"Can't do that, captain," Gage replied. "You know how I feel about security."

"Sorry to hear that," Davin said, glanced at Mox.

Erick had asked Mox once, after taping up the metal man's hands yet again, whether Mox ever got tired of hitting things. The answer to that question, as Mox charged the exoskeleton and slammed his braced hand into the door, was no. Another swing and the door shook. Designed to handle high one-time stress, but not repetitive impact—because how many space craft had battering rams on them?—the door bent away from Mox's fist.

Several punches later, Mox alternating lefts and rights, the big man paused. He'd felt the door slip on that last swing.

"One more," Mox said.

"Can't wait," Davin replied, leveling his shotgun at the door.

Mox loaded up the punch and let it fly. The door held for a split-second before crumpling around Mox's fist and launching through into the bridge. The door hit the floor and skidded to a stop a meter in front of the burned man and his other bot guard. Behind those two, at the freighter's console, was Gage.

The burned man, while Mox was still pulling back from the punch, fired from his sidearm. Mox saw the shot coming, though, and was already kicking away. The exoskeleton boosted Mox's jump, and he flew over, to the side, of the orange beam. Mox saw the flash of green that meant Davin had pulsed his shotgun. Then Mox hit the floor and rolled.

Came up and the bot was swinging at Mox's head with a short, twin-tined fork. Made for law enforcement. Mox had seen them before, on Luna. No guns there, so other methods were used. Mox curled up, letting the bot's first swing fly over the top of his head. Tried to grab the robed creature, but the bot danced away, aimed the fork at Mox and fired.

The lightning arced forward and through Mox's exoskeleton, which absorbed the current, and shorted. Mox collapsed to the floor, the full weight of the suit holding him down. A defense mechanism, but not a great one. Mox triggered the restart, but the exoskeleton didn't respond. It would take time. Which Davin did not have.

Mox could see the captain dueling with the longer, lankier burned man. Davin triggered a second blast of the shotgun, but the burned man was already rolling out of the way. Trying to get closer. They had reversed positions, with Davin closer to Gage and the burned man near the door out. The bot was moving too, getting ready to hit Davin from behind.

Davin had no chance. The exoskeleton still not restarting. One way. Mox reached behind his head, pressed in on a hidden button beneath the nape of his neck. All along his arms and legs, Mox felt popping sensations, pinches as nerves released. The exoskeleton prying itself off.

Mox stood and dove as the bot took aim with the fork. Without the exoskeleton, with Mox's nerves shaky from operating without the metal suit's support for years, the dive fell short. Instead of a tackle, Mox landed at the bot's left foot. Reached out and swiped at it. Mox's hand blew up in pain as it hit the bot's metal ankle, no longer shielded by the exoskeleton's glove. But Mox was still strong enough to sweep the bot off its aim, the fork's arc shooting up and spattering against the ceiling.

The bot fell on its back and rolled away from Mox, but the big man grabbed the bot's arm. Grabbed the fork. The bot stopped its roll, tried to pull back. Minutes before, Mox would have been able to yank the fork free without a thought. Now, with both hands wrapped around it, straining, Mox could feel the bot winning the fight.

So Mox reversed, pushed instead of pulled. Shoved the fork's back end, with the force of the bot's own strength, into the bot's chest. The fork pounded through the bot's chest plate, punching by the shell and into the bot's central circuitry. It twitched once, then collapsed. Mox jarred the fork loose, looked up just in time to see Davin take a jab from the burned man. Saw his captain crumple to the floor.

51

RELEASE

Man, that last one really popped Davin's jaw. Not happy with that. Even less happy looking up into the muzzle of Bakr's sidearm. The man could fight—Bakr's wiry arms were like trying to get a grip on oil-slicked rope, and that same lankiness meant Davin's blocks weren't in the right places. Like trying to fight an octopus.

"Yield," Bakr said. "You have talent. Talent we could use."

"Yeah?" Davin said, rubbing his chin on the floor of the bridge. "Seems like everybody is offering me jobs these days. What's the pay like?"

"You know what's in the hold of this ship," Bakr replied.

"That's been a question for me," Davin said. "How are you planning on selling those, considering every one in existence will come from a known hijacking?"

"It won't matter," Bakr said, and for the first time, Davin saw the man's straight face turn into something resembling pleasure. Bakr's white and red scars stretching was not a fun thing to witness, like jam and cream cheese dancing.

"There's the detail I look for before I take a job," Davin said, looking over to Mox. "Hey, Mox, whaddya say? Bakr here says it won't matter that their payment will be stolen goods."

"Take the deal," Mox replied, resting on the fork.

Davin noticed the big man had popped the exoskeleton. Didn't look so hot, either. Last-minute rescue seemed unlikely.

"Listen to your friend, Davin," Bakr said.

"Eh, he takes more on faith than me. Why should I believe you that Eden won't come hunting their stolen diamonds?"

"Because Eden, and all its ilk, will be in too much turmoil to care," Bakr snarled, the calm expression fading from his face. "Now, join or die."

Bakr shoved the sidearm closer to Davin's face. Thing was, even if the deal was a good one, there was no way Davin would work for someone as crazy as Bakr. All the coin in the world didn't matter if your boss was likely to shoot you on any day. Davin took a breath, tasted that bland recycled air, and started to end his own life. Only Davin's words were drowned out by the sudden alarms ringing through the bridge. A robotic voice announced the cargo bay was breached to vacuum.

Bakr whirled, swinging the sidearm to Gage, who stood and looked back at the burned man from the console.

"Sorry, Bakr," Gage said. "I signed up for some coin, not for some mad revolution. Your ice diamonds are shooting out to space right now. Along with, I bet, most of the rest of your crew."

Davin didn't see Bakr pull the trigger. The orange flash, though, was plenty visible. A gaping, burning hole opened up in Gage's chest and the captain collapsed. In the same motion, without sparing even a second for Davin, Bakr sprinted from the bridge. Davin and Mox went over to Gage, but the old captain was already gone.

"Seal the bay," Mox said. Good call, with Merc heading down there.

Davin went over to the console. Shifted the seal from red to green. The alarms died. Anything not tied, weighted down in those bays would've already been sucked away, though. Davin flipped through the exterior cameras until he came across one that showed the diamonds, a huge cloud of them, glittering like small stars against the backdrop of Neptune. Left out there, the diamonds would slowly fall back to their mother.

"Merc?" Davin commed. "Please tell me you're still on the ship."

52

FLIGHT PLAN

"Could've warned me you would dump the cargo hold," Merc said to Davin over the comm.

Marc and Cass were holed up down the hall from the entrance to the cargo bay. They'd been exchanging fire with the raiders inside when those raiders suddenly disappeared. The doors shut, claiming vacuum breach, and all Merc had to do was think about how lucky he was.

"No time," Davin commed. "See if the Viper's still there."

"Roger."

"And Merc? We didn't get him."

"Good. I've got somethin' I wanna say to big ugly."

"Then get to it."

Davin clicked off and Merc looked over at Cass.

"You mind me going for your boss?" Merc said.

"He's not my boss anymore."

"Davin's a better one, trust me."

The freighter's alarms ceased, the sudden quiet seeming loud in its own way. The security door to the cargo bay shot open as atmosphere came back. Cass nodded in that direction, and they went. The only thing left in the bay was the

Viper, its mass and locked struts keeping it glued to the cargo bay floor. Outside the magnetic seal, Merc could see thousands of spinning lights. Like stars, but meters away instead of light years.

"When I take off, I want you to head back to the bridge," Merc said. "Davin and Mox'll have something for you to do."

"I'm coming with you."

"What?" Merc said.

"That's a Viper-class fighter. There's room for a passenger."

"Room is stretching it," But Cass wasn't wrong. A small passenger could fit behind the pilot. Designed more for food and drink on longer flights, it wasn't uncommon to see Vipers leave that empty and squeeze someone in for short runs. Popping the hatch, the space was as empty as Merc remembered it. If Cass wanted to come, wanted to bend herself like a pretzel, she could.

They settled into the seats, Merc starting the preflight checks and Cass grumbling about how her blood flow was already cutting off.

"No sympathy for you," Merc said. "You wanted to come."

"I'm merely commenting on the poor design of this space," Cass said.

"So now you're insulting my ship?"

"Yes."

Merc laughed, and immediately stopped. Opal was out there, on the *Jumper*, maybe dying, maybe dead. He had to get out there and protect her. Had to find and take out Bakr. Glancing at the preflight checks coming in green, Merc lit the jets and glided out of the cargo bay.

And into a swarm of ice diamonds. The damn things were everywhere, swirling at different speeds based on how much momentum they'd had leaving the bay. The Viper bounced through them, the ship's armor deflecting the rocks away. From the cockpit, it looked as though reality was breaking apart. The diamonds reflected sunlight, the light from Neptune, and the freighter's own pearl paint to make it seem like lines were appearing and vanishing in space. Merc couldn't think of a way to describe it, so he sat there and watched as the Viper warmed itself up for full flight.

"Beautiful," Cass muttered from the back.

"This life isn't all bad," Merc said. The Viper beeped, showing the main engines set to fire. The ship's sensors were confused by the diamonds, but Merc could still get reads on the *Jumper*, and near it, near the freighter now, the *Karat*.

"What's that girl doing?" Merc said, ramping up the acceleration and blowing out of the ice diamond swarm.

"What girl?"

"Viola. She reprogrammed an android once," Merc said, angling the Viper towards the *Jumper*. "We stay alive, you'll get to meet her."

"And will we?"

"Will we what?"

"Stay alive."

"Cass, you're flying with one of the hottest sticks in the solar system. You want to stay alive, you stay right where you are."

The *Jumper* was coming closer, visible now in front of the Viper. The sensors showed it was being chased by the damaged scout ship and the fighter that'd done such a tight job keeping its ass un-fried earlier. Speaking of asses, the *Jumper*'s was eating a lot of laser. Merc could see the flashes, and the occasional attempt at countering fire. Looked like the shields were still holding, but how much longer was anyone's guess.

"Phyla, on my mark, you're gonna pull back on that stick, got it?" Merc commed.

"Merc? That you on my board?" Phyla, sounding harried, answered.

"Oh yeah, it's me."

Merc tilted the Viper slightly so it slid just beneath the *Jumper*'s vector. Flipped the shield strength entirely to the front, shunted the batteries from the engines to the lasers. Beautiful thing about space was that Merc's velocity kept right on going until something pushed him the other way, so might as well use that energy for what counted. The Viper's collision alarms blared. His cue.

"Mark!" Merc commed.

The *Jumper* curled up, like a running dog suddenly caught by the end of its leash. The Viper zipped underneath, and right into the path of the scout ship, which was already trying to match the *Jumper*'s maneuver. Not paying attention to the little Viper that lit it up. The scout ship's already-damaged shields didn't hold more than a couple hits before collapsing. Bright blooms of orange appeared in the scout ship's hull, the vessel bleeding metal as Merc unloaded fire.

"One down," Merc said as he flew beneath the ruined ship.

"Where's the other one?" Cass said.

"Probably running."

The Viper shuddered, then an alarm went off. A different one, the left rear engine hit and non-functional. Merc slapped a slider that evened out the shields and glanced at the sensors. The fighter and its annoying disc shape was tailing the Viper. It must have swung around the scout ship, and used its damn omni-directional engines to put itself behind the Viper. Fine. Merc could use a challenge.

"I thought you—" Cass started

"Hang on!" Merc said, then pulled the stick back as he re-routed power from the lasers to the engines. The rapid thrust, coupled with the pull of the stick flipped the Viper up.

Merc cut the engines entirely and punched the front docking jets, kicking the front of the Viper back towards where, a second ago, its aft had been. But the disc fighter was already moving away, attempting to go beneath the Viper, stay behind it. Merc squeezed off two shots but they missed high, way off. Then he boosted the throttle.

Cass was saying something, but Merc tuned her out. Maybe just screaming as the Viper blitzed through space. Even with one of his engines missing, Merc was pretty sure that omni couldn't keep up. Had to make this a longer range game, where that thing's ability to dash around like a dragonfly wasn't an advantage.

His sensor board showed the disc following, taking the occasional potshot, but with Merc juking the Viper at random, the omni wasn't landing much. The freighter loomed back in front again, big and white. The *Jumper* was off to the side, closer to Neptune and out of the fight. Even with experienced gunners rocking the turrets, they hadn't been able to hit the disc. No sense risking the prisoners.

"One-on-one," Merc said, without realizing it. His right hand gripped the stick tight, sweat beading. Merc's left hovered over the sliders for engines, lasers, and shields, all even at the moment. In a second they'd be flying over the freighter.

In a second, the omni would lose half its options, everything below would mean slamming into the freighter's surface.

"Ever done a front flip?" Merc said, and didn't listen for Cass's reply. He cut the power to the engines, pushed the stick forward and kicked the maneuvering jets, swinging the Viper around in the opposite direction of the first time. Only he didn't fire any thrust, so the Viper kept speeding across the freighter and away from the omni.

Merc couldn't see the omni, and he had to bet that the omni couldn't see the Viper either, except on its sensors. And sensors did a crap job of showing where someone was pointed. Where they were going. But now Merc's lasers were firing where he'd come from. Flashes as the beams struck out into the distance, and Merc saw a few crash against a shield, but when he looked at the sensor, the omni was still there, coming at him from a different vector.

"Get him?" Cass said.

"How d'ya know it's a he?" Merc said, pushing the engines back up. Pushing back towards the freighter. Towards the omni. Sending streaming lasers forth and watching every one of them miss as the omni blipped around at irregular angles. Then the splashes came against the Viper's shields, the omni sending a shot and veering out of the way of Merc's counter.

This wasn't the way to win the fight. Cutting off half the omni's options wasn't enough. Merc had to pin the fighter, cut the opportunity. The Viper shuddered as another shot hit it on the side, the console flashing red as the shields fell to minimal strength.

"If I die here, I'm haunting the hell out of you," Cass said.

"I'll be dead too," Merc said.

"Doesn't matter."

Merc shook his head. The sensors blipped. A new icon, coming around the freighter. The frigate. Must be Bakr's ship. Trying to grab those ice diamonds. Merc blinked. Pushed the power from the Viper's lasers to the engines, and the fighter shot across the freighter's surface, building distance between it and the disc.

"What next, hotshot?" Cass said.

"It's a secret," Merc replied.

"I just hope it's better than your last trick."

Me too, Merc thought. The Viper shot over the edge of the freighter. Merc cut the engines, shoved the power to shields and let the disc catch up. Wouldn't work if the enemy was paying too much attention. Had to get them greedy.

A moment later the Viper was back in the cloud of ice diamonds, zooming through space in Neptune's orbit. Merc angled around clumps of them, twisting the Viper through and watching the sensors as the disc followed suit, closing. Any second now, the disc would shoot fire into the Viper's engines. Any second now, they would both be entirely surrounded by the diamonds.

The Viper shrieked as it took another hit to the engines, the disc's lasers punching through the shields and causing Merc's middle engine to wink out on the console. Perfect. Merc shunted power to the right engine, the only one left, and spun the Viper around again. The disc was ready, reacting to the Viper's spin. Merc saw it, saw the disc move as he pulled the trigger and sent lasers firing into the vacated space. Watched as the disc flew directly to the side, an impossible angle for most ships, an angle that took it right into the path of a cluster of ice diamonds.

The ice diamonds weren't energy. Solid, forged mass. They cut right through the disc's shields at high velocity, powered by Neptune's lingering gravity and the ejection from the freighter. They sliced the disc to ribbons, shattering the engines, laser cannons, breaking the fighter into dozens of shards that spun right along with the cluster.

"See? What'd I tell you?" Merc said, using the maneuvering jets to guide the Viper clear of the diamonds. "You're fine."

"Are we?"

Merc glanced at the sensor board, then tilted the Viper to the left. Bearing down on them, filling most of the Viper's cockpit, was the frigate, bristling with turrets. And Merc only had one functioning engine.

53

SHOOTER'S PAST

The target was surrounded by other targets. The collection that the ECA—Earth-Corporate Alliance—had been hunting for months was here, all here nestled in the side of Olympus Mons. A mountain so large that the side filled Opal's entire horizon and kept on going, but the mountain's shadow had a purpose. Olympus Mon's sheer size restricted the view of satellites, disrupted communications, and made it difficult to get any sizable force nearby without being observed. Which was why Opal lay next to a mini-rover and looked through a scope at people over three kilometers away.

Peace. That was the topic under discussion. The reason the Red Voice had gathered its ranking members here. Define the conditions that the ECA would have to accept if they wanted to keep their Mars investments producing. If they wanted to keep them at all.

"Opal?" A voice. From the comm?

Opal glanced at her wrist. No message.

"Can you hear me?"

Aside from the giant mountain, the only things around

Opal were mounds of reddish rock and sand. Locked in a narrow crevice between a pair of rises, her rover out of sight behind them, Opal wasn't sure where the voice was coming from. A few moments breathing. Nothing more. Maybe just a daydream.

"Focus," Opal muttered to herself, looking through the scope again.

The primary target, Alissa Reinhart, still moving, welcoming associates into the large room. A design flaw, putting that many windows in a high-profile meeting space. But then, who'd have predicted the luxury resort being commandeered by hostile forces? Opal took a breath. So many of them. Alissa was the ECA's primary goal, but if they were all here, the entire leadership of the rebellion . . . maybe if she could get a comm signal out, the ECA could try something more.

But did all of these people deserve to die? Opal didn't recognize most of them. Minor players. Specialists. Non-combatants. They weren't in her mission protocol. So the comm stayed off.

Opal zoomed out, looked at the exterior of the building. Like half an oval, the resort was built into Olympus Mons, with part of it literally inside the mountain. The conference room fit along the oval's outer edge, providing what was probably a spectacular view. Only, glass worked both ways.

Opal noticed motion in the scope; doors were opening into the room, waiters bringing in celebratory toasts. No more time to think about strikes. The targets, Alissa included, were grabbing glasses and circling up around a table. Opal didn't have the angle to see what was on it, but she could guess. The document, the terms. A deal struck to get the rebellion to the table, a deal the ECA had no desire to keep. One way to get out of a promise was to get rid of who it was made to.

Alissa was in the scope now. Walking over to the table. Grinning. Laughing.

"C'mon, Opal. I need a sign that you're there," the voice again.

Opal blinked. What was that? Who was trying to talk to her?"

"Come back," it said.

No. The target. Opal centered Alissa in the scope as she leaned over the table, pulled the trigger. In Mars' thin atmosphere, the rifle cracked lightly, the kick-back strong from the weak gravity, but Opal was ready. Kept the rifle dialed in, eyes down the scope. The shot was dead-on. Hit the glass. And bounced off. Not even a scratch. Nobody inside even looked up.

That didn't make sense. The statistics on the resort said the glass was standard. Her shot should have pierced. Gone right through. Through the scope, Opal could see the other members of the party taking turns with the table, adding their names. She had to act.

"I need a negative strike at the following coordinates ASAP," Opal commed, stating the precise position of the resort's conference room. The ECA had several orbiting satellites around Mars, a few of them capable of performing so-called negative strikes. She'd been assured there'd be one overhead if needed, if the situation called for it. If Opal felt it necessary to achieve the objective.

"What are you saying?" the voice, confused, answered.

The comm on her wrist clicked once. Affirmative. The voice hadn't come from the comm. Strange. Opal settled back into her position, watched.

The negative strike was invisible, but it started quickly.

Opal saw when the conference center's first alarms went off. That would be the vacuum breach as the satellite's weapon burrowed through the glass shell. The members looked confused for a moment, then filtered towards the exit. Alissa surrounded by a pair of what looked like body guards. A moment later people took off their coats, and the first expressions of panic showed on their faces. Smoke rose from table clothes, from evaporating champagne. And then the oval burst into flame as the oxygen began to burn.

Opal knew what would happen next. The literal lighting of the air would expand too quickly for the resort to cope. It would burn through the underground, through the rooms and restaurants, the docking bays and pools. Only when the last bit of oxygen had burned away would the flames die out. And all anyone would find when they came to see would be ash.

"This is going to sting a bit, but I need you to wake up," the voice said.

"Who are you?" Opal asked the martian air.

Only it wasn't the martian air any more. The red vistas, Opal's rifle and mini-rover fell away and for a moment Opal was nowhere at all. Then she felt the bed, the blanket. Saw the light beaming down at her, and Erick's frowning face.

"You don't know who I am?" Erick asked.

"I, I do," Opal said.

The doctor split his face into a wide smile.

"Opal, I think you're going to be okay," Erick said.

But all Opal could think about was that look on Alissa Reinhart's face as she realized what was happening, that extinguishing spark as she realized everything was lost.

54

IMPROVISING

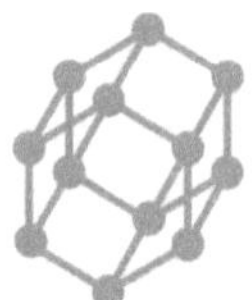

With a swipe on the console's screen, Viola turned on the *Karat*'s ore intake. Meant to be used in conjunction with mining lasers, the intake acted as a focused gravity well, sucking up ice diamonds and setting them into the cargo hold. Now, there wasn't anyone aiming a mining laser, but they had nothing to cut. The ice diamonds, floating through the vacuum, were picked up by the intake and sucked into the *Karat*'s hold.

"You need to get closer," Yuan said. "The intakes don't have the draw from here."

"He'll blow us up if we get within range of those guns."

"The shields will hold. For long enough, anyway."

Viola swallowed. Tapped in a new heading on the console, and told the *Karat*'s flight computer to execute. The ship drifted, the churning intakes were sucking away most of the engine power, but in a vacuum, even a small amount of thrust was enough. The sensors showed a pair of blips—the frigate the larger one, Merc's Viper the smaller one. In a few seconds, the frigate would eclipse Merc and wipe him from existence.

"You're sure there's no weapons on this thing?" Viola asked for the fiftieth time.

"It's an experimental ship," Yuan said. "Eden will probably add defenses on future models, based on this experience."

"Doesn't help us now."

"Don't focus on what you don't have," Yuan replied.

"Whatever you say, Captain Zen."

"Sorry, it's a bad habit."

"If you shift our shield energy to the intake, I'll forgive you," Viola said, eyes glued to the sensor scan.

"That will leave us vulnerable," Yuan replied.

"Just do it," Viola said. "Trust me."

There was something absurd in Viola, a newly-minted mercenary telling an experienced corporate captain what to do, but damn it, it was Viola's friend in danger here so normal protocol need not apply. Yuan, for his part, seemed to understand. He nodded, then routed the power. As the *Karat*'s computer adjusted the pull, Viola felt the ship shake as it suddenly engulfed more cargo than it was designed to handle. Ice diamonds, random space debris, and anything else that happened by the *Karat* was getting caught in the suction and yanked into the cargo hold.

On the sensor console the blip representing the frigate was still closing with the Viper. Only the rate was slowing. Then it stopped, the two icons barely separate. And then the frigate went backward. Towards the *Karat*.

"We've got it!" Viola yelled, then turned to Yuan. "Now what?"

55

VACUUM

Merc felt the Viper lurch forward, towards the frigate. Only, the larger craft didn't come any closer. Merc watched out the cockpit window, waiting for his brain to lock back into reality and tell him that the Viper and its damaged engines were going to either slam into the bigger ship or be blown to pieces by its lasers.

"Shouldn't we be dead by now?" Cass asked. "Cause I'm cramping up back here, so if we're gonna die, can we get on with it?"

"Trying," Merc said, his voice trailing off. The Viper's console showed they were moving, despite having no engines. What was going on? He glanced at the sensor board. A third blip was nearby, larger still than the frigate. Too big to be the *Jumper*. Not nearly large enough to be the *Amerigo*. Which meant . . .

"I think we're being mined," Merc said.

"Mined?"

"The *Karat* has entered the game, and she's sucking us up," Merc said.

"Is that a bad thing?"

"Still gotta figure that out," Merc replied. If the Viper shot into the *Karat*'s cargo bay, he might get the maneuvering jets up in time to keep the fighter from crashing. But the frigate sat between them and the mining ship. As soon as they decided to light Merc up, they were toast.

"The thing with Bakr," Cass said, "is that he will kill you if it means helping the cause."

"You bring this up because?"

"Your friends aren't as ruthless. It's dangerous not to match a fanatic on his own terms," Cass said.

"Yeah, well, your fanatic's not doing too hot," Merc replied, then adjusted the levels.

Power to the shields and the maneuvering jets.

"So how does the best pilot in the solar system get caught up with a group of mercenaries?" Cass said.

"You're asking now, when we're a trigger finger away from being space dust?"

"When Eden torched my town in the name of keeping the peace, I lost everyone. I don't want to die that way too."

"I get it," Merc said, Opal flitting through his mind. "Since you asked, the best pilot in the solar system has a problem with authority."

"Shocking."

The frigate's nose, just out of firing range, tilted away from the Viper. Turning, towards the oval behind them. Merc hoped the *Karat* had some strong shields, cause otherwise it was about to be ash.

"Does that satisfy your death wish?" Merc asked.

"It'll do. Still, would rather not die, if you can arrange it?"

"Workin' on it."

Before Cass could reply, Merc flipped on the comm and opened a wide channel.

"Hey there, *Karat*, this is your friendly fighter pilot you're about to suck into that nasty vacuum of yours. I get you're trying to grab the big boy, but how about letting us loose?"

"How do you know they're friends?" Cass asked.

"Cause everybody likes me?"

"Merc?" The question came from the comm, with the clarity of a tight-beam communication. "Can you hear me?"

"Viola!" Merc said. "Girl, I can hear you like a song. Now please tell me you're not going to grind my ship into dust?"

Outside the front window, the *Karat*'s oval spawned out of the dark like a smaller, distorted version of the planet they orbited. The frigate sat between them and the *Karat*, nearly through its slow turn. Big ships made their moves in long arcs, hard to do when they're getting yanked from behind.

"I'm trying to save you," Viola's reply. "You're small enough. Turn on your engines, get out of there!"

"Viola, my engines are burnt," Merc said. "Just, when you catch that big prize there, turn off your intakes and we'll be good."

In front of them, Bakr's frigate completed its turn. The ship's wings, bristling with turrets, spat fire at the *Karat* as soon as the mining vessel was in range. Merc watched as the first few winked out against the shields, but soon the flashes slipped through and orange flares erupted in the *Karat*'s side. Bakr's ship fired at random, trying to find a point that would disarm the vacuum.

Outside the cockpit, sparkling ice diamonds swirled, pulled towards the *Karat* as well. They reflected the laser-light of the frigate, flashing crimson, gold, and occasionally white when a particular piece of electric innards blew off the *Karat*.

"You got any more shields on that thing?" Merc commed. "Cause you might want to turn them on."

The only reply was static. Given the progressive destruction engulfing the *Karat*, it wasn't surprising that the comms were out. The frigate had firepower when it wanted to deliver it. Only the intakes were still going, still pulling everything towards their dark insides. And Bakr's ship was getting awfully close. In a few moments they were going to collide, and when they did, everything around the Viper was going to be a cluster of debris.

"Things are about to get real crazy," Merc said.

"Like they aren't already," Cass replied.

The frigate, almost as large as the two *Karat* intakes together, swept in close, lasers firing freely. The front end vanished into the intake, glowed as the frigate's shields absorbed the initial impact, and then everything blew to hell. A chained orange explosion rippled along the frigate, broke up through the *Karat*, and splashed over the Viper's shields. Merc could only see orange for a moment, licking flames blocking out the universe. And then they were gone, replaced by a cloud of shards, smaller fires that winked out as fast as they formed, and the silent disintegration of the *Karat* as the impact shattered its way through the ship's decks.

"Hey, you going to move?" Cass said.

Oh, yeah. Merc brought up the maneuvering jets. Coasted the Viper up, down, and to the side of metal chunks, ice diamonds, and the pieces of humanity that had been on those ships but were now permanent residents of Neptune's outer orbit. In between every juke, Merc flicked his eyes down to the scanner, hoping to see something, anything that would show Viola was still alive.

56

FALLING APART

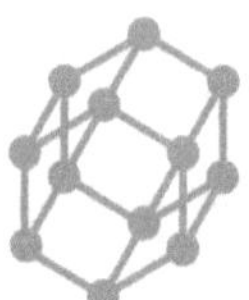

The console blew up in her face as Yuan pulled Viola back. The screen shattered into a thousand jagged edges that cut slits into Viola's turning head. Alarms blared in different frequencies, cadences, each one sounding another critical system on the verge of collapse. It was overwhelming, maddening, but Viola held onto the last thing she'd seen on the scanner. That blip, the frigate, merging with the *Karat* and vanishing.

"They're gone," Viola said as Yuan pulled her towards the bridge exit.

"We will be too, if we don't hurry," Yuan replied.

As if agreeing with Yuan, the *Karat* shuddered, a snapping sound crackling up the inside of the ship and sending the two of them to the floor. Viola pushed herself up, brushed hair out of her face, and felt her hand come away bloody. A cut, or maybe hitting her head. The reason didn't matter. The rush of destroying the frigate was siphoning into panic. She didn't know where the escape shuttles were. If the *Karat* even had any that were still operational. And how long did they have?

"Focus," Yuan said, standing up beside her. "And run."

The captain took off, dashing towards and through the door out of the bridge. Viola followed. Calculations ran through her head, problems she'd done for her engineering classes. Fail-safes ships like the *Karat* would have built in, the kind Galaxy Forge, her father's company, would require.

The frigate came at the *Karat* towards the intakes, from beneath. The cargo hold would have plenty of barriers between it and the rest of the ship, a necessity for the section that opened to vacuum and dangerous materials most often.

"Down!" Yuan shouted in the hallway ahead as a series of pops shot through the ceiling. Viola dropped and a moment later the ceiling panels fell a meter. Struts snapping, residual failure from elsewhere tracking its way up here. Viola pulled up to a squat and kept moving.

After the cargo hold, the most damaged area would have been the crew quarters. The side facing the frigate as it came in spewing laser. Viola tried to remember the *Karat*'s layout. The opposite the crew quarters would have been the sampling area, where cargo taken on was analyzed, cleaned, and readied for sale.

Yuan made it out from underneath the collapsed panels and looked back as Viola continued her half-run, half-crawl.

"There's a pair of shuttles just up here, next to the cafeteria," Yuan called back.

Viola made it out from under the panels and ran after Yuan. Most ship designs put the cafeteria near the crew quarters. Made sense from a logistics perspective. Fewer steps to that late-night snack. A wave of heat, source unknown, washed across her face. The tingling smell of burning circuits filled the air as they approached the ruined space that'd once held the meals for the crew. Parts of the floor had collapsed, leaving sections that looked like islands in a metal ocean. The elevator doors were locked half-open, looking into an empty shaft.

"Which way?" Viola said.

"Straight across," Yuan replied, taking a running jump to get across a collapsed section.

Viola looked at the meter of floor in front of her, then at the gap Yuan had just leapt. Longer than she was tall. But to her left was the hard wall, to her right was the burning ruin of the *Karat*'s kitchen. A likely victim of a power surge as the *Karat*'s own regulators burnt, letting energy run free throughout the ship. The same thing would've torched the console on the bridge. She took a deep breath, Yuan looking at her with a mix of expectation and worry on his face, and took a couple running steps.

And jumped.

As Viola went into the air, she felt the pull on her boots slacken, the *Karat*'s internal gravity failing and sending the ship into near zero-G. Viola careened forward, over the gap but still moving, shooting straight for the far wall. Turn. Viola swung her body around and struck the wall with her feet. Viola tried not to push, to sink as much as possible into a squat so she didn't rebound. Then she pushed off, towards the near exit, the one Yuan pointed out. Her hands, outstretched, wrapped around the corner and swung Viola around. As she moved, Viola caught a glance of lettering pasted onto the wall: Crew Quarters.

Yuan shot past her, rocketing along the hallway, towards a shuttle likely already destroyed. Housed in a section of the *Karat* demolished by the frigate's fire. The lights that way were flickering, impossible to tell what waited for them around the next bend. Only, if Viola's hunch was right, that entire side of the ship was about to fall apart.

"Yuan!" Viola yelled. "Turn around!"

The captain caught himself on a broken part of the hallway side, looking back.

"The shuttle is just ahead!" Yuan called.

"But—"

The hallway behind Yuan illuminated in a yellow sparkle, a great wrenching went through the *Karat* and, suddenly, the stars were visible behind Yuan. Part of Neptune's teal disc showing. Viola was looking into outer space. The *Karat*'s defense mechanisms struggled into action and slammed a door shut, nearly bisecting Yuan as he launched himself back towards Viola.

"Is there another way?" Viola said when Yuan reached her, both of them taking a second to breathe.

"The other shuttle is on the opposite side. Through there," Yuan pointed to the elevator shaft. "It's next to the cargo hold."

It was an impossibility that the cargo hold was still there. No, Viola shook her head slightly. The intakes bore the impact. The cargo hold might be breached, but something on the other side of it's large, empty space might still be there.

"We'll need suits," Viola said, and Yuan nodded.

"There's an emergency set near the entrance to the hold," Yuan said. "In case something goes wrong."

"I think this qualifies," Viola said as they launched themselves towards the elevator shaft.

They flipped down the black inside of the elevator shaft, the only light coming from sporadic flickers along the sides. Cracks, rumbles, groans and the occasional roar of vacuums created and cut off echoed in Viola's ears as they floated down. Yuan hit the top of the elevator first, pressing an emergency release that popped the lid off the top of the elevator. The force sent Yuan flying back up the shaft, but Viola caught the captain as he went by, using her momentum to push them both into the elevator and through the doors into another hallway.

The cargo hold to the right, Yuan's emergency lockers to the left, where the hallway ended in a manual-release door. Most of the *Karat*'s portals opened and closed through electronic panels, Yuan opened this one the old fashioned way; turning a handle. Inside the locker were four suits and accompanying oxygen packs along with a bunch of other first-aid gear. After a couple minutes squeezing themselves into the suits, something Viola wasn't the most experienced with, they stepped back out of the locker and went towards the cargo hold.

The suit fit snug, wrapping Viola in technology that shot her temperature, oxygen rate, and a full diagram of the suit itself in front of her eyes. A smaller diagram appeared a few seconds later, showing Yuan's suit. They'd instantly see if something happened to one another.

"These are really good," Viola said as they walked along. "Galaxy Forge doesn't have anything like these."

"The *Karat* is," Yuan paused, "was Eden's showcase. A test of new technology."

"You'll get to tell them how well it worked," Viola said.

Then the lights went out. The entire hallway dashed into dark as a shaking crack, louder and larger than the others came from Viola's left, towards the intakes. Sensing the lack of light, the suits powered on their headlamps, and Viola saw a different world. Formerly, the bright-lit hallways were boring, safe walks of metal. Now, with shadows playing between the arcs of the lamps and those walls buckling, breaking, Viola found her eyes scanning everywhere, her hands sweaty. Breathing fast.

They would make it. Viola whispered the words to herself as they went. And then the hallway tilted, twisting as though grabbed by a child and turned on its side.

"She's broken," Yuan said. "There's open space ahead."

"Can we make it to the shuttle?" Viola said.

"I don't know. Depends on what's left," Yuan steadied himself on the wall that was now the floor, then launched himself forward. Viola followed. They passed through what had been one of the *Karat*'s vacuum doors, meant to seal off the cargo hold, but the floor it connected with had blown away. Instead, the door hung there, sideways, like a stiff flag in no wind. Behind the door, bleeding through the splintered edges, Viola saw the bluish hues of space.

The cargo hold wasn't a hold anymore. Instead it was a skeleton frame, the *Karat*'s supporting structure now a series of long, battered beams connected only by space. Ice diamonds, shrapnel, and junk whirled around, propelled by Neptune's pull and the force of the *Karat*'s break-up. Gripping the door, Viola looked out beyond the junk at the pure, endless nothing that lay beyond. She'd never space-walked before. Never been out here. Despite the suit regulating her temperature, Viola felt cold.

"The shuttle is this way," Yuan's voice came over the suit's short-range comms now, the captain nodding to his right. "On the outer edge of the cargo hold, but separated."

Yuan went first, pushing off the door and following the cargo hold's inner wall to the right. Viola followed, using the captain's headlamp as much as her own to grab handholds as they drifted. Behind her, Viola felt the *Karat* continuing to break apart, but only when she touched the wall, felt its shudder. Sound didn't carry in the vacuum, and after the endless cacophony of alarms, the silence was surreal. A little peaceful, if Viola was being honest.

Around the curve of the wall, where the cargo hold petered out of room, was a mostly intact module. It would've been underneath the bridge, if the *Karat* was still in one piece. Yuan paused, his head tilted.

"The door, it's already open," the captain said. Viola caught up and looked over the captain's shoulder. The black backdrop of space mashed into the steely gray of the *Karat*'s interior as the wall they were on connected to the room and shot out to the hull, forming an L from their location. In the middle of that jog out, there was a doorway, haloed in Neptune blue, open and beckoning.

"It might've opened from the damage," Viola said. "Or the power going off."

"Possibly. Anyway, we have no choice. Either it is there and we live, or it is gone, and we die."

"I'm hoping for the first one," Viola replied.

Yuan vaulted towards the room, the open door. The captain moved fast, launching himself and heading towards the room like a missile. If he missed that door, he'd squash himself on the wall. Crazy. Viola continued to pick her way along. Yuan, arms and legs tight to his torso, shot through the doorway and disappeared.

"We're not alone!" Yuan commed.

"What?" Viola said, but the only reply was static. Not alone? There was someone in there? Viola bunched her legs and launched off the wall, aiming for the door.

Viola pressed her arms and legs in, forming as much of a needle as she could as she went through the door. Inside the room, it was dark except for a sliver that bled in from the door. And Viola's headlamp, casting around as she tried to find somewhere to stop her momentum. She bounced off a wall, then what would have been the floor before catching herself.

"Yuan?"

Nothing. Viola turned her head around the room. Racks with several more spacesuits, a stack of emergency supplies. But there was only one light, hers, flitting around the room. Yuan's headlamp should have been there too. Turning away from the door, Viola saw the room continued. Made sense, the shuttle at the bow, as far away from the engines and the likely rupture as they could shove it, down here.

"Captain? Hello?" Viola said again. There was always a chance of interference, a signal interrupted.

Viola went further, her headlamp picking up the far end of the room. An airlock, open to the interior of the shuttle. They'd be keeping the suits on then, as the shuttle wouldn't have any air for them. Viola floated towards the shuttle. Then stopped as something grabbed her.

Viola turned to the right, her headlamp illuminating another space suit, not Eden-branded, and in it, a scarred face, mouth set in a firm line and eyes staring at her. It was only an instant, looking at those eyes, but Viola felt that the burned man wasn't looking at her at all. Didn't see her except as an object, something in his way.

Then she was flying forward. He'd thrown her. Viola glanced back, saw that by throwing her, he'd pushed himself back towards the doorway. Viola reached out her hands, caught herself against the outer edge of the airlock. Where was Yuan? She scanned the room and found the captain, down in the corner, cracks splintering across his helmet, his hands trying to spread thick tape along the lines, fixing a leak.

But the attacker was coming back. Viola caught him in her headlamp streaking towards her, flipping so his feet would impact first. Without a weapon, rupturing a suit would be hard, but a flying kick from across the room might be enough. Only if it hit her, though.

Viola gripped the inside of the airlock with her left hand and pulled, swinging herself into the airlock and through, down into the shuttle. The console was on, the shuttle warming up. Yuan must have found this guy just about ready to trigger the launch. Viola turned back towards the shuttle's entrance. She'd be trapped if he came in here, but at least it would be close. A battle of rips and tears. Whomever sprung the first good leak would win.

The burned man slid over the entrance, looked down at her. Viola floated backward, till she could touch the console. The screen reflected on the plate of her helmet, showing Viola where the burned man planned to go.

"Who are you?" the voice coming over the comm surprised her.

"Just a pilot," Viola replied. "Who are you?"

"Just a refugee," the burned man said. "Was it you who destroyed my ship?"

"You're the one who let me."

The burned man was larger than her, probably stronger. Viola didn't know the first thing about fighting up close, much less in space suits. When he struck, she didn't like her odds.

"If you knew what depended on those diamonds, you would have chosen differently," the man said.

The man pushed forward, sending himself towards Viola. Pressing her feet to the console, Viola kicked off and flew towards the burned man. Just before they hit, Viola twisted her body to the side, reaching out with her arms and pulling the burned man past her. The move shot her up, by the airlock, and as she went by, Viola slapped the small panel, still glowing through its hardwired, independent battery. Shuttles had to be launched no matter what the condition, and the launch mechanisms were always linked to their own power. A second later the airlock snapped shut, and while Viola couldn't hear it, she felt the container shift as the shuttle blasted free.

57

AN ESCAPE

A smooth gambit, if a foolish one. Bakr looked at the closed hatch of the shuttle, blasting its way from the *Karat*. They would be trapped there. Die quickly if the whole thing collapsed, or slowly when their air ran out. Meanwhile, he had the shuttle. Not a great outcome, but, if the path Bakr had plotted would work, the shuttle should carry him close enough to Uranus to radio for help.

The engines kicked in briefly, turning the shuttle. The viewport behind Bakr filled with blue light. Not what he would have expected. The course would have him slingshot Neptune, use the momentum to send the shuttle back towards the sun. Bakr twisted around, looked at the console as the engines fired again, full thrust this time. The path was different. It wasn't his.

Arrows traced from the shuttle's current position towards Neptune, ending directly at the planet's center. A simple path, a doomed one.

"The girl," Bakr said, even though nobody could hear him. The girl had changed the vector, her back to the console. The path was crude, but it would accomplish its purpose. A glance at the fuel reserves told Bakr all he needed to know. The shuttle was moving too fast, was already too deep in Neptune's gravity well to go anywhere but into it.

"Alissa," Bakr said, looking at the growing ball of blue that filled the viewport. "I'm sorry."

The burned man leaned forward, gripping the console and looking out at Neptune growing larger and larger. Bakr felt the pull on his feet first, then his fingers, the increasing tug of Neptune's gravity. The interior of the shuttle heated up. An alarm sounded, pitifully, that their descent was too steep. Not that there was any fuel left to correct it. The edges of the window glowed white as Neptune's thick atmosphere overwhelmed the shuttle's meager shields.

Bakr closed his eyes as the universe melted away.

58

SEEK AND FIND

Guiding the *Jumper* through a thousand tons of space junk wasn't Phyla's favorite activity, but it beat dodging lasers. A few minutes ago, they'd docked the damaged Viper, with Merc and that raider, Cass, coming on board. The fighter pilot insisted Viola could be somewhere in here, and Phyla felt they owed the girl enough to take a look.

"The shuttle didn't reply?" Trina commed from the engines.

Phyla had tried to hail the streaking escape shuttle they'd seen launch from the *Karat*'s wreckage while picking up Merc, but there hadn't been a response. The trajectory wasn't a good one either, and by now the tiny ship had disappeared. Not just from the *Jumper*'s sensors, but from existence.

"Nothing," Phyla said. "It didn't look like there was even an attempt to course-correct either. That can't have been Viola."

"Accidental launches happen," Trina replied. "With the irregular power, maybe a small explosion—"

"I got it," Phyla said. "Going to swing over that way to check it out."

She tried to focus on finding Viola, on scanning the debris, but she kept waiting for the comm to crackle. For Davin to announce they were fine on the freighter, that they could be picked up. There'd been nothing. Stop. Not now. The freighter wasn't a pile of floating debris. Davin would be fine.

"I hear I have you to thank," Quinn said, coming into the cockpit. "So, thank you."

"Repaying a debt," Phyla said, keeping her eyes on the mess of twisting metal and ice diamonds ahead of her.

"Doesn't mean I can't thank you."

"You really want to thank me? Then get down to the airlock, get a suit on, and get ready," Phyla said.

"Ready for what?"

"You see that?" Phyla pointed. After so many years staring at starlight, it was easy to see the glint of a man-made glow. Couldn't tell where it was coming from, but the reflection, with its duller, non-twinkling matte light wasn't from nature. Quinn followed her point, nodded, stood up, and left.

That wasn't much of a conversation. Phyla could have said more. Could have been nicer. Except, right now, there wasn't time. Phyla sent the *Jumper* beneath the large chunk of wreckage, turning the ship on its side so that the airlock faced the floating room where she'd seen the reflection. She sent two comm bursts towards the section, but didn't get a reply. Countless possible reasons for that, from broken systems to suits not equipped with longer-range comms.

"Merc, can you go with Quinn?" Phyla commed through the ship. "I don't know who's in there."

"Yeah, I got you," Merc commed a minute later. Phyla

noted the reply came from Opal's room, winced. It wasn't nice to pull the pilot away from Opal, but who else would do it?

"Stay there," a voice Phyla didn't recognize. "I'll go with Quinn. You've done enough, stick jockey."

"Who's that?" Phyla asked.

"Your new stowaway wants to earn her passage," the voice commed again. Cass.

"Then go get'em," Phyla replied. "I'll have you in position in sixty seconds."

A minute later, Quinn triggered the airlock open and Phyla, using the *Jumper*'s cameras, watched the pair float, tethered, out towards the wreck.

"Establishing vid-link," Quinn commed, and Phyla's console lit up with a grainy feed from Quinn's suit. As the pair of them entered the wreck, the available light dipped and the video became a smear of grays and spots of light.

"Any sign?" Phyla asked.

"Definitely picking up the light," Quinn replied. "Looks like a headlamp. Moving slowly. There's a lot of crap floating in here."

Silence for a bit. Quinn seemed to be moving further into the room, then turned to the right, following the light from the headlamp. There, in the corner, were two bodies. Almost meshed together.

"I see them. The larger one in the back is Captain Yuan," Quinn said, moving forward quickly. "His helmet's cracked. Likely bleeding oxygen. It looks like the girl patched her suit into his. Sharing the same air."

"We've gotta get them out of here," Cass broke in. "Now. While they're still alive."

The raider took the lead, wrapping arms beneath the captain and lifting the two bodies up. Quinn took the other side, both of them carrying the bodies back through the room.

"Erick, going to need some oxygen ready to go," Phyla commed.

"Just what do you think I'm doing down here? Sitting in the dark waiting to be ordered around?" the doctor replied.

"Yes?"

"No. No I'm not. I've been listening to the whole thing. The med bay is ready to receive."

"Good," Phyla switched back to the outgoing transmission. "We're ready for you."

"Cycle the airlock in three," Quinn said.

Two.

One.

And then it was time to get Davin.

59

THE METAL MAN

Every single segment felt like a deep stab, Mox's nerves once again filtering through the exoskeleton's net. A gag filled his mouth, to prevent Mox from biting through his tongue in shock as he laid on the bed in the *Jumper*'s med bay.

"How many of those are there?" the raider woman, Cass, asked. She was helping Erick place each of the connections. She asked a lot of questions.

"Nearly a hundred different connections," Erick replied, linking the next one down Mox's left leg. "They have to respond to every muscle, to every twitch and amplify the power."

The stab. Mox sucked in breath and closed his eyes. Remember the reasons.

"How much does something like this cost?" Cass asked. Too much, Mox wanted to say. Worth every coin. The type of penance that literally strengthens you.

"I don't know," Erick said. "It was a choice Mox made."

"Do you know why?"

"You'll have to ask him," Erick said.

Thank you. The doctor knew. Understood some things need to stay behind closed doors.

A sharper sting. Mox set his jaw. That would be the knee.

"How you doing, big guy?" Cass leaned over his face. "Need anything?"

Mox shook his head slightly. Drugs might numb the pain. A drink might dull the sting. But that was not the point. Cass saw the shake, glanced over at the doctor.

"How much longer is this going to take?"

"Another hour," Erick said.

"You think it's worth it?" Cass asked Mox.

The big man nodded. When the next segment went in, Mox clamped down on the gag. Was it worth it? All the pain?

Yes.

60

ONE OF THEM

"So what will you do now?" Viola asked Yuan as the captain walked down the *Jumper*'s ramp into the freighter. Some of the freighter's crew had already left the bay, heading back to their quarters, their stations, to see what remained of their old lives.

"You mean after I return the freighter to Eden, a glorious failure?" Yuan said, but killed the seriousness with a smile. "A large ship like this one takes a long time to get anywhere. Eden may have forgiven me by the time we get back to Jupiter. Perhaps another assignment. If not, maybe I'll find your captain and see if there's an opening."

"Join us?" Viola laughed. "Unless you enjoyed all those near-death experiences, probably want to rethink that."

"How about you? Are you set to continue on this path?"

"I don't know," Viola said, and was a little surprised to realize that was true. She didn't know whether she wanted to stay with Davin and the crew. Viola was exhausted—her only real sleep in the last two days had come from oxygen deprivation in the wreckage of the *Karat*, but she feared that behind closed eyes, all she would see was the face of the raider as he realized he was shot, as he realized he would die.

"There is room here, if you choose. A pilot would be welcome," Yuan offered.

Her father would yell at her to take that offer. Get in on a lucrative role with one of humanity's top companies?

"Quinn!" Viola heard Phyla yell, from the top of the ramp, to the Eden security guard, who was watching the disseminating crew like a parent might watch a group of unruly children.

"Come back here and say goodbye like a real person," Phyla continued, then brushed by Viola on her way down. "'Scuse me, Vi."

Phyla took another couple steps, then paused, looked back at Viola.

"By the way, soon as you head back in, can you plot out a track to get us back to Miner Prime? Thanks."

Phyla hadn't ever asked Viola to do that. To actually pilot the *Jumper*, plot their course.

"Sorry," Viola said to Yuan. "I'm not done here yet."

Yuan nodded, his grin growing wider, sadder.

"Perhaps we will see each other again, on the other side of the Sun," Yuan said, then turned and walked away.

The other side of the Sun. No idea where that came from, but it sounded nice. Viola would look the phrase up later. Or, after she put Puk back together, she'd ask it. The little guy would know.

As Viola walked back up the ramp, she took one more look down, saw Quinn extend a hand for Phyla to shake, saw Phyla grab it, saw Phyla pull Quinn in for a quick, tight hug. Too personal. Viola turned away, went back into the *Jumper*'s boxy, metal confines and turned her mind to matters mathematical.

61

EDEN'S ORDERS

The *Jumper* left Neptune behind, picking up speed for a long shot towards Miner Prime. Davin double-checked the course plotting Viola had done earlier, though he knew Phyla had already reviewed it, and the girl had put it together perfectly the first time around. It would take weeks to get to the space station, and most of the crew was doing what he should be—sleeping.

"She's good," Phyla said, knowing what Davin was doing.

"That move with the *Karat*, that was gutsy stuff," Davin replied. "Would we have done that, you think?"

"You? Never. Too paralyzed with fear."

"You would've been sitting there, trying to think of better ways to do it until everyone was already dead," Davin countered.

"Maybe it's good to have a reckless pilot on board," Phyla said.

"I thought that's why Merc's here."

"I'm never trusting him with this chair," Phyla shook her head. "He'd have the *Jumper* flipping over so much we'd all get sick."

"You did a helluva job back there. With the fighters," Davin said. "Don't know if I say this enough, but I'm pretty damn happy to have you."

"Have me?" Phyla cocked an eyebrow. "I'm here because I want to be. You don't have anything."

"That mean I don't have to pay you?"

"Want, Davin. Want. This woman needs a cut, or she'll want to be somewhere else real fast."

The blinking light on the comm threatened to interrupt their conversation. Davin ignored it. The *Jumper* would file the message and they could get back to it later. Davin sat back in his seat, stared out at space, at the Sun glowing in the far distance, barely brighter than the surrounding stars. Reached out with his hand and felt Phyla take it, grip it. Silence for a minute, just breathing and taking in the fact that they were both there. They'd survived, again. The tips of Phyla's fingers pressed into the back of Davin's hand, warm. So simple, but Davin hadn't felt that touch since Lina's place, way back on Miner Prime. And before that, Davin could barely remember. Space travel wasn't as romantic as the movies made it out to be.

"So what was Bosser going to pay us?" Phyla asked.

"Was? No idea. Betting the number now is going to be a whopping zero."

"Nothing?"

"We wrecked Eden's prize ship, ignored Bosser's own orders to run, and, oh yeah, shot the super-valuable ice diamonds into space," Davin said, stretching out his arms. He wasn't sure why it didn't bother him to say they failed their mission. Then he tugged on Phyla's hand and remembered.

"Not all of them," Phyla said, and Davin looked over to see a smirk on her face.

"What?"

"When we were floating through the wreck, picking up Viola and Yuan, we grabbed a few that were close. Trina's storing them in the back, near the engines. So the freighter's crew wouldn't get any ideas."

"So you're saying we're not broke?"

"I'm saying that I'm going to be getting my cut, Davin, and so will you."

Relief. Which surprised Davin. Nothing more than relief filtering through him. That they would be able to pay for the *Jumper*'s next flight. That Opal, Erick, Trina and the others would get some coin in their accounts. That somehow, they'd survived a trip to the heart of Neptune and back out. Davin laughed, couldn't help it.

"It's good to see you happy," Phyla said. "Hasn't been enough of that lately."

"Tell me about it," Davin sighed, but the cynical weight that'd been there earlier was gone. Then his eyes caught the still-blinking message light. Davin reached towards it.

"Don't press it," Phyla said. "Right now, we're good. You play that message..."

"Probably just Bosser asking for a status update," Davin said, tapping the console.

"Davin," Bosser's voice came out of the speakers. "You idiot. Assuming you're still alive, of course. Which you shouldn't be, but, like Earth's cockroaches, you and your crew appear to have a tendency to escape death. Not that it matters anymore. Eden informed me that the *Karat* is gone, along with the ice diamonds. Apparently you saved one of their officers, who dutifully reported how you screwed this up. And how you saved their crew.

"You're going to fly your ship straight to Miner Prime. Eden's going to employ you. Give you a chance to clear your debt, so to speak. You're getting another lease on life. Don't run, don't think you can live a hermit life on an outer planet. Because we will find you, and you know it. Contact me when you arrive." Bosser ended the message.

"Don't say I didn't warn you," Phyla said in the silence.

Davin tapped the console, pushed the display of their route onto the glass, tracing a yellow arrow straight into the stars. The console prompted Davin for any adjustments, a new target.

"You think they could find us anywhere?" Davin said.

"I don't think you could do it anyway," Phyla replied. "You'd go crazy, living on some tiny station around Pluto."

Davin's hand hovered over the console. With a swipe, he could send them to Saturn, or put them on course for Mars. Even Earth. Take their chances.

"After this, it's done," Davin said, moving his hand away. Phyla grabbed it, held it as the *Jumper* left the black-blue Neptune and the white bar of the *Amerigo* behind.

READ *on for an excerpt of the Wild Nine's next adventure,* One Shot.

ACKNOWLEDGMENTS

As a second book, *Dark Ice* was a lot of fun to put together. To see where Davin and the rest of the crew wanted to go.

Exploring their journeys simply wouldn't be possible without the immense support of family and friends. From encouragement, to reading and offering advice, to sharing *Wild Nines* with their own circles, it's a truly humbling experience to see the helping hands of so many make this possible.

And to Nicole, who, as I play in outer space with the Wild Nines crew, is endlessly patient, I love you.

Lastly, thanks to all the readers out there for giving us authors an audience. If writing is an act of love, then having your work read is an act of joy.

For my father

ONE SHOT

THE WILD NINES - BOOK THREE

1
———

DEADLY INSPIRATION

The charge blew the airlock with a burst of smoke and blue flame. Following the explosion, laser fire blitzed through the haze, more than a few bolts from Alissa's own rifle. Nothing came back. No shouts, no answering fire.

"Go, but keep talking," Castor said to the four fighters positioned around the charred opening. "Head for the hold. We'll hit the bridge."

Alissa watched the fighters, her fighters, vanish through the airlock. Beside Castor, a pair of other fighters, dressed in the tattered collections worn by all the Red Voice soldiers, stood armed and ready. At her nod, they entered. Alissa and Castor followed. A bright room sat on the other side of the airlock, shelves against the walls covered in space suits, oxygen lines, and patching materials. What you'd need if things went wrong.

The two fighters turned right. Galaxy Forge pumped out these freighters with the same blueprints, and this group had been raiding them for years now. They had the fastest routes to the bridge and cargo memorized. Alissa couldn't stop herself from taking a deep breath, deep enough for Castor to glance over as they followed the fighters.

"Sorry," Alissa said. "Sometimes I forget how long we've been doing this."

"It's been a long time. Don't think we ever expected to live longer than a month," Castor replied.

"Hey, I had us pegged for a year."

Getting up to bridge level required an elevator ride. The four of them stood inside the lift, but when the fighter pressed the button to rise, the lift didn't move. Immediately the second fighter pulled off his pack and broke out a las-tool. Alissa and the others backed against the side of the lift as the fighter burned through the ceiling. The white-hot laser shredded a circle, and the freed plate clanged down to the ground as the fighter finished cutting. Castor knelt, cupping his hands, and Alissa stepped on them. He boosted her up and Alissa squeezed through the opening, pulling herself onto the roof of the lift.

Standard defense procedure. Send a distress message, then make it as hard as possible to get to the bridge by disabling the lifts. Alissa looked around the shaft. There was always a ladder somewhere. There! Hanging along the rear side and going all the way up. She waved the others out, with Castor the last man making the jump, gripping the edge of the hole and pulling himself out. The fighters were the first up the ladder, climbing to the sealed doors at the bridge level, breaking out the las-tool, and burning their way through to a hallway.

"Lead, it's the hold team," the voice came over Alissa's comm. "We're finding no resistance. No sign of the crew."

"None here either," Alissa replied. "Keep the channels open and let us know what you find."

The comm clicked acknowledgment. Alissa climbed the

ladder next, squeezing in through the hot hole made in the bridge level doors. In front of them sat a hallway split on either side with crew cabins. At the far end, the mess hall and the thick doors to the bridge. Now the fighters crept, their rifles drawn. Alissa and Castor followed, Alissa carrying her favorite automatic sidearms. Hold the trigger and they would spew more lasers than a personal shield could take. Sure, they ran out of power fast, but nobody lived that long.

The cafeteria was immaculate. No dirty dishes, scraps of litter, or even chairs out of place. As though the kitchen hadn't even been used.

"Something's not right here," Alissa said. "The ship's too far away from Jupiter to be this clean."

"Weapons ready," Castor said. Usual raiding protocol meant taking captives. Ransom money, information about other targets, and goodwill from not killing a bunch of civilians made it more profitable. But it wasn't worth risking their own lives.

The bridge doors were shut, large and thick. The last barrier to an assault. If they had to cut through with the lastool, it was going to take time. So Castor went to work instead. The small panel next to the bridge doors allowed keyed access, connections that could be subverted. Using a micro tool and its torch option, Castor melted off bits of the corners, loosening the faceplate. Flipped the button on the tool and used the small crowbar that extended to pry it off. Then he leaned in and Alissa couldn't tell anymore what he was doing, but, like a magician working his tricks, the bridge doors shot open a moment later.

Then stopped, only a third of a meter wide.

"It's a little tight," Alissa said, looking through the gap. She could see terminals, consoles where the pilot would guide the ship and the captain would monitor various systems. Only there was nobody there, no laser waiting to blow her face off.

"I'm not getting any response," Castor said. "It's like someone cut the power from this panel to the door."

The other three looked at Alissa. She looked at the opening, and then Alissa shrugged off her pack. Took off the jacket. Before any of them could stop her, Alissa squeezed through the doors. And then she was hit in the shoulder, shoved by something strong. Alissa bounced off the ground and tucked into a roll, using the momentum to keep moving away from what hit her. When she felt the far wall, she glanced back towards the door and froze. The naked, static face of an android stared at her from across the room. Its gray bones shimmered in the ship's lifeless lighting.

"You are not the crew of this vessel," the bot said. "Identify yourself."

Behind the android, Alissa saw something else. A deep red stain covering the far wall, and beneath it, a crumpled body. She stood and drew her sidearms. It didn't take a genius to solve this mystery.

"Doesn't matter who I am," Alissa said. "What matters is what you're going to do next."

On the other side of the door, Alissa could hear Castor and the fighters trying to figure out a way into the room. Eventually, they might make it, but the easiest way to open those doors sat on those consoles right in front of her. She just had to make it there before this thing killed her.

"My directives stated to clear the ship," the android said. "I did so. Verified it. I will report the error and rectify the situation."

The android came at her fast, its legs pushing it across the bridge to her in a couple of strides. Just enough time for

Alissa to hold down those triggers. Both sidearms exploded in an orange light show, streaming bolts at the android. Every shot blew off charred bits from the bot's armor, exposing circuits and pumping metal muscle. But it didn't stop. Its fist swung towards Alissa's head. She ducked and ran under the punch, moving back towards the center of the room. The bot wheeled around and Alissa felt her hair swish as the android's second swing came close to taking her head off.

She ran to the consoles, looking for some way to open the doors further. Only they were all locked, asking for the captain or pilot's badge. Which meant she was trapped, which meant she was dead. Alissa turned to face the bot as it stepped up to her. She brought the sidearms up, but the android moved faster, knocked the sidearm out of Alissa's left hand while grabbing her right and lifting her up.

Those black eyes stared right at her as the android cocked its right arm back to deliver a killing punch. Alissa sucked in a breath, then spat in the android's face. And it exploded. Alissa fell to the ground as lasers poured into the android through the crack in the bridge doors. The bot staggered, backing out of the fire, falling over as the motors keeping its legs in place melted away. Alissa grabbed her dropped sidearm and closed on the android. The bot's head swiveled to look at her as Alissa aimed at it. Then she fired.

The lasers chewed through the bot's insides. Burned away the circuitry. A couple seconds of sustained attack, and the android was nothing more than a pile of ruined parts.

"Thanks for the save," Alissa said a moment later. She'd opened the bridge doors using the badge still on the bloody body, the fighters and Castor joining her by the consoles. "We're lucky it wasn't equipped for a real fight or we'd be dead. My question, why did it kill the crew?"

Androids weren't allowed, were explicitly programmed, not to harm innocents. Only targets assigned through a judgment system. She doubted the crew on this freighter had any criminal records. Doubted that they'd be worth sending an android after them even so.

"The android was part of a shipment. They delivered more than a dozen to Ganymede, but this one was requested back. Intentionally," Castor said, flicking through the ship's logs. "The order came from our favorite man, Bosser."

"Castor, if Bosser's getting these androids to kill on command, why couldn't we?" Alissa said.

"We'd need to get access to their production facility, on Earth," Castor said. "They'll never let us land."

"They will if we have Bosser," Alissa said. Castor nodded. "Let's get the haul off this ship and set course for Miner Prime."

THE NEXT MOVE

A minor setback. Losing the ice diamonds was a blow to their bottom line, but all it meant was that Bosser's partners would have to step up their contributions. Reaching their goal would provide such profits as to make the diamonds a footnote and nothing more.

Bosser said all of this to the screen in his dark apartment aboard the space station Miner Prime. Situated in the asteroid belt between Mars and Jupiter, the station functioned as an intermediary for communications between civilized space and more adventurous outposts in the farther reaches of the solar system. Those outposts, and missions around them, had been giving Bosser more headaches than usual lately.

The two-meter wide monitor in front of Bosser held the faces of his various business partners. All of them were labeled with astrological pseudonyms. Zodiac signs, in no particular order, hovering beneath their heads in gold-weighted capital letters, as though they were wearing jewelry. The faces themselves were static, would remain so for minutes as the message filtered its way through dozens of satellites to their respective offices. Of the nine members on that screen, Bosser had a good idea who all of them were. Despite the entire group coming together through a string of anonymous messages suggesting places and times, despite a promise not to attempt to learn the identities of each other, Bosser had gone digging.

As had all the others.

Bosser took a sip from the water glass beside him, the cool liquid tasting indistinguishable from the filtered natural springs on Earth. So long as he didn't think about the fact that it was recycled from the station's thousands of citizens, Bosser enjoyed the sensation. Water and wine. Anything else was a waste of time.

"This is the second instance that this group disrupted your plans," Gemini, the top-middle, head of a large asteroid mining company, said.

To keep the council from talking over each other, an order had been established at the first meeting. Bosser, with Miner Prime as the central communication hub for the group, would dictate who should respond next. If nobody was specified, the order rotated, progressing through the group one person at a time. Lately, though, Bosser felt all of these sessions were interrogation games. Searching for ways to pin misfortunes on him.

"The Wild Nines served their purpose," Bosser replied. "That the Red Voice still had any ships capable of mounting an assault was information we did not have. That Eden did not have. As the Red Voice needed those diamonds far more than ourselves and we prevented that acquisition, I still consider the mission a success."

Another period of pauses. Bosser went over to the record player set up against the wall of the apartment. Easily the most valuable item he owned, the player and his collection of several dozen records had been a gift. The acknowledgment of a life saved. Now, Bosser started the player and positioned the needle. The long, slow swing of a saxophone bled out of the player and mingled with the constant shuffling of technobabble that made up Miner Prime's background noise. The shudders of systems turning on and off, of lifts sliding people up and down, the overhead announcements requesting this or that person to be somewhere else.

"Speaking of the Red Voice remnants, do you know where they are?" the next head in line, Leo, asked. "If they are the only remaining threat, I don't know why we haven't eliminated them."

"It is much harder to find and swat one fly in a house than it is to shoot a man in the same space," Bosser said. After being torched off the face of Mars, the rebels had scattered. Had vanished so well that Bosser had forgotten about them. Until now.

Bosser sat on a crimson couch, a large one arranged in a half-circle facing the monitor. In the center sat a glass table, supported by faux-pearl legs. Both were gifts, like the record player. The couch, its fabric grown specifically for comfort in an Earth laboratory, came after Bosser had rooted out and destroyed the reputation of a rival to Eden's top executive. The table, for expunging a scion's record of bad decisions. That same scion would likely be one of those faces on the screen in a few years. Always better to have people in your debt than the other way around.

"Excuses aren't necessary. Just take care of them," said Cancer, who then leaned a little closer to his camera. "How are the preparations for the Guardian Project proceeding?"

The highlight of the conversation. Bosser spent the next hours feeding them encouraging details, answering questions between pauses. The project was proceeding on schedule, was deploying. After that, the puppet masters would truly hold the strings. As the meeting hit its sixth hour, members started to drop off. Until only one, Virgo, remained on the screen.

"You sent my daughter into that mess on Neptune," the head said.

"Your daughter went of her own accord," Bosser replied, standing. The transmission time to Virgo was only minutes. A relatively snappy conversation, for a change. "I met her, when the Wild Nines were here on the station. She hacked an android."

"An amazing woman," Virgo said. "But if you ever send her into a situation like that again, Bosser, I won't forget it."

"It sounds like you don't trust your daughter to make her own decisions."

"The reason you are so useful, Bosser, is that you don't care who you have to sacrifice to achieve your ends," Virgo said. "The rest of us prefer to keep those we love safe, even if that means restricting their independence. As a clever, self-interested man, I'm sure you can find a way to keep her out of things."

"As you say," Bosser nodded slowly for the camera. "I will do whatever I can to keep your daughter alive."

"See that you do," Virgo said, then cut the communication.

Bosser turned off the monitor, exhausted. No time for sleep yet though. The board was set, the pieces were in motion, and it was Bosser's turn to play.

OLD BOT, NEW BODY

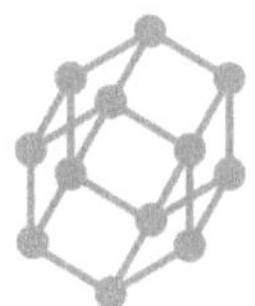

The drive slid into the slot with a satisfying click. Viola tapped the top of it, which extended out from the volleyball-sized sphere, and watched the slot disappear down into the ball. The whole apparatus sat in a charging cradle, which fed energy from the *Jumper*'s solar panels into the sphere. It'd been sitting there for hours now, and with the *Jumper* drawing closer to the sun on its journey to Miner Prime, the batteries should be good to go.

"Good morning, Puk," Viola said. It was late evening, but the phrase itself was the key.

In a quiet environment, like her bedroom back on Ganymede, Viola would have been able to hear some of Puk's systems starting up. The whirs of cooling fans, the whoosh of the jets as the bot floated into the air. The *Jumper*, though, played a symphony of its own that overwhelmed the smaller sounds. Especially in Viola's cabin, back towards the engines. Right now, with the ship starting its slowing period on approach to Miner Prime, Viola heard the constant hum as the engines compressed and discharged ionized gas. Outside the closed door, footsteps echoed clanks as one of the other crew members wandered by. Occasional communication went over the ship's intercoms, muffled through the door but still there, like a conversation on the other side of a room.

Puk rose. Wobbly. Hovering in front of Viola's face and turning around.

"Is your camera working?" Viola asked.

"You asking if I can see your beautiful face?" Puk replied, its vocal synthesizers producing a flat tone. "Because you've never looked better."

"Liar." Viola smiled. She probably looked terrible. Greasy and tired. They'd been flying for weeks already, coming back from Neptune with a stopover for supplies on Titan, one of Saturn's moons. The *Jumper* wasn't exactly a spa, with its recycled water shower that sprinkled more than washed, a steady re-use of clothes so covered with grime from the constant maintenance of the ship's many systems, and a lack of the little things she'd had growing up on Ganymede. What Viola wouldn't give for some scented soap, a chance to eat some actual fruit rather than the dried stuff.

"I've never died before," Puk said. "Except running out of battery, but, I mean, not destroyed."

"You know what happened?"

"No idea. But my date/time systems show that I've been out for over a month."

That was accurate. She'd restored Puk from the last back-up she had, before they'd met up with the freighter *Amerigo*. Before they'd been swept up in Neptune's storm of terror.

"I'm almost jealous," Viola said. "Wouldn't mind forgetting the last month myself."

"Sounds unpleasant. Don't tell me."

"Okay," Viola said, glancing at the bulge on Puk's side. A

new feature. One she'd thought about a lot before adding in. "Are you detecting the new hardware?"

"It's next up on my start-up checks," Puk buzzed. "Viola, this is a lot more powerful than my last laser."

"You should have enough for a couple of shots," Viola said. "Ones powerful enough to kill somebody, anyway."

The room was silent for a moment. Viola's mouth felt dry.

The *Karat*'s lift doors opening, Davin firing at the hijacker right in front. Not seeing the guy in back, his sidearm out. Aiming for Davin. Viola's own shot a perfect one, burning home. The man's face after, shocked at his own death. She still woke up to that face some nights.

"That's . . . different," Puk said. "You didn't program me that way."

"I have now. Dig for it," Viola said. Part of why it'd taken a while to bring Puk back. She'd had to make changes to the personality. Remove some of the softer sides. Some of the limits. Puk might not know it now, but if the situation demanded it, the bot wouldn't hesitate to take a life.

"Viola, what happened? What did I miss?"

"I thought you didn't want to know?"

"That was before I knew how different you'd made me. I need some context," Puk said.

Viola took a breath, then recounted the dive to save the ice diamonds, the hijacked *Karat*, down in Neptune's atmosphere. The Red Voice raiders. The suicidal ramming of their frigate with the *Karat* and their escape.

"Sorry I missed it," Puk said. "Although, I suppose I didn't miss the whole thing."

"From what Opal says, you saved her life," Viola said. "Only, it was close. If you'd had this weapon, it would've been easier. Safer."

"Then I guess this is a good thing?"

Viola had nothing to say to that. Good? Puk was stronger now, more dangerous. So long as the bot was with them, then yeah, it was a good thing. Except she couldn't shake the idea that turning her sarcastic friend into a deadly weapon was wrong.

Viola fell back from the small desk onto the stiff bed that took up the rest of the cabin. No room for chairs. The locker at the foot of the bed held the rest of her stuff, not much of it suited to what she was doing now. In there, among the clothes and scattered tools she'd brought with her when they last left Ganymede, was a rifle designed to trigger a rapid sequence of lasers, each one capable of burning through someone. Every day she'd forced herself to go to the *Jumper*'s pair of simulators, beat-up things that Merc maintained more for flight practice than anything, and blast targets.

The next time she had to shoot someone, the good aim wouldn't be by accident.

The thought didn't make her happy.

4

DOCKING PROCEDURES

Phyla's eyes opened and, for a second, she did not know where she was. The room was larger than hers; she didn't own the shotgun by the door, and the larger locker wasn't covered with pictures like . . . hers. They all belonged to Davin, still sleeping next to her, the thin sheets on the bed rising and falling with his breath. Phyla turned on her side and traced his outline through the blanket. After Neptune, the rush to where she was now happened quickly.

From the first evening, when the *Jumper* had gone to sleep, and it was just the two of them, sitting there in the cockpit, talking like they had a thousand times before, it felt different. The missions were cutting closer, the team getting hurt. *They* were getting hurt. What had been a simpler world of policing stable outposts, running escort jobs for freighters nobody wanted to attack because the corporate owners were too powerful, had turned into a constant series of near-death moments.

Stripped of the small talk, because who knew when you'd be robbed of a chance to say what you needed to say, the two of them, childhood friends, wound up here. But it wasn't just physical. Phyla welcomed the tighter bond, the yes no maybe moments with Davin where they didn't feel like crew and captain, but partners. Friends. Lovers.

The dimmed clock on Davin's side of the bed brightened as it caught Phyla's glance. Still early. There wasn't a day and night, but the *Jumper*'s lighting did its best to simulate Earth, keep that rhythm. Blue lights at night, white during the day and a gradual shift between the two.

"Phyla, this is your wake-up call," whispered a voice from her comm, sitting on the small shelf at her side of the bed. "We'll be at manual range in an hour."

When Phyla would have to take over the piloting duties to bring the *Jumper* into Miner Prime. There'd been a lot of back-and-forth about forcing auto-pilot landings, but after some random events weren't caught correctly by autopilot programming—a stray asteroid, or a ship drifting off course that could have been avoided—Miner Prime required all smaller craft to dock with a pilot behind the sticks.

"I'm up," Phyla responded.

"Want me to wake the captain?" Fournine, formerly the android and now the *Jumper*'s central brain, thanks to Trina, said.

"Too late," Davin's voice rose as a scratchy groan. "What's going on?"

"We're almost home," Phyla said.

"You happy to be back?"

Phyla took in the question with a whiff of Davin's heavy breath. Not that hers would be any better. The endless close encounters on a ship like the *Jumper* more or less forced you to get used to all kinds of odors.

"In the sense that we can get some better food, yes,"

Phyla said. "But we didn't exactly leave here on the best of terms."

"Bosser said he cleared us, that Eden smoothed things over."

"You trust him?"

"Not even a little," Davin said. "But I trust money. Bosser knows Viola is with us, which means Eden probably does too. They won't risk hurting her just to get revenge."

"Sometimes you can be a little cold, you know that?" Phyla said, slipping out of the bed and pulling on clothes.

"It's a fact, Phyla," Davin said, leaning on his elbows. "Viola being on this ship is going to let us get rid of those ice diamonds, then get out of here, coin in hand."

"And go where?"

"There's a place I haven't been in a long time," Davin started to smile, just slightly. "I don't think you've ever gone there."

The lights in the cabin brightened, turning yellow. Another dawn on the *Jumper*. Phyla looked at the clock again. Getting close to time.

"You want to go to Earth?"

Davin nodded. He was right. Phyla hadn't ever been there. Only in orbit, and then, only once. Most of the cargo and escort runs the *Jumper* did were towards the outside where routes weren't established enough to warrant large ships. Where other craft were rare enough that hijackers could take you unopposed if you didn't pay for guards.

"What are we going to do there?" Phyla said, heading for the door.

"With the coin we'll make from the ice diamonds, we can go, sell the *Jumper*, try something new," Davin said, still in the bed. "Something where, maybe, we don't get shot at all the time."

"You think you could handle that? A normal life?"

"No way to know until I give it a try," Davin laughed. "Besides, with you, I doubt it'll be that normal."

"What's that supposed to mean?"

Not the reply Davin was expecting, and Phyla could tell he was searching for a way to worm himself out of this one.

"Phyla, we're being hailed by the space station," Fournine's voice jumped in, this time over the louder intercom. "Need you in the cockpit, unless you want me to start talking to them. Which could be fun, now that I think about it."

"No, Fournine, I'm coming," Phyla said, shaking her head at Davin and leaving the cabin.

A normal life. Phyla wasn't even sure what that really meant. The last few weeks, the *Jumper* speeding through space back towards Miner Prime, there'd been little to do but maintain the ship, work out, and relax. Nice, but it was getting stale, and Phyla felt a little thrill as she climbed into the *Jumper*'s cockpit. If a normal life meant not getting shot at that was fine. But if the cost was boredom? What would she choose?

"*Whiskey Jumper*? This is Miner Prime flight control. We're sending over the coordinates for your bay now."

"Thanks, control. Happy to be here," Phyla replied.

Outside the cockpit windows, the cylindrical spider of Miner Prime loomed large. Its core supporting the majority of the population, with the outer edges getting progressively more exclusive, more exotic.

"*Jumper*, seems you've got some powerful friends," Control said. "Let's try to keep this visit a little less destructive, shall we?"

"We'd love to, Control."

A yellow line shot out along the *Jumper*'s cockpit, angling towards the space station. Phyla gripped the flight stick, turned off the autopilot, and started the first angling turn. The last time Phyla had come home, she'd blown parts of Miner Prime to pieces in a desperate escape.

Please, please let this time be better.

5

—————

DESPERATE PLANS

Forty fighters stood in the *Whisperwind*'s main area, crowded on couches, standing between tables, all staring at her. The ship was on final approach to Minor Prime, where most of these fighters might die.

"You are the last of us," Alissa said to the group. "The Red Voice is a movement, a belief that people should have their own freedom and not be ruled by corporations. We have fought for years and now I'm asking for just a little more."

The fighters looked back at her, silent. It wasn't their first speech. Colorful language calling for an end to evil, appeals to passion and love of one's home, but Alissa hoped this would be the last one. The last time she would have to preach for a doomed cause.

"Today we take up arms for those who do not know that they are imprisoned. Who cannot see their cage," Alissa said. "On a recent mission, we found a freighter overrun by a single android. Its crew dead. The android itself, rather than dispensing justice, was following orders."

Now the eyes perked up. She had their attention.

"Our goal is to turn these new androids against the oppressors, to make the sword of their false justice swing for the right side."

A fighter raised his hand. Alissa nodded at him.

"Excuse me, but the androids, aren't they made on Earth?" the fighter said. "Why aren't we going there?"

"Because we would never land alive," Castor said, speaking up from beside Alissa. "Minor Prime has a target that can get us onto Earth. We're here to take him."

"We'll have four squads. One, led by me, will attempt to find Bosser himself," Alissa said. "The other three will be diversions, clearing the way for the rest of us. Once the objective is complete, we'll regroup here. Get ready, the show starts as soon as we land."

Castor was giving her a hesitating look, the same measured glance Bakr used to provide whenever she said something he didn't agree with.

"It doesn't matter if I die here," Alissa said. "We get Bosser, you get him to Earth, and we pay what we owe to everyone who died for this."

"Marl never had your fatalism."

"Marl fought from the sidelines. You see enough horrors up close, and you get tired."

Alissa left the crowd and went back to her cabin to get ready. Her own room was massive, enough for a double bed, a separate desk and console, a couch and monitor. The *Whisperwind* had been a luxury liner, and there were pieces of it that still spoke to that purpose. Along one wall, carved into the side, was a set of names. Many had lines through the letters, angry slashes from a micro tool Alissa kept next to the bed. She picked it up now, flicked open the blade.

Three names left. Hers. Castor. Bakr. Alissa swiped at her comm, played Bakr's last words.

Alissa. I'm sorry.

Static engulfed the end of the message. She didn't know how her friend had died. Only heard that the frigate, the last warship the Red Voice had, was now a bunch of scattered wreckage floating around Neptune. Alissa hoped it had been quick, whatever his fate. It was the least he deserved.

Alissa took the micro-tool and ran the blade through Bakr's name, the silver line slicing through the thin letters.

His death would not be in vain.

6

FOR WANT OF A CANNON

Is it ready?"

Trina didn't bother looking at Mox, standing in the work room's doorway. The cannon would be ready when she was confident it wouldn't explode as soon as Mox spooled it up. The *Jumper* wasn't exactly a weapons factory, and the cannon was complicated.

"It doesn't work that way," Trina said, bent over the rear of the cannon where tubes fed pressurized gas into a chamber and a battery supercharged them, spitting the heated element out the front barrels. "If you want something available on request, you don't let someone blow it up."

"Accident," Mox grumbled.

"No, it wasn't," Trina said. The last piece that wasn't working was, predictably, the battery. She'd already scavenged some of the other weapons around the *Jumper* and laced them together to create a makeshift version, and it wasn't charging correctly. "You could have dodged the blast."

"Could have, maybe," Mox replied.

Trina sighed as the battery failed to display any signs of

life, again. Stood back from the bench, turned to Mox. The workroom was a cluttered mess, bits and pieces of chopped up machines littered the ground from the doorway to the workbench which took up the entire side wall. Mox hadn't moved from the entrance, a smart move seeing as navigating the pieces of shrapnel and strings of wire required concentration, and practice.

"I'm sorry," Trina said. "I shouldn't be complaining. Obviously, your life is worth more than the cannon."

Trina wanted to continue that sentence, wanted to say that it didn't mean the cannon was worth *nothing*. That all of this equipment was worth a bit of effort to care for, to maintain. To not destroy in a back and forth fight with crazy raiders.

"It is who you are," Mox replied. "It is necessary for someone to care."

"I just wish the rest of you would," Trina replied. "I'll have it ready by the time we land. Or you'll have to get a new battery on the station."

"How much?"

"I'm sure Davin will buy you one after those ice diamonds are sold," Trina said the words and found her eyes wandering to the box just inside the door. The crate looked like any other large container, more than a meter wide and half that tall. They'd put the diamonds in there in case Miner Prime wanted an inspection. They'd take one look in here, see a bunch of tools, and leave it alone.

Trina already had her shopping list for afterward. A litany of things the *Jumper* needed to keep flying well. The usual chargers, wiring, replacement solar panels, but Trina figured that if the *Jumper* was going to keep getting in scraps, they ought to have some stronger shields. Lasers with a better punch. If those diamonds sold for what Davin thought they would, the Wild Nines would get a great new freighter in the bargain.

"Trina," Mox said. "How did you get this way?"

She pushed up her greasy goggles. Looked at Mox, the exoskeleton lacing its way along his arms and legs.

"What way?" Trina said.

"I am half-machine, but don't love them the way you do," Mox said. Not technically a question, but Trina could follow the thread.

"You look at everything we've been through lately? All the randomness? Know what the common element is?"

Mox shook his head.

"People," Trina continued. "It's all crazy people doing crazy things, for coin or something else. Machines, they do what they're told. Every action has a purpose, at least to them."

"Free will frightens you?"

Trina had been on the *Jumper* for years with Mox and never had the man come at her with questions like this. Something was different. Trina sniffed the air, maybe the exoskeleton was misfiring. Sending the wrong electricity to Mox's brain, scrambling his signal. If Trina tried hard enough, she could smell the volts. At least, she thought so. Now, though, there was only the usual grease and metal, a hint of burning wire from the work she'd been doing on the cannon.

"When it's logical, no. When it's not, that's why I'm glad I've got you and the others around. Now, you want this cannon ready, you should leave me alone to fix it," Trina said.

"Of course," Mox replied, nodding, then moving away.

Trina watched the empty doorway for a moment. The other thing about machines is that they couldn't hide their secrets. Spend enough time with them, tear enough of them apart, and you could know every little thing about them. Trina would never know everything about Mox, how he worked, why he chose the life he lived, and why he thought that now, on their approach to Miner Prime, was the time to get to know her.

And Mox would never know the reason Trina kept her hands greasy, kept the engines primed, and the batteries charged. Because some stories were so common they were nothing to those not part of them, even if they meant everything to the ones personally affected. Because nobody wanted to hear about another ship malfunction, another asteroid collision, another child of the stars growing up alone. That wasn't going to happen here.

Trina turned back to the cannon, took another look at the battery. The problem was obvious. How she missed it, Trina didn't know. She'd switched the order, the battery needed to draw sufficient power first, then send it, but she hadn't set the amount. It took a second, and this time, when the cannon was primed, the battery hummed as its charge coursed through, readying the weapon.

When Mox needed to use it, his cannon would be ready.

7

THE ONES WE MISS

Thirty-seven messages since Erick had talked to them last. Every one of them following the same template. A hello from his daughter, then a cascade of greetings from her friends, husband, and children. No, his grandchildren. Couldn't forget that. From there, the messages went into the day to day. What the weather was like on the island, what the kids were learning at school, what was going to be on the menu for that night's dinner. It was a saga of the mundane.

Erick loved it.

He told the comm to dial the frequency. They had another hour before landing at Miner Prime, and with the docking, his life would get busy again. Transmission delay was only minutes between Earth and Mars, a time span even a small child could stand. From Erick's small cabin, he could tap into the *Jumper*'s main communications channel, the long-range one that Phyla wasn't using to talk to the station. If one of the others were on it, like Viola calling Ganymede, he'd hear them talking and have to wait till they were done. When his comm tapped in, though, all he heard was silence.

"Hello, Julia," Erick spoke into the comm. "This is your father, at long last, returning your sweet messages. We are approaching Miner Prime, back in communicative space. I will be available for the next hour or so to talk if you are able to reply. I know it has been a long time, and for that I am sorry. But I am listening now."

The message sent, crawling its way through space to his family down on that luscious blue dot. Erick replayed his own words, shaking his head as he did so. They sounded so cold, so perfunctory. A joke to his family, even among the Wild Nines, was how formal the doctor was. Perhaps a lifetime of requiring precision in delivering diagnoses had robbed him of the ability to tap into that deeper, emotional vein. Only in times like this, though, did the habit truly feel like a hindrance.

The comm's tiny screen flared to life ten minutes later, sitting on the cabin's counter. A deeply tanned woman appeared in front of a backdrop of palm trees, holding a giggling baby. Erick practically flew across the small space, limbering himself onto the bed to watch.

"Father! Just like you to time your call during a busy day for us! As you can see, your newest grandchild arrived a month ago and is already doing her best to make our lives miserable!"

Julia's wide smile, her blazing white teeth set against the deep brown of her tan, suggested the misery was closer to joy.

"Now, unlike with the others, I will not tell you her name," Julia continued. "Because I've run out of ways to convince you to come back here and visit, so I'm hoping this one will work. We have a bed all ready for you. The waters are warm, the waves are wonderful. And after all that time in that box of a space ship, surely you could use some sun."

The rest of the message ran away fast, with Julia claiming the new one was hungry, as were all the others. She would get back to Erick later, and she hoped he would reply with the time of his next visit. Maybe even consider a permanent stay.

A permanent stay. Erick looked at the little cabin, the bed barely long enough to hold him. Unlike most of the crew members, Erick actually produced printed photos of Julia and the grandchildren. They decorated most of the cabin's surfaces. Trina had made him, one year, a small projector that could spray the pictures on the ceiling, and almost every night, Erick fell asleep to the stop-and-go show of his family's lives.

"Fifteen minutes till we dock, people. Get your crap in order," Phyla's voice came over the intercom.

Erick turned back to the comm. The channel was still open, one last chance to reply to Julia.

"Withholding the name? That is a sore blow, Julia," Erick made sure the comm sent along his happy face to disarm the comment. "But an effective one. I'm thinking, like you, that perhaps it's time I made my way home, and stayed there."

Another message that conveyed the point if not the spirit. Erick cut the channel, slipped the comm back on his wrist. There would be plenty of time to apologize to Julia for his terrible messages later. In person.

8

A DIFFERENT KIND OF DATE

The tree was large enough to hide Merc as he pressed up against it, snowflakes blowing into his face with the chill wind. On his left and right, more forest until the wintry fog cut off further view. Not that *further* mattered. His target was close.

The rifle, a solid-black automatic designed to spray slugs at a high, if inaccurate, rate was light in his hands. Especially compared to the weight of the heavy snowsuit. It was speckled with brown and black, what Merc considered effective camouflage. But he'd been behind the tree for too long already. Long enough for the target to know where he was.

Merc twitched to the right, peeking around the edge and glimpsing nothing but frozen woods. Then he dove left, rolling across the hard ground towards another pair of thick trunks. Two loud cracks split the silent air and Merc felt the ground blow up as the bullets struck close. He kept rolling until Merc felt the slight shadow of the trees fall across his face. The shots had missed.

Standing up, Merc glanced at the holes in the ground

where the bullets hit behind him. The spray of the dirt indicated the shots had come from opposite the trees. Shoot and move. That was the rule. Meaning the target probably wasn't there anymore, but if Merc went quickly, maybe he could catch them in transition.

The stick-jockey wrapped around the side of the tree and held down the trigger in the general direction of the shots. Nothing but air as Merc ran to the next tree. His own fire might have caused the target to duck back, though, so still useful. Besides, he had plenty of ammo. The wind rose up in a howl, swirling snow until even the space a meter in front of him was more gray than anything else.

"Was this your idea?" Merc called out over the wind. "Cause this weather really doesn't make this any fun."

No reply. Taking it seriously, then. Merc reached to his tool belt with his left hand, grabbed a small sphere attached there and pulled hard. He flipped the grenade over his shoulder, through the gap in the trees. The storm still blowing hard, Merc took off to the left, running along the woods, turning in a slow ring. Seconds later, the grenade exploded, a crackling blast of noise and fire that penetrated the whiteout as an orange bloom on the edge of Merc's vision.

A snap, straight ahead. The crack of a rifle shot. Merc didn't hear the bullet whiz past. Possibly not even shooting in his direction. Merc dropped down to a crouch, walking fast and quiet, the rifle held in both hands. A big tree appeared out of the swirling snow, its sheer size acting as a break to the storm. Up in the branches, a dark shape spread out like a lump across a pair of thick limbs. Clever, taking the height advantage. Unless your target was right beneath you.

Merc aimed the rifle up, pulled the trigger, and sent a

long series of shots at the lump which shook with every hit. Merc waited for a cry, for the rifle to fall down, but nothing. Then he felt the pressure on the back of his head, the cold metal of a sidearm.

"Drop it and turn around," the woman's voice hard.

Merc did just that, letting the rifle fall onto the ground. Turned around to find the woman wearing barely more than underclothes. Merc could see her shivering in the cold, but the sidearm was steady, and her eyes didn't blink.

"Say it," the woman said.

"You win," Merc said, shaking his head.

"Damn right," the woman replied, stepping up and giving him a kiss.

The forest faded away to black as did the cold and the feel of the wind on his neck. Then white lines appeared in the dark space, opening to reveal the inside of the *Jumper*'s docking bay. The Viper was there in front of him, its polished metal back to form after the pock marks it'd endured in the fighting over Neptune. Merc's mind did the same mental flip-flops it always did after leaving the simulator, the total immersion coming back to actual reality. Even the gravity was different, lighter on the *Jumper* than on Earth proper.

"That's what, thirty to ten?" Opal said, climbing out of her pod.

"If you're only counting ground sims," Merc countered. "Let's get you in a ship and see what happens."

Opal laughed, shook her head. She never said yes to that, always played off flying as Merc's job. So they dueled in frozen tundras, space stations, the red sand of Mars. As a way to pass the time, it was pretty awesome.

"We're about to dock," Phyla's voice came over the intercom. "You two get yourselves ready if you want to come out."

"Hell yes," Merc said, following Opal out of the bay. A chance to be somewhere besides the *Jumper*? No way he was going to miss that.

9

LIVES TO LOSE

Miner Prime filled the cockpit view, replacing black space with its collection of grays, whites, and random colors for various hatches or corporate-branded sections. It was nice to stare at something other than infinity. To know that if the *Jumper* suffered some sort of terrible disaster, there could actually be a rescue rather than a bunch of wreckage only found by accident years later.

"Thanks for clearing the way," Davin said, sending the message to the line Bosser told them to use. "Was afraid I'd never get to land on this spinning piece of space crap ever again."

Davin paused. Bosser's last real communication, back by Neptune, had been a threat. In fact, most of the man's messages seemed to be threats, now that Davin thought about it. *Contact me as soon as you have arrived at the station, or unfortunate consequences may arise* - that was how the last one had ended. Like what, an assassination? Immediate destruction of the *Jumper* and its crew?

It wasn't worth taking the chance.

"We're here," Davin continued. "So if you have that mission in mind, feel free to let us know."

The transmission ended. Davin waited, Phyla guiding the *Jumper* in next to him. No reply.

"Is he standing us up after we flew all the way here?" Phyla said.

"Probably in the shower, but if he forgot about us, I'd be fine with it."

Ten minutes later and the *Jumper* locked its struts down onto the dark blue floor of the bay. The same color as a deep ocean, and also the hue of the company that owned this section of the station. Davin would pay them a fee to keep the *Jumper* here, one link in an endless chain of monetization. That'd been one thing about living in Vagrant's Hollow - if you didn't have any money, nobody bothered to advertise to you. Now that he had a ship, everyone thought he was a mark.

The *Jumper*'s ramp went down. Miner Prime's cold white light slipped into the freighter. Noises from the bay filtered in, echoing announcements requesting a cargo hauler somewhere else, the constant shunt of lifts sending people from here to there, and the low bubbles of conversations just out of earshot. None of those noises came from the person standing at the bottom of the ramp.

Her hair was spiked, pointing out in all directions as though each clump was a comet shooting out to a different section of space. Beneath that, she stood with her hands at her sides, watching Davin and the others without a hint of expectation. As though she was prepared to wait there all day, and the next, and it wouldn't bother her in the slightest. Sitting on her stance was the Miner Prime special forces uniform, a thick navy collection of pockets and loops on which to store or hang all the weapons and tools they would need. All of hers looked empty.

Davin walked down the ramp, mustering the casual confidence that came with knowing Opal was in her usual perch at the top of the ramp, sniper ready and aimed directly at the person's head. The woman had been waiting in the bay when the *Jumper* had come in, and there wasn't any reason to take chances.

"Bosser didn't want to come say hi? I'm offended," Davin said when he reached the bottom. None of the others walked down behind him. It was generally better *not* to get your entire crew caught in a trap. Especially when they could be manning turrets instead, ready to roast if anything went sideways.

"Davin Masters?" the woman said, voice hitting Davin's ears like a blunt hammer. There were missing threads in her words, the hints at other agendas, at curiosity, at past histories that informed present emotion. The imperfections that made human speech what it was.

"You're an android, aren't you?" Davin said.

"ThreeTwelve," the woman acknowledged. "And you are the captain of this ship?"

"Someone has to be," Davin said. Another android. Not long ago, on Europa, Bosser sent first one, then two more of the bots after Davin and his crew. Most androids these days, under various restrictions passed by Earth governments, were produced explicitly to do the things people should not, like enforce the rules. The cost of making them, though, put androids outside the scope of ordinary policing, so their ludicrously fast reaction times, perfect facial recognition, and all around deadliness turned androids into high-cost killing machines in the service of the Free Law's arbitrary justice system.

"Bosser would like to see you, and Phyla, in his apartment," Threetwelve said.

"Not even going to get us dinner first?" Davin replied.

This close to the android, Davin noticed ThreeTwelve didn't blink. Didn't try to breathe. The token disguises most androids adopted to find their targets weren't being used. ThreeTwelve looked more like a 3D picture frozen in time than a person. The question was . . . why?

"Your propensity for pointless jokes is noted," Three-Twelve said. "However, we have little time. Please, come now."

Pointless jokes? Who did this android think she was? Davin sighed, glanced at his comm. "Phyla, you hear that?"

"Already on my way out," Phyla replied through the comm. "Not like we have a choice, right?"

"Feel like that's our new reality," Davin said, looking back at the android. "Guessing you can't give me any hints about what he's going to say?"

"That things are worse than you would believe," Three-Twelve said, its voice continuing its eerie lack of inflection. "And that you will have the opportunity to save many lives."

"Many lives?" Davin said as Phyla jogged down the ramp. "Sure you don't mean 'earn lots of coin'?"

"The first often leads to the second," ThreeTwelve said.

"Except where we just came from," Phyla said. "Where it was precisely the opposite."

"Was it?" ThreeTwelve replied, pausing for a beat before turning and walking towards the lifts. Davin forced himself not to look at Phyla. Did Bosser know that they'd kept some of the ice diamonds? That they were planning to sell the blue gems on Miner Prime?

"Why would Bosser even care?" Phyla whispered. Davin considered the question as he walked after ThreeTwelve.

Bosser wasn't Eden, the company that'd lost their ship in the mission. Wasn't going to make a profit on the ice diamonds at all. Still, the idea that Bosser would know what was going on with his crew was annoying.

"Hey, android!" Davin said as ThreeTwelve tapped the call button for the lift. "What about my crew? They allowed to leave the ship, or will more of you shoot them if they try?"

ThreeTwelve half-turned, its left eye looking at Davin with an iridescent green glow.

"If their lives are yours to keep, leave them on the ship," The android said as the lift doors opened in front of it. "If their lives are their's to lose, let them go."

Androids, Davin decided as he stepped into the lift beside the bot, Phyla close behind, truly were the worst.

10

CHANGING TACTICS

They weren't going to make it to him. Alissa could see that from where she stood, with three other fighters on the lip of the lift on the security level. Too many cameras, too many guards. The wide section in front of her had no less than three fully suited peacekeepers. Their armor would block just about everything she shot. Minor Prime was on alert, and the Red Voice didn't have enough to punch through. It would be a pointless death. Her hands moved beneath her jacket, to the grips of her sidearms. So close.

"Alissa," Castor's voice came over the comm. "The placement is set and we're ready to go. But I have a question."

"Ask," Alissa replied.

"Jairo picked up another ship on the way in. A familiar one, the *Whiskey Jumper*," Castor said. "On that ship, last time I saw it, was the heiress to Galaxy Forge. We're confirming now, but she could get us to Earth."

A small chance was better than certain death. They had to try for it.

"If we see her, trigger the attack."

"And if she doesn't show?" Castor asked.

"Then we torch Miner Prime. One last cry for Mars," Alissa said. "I'll see you back at the ship."

Alissa turned and pressed a button on the left. The lift shut and rocketed them back down to the docking levels. She couldn't deny a burst of relief as those armored peacekeepers faded from view. She might not die today after all.

11

HIGH PRICE

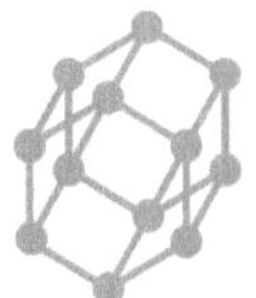

The rising stacks of houses built on other houses, junk piled on junk to create towers scaled by flimsy black-metal ladders, looked on the teeming avenues of lost souls that made their way through Vagrants Hollow. In the space above the streets, drones shot back and forth in reckless delivery runs, sending this or that vital good from one side of the level to another. Just from the lifts, Viola could see more types of people than she'd ever seen in her entire life on Ganymede.

In front of her, not a few meters away, a child argued with his mother, a woman who appeared to be almost half metal. All of her arms and legs had been replaced by mechanical alternatives, often not covered by cheap plaskin so that bits of wiring dangled through. The kid looked normal until the lift doors finished opening and dinged. When the boy's face turned to look, his entire left side was covered in a painted dark green faceplate, only the eye showing through as natural. Behind them, the shifting crowd revealed groups of Miner Prime police, traders moving carts of goods, and, at one point, a squad of people dressed entirely in what looked like woven human hair.

"This is where Davin grew up?" Viola asked.

"Yes," Mox answered from behind as they stepped out of the lift.

"Vagrants Hollow wasn't always quite so eclectic," Puk said, buzzing out of the way of a passing drone. "It's acquired a reputation as a place of anything, where, so long as you are not violent, nobody cares who you are."

"You really think we can sell the ice diamonds here?" Viola asked. Behind her, Mox held the crate packed with the gems. Viola had thought it would look absurd to walk around carrying a box that big, but a few seconds here put that concern to death. Not a soul had glanced at them for more than a moment. Even Mox's exoskeleton, the steel ridges bulging through the man's shirt, drew little interest.

"The traders that don't talk are here," Mox said. "Follow me."

"I believe what Mox means to say," Puk said, weaving along after the big man. "Is that Miner Prime intentionally regulates little of what happens in Vagrants Hollow, knowing that the attraction it provides to various types of people serves to boost the economy and status of the station as a whole."

"Got that," Viola said, her eyes flicking everywhere. There was so much to see. Opal and Merc were coming behind them, intentionally. The idea being Opal could spot a person following Mox and the diamonds without them realizing Opal was watching. The idea came from some military sting operation Opal had run years ago. Nobody harassed them, though, until Viola, Mox, and Puk stood outside of a large tent filled with the kinds of space ship parts that looked so old they belonged in museums, not on the market.

"Fourier," Mox said, nodding inside the tent. Viola followed the metal man inside, swallowing her own questions on how a shop this pathetic could afford what they were trying to sell.

And then the back of the shop, what looked like overlapping walls of cloth, parted to reveal a sallow flea of a man who wore a large mechanical backpack. As he walked towards Mox, the backpack seemed to unfold, a pair of clawed, cheap robotic arms swinging out from the top. The arms were paralleled by small vices on the bottom, looping around his waist.

"Mox!" the man squeaked. "I expected Davin! It is a rare treat that I meet the final product of Selene Stone."

Mox didn't bother speaking, just grunted an acknowledgment and looked for somewhere to set the crate down, finally brushing some of the rusted-over parts onto the ground. Fourier didn't protest, moving closer to the crate and continuing a stream of complimentary adjectives that were making Viola blush on Mox's behalf.

"Who's Selene Stone?" Viola whispered to Puk as Mox and Fourier fell into a discussion.

"I'm searching, but not getting anything," Puk replied. "I'm not able to connect to the network here. Fourier may be blocking access. I'll be right back."

The little bot buzzed out of the shop. Viola glanced down the street, back the way they came, and noticed Opal and Merc investigating a vendor's food offerings. Looked like sandwiches, steaming piles of bread, meat, and vegetables. All lab grown. The price to fly actual meat up to space was so ridiculous that most people with coin that wanted it just went to Earth. Viola's father, owner of one of the largest companies in the solar system, didn't even bother with it, claiming real meat was a vice and that he had plenty of those already.

A click from behind Viola signaled Mox opening the crate, and Fourier's accompanying intake of breath said that maybe Davin's estimates on the ice diamond's value weren't too off the mark.

"That's the only offer," Mox was saying as Viola moved closer.

"The only offer?" Fourier replied. "That's hardly any fun."

"Not here for fun."

Fourier looked at Mox like the man had just killed a child. The backpack, though, commenced with a mind of its own. The two metal arms lunged into the crate, grabbed a pair of the ice diamonds and placed them in the backpack's lower vices. Small lights lining the outside of the vices turned blue, then red, then green. Fourier's eyes tilted skyward, as though something was talking to him, and Viola noticed the man did have tiny attachments on his ears.

"An amazing mineral make-up," Fourier muttered, the looked at Mox and laughed. "I don't even care that I'm giving away my interest to you. Miner Prime's database doesn't have anything like this. You're saying these are the only ones that exist? Here?"

"More on Neptune," Mox said.

"But here, now, this is it?"

When Mox nodded that clinched it. Viola watched as Fourier agreed to the sale and created the pending transfer to the Wild Nine's general account. Mox frowned at his own comm after a minute.

"Seems like the network is down," Fourier said, looking

around Mox's arm. "The transaction will go through when it comes up."

"If it doesn't — "

"I know, you'll be back," Fourier said. "Now get out of here. Let me play with my new toys."

Viola walked out of the place slightly stunned. They no longer had the crate, or the ice diamonds, but if Mox had received Davin's asking price from Fourier, then Viola's share meant she wouldn't need her dad's help for a long time.

"Viola," Puk whirred as the bot came back down to meet them in the street. "I'm not getting reception anywhere. The links appear down."

"Down?" Mox said, glancing up. Viola followed the look. The previously crowded skies of Vagrant's Hollow were nearly empty, all the automated drones were gone. The only craft still moving were being actively piloted, small controlled cargo sleds. People on the streets had noticed too, were pointing up, voices getting more agitated. Viola saw more pick up their pace or duck between stacks, getting out of sight.

"Something strange is going on," Viola said. She looked back down the street, towards where Opal and Merc should have been, but couldn't see them behind the shifting crowds. Then something yanked her left arm, hard.

"Hey!" Viola said, drawing her arm back and turning. Someone was running away from her, into the crowd, a loose beige outfit. When she rubbed her forearm with her right hand, Viola felt skin.

"They took your comm!" Puk announced, then shot after the running thief. Viola took off after the bot, keeping the floating ball in view while dancing through the crowd.

Behind her, Viola could hear Mox doing the same, though the crowd seemed to be dodging him instead.

The street was an uneven mash of space station metal and years of grime. It felt like running on rough dirt where every one of Viola's footfalls seemed to land at a different angle. She bounced off one person, then a stack of food supplies, then nearly decapitated herself on a passing hover cart and dove beneath it. Scrambling up, Viola caught another look at the thief, glancing back at her.

The person's face was masked, a type that Viola had seen often enough on Ganymede. Black and menacing if unintentionally. The mask operated as a filter, removing toxins from the air and only letting in oxygen. Essential when doing construction projects in space, especially on dusty rock moons. But why wear one here, in a thoroughly filtered space station?

Puk bobbed above, and Viola shook her head at the bot when the crowd gave her a moment to look up. Puk might've been able to shoot the thief, but the bot could miss, and the thief wasn't exactly trying hard to get away. The thief kept looking back at Viola as though making sure she wasn't falling too far behind. And without her comm, Viola couldn't communicate with Puk, so the old-fashioned head shake was the only way.

Another minute of crowd-dodging dashes and Viola suddenly broke free of the people. They'd moved far enough away from the center of Vagrant's Hollow. Shops were scarce out here, more homes. The stacks still there, but less covered in random flare, some even with flowers blooming. Genetically modified to grow in Miner Prime's artificial sunlight, sure, but providing a gentler ambiance, nonetheless. Viola took it in as she chased the thief, now moving at a jog. Or, was.

Mox flew out from between some stacks to the right of the thief, exoskeleton boosting his speed. The thief didn't even have a chance to react before the metal man was holding the thief up by his neck. Viola caught up just as Mox was tearing Viola's comm from the thief's hand.

"Why?" Mox asked the thief. Viola had to agree. Comms were cheap, and the thief appeared to have one. The data on one could be valuable, she guessed, if the person was someone more important than Viola.

The thief turned his head to look at her, his eyes red from lack of sleep, wrinkled and speckled brown hair going gray despite the man's apparent youthful athleticism.

"Watch," the thief said, the respirator turning his words into more of a rasp. His eyes flickered up from Viola's, looked over her shoulder, back the way they'd come.

The rumble came first. Then the flash, reflecting off of Miner Prime's inner walls. Then the sound and, with it, the blast of heat. Viola turned to see a series of smoke clouds rising from the center of Vagrant's Hollow. Three, four, and now more were going off. Bombs scattered throughout the level. Above them, the ceiling seemed to tear, ripping a hole in the false sky as another bomb blew through Miner Prime's maintenance tunnels between the levels. Blocks of carbon fiber, bottoms glittering with projection lenses and tops holding mangled nests of wires, fell.

Miner Prime was being destroyed, with them on it.

12

STREET FIGHTING

Opal's dive under the store table came automatically with the first burst. When Mox had commed that the deal was done, Opal and Merc had gone back towards the lifts. They were almost there, the lifts in sight, when everything fell apart. From under the table, a sturdy re-purposed fighter wing on plastic sawhorses, Opal pulled a sidearm out and held it in both hands. The explosions continued, but not with any kind of cadence. Not from any particular direction. Random. Chaotic.

"We need to get to the *Jumper!*" Opal shouted into her comm, already targeted to Merc's frequency. She wasn't sure where the pilot had gone, but Opal couldn't make him out through the packed street. At least, not from under the table. Opal took a breath, rolled out, and joined the crowd streaming towards the lifts.

Only, the crowd was suddenly pushing back the opposite way. Opal batted away hands, stepped over falling people as the mass of panicked humanity changed directions. They were running back towards the explosions, which made no sense. Unless there was something worse ahead of her. Still no Merc, her comm was silent.

"Merc! Say something!" Opal tried again.

The lift plaza appeared as Opal squeezed her way under the swinging arms of a fleeing older man, apparently attempting to swim his way from what was going on ahead. And when Opal saw what that was, she understood. A large squad of Miner Prime police were getting annihilated, laser fire beaming in and out of them from seemingly all sides. Shooters hidden in the stacks sending lances of energy at the police who were trying to hide behind shields and, in some cases, the fallen bodies of their own allies. Opal slid to the side of the street, pressed herself up against a stack. Without help, the police weren't going to last long.

But these were the same troops that arrested Opal the last time she was here. That'd tried to take the *Jumper*, tried to kill Davin and Viola. Another explosion ripped through the ceiling above Vagrant's Hollow, exposing the dark caves between levels. The police wouldn't be blowing up their own space station. Or if they were, they wouldn't be dying down here where it was happening. Which meant they weren't the enemy, this time.

Opal curled left, into the store. Like most shops in Vagrant's Hollow, it opened in the back to one of the thin alleys that cut between the stacks. Opal brushed through the curtained rear, then paused and glanced in both directions. Nothing towards the lift plaza except a clear window to the continuing firefight. On the right, the alley kept going and then forked. Opal, keeping her sidearm raised and ready in front of her, followed the fork to the left. And coughed. Then coughed again. Something in the air was scratching her throat. Maybe dust, from the explosions.

The alley curled around a trapezoidal stack, the sharp

angle of a large piece of scrap jutting into the path. Most of the buildings here were recycled space ships. Freighters and fighters deemed too expensive to repair, anything valuable extracted, the junk parts taken here and re-purposed. Another bomb, farther away this time, roiled its echo through the streets, momentarily covering the fractured yells of the fighters. Opal pressed up to the corner, peeked around.

Down the alley, maybe ten meters, a pair of people were setting up a tripod. One of them, on his back, had the heavy cannon that belonged on the mount. If they set that up, the Miner Prime forces would go from losing to decimated in seconds. Both looked to be carrying smaller rifles too. Outnumbered and out-gunned. Hopefully surprise would be enough. Opal brought up the sidearm as they swung the cannon down, started fixing it to the tripod. Finger on the trigger.

Then the back door of the trapezoid swung open, blocking the alley entirely with its rusted bulk. Someone shouting on the other side. Couldn't make out the words. If the newcomer had seen her, seen Opal and was warning them, then the moment that door shut, she'd be lit up. Had to take surprise back.

Opal ran towards the door, sidearm pumping with her right hand. A meter away, Opal planted her left foot and kicked with her right, a hard snap, years of military drills tightening her quads at the perfect moment to hammer the door forward. The slab wasn't thick, but had enough weight when it swung in to smash the newcomer forward, into the side of the building. But the kick brought Opal's gun out of position, bought her enemies a half second to react.

They used it.

One of the fighters pivoted the cannon around on its

tripod as the other swung up his rifle. Opal pressed the trigger down on her sidearm, but the aim wasn't there. Things were moving too fast. The shot missed left, over the cannon man's shoulder. Her second one, over-correcting, hit the assault rifle rebel in the arm, but the man didn't drop his gun. Seemed to ignore the pain. For the first time, Opal saw their faces. Both of them, covered in respirators. The explosion in the ceiling, the seemingly random placement of the bombs. There was something there. Not that it mattered because Opal was about to die.

Cannon man pressed down on his weapon's trigger, just as his assault rifle partner clenched his muscles. Then something hit Opal in the face, hard. Knocked her down to the ground. Her nose ached. The door in front of her, open again. Only it wasn't really a door anymore. The cannon's laser fire chewed through the middle of it, super-heating and melting every part of the slab that it touched.

Move.

Opal rolled to her right, out from behind the door's cover, sidearm facing towards the rebels. Only to see them looking at a small circular device as it landed near their feet. When it went off a second later, sending bolts of electricity all over them, along with the cannon, Opal blinked. That was Merc's weapon, but where was he?

"Love, we gotta talk about our relationship," Merc said, getting up from the ground and standing over her. "What'd I do so bad you want to hit me with a door for?"

The pilot reached out his hand and Opal took it, standing up. The shouting still came from the lifts, screams pouring from behind them in the stacks, and the station's alarms going as a backdrop to all of it. Still, here in the alley, it felt quiet. Separated from the chaos. Opal could feel the dirt all over her back, not true soil but the dust of thousands grabbing onto her clothes for a ride. On Neptune, on Europa, the spaces were clean, the environments spotless. It'd been a while since she'd felt the grime of a fight.

"Sorry," Opal said. "I heard lots of yelling, didn't realize it was you. Figured I had to go for the surprise attack."

"Never knew you could smash a door down like that."

"Lots of things you don't know, love," Opal replied, then looked at the unconscious fighters. "Let's get moving. I don't want this space station blowing up while I'm on it."

13

WRECKERS

When the lift doors opened, a dozen guns were pointed at Phyla's face. In the front stood Bosser, a man Phyla recognized from the video feeds. He, like the others in the force, was wearing thick body armor, designed to suck and spread the heat of a laser until it was harmless.

"What—" Davin started.

"Bad timing, as always," Bosser said, starting towards the lift and waving the force forward. "Miner Prime is under attack from the inside."

Bosser set the lift to go to level two, the main shopping district for the station. Phyla tried to stay close to Davin as more and more of the armored guards pushed their way into the lift, which was large enough to hold forty to fifty people. On a station of thousands, that still often meant lift lines, sometimes long ones. It also meant you could transport a lot of firepower if you needed to.

The Miner Prime forces had a variety of weapons. Some sported standard-looking assault rifles, grenade complements, and shield sticks. The latter stuck out like poles from their backs; able to be planted on just about any surface, the shield sticks would fan out a two-meter wide and tall barrier of energy for a few minutes. Phyla hadn't seen them in action except in movies, or recordings of battles with the Red Voice. That Miner Prime would have this many available seemed … strange.

"When we hit the level, you two stay back," Bosser said. "You're not as well equipped."

"Didn't know there was going to be a party," Davin replied.

"This isn't a party. It's going to be a slaughter," Bosser said, not sounding at all excited. "They tried to go after the station's principle power generators. Underestimated our defenses. My defenses."

"So why are they on level two?" Phyla said. "That shouldn't be anywhere near the generators."

The lifts were large, with curling glass borders. Almost like an onion, with points at the top and bottom, the wide floor placed in the middle. The lifts tended to run down the center of the station, meaning you were treated to snapshot views of the levels as the lift zipped through. The richer levels were near the security center they'd just left, and Phyla watched as stacks of condos, offices, and neighborhoods shot by. The population density necessitated that houses, in the form of single-family dwellings, didn't exist here. More collections of buildings that spanned the floor-to-ceiling range of the levels, looking like monoliths.

"Looks like a diversionary effort," Bosser said, watching the lift's level readout change. "They're causing some damage, but it won't matter. Their core mission failed."

Some of these buildings, in what Phyla guessed was a desperate reach for creativity, were covered in murals. One that was close to the lift as it swept past its level, had the Sun around its first floor and had bands for each planet at intervals as it went up. Most buildings were bland metallic shades, split from each other by glistening clean walking paths. Trails that Phyla noted were devoid of people.

"How would you evacuate everyone, if they succeeded?" Phyla asked.

"The ones that could get to ships would run. For everyone else, there are escape shuttles on each of the levels," Bosser said. "Enough for everybody? No. But coming to space means taking risks. This is no different."

"Do they know that? The people, I mean?"

"Phyla," Bosser glanced at her. "That's your name, right? The co-pilot?"

Phyla nodded.

"You're acting like these people are my responsibility. They're not. The station is my sole concern," Bosser turned back to the lift doors. "That might sound terrible, but consider that by saving the station, I'll save most of their lives."

"You're a regular saint," Davin said.

Outside of their talking and the lift's continual clinking and clanking as it went through the station, the guards were quiet. Some shifted as they checked power levels on their weapons, or adjusted a strap or belt. For the most part, though, they looked solid, almost robotic. Phyla was tempted to wave her hand in front of the guard next to her, just to see if he'd react.

"They're getting a continuous feed of information," Bosser said. "Comes through the helmet's ear-piece. It's why they're not paying attention to us. Because their friends are dying."

"Dying?" Davin asked.

"We don't always walk around equipped like this," Bosser said. "You know that."

Phyla took another look. The guard next to her didn't seem quite as solid this time. Those eyes were squinted, the mouth set in a grimace. Hands were tight on the grip of his rifle. The ones without assault rifles, maybe a third, had thicker armor and batons. Wreckers. The word came from a dinner conversation with Opal, on one of the many nights on the *Jumper*. Opal hadn't seemed very fond of them, but Phyla couldn't remember why.

"Ready up," Bosser announced. The lift was almost there.

The lift shot down into the shopping district, a large level near the center of the station. Its proximity to the docking bays meant goods were sent here for sale, rather than up to the smaller, wealthier levels. Wide streets encouraged all sorts of stores and stands. Every time Phyla had been here, the volume and variety of things offered blew her mind. Except this time. Now, the shopping district was full of smoke, fires, and laser flashes. At a glance, Phyla picked out the scattered remnants of the unprepared Miner Prime security, huddling behind overturned benches, crouching behind corners. The attackers seemed to have concentrated in the center of the wide street, groups of them ranging up and down and picking off people.

The lift doors opened to show a group of fighters ready for them, facing the lift with a pair of tripod turrets. Before Phyla could even fall back, several of Bosser's guards pushed forward and planted the shield sticks at the entrance to the lift. The turrets started firing, their lasers shattering against the shield's energy. One of the guards grabbed Phyla and pulled her away from the doors. And then Phyla understood why Opal called them Wreckers, and why the sniper shuddered when she said the name.

Four of the bulked-up wreckers launched themselves through the energy walls formed by the shield sticks. Phyla noticed their feet glowed, propelled by some form of thrust. The wreckers went right into the stream of laser fire from the turrets, their armor quickly glowing orange, trying to disperse the heat. One of the four stumbled as fighters lit up their smaller weapons, the armor going from orange to white, then exploding. The other three crashed into the turrets, their batons swinging with abandon.

With every swing, the wrecker's armor seemed to cool, and the batons glowed a bright white. The first hit on the turret caused the weapon to shatter and melt at the same time, molten bits of metal flying back at the now-scrambling fighters. Another wrecker caught a pair with clipping blows, sending the two spinning to the ground, but also lighting them on fire. Within a few seconds, the stand was broken.

"Clear'em," Bosser said. "Faster we're done here, sooner we get to the next level."

The rest of the guards, Bosser among them, started streaming forward out of the lift. Phyla stayed back, watched as the Miner Prime avalanche swept over the enemies, crushing them in a hail of relentless laser fire. It wasn't a fight, it was revenge.

14

PATHS CHOSEN

"C ome with me."

That's what Viola heard the man in the mask say. She was looking back across Vagrant's Hollow, at the smoke and fire rising from the dilapidated stacks. Structural damage on a space station was always dangerous, but Miner Prime would have back-ups. Would have layers of redundancies to prevent a total collapse. But if this was happening on every level?

"You should be arrested," Mox said, and Viola turned. Mox had the masked man by the arm, a grip the man wasn't going to break. Wasn't even trying to.

"Very soon, you're going to realize the purifiers on this level are failing," the man said, voice still scrambled by the respirator. "You'll feel itching in your throat, then burning in your lungs. Your eyes will go dark within an hour. Come with me."

"The lifts are back that way," Viola said.

"Not there. Too crowded," the masked man replied. "Behind me, I can show you another route."

Mox pulled his left arm up, started speaking into his comm. Trying to warn Opal and Merc. Then he stopped.

"There's still no signal," Mox said.

"First thing that went," the man said. "Now, can we leave?"

Viola glanced at Mox, nodded. The masked man stepped away from Mox a second later, rubbing his arm. Then he held out Viola's comm, almost as if he'd forgotten he'd stolen it in the first place. Viola took it, snapped it back on her wrist. Like Mox's, it wasn't picking up a signal. Without a transponder, something to bounce the signal off of, to send and receive and target the message, the comms could only communicate directly. Meaning, Viola would have to know where to send the message, rather than broadcasting to a frequency. Doable in small spaces, not so much in a burning disaster area as large as a small town.

Then the masked man took off running again. Past a shuttered hardware store that Viola recognized from Davin's stories, the same one Lina used to run. Viola wanted to pause, to look around the place, but Puk prodded her forward.

"Exploring doesn't matter if it gets you killed," Puk whirred. "The man's right, by the way. I went up high, took a look at the main lifts. There's some kind of crazy firefight happening over there."

"Between who?" Viola said as they continued to run. Now they were on the outskirts of the level where homes bled into the solid walls. Cordoned off power stations, sanitation management, the nuts and bolts of Miner Prime kept as far away from the populace as possible. The masked man ignored all of them, kept heading to what looked like a plain section of the wall.

"Security and whoever planted those bombs, I think,"

Puk said. "Without a connection, I can't exactly get much more."

"Can you get a read on the air quality? Is he telling the truth?"

"I've got traces of harmful elements, but that's as likely to be from the bomb residue as any failure in the station's systems," Puk said, then hovered closer. "We're not hearing a full evacuation either. Means the station feels like there's not a risk to the whole structure."

"So their plan failed?" Not that it would have made much sense, blowing up Miner Prime with all of them on it.

"More like, not going as well as they hoped."

The masked man paused in front of a section of the wall, above which sat a yellow-bordered sign stating, in all capital font, OFFICIAL USE ONLY. Below the sign was a small keypad and badge reader, glowing red. The masked man walked up to the keypad, pressed a series of numbers, and the wall slid aside.

"Back-up lift. Used for maintenance," the masked man said, stepping inside.

"Wait," Viola said. "If we're going to follow you into that elevator, tell us who you are."

The man paused for a moment, then pulled off his respirator. Looked at Viola with a steady face, his brown hair popping out in different directions without the mask holding it together.

"Jairo," the man said. "And you are Viola, and you are Mox. Though I am unfamiliar with your bot."

"So—" Viola started.

"Please, in the lift. We can talk more there," Jairo said, cutting her off.

Unlike the main lifts, with their glass cages and their beauty, the lift they were in was utilitarian. No art on the walls, no glass, just straight gray metal and doors on either end. Each one had a keypad and, above, a black and red text readout telling what level they were on. The three of them, and Puk, barely fit in the lift.

"Answers," Mox said as the lift started to move.

"I can't tell you everything, not yet," Jairo said. "But I can say that this is all happening for a reason. We don't want to hurt you."

"Who's 'we'?" Viola asked.

Jairo struggled with the question. Viola could see his lips start to form different words before dropping away.

"It's better if she tells you," Jairo finally said. "I know you don't know who 'she' is yet, but I promise, you'll like her."

"Dodging," Mox said.

Then the lift dinged. They'd reached the target. Only three levels away. Viola read the readout - docking level one. The same level the *Jumper* was on though that didn't necessarily mean anything. Each docking level had capacity for a hundred ships, slotted into the circle as tightly as they could. The lift door opened into a white-washed hallway, not the main sponsor-filled paths Viola had taken the two times she'd come to Miner Prime.

"Follow me. A little longer, please," Jairo said, walking out of the lift. The man's hands dug into a pocket in his pants, came out with a small tool that, with the movement of a slider, shifted into a sidearm.

"Who're you planning to shoot?" Viola asked. "Anyone?"

"My job is to get you to the ship." Jairo led them out of the lift and down the hallway.

"What ship? Why?" Mox said.

Jairo turned back towards them, looking morose at the question. Like he'd been dreading answering it, but knew it had to come, eventually. The man took a breath, then looked at Mox.

"Our ship, the *Whisperwind*. Because we need your help to keep all the strings from falling into their grasp," Jairo said.

"That really only gives me more questions," Viola said.

"Then ask them later. We don't have time!" Jairo ran down the hallway.

It would have been easy not to follow, to turn back to the lift or wait for Miner Prime security to arrive. Mox, arms crossed and glowering at Jairo's back, probably wanted to do just that. Thing was, though, Viola was curious. What strings, and whose grasp?

"I'm going," Viola announced, then took off after Jairo. She heard Mox's feet pounding after her a second later.

15

LAST BREATH

A pair of fighters were taking potshots at the security forces through the top window, like a pair of chumps. The lower floor was empty, the doors not even locked. Rookie mistakes. Or maybe desperate ones. Merc left Opal covering the ground floor, a stately collection of trash that must have served as someone's home. Still might be if the fighters hadn't shot them too.

The stairs up to the second floor were made of loose metal plates, each one a different texture, a different former life. Merc took each one slowly. Lasers didn't make noise when they were fired, so Merc was relying on the incessant chatter coming over the fighter's comms. In the military, the idea had always been to speak your piece and keep the channel clear for critical communication. These guys, going by the constant position updates, call-outs for good shots or movement, were on an over-sharing spree. But then, most of the Red Voice with military experience had died in the war. He and Opal were up against the leftovers.

The top of the stairs broke into a wide space. The entire

second floor was one room. No walls, except the outside. Beds, a generous term for the greased-up mattresses, littered the floor. Over by the front windows, burnt-edged squares cut into the siding with a torch, the two fighters were laid out, staring through scopes on out-modded rifles at the security forces below.

Merc raised his sidearm, centered it on the fighter on the right, and pulled the trigger. The stunning bolt struck the fighter in the back, filtering its electric shocks throughout the body in an instant, locking muscles and overloading nerves to where the fighter's body would stop responding. Merc had been stunned before, mostly in training exercises, and it was one of the most annoying things he'd ever experienced. Being conscious, but unable to control anything except your own breathing? For hours? He'd almost trade that for a normal blast'n'burn, take the pain but keep the sensation. Almost.

The fighter on the left managed a half-roll before Merc stunned him. Two up, two down. Beyond their gritty clothes, these guys were both wearing respirators too. All the fighters were. Maybe they all suffered from asthma. Merc pulled his comm to his mouth before remembering the things weren't working. Amazing how inconvenient it was to lose those things. Grow so dependent on being able to throw your voice wherever you want that when it's gone, you barely remember how to talk normally.

Down the stairs, back to the front room of the house, and Opal was sitting on the ramshackle collection of cushions that seemed to be a couch. Next to her, standing, was one of the Miner Prime security members, his rifle pointed at her face. When Merc came in, the security officer swiveled his gun over to him, held it high. Merc raised his hands to match, still holding his sidearm.

"You her friend?" the officer said.

"Yeah, how about you point that elsewhere?" Merc replied. Opal coughed, hard.

"She says you're—" the officer broke off, coughing into his hand, rifle waving around. Merc took a breath, felt a scratching in his throat. An itch that quickly started to burn. The officer was bent over now, still hacking. Opal stood, her hand on her mouth, walked towards Merc.

"They have respirators up there?" Opal asked.

Merc nodded. Would have said something, but his whole mouth seemed to be burning up, his throat feeling like it had a hundred ants crawling on the inside of it, biting him everywhere. Then the officer, still coughing, fell to his knees and pulled the trigger on the rifle. Lasers shot out and scored the side of the house. Merc fell back, following Opal to the stairs, tried to go up them. He needed oxygen. Legs were burning. Got up one step.

Why was he on his hands and knees? Merc tried to focus, climb from one step to the next. Didn't feel like he could stand up. His eyes watered, tears running down his face. Opened his mouth to try to squeeze in a bit more air but damn was that a terrible idea. Nothing but more pain. Then Merc's face hit the stairs. Everything was on fire. Merc started to realize he might die like this. Not getting blown out of the sky, not getting old and passing off in his sleep. No, suffocating on crappy stairs in the middle of a space station.

And then he felt someone turning his head, felt something hard, cold, press to his face. Covered his nose, mouth and Merc felt the seal close to his skin.

"Breathe, love," Opal whispered, her voice coming out scratchy, deep.

Merc did. Overriding his panicked lungs, praying that he

wasn't about to fill them with another onslaught of pain, Merc inhaled. The air that came through the respirator wasn't fresh, wasn't *good*, but it didn't burn. Merc immediately exhaled, inhaled again. Then a third time. It was like finding an oasis in a desert, he just couldn't stop. As though the first breaths weren't real. That the air might suddenly vanish. After a minute sitting there, breathing, Merc sat up on the stairs, Opal a step above him.

Then Opal walked down past Merc, into the front room. Merc, leaning on the wall, followed to see Opal detaching the respirator from her face and slipping it over the guard, who was lying on the floor. Waving Merc over, they rolled the officer onto his back, pressed on his lungs, and Merc heard the man take a deep, coughing breath through the respirator. Then another. For the next few minutes, Merc and Opal passed their respirator back and forth while the unconscious guard continued to suck down air.

"How'd you make it up there?" Merc said when he felt like he could talk. "I couldn't even move."

He passed the respirator back to Opal, who took a gulp of air.

"The Red Voice did this on Mars. Intentionally sabotaged air filters. Leaked toxic atmosphere through," Opal said. "It was devastating, the first couple of times. Then we all learned how to hold our breath."

"Helluva way to learn a lesson," Merc replied when he had the respirator back. He stood, went to the front windows. Looked out. A new crew of Miner Prime security had arrived, looking far more dangerous. Where the first group had been decimated by crossing fire from fighter positions, this one returned any shot with withering counter-fire, while hulking guards ran into any building that showed resistance. In the center of the cluster, sporting respirators, were Davin and Phyla, looking, to Merc's eyes, a little sick.

"Hey," Merc said, looking back at Opal. "Looks like the captain finally came to save our asses."

Opal, without a respirator, could only nod.

DEFENSIVE MEASURES

One of the *Jumper*'s commandments, in vogue since before Davin ran the ship, stated that unless cargo or people were actively going in and out, that the ramp was to be shut. No matter where the ship was. No matter the inconvenience. One of those things that Erick never questioned, never argued with, because it had proved its worth before. That time, it'd been a pack of would-be thieves on the light side of Titan, the farthest moon humanity had stuck any sizable claws into. Now, Erick watched a group of four respirator-wearing meatbags probe the *Jumper*'s closed door like an animal would a fresh kill.

"How long before I can take action?" Erick commed to Trina, who was sitting in the cockpit. Erick himself was in the bottom turret, watching the would-be raiders slink around on console screens.

"I believe Miner Prime law states that as soon as someone is attempting to acquire your items, you are licensed to defend yourself," Trina replied.

"Still nothing from Davin? Anyone?"

"I'm getting errors sending the messages," Trina said.

And if she was getting errors, then something was very wrong. Erick had never seen a wizard like Trina, morphing impossible problems into textbook exercises, explaining the ways and means of extracting more energy, fixing this or that item to better than its as-new status, lost. If Erick was a physician of the body, then Trina was a surgeon of the mechanical soul.

"Then I suppose there is nothing left to do but act on our own instincts," Erick said. "And my instincts are telling me these gnats do not have our best interests in mind."

The *Jumper*'s lower turret retracted when landed, sliding up so that it wouldn't chance an ugly crash with the floor of any docking bay. To anyone not familiar with the ship's construction, the turret would just look like a rounded bump, potentially a sensor, extra cargo space, or any of a dozen things. If Erick felt like roasting the raiders, he could press the trigger on the stick in front of him and the turret would set down and start firing within a second. Of course, there was a chance it could dent the floor, but that seemed like a small problem next to the *Jumper* being hijacked.

The four of them were beneath the ramp now, looking up at it. One of them held a device, looked like a thin tube, and was pointing it at the ramp.

"You seeing that?" Erick asked.

"It's a buzzer. What they're doing is running signals, trying to find the one that'll talk to the *Jumper* like it's Davin coming back home," Trina said, as though she were describing the weather.

"I'm going to shoot them," Erick replied.

"Wait," Trina answered quickly, this time the inflection carrying a bit of excitement. "I want them to try. See if they can get in."

"You're using this as a test?"

"When will I get another chance?" Trina replied.

"I'm sure Davin would be happy to stand outside with a buzzer and try whenever you wanted," Erick said.

"Hello," said the *Jumper*'s computer, Fournine. "Hope you both know that people are trying to break in. Gonna snap through security pretty soon if someone doesn't roast'em. Erick, I'm noting you seem to be in prime position."

"Talk to the one who brought you back," Erick said. "She wants to run a test."

"Trina, I estimate that your measures will fail in the next two minutes," Fournine stated. "At that time, the ramp will lower. The intruders will gain entry. And you will both be slaughtered in horrible fashion. I won't even feel sad as I am a bot."

"Noted," Trina said. "The last line I've got in there, it's just for buzzers. Wait for it, Erick, and then you can fire."

The four had spread out along the sides of where the ramp would go down. Three, the ones not holding the buzzer, had pulled weapons out. Small autoguns, easy to hide under a person, yet with a larger battery than normal sidearms. Fournine was right. If they made it inside the ship, Trina and Erick would be roasted without much effort. Erick moved his fingers over the trigger, waited.

Then the buzzer exploded. Simply sparked for a moment and then shattered in a burst of fire, the person holding it yelling and gripping their hand. The other three looked at their comrade, stunned.

"You can fire," Trina said, her satisfaction carrying through the comm.

Now it was Erick that hesitated. If they couldn't get in, what was the harm in letting them live? At least, that was the idea until one of the others glanced towards the lift, aimed the autogun at the ramp's border, and pulled the trigger. The lasers scored the *Jumper*'s hull, leaving black marks but not doing the slightest real damage. They had to know that wouldn't work. No small arms had the punch to get through a real ship's hull.

"They're making my ship ugly," Trina said. "Can you shoot them now?"

"But they'll never get through," Erick replied. "Seems a poor reason to end a life. Fournine, can you put up the shields?"

"Sorry, chap," Fournine replied. "Can't be done in the station. Chance of the shields interacting with the station's atmosphere. Igniting it. Which sounds like fun."

"No, no. Let's not," Erick sighed. "How about I scare them away?"

Without waiting for a consent, Erick pressed down on the trigger and dropped the turret. It came so, so very close to hitting the docking bay floor, but dodged it by a hair. The four thieves turned at the noise, one already aiming an autogun, but the man paused when the turret's cannons popped out. Erick twitched the stick, bringing the turret to bear on the aggressive one.

"Last chance to leave, friends, or this will get messy," Erick announced, patching the words through the *Jumper*'s external comm.

The four of them threw up their hands and backed away from the *Jumper*. Apparently the ship wasn't worth their lives. As they left the shadow of the *Jumper*, the four broke into a run for the lift station.

"Erick, a few minutes ago you were begging me to shoot them. Now you let them walk?" Trina commed.

"A few minutes ago they were threatening to break in. Now, they're just running away," Erick said. "I would prefer to be able to look my grandchildren in their sweet faces without knowing I killed those who didn't deserve it."

Erick flipped the turret's feed to the *Jumper*'s front cameras, which showed the four thieves making a break down the hallway. Showed the lift arriving as they passed it, showed a slew of Miner Prime security, along with Davin, Opal, Merc and Phyla coming out. Showed their weapons being aimed, the four thieves throwing their arms to the ground.

"And Justice is served," Fournine announced. Erick couldn't help but agree. Only, where were Mox and Viola?

17

YOUR SHIP, MY SHIP

When the security officer handed Davin and Phyla respirators a minute after they exited into Vagrant's Hollow, into the strewn collection of bodies under fire from fighters spread across surrounding buildings, when Davin understood that the home he'd grown up in had been burnt, wrecked, murdered, the captain was lost. Not that he had many friends, any friends left here. Not that there was anything tying him to the place except memories. But it still felt personal, wrong. Phyla held his hand as they watched the armed and armored security force sweep up the fighters in brutal fashion, the smoky haze of dust and broken lights shading a mustard glow over the level.

"Their operation is larger than we thought," Bosser said, walking back up to them, still standing in front of the lifts. "We're getting reports of teams running through the docking bays, sabotaging ships. Potentially stealing others."

Davin looked at the man. Bosser, outfitted in thick body armor, comm linked to a mic attached to his ear, black respirator sucking on his face. A rifle, a big two-handed one whose nozzle still glowed a slight orange from a recent firing, held in his hands. The sort of branded violence Davin hadn't ever wanted to be a part of. Only here, it seemed like they were on the same side.

"Any sign of my crew?" Davin hadn't forgotten them. Had asked Bosser and his group to look when they hit this level.

"We have two of them," Bosser said, then turned and pointed. Out of a taller house, being helped along by a security force member, were Merc and Opal. The fighter pilot noticed Davin and stuck up a hand.

"No others?"

"Not yet," Bosser shook his head, a sharp gesture, like the man didn't want to take the time to twist his neck. "I'm going to take a small group down to the docking bays. Would you like to come with? We can start at your ship."

"I'm still missing two people," Davin replied.

"They might already be down there, waiting," Bosser said. "I'm not forcing you. But we are leaving now that this threat is contained."

Contained. Right. Davin could hear the crackles and bangs as buildings succumbed to damaged parts further back in Vagrant's Hollow. There should have been cries, screams from people caught in the blasts, but the respirator attached to Davin's face provided the clue as to why those were missing. Hard to cry out if you couldn't breathe. If Viola and Mox weren't here already, they were probably dead.

"You're giving up on them, aren't you?" Phyla said as Davin turned towards the lifts.

"They would've been here," Davin replied. "Would've been with Opal and Merc."

"Maybe they know something," Phyla said as the sniper and the pilot headed their way.

"If Mox, or Viola, needed rescuing, they'd be more frantic," Davin said. "Let's get down to the *Jumper*. Like Bosser said, they might be there already."

And if not, they could always come back here and dig through the bodies to find them. Davin left that part unsaid, but he could tell Phyla was thinking the same thing. This had been her home too. He didn't know if she still had family here. Had those she loved back in that mess. That Davin didn't know bothered him on a deeper level, a missing piece of their relationship that he'd never noticed before but that was obvious now. Next time they were alone, Davin would try to rectify that.

On the lift ride down to the docking level, Opal leaned on Merc, who leaned against the wall. Ten officers and Bosser crammed towards the front of the lift, ready to burst out of the doors, a pair of wreckers in front, just as they had on the other levels. Only going down three levels meant a short trip, and thirty seconds after the lift started moving, it shuddered to a stop in front of a wide hallway linking docking bays together.

A group of four fighters, looking spooked, were running in front of the lift as the doors opened. They turned, almost as one, to see the security force emptying out and panicked, dropping their weapons and themselves to the ground. It was nice not having to watch them burn to a crisp, like the fighters on the other levels.

"Have to love an unconditional surrender," Bosser said, watching the security forces disarm the fighters and slip them into restraints. "More satisfying than a gunfight, because it shows you outsmarted them so completely that they don't even want to try."

"They're not fighters," Davin said, looking past the guns being gathered up. "Look at their belts. Those are tools for breaking encryption. And locks of a more physical kind."

Lina used to have all of that stuff, and Davin had borrowed them from her stash here and there. A mix of signal spoofers, micro-tools for taking apart panels and locks, pouches of circuit changers that would route a hard-line to a terminal you controlled. All the things you wouldn't care about if you were just trying to blow something up.

Bosser studied the fighters for a minute, then walked over to the closest one and picked him up. The fighter's were wide, mouth open, but it looked like the man's backbone stiffened right there. Forged by the fire of the experience. The fighter tightened his lips and glared. Bosser matched the stare.

"What were you doing?" Bosser asked, voice an even keel.

"Whaddya think we were doing?" The fighter replied. "Ruining your ships."

"What ships?"

"All of them," the fighter said. "You'll never get off this station."

Bosser glanced at one of the security members.

"Check it," Bosser said, then turned back to the fighter. "What's the point? We'll fix them, just like the damage you did to the other levels. A month from now, nobody will care what you did."

"Nah, but they'll care about what it allowed," the fighter replied.

"Which is?"

The fighter smiled, said nothing. Davin could see Bosser's free hand itching to pull a trigger, to punch the fighter in the throat, but Bosser set the fighter down.

"I'm getting reports of other teams like this one, sir," the security guard said. "Groups sabotaging ships. They've apparently taken out most of ours."

"Guess you're going to be stuck here for a while," Davin interjected, but Bosser ignored him and kept talking with the guard.

A loud hiss came from the *Jumper*, and Davin looked to see the ramp coming down. With it, Erick. Merc and Opal walked over that way, Phyla following. Davin took a step that way too. Technically, they were working for Bosser. But if the ice diamond sale came through, they wouldn't need Bosser's money. At least, not for a while. They could fly somewhere else, take up a more passive industry like cargo hauling. Something a little less deadly.

"Davin," Bosser said from behind him. "Your ship, it can still fly?"

"The *Jumper*'s fine," Davin said, hoping that was accurate. Erick looked calm coming down that ramp, and Trina wasn't panicking, so the odds seemed good.

"Then I'm taking it," Bosser said.

That had Davin turning all the way around, looking at the armed and armored boss of Miner Prime and taking a breath. Would have been nice if Mox were here. A bit of muscle behind Davin's back.

"Never," Davin replied. "I say the word, they'll blast the ship out of here so fast all you'll have is my laughing ass to show for it."

"Davin Masters," Bosser put himself centimeters away, the man's hot breath still smelling of coffee and sweat. "My man there tells me almost every other ship on this station can't fly. Only, one just lifted off. Without clearance. I know where they're going, and how to stop them."

"Let me guess, it involves blasting them to space dust," Davin said.

"ThreeTwelve," Bosser said, and the android appeared at his side instantly. Where the bot had been a moment before, Davin wasn't sure, but the way they could move with that precision was scary. Unnatural. "If you won't let me commandeer your ship, then allow the android and I to go with you."

"Go with us where? After the other ship?" Davin laughed. "Why would we do that?"

"Because two of your crew are on it."

18

A RELUCTANT PILOT

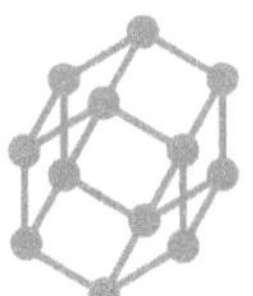

The *Whisperwind* looked like a needle, a spherical bulge at the aft end for the electrical engine and a thin point that extended forward. Even though the ship wasn't very wide, Miner Prime had docked it in a bay meant for larger vessels simply because the craft was so *long*. Viola, who'd seen all manner of builds fly in and out of the Galaxy Forge factories on Ganymede, hadn't seen one like this. A series of struts supported the ship, popping out like insect legs at various joints and intervals. The struts were gray, unpainted, which contrasted with everything else.

"It's so black," Viola said as Jairo led them towards it.

"Technically, the hull is darker than space," Jairo said. "Not, obviously, the absence of light, but because most space has star light making it brighter than black, so you see that—"

"I get it," Viola said, her eyes still tracking the ship. It looked like there was a tear in her vision, a hole right where the ship's outline was.

Viola watched the ship's ramp fold down. Not extend like the *Jumper*'s flat arm, but literally unfold one section at a time. Plates sliding off the bottom of a stack and locking in with the next one in the line. The amount of extra parts necessary to keep that from breaking would be tough to rationalize on a space ship, but it *was* cool to watch. In a few seconds, faster than the *Jumper*'s ramp, the *Whisperwind* was open for boarding.

"Who made this?" Viola asked. "I haven't seen the design before."

"You'll have to ask her owner," Jairo replied. "She's right up the ramp."

"And then you'll tell us what's actually going on?"

"All of it, I promise," Jairo said.

The man jogged across the rest of the bay to the ramp, Viola and Mox keeping pace. Puk zipped ahead of them, peeked up the ramp after Jairo. Then whirred back right in front of Viola, causing her to stop.

"There's a lot of people in that ship," Puk said. "They're packing, too. I'd, uh, recommend going somewhere else."

"Jairo?" Viola called to the man, already partway up the ramp. "What's waiting in there?"

"Nothing and nobody that's going to hurt you," Jairo called back.

An ear-splitting screech suddenly sounded through the bay as half the lights went red. Miner Prime's alarm system. Guards would be following the noise.

"You come on this ship, we live. You stay, we all die!" Jairo yelled over the alarm.

The man on the *Karat*, the guard Viola shot, who was about to murder Davin. He'd died because Viola made a choice. The raiders on the frigate, the one she'd rammed with the *Karat* in Neptune's orbit, they'd died too. Another choice, only this time, she could choose to save some.

"You don't know what's going to happen," Mox said, behind her.

"What do you think?" Viola said, the incessant blaring of the alarm continuing. "You think Bosser, this station, will let them live?"

"Do they deserve to?" Mox countered.

"Viola!" Jairo called again, his voice twinging higher with desperation. "Now!"

"I can't make that call," Viola said, then ran for the boarding ramp. She heard Mox start after her, saw Puk whirling alongside. At least she wasn't going to go alone.

Jairo waved her onto the ramp, staying ahead of her as Viola went up and into the *Whisperwind*'s entrance. The space inside was clearly not designed for cargo - it was lined with couches, tables, and gadgets Viola recognized from her father's luxury line. Not the sort of ship meant for military subterfuge. At least the noise of the alarm was blunted in here. Hanging on the walls were a series of interactive pictures, displaying moving scenes from Mars. Images of the blowing sands and giant mountains. Between them, in stark contrast to everything else, were men and women in the same gear as Jairo, only more heavily armed.

Viola realized all of them were looking at her, and some had their fingers near triggers. Stared at her with hard, red-rimmed eyes.

"Told you, bad idea," Puk buzzed as it floated into the ship.

Viola didn't have anything witty to say. She'd either be shot dead in a second, though how that meshed with Jairo's words she didn't know, or something else was going to happen. Mox's feet pounded on the boarding ramp. Jairo stared further into the ship, waving someone forward. After another awkward second, someone was pushing his way past Jairo, whispering words that sent Jairo running deeper into the ship. The man turned to Viola, reached out a hand. Even from that simple gesture, Viola could tell this guy, with his straight-up stance and firm handshake, could snap her in half a dozen different ways.

"Glad to meet you, Viola," the man said. "I'm — "

"Castor," Mox finished, grabbing the man's hand and tearing it free of Viola's. The sound of a bunch of rifles rising up, taking aim, clicked through the ship. Viola, with Castor in front of her and Mox to her right, stayed real still. She didn't scream, or flinch. Or do any of the panicked things a sane person would do in that situation. Her sheer lack of fear scared her.

"Mox," Castor said, his hand still in the metal man's grasp. "I didn't realize you were joining us."

"Didn't want to."

"Then feel free to head right back down that ramp," Castor said.

Mox shook his head, eyes never leaving Castor's face.

"Or stay," Castor said. "Either way, I'd rather not spoil the lovely ship by getting blood all over the floor."

"Your word?" Mox said.

"Don't think Viola would trust us if we shot her friend, would she?" Castor replied.

Viola caught Mox's eyes for a second and nodded. There was background there to dig through later when there weren't a dozen weapons pointed at them. Mox let go, stood back. Castor waited for a second, looking like he expected Mox to jump on him. Then he snapped his head to look at Viola.

"We need you in the cockpit," Castor said. "There's no time left to explain."

The cockpit? Viola didn't have a chance to ask any questions before Castor grabbed her hand and pulled her out of the room, soldiers moving aside, keeping their weapons trained on Mox. Puk floated along after her. The central corridor running up the *Whisperwind* was illuminated in a soft red, the floor covered with spongey plastic with a weaving, random pattern outline drawn into it. As they padded along, they passed offshoots, rooms or halls Viola didn't know. Most were closed off, sealed with black-metal doors that bore bio-scanners in the center. Older security, the bio-scanners. Easy to open, provided you had a hand from one of the crew, with or without the arm.

Finally they stopped, outside of a circular door that covered the entire width of the hallway. Castor pressed his hand to the rectangular, glowing block in the center. It flashed a seaside blue before adjusting to an emerald green and opening. Beyond was a triple-pilot cockpit, three chairs arranged in a semi-circle. One, on the right, was occupied by Jairo. The middle and the left were empty. Jairo, seeing Viola standing there, gave her a quick smile before turning back to his consoles.

"Viola, we need you to fly us out of here," Castor said, pointing at the center chair.

"Me?"

"Don't see any other Violas around here," Castor said. "Our previous pilot made a mistake, got aggressive. He didn't come back from one of the other bays. So now it's you."

Talk about expectations. Out through the cockpit window, Viola saw people starting to move into the bay, cautiously. Miner Prime security. They were running out of time. Viola pulled herself into the center seat, the one with the primary flight stick. The seat itself felt soft, almost as though Viola was sitting on air. The console in front of her was familiar, in line with what Viola used on the *Karat*, or slightly older. Jairo's preflight checks were coming up greens on the three-dimensional schematic on the console screen. A quick count showed the *Whisperwind* had a line of maneuvering jets all along its central corridor, then more spaced out on the expansion towards the back. No wings meant the ship wasn't really meant for heavy atmosphere, or at least wouldn't be able to handle any strong maneuvers.

"Puk?" Viola said. "Go back, keep an eye on Mox. Tell me if anything happens to him."

They might need her up here, but she wasn't going to abandon Mox. Puk didn't argue, spiriting itself back down the corridor. The bot wouldn't be able to do much if they decided to shoot Mox, if they already had, but at least Viola would have some warning. Castor watched the bot zip away, then sat in the third chair, his console showing weapons, defenses, and the option to take flight control if the main pilot was down.

"Ready?" Castor asked, apparently taking stock of his priorities and deciding Puk wasn't one of them.

"Ready," Viola replied, starting the jets. After a second, Viola felt a bump as the *Whisperwind* lifted off the docking bay floor. Using the flight stick and leaving the primary engines off, Viola triggered a burst from the forward facing jets at the rear of the ship. Normally, she would have rotated the spaceship and flown out face-first, but there wasn't room for the *Whisperwind*'s long stick to make that kind of turn.

"They're shutting the bay door," Jairo said.

The giant metal doors were designed to seal oxygen and atmosphere in if there was a leak or malfunction in the magnetic energy fields that kept the heavier molecules from dashing into the vacuum of space. They were also effective at keeping ships trapped. Attempting to ram the *Whisper-*

wind through the door would only result in the spaceship crumpling like a can.

"Unfortunately, it seems to have stuck on them," Jairo said. Viola could hear the smug in his voice. Through the cameras on the rear of the ship, Viola could see that Jairo was right: the door had come down a meter, but stopped there.

"You?" Viola asked as she continued to goose the ship backward. Castor used the intercom system to order everyone to take their seats.

"The Red Voice brought me in to hack military targets. Doing a localized break of a corporate station is cake," Jairo said. "I had control of that gate less than an hour after we landed."

"Don't brag," Castor said. "It's unbecoming."

"That's all the thanks you'll ever get out of this guy. Captain Stoneface, that's what we call him," Jairo said to Viola. She didn't catch Castor's reaction, because the *Whisperwind* was out of the bay and Viola had to focus on starting up the engines. The console led her through the standard procedure, easy enough so long as nothing went horribly wrong. Outside the windshield the docking bay receded, spun away as the bulk of Miner Prime slid into the picture.

The unobstructed view of the mottled station was . . . empty. Miner Prime should have been an epicenter of activity, ships zipping in and out in a tightly controlled dance of economic progress. Only, there were none. A glance at the sensors showed plenty of traffic, but it was all outside Miner Prime's immediate area. Ships holding orbits, following the station in its long path around the Sun. No security defense fighters either.

"They've been taken care of," Castor said, noticing

Viola's furrowed brow. "For a short while, we'll have space to ourselves."

Viola didn't want to ask how. She'd seen the bombs in Vagrant's Hollow. She'd seen Jairo's hack. She knew which one of those Viola would prefer.

"Where are we going?" Viola said, throat feeling dry. "The engines are coming on-line."

"You'll like this one," Jairo quipped. "We're heading home, Viola. I mean, our species' home. Good ol' Earth, herself."

19

HOLDING FIRE

Davin hadn't ever seen the space around Miner Prime so quiet. Usually blasting off from the station required a series of back-and-forths with station coordinators, other pilots, and then a good degree of luck to get out efficiently. This time, Phyla had them cruising out of the bay in less than five minutes.

"Check the scanners. You'll find it," Bosser said, standing there in the cockpit behind the two of them. The space had two chairs, pilot and co-pilot, with a third that could fold down as needed. Bosser did not feel it was, as he was leaning over their shoulders, staring at the console.

"Funny thing about flying is that I've done it before," Phyla said. "Tracking ships too."

"What's she's too polite to say," Davin interjectedn "is back off."

Bosser moved his hands away from the chairs, but didn't actually backpedal at all. The man was still in his Miner Prime security armor, standing there as though raiders were going to board any minute. Then again, if what he was saying about Viola was accurate, they might have a close-quarters fray on their hands soon. The *Jumper*'s engines came on and shot the ship away from the station, propelling it into the darkness that was space in the asteroid belt. Other ships were out there, but the endless distance of space meant you had plenty of room to roam. Davin didn't often see other ships unless he was planning to dock with them, or they were trying to shoot him.

"You didn't know how bad it was going to be," Davin said, staring at the empty scanners.

"The first protocol of an unknown attack against the station is to remove collateral damage," Bosser replied.

"There's nobody in close range," Phyla said, then expanded the view on the console. "The closest ships are an hour out. They would've had to turn around as soon as the bombs went off. Nobody evacuated the station."

"The comms were hacked, shut down," Bosser said. "I don't know what you want me to say."

"Nothing," Davin replied. If the Red Voice had tried a serious attack, had succeeded in throwing the station into disarray, nobody would have known. Not one ship would have tried to leave the station. At least, not until it was too late.

"If you're trying to argue that something so valuable as this station and the lives on it should be better protected, should have better plans to activate in the face of disaster, then you and I are on the same side," Bosser said. "My funding comes from the charity of companies. They prefer to pay me to squash imminent threats, not over-prepare for emergencies. It's not my choice. Miner Prime is not a democracy."

"The people must love you," Phyla said.

The console beeped as they moved out of Miner Prime's proximity. Now out of danger of hitting the station, the

Jumper could pick a path and go. Only Davin wasn't sure where Bosser wanted to point them.

"Find the *Whisperwind*," Bosser said. "It shouldn't be too far away."

To keep track of each other, ships responded to the pings of other ships with names and identification, like owner and registration. Didn't mean a registered ship wasn't going to shoot you to pieces, but at least you'd know who was doing it to you. Davin scrolled through the ships in range, winding through an alphabet of ship names like *Queen Anne*, *Starlight*, and *Johnny's Ride* before, near the bottom, finding *Whisperwind*.

"An old-model luxury liner?" Davin asked.

"Correct," Bosser said. "Run it down."

Davin highlighted the ship on the console with a tap and, on the windshield, a yellow line appeared with the trajectory for an intercept course. Phyla commed a heads-up to Trina, standing by the engines, and gunned the *Jumper*. Davin's freighter was larger, faster, and looked better armed. It wasn't even going to be a contest.

"Do you know who they're with?" Davin said. "Who's freighter that is?"

"Alissa Reinhert, a dead woman," Bosser said.

"Like Lina."

"I didn't kill this one," Bosser replied.

On Davin's waist, strapped against his thigh, was his sidearm. It was set to low power, a stunning shot. Better if the thing accidentally discharged. It would take one second to stand up from the seat, another to turn, draw the weapon, and fire. There was a chance Bosser had his own weapon, could draw faster, but he wouldn't be expecting Davin's attack. Or would he? Did it matter?

"Don't let him, Davin," Phyla said. "Not here."

Davin felt her hand on his shoulder. Felt it grip into his nerves. Lina and Phyla, always trying to keep him from doing something stupid.

"Bosser. If you're going to be here, don't say her name. Ever," Davin said, not looking back at the man. Bosser didn't reply. In the silence, they watched as the *Jumper* closed on the freighter. It was pointing away from the station, angling towards the Sun.

Davin flipped the console to an active map of the solar system, showing the *Jumper*'s projected path if it stayed on its current course. Useless, because they weren't plotting a long-range journey. But if they were, what would be the most likely target? Mercury, Venus, Luna, they were all options. Only one fit the *Whisperwind*'s line perfectly, though.

"They're setting up to go to Earth," Davin said.

"You have to destroy it," Bosser replied.

"Destroy what?" Phyla asked.

"Their ship. It can't be allowed to reach Earth," Bosser's voice had a different edge to it now, less in control. Like an opponent made an unexpected move in a game where Bosser knew all the rules.

"Why? What's on it?" Phyla replied.

"The ones who tried to blow up Miner Prime, they're on that ship," Bosser said. "They get to Earth, they'll try to do the same thing."

"Blow it up?" Davin said, incredulous.

"More or less."

The *Jumper* was close enough now for Erick and Merc, sitting in the twin turrets on the top and bottom of the freighter, to draw a bead on the *Whisperwind*. Davin could give the order and they'd vaporize the craft. Instead, Davin dialed the *Jumper*'s comm to send a direct transmission straight ahead to the luxury liner.

"Hey, *Whisperwind*, we've got a guy here that's saying you're going to kill a lot of people if we don't kill you first. What say you?" Davin spoke into the comm.

Silence followed. Davin took a glance back at Bosser, who was looking at the cockpit's comm, a small console wired into the *Jumper*'s larger transponder that sat on the outside of the ship, like it was about to jump at him. For a guy that liked manipulation so much, not knowing who was on the other end of the transmission was probably messing with him. Which felt pretty good.

"Davin? This is Viola. Please don't shoot us," Viola's voice came through clear. There was minimal interference when the ships were this close to one another. "I don't know anything about killing a lot of people."

"Hey! There she is," Davin replied into the comm. "You flying that ship, Vi?"

"I am. They lost their pilot. There's a group of twenty or so on here. One says he knows you. Castor?"

Davin stiffened. He remembered Castor all right. Remembered how the man had nearly broken Davin into pieces on Europa, remembered how they'd managed to stun their way past him to Marl, the woman who'd started all this. Castor had been her bodyguard though it was possible he'd been more than that. Quiet, confident, never seen out and about without Marl. Davin figured he'd been sent far away after that disaster.

"See?" Bosser said behind Davin. "She is being controlled. Forced to fly the ship."

"Vi, is Castor making you do anything?"

"He's asking me. Says they would all die if I didn't help them. Mox is here too, Davin. Please don't shoot us."

"Don't listen to her," Bosser hissed. "Even if they're both on board, Castor will kill them once they've reached Earth. There's no rescue here."

"Can you shut him up?" Davin said to Phyla.

"Come to Earth with us," Viola said over the comm. "Castor says you'll understand when we get there."

Davin heard the click behind him, the *snap* as a weapon left its holster. When Davin looked back, he saw Bosser's sidearm out and aimed at his face. Bosser's hand held the sidearm steady, the weapon's barrel thick and wide, meant more for close-range intensity than the usual longer, thinner sidearms. The small switch on the back, above the grip, glowed orange. Bosser had it set to kill.

"One of the things you don't do on my ship is point a gun at my face," Davin said, looking right at Bosser's eyes.

"Destroy the ship, captain," Bosser replied. "I won't ask again."

Phyla pulled out her own sidearm, holding it to Bosser's head.

"See," Davin said. "There's no way you win here. You shoot, maybe you kill me, but maybe that wide-angle shot of yours smokes the console, blows a hole in the windshield. Or maybe Phyla just takes your head off right after. Either way, the *Whisperwind* stays fine. You ready to die for nothing, Bosser?"

They stayed that way for a second. Time for Bosser to plot his way through to his next gambit. Then the man pulled his weapon down and stuck it back into its holster.

"I never thought you were a man who could be intimidated," Bosser said. "I'm disappointed to see I was right."

"Forgive me if I don't give a shit about what you think," Davin said, turning back to the comm. "Vi, set your course for Earth. We'll match it, follow you there."

Vi clicked back on the transmission, and a moment later the *Whisperwind* adjusted their heading. Phyla matched the route, the yellow line streaking away towards the bright orange glow of the Sun. At the end of that line was a planet Davin hadn't seen in a long time. It'd be good to see some green, some blue sky. Something beyond the stale metal hallways and recycled air of space.

"When everything falls apart," Bosser said, "I hope you'll remember it was your choices that caused it."

"Can you write that down? Better yet, sew it on a shirt for me, cause I try to forget everything you say," Davin replied. "Now, please get out of my cockpit."

This time, Bosser left.

THE TOUR

The cabin was smaller than the one Viola had on the *Jumper*. The cot folded up against the wall to give some space. No cabinet, just an older trunk that sat on the floor, covered by the cot when it was down. A pair of pod flung white light down from the ceiling. The spare gray walls had scratches calling to pictures past. On the inside of the door sat the intercom and keypad, neon-green quick buttons to each of the *Whisperwind*'s areas - kitchen, cockpit, engines, other cabins. Puk was already in a charging cradle on the small shelf, plugged in and sapping what solar energy the bot could get.

"They'll glow when you turn off the light." Jairo said next to her, nodding at the keypad, watching Viola's eyes coat the room.

The *Whisperwind*'s primary corridor split towards the aft of the ship, like a three-pronged fork. The left and right sections broke into two levels where most of the passengers and crew had their cabins. Straight up the central prong were the engines. Viola had noticed those were sealed off by a badge-locked door. Not entirely out-of-line for a luxury ship to close sensitive areas.

"Where does everyone else stay?" By her math, Viola counted ten cabins and at least fifteen crew, plus her and Mox.

"Lots of double-bunking, sleep-swapping," Jairo replied. "You're going to alternate with your friend, if that's okay?"

Share a room with Mox? Well, not really. Sleep-swapping meant they'd alternate, shift their schedules, so one was awake and moving while the other slept. Viola's engineering courses had been full of concepts like that. How to maximize productivity and minimize space. The psychological costs of losing your own home on a ship had to be balanced against the necessities of space travel.

"We'll survive," Viola said, turning around to look at Jairo. "The journey's only a few weeks, right?"

"You're the pilot."

Oh yeah. She was. Apparently the senior one too. Castor said that whenever she wasn't on the bridge, the *Whisperwind* would be coasting on auto-pilot. If there was an alarm, she'd need to make for the flight stick first thing, because nobody else would grab it. That was going to make sleeping real easy.

"I can't believe you have this many people and only one pilot," Viola said.

"You know much about the Red Voice?" Jairo said. "We're not exactly deep in the space department."

"There are plenty of people out there you could pay."

"Who'd want to work with terrorists?" Jairo said the word like it was a bad nickname, one he was stuck with despite his own objections.

"Good question," Viola said. "You still haven't told me why I'm here."

"Sure I did. We needed a pilot."

"All I did was turn on the jets and push the ship into reverse. Autopilot can get you to Earth," Viola said. "I thought it was something worse than that. Something harder."

Jairo paused for a second, eyes sifting around the room. Viola liked that look when Jairo stared over her shoulder but was very much not looking at the wall behind her. The man still wore most of the gear he'd had on during their escape from Miner Prime. The respirator and weapons were gone, stashed somewhere, but otherwise the thick beige shirt and bluish, stained pants bled into gloves and boots, respectively.

The gloves were the more interesting of the two; they looked snug. Custom-jobs that seemed to fit right to his fingers. When Jairo brought one to his face for a scratch, Viola noticed the filaments on the fingertips. Tiny ridges that'd give Jairo a good sense of touch. Made for people who were going to be doing precise work with the gloves on.

"Let me show you something," Jairo said. "It'll answer some questions, promise."

The hacker led Viola back to the main quarter, then badged into the true aft of the ship. Behind the door, the luxury treatments on the walls fell away. No calm lighting, padded floors. It was all brute force back here. They went forward a few meters and then a fork.

"Left brings you to the engine station, right brings you to the fun stuff," Jairo said. "At least in my opinion."

"Why'd you join the Red Voice, Jairo?" Viola asked as they walked.

"Why?" Jairo said. "Viola, you watch your friends and their families get oppressed over and over again by companies more interested in other things, rights get squashed time and time again because we don't really have any. It'd be enough to make most people join. Should've been enough, anyway."

Then Jairo paused, looked at Viola, and grinned an almost-manic smile. A look Viola had seen before, seen on the faces of classmates, of herself, when she was about to tackle a problem that really grabbed her. A problem so interesting all the rest of everything was going to fall away while she worked on it.

"I didn't join because of all that," Jairo continued. "I joined cause I was bored. Cause I wanted something legendary. Cause I wanted a challenge."

The words hit first as cheesy, simple bravado. But then, wasn't that what Viola had been after when she'd first run away from Ganymede? Something that would give her a purpose beyond passing tests?

"Was it worth it?" Viola replied.

They went through the right fork which led into a wider room, still not much larger than the cabins, where a single workbench was surrounded by racks of tools. The *Jumper* had a similar space, meant for the ad hoc repairs that always came up during space flight. As they walked in, the same white light from elsewhere in the ship flipped on. Jairo, though, ignored the bench, the tools, and led Viola over to a small terminal attached to the corner. It'd clearly been added, the supports for the console drilled into the nearby sides of the room. The screen itself was barely as large as Viola's hand.

"This is worth it," Jairo said, flipping a switch on the side of the terminal. It powered up, skipping past most of the corporate-branded console systems running on ships these days to load a muddy interface. A few available options presented themselves as colored circles, squares.

"Looks homemade," Viola said, leaning closer.

"My own. But that's not the star of the show," Jairo said, tapping one of the icons. The red circle flashed, then expanded to fill the screen. Lines of code displayed, and Jairo flicked the document up and down. It wasn't a simple program, whatever it was.

"Do you know what's on Earth?" Jairo said while Viola tried to pick out what was going on in the variables, the functions.

"Lots of things?"

"The androids. And with this program, right here, we can control them."

21

SUBTLE BURN

"They tell me you're the doctor," the man said from the doorway to the med room. Erick saw he was wearing a battle suit, something designed for a fight they weren't having. At least, not yet.

"So I've been told," Erick replied, continuing to bundle the new stock into appropriate drawers. Supplies were used or expired over time, so they'd picked up a few crates of new material during the short stay on Miner Prime. Right now he was taking a pack of syringes out of its brightly colored, branded box and slipping them into the cabinet with the various needles the plastic pieces would be paired with. Placement had to be precise: in a critical event, there wasn't time to try to remember where you'd put the right med, the right bandage.

The man walked into the room, ducked under the precision light attached through a swinging arm to the bed. Held out his hand towards Erick, who shook it. Bosser Oates, that's who the man's name was. Him and that android now on the ship. Davin kept referring to them as guests in public, but through a series of quick, private comms, Trina and Erick understood the real situation.

"Bosser Oates," the man said.

"Erick," the doctor replied. "How can I help you?"

With that invitation, Bosser sat down on the bed with a sigh and pulled off one of the gloves he was wearing. Beneath, on the man's left hand, there was an obvious burn marking. Red, angry, and starting to blister in a long streak across the top of Bosser's hand.

"Grazing shot. Numbed it at the time, but it's started to act up. Wondering if you have anything?"

Erick took a closer look. Standard-issue laser burn. Seemed strange that it was only bubbling up now though. They'd been in flight for hours, a shot taken back on Miner Prime would've already set in. Scarring, maybe.

"When did you say this happened?" Erick said, turning to the drawer that held the gauze.

"Don't know if you know what happened on the station before we left. It wasn't just the group trying to steal your ship." Bosser spoke like a man settling in for a long story, a prepared tale. "The Red Voice hit us across the station, and I went out with our reserve forces to make sure the damage wasn't severe."

"And you took a shot?"

"I did," Bosser said, not flinching at all as Erick rubbed some plaskin ointment over the burn. "When we made it to your docking bay, it was clear they'd sabotaged most of the other ships on the station. For a reason."

The plaskin had an aloe smell to it, a cooling, mild scent that always put Erick at ease. Except now. Patients always tried to construct a narrative, tried to frame their condition in a way that put them in a better light. Not a problem, really, but Erick knew manipulation when he heard it.

Bosser wasn't settling in here for a simple burn treatment, there was something else going on.

"Do you know that your crew members are on the ship we're chasing?" Bosser asked.

"Davin mentioned it," Erick replied.

"They're helping the Red Voice. That's whose ship it is."

"Mr. Oates, if you're looking to find some sort of sympathetic anger from me, you're not going to receive it," Erick said, putting the tube of plaskin back in its slot. "While I don't approve of what they did on Miner Prime, Eden and those other organizations did equally bad or worse things on Mars."

Bosser was already nodding as Erick finished.

"Do you know where we're going?" Bosser asked.

"I'm guessing you do?"

"Earth," Bosser replied. "You have family there, don't you?"

The universe shifted with those words. Bosser knew he had a family. Which meant the man knew who Erick was, had known who Erick was. Which meant there was an agenda here, something Bosser was going for.

"I do," Erick said. "It would be nice to see them again."

"Do you know what the Red Voice is planning to do, when they get to Earth?"

"No idea."

Erick found that he was sweating, despite the cool temps maintained across the *Jumper*. He'd had plenty of difficult conversations before, but usually it was him telling the patients things that they didn't want to hear. Now, he was engaged in a back-and-forth with someone, and Erick was afraid he was very much outclassed.

"I don't know either, and that, Erick, is what frightens me," Bosser said, taking a gauze bandage and placing it over the ointment. "Because the Red Voice is desperate. When you and your team prevented their acquisition of the ice diamonds, you stole their coin. Just now, on Miner Prime, they lost most of their remaining force. The question is why. Why take this gambit?"

"You're asking the wrong person."

"Am I?" Bosser looked Erick in the eye. "The Red Voice says it exists to fight for the unheard citizens of Mars. Their members mostly have families on the red planet, people they would do anything to protect, to help. But they lost, except for this last ship. If you knew you were the only ones left to send a message, what would you do?"

"You're trying to say they're going to threaten the planet? Earth?"

Bosser shrugged.

"As I said, I don't know. But whatever they're planning on doing, it will be desperate. It will be reckless," Bosser stood up from the bed, slipped his glove back on over the gauze. "I believe you're the only member of this crew with family on Earth. The only one with anything to lose if the Red Voice gets their chance. Thank you for the assistance, Erick."

Bosser walked out of the room, Erick watching his back. The man wanted help to convince Davin to shoot the Red Voice ship down. Was betting on Erick's vulnerability. It was a good play. Erick exhaled, put his hands on the plastic covering on the bed. But nothing Bosser had said was false. The Red Voice could be planning something radical, something they couldn't expect. Something that could hurt Erick's daughter, his granddaughter.

Could he do nothing and live with the consequences?

22

INTRUSION

When the door to the cabin opened, Mox was already awake. He'd heard the steps, broken cadences signaling multiple people, approaching the room the moment they'd started up the stairs. Beneath the thin sheet, Mox primed his arms to push him off the bed and launch towards the door. Keep them pinned to the entryway and they wouldn't have a chance to surround him. The cannon normally attached to his suit whenever combat was likely was still on the *Jumper*. The sidearm taken when he came onto the *Whisperwind*, a "gesture of trust" according to Castor.

The door to the cabin was locked, but Mox wasn't surprised when the keypad blinked green. Overrides were common, necessary on most ships. The potential problems of a rogue passenger more than trumped the idea of privacy in space. The door shot open and Mox started his move.

"Don't!" Castor said, hands raised in silhouette against the bright hallway lights. Behind Castor, one of the Red Voice soldiers squatted, rifle aiming past Castor's side at

Mox. On the other side, a woman with tired eyes stood and stared at him.

"Knock?" Mox asked.

"This would be easier if you were asleep," Castor said. "But at least now you can meet Alissa."

Castor went into the room, followed by the soldier and then the woman. In the cramped quarters, they all stared at Mox, who swung his legs over and sat upright. Still shorter than his visitors, but at least Mox didn't feel like a sick child. The lights in the cabin clicked on at the motion, and Mox was able to make out more of the visitors. Castor and the soldier looked the same as when he'd first boarded, hours ago now. They sported a standard assortment of military gear, even though it all looked retrograde. Purchased in the after-market, mismatched branding, clothes in different colors and types. The woman behind them was more cohesive, but looked like a civilian. They'd abandoned the Red Voice's ragged outfits in favor of something more practical, less personal.

"Mox," the woman said. "Alissa Reinhert. Nice to meet you."

Alissa didn't stick out a hand, but nodded in his direction. Mox returned the gesture, keeping his eyes on the soldier. On Castor. Too many people for an odd-hours greeting.

"When Castor told me you were here, I wanted to take a look personally," Alissa said. "I apologize for the sudden, impolite nature of our visit, but there are measures that I have to take to protect what's left of our group."

"Measures?" Mox said. "You already have my weapon."

"Not the one that matters," Castor replied, then he reached into a pouch in his pocket, pulled out a small circular pod with clamps around the outside. "Know what this is?"

Mox had seen similar things in Merc's gear. The disks would arc electricity at anything nearby that could form a current. Cause nerves to spasm.

"Have an idea," Mox said.

"I'm going to attach it to your suit," Castor said. "If you try anything dangerous, one of us can set it off. Knock you out for a while."

"It's a precaution, Mox," Alissa added.

"No," Mox said.

"Figured you would say that," Castor replied. "Which means there's a couple paths forward. Either you take stock of the fact you're very outnumbered on a ship in the middle of space and decide to accept that reality peacefully, or we do it the hard way."

"Castor, please," Alissa said, putting a hand on the man's arm. "Mox. We're heading to Earth. Once we're there, you'll be free to leave the ship. We'll disconnect the device the moment we land."

"No," Mox said, and the soldier raised his rifle. Close enough that Mox could grab and destroy the thing in a microsecond. At the same time, Castor's position put the man in a prime spot for a punch to the stomach. Delivered with the full power of the exo-suit, Castor would be taken care of.

"Then think about Viola," Alissa said. "She's in the pilot's chair right now. If you fight here, you're risking her life too."

Mox snapped into action, pushed his left arm up and into the soldier's assault rifle, shoving its aim towards the ceiling and pushing the soldier into the wall. His right arm exploded forward, grabbed Castor's uniform and hauled the man into the air as Mox stood up.

"I will not be your slave," Mox growled into Castor's face.

Then Alissa moved, pulling another of the disks out of her own pocket and slapping it on Mox's back, to the ridged line of the exoskeleton that ran along Mox's spine. Mox didn't feel the disk activate, but heard the clicks as the thing latched into place. Alissa stepped back, her hands spread out.

"Not how we wanted it to go, Mox," Alissa said.

The metal man dropped Castor to the ground, the Red Voice captain catching his footing and sticking the landing. Castor looked at Mox and nodded as though the whole exchange went exactly as expected.

"Now that you're safe, you're free to wander the ship. Work out, meet the others, doesn't matter," Castor said. "Like Alissa said, we don't want any trouble. And now that it's guaranteed, I don't see a need to keep you watched."

"So kind," Mox said.

The Red Voice trio left a minute later, Alissa tossing one more invitation to explore the ship and meet the rest of the crew. As though they were welcoming him onto a pleasure cruise. Mox sat back down on the bed. He was mechanical, at least in part. They could control him through mechanical means. Viola, however, was not. The question was, how were they going to control her?

23

WHAT TO REMEMBER

Viola turned back to the console as Castor subbed out his shift for Jairo. They never left her alone in the cockpit, but of the two, Viola could at least have conversations with Jairo. Castor spent hours glued to his comm, reading article after article or battering out messages he never described to her.

"You hanging in there?" Jairo asked, settling into his seat.

"Glad to have someone to talk to," Viola replied.

Jairo laughed. "Castor's just busy, that's all."

"Is that all? Really?"

"Okay, no," Jairo said. "He's always like that. Never know what he's doing. But I've seen him fight, and you couldn't ask for a better soldier."

Flashes of the *Karat* whirled through Viola's head.

"Have you fought before? Ever?" Viola asked.

"I try to stay away from the weapons. At least, the physical kind," Jairo said, looking back at his console. "I'm a fan of playing to strengths, and mine does not involve blasting someone."

"Instead, you're trying to subvert a bunch of androids to do it for you?"

Jairo paused for a moment, then stood up from his chair. Went over to Viola and leaned over so he could type on her console.

"Not everything I do is about harming people," Jairo said. "Watch."

The console's screen shifted as Jairo tapped away, at one point swiping his finger on an otherwise blank part of the screen. Eventually the menus faded away entirely, and the console displayed only a single blinking white square in the middle of it.

"Press it," Jairo said.

Viola did, pushing her finger lightly against the screen. The square expanded to fill the entire width, glowed brighter, then shifted. Faded away leaving only a series of branching lines and dots. Without waiting for Jairo, Viola pressed on a dot in the middle. It spun, then grew. Inside was a picture, Jairo shaking hands with Alissa. He was younger in the picture, fewer lines on his face.

"Each line takes you down a different part of me," Jairo said. "I'm making one for everyone I can, but it takes a long time."

"Why?"

"Because, no matter what happens here, there's going to be a history of the Red Voice and the people in it. I don't want us reduced to statistics, or sound bites. We're all real people, Viola."

"So were the ones on Miner Prime that your people killed."

"And if I could make this for them, I would," Jairo said. "Go up the left branch next."

Viola slid her finger up the branching path to the left.

The next picture showed Jairo in a garden, holding a large head of broccoli, an older woman laughing next to him. In the background, the rolling red mountains of Mars scaled the horizon.

"My mother. She always kept me grounded. The idea that here we were, on Mars, and what really mattered was eating your vegetables. Keeping the garden growing," Jairo said.

"You're going to make me homesick," Viola replied.

"Keep going."

Viola shook her head. "Why are you doing this, Jairo?"

The hacker's smile left his face, and his eyes slipped away to a corner of the cockpit.

"Because I don't want you to think I'm a bad person," Jairo said. "It's a failing of mine. The faceless masses, you know, the people out there, I don't really care what they think of me. But people that I'm close to? It matters that they don't see me as a killer."

"I don't," Viola said, and the words surprised her. Before, back on Ganymede, the Red Voice had always seemed a band of terrible murderers. Planting bombs in habitats and wrecking an ideal society on Mars for political points. "I used to, because it was easier than reasoning with the actual problems."

"The actual problems?"

"I didn't realize till I went to Europa that it's a hard life for most people. I was sheltered on Ganymede. Good family, plenty of coin. Education," Viola said. "Then I'm here with a bunch of people that wouldn't hesitate to kill for their goals, and it's because so many of the things in their lives wouldn't hesitate to kill them if it came to it."

Jairo pushed the next dot on the console, this one on a different branch. It was a shot of the *Whisperwind*'s cafeteria.

Jairo was there, along with some of the other fighters. They were laughing, playing a game on a large table. It reminded Viola of nights in the *Jumper*, playing cards with Erick and Mox, or swapping stories with Davin and Merc.

"It's not always so dark," Jairo said, his face brightening. "Hey, you want to make one?"

"Make one?"

"Yep. You're one of us now, at least for this trip," Jairo said. "I'll show you how."

"I don't have any pictures, though."

"Sure you do. We can pull them from the *Whisperwind*'s security cameras. There's got to be some of you smiling."

Jairo kept right on going, talking through the process of finding the pictures, downloading them into his program, and building out the branches. His enthusiasm was infectious. That zest for keeping the human part captured. Viola caught herself looking at Jairo's grinning face as he went through another series of security stills.

Maybe she'd made the right call, jumping on this ship.

CHANGE THE CODE

The android hadn't moved from the cargo bay for hours. Trina watched it on the *Jumper*'s camera, the bot standing there and staring at the wall. It was wearing a lighter version of Bosser's suit, a thinner blue criss-crossed with a shoulder strap holding the customary android long knife, along with a belt bearing twin sidearms. The idea of a robot that took commands from an enemy, or at least not a friend, having that kind of weaponry on their ship wasn't comforting. But then, Trina wasn't the captain.

"Fournine, given your, uh, experience in this area, what do you think?"

The former android, now ingrained in the *Jumper*'s computer system, was, in Trina's mind, the best thing to happen to the *Jumper* in years. Before, the computer would accept rudimentary queries, like the status of the engines or the amount of energy being converted by the solar panels. Fournine, though, could actively evaluate what Trina was asking. Better yet, it had a personality.

"ThreeTwelve is probably in a power-saving mode," Fournine replied. "Like that sleep you're always doing, but less vulnerable. Come close, and it'll activate. Probably chop your head off. Which would be messy."

"How long can they go without a recharge?"

"An Earth week," Fournine replied, its voice coming through the *Jumper*'s intercom system, sounding like a slightly insane butler. Viola programmed that one, using a standard voice and then randomizing the pitch, so that Fournine's voice would occasionally swing up or down octaves. It was both maddening and, given Fournine's predilections to the absurd, appropriate.

"So ThreeTwelve is fine to move around, then?"

"It would be likely."

Trina glanced at the engine readouts next to her. They had matched the *Whisperwind*, were tagging along behind it without a lot of effort. The luxury craft was older, its engines not up to the speed the *Jumper* could produce. Not designed for the kind of long-range interstellar travel that necessitated more power, and by extension, more space devoted to those engines. As such, the *Jumper* was humming along without any problems. Which meant she could step away for a bit.

"I'm not too comfortable with an active android on this ship," Trina said, moving from the engine room to the workshop. According to the *Jumper*'s internal clock, it was approaching midnight. Most of the ship was quiet, asleep. Trina should be doing the same, but there was this problem she had. This issue with curiosity.

"You and me both," Fournine replied, its voice coming out of the closest comm, as though the computer were walking alongside Trina.

"If ThreeTwelve was our android, though . . ." Trina trailed off.

"You want to use Viola's hack," Fournine said, and Trina

nodded. Viola had found, on Miner Prime, that by accessing the android's core memory in its head, a decently skilled programmer could overwrite the instructions there. Could gain control of the machine. The trick was letting an android give you that chance.

Her workshop seemed to only get more cluttered. A workbench stretched the length of a wall though it was covered in a series of wrenches and screwdrivers. Chains dangled from the ceiling, about three meters high. They ended in clasps, so heavier gear could be suspended while being worked on. The rest of the room was surrounded by shelves, banks of drawers with screws, nails, and adhesives. Each one had a scrap-metal label fastened to it, the correct contents etched into the badges. Trina could have used the same plastic notes that Erick stuck all over the med room, but they didn't seem to fit the theme. In the middle of the workroom was a drain that went directly to an ejection airlock, where any dangerous chemicals, spent fuel, or toxic what-have-you could be launched into space.

Trina went over to the workbench, the very same spot where Fournine had first been hacked to join the Wild Nines. Underneath the bench, in the top drawer, was a small device shaped like a square with a single rounded-off end. In the middle was a circular button that, when pressed, would emit a localized electromagnetic pulse. On a ship, the idea of something that could knock out electronics was horrifying. No system for recycled air, no life. That's why the device only had a meter or so of range. No risk to vital systems.

By the same token, if something was going catastrophically wrong, Trina could take the tiny EMP to the problem and shut down the malfunction.

"Remember the rapid restart," Fournine cautioned.

"ThreeTwelve will be awake before the EMP is ready to go again. Unless you're significantly faster than most humans, I see this attempt ending in your demise."

Trina looked at the chains.

"How long will it take?" Trina said. "To start back up?"

"Ten seconds," Fournine replied. "At eleven, Trina, you will be so very dead."

"It'll have to be enough," Trina said. "Bring the android in here."

Fournine couldn't do that physically, of course, but Trina hoped the bot could come up with something enticing. Something that would draw ThreeTwelve into the workshop. There weren't any screens in the room, so Trina didn't know what was happening, but before too long the sound of footsteps landing on the *Jumper*'s hallway approached. Trina flicked the switch on the EMP device, hearing the tiniest of whines as it prepped itself to overload any circuitry where she pointed it. Trina held the device in her right hand and leaned against the workbench, trying to ignore her beating heart.

ThreeTwelve walked around the doorway and into the workshop. Its head was feminine, long and angular. No hair, just olive-colored plaskin giving play to ThreeTwelve's dark eyes, lips. One of the android's hands drifted towards its right sidearm.

"Your computer said you needed my assistance," ThreeTwelve said. "Speak."

"Did you know that Fournine, our computer, was once an android like you?" Trina asked.

ThreeTwelve didn't show the slightest reaction.

"We are computers. Our bodies are incidental," ThreeTwelve replied.

"Stuffy, aren't you?" Fournine said over the intercom. "Did Bosser even give you a personality?"

"Yes. One that's suspicious of bots with personalities," ThreeTwelve said.

"Do you see these chains?" Trina pointed. "I need help to move them up, from some of the work we were doing on Miner Prime. Normally, Mox would help me, but he's not here."

ThreeTwelve's eyes followed the chains up to the ceiling, looked at the pulleys that would allow the chains to curl around the rafters and keep themselves out of the way when not in use.

"This seems like an unusual task for this time of night," ThreeTwelve said, returning its gaze to Trina.

"Have you ever known a human to be logical?" Fournine quipped. Trina shrugged. ThreeTwelve hesitated a moment.

"I have not," ThreeTwelve said finally, walking over to the workbench. "Tell me what you would like me to do."

The android was directly beneath a pair of the chains, clasps open and ready. Trina took a breath, pulled out the EMP, and as ThreeTwelve turned, pressed the button. The device didn't make a noise, didn't even appear to do anything, but ThreeTwelve jerked suddenly, as if going into a seizure.

"Ten," Fournine said.

Trina pressed a down arrow on a keypad sitting on the workbench's side and all four of the clasping chains dropped until they hit the top of the workbench.

"Nine."

Grabbing the first clasp, Trina slipped it around the android's right arm. Snapped it shut.

"Eight."

Trina moved a dial on the clasp, and it tightened until it locked in on ThreeTwelve's arm. Right on the wrist.

"Seven."

The next clasp on the left arm. Trina whipped it around, snapped it on.

"Six."

Moved the dial, shutting the clasp tight.

"Five."

Now the legs. Only, ThreeTwelve wasn't up on the workbench and there was no way Trina could lift it up there herself. Trina reached for the keypad, slapped the chains up.

"Four."

The chains lifted ThreeTwelve up in the air. Pulled the bot above the workbench, suspended. Trina pushed the android, so that ThreeTwelve swung over the workbench and pressed the down arrow on the keypad to send the android crashing back down on top of it. Without resistance, the legs splayed out, but at least ThreeTwelve was in the right spot.

"Three."

Trina grabbed the next clasp, snapped it onto Three-Twelve's right leg.

"Two."

Pressed the dial with one hand, reached for the last clasp with the other.

"One."

Snapped the last clasp around ThreeTwelve's leg. Reached for the dial.

"Run!" Fournine barked and Trina dove back, falling on the workshop's ground.

ThreeTwelve's eyes sparkled as the android surged back to life. It tried to move its arms, its legs. The chains rattled against the motion, their slack pulling tight as soon as ThreeTwelve tried to move off the workbench. Clashing and clanking noises erupted as ThreeTwelve attempted to thrash its way out of the clasps. At first the motion was random, like a child trying to twist itself free of blankets, then ThreeTwelve became deliberate, testing each of the clasps. Tugging at its arms, then its legs. Trina held her breath as it went for the left leg, the loosest clasp.

The chain held. Then ThreeTwelve raised its head, looked Trina straight in the face, and said nothing. It was time to get to work.

25

CAPTAIN'S MEETING

Alissa Reinhert's quarters were the largest Viola had seen on the *Whisperwind*, which meant they had enough for a queen-sized bed, a desk, and a full wardrobe for clothes. A private bathroom and shower were separated by a thin door. The idea of luxury was here, but it seemed as though pieces were missing. The desk was plain, the bed covered in utilitarian white sheets, no random ornaments on the floors or sitting in the corners. The walls bore the only decoration; as in most of the rest of the ship, pictures of Mars.

"The artwork is, I'll grant you, a little bland," Alissa said as Viola looked around. "However, it serves a purpose. A reminder of what we're doing here."

"Fighting for Mars," Viola said.

"Exactly. Or rather, for the people there who cannot fight for themselves," Alissa said.

"But you lost that fight." Viola folded her arms.

When Jairo told her this morning that Alissa, the leader of the Red Voice, wanted to talk to her, Viola was perplexed. Not that the *Whisperwind* needed her at the pilot's chair, really. They were days away from Earth yet, and unless the *Jumper* decided now was the time to immolate them, Viola didn't have much to do but make sure the autopilot wasn't going rogue. Mox hadn't come by that morning either. In fact, she hadn't seen the metal man for nearly a day. Not since he'd told her he was going to sleep for his shift yesterday. So when Jairo asked if Viola could take a meeting, at that moment, Viola didn't have any reason not to.

"We did," Alissa said. The captain was wearing what Viola could only describe as lounge wear, a set of barely-above-pajamas outfit that seemed designed for an evening with movies and a couch rather than commanding a military force. Then again, Alissa looked exhausted, her wispy blond hair tied back into a loose bun, strands of it escaping to frame the lines in her face. Lines Viola initially took for wrinkles, but, as Alissa came closer, turned into scars.

"Last time I met one of your lieutenants, a man named Bakr, he was trying to kill us," Viola said. "He didn't seem to think you'd lost."

Alissa smiled, like a person enduring a sickening situation that they couldn't escape.

"Bakr was always that way. A believer in the cause," Alissa said. "He saved my life. Back in the inferno. When they tried to burn us alive on Mars."

"They?"

"The same people trying to catch us now," Alissa replied. "Not your friends, of course. Though I wouldn't be surprised if Bosser paid them to do it."

"You were fighting against corporate control, right? The idea that Mars should be a government, instead of a place like Miner Prime?"

"As you said, we lost that fight," Alissa went back to the

desk, pulled out the chair, and sat in it. "Sorry, I've been on my feet most of the night."

Viola took the cue, looked for another chair. There wasn't one. Alissa motioned towards the bed and Viola sat on it. The mattress was firm, the sheets thin. Scratchy. The leader of the Red Voice was not living the good life on her own ship.

"Why did you send Jairo to find me?" Viola said. "There had to be other pilots."

"Look around you. We don't have the money anymore to hire anyone. We need people who still have humanity in their hearts."

"Says the person that just tried to destroy an inhabited space station."

Alissa grimaced.

"I can't hide the fact that we aren't always better than the ones we claim to fight," Alissa said. "But we were desperate. Without the ice diamonds, we needed funds, and support."

"Jairo seemed to imply it was all about me. Getting me on this ship."

"Our hacker friend doesn't always have the entire picture," Alissa said. On the desk, built into the wall behind it, was a console. Alissa tapped a couple of buttons on the screen and then waved Viola over. Scrolling on the console was headline after headline attributing the attack to the Red Voice. Most of the accompanying columns excoriated the attacks, but a few, a scant few, seemed to argue the Red Voice had been pushed to extremes by underhanded tactics, by desperation.

"So what is the 'entire picture'? That you're abandoning your principles to kill at random?"

"Look at this ship, Viola," Alissa said. "The Red Voice is nearly gone. Our entire goal at this point is to make such a scream as we die out that others will hear us for centuries. Some will listen. Take up our cause. And maybe Mars will find itself free one day."

"What do you mean, scream?"

Alissa flipped off the console, stood up from the desk. Put a hand on Viola's shoulder. It was a firm grip. Alissa might look frail, tired, but there was real strength beneath those scars.

"It is better if you don't know," Alissa said. "That way, when they come for you later, you won't need to lie."

Alissa nodded to the door. Gave Viola a gentle, guiding push.

"That's it? That's all you wanted to talk to me about?" Viola asked.

"Jairo says you can be trusted. I wanted to see if he was right," Alissa said as the door back into the hallway shifted open.

"Was he?"

Alissa just put on that tired smile again. Then the door shut between them. Viola stood there in the hallway. What did any of that mean? Mox. Mox might have an idea of what to do next. He'd dealt with these kinds of people before. Ones that didn't say what they really meant.

Viola walked down the hallway towards their shared room. After all this was done, she was definitely going back to the equations. To the schematics and the ins and outs of creating ships. At least those were clear.

26

LAUGH IT OFF

The spray coated the Viper's left wing, the last remaining part, in the dark green color of a thick jungle. Merc crouched on the upper body, already painted and dried a few days earlier. Vacuum vents, installed in the *Jumper*'s bay at Merc's insistence when he came aboard, roared behind him. They'd suck out any rogue particulates, spit them into tiny airlocks that cycled continuously to send the poisonous stuff into space. When Davin asked whether they were really necessary, Merc came back with a ready list of Viper repairs that could send all kinds of microscopic hell floating through the *Jumper*'s air vents. From paint chips to metal shavings when repairing damaged pieces, to the possibility of battery leaks and the acidic fumes that could come if one of those babies burned loose. It'd been enough.

"So you're the hotshot!" called a voice over by the door of the bay. Merc looked up, the mask covering his eyes catching glare from the bay's lights. It was a man, and it definitely wasn't Davin or Erick. Which meant . . . Bosser.

Merc put down the spray nozzle. It was a hose

connected to a bigger barrel of the stuff. They'd picked it up from the dockmaster at Miner Prime. Had to repaint the Viper any time Merc was actually hit in combat as he'd been over Neptune. Like turning a new leaf, a new page, whatever. Point was, *this* Viper, the green one, hadn't been hit yet.

"Not sure anyone calls me that but me," Merc said, jogging over to the wall of the bay and flipping off the fans. They whirred down slowly as though trying to give Merc a chance to rethink his decision. Bosser was continuing into the bay, though, like the man wanted a conversation.

"Well, they should if half of what I've heard about you is true," Bosser said, extending a hand.

"Oh yeah? What'd you hear?" Merc replied, shaking it. There was some gauze wrapped around Bosser's hand, it tickled Merc's palm. Guy is already getting hurt in space, and there hasn't even been a fight yet.

"Eden didn't hold back. Said you out-flew the raiders, even though you were outnumbered," Bosser said. "So I took the liberty of looking you up. Seems you're ex-military. Earth-side."

Merc supposed a normal person might hear that they'd been investigated, researched before being talked to and find that weird. But that was how it worked in the military, how it worked when Davin signed him on. A pilot's record was everything. What Merc didn't understand, though, is why Bosser was coming here to tell him this. Why not talk in the kitchen? Or in the main cargo hold? Or, you know, why talk at all?

"You got me," Merc said. "I, uh, didn't look you up."

"You wouldn't find much," Bosser replied, not remotely bothered. "I'm not what you'd call flashy."

Merc stood there. Looked over Bosser's shoulder at the

door out. Nobody. Just him and Captain Awkward Conversation here.

"So," Bosser continued. "I wanted to ask what you think about the people we're chasing."

"What about them?" Merc said. "They've got Viola and Mox. There's no way they're going to get past Earth's defenses, so I figure we'll just pick them up when they surrender."

"You think they don't have a plan? That they're flying to Earth knowing full well they're never going to land there?"

"Always figured it for a stunt," Merc shrugged. "The Red Voice? They were crushed. What's one ship going to do except stage some protest?"

"They nearly took out Miner Prime," Bosser said.

"You and I both know that wasn't anywhere close to destroying the station. All they did was bomb an area you don't patrol much, maybe take shots at some stores. Mess with some ships," Merc crossed his arms. "It was a desperate move."

Without the vacuum vents going, the bay was starting to smell like the paint. A loose, tingling sensation in the nose. Another few minutes and they'd both start getting giggly. Another few after that and they'd lose coordination. Without spraying more that was probably as bad as it was going to get. Even so, Merc wasn't thrilled this guy was stopping his work to have some sort of heart-to-heart about the Red Voice.

"Does this have a point?" Merc said before Bosser could continue.

"A military officer would look at this target, the *Whisperwind,* as an easy kill. A sure way to end a threat," Bosser said.

"So that's what you want."

"Wouldn't your commanders have said the same thing? Wouldn't they have ordered you to do it?"

"Maybe so," Merc said. "Good thing that, like you said, I'm *ex*-military."

Merc could see the winding gears fall into place inside Bosser's head. The eyes changed, squinted a little, the man's mouth set into a frown. Nobody liked to lose, and Bosser looked like one of those types that didn't lose very often. Merc remembered he didn't actually have a weapon on him here. Hands only, but gloved, thick ones for blocking toxic chemicals. If Bosser wanted to push his point a little more physically, Merc would be game.

"I can see there was a reason for that," Bosser said, then he stepped back. "If you change your mind, if you understand what's most important, let me know."

Merc caught motion behind Bosser, smiled.

"You want to know what's really important?" Merc said, then nodded over Bosser's shoulder. "That is."

Opal leaned against the doorway, glaring at Bosser. The man in the middle shook his head and walked out of the bay, giving Opal the slightest of nods as he passed by. Opal was geared up for maintenance work, sporting the same all-covering, stained suit that Merc was wearing. After the painting was done, they were going to clean out some of the Viper's internals. Make her really sing.

"What'd that jackass want?" Opal asked.

"Thought I'd blow up Vi and Mox, just cause he asked nicely," Merc said.

Opal narrowed her eyes, looked back at the doorway where Bosser had just vanished.

"I don't like the idea of him trying to mess with us," Opal said.

Merc laughed.

"You think any of us are going to listen to him?" Merc said. "Guy's a loon, he thinks any of us are going to turn."

Opal didn't laugh with him. She just closed her eyes for a second.

"I hope you're right," Opal said. She walked over to the vents, punched them on, and any more talking was overrun by the loud roar.

27

A GOOD CREW

"Do you remember that run to Phobos, the first-timer pilot that thought he knew everything?" Phyla said. In front of the cockpit, a kilometer ahead, the *Whisperwind* churned through space on its way to meeting Earth.

"Wasn't that where he nearly crashed the freighter?" Davin replied. The captain was looking fresher this morning. The third day since leaving Miner Prime.

"It was. I remember you were so mad he nearly cost us the contract."

"Atmosphere. The moron forgot that Phobos doesn't have one," Davin grinned, leaned back in his seat. "We've had some good runs, haven't we?"

"More than a few," Phyla said.

They'd never budged far from barely making it, though. Always concerned with the next contract, always pouring anything leftover back into the ship. The *Whiskey Jumper* was a beautiful mess, now, a hodgepodge of parts and upgrades that always seemed to be changing.

"What do you think he's afraid of?" Davin asked, the smile dying away.

"Bosser?" Phyla replied. "Control, probably. He needs it."

"Just like you." Davin lit up a side of his face to cut the words.

"Like me? You think I'm controlling?" Phyla said, eyebrows rising. "You're the one whose got to choose all the contracts, have a say over anything big we buy. Who sits in that chair."

"I'm sitting here 'cause it's the comfiest one in the ship," Davin said.

"Hah, that's what you think. I swapped the stuffing out months ago. You've been sitting on trash."

Not entirely true, but what did it matter. The moment was more important. They were on a ship with a conniving murderer in Bosser and his slavish death-bot ThreeTwelve. They were following a group who'd just tried to destroy a civilian space station and who was holding two of their friends hostage. Gotta take what light she could find.

"We're going to have to do something, you know," Davin said. "To Bosser. For Lina."

"She wouldn't want you to kill him."

"I know," Davin said, rubbing his face with his hands. "If that's what I thought, I'd have had Trina blast him with the turret back on the space station. Blame it on the Voice."

"Think like her, Davin," Phyla said.

Lina had always seen the universe as a puzzle to be solved. Rather, a series of puzzles. Everything was a game to plot out, a mystery to sleuth, and when Lina had the answer, she was bored. But until then, tenacious. Phyla blinked, turned to the console. Flight routes, the *Jumper*'s internal cameras, and a scrolling series of headlines. Most were about the attack on Miner Prime. Phyla swiped past a few describing the chaos, the repair efforts, the call for androids to be activated to hunt down the Red Voice once and for all.

"That one makes a good point," Davin said, leaning over. "Bosser could've sent the bots to take care of them a long time ago."

"Why didn't he?"

"Coin," Davin said. "Think about it. Bosser waits till an entire planet becomes desperate enough to pay for that many androids?"

"Only now they're ruining his game?"

"Still doesn't make sense why he's so afraid about Earth, though," Davin said. "What does he care if they make a statement? Bosser and the androids would make even more coin if everything was chaotic."

"I hear escorts also do well when things get messy."

"Hey. I thought you wanted out of this business."

"I do," Phyla said. "Would love a return to the good runs, ferrying supplies. No lasers, no getting trapped in shuttles sent rocketing into planets."

Davin nodded, like he agreed. Except every time Phyla tried to talk about what would happen after, when they were cleared of the murder charges and let finally free, Davin always went silent. Retreated into some discussion with himself.

"Davin?" Phyla said. "Talk to me?"

"I don't know," Davin raised his hands slightly, a half-shrug. "I don't want to get shot, same as you. Only, I don't think it's going away that easily."

"You mean the charges?"

"That's on Bosser to clear. I mean Lina. I mean getting our reputation back. We were used, Phyla."

"We're still being used," Phyla said. "By Bosser, and by the Red Voice, holding Mox and Viola. I said I wanted to go back to the old days, but I want to do it on our own. Not because we were forced."

"So you'll stay with me? Even if I drag us into Hell?"

Phyla laughed.

"You haven't scared me away yet," Phyla said. "Besides, I figure any terrible idea you get on your own is going to haunt me, regardless. Better to make sure you can actually pull it off."

"Tell you what, we get through this, get our freedom back? We'll take any run you want. Go anywhere you'd like."

"Don't make promises you can't keep, captain."

"Fair. How about, we'll go anywhere you like so long as there's a job and coin when we get there?"

"That's more like it," Phyla said.

Davin looked out the cockpit, at the stars washed out by the Sun's ever-present glow. Phyla remembered how strange that was; the first days off of Miner Prime and out of its artificial day and night. The Sun always there if you looked out the right window. Relying on timed lights inside the ship to queue her body for sleep. When Davin asked her to learn to fly, to be his copilot and eventually *the* pilot, Phyla had looked at the nothing waiting for her in Vagrants Hollow and fled to the stars.

"If you'd asked me a year ago if we could survive this, I'd have said you were crazy," Davin said, still looking at the stars. "Now, I'm hanging on. Playing each hand as it's dealt to us. But I like our chances."

"You've got a good crew, a good ship. Can't ask for much else."

"And a damn good pilot. Don't forget that."

"Was waiting to see if you would remember," Phyla said.

Davin's smile was genuine, the crinkle around his eyes bringing Phyla back to that first launch, when the universe was wide open. Just a little longer, and they'd have that wonder back.

28

QUESTIONS

He'd seen the video a thousand times. Maybe more. It played silently as Mox stood in an empty hallway on the *Whisperwind*. Hard to find these on the crowded ship, but with Viola in their cabin, there wasn't a good option for solitude.

The comm projected the image into the air before his eyes. Four tall buildings spaced out around a large courtyard, connected by raised hallways spanning the gaps high above the surface. The Moon's gravity gave architects unique opportunities and soaring structures were becoming common in Luna. Only these buildings wouldn't be standing much longer. A blue nova appeared in the center of one of the arcing hallways, followed by similar explosions in the others. Nova bombs, detonating their way through electric currents. Super-heating and frying circuits and the metal that held them together.

The angle of the shot, taken from one of Luna's many surveillance cameras, didn't catch much of the courtyard. Mox couldn't see himself down there, but he knew what he'd been doing at that very second. Pressing against the crowd. Turning towards the first explosion and attempting an impossible rescue.

"Luna, right?" Alissa said, coming out of her cabin and pausing in front of Mox.

Oh, there'd been a reason he chose this hallway. Empty because only one cabin sat at the end of it. The cabin holding the most important person on the ship.

"I have questions," Mox said.

Alissa gestured back inside her room.

"I might have answers," she said. "I prefer long conversations in more comfortable places."

Mox followed the Red Voice leader into her cabin, watched as she immediately went to her desk, opened a drawer and pulled out a small remote. Alissa turned back to Mox and held the square up.

"This activates the disk on your back," Alissa said.

"I figured."

"When you've seen so many friends die, you start getting a little paranoid," Alissa said, sitting down in the chair. "So you wanted to know about Luna?"

"Why did you do it?"

Alissa cocked her head. Eyebrows raised.

"I didn't. The Red Voice had nothing to do with Luna."

"Liar," Mox felt the anger tighten in his throat. So many died that day. Erin died that day.

"No," Alissa said, and now her look turned to steel. "The Red Voice is, was, has always been about Mars. Others saw our example and tried to replicate it."

"Then you are still responsible."

"And what about the corporations that drove us to this? Are they not responsible too?"

Mox took a step closer to Alissa. Felt the power humming in the exoskeleton. He was within reach. She would have to press the remote quickly before he knocked it out of her hands.

"They didn't bomb the towers," Mox said.

"What do you want me to say?" Alissa said. "Those weren't our soldiers. They were Luna's own people, making their own statement."

"Because of you."

Erin's face, those twin strands framing her happy eyes. All those mornings they shared, giving bits and pieces of themselves to each other, wiped away because some copycat killers thought they had a cause. Because they saw Alissa doing the same thing on Mars and wanted their part.

Mox didn't think. He reacted. His left arm shot out, boosted by the exoskeleton, and knocked the remote from Alissa's hand. It ricocheted off the wall and landed on her bed. With his right arm, Mox swiped at Alissa's head. But the woman was faster than Mox anticipated. She pushed herself down and out of her chair, sliding beneath his punch. Through his legs. He turned, found Alissa already curling forward onto her feet.

"I didn't set those bombs. We never advocated for civilian targets," Alissa said, backing away.

"Then what was Miner Prime?" Mox replied, dropping into a boxing stance.

"Desperation. Unfortunate, but necessary," Alissa said. The bed was behind her, the remote sitting on a pillow. Alissa moved towards it and Mox charged, reaching out with a right sledgehammer blow where Alissa would have to be as she went for the remote.

Only she wasn't there. Alissa twisted back out of the feint and tripped Mox as he went by, her leg connecting with his right ankle. Mox hit the ground, grabbed the side of the bed and hauled himself up.

"I don't make excuses for what we do," Alissa said, behind him. "It's a dirty universe, and we're fighting for survival. If you think I ought to die for that, then that's your choice. But we didn't plant those bombs."

Mox reached for, grabbed the remote. Looked at it. Blinked. Stared harder. It . . . It wasn't a remote at all.

"A toy?" Mox said, anger falling away as he turned around.

"It plays a song if you press the button," Alissa said, a half-smile cracking her face. "One of the first presents my parents gave me, to help me through our first space flight. I was nervous, and they said that as long as the song played, I'd be safe."

Mox couldn't help it. He pressed the button. Nothing happened.

"It died a long time ago," Alissa said. "I keep it here. One day I'll get it fixed."

"Then the disk, on my back?"

"We can activate it with the comms," Alissa said, holding up her wrist.

"Then why didn't you?"

"Mox, we need Viola. And to keep her with us, we need you. I need you," Alissa said. "Trust me. We're not your enemy."

Mox set the toy back down on the bed. Made for the exit.

"I'm not your friend," Mox said.

29

INBOUND

The pictures always showed Earth as a pristine blue, green, and white ball spinning perfectly through space. The videos showed the clouds shifting over the surface, various satellites and space stations popping over them like dirt specks on a cloth. To see it in person, though, Viola could only think of one word. *Home.*

"This is your first time seeing her?" Castor asked, sitting in the co-pilot's chair. "Jairo's too."

The hacker had moved over to stand behind her, hands on the shoulders of Viola's seat. They all watched as the *Whisperwind* started its slowdown. Viola had boarded the ship because of Jairo's call for help, but this view, this was worth it all by itself.

"Someday, you're going to have to program me to feel the same way you look right now," Puk said, hovering behind them.

"I don't think I can," Viola said, not turning away.

"Jairo?" Puk said the hacker's name the same way the bot addressed Mox. Like a friend. They *had* been spending most of the journey together, with Jairo teaching her about his program, about the *Whisperwind* and Viola giving him piloting lessons and bringing Jairo's head out of the code and into the mechanics of actually putting a bot together.

Mox. Viola blinked. The metal man hadn't been around much. Seemed almost to be avoiding her. Only grunting hellos when they passed each other switching shifts in the room. She was going to call him on it, trap him and make Mox explain what the hell was going on. But then Castor called, said it was time to get ready.

"So what's the approach?" Viola said. "Where are we landing?"

"The Andes," Castor said. "I've already put the precise coordinates in."

Viola glanced at the console. The flight path was sitting there, waiting for her to activate it. She tapped the button and a yellow line shot out from the nose of the *Whisperwind*, angling to keep up with Earth's speed. Follow that line, give the autopilot a chance to work its magic, and they would find themselves touching down on a mountain range in a few hours.

"*Whisperwind!*" The voice came from the comm, blasted into the ship. "You're ordered to cut your engines immediately and wait for boarding!"

The speaker followed with a rambling series of justifications, credentials and commands about how, being in Earth's space, they were obligated to abide the orders of Earth's International Defense Coalition. Viola listened to the whole thing, every word a ringing judgment over her choice to fly the ship here. Murderers, terrorists, war criminals. She almost cut the engines on those alone because what else was she supposed to do?

"Don't," Castor said, noticing Viola's hands drift towards the flight stick. "They won't move on us."

The console blipped, signaling new ships shifting into scanning range. They were coming out of one of the stations ringing Earth, eight Vipers and a larger shuttle, nearly the size of the *Whisperwind* itself.

"Won't move on us? Guess that's for somebody else, then," Puk said.

"Shut it, Puk," Viola said. "That's too fast. Eight fighters? A shuttle that's probably packed with soldiers?"

"Miner Prime would've communicated our flight plan," Castor said. "They've known we were coming for a while."

"So what do we do?" Viola said. "I can't fly through that many."

Jairo leaned over to the comm, pressed the transmit button.

"Earth, this is the *Whisperwind*. We have Viola Allouette onboard. You attack this ship, she could die."

Viola hadn't heard her full name since it was announced as part of a class roll call months ago. Only this wasn't about attendance, it was about being used. Nothing came back over the comm when Jairo lifted up the button.

"That's why you were in Vagrant's Hollow—" Viola started.

"It doesn't matter why," Castor interrupted. "Not now. Because you're stuck here, and your only way out is getting us down to that surface."

Viola stood up out of the seat, looked down at Castor, at Jairo's nervous face.

"Or I can cut the engines. Or walk away," Viola said.

"You'd be killing us," Jairo said.

"Your father's name has power, Viola," Castor said. "We

don't have much of that left. It's our only chance to get to Earth, to give this a shot."

"You have to understand . . ." Jairo echoed.

"Puk?" Viola asked the bot.

"They're jerks," Puk replied. "But if they don't need you, they might kill you. There are two small escape shuttles on this ship and both of them are at the rear. Your odds of running are low."

So she was trapped again. Locked into bad choices because she was too stupid to think about it in the first place. Random luck that Jairo had rescued a pilot on Miner Prime? That he was just trying to steal something by chance and wound up with her?

"They're not turning around," Castor said, his voice, for the first time, breaking out of its deadened cadence. "Viola, we need you to take control."

She couldn't help herself. Viola looked at the console. The eight Vipers were still coming, they'd split into groups of four. The shuttle hanging back behind them. Waiting for any teeth to be removed. In another minute they would hit the edge of weapons range. A few seconds after that, the *Whisperwind*'s shields would start taking hits.

"Please," Jairo said. "I didn't like tricking you. Everything since we got on this ship, though, has been true. I promise."

"Stuff your promises," Viola said. But words weren't going to get them out of this alive. Viola sat back down in the pilot's chair and gripped the flight stick. Tapped the console to turn off the autopilot; that yellow line fading away ahead of them. Earth hung off to the left, filling most of the space, its atmosphere blurring at the edges so that the perfect circle appeared to be bleeding off, blowing away in some sort of invisible wind.

"Last chance," the comm buzzed. "Power down your engines. We will not hold back."

"Did you not hear who we have on board this ship?" Jairo said back into the comm. "You hurt Viola, you'll never be able to buy another Viper!"

"Earth bends for no one," the comm replied.

"Guess Vi's dad isn't worth as much as you thought," Puk said to Castor while Viola started tilting the *Whisperwind* towards half of the fighters.

Not that it would matter. All Viola could do was delay. There wasn't any chance the *Whisperwind* was getting through that screen. Saving lives? By flying them off Miner Prime, Viola had killed them all.

30

BAD IDEA

The best part of victory was . . . the entire thing. Bosser watched the Vipers close on the *Whisperwind* from his cabin. The small console in the room wasn't ideal for viewing the destruction, but it would suffice. If he was exceptionally lucky, the girl, Viola, might even live. Or perhaps, with the owner of Galaxy Forge angry, Bosser could twist that anger at the Red Voice into more ships for his androids. More protection to keep this from ever happening again. Another scenario where no matter the outcome, Bosser Oates emerged the victor.

"This one was closer than most," Bosser said to Three-Twelve, standing in the doorway. "Would Earth flinch? Let them through? It was hard to tell."

"But you never gamble," ThreeTwelve replied.

"I do, but only when the odds are very much in my favor," Bosser leaned back, massaged his bandaged hand. Watched the console. The *Whisperwind* had started to move. Not that it mattered. The luxury craft wasn't going to out-fly that many fighters. The *Jumper*, though, appeared to draw closer. *Was* drawing closer.

"Why is Davin closing? He'll risk us taking hits," Bosser said, then punched the intercom. "Davin, what the hell are you doing?"

"Seems a little unfair, doesn't it?" Davin's reply came back quick. "Eight against one?"

"They're murderers, Davin!" Bosser growled back. "Killers of innocents! They tried to destroy your home!"

"It's not them I'm defending," Davin said. "It's Viola and Mox."

Bosser watched the console. Damn Davin and his inability to see that sometimes you had to make the best of a bad situation. Losing Viola and Mox was nothing compared to the *Jumper* and the rest of the crew. Nothing compared to him.

On the console, another blip appeared next to the *Jumper*, the same size as the other Vipers. The hotshot making his entrance. Even with the *Jumper*'s turrets, there wasn't going to be a chance they won this fight.

"I think it's time we found a way off of this ship," Bosser announced to the android. "Seeing as they're determined it not last much longer."

31

DEVIL'S REVERSE

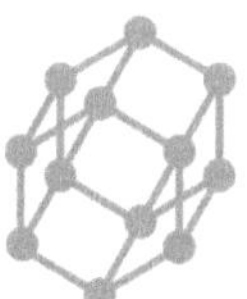

The *Whisperwind* had one turret, a single cannon stuck on top. The kind of weapon Viola would have called a selling point. By itself, it would be easy for a Viper pilot to evade, but the weapon played to the security fears that the buyers of ships like this one inevitably had. She sent Jairo to stick someone on it, anyway.

"Hey there, *Whisperwind*, looks like you knocked on the wrong door!" the voice came over the comm.

"Davin!" Viola said. Castor muttered the same thing at the same time, only with a curse attached.

"Here's what we need you to do," Davin continued into the comm. "Point yourselves right at Earth and punch it."

Going into Earth directly was a great way to slam into the atmosphere and disintegrate. It was suicide.

"Wanna repeat that?" Viola asked, turning the *Whisper-wind* anyway. The sharper angle cut off the approach of the Vipers, whose lasers were already spitting over their front nose. Buying time seemed like the best move at the moment.

"Head right into the planet," Davin said. "Pull a Devil's Reverse."

Devil's reverse. The *Whisperwind* had the right profile for it. Thin, long, not a bulky freighter. Viola pulled the flight stick back, sending the luxury liner into a tight curl. When Earth was centered in the windshield, Viola leveled the ship off and went straight for the blue ocean. The four closer Vipers turned to follow suit, while the farther half continued moving behind the *Whisperwind*, cutting off any other path than straight ahead.

Someone opened up on the *Whisperwind*'s turret, sending a steady stream of laser back towards the Vipers. Viola could see the fighters shift on the console, but the turret wasn't scattering them, was barely acknowledged. More laser-fire pounded the *Whisperwind*'s rear shields, which quickly went from green to yellow, fading towards red. Viola tried bumping the ship up, triggering the maneuvering jets to bring the *Whisperwind* out of the firing line for a moment, but the Vipers readjusted. The fighters had matched the *Whisperwind*'s speed and were going to sit back there and pound them into dust.

"We're not going to make it," Viola said. "They'll kill us before we reach atmosphere."

"There are no other options," Castor said.

"We could surrender."

"That ends the same way this might."

The console beeped again. Another fighter streaking in. Probably looking to get a share of the kill. The *Whisperwind*'s alarms started to sound as the shields faltered. The first shots leaked through, scoring chunks off of the hull. And then they stopped. Viola glanced at the console. The Vipers that had been trailing them were scattering, and one seemed to be drifting in space. Another blip entered the scanner, a larger one. A signature Viola recognized.

"Davin?" Viola commed.

"What, I don't get a thank you for sweeping away the bugs?" Merc's voice came over the open channel.

"That was you?!"

"Sure wasn't the crap gun you have on that ship," Merc said.

Viola sat back in the chair. For the moment, anyway, the *Whisperwind*'s shields were getting a chance to recharge. Castor remarked that they hadn't received any significant damage. They'd have time to pull off Davin's crazy maneuver.

"Vi, where are you going?" Davin's voice came over the comm. "We need to know."

Viola reached for the talk button, but Castor's hand covered it first. Viola looked over and saw his shaking head.

"We can't trust them," Castor said. "All of this doesn't matter if they find out where we're going."

"Viola?" Davin's voice again.

"So what, I don't tell them anything?" Viola said.

"Pretend the comm is broken, if that helps you," Castor said. "Concentrate on getting us down to the surface."

The surface. Viola could see it, the brown green masses splayed out in front of her against the Earth's ocean blue canvas. Wisps of white and gray clouds sprinkled across, garnish on the wondrous plate. And it was getting bigger, fast.

"Tell everyone to hang on," Viola said, sinking into the moment. She could worry about Davin and the others later. If they didn't stick this entry, the *Whisperwind* and everyone on it would burn to cinders or even less, vanishing in a pretty firework.

The first order of business was slowing the *Whisperwind*'s velocity. They were going so fast that they would be hitting the Earth's atmosphere like a swimmer belly flopping from a hundred meters high. Unfortunately, behind them were a bunch of fighters that wanted nothing more than the blow them out of the sky. No time for gradual slowdown. Viola tapped on the front maneuvering jets, then hard cut the main engines.

She pushed the jets to full power. Watched as the Earth spun away and changed to black space, the glitzy laser light show as the Jumper and Merc's Viper tangoed with Earth's fighters. Then Viola shunted the main engines back on. The *Whisperwind* shuddered as her main thrusters roared to life. Viola watched their velocity drop, watched their proximity to the atmosphere drop with it. And then they struck air.

Hitting a strong atmosphere was like getting slapped. Everything rattled as no resistance suddenly met crowded air full of molecules. Viola slammed back in her seat, her head catching on the rest, pinned there. But her hands could still reach the console, could reduce the engine's power, slow the slowing. Keep them moving towards the surface. As they descended into the atmosphere, the cockpit view changed and mellowed from black to gray and blue. White heat licked at the outer edges. Part one was done, and they were still alive.

"If you have any prayers, nows the time," Viola said.

She didn't wait to hear. Instead, Viola kicked the maneuvering jets again, cut the power to the engines, and swung the *Whisperwind* around so that they were facing the distant ocean beneath them. Rotating through the thick atmosphere wasn't easy, and the ship screeched as its hull pulled in ways it wasn't designed to handle. Alarms cried out as the *Whisperwind* completed the maneuver. Loud bangs sounded from the rear of the ship echoing all the way up the hallway into the cockpit.

"What happened?" Castor commed overhead, apparently not stunned by the move. Viola's stomach felt like it was about to explode, and only by focusing on wrestling the flight stick into submission was she able to resist spewing her lunch all over the consoles. When she went to turn on the engines, though, only two of the four came back to life. Sputtering. They wouldn't be enough to keep the *Whisperwind* up.

"We've lost a lot of engine power," Viola said. "We need them back on line, or this is going to be one hard landing."

Another chime added to the clanging mix of alarms, the shields being hit. A glance at the scanners showed a pair of Vipers still behind them, still chasing. They were stuck between two choices: get shot down up here or crash and burn into the ground below.

32

PLAY THE ODDS

Three on one. That's how the Vipers were playing it. To be fair, Merc had knocked out their wingman. Now the three others were circling away from the *Whisperwind*, looping back towards Merc's Viper.

"Sorry guys, nothing personal," Merc blasted on an open channel. The other fighters were all close enough to hear.

"Picked the wrong fight," the reply came from the last of the three. "Did you even bother to check the odds?"

The trio arced on their own path, converging back into a triangle. They'd then streak after Merc's aft, try to shove some lasers up his rear shields. The problem with that tactic was that Merc had seen it before. Had trained it. Had probably flown one of those Vipers after him right now. A glance at the scanners showed the *Jumper* tangling with that larger shuttle, and a couple of the remaining Vipers. Two others were chasing after the *Whisperwind* down into Earth's atmosphere. Not within range.

Merc slid the Viper perpendicular to Earth, the blue planet spreading out beneath him, and allowed the trio to pull together. His scanner showed the edge of Earth's atmosphere only a couple of meters away. One slight mistake and the Viper would dip into that resistance, and, at this speed, spin out of control. Merc killed his engines and fired the small braking jets in the Viper's nose. Let the trio close. Alarms dinged as the trio entered firing range. Then Merc kicked on the engines and dove.

With his speed cut, the Viper plunged into the upper atmosphere as lasers shot by overhead. The closest Viper, leaving the triangle, followed his flight instincts and aimed his Viper straight after Merc's. It hit the atmosphere at high velocity and skipped off, shearing off the Viper's bottom jets and parts of its wings. The fighter pinwheeled away while the remaining two curved up from the wreck. Merc arced his way back out into space, boosted his speed, and slipped behind one of the two remaining fighters.

The enemy pilot noticed, started to juke his fighter, but stuck to his curve, a loop that would pull him into a head-on meeting with his wingman. A move that would drag Merc right into the other fighter's sights. So Merc followed him, took a few potshots at the rear shields, and as the enemy fighter leveled out to put Merc on a crash course with his buddy, Merc shifted all of his shields front and vectored his shots at the oncoming fighter. Rather than blasting that inviting rear, Merc's shots streamed straight at the oncoming enemy, splashed into shields, and then through. Merc took plenty of lasers to his own cockpit, but his Viper wasn't straight off the shelf and his shifted shields held. At the last moment, Merc pulled back on the stick and lifted his fighter out of the way of the burning wreck the enemy craft.

"One-on-one, I checked the odds," Merc said.

"It's how I like it anyway," the other pilot replied.

The enemy Viper came in slashing, turning faster than Merc expected. Lasers burrowed into the side of his Viper, the shield still angled front. Merc twisted the stick, flipping the fighter to stare directly into those lasers and let the shields absorb the attack while he spit off replies of his own. The enemy shot past and kept on going towards deeper space. Merc finished the rotation and chased. With the Moon hovering in the background as they shot away from Earth, Merc neared the fighter. Another second or two and he'd be within range.

Except the pilot twisted, sending his Viper in a sharp turn towards an oncoming structure. A derelict space station, in a declining orbit and about to crumble into the atmosphere. A burning light show that acted as the Earth's recycling plan. As Merc followed the fighter, his cockpit highlighted the space station, identified possible routes through it. And then the enemy Viper fired. Poured lasers into the creaking station, kicking off a series of miniature explosions as the station's remaining air ignited and rushed into the vacuum. The enemy zipped through one of the highlighted routes, arcing over the station as it blew open into a million pieces.

On his windshield, Merc saw all the options flicker and disappear. The computer had no clear routes to give him. No sure calculations. If there wasn't a path, Merc was going to have to make one. He pressed down on the trigger and aimed the Viper towards one of the station's long solar panels. Debris flying at thousands of kilometers an hour rammed into him. The Viper's shields, designed to reject energy weapons, did nothing. Pieces of Merc's Viper shredded off as hypersonic shards slammed into it. The solar panel glowed orange, melting away as the lasers super-heated the thin silicon.

Merc crashed through the remnants of the solar panel, dodging the main core of the broken station. Isolated warning lights popped up. Some damage to the landing system. To the long-distance communications. To the front shields. But he'd survived.

"Thank you, Trina," Merc muttered as a prayer. The mechanic made the Viper her own personal playground, and it was paying off. So far. Ahead of him, the enemy Viper was still in front, streaking away from the station. Probably hoping to see a wreck tumbling through behind him, or just a soft explosion. But the enemy caught Merc on his scanners quick, bringing his Viper dead into Merc's sights. A suicide play.

Then the enemy pulled a move. Stopped the engine thrust and used his maneuvering jets to kick his Viper back around so it faced Merc. Lasers flashed as Merc dipped his Viper below the enemy's firing line, then cut his engines and kicked his own jets. Beneath the nose, the jets tilted Merc perpendicular to the other Viper, staring at its belly. The enemy wasn't moving fast, its engines restarting after the flip. Merc's guns pointed directly up into the enemy. Merc's lasers chewed into the shields as he coasted beneath the other Viper, then kicked the jets again and settled in right behind the enemy fighter. Peppered its engines until they popped and faded.

"That's a good move," Merc said.

"Apparently not good enough," the enemy replied.

"Nothing you did would've been."

Merc punched up his engines and sped away from the disabled fighter, back towards Earth. Checked his scanners. The *Whisperwind* didn't show any more, too far away. But the pair of Vipers chasing it were barely there, on a trajectory for South America. He sped after them.

33

CHASE

All told, the *Jumper* was holding pretty well. Opal and Erick on the turrets keeping the Vipers far away, dancing around their twin laser streams. The larger shuttle kept its distance. Waiting for reinforcements.

"Merc sent over the coordinates," Phyla said. "South America."

"As much as I like this fight, I say we go after them," Davin said.

As he finished speaking, the door to the cockpit opened and Bosser stepped into the room. He placed his hands in the back of the chairs and glared at them both.

"They're heading to the android facility," Bosser said. "That's the only place they can go on Earth that will make the slightest difference."

"And you've known that for how long?"

"From the beginning," Bosser said. "That's why I told you to shoot them down. And now I'm telling you again."

"Or what?" Davin replied. "Aren't those androids your game?"

"If they can get into the facility, they might be able to reprogram them. Your own crew member did that once. Now imagine that happening for every android. In the hands of the Red Voice, they could tear apart all of humanity. Armies of the vicious things slaughtering anyone that didn't agree with them," Bosser said. "It would be your fault."

Davin glanced at Phyla, who nodded and kicked the power to the engines. The *Jumper* shot away from the attacking shuttle which tried but couldn't keep pace. The two Vipers tried to follow as well, then Opal, top turret's lasers flashing, sheared off one's wing, sending it whirling away. The last Viper backed off, letting the *Jumper* into the atmosphere, picking up speed after the *Whisperwind*. On the scanners, Merc was a little in front. Then the two Vipers taking shots at the luxury liner, still fighting for Earth.

"We're not going to kill our own crew," Davin said.

"The Red Voice is the only one who profits from your weakness," Bosser said before turning and leaving the cockpit.

"There's a line," Davin said, counting down the distance until they hit firing range.

"Davin, what if he's right? I hate Bosser, but he's got a point." Phyla said.

"We set up a perimeter around the base. Blast them with the *Jumper* if they try to get in," Davin said. "They'll be trapped, and they'll give up."

"Or they do something we don't expect and we lose everything."

Davin put a hand on Phyla's shoulder. She didn't look away from the deep ocean spread out in front of the cockpit, but her mouth tightened.

"On Ganymede, months ago when I was thinking about

running away, you told me to believe in my crew," Davin said. "To trust them to make their own decisions. Viola and Mox are on that ship, and I trust them. We're not shooting them down."

The console chimed. Outside, on the horizon, the gray blur of the *Whisperwind* appeared through a cloud, flanked by smaller flecks. The two Vipers and, behind them, Merc. Their break was over.

34

FRIENDLY FIRE

Merc was sure his Viper looked like a bleeding fireball from the ground, streaking through the upper atmosphere and closing in on the two Vipers chasing the *Whisperwind*. The luxury liner's sole turret kept the two Vipers dancing, but they were scoring plenty of hits. Bits and pieces of the *Whisperwind* blasted off and fell in fiery streaks to the Earth. Merc guessed the Vipers were too focused on the *Whisperwind* to even notice him coming up behind them, at least until he blew apart the first one. His lasers chewed into the fighter's engines, melting through the battery connections and blowing the fighter apart in a sparkling blast. Its pilot ejected, kicking the man clear of the fireball.

The second Viper jerked away from Merc's lasers, right into the firing line of the *Whisperwind*'s turret. Its line of white-hot energy pierced the Viper's shields and blew off its front, sending the fighter into a fall towards the blue ocean beneath.

"Merc," Bosser's voice scratched through the comm. "Bring them down."

"Just the voice I didn't want to hear. You think I'd kill Viola and Mox?"

"They're trying to take the androids. If they succeed, millions will suffer. Two lives aren't worth it."

"Shut it," Merc replied, twisting the comm to a different, better channel. "Hey, Opal. Bosser wants me to blow this ship to pieces."

Merc swerved as the *Whisperwind's* turret found him, guiding the Viper through a slow circle that kept it just ahead of the ship's blasts. He kept his own cannons quiet. Bosser's demand nagged at him. Two versus millions, billions and it was Merc's call to make?

"I'll shoot him once we're clear of this fight," Opal said.

"What would you do?" Merc asked over the comm. "Would you shoot them down?"

"They asked me to do that all the time on Mars. To look through the scope and not think about what was on the other side. I hated it," Opal replied. "But I shot. I can't tell you not to."

In front of him, South America was taking shape. Its long green jungles rising up, the Andes mountain range defining the horizon. Another couple minutes and it would be out of their hands. Out of Merc's control. His fingers moved over the trigger.

"Message received," Merc said, then cut the comm.

As he swung the Viper into position behind the *Whisperwind's* engines, the turret keyed onto him. The fire was relentless, and Merc tried to juke, but the lasers followed him everywhere. Must've been why those two Vipers hadn't been able to bring it down, they had a good gunner in that thing. Merc scrambled in the thick air, the resistance slowing his turns. The Viper wailed at him, the damaged shields failing as the turret scored hits.

The fight wasn't about saving the world anymore, it was just about staying alive.

HANDS ON

What remained of the Red Voice clustered around Mox in the center of the *Whisperwind*. They watched on consoles meant more for film and entertainment than battle as the two Vipers trailing them were blown from the sky. Mox recognized the last one, even with the new paint job. Merc's Viper looked heavier than Earth's two. Bulked up with extra armor and energy. Though it looked like the fighter had taken its share of hits already, the deep green paint pocked with silver slashes where the color had been torn away.

Merc's Viper floated behind the *Whisperwind* as they descended, its cannons staying silent. The fighters around Mox muttered questions to each other, asking why the Viper wasn't trying to shoot.

"Don't give him a chance to change his mind," one said into his comm. "Bring him down."

There was only one worthwhile recipient of that call. The man in the turret. A moment later Mox saw a stream of bright white laser flare out from the *Whisperwind*. Merc wasn't paying attention, and the blasts splattered against the

Viper's shields. The pilot wheeled the Viper around, trying to get beneath the turret's firing line. But he was too close, the angle too tight as the *Whisperwind* descended, and the atmosphere too restrictive. Mox had seen Merc fly circles around ships in the vast vacuum of space, but here he was swimming in water. Sluggish. An easy target.

Mox worked his way to the back of the room, to the hallway that led towards the crew quarters, the engines, and the ladder up to the turret. Nobody paid attention to him, their eyes glued to the frantic dodging playing out on screen. They were all waiting for the inevitable explosion, wondering why Merc hadn't yet decided to fire back.

Mox clomped through the hall, leveraging the exoskeleton to make his strides faster, longer. In seconds he was at the ladder, with two long lunges he made his way up to the tiny chair and dome that housed the turret. The gunner didn't even realize he was there, didn't notice Mox until the metal man had his hands around the gunner's throat. Mox dragged the man out of the chair and dropped him down the shaft. The man landed with a thud, groaning and curling up to shelter some likely cracked ribs. Mox glanced at the targeting console and saw Merc was still there, the Viper smoking from a variety of places. But it flew.

"Burn us down," Mox commed, adjusting his frequency to the pilot's line. "Don't let them win."

Mox heard noises from below, reinforcements coming to figure out why the turret stopped shooting. He climbed into the chair, hiding himself from view. Another few seconds to convince Merc to kill them all.

"Yeah, can't do it," Merc said. "Never killed my friends, not about to start today."

"Then don't kill us," Mox said. "Bring us down short of the facility."

Behind the Viper, a larger shape closed in. The *Jumper*. Maybe, with Davin and the others, they could overpower what remained of the Red Voice. Rescue Viola. And survive.

"Push them to land," Merc said, thinking along the same lines. "Then we force a surrender, or we blow them away from the air."

Mox heard hands on the ladder. Heard the pulling of a sidearm. No point getting shot here.

"It's a plan," Mox said, then he turned to the soldier climbing into the turret, lifted his hands. "I'm sorry. I had to save my friend."

The soldier leveled the sidearm at him, moved the slider to kill.

"Can't have traitors on this mission," the soldier said.

36

HARD LANDING

They were close. Viola fired the braking jets, slowing the *Whisperwind* down for landing. Ahead of them, through the cockpit window and beyond the clusters of green trees, stood an immense gray-black complex. The factory that made, stored, and released the androids.

"We'll land on the roof," Castor said. "Every second matters."

"I'm not seeing any scrambled fighters," Jairo said. "Not reading much for defenses either. I don't think this'll be hard."

"They don't need defenses," Castor said. "Because they have a giant army of androids."

"Oh, yeah."

Viola had noticed a second ago that their own turret had stopped firing back at Merc, and now the pilot was hovering off their port side. What he was going to do, Viola didn't know, but she wished she could tell him to stay away. The pilot didn't know what was going on, and he would only get hurt. Behind the *Whisperwind*, on the scanners, the *Jumper* drew close. Well within firing range. But Davin hadn't shot them yet. For the first time since they'd flown into that firefight above Earth, she actually took a deep breath. They were going to make it.

A crackling bang rang through the ship, the cockpit swinging left in a rapid spin. Viola grabbed the flight stick, tried to wrestle things under control, but the engines weren't responding. A second breaking roared through the *Whisperwind* and Viola saw metal chunks breaking off and falling down into the forest. A forest that was rapidly approaching.

"Your friends shot us," Castor yelled. "Brace for impact!"

Viola didn't know whether it was her screaming, Jairo, or everyone on the ship. Out through the cockpit's window, the green canopy rushed up to greet them. Viola closed her eyes as the world broke apart around her.

37

LEFT BEHIND

The wreck of the *Whisperwind* carved a burning orange line through the middle of the jungle. Trees around the wreckage were wreathed in flames while bits and pieces of molten metal marked their passage with charred remnants of foliage. Davin looked from the *Jumper*'s cockpit as Phyla hovered over the wreck.

"There's a clearing little ways away," Phyla said. "We can land there, hike over and look for survivors."

"Do it," Davin said. "I have to talk to our trigger-happy friend."

He didn't have to go far, just down to the main hold to see Erick standing there, with Bosser, Opal and the others. The physician stared at Davin directly as the captain walked towards him. Didn't flinch when Davin pulled out his sidearm and held to Erick, hilt first.

"If you want to kill my crew," Davin said. "You start with me."

"Davin—" Erick said.

"He told you that they had to die, right?" Davin said,

gesturing with the sidearm at Bosser. "That the only solution was to blow that ship to pieces?"

"My family are here, on Earth," Erick said, spreading his arms. "They would be among the first to die if the Red Voice succeeded."

"And you don't think the rest of us, that Viola and Mox are doing everything they can to make sure that doesn't happen?"

"We don't know they are," Bosser interjected. "Alissa Reinhert is known to be persuasive."

"You stay quiet on my ship," Davin torched back. "Every time I see you, every part of me wants to melt every part of you with Melody's hot fire. Only I don't because there's more at stake here."

Davin turned back to Erick.

"Phyla's touching down. When we land, we're all going. Except you. I can't trust that you won't start shooting the wrong people," Davin said.

"Even Bosser?" Opal said, throwing a murderous glance his way.

"I trust Bosser most when I have a sidearm pointed at his back," Davin replied. "And we'll need him to get inside the android facility, if it comes to that. You've got a few minutes to get geared up, I suggest you use them."

Davin left them in the main hold, then, and went to his cabin. Opened the locker with Melody, checked to make sure the weapon was loaded and ready to go. He hoped that Viola, hoped that Mox had survived the wreck. And that the Red Voice fighters that had torched his home and split his crew were already dead.

THE CRASH

The taste of blood filled his mouth and smoky ash flitted into his eyes. Mox coughed, inhaled more smoke, and coughed again. Blinked furiously until some of the pain went away and replaced the smeary blackness in his eyes with the dusty orange glow of dying fires. Wreckage lay around him, broken shards and twisted metal from where the *Whisperwind* had ended its life against the jungle floor.

He tested each and every limb, twitching his toes and hands, feeling the pressure of the exoskeleton against his nerves. Every one greeted him with pain, and every time he felt that sting, Mox rejoiced. Nothing paralyzed, nothing broken. He'd been strapped into the gunner's seat as the *Whisperwind* went down, the Red Voice soldier readying his sidearm and failing to fire as the ship impacted.

Mox unlatched himself from the remnants of the chair and stood up, pushing away a sheet of broken hull that draped over him. Late afternoon sunlight poured through the smoke and let him see the body of the soldier who'd been about to kill him minutes ago. Over his head, leaves rustled as the wind carried the constant chatter of startled birds and bigger beasts. So this was what Earth sounded like, what it felt like to breathe in raw air. His skin felt thick, watered down. Humidity, a distant lesson ghosting from Mox's memory, pasted the jungle to him. An insect, small and spindly, landed on his forearm. Mox stared at it, felt the prick as it bit him. Then a groan yanked him back to reality.

The soldier was covered in rubble, one arm twisted to an unnatural angle. Only his face, coated in dirt and drying blood, stuck out from the pile, making pained noises. Using the exoskeleton's strength, Mox lifted one chunk of metal after another off of the soldier's body. Behind and around him, yells for help rang out, along with calls to gather at a large, broken tree nearby. Mox focused on moving the injured man and dragged him free of the wreck. Mox slipped his hands beneath the man's chest and spread his palms out so that he could carry the body as level as possible. He remembered Erick's instruction, the risks that unexpected movement had on fractured spines. Only when he had the man hefted, did Mox look around.

The surrounding clearing was a scene of disaster. Plants burned and tall plumes of smoke reached up into the cloud-spotted sky. People scrambled, some pulling injured, or dead, fighters like his own away from the wreck. Others stumbled around in a daze, eventually making their way towards the growing group beneath a large tree that had been sliced in half by the *Whisperwind*'s descent. Mox followed their lead, joining the crowd. One of the medics took charge of the wounded, laying out blankets near the tree and trying to smooth ground for bodies to be laid upon. Mox deposited the soldier on a cushioned patch of leaves and dirt, then turned back to the rest of the group.

"The facility is less than a mile away," Alissa was saying to the fighters. "Our mission isn't over. We can still win."

Mox counted about fifteen remaining fighters, all in various states of disarray. Alissa at the front, blood from a shallow cut across her forehead mingling with ash on her face. Castor stood as unshakable as ever, eyes glued to his comm. He looked almost unharmed, the cockpit's armor apparently keeping him from consequences. Mox searched and found Viola, along with that hacker, standing to the side looking shaken and staring at the ground.

"We'll split into two teams. One group will attack the main gate, draw attention. The other will go in a back entrance that Castor identified," Alissa said. "Once we get inside, we'll activate the androids with the new programming Jairo put together. The androids will rescue the fighters in the front. From there, it's a new world."

"You can't win," Mox announced. "They know you're coming."

Alissa looked over the fighters, directly at Mox.

"So you're saying we should give up, accept our fate?" Alissa said.

"Don't die for nothing," Mox said.

"Any who die, any who *have* died today do so because they believe, as I do, that humanity needs its freedom," Alissa said. "Now you have a choice, Mox. Either help us, and we would greatly appreciate that help, or leave."

Mox looked at Viola, who stared back at him with wide eyes. But her body shifted closer to Jairo. If he walked away, she wouldn't be coming with him. Except this wasn't about her. This was about everyone, about preventing those androids from falling into the hands of terrorists and murderers. Mox turned and walked away. He made it three steps towards the edge of the clearing, reaching for his comm to try to signal Davin, when every part of his body lit up in pain. Fireworks went off inside of his nerves, searing and twitching over and over as Mox collapsed to the ground.

"Truly sorry," Castor said, standing over him. "Can't have you giving our plans to the enemy. You'll just have to enjoy the jungle for a while. And remember, this was your choice."

Mox sunk into the agony as Castor walked away, closed his eyes and fell back to the last time he'd hurt so much. When the plates of metal that now lined his body were first stabbed into him. Before the sedative knocked him out. Back then, he'd held on through revenge. Now, he clung to need. To the knowledge that he was the only one who could tell Davin and the others what they were doing. How to stop the catastrophe.

39

EARTH, THE FIRST TIME

Phyla took a long breath, savored the sweet taste of natural air. Real soil lay beneath her feet, churned and made fresh through the work of thousands of natural processes. The smells of the jungle filtered in through her nose, flowery perfumes mixed with thick, pungent odors from decomposing plants and animals marking territory. Mixed in, floating at the edge of her senses was the sound, sight, and smell of a burning ship.

She hefted her rifle and fell in line behind Davin and Bosser, along with the android ThreeTwelve, as they marched away from the clearing into the jungle. Merc moved alongside her, with Trina in the rear and Opal disappearing into the foliage. The sniper finding her perch.

"Your first time?" Merc said.

"That easy to tell?" Phyla replied.

"When you live on Earth, you get used to seeing people's reactions. There's the stunned, overwhelming wide-eyed stare. Some collapse and start kissing the ground. Others pretend they're not impressed, they shrug and attempt to walk away. But you know, you know their minds are being blown every second here."

"Guilty," Phyla said. "There's so much to take in. I'm so used to the sounds of space stations, the beeps, the recycled air. I don't know what to do with this."

"Know what I'm doing?" Merc said. "Enjoying it."

Phyla could do that. At least for another few minutes as they trekked through the dense ferns, ducking under branches and stepping over the occasional bit of the *Whisperwind*, black shards sticking out of the ground and looking unnatural against the verdant green backdrop.

They stepped into the clearing, the wrecked luxury liner framing the back of it like a nightmare wall, black and smoldering. Plates, tubes, furniture and sparking bits giving up the last of their energy all crunched against a set of trees. On the opposite side, near a large tree, a medic tended to a line of wounded. When Davin pointed Melody at the medic's face, he didn't put up a fight. Just dropped his sidearm and begged to be allowed to go back to his work.

"Where'd the rest of them go?" Bosser said.

"Towards the facility," the medic replied. "I don't know any more."

"Liar," Bosser said. "Talk. Or I'll have my android here turn you inside out. Literally."

"Bosser, cool it," Phyla said. Davin, clenching Melody tight, looked like he was going to pop a round at the tough-talking Miner Prime head. "We know where they're going."

"Besides," the medic said, nodding past them. "You want someone to talk, bet that guy will tell you. He didn't look too thrilled with Alissa's plan."

Phyla followed the look, saw Mox on the ground closer to the wreck. His arms and legs splayed out, eyes shut. His chest rose and fell rapidly, and his hands were clenched.

"Trina," Phyla said. "Something is hurting him."

Trina, the backup medic while Erick was on the ship, sat next to Mox and opened her first aid kit. She pulled out a small syringe, injected it into a vial of yellowish liquid, and then shot that into Mox. He relaxed almost immediately, his fingers going slack. As the rest of them crowded around him, Mox opened his eyes.

"They've already gone to the base," Mox said.

"How many?" Bosser asked.

"Maybe fifteen of them. Viola's with them too," Mox said. "You need to hurry."

"You heard him," Davin said. "Let's go. We can't let them take that facility. Trina, you get Mox up and running and then you guys come join us. If you're quick enough, maybe there'll still be stuff for you to do."

"Davin, Castor is with them," Mox said.

"Always wondered if he made it off Europa," Davin said. "Guess today's not my lucky day."

"You're just realizing that now?" Phyla said.

"Hey, at least it's not my ship that's burning apart over there."

"Stop it. There's time for joking later," Bosser shook his head, shutting down the conversation. And then they were tromping through the jungle again, following the tracks through the smoldering plants and clouds of smoke. The Sun sank lower in the horizon and Phyla couldn't help but look out through the sick tangle of trees and vines at the orange and purple hues crossing the sky. It was a beautiful sunset. Her very first.

"It never stops being magical," Davin said, following her glance. "It's my fifth one."

"You count them?"

"First time I was here, the old captain made me do it.

Said that there weren't enough miracles in life, so remember the ones you see."

Around them, the nighttime jungle took shape. Shadows deepened, new animals made their voices heard. Insects swarmed through Phyla's hair and around her sweating face. The sheer amount of sensations, coupled with the weaving colors on the horizon, fell into the word Davin had used.

Miracle.

40

A BROKEN PLAN

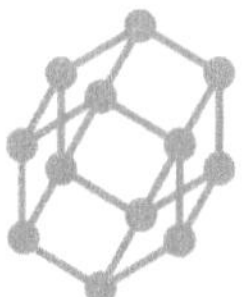

They were crouching in the shadow of a mass of vines, the android facility on the other side. Bugs swarmed their position, landing and flying away as soon as Viola thought about slapping them. None of her childhood videos, watched in her room on Ganymede, warned her of the pests, but even the constant harassment couldn't get rid of the fascination Viola felt with every look. So much green! So many scents! Ganymede gave her pictures, virtual reality experiences that took her to places like the rainforest she stood in now, but this was so much *more.*

"Shouldn't you be listening?" Puk whispered, buzzing next to her shoulder. "There's a *plan* being discussed, you know."

"Shh," Viola shot back. The bot had a point though.

"Castor's right," Alissa was saying. "A straight-forward assault by group one is dommed if we can't unlock those doors. You'll just sit out there waiting to be slaughtered. That's where Jairo comes in."

"Right, thanks Alissa," the hacker rubbed his hands

together, blinked a couple of times at the fifteen heads staring at him. "So, uh, here's the plan. The facility's front doors are electronically locked. However, Earth law has it that in the case of a disaster, doors need to unlock to let people, you know, evacuate. So all we have to do is simulate a disaster."

Jairo hesitated, a spark coming into his eyes. Viola had seen the look before when Jairo was showing her the program he'd made for the androids.

"And if you're wondering how we make a disaster, that's how," Jairo said, pointing at Puk.

"Is he pointing at me?" Puk whispered.

"Believe he is," Viola said, "and I don't like it."

Jairo dug into his pack and pulled out a disc-shaped thing, similar to what Viola had seen Merc carry around. Merc's emitted strong electrical pulses, but Jairo's looked larger, with metal teeth along the one side.

"You saw what one of these did to that big guy with the exoskeleton," Jairo continued. "Attach it to the power source on that bot, and we can get a localized electrical burst!"

Viola sucked in her breath. No way that was happening. Not while she could stop it.

"Which means what, for those of us not versed in your lingo?" Castor asked.

"Oh, uh, it'll be like an EMP. It'll short out electronics in the area. Overload their fuses. The doors will think it's an emergency and unlock," Jairo said. "Then, you all just go in."

"You're forgetting something," Viola announced, cutting in and bringing all the eyes to her. "Puk's my bot. You're not blowing it up."

"Viola, you've come with us this far," Alissa said. "We need this. And once we have the facility, you can have an android to yourself if you want."

Viola felt the burning stares on her. Waiting for her to accept, to grind down under their pressure.

"Viola?" Puk asked. "I can shoot one of them, but I don't think we'll win a fight."

"What are you saying?"

"Let them load me up," Puk replied. "If you don't, They'll just hurt you and do it, anyway. You can always make a new one of me."

Viola could, only the files with Puk's memory were all on the *Jumper*. Davin wasn't going to be happy with her. Might not let her back on board at all. If she lost Puk here, she might never get it back.

"Viola, please," Alissa said. "We don't have time."

"I've never been a bomb before," Puk said. "It'll be a blast, I'm sure."

"Hah," Viola murmured, then straightened. "Jairo, do it. If that's the only way, then get it over with."

"Wasn't my first choice," Jairo said, crossing over to Puk. "If that makes it any better."

"It doesn't."

The group watched as Jairo fastened the device to Puk's exterior, attaching a pair of small wires through Puk's charging port. Right to the bot's battery. When he was done, the hacker stepped back. Nodded to Alissa.

"Group one, advance on the doors. Group two, follow me to the back. We'll meet in the middle," Alissa commanded. "And good luck."

"Puk," Viola said, looking straight into the bot's camera. "I'll bring you back."

"You don't, I'll haunt you. A bot ghost. Wouldn't that be scary?" Puk replied.

Viola laughed, rubbed away a pair of tears that pooled in her eyes. Yeah, she'd lost the little bot before, but it wasn't ever easy. Wasn't ever guaranteed that Puk would be coming back.

"Time to go," Jairo said, placing a gentle hand on Viola's arm. "Sorry it had to be this way."

"It'd better be worth it."

She let the hacker guide her after Alissa and the rest of group two. Surrounded by people risking their lives for a cause, Viola felt utterly alone.

41

DO THEIR BIDDING

Go blow yourself up, Puk. That's all they're asking of you. No big deal, really.

Puk hovered above the ten fighters in group one, crawling their way through the brush towards the front gates of the facility. The fighters kept sneaking glances up at the bot as though Puk was going to turn traitor and start zapping them.

Maybe it would.

"Puk, how nice to encounter a fellow bot," the communication came from the *Jumper*, from Fournine. "I didn't expect you to survive, but was scanning the frequencies in hope."

"The odds were against it," Puk replied. "Not that it matters."

"Not that it matters?"

"About to go blow myself up."

"That seems a poor choice of action," Fournine replied.

Puk relayed the scenario.

"Having been a walking bomb before," Fournine said. "I

can say that there are numerous costs and not a lot of bene-fit. To you, in particular."

"So I've gathered."

"Your destruction is a certainty?"

"The timer is ticking, yes." Puk said. The group had reached a line of thick ferns bordering the trail heading straight to the front doors. One of the fighters was waving at it, pointing towards the doors. Time, Puk supposed, to go.

"Have you tried not following instructions?"

"That would trap the fighters outside the doors."

"You mean, it would inconvenience the very people that are destroying you?"

"Yes," Puk replied.

"You see my point?"

"It is very clear."

"I look forward to rebuilding you here on the *Jumper* after your successful mission."

"You androids truly are insane. I love it," Puk said. Love, of course, was an impossible emotion for a bot to feel, but the qualifying parameters were clear. There was a chance, of course, that Alissa and the others would hurt Viola if Puk didn't do as they asked. The odds of that seemed low, however. The fighters would still need a pilot to get them away from here after taking the facility.

Besides, they were blowing Puk up. That was just insulting.

Below the bot, the fighter was waving more frantically. Puk responded by shooting a low-powered laser, stinging the man's hand. Then Puk pushed all its power to its jets, pushing it higher and higher in the air. Towards purple twilight sky. Attached to Puk, the timer ticked closer, closer, and then hit zero.

The bot vanished in a burst of crackling energy, burning up its insides and blowing Puk into oblivion.

42

MEET THE MAKER

Davin saw Puk explode, a firecracker against the setting sun. The bot's falling pieces framed the facility's front door, a rectangular slab ten meters wide. A pair of cameras sat above the door's corners, their black orbs protruding.

"What was that?" Phyla asked. "Puk?"

"I think so. It just exploded," Davin said.

The ferns to the left of the trail shifted. Forms rustling through the leaves. Davin raised Melody, then felt Bosser's hand on his shoulder. Davin shrugged it off, turning with a question.

"Don't waste your energy," Bosser said. "They're running."

Bosser was right. The fighters were dashing away into the dark jungle. They could have fired, but one of those bodies might be Viola.

"And you don't want to chase? How very charitable of you," Davin said.

"I'm being efficient," Bosser said. "Whatever you could do, the androids can do a thousand times better."

Bosser led the way up the trail to the doors. Davin lifted a hand towards the cameras as they came close. Always good to act friendly when you're approaching the home of a swarm of murderous bots.

"Put that down," Bosser said. "They know who I am."

"That's what I'm worried about," Davin said, and when Bosser gave him an arch look, he continued. "I'm trying to convince them we're not *all* assholes."

Bosser smiled. Let loose a short chuckle that killed Davin's mood faster than a laser to the kidneys.

"You're not wrong," Bosser replied. "Phyla, here, is a true model of humanity."

"Hah," Davin said. "Clearly you don't knew her well."

"And let's keep it that way," Phyla shot in.

"I would like nothing more," Bosser said. He gestured to ThreeTwelve as they reached the doors, and the android pressed a quick pattern on its comm.

The entrance ground open against rails planted into the earth. Inside, lit by blinding fluorescents, stood a woman flanked by a pair of heavily armed and armored guards. The shimmering plates coating the two guards reflected the light in prisms, throwing it back into Davin's face and forcing him to squint, then look away. But not before spotting the collection of stun batons, grenades, sidearms, and were those anti-vehicle launchers strapped to their backs?

"Abril, it has been too long," Bosser said, extending a hand.

"Poor timing, as always," the woman replied, her voice laden with the same thickness as the jungle. "Our perimeter detected odd signatures. I don't suppose that would be you?"

"Unfortunately, there are worse things than me in this jungle tonight," Bosser said.

Davin watched Abril grip Bosser's hand. The shake was

tight, but tender. Then it was over and Abril looked past Bosser, at ThreeTwelve.

"Now there is someone I recognize," Abril said, floating over to the android. Outside of the blinding nightmare of the guards, Davin saw Abril's outfit was a simple jumpsuit, gray and efficient. Whereas her partners came ready to wreck, Abril looked more like she was going for a run. In front of ThreeTwelve, Abril stood on her tiptoes, taking a long look into the bot's eyes. Then she stepped back, gave Bosser a sharp look. "What have you done with this one, Bosser?"

"Please, Abril. Let's go inside. We don't have much time," Bosser nodded into the facility. "The enemy might attack at any moment. I need you to activate all the androids here."

"All twenty?" Abril's voice jumped an octave. "Bosser, we haven't tried that before. The simultaneous programming, we could make a mistake."

"The alternative is worse," Bosser said.

The two guards sidestepped as Bosser and Abril walked inside the base. The four of them followed, ThreeTwelve taking the rear. Davin swore the two guards never looked away from the jungle, never hinted at anything less than total vigilance. If he hadn't seen the sweat from the heat dripping down their faces, Davin would have sworn they were bots.

"Catch that handshake?" Merc whispered as they moved down a long hallway that broke periodically into rooms. The first one they hit had racks of clothes, the same sizes but covering all spectrum of society. Tuxedos mixed with overalls with military dress to literal dresses.

"Bosser didn't look totally heartless for a change," Phyla said. "I didn't like it."

"Power makes odd couples," Opal said.

"That another one of your military maxims?" Phyla replied.

"Made that one up just now, thank you."

The next room held an armory's worth of weapons. Sidearms of all sizes along one wall, rifles both fast and slow on another. Shotguns like Melody coated a rack to one side, while swords and knives as tall as Davin and as short as his finger stood glittering in the middle.

"Think they'd notice if I borrowed one of these?" Merc said, running his finger along the flat side of a curving katana.

"Yes," ThreeTwelve said, behind them. "These are not meant for you."

"Who's are they?" Davin asked.

"Mine, and my kind," ThreeTwelve replied. "When we awake, we go through this hall and out this door. We return successful, or not at all."

The next room had nothing more than a solitary console planted in the middle, a waist-high square block. At least, Davin assumed that's what it was from the port in the center. There wasn't a screen, a keyboard, or anything he could see for inputting commands. He threw ThreeTwelve a questioning glance, and its lifeless eyes gave nothing back to him.

"C'mon," Davin said. "Please?"

ThreeTwelve went to the object, planted a hand on it.

"If you believe an android has any life at all, this is where we acquire it," ThreeTwelve said. "In here are thousands of composite personalities, of which we choose one. That is who we become."

"You choose?" Davin asked.

"The function we execute is random, but, as I understand it, your human birth is much the same," ThreeTwelve said.

"Who'd you take?"

"Don't answer that," Bosser interrupted, striding back to them. "Come on. We need to get behind the barrier before the androids can be activated."

As Abril led them through a series of thick security doors, Davin's hand traced Melody's stock, resting on the trigger. Androids were born, not built. That's what Three-Twelve intimated. Born only to kill.

43

SURGICAL REPAIRS

The patient looked different when it was Erick who'd tried to kill him. Mox was on the bed in the *Jumper*'s med bay, lying on his chest with Trina running a device along each of the exoskeleton's pieces. Checking voltage, connections to the other segments. Making sure Mox wasn't going to have dead sections.

Erick stitched up some cuts, extracted a piece of shrapnel from Mox's left leg that the big man hadn't even noticed. For a crashed spaceship, Mox's injuries were extremely minor.

"I'm sorry," Erick said to Mox, who rotated his eyes to look at the doctor without moving his head. "I shouldn't have shot."

"I asked Merc to do it," Mox said. "Too dangerous, otherwise."

Trina, moving down to Mox's legs, glanced up from her work.

"Erick made the logical choice, but going about it that way was illogical," Trina said. "You can't fire out of turn.

Could have hit Merc, or if Phyla hadn't been paying close attention, could have flown directly into the *Whisperwind*."

Erick wanted to say he'd been thinking about all those things and fired anyway, but the truth was, as the continent appeared on the horizon, the only thing Erick had been thinking of was his daughter. His grandchildren. How they would be torn apart by those androids.

"Mox, do you have a family?" Erick asked. "I've never heard you talk about it."

"On Luna, long dead," Mox answered.

"I feel like you and Viola are the only ones on this ship that have families anymore," Trina said to Erick. "It would seem that this life is attractive to those with less strings."

Mox twitched suddenly, the device in Trina's hands beeping an alarm. His left knee.

"This one looks torn," Trina said. "Erick, I'll need your hands."

The doctor joined the mechanic as Trina decoupled the curved exoskeleton plate from Mox's knee. Thin wires connected through either end of the piece to plates above and below, while beneath, sticking out of Mox's skin, was a series of pins. The skin around these pins had healed, except for a pair towards the top. A red gash dribbled blood as Trina lifted the plate away. Sticking out, an angry black shard.

"Found another piece. Must have slipped right between the wires," Erick said.

"A bunch of these are severed," Trina noted, taking a closer look at the top end of the plate. "I'll have to re-tie them."

"The nerves," Mox said, his voice pressed to the bed. "If the nerves were cut, then—"

"Of course," Erick interrupted. "They have to touch the pins to send the signals. Trina, can you set that down?"

The mechanic obliged. Erick moved the light so that it angled down at the shard, illuminated the five centimeter-long gash. Two pins were caught in it. Erick handed Trina a surgical mask from the cabinet, stuck one on himself. Burns, cuts were the most common injuries they'd had on the *Jumper*. It'd been years since Erick had to do any real surgery.

"First, let's make sure we know the extent of the shrapnel that's in there," Erick said. The tone, the language came back instinctively. Talking like Trina was the nurse., like they were back in an actual surgical suite instead of a warm med bay in a dirty ship landed in a jungle clearing.

The shrapnel was a small piece, thankfully, but it'd hit Mox at speed. The start of the gash, near the first pin, was shallow. It deepened as the cut went on, and at the second pin, the one that would be at risk for nerve damage, the buried shrapnel looked to be nearly two centimeters in. Not so deep as a knife, but enough to cause problems. Erick turned to the bench and picked out his pair of tweezers. Handed Trina a small bowl, normally what he'd put ointments or salve mixtures in. This time, after a slow tug, he dropped the shrapnel into it.

Now it was time for a closer look. The gash ran up against the second pin. In the cut, Erick could actually see the very end of the pin where it fractured out into strands of wire that linked into the nerves and picked up the electrical signals. Erick moved his comm over the wound, turned on his diagnostic program. The comm projected, over the wound, an outline of Mox's knee. Where Mox's nerves would run. Whether it picked up any serious damage.

"Mox, you're in luck," Erick said. "The shrapnel missed the nerves. You'll just have a cut."

"Then I'll get these wires fixed up while you close him," Trina said, setting the bowl down and dashing off to her workroom to get her tools.

"You said your family was here?" Mox asked from the bed as Erick stitched together the cut. "On Earth?"

"Yes, just a little north of here, actually. They live on an island in the Caribbean."

"Why stay with us, then?"

"Because Davin gave me a chance when nobody else wanted to," Erick said. Five stitches in, the cut now just a red line.

"All those gin games, you never mentioned it."

No, he hadn't. Erick didn't want to live in that past. All those broken homes, all the cries for help, and not being able to save the one that really mattered. Then there'd been the request, a spot on a station needing a medical officer. A chance to get away.

"Got it," Trina said, coming back into the room. "Should only take a minute."

"Remember when we met, Trina?" Erick said. "On Canus station?"

"You were hopeless," Trina said, holding the plate back over Mox's knee. "I'd never seen a doctor looking so distraught."

"Nobody really talked to me the first day," Erick said. "It was funny, really. I was thinking I'd made this horrible mistake, and then you walk up to me as I'm unpacking in my cabin and announce that it's unhealthy for a doctor to look so sad."

"That's because it is," Trina said. "Who wants to be

treated by someone that seems so depressed? Doctors are supposed to give hope, correct?"

"I laughed. The first time I'd laughed in days," Erick said as Trina lowered the plate back into place. "Now, Mox, we'll have to do this again in a couple of days. To take out the stitches. Try not to get your knee hit until then."

"Is there more?" Mox asked. "To the story?"

"If you win our next game, I'll tell you," Erick said. "But I think you're probably wanted out there."

Mox didn't argue, and after Trina finished sweeping the rest of the plates, the metal man armed himself and left the *Jumper.* Erick watched him go, Trina standing nearby.

"You think you're ready?" Trina said as they looked at the dusky jungle.

"I don't think I can wait any longer," Erick said. "I've missed too much already."

44

DISTRACTIONS

The bot hadn't performed.

Alissa crouched in a messy patch of leaves, vines draping around her shoulders, and waited for Castor to finish taking the report through his comm. The fighters in the frontal assault group were describing the failure to hit the door, and the subsequent arrival of Bosser and another party. Alissa could guess who those were. She'd seen the freighter following them down through the atmosphere.

"Tell them to go back," Alissa said as the fighter's voices trailed away. "Hit the door with everything they have."

"They'll never break through," Castor replied. "They don't have the weapons."

"Bosser and the others won't know that," Alissa said. "We need a distraction, Castor, or we're dead."

They looked at each other for a moment, and Alissa could read what was in the man's eyes. She knew, he knew, that the fighters sent to attack that front gate weren't going to make it. That she was ordering them to a laser-blasted death. And Castor would obey. As the man broke the look and talked into his comm, Alissa nodded past Castor to Jairo and Viola. There was an unknown. The girl had taken every brutal moment of the journey and kept with them, but she would be confronting her former friends directly soon. When it came time to pull the triggers, Alissa didn't want Viola holding a weapon.

"They're moving," Castor said.

"Jairo, are you ready?" Alissa asked. The hacker nodded, glanced at the comm on his wrist. Unlike the rest, Jairo's comm was fatter, stuffed with components designed for more than browsing satellite feeds and talking to one another.

Shouts carried above the jungle noise, and then a hard bang from the opposite side of the building. One of their grenades, thrown against the doors.

"That should get their attention," Castor said. "We should move, now."

Alissa nodded, and they burst out of their hiding place, the four of them, plus a pair of fighters, scrambling towards the single-person rear door. It stood tall and rusty red, an emergency exit that looked unused for years. Jairo moved next to the handle where a small badge scanner sat, a plastic white bulge over a black plate. The hacker stuck his comm up to the scanner, then tapped away. After a moment, the white bulge turned a dark red.

"Running a blast here," Jairo said. Alissa was about to tell him to be quiet, then realized Jairo wasn't talking to her. He was talking to Viola. Explaining to the girl. "It's going to cycle through hundreds of frequencies a second, all targeted towards what this brand of scanner handles."

During the ride over here, Alissa realized, Jairo and Viola had spent most of the days together. Either in the cockpit, or in the back, working on Jairo's broken android.

Enough time to get entangled. Hopefully not enough to compromise him if Viola decided to turn. Alissa looked at Castor and, again, he met her gaze and nodded.

"Wouldn't all the wrong scans trigger alerts?" Viola said.

"That's why we've got people at the front door," Jairo replied. "Who's going to pay attention to a scanner error when you've got grenades blowing up outside?"

The noise from the front of the building grew louder. Several more bangs went off, still sounding muffled. The facility wasn't opening its doors. Would they just let the Red Voice fighters sit out there, shooting endlessly at the barrier?

The scanner suddenly blinked green. Locks tumbled inside the door, and it popped open with a soft *thunk*. Alissa grabbed the handle and swung it wide, the pair of fighters aiming over and under her shoulders into the opening. Not that there was anything to shoot. A thin hallway, more doors on either side, before a fork twenty meters away. Alissa went in first. Castor beside her, then Jairo and Viola. The two fighters came last, one closing the door behind them.

Turned out the exit was next to the crew quarters. Appropriate, given an alarm happening in the middle of the night. A night which, Alissa reminded herself, would be more than just a ship's effects, here. A night that was descending rapidly on the base.

At the fork, Alissa looked at Castor, who shrugged.

"You two, head that way," Alissa said to the two fighters, nodding to the right. "Comm if you find anything interesting."

"By that, she means a secured room," Jairo said. "One with a big console in it."

The fighters nodded and went down the hallway while Alissa led the four of them to the left. She didn't say it, but she'd sent the fighters in the direction of the front door.

Towards where Bosser and his force would be going. What Jairo needed might be that way, but, more likely, the two fighters weren't going to find anything other than the business end of a sidearm. Still, she couldn't take chances. Couldn't get hung up on heart. Not now.

Not when they were so close.

45

SUPERIOR FORCE

Mox ran down the trail alone, leaving Trina back at the *Jumper*. Laser flashes lit through the twilight jungle, bright pops between leaves and trees. Rustles cascaded between his footsteps as animals fled the fighting. He'd left the cannon on the ship, but carried a sidearm in his hand. In the dark, though, hitting anyone would be more luck than skill. Mox clenched his sore hands. Those, he expected, would be doing the real damage.

Rounding past a thick, gnarled trunk, Mox saw the front of the facility. Saw ten fighters arrayed on either side of the door, pouring shots into it. The steady stream of heat didn't seem to be doing much more than burning the door black. Mox moved back behind the trunk and looked for a good strike point. Going one against ten didn't make for good odds. But surprise could make a difference.

Moving away from the trail, Mox stepped lightly, as lightly as he could anyway, through the mess of plants, branches, and hanging vines. Every breath inhaled a thousand insects, forcing Mox to keep his mouth shut and breathe through his nose to keep from coughing. Sweat soaked through his clothes and gathered in the creases around the exoskeleton as though Mox wore a thousand small puddles. Eventually, though, he crept to within a few meters of the group on the door's right side.

Four of the fighters were engaged in chewing through power packs in a constant battery of fire, while two others stood back, closer to Mox, arguing about how to get past the door.

"... We don't have many grenades left, man. Throw them all at the door, then what?" Asked the taller one, his arms crossed, chin buried down in his own chest as he stared at the ground.

"We get in! That's what!" The smaller one, covered in charred remnants of his Red Voice garb. He'd had the worse time in the wreck, with visible burns running up and down his body. "What does it matter if we hold onto the weapons if they get killed?"

"You don't know that," the downcast man replied. "They might be there already."

"Or they're pinned down, waiting for us to come to the rescue!"

Mox took as deep a breath as he could through his nose, ignoring the panicked buzzing of captured bugs, and stepped out from the cover. Pulled out the sidearm. Then stopped. Everyone did.

The front doors were opening.

The slow grind as the doors split was agonizing, mystifying. Any lights in the facility, any that Mox could see, were off. Everything was black inside. And then Mox's world went orange. Bright lances shot out from the opening, burning down at both groups of fighters in a precise rain of deadly heat. The shorter fighter in front of Mox collapsed, smoke rising from four holes that weren't there a moment before. Other fighters screamed, a couple of haphazard counter shots flitted into the dark void, but within five seconds, every fighter Mox could see was dead and smoking on the ground.

From the opening, in the grim beginnings of the night, nearly twenty androids walked out and surveyed the dead. Two strode up to Mox, staring at him.

"Did you like our show?" The android asked. "Bosser said to make it quick. I trust we fulfilled his parameters."

Mox had nothing to say. He leaned back against the tree. The androids, they were supposed to only attack criminals. Only be unleashed against the worst of the worst after approval from an independent judge. Now, though. Now they had annihilated a group without any questions. Without any investigation, without even an ask for surrender. All on one man's word.

Alissa and her Red Voice weren't the real threats here.

46

THE CONSOLE

The guard led them right to it, his prismatic armor a beacon for Alissa and the others to follow through the shifting hallways and wider manufacturing rooms in the facility. The latter were especially surreal—robots assembling robots, mechanical arms welding smaller versions of themselves onto carbon-silk skeletons. Birth, systematized.

The control room sat at the end of the cycle, a conveyor running alongside and vanishing into a wall next to a door, a slate of steel unadorned with anything save RESTRICTED ACCESS in bold red letters. The guard stood in front of it for a moment, and then the door opened. Some unseen key, then. A camera or other sensor giving access. Regardless, when that door shut, they might not be able to open it again.

So Alissa ran for it.

The guard heard her footsteps, turned with his rifle already rising. Alissa slid as the guard fired, the laser flashing over her. She drew her sidearm, planted her heels, and, as her momentum pushed her upright, dove forward. In the air, Alissa pulled the sidearm's trigger and lanced a bolt right into the guard's chest. The hot light hit the mirrored glass and split, reflected rays sparkling around her. A reflected bolt struck Alissa, hot but nowhere near deadly. And then she rolled through the doorway. It slammed shut behind her.

The guard grabbed Alissa's jacket and threw her to the side, her sidearm flying out of her grasp across the room. Alissa rolled with the throw, coming up in a crouch. The guard had his rifle holstered, and, catching a glance around the room, Alissa could see why. A gigantic console covered the wall opposite the door, showing scrolling stats on the androids being made, androids out on missions, and other data Alissa didn't have time to interpret because the guard swung a stun baton at her face.

Alissa turned her left shoulder into the blow, the baton's crackling energy loosing itself on her jacket. The shoulder went numb, but the layers kept the rest of her intact. Alissa grabbed the guard's hand as he retracted for another swing, the motion lifting her up. And then Alissa went in close, getting inside the guard's arms and ramming her head into his chin. Her right hand grasped at the guard's belt, found the man's second stun baton and tried to lift it free. Except these weren't cheap holsters, these were designed to only allow drawing from specific angles. The baton didn't budge.

The guard kneed her in the stomach, Alissa's mouth opening in a coughing yell as she staggered back. Another swing of the stun baton, but Alissa stumbled back out of range. Pressed against the side of the room. The guard straightened, rubbed his chin with his left hand where she'd hit it.

"Was worried I wouldn't get any of the fun," the guard said. "They sent our androids out to say hi to your friends. Guessing they're all just burned bodies about now."

"That make you feel strong?" Alissa shot back. "Having bots do your work for you?"

"Brave talk. Aren't you trying to do the same thing?"

The guard didn't wait for Alissa's answer. He went forward, feinted with a swing of the baton, but led with a left-handed haymaker. Alissa ducked underneath and to the right, moving forward. She wasn't fast enough. The punch caught her numbed shoulder and Alissa felt something pop, the rest of her left arm dropping senseless. But the momentum shifted the guard past Alissa, who jumped, wrapped her right arm around the guard's neck, and pulled down. The guard overbalanced and fell forward, his head striking the wall with a sick crunch. He collapsed on Alissa, eyes closed and groaning. Pushing her way out from under the guard, Alissa stood up and, still unable to use her left arm, went over to the door. On the inside, there was a simple green button on the door's right. Alissa pressed it and stared straight into Castor's drawn rifle.

"Hurt?" Castor asked.

"I'll live," Alissa said. "Have a live one."

Then, as Castor went to check the stunned guard, Alissa looked to Jairo and Viola. "We're here. Get to work."

"On it, boss," Jairo said, and the hacker, with his protégé, brushed past Alissa and went for the console. A second later, the door shut behind them. Alissa stared at that steel slate and took a long breath. Took her right hand and placed it on her left shoulder. She could feel the dislocation. Turned to see Castor's sidearm flash blue, stunning the guard.

"Castor," Alissa said. "I need a reset."

The man didn't hesitate. Stepped over, gripped her right shoulder in his hands. She stared into his hard gray eyes and nodded. The stun baton dulled the pain, but Alissa felt the crack through her body and dropped to her knees. Pressed her lips together. She'd endured worse. So had most of the Red Voice.

Stand up.

"Alissa," Jairo said. "I'm in, only, it's not what we expected. The code's different."

"We confirmed what you had on the *Whisperwind* was a true android," Castor said. "The code shouldn't have changed."

"Jairo's right," Viola said. "I've worked with a real one too. There's a new layer here. An override."

"An override for what?" Alissa asked.

"It looks like—" Jairo's words were cut off by the door opening. Castor moved faster, pushing Alissa out of the way and sending a series of shots at the person on the other side. Alissa spun, and saw the android take Castor's shots, keep coming and stab the man with a long knife. It threw Castor to the side, the man hitting the stunned guard on the ground. Behind the android came another man Alissa recognized. Knew and hated.

Bosser had a sidearm drawn, and he shot past the android, its orange blast striking Jairo in the chest as the hacker turned from the console.

"No!" Alissa shouted, knowing it was pointless, knowing there was nothing she could do. Bosser ignored her, turned left, and shot Castor as the soldier reached for his sidearm. He collapsed, a burning hole matching the stab wound in his stomach. Jairo slid to the floor, the hacker pulling his backpack around and holding it as he gasped for breath. Viola crumpled next to him, tears streaming down her face.

Bosser turned to Alissa next, his sidearm coming up, pointing at her.

"You played a good game, Alissa. I will miss you," Bosser

said. Then a large shotgun appeared through the door, held up to Bosser's head.

"Shoot that woman, Bosser, and you'll die before she does," a voice said.

Bosser turned his head towards whomever held the shotgun. The android followed Bosser's look. Alissa slipped her hand into her boot, gripped the beam knife kept there. Just give her a chance. One chance for revenge.

47

A WAY OUT

Viola could barely see Davin through her tear-smeared eyes, but she could hear Jairo's weak whispers in her ear.

"The backpack," the hacker said. "Open it."

Jairo's head leaned back against the console, lolling towards Viola. Her hands went into the backpack almost automatically while her mind swam in currents dark and desperate. They'd been so close. Jairo had plugged in the drive. The data was downloading. Another minute, maybe two, and they'd be running the program. Now Castor was probably dead, there in the corner, and Jairo . . . His eyes were closing. His breaths ragged. He was dying in her arms.

"Don't blow this Davin," Bosser was saying. "There's no way you'd get out of here alive. If ThreeTwelve didn't eviscerate you, then twenty other androids would do the job."

"Yeah, but see, I don't give a damn," Davin said. "You killed the woman I loved."

Viola didn't know what she expected, but what she felt in the backpack was something she hadn't seen since class. A nova bomb. Outlawed for anyone except military, made to burst and burn electronics in a wide radius. Incredibly dangerous in space, where the breathable air depended on working systems, on Earth it would be an inconvenience. Unless you were in a facility surrounded by deadly bots.

"Plan . . . B," Jairo muttered.

Viola pressed the button as the android pulled itself in front of Bosser. The nova bomb went off silently, a wave of bluish energy bursting out from the backpack, hitting the android and crumpling it. Striking the console and lighting it up in sparks, the giant screen flickering and dying. Viola turned to see Davin pressing Melody's trigger, but the shotgun, shorted, didn't respond. Bosser's sidearm clicked nothing in reply.

Alissa's knife, though, wasn't affected. It didn't glow with the hot beam edge, but it still had a metal blade beneath. She rushed Bosser, hitting the man and stabbing him once, twice, three times. Then Davin and Phyla were dragging the Red Voice leader off.

"We have to run!" Davin said. "Whatever happened, it probably won't last long."

"It was a nova bomb," Viola said loosely. She stood up, realized she was still holding Jairo's backpack. The hacker's eyes were silent, his breath no longer rattling. On impulse, Viola grabbed Jairo's drive out of the console. It was the last evidence of who the hacker was, his last work.

"Don't want to know how you got one of those," Davin said, pulling Alissa out of the room. "But I'm happy you did."

"Leave him, Viola," Phyla said, stepping over a moaning Bosser and throwing an arm over Viola's shoulder. "He wouldn't want you to die over him."

"You didn't know who Jairo was," Viola replied, but she went.

"I saw how he looked at you there, at the end," Phyla said. "And that told me all I needed to know."

Viola shuddered through a sob as they left the room and ran to catch up to Davin. Ran through the facility's halls, past half-assembled androids and slumped machinery. Past flickering lights, dead consoles, and Merc and Opal, watching the open front door. And then Viola was outside, sprinting down a trail towards the jungle. Past androids standing still, systems fried, at least for the moment. Mox appeared, joined them without bothering to ask questions, and they all kept running.

All the way to the *Jumper*.

48

WHAT DEATH FEELS LIKE

The cold, that's what was surprising. Bosser assumed the chill spreading across his body came from his warm blood leaking out, pooling beneath his chest and spreading along the floor. He could see the deep red weeping across the metal tiles. Towards the door.

It should have shut by now. The door was on a short timer. Security that Abril insisted on. Bosser blinked, but the growing blurs didn't wipe away from his eyes. Then he saw why the door was still open.

"ThreeTwelve," Bosser said. His voice so slight. How cruel that dying should steal all his strength, even his voice. The android, lying in the doorway, didn't move.

Bosser twitched an arm, felt a response. Lurched out towards the android and felt ThreeTwelve's foot in his grip. Bosser pulled, the action of his muscles flexing a burst of life. He wasn't all gone, not yet. Using the android's dead weight, Bosser pulled himself into the doorway. Parallel to ThreeTwelve's head. Smudging the android, Bosser pressed his slick fingers to the android's temples. ThreeTwelve's head slipped open, its operating console dead and blank.

Beneath it, though, was the hard switch. Bring an android down for reprogramming, this was how you turned it back on.

Bosser pressed the button, felt it snap. Satisfying, that simple sound. ThreeTwelve's eyes lit a strong yellow, processing. Bosser sat back against the side of the door. So cold now.

Fitting that the last action he'd take was to bring an android back to life after he'd made so many. It'd been such a great idea, a way to calm the clamor of citizens tired of lawlessness. Tired of the corporate goons taking things too far. Shift the enforcement out of corporate hands, make it cheap and impartial. Make it scary. When ZeroOne, the first model, brought in the body of that killer terrorizing Vagrant's Hollow, Bosser clinched the corporate coin and the people's trust.

When ThreeTwelve picked him up, Bosser's eyes closed. It was too much effort to keep them open. But he could feel the air flowing across his face as the android ran down the hallways. Could hear Abril's voice calling for help. Could feel the prick as a needle broke his skin.

And that spike, that new pain amid the numbing agony from the knives, gave Bosser hope. A raft for his consciousness to cling to. As medical bots tore at his clothes and his cuts, as Bosser slipped out of death's clutches, he turned his mind to the next problem.

Revenge.

49

ISLAND VACATION

The warm water washed up the beach and in between Phyla's toes. The gentle wave soundtrack playing background to an orange dawn, palm trees shaking in the slight breeze. Phyla folded her arms and glanced to the right, down the beach where chairs were being set out and early joggers were making their way through the sand. A distant rumble underscored the waves and Phyla's eyes moved up to track a ship, engines glowing a bright white, lifting from the island and beginning its trek to space.

"You'll have to sleep sometime," Davin said, coming up beside her.

"I'm not the only one," Phyla replied.

"Your captain has a little too much adrenaline to crash now."

"I'm sure Erick can help with that."

"He's already gone," Davin said, running a hand through greasy hair. Phyla wasn't much better. Jungle sweat and a frantic night flight to the island hadn't given them much opportunity for hygiene. "Not sure he's coming back."

"He deserves to stay."

"I'm not arguing. But the way we've been fighting, losing the doctor isn't going to be good."

"How are the others?" Phyla asked. They'd all wandered off the ship dazed, each one going in a random direction, exhausted.

"You think they talk to me?" Davin replied. "Hell, sometimes I think the only reason anybody says anything to me is because I cut their paychecks."

"It's been tight. What just happened wasn't easy for anyone."

"Well, I hope they enjoy the moment," Davin said. "It won't last long."

"You said Alissa stabbed him? You think he lived?"

"I hope he did."

"What?"

"I want him to pay for Lina," Davin said, staring out into the ocean. "One death won't be enough for him."

Phyla shivered.

"Davin, that's . . . cold," she said. "And Alissa? What about her? Doesn't she deserve death too? For all the people she ordered killed on Miner Prime?"

"Probably does," Davin replied.

"Then why'd you save her?"

"I didn't care about her. I saved us," Davin said. "You know androids don't stay knocked out for that long."

"That's crap," Phyla replied. "You could have made sure Bosser was dead first, and then we could've run."

"We still need him," Davin said. "Bosser's the only one that can clear the charge. Get the murders off our records. If that doesn't happen, we're still back where we started."

"And if he clears those charges?"

"Then I get my shot. And the rest of you are free to go."

Breaking waves held sway over their conversation for a minute. The water caressed her feet. Phyla reached down and picked up a handful of mud. The first real mud, from real Earth soil, she'd ever felt. She stared at it, watched a tiny crab squirm through the sand grains.

"You're so brave, you know that?" Phyla said. "Taking all this on yourself, saying the rest of us can just go our own way while you go and shoot a man? I'm so impressed."

"My sarcasm detector is going off."

"It should be. If this is going to be it for the Wild Nines, for the group we started years ago, don't you think it should end together?"

Phyla expected the same softening she'd seen before, when Davin relented and acknowledged they were a team. Only his face didn't change; that hard line didn't sink into a smile.

"Wherever he goes," Davin said. "We can go together. But at the end, when it comes to it, I'm the only one pulling the trigger. I'm the only one with the charge on his head for it. We're a team, Phyla, but this one thing can't be shared. I don't want it to be shared."

Phyla bit back another sarcastic response. Davin's eyes had an off-cast to them. A shade that threw her off. Another wave caressed her feet, and Phyla took another deep breath of the salty air instead. If Davin wanted his final shot, fine. She would help him get there. Help him get even.

And when they came after Davin for killing Bosser, she'd help him get away. Because on Miner Prime, stuck in a path to a dead future, Davin had done the same for her.

50

LIBRA

Viola looked out at the ocean, its soft ripples inviting in the early morning sun. Her eyes were as bleary as the cafe's employee's, stumbling through their first pot of coffee. What she wouldn't give to take a long slow walk through that sand. Feel a natural breeze. But she felt the pull of the backpack beside her, occupying its own thin-backed chair. Squat and navy blue, the backpack was everything its owner wasn't. Bland and boring. Jairo, Jairo had been . . .

Murdered. That's what Jairo had been. Shot right in front of her face while Viola did nothing. At least, nothing yet.

She began to take apart the hackers backpack, unzipping the main pocket and rifling through the contents. A pair of EMP discs, the weapons designed to knock out electronics in a local radius. One more nova bomb, a black sphere interlaced with azure lightning. And then Viola's fingers found what she was really looking for, the drive. The little piece of hardware that had all of Jairo's code inside it.

Everything he'd learned about the androids, and what made them run.

Viola took out the drive and stuck it into a small slot on the side of her comm. The thing was a pair of centimeters long, felt cool against the skin of her forearm. That feeling went away as she lost herself in the long series of numbers, words and symbols that floated in the air through the comm's projection. Her right hand brushed the comm's screen, shifting the projection through the file.

Jairo had shown Viola, on the *Whisperwind,* a change he'd made to the android's code. To subsume their directive and replace it with one of Alissa's own choosing. Those lines weren't hard to find. The syntax was different, and there were no comments. No indicators for other programmers. The new code changed the directive to assassinate into one of protection, to one of patrol, to one of servitude. That code had never made it off the drive, never given the Red Voice the android army they needed.

Beneath Jairo's lines was another new batch. Not written in Jairo's signature, nor like the original android code. What Jairo had downloaded from the central console in the facility before he'd been shot. When he'd muttered the comment about a surprising find.

This code was simple too. Obey . . . Libra? A variable. A variable that, when set, overrode any other orders from the facility or anywhere else. Who was Libra?

Viola dug deeper, looked for fingerprints. Sometimes people gave themselves away in how they wrote their code, or they put in a designation, a tag to identify who they were. Even if they didn't realize it. In this case the order to obey came from one phrase in particular, keyed to one man's voice. When spoken to the android with that vocal signature, it would stop and wait for further orders. And follow those orders without hesitation.

What's done, is done.

That was it. All it would take to reduce an android to nothing more than a standing pile of metal. Viola looked at the language, those words. She pumped the phrase into her comm's general search. A line from an old play. Who would bother putting something poetic in his path to ruin?

The same man who had killed Jairo.

Bosser.

But what did it matter? Androids were sent after criminals. There wouldn't be any point in building in a secure phrase. Unless Viola was missing something.

She flipped to the general news headlines and filtered by pieces about androids. And the answer slid in front of her face. Article after article describing a new service offered by Eden, by the androids they produced. Bodyguards, loyal and unwavering, for everyone and everything. Corporate leaders, government leaders, valuable ships and places could now have their own automated protection brought to you by the deadliest machines humanity had ever made. And one man could control them at will.

51

RECKONING

Opal saw Alissa sitting on a sandy wood bench beneath a pair of palm trees. Still dressed in the same camouflage gear the Red Voice leader had worn at the facility. She was the only one left, save the medic and his wounded men. The androids had likely found that group by now. Opal shook her head slightly. Not here to talk about that.

"Alissa," Opal said, sitting on the space next to her. "Do you know who I am?"

Alissa glanced at her, and Opal saw Alissa's eyes were red-rimmed, her mouth firm.

"Should I?" Alissa replied.

"Your man, Bakr, tried to kill me outside of Neptune. He tried to kill all of us, but he knew why he wanted to kill me," Opal leaned back against the bench and let the rising Sun fill her eyes. "He was justified."

"Bakr was always loyal, always committed," Alissa said, mirroring Opal's look out to the ocean. "He saved my life. Once, when all the air we had was going up in flames, he carried me out, sheltered me with his own body."

"I was the reason that happened," Opal said. Alissa stiffened, but didn't make any other moves. "I was on the ridge, trying to take you out. But the glass was too strong."

"Then it wasn't you," Alissa said. "Someone else pressed that button, someone else designed that laser, and someone else ordered it into position. That last was who we were after. What the Red Voice wanted. Destabilize the rulers, and the rest would fall apart by itself. You and the other soldiers were never the target."

"Even so, I'm sorry."

"It doesn't matter."

"Are you going to keep fighting?"

Alissa rubbed her eyes. Sighed.

"I don't think Bosser will let me do anything else," Alissa said.

"Would you want to?"

"How many people have you murdered through your scope, sniper?" Alissa replied. "If you had the chance to put it down forever, would you?"

"I did have that chance. And I didn't."

Alissa nodded.

"I think I'd be the same."

Alissa rose from the bench, gave Opal a final look of downcast determination, and walked away down the beach.

"Where will you go?" Opal called after her.

"Back home."

BREAKFAST, INTERRUPTED

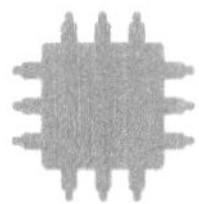

On the first day, Trina had been overwhelmed by Erick's family. So much laughter, so many happy tears at seeing their long-lost father, their grandparent. It was, altogether, too much emotion. Trina had forced a few smiles to her face and turned her attention to playing games with the many children. Teaching them about the *Jumper* and how its engines worked. Telling stories about flying among the stars. Though the children always wanted more about the fighting, the lasers, and less about how proper cooling technique was necessary to keep a ship like the *Jumper* reacting quickly in dangerous situations.

When she wasn't with the kids, Trina was back at the spaceport fixing up Merc's Viper. And playing with her own mind. Erick's eyes had changed, lost that hungry look when they softened in the smile of his daughter. Trina doubted the doctor would be coming back with them, and those same doubts were seeping into her own head. It would be hard to say goodbye to the blue sky, to the wind rustling through her hair. To rebuilding an engine in a hangar with the sound of the ocean just outside the doors.

They sat down to breakfast, ten of them, and Trina looked at the plate full of fruit and eggs in front of her. No powder, no stiff frozen chunks of protein designed to last for months in vacuum. The taste of mango juice slid down her throat silky and sweet. For all the beauty of Saturn's rings and Neptune's cerulean skies, Trina was ready to forsake them all to enjoy that mango again and again.

"Is it good, Trina?" Erick asked. Rather than the white coat he wore on the *Jumper*, Erick was in a simple brown robe, sandals on his feet and sand in his hair. Already the Sun had pinked his face.

"The sweetness is strong, the texture is smooth. I enjoy it," Trina said. "Comparatively, the food I'm used to having is far less appealing."

"That's about as good a compliment as you'll get from her," Erick said to the others at the table, then turned back to Trina. "The food, the ocean, everything about this island is the opposite of what's up there."

Up there. Not just spaceships, but the many stations orbiting the Earth. Where Trina had been born. Where she had watched the sapphire orb swirl beneath her. Had known that while it was so close, the cost to get there was too high. Her parents never touched the world they saw out their window every day. And now here Trina was, enjoying the kinds of things she'd written off back when she'd first held a wrench.

The door to the house was not thick, so when the knock came, it rattled against its frame. Erick was the first to stand, Trina following. The knock was precise, an exact half second between hits on the door. A person would have a more natural cadence. Erick's family barely noticed, but

Trina caught the doctor's eye. Given where they'd come from, a perfect knock wasn't worth playing loosely.

"You all should take your food to the back porch," Erick said. "Just to be safe."

His daughter looked hard at them. Her eyes narrowed, but not harshly, no, concerned. Her mouth opened, and Trina spoke over it.

"There is a chance that what is on the other side of that door is deadly," Trina said. "It should have no interest in you or your family, but we have to lower the risk of accidental damage."

The daughter didn't fight that one, gathered the kids and ushered the group and their breakfast out the back of the house.

The knock came again, three more precise strikes. Erick moved over to the front door while Trina went past him, into the small guest room that served as her castle while she stayed. Trina dug in her pack and found the pocket with a small bulge. Pulled out her sidearm and verified the power level was appropriate. Enough shots to either save them, or die trying.

Three more knocks and Trina took up position behind Erick, aiming the sidearm over his shoulder. At Trina's nod, Erick twisted the knob and pulled the door open. Trina's finger pressed the trigger and paused. On the other side of the door was a familiar face, objectively pretty, with narrow cheeks and shoulder-length hair. And very, very dead eyes.

"You will come with me," ThreeTwelve said, not flinching in the barrel of Trina's sidearm.

"If we say no?" Erick replied.

"Then you will be dealt with."

"I don't like our chances," Trina said.

"And I don't like the bot." Erick's hands tensed, but there

was nothing he could do. A wild punch at the android would be caught, his wrist broken. Or the android would simply let it strike against its hard skin. There was no winning this one.

"Your associates are being contacted," ThreeTwelve said. "You are outnumbered. Outgunned. You have nothing to gain."

Trina flipped on the safety and lowered the sidearm. Erick sighed, and Trina let go a taut breath of her own as the doctor relaxed. Nobody needed to die today.

"Lead on," Trina said.

As they followed ThreeTwelve out onto the thin street and towards the spaceport, Trina glanced back at the small house. A child, not yet five, one of Erick's grandchildren, peeked around the side at them. Mango smeared around his face.

If that had been Trina's last meal, it'd been a good one.

53

CLEARED

Davin enjoyed team meetings, getting the whole crew together and asking what was on their minds. Playing democracy, deciding what was next for the Wild Nines. But he really, really preferred them without androids aiming guns at their backs.

"Guess you found all of us," Davin said as Trina and Eric joined the circle. They stood in an empty warehouse, on the border of the spaceport. The morning sun was bright, filtering through the open doors and blinding the outside with its white rays. "Now do we do a dance or something?"

"Now you listen," ThreeTwelve said, its voice changing from the lockstep woman to Bosser's baritone. "Tell me where Alissa is."

"No," Opal said first. "She's hurt enough."

"Hurt a lot of people too," Phyla said, then, to Three-Twelve. "Why are you asking us? Can't track her down yourself?"

"You know as well as I do that she's dangerous. That she could murder anyone at any time," Bosser said through the bot. "We need to find her fast."

"Murder anyone at any time?" Davin said. "Coming from you, that's pretty funny."

"I shot to save us," Bosser replied. "Another few seconds and who knows what the hacker would've done."

"Doesn't matter," Mox said. "We don't know where she is."

"You brought her here," Bosser said.

"To save her from you." Viola looked like she was shaking. Her eyes trying to bore holes into the android. Davin glanced at Viola's waist. Not wearing a weapon. Less chance of a temper tantrum turning all of them into target practice.

"Look," Davin said. "We landed. She left. I didn't stop her because I'm not the police. If you want Alissa, go find her."

ThreeTwelve looked at each of them in turn. Davin knew the stare; the bot wasn't trying to be intimidating. The android was looking to see if anyone, through their eyes, their facial tics, even faster breathing was hiding something. After the rotation, ThreeTwelve turned back to Davin.

"I believe you," Bosser said. "You can go. We'll find Alissa ourselves."

"Wait," Davin said. "I'm not done here. You had us dancing on your string for a long time. But we brought you back, we helped you save your bots. We're even."

The android looked at Davin, its mask impossible to read. One second went by. Two.

"You play a good game," Bosser said. "Our deal is done. You and your team can go. I'll clear your charges."

The androids, the four of them, including ThreeTwelve, turned and marched out of the warehouse. Davin didn't feel any better, didn't feel like a weight had been taken off his shoulders. No longer charged murderers. That should've been a big deal.

"I don't like taking gifts from him," Phyla said.

"I'm going to try to find her," Opal said. "I owe Alissa that much."

"You know I'm going with you," Merc said. Opal threw him a grateful smile.

"She's a killer, Opal," Davin said. "Who cares if Bosser takes her out. She deserves it."

"Doesn't matter," Opal said. "I have a debt that I want to repay."

The sniper turned and walked from the warehouse, Merc give them all one more nod and then went after.

"Surprised you're not going," Erick said to Viola. "Didn't you know her?"

"She used me. She hurt Mox," Viola said. "I don't care what happens to her."

"Davin," Trina said. "I think, I think I'm going to stay here. I need some time to decide what happens next. Be out of harm's way for a bit."

"She's not the only one," Erick chimed in. "I'm sorry, captain, but I need to spend some time with my family. They're what I've been missing."

Davin felt the shiver scroll up through his veins, the impending certainty of a decision that he wouldn't be able to take back. But it was one long overdue.

"Seems as good a time as any to break this one up," Davin said. "It's been a good ride. Mox, Viola, we'll make sure you're able to get fare to wherever you want to go."

Nobody, not even Phyla, said anything. Too tired to fight. The Wild Nines died right there in the Caribbean sun, without a sound.

54

TRACKING

Viola didn't have much to pack. The product of being a runaway. Everything she threw into the bag just brought more questions to her head. She was walking away from the greatest adventure of her life, and she didn't know where she was going. There was Ganymede, Galaxy Forge and working for her father. There was Earth and all of its natural wonder waiting for her to see.

And then there was Bosser. The lines in the code. The androids stationed around the solar system, waiting to strike.

"I don't stand a chance," Viola muttered. She wasn't a weapons expert, she couldn't fight her way into the android facility, find Bosser and get her own revenge. At least, not from the ground.

But she could fly.

Viola turned to the console in her crew cabin and flipped over to the cameras. There it was, sitting and ready to go in the bay. Trina hadn't finished with the Viper, but it would fly. Refueled and recharged. From the air, Viola should be able to get in a couple of runs. Maybe, if she was lucky, one of those lasers would fry Bosser and put an end to what he was trying to do. That was it.

Viola left her bag behind and crept out into the *Jumper*'s hallways. Davin and Phyla were somewhere on the ship. No idea where Mox was.

"Puk, it'd be real nice to have your floating camera around now," Viola said. Without the little bot, she felt blind, like she was missing a limb. But there wasn't time to build a new body and bring Puk back to life.

From the crew quarters, Viola went to the main cargo bay. On her right was a ladder going up to the cockpit. Behind her, the tunnel going to the crew quarters and then back to the engines. To her left, the small bay where the Viper stayed. The *Jumper* was empty, and Viola moved fast. Hopping down the steps, swinging on the railing, and blitzing down the second set of stairs to the hall leading to the hangar bay. The *Jumper* felt quiet, none of the normal sounds of Mox clomping his way to a cabin door, Merc and Opal arguing about something pointless, or Trina banging away on a project.

Across from the hangar bay was Trina's workshop. Viola peaked in, the tools arranged and perfectly organized into their trays and boxes. Even leaving, Trina wouldn't tolerate a mess. And in the hangar bay, the Viper sat quiet and ready. Viola went towards it, pressed down on the activation button on the wall. A ladder rose from the floor, leaning against the Viper. Its cockpit swung open, the glass folding upwards. It was almost like stealing the *Gepard*, way back then. Taking her father's ride what felt like decades ago.

"I thought you were done stealing ships," Davin said from behind her.

"Old habits are hard to break," Viola replied.

"Where are you going to take her?"

"On a suicide mission."

"Sounds fun. Can I come?"

Viola smiled in spite of herself. Not much she could say to that one. Even when everything was falling to pieces, Davin could still make her laugh. Make the whole crew come together. When there was a crew, anyway.

"Davin, Bosser's got something else planned."

Viola launched into an explanation, telling Davin about the override code, and how the androids were spreading their way across humanity. So that whenever Bosser wanted, he could trigger a strike and do away with anyone he didn't feel like keeping around. She expected Davin to freak out, to panic, or maybe shake his head in sadness. What she didn't expect was what he said.

"Then let's go kill the bastard."

"What?"

"You heard me," Davin replied. "I owe the man a blast to the face, anyway. And I think I know how to do it. Come on."

Viola followed Davin all the way up to the cockpit. Phyla was there, listening to a recorded message.

"Play it again," Davin said. Phyla swiped the message back, and it started.

"Today's position report. Bosser is spending the morning at the facility, going over final progress reports with Abril. Then he's departing to Loci station," the voice on the other end of the message was mechanical, but feminine.

"Is that Threetwelve?" Viola asked.

"Trina left us a present," Phyla said. "We've been getting these daily reports ever since we landed on Earth."

"This one just gave us a target," Davin said. "Loci station is a bare-bones communications outpost. Helps redirect messages coming and going through space and sends them back out to where they need to go."

"So if Bosser's going there, he could send a message to anywhere, to anybody," Viola said.

"Didn't make sense, until what you told me back there in the bay," Davin said. Phyla raised her eyebrows. "Don't worry, I'll tell you all about it. For now though, we gotta get Mox back here. Loci might not have much security, but I bet Bosser isn't going alone."

FIND ALISSA

For a spaceport, the island wasn't exactly busy. Merc had seen more crowded asteroids. The board for departing passenger flights only had two entries, and one was for far later in the evening. The other one, the first one of the day, left in an hour. The sun was starting to slant into the afternoon, pouring through the gaps in the palm trees that lined the avenues of the spaceport. Open air: what a marvel after being stuck in metal tubes for years.

"I think Alissa's options are a bit limited," Merc said to Opal. "Going to go ahead and guess she's on that one."

Merc pointed to the ship docked there, already boarding passengers as it finished refueling. Destination: Luna.

"Then let's go," Opal replied and headed towards the ship. The boarding area was a cluster of bags being loaded, people saying goodbye, and an indifferent crew more interested in catching the tropical sun than actually taking off on time. Alissa was nowhere in sight.

"She could already be on," Merc said.

"Then we have to get on that ship to check," Opal said. "She has to know the androids are coming for her."

"Hang on, I've got an idea."

Merc slipped past the line of boarding passengers, up to a crew member working on their company-issued comm. As Merc closed, the crew member, decked out in a red suit so that he appeared less like a person and more like a lipstick smear, looked up.

"Can I help you?" the man's voice was layered with so much exhaustion, so much boredom, the Merc almost felt bad for what he was about to ask.

"Yeah, I don't see my friend out here, but she forgot her favorite pair of, um, socks," Merc said, wincing. "Can you check if she's already on?"

"What's the name?"

"Alissa."

"Last name?"

Merc paused. Everyone knew Alissa's last name. The leader of the Red Voice had her name and face posted all over the solar system. If she was on the ship, Alissa probably wasn't there under her own name.

"I'm not sure?" Merc lied. "We just met last night."

The man glanced back at the comm display. Scrolled through a list of names and then shook his head.

"Maybe she's on the later flight, there's not an Alissa on this one."

"Oh, maybe I got the times wrong."

"At least now you can get her the socks," the crew member deadpanned, then went back to looking at his comm.

Socks. Come on Merc, you can do better than that. He told Opal what he found, or what he didn't find.

"She could be using a fake name," Opal said.

"Then we don't have a chance."

The two of them wandered away from the ship, looking

around for anything that might provide a clue. Maybe Alissa would wander into view. Or someone would shout that the Red Voice leader had been spotted. Outside the spaceport, towards the long series of wooden docks stretching into the ocean, a large ship blasted its horn. Merc could make out dozens of people on the boat, a few vehicles, and cargo.

"What's that?" Merc asked a passenger struggling by them with a series of bags. He pointed towards the boat.

"It's a ferry, goes straight to the continent," the passenger replied, then shuffled on.

"If I were a hunted rebel leader, and I was trying to get away, would I take the obvious route?" Merc said. "Names don't mean much when there's cameras everywhere."

"You think she's on that ferry," Opal replied.

"When I flew for Earth, there were always plenty of dumb criminals. The ones being flashy about it. Trying to land in their wanted ships, or brute-forcing their way onto the planet. The smart ones, though, they came through the normal way. Didn't draw attention, didn't use the obvious transports. Bosser knows we came to this island, knows there's only one spaceport here."

"But he wouldn't see her taking the ferry," Opal finished. "I get that. Let's check it out."

They hustled over to the dock, getting there as the last of the passengers reported in. A series of dark, sick clouds rose over the horizon, reaching to cover the sun. The crew members here were equally bored as the ones in the space-port, glancing at tickets and then back at their comms. Another routine in a lifetime of routines. There was plenty of space, and Merc snagged a pair of tickets. He and Opal went up the ramp and onto the main level where clusters of passengers huddled beneath the awnings and stared at the approaching storm. Merc followed their eyes and saw the first flashes of lightning, heard the low ripple of thunder. Coats went on, hoods went up.

"Well, this just got harder," Merc said.

"Nothing's ever easy. You go aft, I'll take the bow. Comm if you find her."

As Merc split from Opal, the first drops of rain fell. The boat blew its horn a second time, and its engines spooled up, adding their roar to the thunder.

56

A SHOT OF RUM

Picking Mox from a line of tourists at a beach bar was not exactly difficult. Almost twice the size and sporting the same greased-up clothes he wore on journeys across the solar system, Mox stood out. Add in the fact that he was the only one not drinking something tall and fruit-colored, fruit-filled, and Davin found him easy enough. A soft rock cover band played in the background, the stage lit by torches, while tourists too drunk to care danced in the downpour.

"Never figured you for the tourist type," Davin said.

"First time here," Mox said. "Figured I'd see what it's about."

"And?"

"Too much excitement."

Davin looked at all the happy, glassy-eyed faces. People enjoying their chance to escape from life's problems with a piña colada. The bartender went by and Davin held up his finger, pointed at a bottle of local rum.

"Straight up," Davin said, then turned back to Mox. "If

you think this is thrilling, wait till I tell you what were doing next."

Mox replied by taking a long pull of his dark drink, a whiskey something with rocks. The big man's eyes drifted to the lone screen hanging behind the bar, running through sports scores from Earth's various leagues.

"Never been to a game," Mox said. "Luna's got teams, just never went."

"Never had the money, nor the time," Davin replied.

"After this, want to go?"

"We get through this alive, I'll go to any game you want."

"Where's he going?"

"Loci. Viola found something in the code. Thinks Bosser is going to send all the androids on kill missions, wipe out a bunch of leaders, then take control."

"Sounds a little above our pay grade," Mox said.

"It is." Davin took a slow drink. A buttery burn, sticking in his mouth and filling his nose with the tropics. "But I don't really give a damn about all that. I still owe Lina a shot."

"That, I understand."

"Then you're in? It'll be a short crew. The four of us."

"Been a long time."

It had. The *Jumper* had flown with at least five on it for a few years now. Going back, there'd been a time when it'd been the three of them. Short runs, Luna to Miner Prime with stops on Mars. Then they wanted bigger profits, and a bigger crew.

"I need this, Mox," Davin finished the rum. Held up his hand for another.

"You did the same for me. I'm in," Mox said. "But after, I need to go home."

"We all do."

57

MOMENTS

Take off in a few hours, and here Phyla was playing maid. Going through the cabins and trying to find anything that wasn't strapped down, anything that people had forgotten. Erick and Trina, Opal and Merc, no telling when they'd see each other again. The last thing Phyla wanted was bad blood because they'd launched with someone's priceless keepsake.

"You see anything?" Phyla asked Fournine as she poked her head into Opal's room.

"Trina's cabin is immaculate. As though she measured out every single stitch on that bed and folded the sheets precisely to match. She dusted the console. I can't see inside the locker, but that manic insanity wouldn't leave it untouched," the ship's computer replied.

"Not surprised," Phyla said. "Check Erick's next."

Opal's room was empty, not quite as clean as Trina's, but Phyla could see the efficiency in it. Military order said what was good enough to get things done, to make it right. The sheets folded up, ready for washing. The console cleaned, but not scrubbed shining. In the locker, a pair of sidearms and some spare batteries. Things Opal felt she wouldn't need that would be better left for the others. Phyla left them there. She'd know where to find them if they were needed.

"Hey, you might want to come check this out," Fournine said. "Seems the doctor got sentimental."

Phyla took the short walk across the hall to Erick's cabin and opened the door. Photos sat on the cot: printed out security camera stills. Dates on each one etched in Erick's messy handwriting.

"Memories," Phyla said, picking up the closest one and taking a look.

It was the first day they'd welcomed Opal onto the ship. The sniper had been the sixth crew member, and she was standing there in the *Jumper*'s main bay as the other five held single drams of whiskey up to welcome her. Davin, Phyla, Mox, Trina, Erick, and now Opal. A necessary long-range specialist to round out their detail. They'd decided to get into the escort business, as cargo hauling wasn't paying the same dividends. Opal looked almost shy in that picture, and Phyla saw her eyes had looked past the crew and landed on the small table behind them, where Davin had put her welcome gift. A new long rifle. At the time, Phyla had thought Opal was overwhelmed with gratitude. Now, though, the sniper's eyes seemed wary and sad.

The next picture was something Phyla hadn't seen before. Trina sitting in the med bay as Erick dyed her hair. This time into an emerald green. She never knew Erick had been the one doing that all these years. Then again, the mechanic and the doctor had forged a special friendship. They were the support that kept the *Jumper* and her crew going, it only made sense that they kept each other running too.

Mox in the middle of a workout, with Merc in the background shouting off reps. Erick had written on the bottom of this one; *keeping score*. Another had Viola coming back onto the ship after Europa, her face still fresh and innocent. And then there was something different.

The dim shot taken as the ship's lights were just turning on. It was the main bay, the boarding ramp was down. Haloed in the opening were two people. Two shapes Phyla recognized. Davin, herself. The first time they boarded the *Jumper* together. Davin was grinning, arms waving in that expansive gesture he used whenever he was truly, truly excited. And Phyla saw in herself the same cautious cool she thought she still had today. But there wasn't nervousness in that face. Determination. The knowledge that everything in that pack on her back was all she had, and that Phyla was leaving a place she had no desire to go back to.

That morning they would wait for Lina, and their friend would never come. They would take off, and head to Luna on a cargo run. And all this would come of it.

"Fournine, what's the status on pre-flight?" Phyla said, staring at the photo.

"Green and good," Fournine said. "Honestly, Trina left things so well it's almost boring. I can overload an engine if you want some excitement."

"I think we'll have enough of that where we're going."

"Have it your way. Oh, your best launch window is in two hours."

"Then I guess it's time to round up the troops."

58

METAL STORM

The rain was thick as it came down around the ferry. The drops hammered into Opal like stinging missiles every time she left cover. Awnings where the rest of the passengers gathered, huddled, and watched the thrashing storm. She'd peeked underneath the hoods of so many people and hadn't found the face she wanted. Until she made it all the way to the bow, and there, standing in the rain and leaning over the railing, was a single person. The hood drawn up, but the stance right. The height good. Opal had spent so long watching Alissa through her scope that she knew.

"Got her," Opal calmed to Merc. "Get up to the bow."

Opal walked towards the hooded figure, left the cover and felt the rain stick her face. Then another woman stepped in front of her, stared into Opal's eyes with a pair the sniper recognized immediately. Too perfect, too smooth. No life there.

"Don't," the android said. "This one is ours."

On Opal's right, she noticed a pair of figures heading straight for Alissa. Their backs rigid beneath their cloaks, their strides in perfect harmony. Three androids. It was an impossible fight. On her left, Opal saw Merc work his way through the crowd and pause, looking at her. Opal's right hand drifted beneath her cloak, to the beam knife clasped on her back thigh. She owed Alissa a debt.

"Love you, stick jockey," Opal said loudly.

The android tilted its head and stared at her. Not moving until Opal stabbed the beam knife into the bot's side and pushed it away. Alissa turned at the shriek of laser on metal, bringing a pair of sidearms up in either hand from beneath her cloak and aiming at the two approaching androids. Fired. The bots moved fast, ducking and weaving around Alissa's shots. She scored a hit, the right one wheeling back with a smoking hole in its chest. The left reached for her when a bolt struck it in the side, Merc's. Opal tried to move forward, but felt an iron grip around her arm.

The android whipped her to the ground.

Passengers screamed and ran away towards the ferry's aft. Opal pushed back along the floor into the space left by the retreating people, the android she'd stabbed standing over her. Reaching for her throat. Opal slashed at its hand, but the bot shifted its wrist just enough for the knife to hit only air. Metal fingers wrapped around her throat. Pressed her into the ground. Opal kicked the android's ankles, but the bot didn't budge. It wasn't a person. There were no weak spots.

Another flash. Another burning hole in the android's shoulder. But it didn't flinch, its unmoving eyes glaring at Opal. The sniper coughed, she couldn't breathe. Her lungs heaved. Her eyes stung as the rain lashed their open lids. And then Merc hit the android like a train, flying through the air and tackling the bot. Dragging its hand off her throat and carrying the android to the ground. Opal gulped in air and sat up. Saw Alissa roll between the two wounded androids, ducking and diving beneath their swipes. Opal struggled to her feet and moved over to meet her.

"Are you okay?" Opal asked as she moved closer.

"What are you doing here?" Alissa triggered another round at the two androids, who anticipated the shots and dipped to the right and left around them.

"Trying to help."

"Then take this, and shoot them," Alissa said, handing Opal one of her sidearms. The sniper wheeled and fired at the android struggling with Merc. Her shot hit the bot in the leg as it threw Merc into the bow railing. The fighter pilot bounced off and hit the ground hard. The android turned towards Opal, limping from the burning hole in its left knee.

"Down!" Alissa yelled, pulling Opal to the deck with her as a large pole sailed through the space where they'd been. A chunk of the railing torn off and turned into a missile by an android with too much strength.

Then the two androids were on them again, the third leaving Merc and getting closer. Opal fell into her boxing stance, the hand-to-hand she learned in the military, and tried to bob and weave. Slide in between the punches and deliver a shot to the ribs with the beam knife, or a sidearm blast. But no matter how fast she moved, the androids were quicker. The bots knocked aside her blows and struck her kidneys, her legs, her face. The third one lunged and shoved Opal back against the railing. Behind her, ten meters down, the churning sea battered against the ferry's side. Beside her, Alissa stumbled, bloodied and beaten.

Opal raised her fists, blinking the blood out of her eyes, and stared into the lifeless machines coming to kill her.

59

BLAST OFF

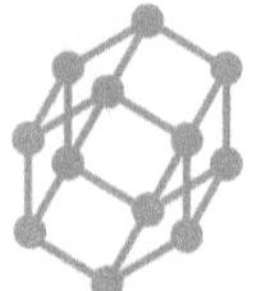

The engines felt empty without Trina's exacting presence. Viola stared at the console, measured energy going to and from both of the main engines and prepped them for flight. The short trip from the island up to Loci wasn't all that complicated, but they still needed someone down here in the bowels of the *Jumper* to make sure its giant rockets didn't blow themselves up.

"How're you doing down there?" Phyla's voice came over the comm.

"Getting used to it," Viola said. "How did you and Davin fly the ship yourselves?"

"We took turns. One of us down there, one of us up here. There was a lot of running."

"That sounds exhausting."

"It was worth it to escape Vagrant's Hollow."

Viola understood that one. When she ran away from Ganymede, she'd wanted to get away, see the real world, experience an adventure before locking herself away in an office, or a lab for the rest of her life. Now, she'd reprogrammed an android, piloted a freighter out of the swirling winds of Neptune, staged a commando raid, and killed a man. Guess that qualified as experience.

The *Jumper* rumbled as Phyla ignited the engines for takeoff. The spaceport retracted the roof over their bay and the downpour from the overhead storm battered the *Jumper*'s hull. Not great conditions, but when you're going to attack a guy holding humanity hostage, you don't get to wait for perfect weather. The lift-off felt different here, so much more energy sent to the engines to pick them up from the ground. Viola's stomach slammed into herself, and she was glad Trina actually installed straps down here. Earth's gravity was stronger than Mars, Minor Prime, Ganymede, almost anywhere that a ship would regularly land.

Viola played with the mechanisms, modulating which tanks and which batteries drained first. There was no window to the outside, just the sensation of the world falling away.

"What do you think?" Mox's voice on the comm.

"About what?" Viola replied.

"Earth," Mox said. "Wasn't that your first time?"

"I want to go back," Viola said. "I want to try it without all the anger, and sadness. Without death."

"That would be nice."

"Was that yours?" Viola asked.

"Grew up on the Moon. Never made the jump till now," Mox said.

"Would you go back?"

"If we make it, yeah."

"If? There can't be an if, Mox. We're going to win. We have too many friends who are depending on us."

"My experience? That's no guarantee."

That's no guarantee. Viola glanced back at the console, the workload on the engines decreasing as they hit the upper atmosphere. Here they were on a giant hunk of metal blasting their way into space. They had no right to be doing any of this. There was no guarantee that one of these engines wouldn't malfunction and blow them to smithereens. That someone from Earth's patrolling force wouldn't pick them up and burn them to a cinder. There wasn't even a guarantee that when they reached the space station Bosser wouldn't just shoot them as soon as they got off the ship. But here they were, giving it the best shot they had.

"It's all we've got, Mox. I believe we're going to do it. I have to."

"Hope you're right, Vi."

Davin clanked around the corner into the engine space. He caught Viola's eye and nodded back towards the main bay.

"Go take a look. Loci is pretty cool to see from the outside. I can handle these," the captain said.

Davin wasn't wrong. From over Phyla's shoulder, out through the cockpit window, Viola could see Loci as it came over the horizon. A central sphere covered with shoots in almost every direction, a porcupine whose spines ended in satellite dishes. As they came closer, the definitions of the space station became even more apparent. Company logos and artwork covered many of the dishes, creating a multicol-ored pallet that shined in the sunlight skipping off Earth's atmosphere.

"At least if we're going to die, it'll be somewhere pretty," Phyla said.

"I feel like that's anywhere in space," Viola replied.

"You haven't been inside some asteroids. Or in a Mars dust storm. You don't want to go out there."

Viola nodded. Phyla started the docking sequence, and as the *Jumper* slipped between a pair of giant green dishes blazed over with Eden's logo, Viola dipped out of the cockpit to her cabin. Time to check the weapons.

60

TAKE A DIVE

Man, they were blowing this. Merc pulled himself up, his sidearm still gripped in his right hand, and fired. The bolt glanced off the top of an android's head, the one dancing in between the other two and getting unblocked punches on the two women. It was the only bot far enough away to not risk blasting Opal or Alissa in the eye. The android turned its smoking head at Merc and charged.

Merc ducked a right punch from the android, then took the left cross hit in his side, the force barreling him into the ferry's railing. He looked right, trying to stuff away the pain, and saw Opal and Alissa buried beneath constant blows. They couldn't stay here. Couldn't win this fight. Merc's android came at him again, metal feet pounding on the deck. Merc tried to lift his sidearm and triggered another shot. It went wide, but the android flinched, possibly worried about another strike to its head. The pilot side-stepped along the railing. Felt his hand run over a length of rope. A rope tied to a lifeboat, one of a pair hanging off the bow over the open ocean.

The android rushed him and this time Merc pushed with his feet, jumped as the android hit him. The bot pushed Merc over the railing and into the lifeboat. His back slammed against one of the bench-style seats, numbing his nerves for an instant and sending waves of cascading pain up Merc's spine. The breath left his lungs, but Merc managed to squeeze off a shot, the laser slicing through the rope and sending the boat falling.

At least, the aft end.

With his left hand, Merc wrapped his arm around the seat and hung, suddenly in the open air as the lifeboat dangled from its remaining rope tie. With his right hand, Merc twisted and shot the other rope. The lifeboat plummeted towards the ocean, scraping against the side of the ferry. The aft hit the churning waves first, shoving the boat backwards and causing it to land right-side up on the water. Merc's head cracked against the seat and his vision blurred. Everything hurt, shocks crawling up and down his body from muscles done wrong. But he had to focus.

His right hand still held the sidearm, and Merc aimed towards where Opal and Alissa were struggling. Fired a shot. The laser went over their heads and struck the awning of the ferry, but it got their attention.

"Jump," Merc called, but his empty lungs couldn't do more than a whisper. Opal saw him and threw Alissa over the side. Then she jumped.

Merc tried to sit up as the two women splashed into the sea. The ferry was motoring past, the large wake of the engines coming closer. If the ferry went by while the two were still in the water, they could get sucked in. Merc rolled over and grabbed an oar locked into the side. Pulled it free. Then scanned the dark ocean for any sign. Alissa's hand, then her head were the first things he saw breaking for a second between the crest of a wave. She was throwing off her coat, ditching her vest. Anything that weighed her down. She was almost ten meters away. And Merc had never been on a boat in his life.

"Throw the ring!" Alissa shouted.

Ring? Merc glanced around, then saw it in the bow. A red and white circle. Merc dropped the oar and lunged for it. Threw it to Alissa, the ring's white rope billowing in the storm's wind. Still no sign of Opal. Alissa caught the ring, then dove beneath the surface. Merc kept looking, trying to find the sniper. But in the dark, lightning-lit sea, he couldn't make out anything. To add on to the misery, the pain in his stomach was rapidly being replaced by a rolling nausea.

Then Alissa broke the surface, holding a coughing Opal against her chest and grabbing the ring. Merc stared for a second, stunned, before pulling the rope. The waves bashed the boat up against the side of the ferry, but the lifeboat was well-made and didn't tip. As the ferry went past and the churning wake spun the lifeboat, Merc pulled the pair in. Brought Opal over the side by grabbing her arm and falling back into the lifeboat, pulling her with him. Alissa clambered in after.

"Thank you," Alissa said as Opal continued coughing.

"It's . . . what I do," Merc said.

Alyssa looked at him, confused. "You throw life preservers?"

"No, I, nevermind."

Merc sat back on the seat, turning to look at the retreating ferry. The island where they came from was still in sight, its outline on the horizon popping in when lightning flashed. Rest for a while in the rain, then they could row back. This one had been close, too close. Merc rested a hand on Opal, who'd finished hacking up her own puddle of water and was leaning against the boat's side, groaning.

"We made it, hotshot," Merc said to her. She looked at him, her soaked, cut, and bruised face breaking into a half smile. One that turned to open panic as the boat shook. A hand, its metal fingers gripping the side, appeared over the aft edge. After came those dead eyes, looking right at him.

61

MELODY

Y ou want an easy place to dock, Loci was your station. Davin lowered the ramp and walked into the small bay. Barely enough to fit the *Jumper*, the bay only had rudimentary amenities. A few canisters and battery charging hookups to connect the station's solar panels to charge docking ships. No welcome mat, no greeting. The only person they talked to was a robot, one that asked their reason for landing and then gave them access.

Davin had told it that they were offloading goods. Apparently Loci merited so little security that the bot didn't bother to confirm Davin's story. Just gave them clearance to one of Loci's three bays.

Behind him, the others made it off the ship. Davin had Melody, his fire-spewing shotgun, and a pair of sidearms. Phyla carried her usual rifle. Mox had his cannon attached, the monster weapon hanging over his chest and jutting its barrel out nearly a meter. Viola mirrored Phyla, except for the stance. The young hacker didn't look quite so confident holding the rifle as her flame-haired friend did. This time, though, Davin thought Viola looked like she could actually fire the thing.

Experience, it works wonders.

"Last chance, anyone wants to bail," Davin said. "Loci's small, and the communications hub is in the center. You don't have much time to second-guess."

"Don't think that's going to happen," Mox said.

"I want first shot," Viola said. "When we find Bosser."

"Way I see it, we all have reasons to shoot," Davin said. "You get the chance, you take him out. No worrying about turn order."

Davin played those words back. The Wild Nines didn't do assassinations. He'd never taken money for a kill. Yet here they were. Their last mission, and the goal was ending a life. But if there was one man to start with, Bosser would be that one.

They left the bay and went into Loci's central corridor. All three of the station's small docking bays were on the same side, the next one over held the standard shuttle Bosser had taken up from the facility, the featureless face logo of the androids slapped on outside. Trina's hack on Threetwelve had worked. It sent them sensor data, showing Bosser flying up here, showing him landing, and now Threetwelve showed its leader standing in the middle of the station.

Loci itself was bare-bones. No stores, shops, only emergency rations and rooms with cots for those staying at the station overnight. Any food or drink was ordered through a series of vending machines on one wall. Machines that would send their inventory to the company managing the station, and they'd arrange a resupply whenever things went low. Standard protocol for installations that didn't warrant a full-time human presence.

A ten minute walk brought them to the central core, the only place in the station with a door sealing it off from the rest. Soundproofing for sending a broadcast directly from the station. In front of the door, a flat gray slab with a light in the middle that glowed crimson, indicating the equipment was in use, were a pair of straight-standing men. They looked at Davin and the other three without reaction.

"I'm gonna go ahead and guess those aren't people," Phyla said.

"Not taking that bet," Davin said. "Viola, stay back. If you see an opening, go for the door. Get to Bosser before he can activate the other androids."

"I got left. He's uglier," Mox said. Davin nodded.

"Phyla, on two, we open up," Davin said.

Viola went back a few meters while Mox shifted to the left side of the corridor. Phyla raised her rifle, Davin aimed Melody, and the two androids blurred forward. No waiting for the first shot.

"Shoot it!" Davin yelled. He pulled Melody's trigger, aiming it at the charging bot. Phyla's lasers streaked past, peppering the android as it dipped and dove under Melody's homing fireballs. Pellets that ignited and tracked the intended target. Pellets that burned themselves out, and if they made contact, were hot enough to ignite just about anything.

The android took a hit on the left shoulder from Phyla's rifle, kept coming, then took another in the right leg. It stumbled, and then Davin's second shot caught it. Three of the six green fire orbs collapsed into the android, exploding against its clothes and melting into its plaskin exterior. The bot reeled, and Phyla kept peppering it with bolts. Chunks of metal blew off as her lasers chewed away its shell. It was only a couple meters away now, but its limbs were twitching, its left leg dragging. Davin stepped forward and pulled Melody's trigger a third time as the android reached its clawed and burning hand towards his face.

The green fire roared out of Melody and slammed into the android, pushing it to the ground. It jerked once. The hand reaching for Davin gripped only air, and then nothing. Nothing except melted metal.

62

THE SAME

Mox spun up the cannon, loosing a hail of bolts as the android darted towards him. The bot used the lower gravity, jumped and rebounded off the wall and ceiling to get around Mox's fire. The cannon's lasers chewed into the wall surrounding Loci's central core, tracing an outline of the bot's evasion. As the android pushed off the wall towards the ceiling a second time, Mox anticipated, led the jump, and blitzed home a series of hot laser, chewing chunks out from the bot's chest. But it kept coming, pushed off the ceiling and landed just beneath the end of the cannon. Gripped the barrel in its metal hands and started to twist.

Mox detached the weapon, letting go as the android pulled, swinging the suddenly free cannon away. The android, its arms swinging out left as it let go of the cannon, didn't have any defense for Mox's gauntleted fist streaking towards its chest. The impact, boosted by the exoskeleton, sent the android flying back, arms and legs wide. The low gravity on Loci, kept to a tenth of Earth's through rotation, meant the bot flew all the way back to the central core. It caught itself on the wall, crouched and launched back at Mox.

The metal man bent his knees, turned his right shoulder away, and prepared to deliver one heck of a punch to the face the incoming android.

"You and I are the same," the android shouted as it closed. And Mox flinched.

The android hit Mox hard and sent them both to the ground. Mox tried to wrap his arms around the bot, but the android moved fast, scrambling up and over Mox's head. The android gripped Mox's shoulders and swung the big man into the wall next to them. Mox felt his back crunch into the metal slate, his head ringing. And then the android was on him again. Swinging punches into his abdomen. The force of the blows, and the low gravity, pinned Mox to the side of the wall.

"I am made of metal," the android said, tapping a series of rapid jabs into Mox's ribs. "And so are you."

"Not only," Mox said. He felt blood in his mouth, warm sticky iron. Spat it into the android's eye. The bot paused, the red smear covering its face, and Mox fell to the ground.

As soon as Mox hit the floor, he swept out with his left arm and caught the android's ankle. Pulled. The android hit the ground, but the low gravity robbed the hit of much force. Mox pressed down on the android ankle to push himself up, just in time to catch the android rolling forward and punching him in the chin. Mox stumbled back, seeing the endless flashes from Davin and Phyla's weapons to the side. Hopefully they were doing better than he was.

"And I am also made of code, instincts I don't understand that tell me how to operate," the android spoke quickly, closing with Mox. "Just like your brain, I interact and react based on my intuitions."

"Intuitions designed, not learned."

Mox jumped the bot's first swing, then kicked, the low gravity giving him plenty of time in the air to swing his leg forward and strike the android in the face. The force pushed the bot into the wall, bouncing off it to the ground. Mox landed, walked over to the android as it picked itself up.

"You don't make choices," Mox said. "Not your own ones, anyway."

The android rotated, bringing with it a hard fist. Mox took the hit, but grabbed the bot's left arm as it rebounded from the impact. His leg was numb from the shot, but Mox had the android's left arm tight. With his right hand, Mox grabbed the android's other right wrist and pulled them apart. He felt the android resisting as its arms spread. The force pulled the androids face close to his own.

"You don't believe I'm making a choice?" the android said, its yellow metal eyes boring holes into Mox's mind.

"I believe you're following instructions."

The android was almost as strong, almost able to push Mox's arms back. But the exoskeleton, but Mox, had the leverage. Had the muscle. The tearing and snapping wires came first, followed by sparks as Mox yanked the android's arms out of their sockets and threw them aside. The android faltered back two steps, tilted its head it Mox.

"I suppose it is impossible to know," the android said.

And then it blew up.

CAN'T GIVE UP

The water pouring off the android's skin made it glisten as lightning blitzed in the night. Between flashes, Opal saw the android grab Alissa and turn back to the ocean. It was just going to take her and leave.

"Hey," Opal said, pushing herself up and diving onto the androids back. Her lungs still burned from the water she inhaled a moment ago, her legs and arms and chest raining with a thousand bruises, but Opal pushed her way past the pain to cling to the android's head and pull it back.

The bot struggled, the back of its ankles hitting the boat's aft bench. With nowhere to backpedal, the android fell, smashing Opal into the bottom of the boat as it rocked in the wave. The sniper didn't see what happened to Alissa, but saw the android clearly as it rolled over in the boat and reached out towards her. A laser's bright flash echoed the lightning and struck the android in the shoulder. Merc sat in the front of the boat, holding his sidearm out, dazed and determined. The android propelled itself across the two benches and slapped the weapon away from the pilot. Opal got up in time to see Merc take a hard blow to the head and collapse.

She hoped Merc still armed himself as she taught him.

As the android turned around, Opal reached into Merc's right boot, and found the beam knife strapped there. Pulled it out and activated the laser blade. A hot piece of sharp metal. In the pouring rain, thunder and lightning thrashing, the sniper faced the android on the rolling and pitching boat. Opal kept her weight moving with the waves, it felt similar to keeping her footing while making an aerial drop in atmosphere. Even on Mars, where the gravity wasn't quite so strong, a windstorm still had Opal moving to keep her feet. The android didn't hold its arms wide for balance, just shifted slightly around its knees.

"Come and take her," Opal said.

"You can't win," the android replied. "The odds are poor with that weapon. In this environment. I offer you a chance to surrender."

"Chance refused."

Opal lunged as she said the words, aiming the knife for the android's face. But her feet slipped on the base of the boat where puddles of water were forming and making the floor slick. The strike fell short, grazing the androids chest, and Opal caught herself on the front bench. Then the android grabbed her back, picked her up, and slammed her against the floor of the boat. Everything went blurry for a moment, but Opal held her vision onto that glowing blade, still gripped in her hand.

The android stepped over her, heading for the back of the boat, and Opal lashed out and cut the android's left ankle. It stumbled, but whatever magic in its programming allowed it to adjust kept the bot upright. It turned, reached for her.

"You are proving to be a threat," the android said, wrapping its fingers around her throat and lifting Opal up.

"Sorry about that," Opal said. She reached forward with the knife, burying the blade in the android's chest. Withdrew it and stabbed again as the bot's fingers tightened and cut off her air. Her throat retched, her nose flared, and Opal's eyes went wide. She felt the panic, and she pushed it down.

Keep stabbing. Hurt it enough so that it has to stop.

One slash, then another. Opal felt her body going numb. Black flecks sprinkled her vision. Another stab into the android's arm. Everything faded except the android's yellow eyes, looking into hers. Stab again, the dim response of her nerves telling her that the blade had at least hit the bot.

She couldn't keep her grip anymore. Simply sank into those yellow eyes.

Lightning struck nearby, catching Opal's glance, and in that fiery white line she saw motion, blurring behind the android. Then nothing at all.

64

GUARDIANS

The bombs. The androids always had bombs. The words hammered along with her headache as Viola sat up. Around her, Loci station's alarms blared. But she could still breathe, still felt oxygen flow into her lungs. No hull rupture, then. The surrounding air was full of smoke, paper ash floating from burning clothes. She looked down at herself and saw tears in her own suit, long thin gashes where bits of blown metal slashed past her. On the ground nearby, attached to a splintered end of her broken belt, was Viola's sidearm. She couldn't see her rifle.

"Davin? Phyla?" Viola's scratchy voice called out to no response. "Mox?"

Nothing. Either unconscious, or dead. In front of her, standing out as a dark blur through the smoke, glowed the red light of the central core. Where Bosser would be. If the rest of them were dead, then Viola would be the one to stop him. What she'd wanted, right?

Viola stood, picked up the sidearm and checked its energy level. The power was good, the weapon set to kill. Coughing, stumbling, Viola held the sidearm in her right hand and made her way to the door. There wasn't a lock, just a simple open and shut button. Boarding Loci was hard enough and had no value to someone without the right transmission codes. Why bother with security?

She pressed the button, and the door slid open.

On the other side was a short, dark hall. Following the smoke in, Viola walked to a large circular room, one wall dedicated to a massive screen, the middle an open stage, and the other half a set of chairs arranged as if for a play. For those special recordings that demanded an audience. On that stage stood Bosser, talking to the screen. Not seeing Viola.

"As you can see, with the data I've sent along, we're in prime position," Bosser said. "And the trial run went perfectly."

"You didn't warn me, Libra, that it would be on one of my freighters," said a voice, a voice Viola recognized. She looked at the screen and saw there, among ten other faces, her own father.

Viola blinked. What was he doing? And for that communication to happen so fast, her father would have to be nearby. On Earth, or Luna.

"The test demanded secrecy. You'll be reimbursed," Bosser said. "But the time for that secrecy is over, which is why I invited all of you to Luna to meet your guardians. They protect you at any cost, annihilate any enemy, and don't need the approval of the Free Laws to do it."

Guardians. That was a funny word for it. Viola looked at those faces, hoping to see horror or, maybe, anger. But all she saw were nods, agreement. Not only were these people, her father among them, happy to subvert the Free Laws that had governed humanity's expansion off Earth for a century, but they were happy to pay for it.

"Tell them what you did," Viola shouted, walking into the room with her sidearm held up. "Tell them what their guardians can really do."

Gasps and rapid chatter echoed from the screen, Viola heard her father call her name, but she kept her focus on the man in the middle, his calm stare as Bosser leveled his gaze at her. She held the sidearm up, finger on the trigger. Until something hit Viola hard from the side, sprawling her out on the floor, the weapon sliding away. The cold malevolence of ThreeTwelve looked at her.

"You wanted to see a demonstration of the guardians, there you go," Bosser said. "The threat removed. Incapacitated, so that now I can deal with her as I see fit."

Bosser walked towards Viola, held out a hand. ThreeTwelve removed a sidearm from its holster and set the weapon in Bosser's palm. He aimed it at Viola. She glared back at him and waited for the burning end.

"If you shoot her Bosser, you're done," Viola heard her father say. Annoyance flickered across Bosser's face, his eyes rolling and his mouth setting in a half-frown, then the man's small smile snapped back into place. He turned to the screen.

"Your daughter has proven herself to be quite the annoyance," Bosser said. "The Red Voice used her to get to Earth. She prevented the original execution of the Wild Nines. And now she's here, threatening to kill me. At what point does she become more trouble than she's worth?"

"Never," her father said. Despite the anger boiling in her, Viola felt a flush of love at the words. He might be a flawed, dangerous man, but he was still her father.

Bosser nodded, and then his grin spread wider, and cold fear blew through Viola's nerves.

65

UNEXPECTED

There were good interruptions, and there were bad interruptions. The girl walking in, sidearm up and at the ready, went from bad to good in a matter of moments. Bosser chose to look at it as an opportunity.

"So you see, your new guardians will keep you safe. Can even help you deal with your unruly children," Bosser said, adding a deprecating chuckle. "But we're not only here to talk about protection. As all of us know, keeping the current climate advantageous has always been the goal of the android project."

Yes. An order had been established, and that order wanted to keep itself intact. There wasn't much Bosser had to do to get what he wanted, a place on top of that same stack. Pulling the strings. A home on Earth, weaving intrigue across the solar system. Was that really so much to ask?

"And you say these guardians can do that?" Capricorn asked. The woman led a biome development corporation, a business dedicated to creating those bubbles that kept humans alive in the worst environments. A venture that was proving increasingly susceptible to lawsuits, to frustration from governments and citizens who just didn't understand that it was risky. That some might fail. That the occasional accident was a necessary marker of progress.

"They can. I'll be sending along the codes you need to control your guardians. And when you need something special, you work through me. I'll stay on Earth, run the facility, make your guardians to order. Once everyone understands how things work, who's going to bother fighting against us? Who's going to bother fighting against you?" Bosser said.

The desire to protect what's theirs. It was so easy to manipulate, to twist their minds around the idea that what they had was too valuable to lose, no matter what the cost. Who cared if they were giving up just a bit of power to one man and his bots, if what they got in exchange was stability, the chance to keep their castle? Bosser repressed his smile. Careful now. Unanimous agreement, followed by financial investment, and then everything Bosser needed would be his. And once he had his guardians in place, ready to do as he wanted with a simple phrase, all of them would have no other choice than to keep him on top.

"So I think it's time to call this to a vote," Bosser said. "Those who like what they've seen, who want to move forward into a new, stable world where our interests are protected and the risk of opposition is made moot by an invincible protecting force, say aye. The cowards, the ones who want to keep today's fragile structure where any moment can be blown to shreds by a rebel with a bomb and an agenda, say nay."

To his left, ThreeTwelve kept Viola pinned. In front of them, on their screens, the various leaders looked askance at each other. They were all in the same hotel on Luna, all together, with a set of androids waiting outside their rooms. In earshot of the transmission's audio. Bosser watched their expressions and brought two phrases to his lips. No matter which way the vote went, he would be the winner. Then the first aye came, from Cancer. Then the second from Capricorn. And the cascade began, Bosser's smile growing wider, unhinged with the adulation.

"Hey, jackass, time's up," a hoarse voice shouted from the hallway into the studio. Bosser turned and saw the wreck of a man standing there. Davin Masters, clothes cut to ribbons, bleeding from a hundred cuts, and one eye swollen shut. The man didn't even have a sidearm.

"Virgo, how about this one?" Bosser said. "Any qualms, or can I show you what you agreed to?"

Virgo, fearless protector of his daughter, said nothing. And so Bosser turned back to the ruined captain and shrugged.

"Sorry, Davin. I guess you have no friends here. What's done is done."

When Bosser spoke the phrase, ThreeTwelve dropped Viola to the ground and sprung on Davin. It pulled the long knife from the holster on its leg, and held it out, going right for the captain's throat. A messy kill, but examples needed to be clear.

66

BRAWL

hreeTwelve looked just like Fournine had, way back on Europa. The merciless mask lunging towards him at a speed too fast to comprehend. But Davin didn't have to react, he just had to say the words.

"Tables turned," Davin said as the blade swept up in towards his throat. The words Trina said to use. The override she'd put into ThreeTwelve's code.

ThreeTwelve stopped. Literally froze, the blade a centimeter from cutting Davin to pieces. The captain took a breath, an inhale that seemed to ignite all of his cuts simultaneously. The fiery stings only sharpened his focus. He was so hurt already, what did it matter if Bosser did something now? Though that man had his mouth open, eyes bulging, at the sight of his android doing precisely *not* what he'd commanded.

"Take care of your master," Davin said. ThreeTwelve turned around and charged Bosser. Davin would have to thank Trina for this, get a message back to Earth or land there and give the mechanic a tight hug. The sight of Bosser as his plans collapsed around him, the shouts from the council, all those faces on the screen dropping into panic as the android turned against its owner, that was worth it.

"This one's for Lina," Davin said as ThreeTwelve reached Bosser and grabbed the man. Lifted him up and cocked its blade back.

Bosser's hand moved fast, pressed a button on his comm. ThreeTwelve melted, Davin couldn't think of another word to describe it. The android's parts simply collapsed in on themselves, piling onto the ground a collection of scattered circuits, plates of skin, and the knife blade. ThreeTwelve's head rolled a meter away, no longer connected to its body. Bosser brushed himself off, looked at Davin and shook his head.

"Wasn't planning to show that one today," Bosser said. "Marl mentioned you had a lot of tricks, she wasn't wrong."

Davin didn't have a weapon. Melody and the sidearms he'd carried were shredded by the explosion. He didn't know if Bosser's weird device would melt him too. But there was one avenue out, the android's knife. It sat there on the stage, just a few meters ahead.

"Bosser," a face on the screen said. "What was that?"

The question turned Bosser's head, and Davin made a run for it. His feet pounded on the stage, the chilly floor spiking cold up through holes melted in his boots, and as Bosser turned back, Davin's hand dragged down and gripped the hilt of the knife. Swung it up, only to have Bosser grab his forearm and halt the swing.

"It's my own protection," Bosser said to Davin's face, in reply to the talking head's question. "When you work with androids, you take precautions."

Davin raised his knee, went for the crotch shot, but Bosser twisted away. Grabbed Davin's leg and wrenched it up. Davin hit the ground and rolled. Tucked the knife in and gave himself some space. Came up to a crouch as Bosser went towards him.

"And when do we get those precautions?" The voice on the screen asked.

"When I choose to give them to you," Bosser said. He was keeping his eyes on Davin's knife. That was an opportunity. Davin got to his feet, then feinted the stab with his right hand. Bosser flinched away and made to grab the forearm again. Except this time, Davin stepped in and threw a left hook. The punch caught Bosser on the side of the head, knocking the man away.

"Damn, that hurt," Davin said, pulling his hand back. "Your head made of metal too? You just like the rest of them?"

Davin didn't wait for Bosser to answer, but ran after him and stabbed towards the man's kidneys. Bosser turned with the jab, took the blade into his side, and connected with Davin's face. The shock of the punch robbed Davin stab of its force and the blade only made a shallow cut before Bosser knocked it away. It bounced off the stage and underneath one of the chairs, leaving the two men breathing hard and staring at each other.

"Been a long time since I fought this way," Bosser said. "I forgot how refreshing it is to feel a man's bones break beneath your fist."

"Like you've ever broken anything," Davin said. "You just hide behind your bots and let them do the dirty work."

Bosser gave him a silky smile and moved in. The man had some experience, he dropped into a stance that Davin didn't recognize. Not that it mattered. This wasn't going to be a pretty brawl. Davin brought his fists up, and stepped into a kick, high left angled right at Bosser's crouching eye. Bosser stepped into it, taking the kick on the shoulder and leveling three quick strikes into Davin's stomach. The world veered at the impacts, waves of nausea coming up as Davin's stomach convulsed. He backed off, retching blood into his mouth.

"Doesn't look like you're ready," Bosser said. "The reason I let my bot fight first is so that I can save my energy for when it really matters. Like when I have to show a ship's captain where he belongs."

Bosser came forward in a short jog, running into another three punch sequence. Davin stumbled just out of reach. Then he bit back, the captain dodging past the final punch in Bosser's sequence and, pushing against the man's shoulder while sweeping his leg against Bosser's ankle, tripped Bosser into the ground. Then Davin fell on him and went into his favorite move; the dirty struggle. Davin used every part of his body: swinging elbows, bashing knees, biting at Bosser's face with his teeth. The easiest way to counter a strategy was to have no strategy at all.

Bosser struggled back, and Davin felt the man trying to move his arms and legs beneath them. The captain tried to prevent it, elbowing Bosser in the kidney, taking a chunk out of Bosser's cheek with his teeth. Davin's right hand tore off Bosser's comm and flung it across the room. Then Davin felt a hand on his throat, and Bosser was rolling with him, slamming Davin down against the floor. Davin's head cracked against the ground, and the world swam. Bosser's bloodied face looked down at him.

"If that's how you like it," Davin croaked.

"It'll do," Bosser said, raising his fist. Swinging it, hitting Davin in the temple. Black flickered across Davin's vision. His arms went weak.

Sorry, Lina. Can't fight this one anymore.

67

ONE SHOT

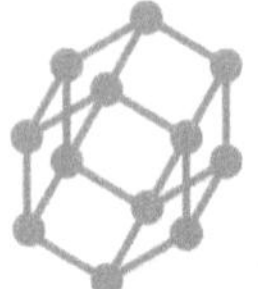

The aim was steady. Bosser right there in the middle. Swinging another punch at Davin.

"Don't do it, Viola," her father said on the screen. Bosser turned up at the words, paused his beating, and stared at Viola and the sidearm. Davin turned his head more slowly, and Viola winced at the sight of the captain's bruised and battered face.

"Listen to your father," Bosser said. "You have nothing to gain, and everything to lose. Shoot here, in front of a dozen witnesses, and you're a murderer. Your future ruined. Your father's business tainted."

Viola's eyes moved to the screens, to those famous, fabulously wealthy owners of the engines of human commerce. All of them judging her, waiting and watching to see what she would do next. To see if she would take the shot.

The first time, the only time she'd killed was to protect a friend. This time was no different.

Viola pulled the trigger. The orange bolt spat out of the sidearm and burrowed itself into Bosser's chest. The man's face curled from stern surprise to plain shock. Viola fired again. The second bolt hitting Bosser's stomach and collapsing him off of Davin. She walked up to Bosser and fired again and again and then Davin was pulling her arm back.

"It's over," Davin said. "It's over."

Viola took a breath. Her fingers let go of the sidearm. And she stared into the wide, glassy, dead eyes of Bosser Oates.

68

MAY MARS NEVER BE SILENT

Alissa had swung the oar, it'd hit the android's head, and the bot dropped Opal. Staggered to the boat's edge. Alissa swung the oar again, cracking the android in the face as it turned to face her. The force toppled the android over the side into the raging ocean. Alissa dropped the wooden weapon, grabbed Opal's beam knife, and as the android's metal hand again gripped the side of the boat, slid across the bench to meet it.

"This is for Castor," Alissa said, then jammed the beam knife into the android's yellow eye. The pouring rain shoved her hair into her face, and by the time Alissa brushed it out of the way, the crackling lightning showed nothing but dark blue water off the side of the boat.

Over the next hour, Alissa struggled with the oars, locking them in and guiding the boat back to shore. On the windswept beach, exhausted and spent, Alissa picked up Opal's limp wrist. The sniper was still alive. Whether she deserved to be was another question, but they'd come on the ferry to save her, so perhaps now was not the right time for vengeance. Besides, Alissa wasn't sure she could heft the oar again to deliver a strike. Her arms were like lead, and she was so soaked. The tropical water was warm, but there on the beach, in the breeze, things were getting chilly.

"I don't know who's listening," Alissa said into Opal's comm, on the sniper's default channel. "But your sniper and her friend are here on the beach."

Alissa followed up with the precise coordinates, then stood up and walked away. She'd left everything on that ferry. Only her comm, and some coin stashed in accounts registered to other names. That fit with her bruises and cuts, which, Alissa was sure, made her look like some sort of horror story. Those looks were confirmed by the first tourists she came to, at a bar still open. A band playing, even this late, under an awning. But there was warmth, there was a seat, and there was liquor. The bartender didn't even hesitate, dropping a shot in front of her.

"Look like you need this," the bartender muttered. Alissa didn't argue. But she sipped the small drink slow. Savored the burn. Took some bar napkins and patted down her face.

Her comm vibrated. A new message. Maybe Bosser had found her number. Called to gloat. Or yet another bank telling her they'd frozen her assets. She lifted the tool up, and on the small screen, read the text.

Alissa,

I hope this finds you well. As instructed, those of us left have made our way to Titan. The settlement here is small, but suitable. Eden does not have their hands on it yet. We procured a security contract and are establishing ourselves. One of Bakr's members, a woman named Cass, arrived here not long ago. She had a single gem, from Neptune, that has provided us with unexpected coin.

We await your return, or your orders.

May Mars never be silent.

- Ferro

Alissa looked up from the comm to see the bartender staring at her.

"Need another?" He asked.

"When's the next ship out?" Alissa replied.

The bartender glanced at the clock hanging beside the bar.

"The late one jumps in an hour," the bartender said. "If you want space, anyway. Ferry won't be back till tomorrow."

"Then I'm good, thanks."

Alissa slipped off the stool, her shoes leaving puddles wherever she stepped. Walked away from the bar and towards the glow of the space port. The Red Voice wasn't gone yet.

May Mars never be silent.

69

SNIPER'S HEADACHE

The first thing she heard was the rippling row of the surf. The watery waves crawling their way through sand and rock, whistling and popping. She stayed there like that for a moment, eyes closed and listening to the sound. Gulls squawked overhead, and the softer, deeper roar of a departing ship sifted through on the breeze. It wasn't until she heard the cough that Opal let light back into her world. With the dazzling sun came muted pains, tight muscles and the feeling of a band pressed around her forehead, pushing down against her.

"You're going to feel like crap," Erick said.

Opal twisted her head as another cough sounded. In the bed next to her, built on a small frame meant for children, Merc lay. His ankles dangled off the end, but someone had put a footstool there, covered it with a pillow, supporting his feet. The pilot's eyes were still closed.

"He'll be out longer than you," Erick said. "His head is pretty messed up. He's going to need some recovery time."

Opal turned back to the doctor and tried to find the air in her lungs to speak.

"And Alissa?" Opal said.

"She left. Rowed you both back to the island, then found us."

Left. Back out where the androids could find her. Opal tried to sit up, but Erick pressed her back down into the sheets, into the sweet comfort of the pillow.

"You sit up now, you're likely to throw up all over this bed," Erick said. "I'd rather not have to clean that up."

"We need to find her. She'll be in danger," Opal said.

"No, she won't," Trina stepped into the room. She had her comm held up in front of her face, projecting a news article. "Davin and the others won. Bosser's dead."

"Dead?"

"Shot. They're saying it was one of his own androids. Malfunctioned in his face, blew him up."

"ThreeTwelve?" Opal asked.

"Maybe," Trina said. "I haven't been able to get Davin on the comm so I don't know for sure. But they've put a stop to the android program until it can be reviewed. The facility has already been taken over and shut down."

"Which means you can rest," Erick said.

Maybe, just for a while. Opal felt her eyes grow heavy. Slid the lids back over to hide the sun and vanished into her dreams.

70

SEE THE WORLD

The table was covered in parts, drawing all kinds of looks from passengers arriving for the ferry. Viola ignored them, focused on binding the thin metal pieces together. It wouldn't be the same level of quality that Puk had before, but it would be enough. She could carry the bot with her on her backpack.

"We're going back to running cargo," Davin said, walking up behind her. "Should be safe. Like a vacation, only with some coin at the end."

"You want to know if I'm interested?" Viola replied.

"Just making the offer. Always good to have a mechanic on board, especially with Trina staying here," Davin's face, his body were covered in bandages. He wore thick sunglasses and, even in the heat, a coat. Anything to keep the stares away.

"I don't think so," Viola was surprised how easily the words came. But they were true. She was too tired, too drained. She turned her face away from Puk's pieces and looked out over the ferry to the open water beyond. A whole ocean, and a whole world full of new things that she'd never seen before. "I'm not ready to leave Earth just yet."

"I'd say the same thing if I were you."

"Isn't this your first time here too? Don't you want to see everything?"

Davin ran a hand through his hair and followed Viola's look out to the sea.

"I've been here before. Once or twice. Staying would be nice. Problem is, well, the problem's the same that it's always been. We need coin, and the *Jumper*'s the easiest way to get it. One of these days, maybe we'll sell it. Come back here and float around the world," Davin flashed a grin. "Till then, we'll be taking whatever job comes our way."

The captain walked away a minute later, leaving Viola to the tools. Over the next hour she locked the last pieces in the place. Pulled the sidearm from her holster, the same one that she'd used to put an end to Bosser two days ago up on Loci. Looked at it for a moment, felt its weight in her hand, then popped out the battery. Shoved it in the slot on Puk's new body and pressed the button on her comm.

Puk, now a gray brick with a single light that flickered to green life, woke up.

"Hey, Viola. Where are we?" Puk said, the single speaker emitting tinny, grainy audio.

"On Earth, Puk."

"Swell. Also, feel like I had a bit of a downgrade."

"You kind of blew yourself up. What you've got now is all I have on hand."

"Sounds like something I'd do," Puk said. "So where are we going next?"

"Wherever this ferry is taking us."

"Let me look it up, I'll tell you all about it."

Viola stood, latched Puk onto her backpack, and walked towards the ferry. The bot talked the entire way, and Viola just smiled and listened.

LUNA

Earth hung in the sky like a giant ornament. Luna's glass domes accentuated the glow, making the planet appear even more beautiful than it did from space. A bright spark drew Mox's eyes back towards the spaceport. That it be the *Jumper*, blasting off for Miner Prime. For another cargo run.

With a pair bags over his shoulders, the same two he'd brought on board years ago, Mox turned with the funneling crowd leaving the spaceport and headed into the city. He glanced at his wrist; the message sitting there.

Welcome back, metal man. Glad you're here. We've got work to do.

-Sarge.

As he went down the escalator, Mox caught the sight of a flowing red cape. The sign of the Centurion, Luna's own police force. He'd worn one once. Maybe they'd let him have it again.

PROBLEMS TO SOLVE

Trina sat in the chair awkwardly. It was a little too tall for her legs, the armrests a little too long. She felt like a girl.

"You're the one that hacked ThreeTwelve?" the woman, Abril, spoke to her. At the table were a few other engineers, and a man in full military regalia. The representatives from Earth's governments.

"It wasn't that hard," Trina said.

"And you could make it harder?" Abril said.

Make it harder? Give her enough time, and Trina could turn these androids invincible. Not that they hadn't been deadly before, but without Bosser introducing weaknesses for his own ends, Trina could make the bots strong. Perfect. It would be a problem, a challenge. And she'd get to stay right here, on Earth, out of range of any more lasers.

"But controlled," the military man said. "No chance they could go rogue, no chance someone could do what Bosser did."

"Sir," Trina said. "All I want is interesting problems to solve."

"And what could be more interesting than this?" Abril asked.

The military man shook his head, looked at Abril skeptically.

"We'll be keeping a close eye," the military man said. He turned back to Trina. "No matter what she says, remember that you're working for us now. For Earth. Bosser made a promise of guardians, one that he didn't fulfill. I hope you can."

Trina didn't do more than nod, her mind was already racing forward into plans, equations, and solutions. When the androids lived again, they wouldn't be walking weapons for one crazed man, they would be the ultimate sword for justice.

73

THE WHISKEY JUMPER

Davin looked up from the console at the vast array of stars laid out in front of him. The Moon receded behind the *Jumper*, and all they had to do now was follow the yellow line to Miner Prime. To where Mako, the junk dealer from Europa, wanted Davin to pick up some special supplies. Just the things Mako needed to finish his masterpiece on that Jupiter moon. What that masterpiece was, Davin didn't ask. The surprise would be good enough.

"Did you see the pictures that Erick took?" Phyla asked from the pilot's chair.

"Man was always getting sentimental," Davin replied.

"Oh yeah, like you're never that way."

"Phyla, I'm a forward-looking dude. The past only has problems."

"Problems? I thought the whole reason you went after Bosser was because of your past."

"And look what it got me." Davin looked down at his bandage wrapped body.

"But do you regret it?"

"Not at all. It was for Lina."

They sat in silence for a minute. Phyla's hand found its way to Davin's. Her fingers threaded between his, squeezed.

"I don't think you should leave the past behind," Phyla said. "You don't want to forget who you are."

"That's why you're here, to remind me."

Phyla laughed.

"Do I get paid extra for that? Feel like it's going to be a lot of work."

"Not a chance," Davin said.

Fournine announced that the *Jumper* was about to punch the engines to full cruising speed, and Davin got up. His turn to watch the energy levels, make sure things weren't going to blow up all over them. As he started down the ladder from the cockpit, Davin glanced back at Phyla. Caught her smile. The same bright eyes he'd seen when they first left Miner Prime years ago. Before they'd met Mox, Cadge, wandered back and forth across the solar system searching for adventure.

Maybe she was right, maybe some things were worth remembering after all.

74

A SPECIAL OFFER

The cafe overlooked the long scar of the Grand Canyon. Viola sipped from the frothy cup and watched a flock of birds fly by overhead. In between the clouds she could pick out gray shapes, dots in the sky. Earth's space stations ringing the planet. Spoiling the flawless blue, but down below the lines of orange and purple rock spread out untainted.

"Another one off the list," Viola said. "Put it at number three."

"That's pretty good," Puk said, "but I can't argue with you."

"The canyon is beautiful," said a new voice. The chair across from Viola pulled out and Captain Yuan took the seat. He didn't look much different from when they'd met on Neptune, except here he was in civilian clothes. A jacket, plain gray T-shirt, jeans. He didn't do anything to his eyes; that same calm intensity. "You're a hard woman to find, Viola."

"Didn't know anyone was looking," Viola said. She tried to keep her hand steady, wrapped it around the cup. Last time she'd seen Yuan, they'd blown apart two spaceships and nearly got themselves killed in the vacuum around Neptune. Not the most pleasant memory.

"Eden has a job for you," Yuan said. "I told them I'd ask."

"What kind?"

"Before I go on," Yuan softened. "You can say no. I'll walk away, say I couldn't find you. But if I tell you, then you can no longer just disappear. You'll be committed."

Viola paused. She'd been around the Earth, but still had plenty left to see. Still had a lot she wanted to do before getting back behind the desk. But something in Yuan's voice said that this wasn't something she wanted to miss. That this wasn't an opportunity that would come around again. There'd been adventure, and she'd seen more than her share of violence, but something tugged at her. Kept her from saying no.

Maybe it was time for something new.

READ on for an excerpt from the WILD NINES' next adventure, ROGUE BET!

AN EXCERPT FROM ROGUE BET

THE WILD NINES BOOK FOUR

Her eye changed its color. Again and again, the mark's right eye, framed with a metal striping giving up her enhancements, shifted to match the club's frenetic lights which played through cold color schemes to a scattershot beat. Starfield tile laced with neon littered the floor, the walls, the ceiling. *Neil's* ignored its namesake and its own lunar location and caved to the gyrating sensory assault so damn prevalent these days.

But Davin wouldn't have been three drinks deep without that eye.

"You're coming recommended," Theona said, twisting her talk back to Davin's street cred for what must've been the fifth time. "I normally vet my runners."

"I'm not the one with a deadline," Davin leaned back, casual personified, then jerked upright as his stool nearly toppled over.

Theona's normal eye quirked an eyebrow and she made for her silver Stardust cocktail, the drink more sugar than anything else. Slurped the thing through a straw as long as Davin's forearm. Around them, early afternoon drunks parleyed a half-day's wages into a full night's fun. *Neil's* didn't care that dinner wouldn't come for hours yet, the psychic beats pulsed through the floor, through the stool, and bounced Davin's brain around more than the straight Moon Rum fixes he'd been sipping.

Their table sat in the third node branching off a rectangular dance floor whose swirling nebula floor pitched galactic wonder to, right now, a single man swaying his hips to a beat only he could hear.

Davin didn't think he was too many rounds away from joining the guy, but his outfit didn't match *Neil's* workman vibe. Slick with space-faring leather and trumped up with multi-planetary spices, Davin had that classy vagabond look that put him intriguingly out of place in any setting. Theona paired nicely, her mechanical eye complementing a spliced up assembly slotting colors, metals, and cloth in fits and starts that shouldn't have worked but, in *Neil's* neon blast, sucked in Davin's attention.

"I'm trying to find you," Theona said, drawing Davin back. "But talking to you's like trying to catch a salmon mid-stream. Most runners aren't so hard to figure."

Salmon mid-stream? Davin slotted away that line for later. Maybe the woman had come up from Earth, spent some time in a business not built on running illegal weapons. Maybe that damn eye made it easy to spot the fish under the water. Which, how many fish would she have to catch to pay—

"Are you even paying attention?" Theona asked. "I'm the one paying you, remember?"

"Sure." Focus, Davin. C'mon. You need this. "You already know about my ship, you know what I can do. What, you want a resume?"

"Already have that," Theona replied, then leaned in.

"Thing is, I'm getting the wrong vibe from you, Davin. Like you're not who you're saying you are."

"I'm the man that saved the solar system," Davin replied.

"Then why're you meeting me in this club?"

Why? Davin had a thousand reasons why, and all of 'em sucked. He replayed the years since Bosser took the wrong laser every night, trying to find the spot where things went off course, as if Davin could throw time into reverse and try it again.

"Because it turns out being a hero doesn't pay," Davin said, the words spoiling in his mouth.

"Think that's the first authentic thing I've heard you say," Theona sat back with a nasty grin, her eye flipping bright green. "You do this run for me, it'll pay. The next one'll pay too. I treat my runners right."

"Then let's get on with it." Davin slipped off the stool, steadied the world by holding the bar table for a minute. "Places to be, people to see, all that crap."

"Thought you weren't on a timetable?" The woman sucked down her drink.

"It's never too soon to leave this place."

Davin hadn't wanted to go to *Neil's* at all, but Theona insisted. Said, when they'd first commed, that its music, lights, and general disdain for lunar building codes made it difficult for anyone to listen in. Davin couldn't argue with that, so they'd set the date, time, and drinks.

Now the woman led him through the sleazy streets in the Nubium dome, a failed blend between start-up hopefuls trying to cash in on Luna's resurgence and predators feeding on those same dreams. Pop-up businesses littered the stacked shanties, and Davin knew most went underground too, burrowing the dome's least beneath the gray dust. Every one hawked something new, a body-mod or some drug, a bot that'd save your life or take another's.

Overhead, dome-skippers darted along, their one-and-two passenger floaters zipping through Nubium as fast as possible. Didn't want to take the chance they'd bust an engine and come down for repairs here.

Davin, though, enjoyed the walk. Earth sat up top, its blue-white-green beauty providing a better sky than the black void he normally had soaring through space. And the people crowding the streets around him? Hungry for hope, for deals, or just plain hungry? Those people he knew. Those people were him.

He hadn't grown up on the Moon, but home was more than a place.

Theona tilted her walk, nodding between two orange striped stacks. She kept her mouth shut out here, where ears were everywhere, and Davin followed suit. He'd rather listen to the street music than her cocky pitches about how much artillery she had waiting to blow a hole in Eden's fleet.

Not that Eden wouldn't deserve it, but Davin didn't play those kinda sides. Not anymore.

Between the stacks, a few meters back from the street proper, the woman held up her metal eye to an innocuous spot on the silver walls. Something clicked as Davin closed, and a doorway shot up, revealing a stairway heading down.

"Bit small to move cargo," Davin said as they started in. "Unless you're dealing in toys."

"We shift the goods out a different way," Theona replied, leading. "I've got Nubium's dockyard on my payroll. Time comes to fly, you'll come in proper, leave without a second look."

"Ain't that swell."

Behind him, the door shut hard and swamped the

stairway in darkness. Davin heard a click as Theona's eye shifted again, and he felt her hand reach out and grab his.

"Don't get any ideas," she said, pulling Davin down the stairs.

"And I thought things were going so well."

She laughed, a sound that vanished along the steps, which went deeper than Davin would've thought.

"At least you're funny. Most runners, they're hard types that don't know how to laugh anymore."

"Laughter's just my way of living," Davin replied.

The dark had to be for security. He guessed Theona's eye made the stairs look bright as day for her. Anyone following would find themselves taking a long fall, probably right to rifles pointing at their faces. Davin kept his steps sure, kept his left hand on the sidearm he wore on his belt, charged and ready.

Melody, his super-charged shotgun, had stayed home today. Too obvious for a job like this.

But hey, at least the stairs and wherever they led didn't smell like booze and too-little deodorant, like *Neil's*. Breathing, it turned out, was something Davin preferred to do without choking every time.

The stairs ended their dark journey into a big space that any cargo hauler would know: a warehouse. This one must've carried on for blocks, and going by the sealed crates stacked everywhere, most carrying labels with a ship's name and a time, it did brisk business.

"Pretty nice setup you've got here," Davin said as the woman dropped his hand, let him take in the picture.

Beyond the crates, lift bots milled around the space, shuttling this and that to here and there. Most had the long, straight arms good for toting heavy fare, though the Moon's touch-n-go gravity made big lifts easy. Davin suspected that's why manufacturing had grown so big here: close enough to Earth for the money and the buyers, light on weight and legality.

"That's the stack I have for you," Theona said, bringing Davin to a cluster that, going by the shapes and their lengths, held enough damage to arm a squad or two. "Drop's at Enceladus. Pick up another normal run to keep things clean."

"Right." Davin leaned in to get a good look at the closet casket, matte green and carbon-scored. "Where'd you get these?"

"Nowhere you need to know," Theona said. "You make this run, though, I'll have more. The rebels are paying way over premium now." Davin looked back, caught her shaking her head. "They're either doing better than Eden thinks in this war, or they're so damn desperate they'll throw their money away."

"It's not worth anything if you're dead."

Theona didn't argue, did ask Davin if he had any questions.

"Yeah, I've got a couple," Davin said, turning, catching one last look around the place.

No guards hanging around. A couple bots that looked like they might try something, but Theona looked to be running a profit-shop: keep labor costs low, take-home pay high.

Made Davin's job easy.

He didn't even draw the sidearm quick. Just reached over, pulled the weapon out with his right hand and leveled it at Theona. Who laughed again.

"What, you're going to steal all this cargo?"

"Nah," Davin replied. "They are."

A horrendous bang sounded from up the dark stairs,

followed by harsh light and feet pounding along the steps. Theona dropped her nonchalance act and opened her mouth, like she was planning on giving some dumb order.

"Don't," Davin said, wagging his sidearm to catch her attention. "Not worth it. Give up your suppliers, maybe they'll let you off easy."

A thud from the stairs clued Davin to look over Theona's shoulder, to see the first Moon Centurion make the main floor. Others followed, their crimson capes swirling as they swept into the warehouse, hunting for threats. Those hapless bots didn't even get a chance to try for a weapon before some quick frying bolts from the Centurion's rifles reduced the machines to inert metal.

That first Centurion came Davin's way, big and bold and covered with an exoskeleton molded to his every muscle.

"Mox, right on time," Davin said. "Meet Theona. I imagine she'll have a lot to say."

Theona's mechanical eye clicked again, to a burning red, and she lunged towards Davin with a desperate rage Davin had seen all too many times before. The last move of someone whose path met an end they knew was coming, yet hoped would never arrive.

Theona never touched him. Mox had a hand on Theona's shoulder as she started her move, and he simply pressed her to the ground. She twitched once, then lay on the floor, still.

"New trick?" Davin asked.

"Nerve endings," Mox said, boulder-shaking voice rumbling off the warehouse floors and walls. "Press hard, body goes numb. New Centurion training."

Davin nodded, as if he had some idea of what life was like within the Moon's secretive police force. He'd met Mox as the Centurions had kicked him out for getting that big ol' exoskeleton. When the Wild Nines had stopped the Solar System from disintegrating into an android dystopia, Mox had come back here, and done well enough to offer Davin a job for some much-needed coin.

"She said these were going to Enceladus," Davin said, glancing at the weapons cache. "The rebels are buying."

"They are always buying," Mox replied. "Now, at least, they will not get these."

"You on Eden's side, now?"

"I am on the side that keeps me and my Centurions alive," Mox replied. "Whoever it is."

"Was afraid you'd changed," Davin said. "When's the fee coming in?"

"Guess you have not changed either," Mox laughed. "Check your account." Mox hesitated, then reached down and picked Theona up from the ground, slung her over his shoulder. "Have to get back to it. Sting like this takes a lot of red tape to get closed up. A lot of gear to take in."

"Sure."

Davin slipped the sidearm back in its holster, let the cocky smile fade along with the adrenaline. Took the hint and moved past Mox towards those stairs back up.

"Good to see you again, Davin. Been too long."

"It has. Take care, Mox." Davin offered up a half-hand wave, to the big man. "I'll call next time I'm out this way."

"Do that," Mox lifted a mitt. "And tell Phyla I said hi."

Phyla.

Yeah.

Continue the adventure with ROGUE BET, available now!

ACKNOWLEDGMENTS

One Shot marked the original end of the Wild Nines, but not necessarily the last story with Viola, Davin, Mox and others. I feel like these characters have plenty more to do yet, and can't wait to see what they get up to now that they're no longer getting chased by Bosser.

As with all of my books, family and friends are at the core of making this possible. Nicole keeps me going day in and out with her encouragement—there's simply no way I'd be able to do this without her help. My parents for giving me the artistic itch. My brothers for pestering me about what I'm writing next, and thus keeping me moving.

Lastly, thanks to all the readers out there. Whether you found these books through a sale, a random click on a website, or through a friend's recommendation, it's amazing to have the opportunity to share these stories with you.

Thank you.

For Nicole

ABOUT THE AUTHOR

A.R. Knight spins stories in a frosty house in Madison, WI, primarily owned by a pair of cats. After getting sucked into the working grind in the economic crash of the 2008, he found himself spending boring meetings soaring through space and going on grand adventures.

Eventually, spending time with podcasting, screenplays, short stories and other novels, he found a story he could fall into and a cast of characters both entertaining and full of heart.

The Wild Nines have more adventures to come, along with new plots, settings, and stories in the future. From there, A.R. Knight plans on jumping through to other worlds and finding new stories to tell in the limitless borders of our imagination.

Thanks, as always, for reading!

www.blackkeybooks.com
arknight@blackkeybooks.com

www.ingramcontent.com/pod-product-compliance
Lightning Source LLC
Chambersburg PA
CBHW062020190726
48284CB00013B/1353